CAROUSEL

SQUARE

for Heidi Kaim, the Sun,

the Moon, and the Stars

forever

outskirts
press

Outskirts Press, Inc.
http://www.outskirtspress.com

ISBN: 978-1-9772-4904-3

Cover art and illustrations © by Keeyonna Fox. All rights reserved - used with permission.

Outskirts Press and the "OP" logo are trademarks belonging to Outskirts Press, Inc.

PRINTED IN THE UNITED STATES OF AMERICA

"Carousel Square is not only a cool positive vibe, and a compulsively hilarious kaleidoscope, and the funniest book on Minneapolis I have ever read, no kidding, but it's like an entire space I left feeling inspired and uplifted."
—*Beej Chaney, lead singer of The Suburbs*

This is the tale of Chitchee Chitchester whose aim is to open his own used book store in Minneapolis, but first he must learn the ropes by working at BookSmart, a book store slowly being strangled to death by the local developers, who own nearby Carousel Square and have set their sights on Uptown and beyond. The developers' plot to overthrow and possess Minneapolis is set in 2009 against a background of economic recession, political greed, police vendettas, and ongoing criminal mayhem. Chitchee and a small band of bibliomaniacs, yokels, and book lovers keep the shop doors open, while the powers that own the building try to sweep and scatter their community of letters into the sewer grates. Because of an epiphany Chitchee had as a child while reading a Little Golden Book about a squirrel, Chitchee thinks himself a squirrel with the magical power of ordinary acorns. Within an allegorical frame of Islamic mysticism, Gangelhoff evokes a situation comedy for everyone who has ever sought refuge in a book store or a book in a book store—in fact, this book is a book store, whose doors readers will be going through years from now.

MINNEAPOLIS

The first book Chitchee Chichester ever read was a Little Golden Book. The book was about a squirrel and was called: *Perri And Her Friends*. As from a past life Chitchee reviewed the photographs that illustrated the text when he flashed on the emerald and silver-spined children's book. A kaleidoscopic bliss cascaded onto the iridescent grass and the rainbow gardens outside. The very act of reading symbols triggered a tiny serpent's coil to loop around itself at the base of Chitchee's spine. A tingle from this tickle emerged as an "I." "I" itself became "We" and added depth to his consciousness. The empty plenty of an acorn flowered into a forest of books, outside and inside. Reading the Little Golden Book illuminated Chitchee's mind, and the image of a candle in his mind, lighted by a book, served to illuminate the path he shone on forever. He heard the blissful song of a red-breasted robin on a berry-branched juniper tree in the backyard. For a timeless moment, the living room, with its lamp of understanding, bedazzled him, uplifted his heart, and stamped him with an unforgettable joy. So, *from the womb of a book, his soul was born, and his soul became conscious of consciousness.* As from a kit of unfolding proteins, from seed to consciousness (Sanskrit: चिति *chit*, *citta*), a Self-assembling Self of one Charles Chichester opened warm-blooded eyes on the observable Universe. He became conscious for the first time while reading a book about a squirrel.

Chitchee discovered later that the Austrian author of *Perri And Her Friends*, Felix Salten, was Jewish; Salten was also the author of *Bambi*, and Hitler banned his books. The little book, סֵפֶר, *sefer*, recounted how Perri the Squirrel (Perri the Rabbi?) had a rabbit friend, Danni (Danni the Rabbi?). Danni lived next door, and when Marty the Marten patrolled the woods for breakfast, Danni alerted Perri, and Perri screeched to the neighboring woods: "Chee chee chee!" That is the plot of the book.

Paisley Chichester clasped her only son Chitchee to her bosom with all her heart. She cleaned, fed, and clothed his helpless body, watched over him, pulled the poisons from his mouth, and dreamed what he dreamed. In turn he beheld his mother's beautiful face and the caress of her eyes. Only one mother had ever been born, and she gave birth to everyone.

Young Charles is in the living room, holding open the Little Golden Book—his mother Paisley enters from the kitchen. Charles splays the book. He sits on her lap, and she sits in her Windsor rocking chair.

"Oh my goodness . . . are you reading?" asks Paisley, spindling a seven-inch 45 on the stereo console.

Wearing summer Bermuda shorts and a floral shirt—martini and Kent cigarettes on the coffee table, Paisley snuggles back into her Windsor rocking chair.

"My word, my little scholar, you're reading whole books now. Charles, I'm so proud of you."

"Chee chee chee!" he reads from the book and smiles strenuously.

"We will call you 'Chee chee chee,' from now on!" says his mother. "Chim chim Che-ree!"

The phonograph plays Doris Day singing "Red, Red Robin Comes Bob Bob Bobbin' Along."

"Now," says Paisley, "it's your friend's turn to rock in the Windsor rocker—you have to share!"

Chitchee jumps off his mother's lap, and falls into the arms of the neighbor girl his own age. She has bangs, sundew-red curly hair, and freckles. She wears a Peter Pan-collared, blue bell-shaped dress and she stands on crooked twigs. So close to her clematis-mouth and sparkly hazel eyes is Chitchee, she kisses him. Her kindergarten smile in the surrounding heat of summer he forever associates with Danni the Rabbit.

Ever after, Paisley spread the fairy tale that Chitchee was born, book in hand.

And then the new hire Chitchee recalled his first day (in the summer of 2009) on the job at the used book store BookSmart in Minneapolis, Minnesota.

That was the day his ex-wife Donna Jensen, who later changed her name to LaDonna DeLaVelle D'Galactica, made a scene that almost got him fired.

Chitchee strolled happily haphazardly (zigzagging to see what new stores were always opening and closing) on Lagoon toward Hennepin Avenue South, half singing the finale from Stravinsky's *Firebird*. While pedestrians, bicyclists, and vehicles adjusted to the traffic lights and thoroughfares open for summer business, Chitchee, thinking of whistling that Russian tune, halted, stooped, and pocketed an acorn and acorn's cap he particularly fancied. The cap's intricate, minaret design—as he had seen in D'Arcy Thompson's *On Growth and Form*—drew him in at once.

"Every acorn," Chitchee prefaced himself, "has the magical ability to fetch from afar the far-fetched."

Hot, buzzing prairie grass and petunias sugared the purpled air of the Uptown side streets. Guilds of honey bees worked like farmhands on the wild roses, hummingbirds vibed with purple lupines and gold honeysuckles, and a Baltimore oriole jostled past Chitchee's thick, blue-black unkempt hair—a little greasy under his black beanie. Although the sun was torrid hot on the pavement and buzzed like a chainsaw, Chitchee wore a black leather jacket over a red and black flannel shirt, tucked out, black Levis, and a black T-shirt, his clothes for all seasons—Minnesota's seasons don't proceed in order and can all happen on the same day. Somewhere about his person he had jammed in a paperback (Mandarin: 书), so that when trapped at a boring bus stop you might catch him reading Chinese poetry—Li Bai, Du Fu, or Bai Juyi.

That guy would be reading a book on the way to the gallows pole.

He hadn't showered or changed his white socks for the job interview, knowing he had the book store job in the book bag. He understood that the interview would follow sometime after his first day of work. And the boss understood that the new guy was nice and would make book about books, الكتب كِتاب, to aid the overburdened staff with their overwhelming body load.

Minnesotans detested being called "Minnesota nice." The despised epithet produced comments of unforeseen outrage, fisticuffs with jackanapes, and indignant Aristotelian lists of refutations—so Chitchee avoided its usage and instead smiled at everyone who smiled at him, and the others too. He imagined loving everybody. He was another very public Idiot. From the sunny side of the street, he greeted the house sparrows that flew overhead. The squirrels he gave nods, the rabbits hellos. A bed of crimson-lipped tulips folded themselves into meditation. The mauve coneflowers intoxicated his cheerfulness.

So what if Minneapolis wasn't the best of cities? It wasn't the worst of cities; it was a *Midwestern* city. Brick after brick like *pustak* after *pustak* (पुस्तक after पुस्तक) told Chitchee: this is the mean average, the median, the middling middle, and the *Mulamadhyamakakarika* of Nagarjuna. Not so large as to lose you, nor so small as to never find you. Sure, for nine months you grew weary of winter, and some years, you couldn't scrape together three months of summer; however, every spring the rains came roping down and the sallow willows beat their breasts with the thunderclaps, and the rain felt good enough for children to play in.

Today, all Chitchee had to do was show up on time for a non-existent interview and sell books to the circle of customers. Relax, breathe deeply he told himself, but the noise deepened. The traffic looked like loose, moving maple leaves on a brightly moving stream. Pieces of the sun had been hammered down on the hot pavement into gold sheets all the way down Hennepin Avenue. Chitchee happily yawned half-way, then terminated the yawn early. He stretched his stretches. Relaxed. He had volunteered at BookSmart in the past for free because shelving books was a delight. Shelving calmed his nerves, slowed his heart beats, and fed his browsing curiosity. He shook his arms and legs as if getting out of a hot shower onto cold bathroom tiles. And then he unleashed a downwardly-facing dog (cribbed from B. K. S. Iyengar), jumped up, saluted the starry sun, and resumed his walk. "*And thus he moved more beautifully in the blue,*" said one of his his favorite poets Georg Trakl on Cloud Nine. The sun's warmth on Chitchee's face had the aroma of sweet corn, his face a kernel of corn. Petals of sunlight lay strewn over the city's metallic surfaces and the cars' chromes. An enamel-white Dodge van parked across the street from BookSmart, vaulted open its back doors, and slammed them shut—changing its mind. A purple martin with a bug in its mouth landed in front of Chitchee, and Chitchee watched the purple martin startle off and fly toward a second white Dodge van parking itself clumsily behind the first. Chitchee, with bumpered eyebrows, braked in front of a flyer on a utility pole.

A marijuana cloud floated by with a minty, peony, and rosemary fragrance.

He shivered and trembled with owl-eyed, buggy eyeballs: Chitchee saw *himself*. He was on the flyer and he heard the suspicious police sirens' thorny wailing. He regretted getting high earlier. He melted as in an R. Crumb comix through the cracks in the sidewalk. A bounty hunter wanted his head? Eek! He looked around in wonder and read:

WANTED BY FBI: CHITCHEE CHICHESTER
For Violation of Anti-Riot Laws, Conspiracy, Intent to Distribute
Un-American Literature.
Chitchee Chichester should be considered dangerous because of known propensity to incite
violence, class conflict, and mayhem. Capable of explosives. Last seen wearing a hijab.

"What does that *mean*?" thought Chitchee. "Maybe it's a message from the future!"

Although he heard a strange *click* (single action?) behind him, Chitchee examined the posted photograph: a grainy, Xeroxed version of himself in Minnesota pine and birch woods. He stood next to a figure who had been cut out, but what woods? The mugshot from his high school yearbook? *Click.* (A cocked revolver? Hammer poised. Flash?) When Chitchee turned slowly around with his hands well above his jug-eared, eyeglassed skull, he faced Sausage Man, who had a rose of a thorny Cyranose and raspberry pimples for planets, obscuring his face. He wore a faded, shapeless, bib Oshkosh overall beneath which denim he braved a checkerboardish, black-on-white plaid flannel shirt, the top button buttoned creating wattles out of his chicken neck. Chitchee caught a whiff of his skunk ass. Ugh, sausages! Puzzled forehead creased, Chitchee watched Sausage Man, who tapped at his cellphone screen and walked away.

"Hey, man, did you take my picture?" called out Chitchee. "Hey, hey where are you going, there . . . Sausagey?"

Chitchee strode toward the foul, meaty breath in clouds, stopped, and looked at where his watch should have been (he forgot to strap it on—it usually felt like a giant deer tick sucking his blood). He looked skyward as if at a trade show for stealth bombers and guessed the correct time from the sun.

"*Ja* and," said Sausage Man, parroting, winking, and blinking bluet-flower eyes a-twinkle. "And I'm going to go get me some Vienna sausages from Lunds there. And I plan to eat them too-hoo."

Sausage Man, well everyone knows he's crazy, Chitchee thought—I didn't know he had a cell phone though. Chitchee hurried back to the totemic utility pole.

"Okay, *this* must be a prank," thought Chitchee. "It must be the guys at BookSmart! Initiation into the hazey brotherhood of books. Must be! Last seen wearing a hijab? لا. Ha, *ha*. No. That ID seems a trifle mistaken . . ."

He paused and added:

"إِنْ شَاءَ ٱللَّٰهُ!"

Two Minneapolis thumpers in a squad car turned on their siren and raced toward Lake Street through the red light on Lagoon Avenue. Other mad sirens chimed in with ululating red tongues of fire. Chitchee, as if tied to a mast, cupped his ears.

He ripped the sheet off the utility pole, slipped the paper into his back pocket, plucked one of his own poems (and a roll of 3M packing tape) from his black JanSport backpack, and switched in his poem:

The trees have agency, cleaving to grammars, where leaves are verbs
Present participles are running like non-binary lions that perch on
The backs of butterflies, flowers falling out of the mouths of
Grad students, who speak with a single tongue of ice,
But we are the squirrels without blessings, the squirrels of ٱللَّٰه .

"There, perfecto!"

He admired himself and read aloud the whole poem with an open heart.

"Even the haters should be turning cartwheels over *that* poem soon. Or my name isn't Perri the Magic Squirrel!"

Leaving BookSmart's front door, a man resembling Sausage Man wore a Brooks Brothers black suit (his well-ironed suit matched the expressionless look on his face), white shirt, and an almost wooden black tie. And Chitchee's mouth opened, shaped with an unspoken: What? This new edition of Sausage Man: first impression: from pariah dog to hedge-fund investor. Is this so large a step? Even the scar above the refurbished Sausage Man's right eye was so precisely carved as to have been ordered from Neiman Marcus. The re-packaged Sausage Man checked messages, his left hand poked the screen, and his right hand gripped the oblong iPhone 3 by his broken thumb in a crooked, vise-shaped hand. A no-nonsense, no-smile-from-me, don't-mess-with-me look fell flat as a flapjack on Chitchee. Indeed his furry eyebrows climbed up the ridges to his intact hairline when he asked the man:

"So, how's your sausage?"

"Have a nice day," said he, his speech clear as the sunny water clipped by the stones in Minnehaha creek.

"Hey, man!" said Chitchee. "I'm not a National Security risk!"

With his shoulders pulled back as if there were a steel rod in his spine that turned his S-shape into an I-shape, the man about-faced and marched off.

"Did I say something wrong?" Chitchee scratched his head, mussing up his wayward hair, more windswept than ever. "Sorry! Oh, *habibi* . . . yikes, arg, wha-? It wasn't even Sausage Man, was it? This day is off to a terrible start with my losing the ability to recognize faces."

Chitchee felt so stung, Cobra-bitten, and guilty, he wanted to bite the bite. His face flushed as if there were a prickly pear inside him trying to get out. He was always saying the wrong thing. Saying the right thing for Chitchee was like the clay pigeon up in the air for an expert skeet shooter to shatter. But was Immanuel Kant right or wrong when he wrote: "All stiff regularity is inherently repugnant."

Finkle and Paisley Chichester sensed at Chitchee's birth something might be "inherently repugnant" about Chitchee. Chitchee didn't open his eyes until he was a month old and when he opened his eyes he was color blind for life. Another anomaly: he was unable to grow facial hair. He remained pink and bald long enough to cause some concern; his father Finkle feared that Charles Chichester would always be a square peg in a round hole! For the longest time, with the face of an overripe cranberry, Chitchee lay in his rocking crib like a big pink rat, weighing four pounds, failing to thrive, and endlessly reading his own mind. But Paisley scooped him out of manure, picked him out of the thorns, licked him, kissed him, and shielded him from the world's eagle hawks, coyotes, and weasels. A bit of a do-nothing baby, thought Father Finkle, and how will his only son, who kind of looks like a giant broken thumb, ever hold down a real job with the face of an overripe cranberry? Mother Paisley swaddled the pink rodent and kissed the thing while Finkle made precise mental observations: *Son Charles slower than Karo syrup: to walk, talk, grasp, and must be poked to respond. Very slow. For about a year, Chitchee stared upward at a point on the ceiling above his head where the ceiling fan spins. Anything that revolves fascinates Chitchee for no reason: bicycle wheels, hand-held rotary egg-beaters, and vinyl 33 ⅓ record albums, for example, my Perry Como, Andy Williams, and especially my Burl Ives's American Songbag collection, which makes him cry.*

True, these crooners stacked on the Hi-Fi's spindle turned Chitchee into blubber and his fresh buckets of blubber churned up fat tears of wax, but Chitchee prefered Peter, Paul, and Mary's "Puff, the Magic Dragon" until Finkle flung it over the backyard fence after he realized it was as communist as *The New York Times*. The song concealed a Soviet plot to drug Republican Senator Barry Goldwater with drugs, or "Puff," to Goldwater, code-named "Little Jackie Paper," who, once drug-addicted to the "Magic Dragon," could be as easily brainwashed as a Democrat. Chitchee moved on and settled for the howl of the Chichesters' celadon-glazed, canister vacuum cleaner at which he clapped at gleefully as at bagpiping bagpipers on a kilted parade.

Churched at sixes and sevens, Chitchee squirmed loose from the pews (mass said at Saint Therese's Catholic church in Deephaven). The little Golem trod down the nave aisle, pulled the tablecloth off the altar, and asked the insulted Father Stryckinzki, celebrant, if he were a woman, and had milk for all his babies. No one laughed and Finkle spanked him in front of everybody in the church.

What rankled worst of all (for Finkle anyway), Chitchee had epicanthic folds over the corners of his eyes. Finkle, shocked at the monstrous growth, disowned those folds, forcing Finkle to lessen eye contact with his own son, *if* it were his son.

"I do not know how these eyes came into the family," said Finkle. "And we can't have him diagnosed, Paize. He'll be stigmatized. He'll be put in some welfare hospital, somewhere with handicaps, Mongols, basket cases—and basket races."

"Yes," said Paisley, "but if he cannot keep up with the other children at school, wait, where is that *Baby and Child Care* by Dr. Benjamin Spock?"

"Oh, *he will keep up*," claimed Finkle. "We don't need that pinko quacko spocko to tell us what to do with our own son. Charles is going to learn to be a man! If I have to break out my father's Everlasting boxing gloves and put Charles in the ring with that Jacky Mattson boy down the street. He'll learn to defend himself like I did, Paisley, when I was at DeLaSalle in my boxing shorts."

"You don't have to yell, Finky," said Paisley. "I'm right here. In our separate beds, next to you. Why are you so angry? Who are you angry with really?"

"Okay, sorry, Puggles," said Finkle in a sweat. "Don't spoil Charles with extra attention. And no more hugging. All that friendly hugging is making him weak. People are always saying how great a father I am to put up with his strange eyelids, but, Paisley, I'd give my left nut, pardon my French, to be a bad father with a normal son, instead of a great father with a son who looks like he just got out of a Midway freak show at the State Fair in Shanghai."

"You're awful! I love Chitchee," said Paisley. "Whether he is like all the rest of the normal kids in the neighborhood or not,

God loves all his children."

"No, he doesn't! Who said that?" countered Finkle. "Probably a big-spending Democrat."

"What are you saying, honey?" asked Paisley. "God is a tightwad God?"

"You're twisting my words around *again*!" exclaimed Finkle, tearing off his bedsheets angrily. "You take one small thread and twist it into a thousand knots. I'm saying God has very frugal characteristics with regard to government outlays. When Eve subsisted on the tree of welfare and ate from it, that was the end of free enterprise altogether."

"Waldorf salad," said Paisley, no longer listening when Finkle raged in one of his storms. "Maybe I'll make a Waldorf salad tomorrow."

Indeed, Chitchee didn't look *at all* like the rest of the kids in the neighborhood, according to Finkle. Chitchee looked Asian, almond-eyed, and the almonds followed Finkle around almost all the almond time. Almonds always reminded Finkle not to eat almonds. He *might* have been cuckolded by a giant almond, but when? Well, there was a time when Finkle lived from job to job, on the road in his shiny black 1970 Ford Falcon, struggling to stay ahead of the mortgage, the bills, and the vertiginous axe of the taxman.

Chitchee, the variant of a random deletion of a few genes he never noticed he lost, tried to be like all the other kids, except he couldn't keep track of his evening paper route (*Minneapolis Star*), which started on Vine Hill Road in Minnetonka and went so far as to touch the border of Excelsior township. Without a bike, the paper route took even longer in winter, when he dragged his toboggan of newspapers behind his snow-caked, tromping boots, squinching through the breaking snow. Old ladies, rich and poor, loved the hapless mite, the little snowman; they invited him into their kind kitchens, his nostrils inhaling the butterscotch, strawberry preserves, banana nut breads, fudge brownies, and chocolate chip cookies freshly sprung from the oven . . . next to which he thawed his stinging, curled, frozen mitten hands.

Whomever Chitchee met at random, he invited over for dinner, especially elderly women wrapped in ACE bandages constrained to crutches because of polio. He loved playing Montana Red Dog with long-haired grease monkeys on Ducatis who he met at Tony's Mobil or the Sinclair station on Minnetonka Boulevard. Much to the chagrin and surprise respectively of Finkle and Paisley, fancy motorcycles roared into their driveway, followed by old diabetic church ladies falling out of gouty Oldsmobiles and other behemoth Buicks.

Meanwhile the *Stars* never arrived. Somewhere in the recesses of his hippocampus, Chitchee heard Finkle shout his name—his blood vessels narrowed and stiffened.

"Charles Chichester!"

"Honey, the papers are late, people are complaining," said Paisley politely from their second best car, a red 1965 Chevy Bel Air station wagon.

"Is everybody mad at me, mom?" asked Chitchee with a smile as broad as a Sabean moon beam. "Why?"

Finkle and Paisley had trundled around the neighborhood, shouting at the neighbors' dogs. Finkle looked the fool. They would throw Chitchee's sled or bike into the back of the station wagon and deliver the evening *Star*s to the doors of the subscribers themselves.

"Here's your goddamn liberal fish-wrap, Jensen!" bellowed Finkle, spearing the bundled news hard at the route's door stoops. "He's got a McGovern sign in his front yard? Can you believe it, Paisley? East Coast all the way! Sends his kids to private schools too! Cocksucker!"

When Finkle discovered that Chitchee himself paid for his customers' newspapers and that Chitchee shredded the tickets that served as the bills in exchange for brownies, cookies, and a warm house, Finkle backhanded Chitchee with a punch across the mouth, giving Chitchee a bleeding fat lip (and a slightly fractured mandible). His poorly aligned teeth cut into the soul of his flesh. Chitchee went to his bedroom and cried. He pulled out a book he had shoplifted from the B. Daltons book store at Southdale Mall, Ludwig Wittgenstein's *The Blue and Brown Notebooks* (he had read a review of it in his bible: *The Whole Earth Catalog*). He couldn't read it through tears. He wished he were dead in his striped pajamas in his comfortable bunk bed with the reading lamp clamped to the headboard. A prodigious failure at twelve.

He entertained thoughts much about death, imagining his life as something he needed to throw away or hang in his closet with his windbreakers, knit shirts, and corduroys. He was an outsider at twelve and then he read *The Outsider* by Colin Wilson, and then he was confirmed as an outsider. He read *The Stranger* and then he was even more of a stranger. And he loved *Quixote*,

Gargantua, *Metamorphoses* . . . He read the Rouse, the Lattimore, and the Fitzgerald *Odysseys* when he was fifteen, Joyce's *Ulysses* when seventeen. He treated his books as if they were love letters from his best friends: all his friends fit neatly on two plywood shelves.

Could he own his own book store someday? Or at least conceive a book that was, in effect, a book store?

His book would be a book store a friendly book *island* to all once and future mariners, battered by their seas of isolation; he would plant a memorial acorn to all the book stores that ever were to be. He would call his universal book store "Ulysses & Sons" in honor of James Joyce, and it would be like Plumtree's Potted Meat, another "abode of bliss" with Leopold Bloom in it, squaring the circle.

Finkle blamed Chitchee for the "new permissiveness." Finkle had to cover the losses on the uncollected newspaper subscriptions, and if every American father did that there would soon be a One World State. That was *The Plain Truth*. That was what *U. S. News and World Report* was all about. Soon the Federal Reserve would send out its G-men to confiscate all the hunting rifles, grenades, and home-version bazookas, and deliver them to the United Nations, which would forward them to Rothschild's of London—the real *sonsabitches* as imagined in Finkle's bedside book *None Dare Call It Conspiracy*.

Back when puberty attacked Chitchee with pimples and his pimples resembled burnt caps from a cap gun, Chitchee suffered a kind of bourgeois leprosy. From behind his ear a rash spread down his neck, forming huge paisley-shaped islands of scab (his scabs had scabs), turning him into a human gila monster diagnosed as acute psoriasis. Besides this bayonet through his self-esteem, he had to sleep in modified Hefty bag suits to keep the ointments on the affected areas and *not* on the bed sheets. For most of his adolescence he didn't have skin as we know it. He had a tectonic crust with bloody rifts in it when it dried like salt flats and peeled off from nervous itching. Finkle interpreted this as a judgment handed down from God who tested Chitchee all the time and made him itch unless he slept in an oily Hefty bag.

But he had his arms and legs. And he was a light in this world, which shone with the *satcitananda* (सच्चिदानन्द) on all that there is and all that there was.

UPTOWN

By day, a fat sun with a shiny, full, tight belly, looked out over Minnesota's green, singing streams and brooks that suckled the state's grasses, mosses, prairies, pink lady-slippered parks, daffodil bulbs, fresh tulips, bee balms harboring hoodwinked honeybees, cedars, hyacinth meadows, halcyon heathers, maples, oaks, apple orchards, wild rice swamps home to nests of whistling blackbirds, urban lots of elephant-eared catalpas, balsam and blueberry bogs, amazing lakes and mazes of maize, and seas of pollen in the brilliant air.

The moon, tossing and turning, lay awake a-nights until finally dreaming the metropolis below:

And the metropolis below was downtown Minneapolis with its IDS Center, a sky-reflecting, steel, blue glass, saw-grooved, oblong tower in the Minneapolis skyline. The Capella Tower had a rooftop like a giant, lidded chimney pot. The US Bank Center had Art Deco setbacks rushing upward and backward. The Campbell Mithun Tower progressed skyward like a giant staircase. Then the endearing Foshay in the center, a granny materfamilias, a beloved alpine flower, and an architectural echo from the era of Art Moderne.

Chitchee reflected that the deckled Minneapolis skyline resembled a bookshelf of folio-, quarto-, and octavo-sized books, urging Chitchee to alphabetize the skyline or group the skyscrapers by size and then alphabetize. It stood all out of order. Whenever Chitchee glimpsed printed matter of any kind, a chemical volley of neuronal nets compelled him to lunge after the stray text, pick it up, read it, and squirrel it away in an Edward Hopper-era file cabinet under "miscellaneous" because everything on paper had to be saved, filed, and color-code foldered.

Chitchee skipped toward the Uptown Theater with its neon minaret that used to spotlight the night sky for premieres like a muezzin's call to art house movies, which Chitchee remembered with tenderness—especially the giant fold-out schedules when the foreign films changed every three days and he and LaDonna smoked weed in the cloudy balcony and watched *Juliet of the Spirits*.

An "I" bounced onto, into, and across Hennepin Avenue South. "B" and "J" fell. The English alphabet rained from the sky in a shower.

Chitchee looked up at the glinting movie marquee.

BLACK SWAN SHOWING KNIGHTLEY IN HER NIGHTIE TONIGHT

"Sorry about that!" said Felix Weatherwax from the top of a rolling extension ladder, which leaned at an ungainly angle.

Felix reached for his water bottle awkwardly and dropped more letters.

"Felix!" hollered Chitchee. "*Natalie Portman* is in *Black Swan*, not Keira Knightley!"

"Whoa!" said Felix. "You're kidding!"

Felix Weatherwax's framed eyeglasses were round as the eye spots on a moth. He had a pancake face, short pointy nose, and a grinding lower jaw whose bottom incisors nibbled his dried upper lip and made his chin quiver constantly. This assemblage was linked to the sweat on Felix's forehead, explaining his constant dehydration. Felix thoughtfully reviewed his water bottle, sipped, fumbled the screw cap, dropped the cap, and then the bottle. He dropped a lot of things because when he was a kid, he found his father's .44 revolver in a closet. And the revolver went off when he dropped it. It blew up in Felix's face. It had a hairline crack in the barrel. Then his father attacked his mother in a drunken rage and then she disarmed, shot, and killed her husband Arminius with his own .22 pump. While Felix's mother served time in the Shakopee Correctional Facility, Felix grew up with his grandfather Michael, but Michael suffered a concussion when he attempted to clear the gutters of his sister-in-law's house, slipped, and fell off the roof, which led to his going on disability. Felix's grandfather Michael submitted to a nursing home in St. Louis Park, whose bedroom window he crawled out of at night to chase Canadian geese back to Canada.

"Hey, Chitchee! Aren't you wanted by the FBI?" yelled Felix.

Inexpertly perched, Felix looked at his water bottle on the sidewalk. Then somehow he kicked the ladder out from under him, which crashed sideways to the sidewalk.

Felix clung to the cliff face of the marquee.

"Whooa-a-a-a!"

Chitchee picked up one end of the ladder and Emily, the Uptown Theater manager, the other, having run outside expecting an accident. Felix, breathing heavily and flushing in the cheeks with two rose blooms, finally descended the ladder.

"I almost fell out of my tutu! Pretty funny, huh you guys? Maybe not."

"Can you work the counter now and make the popcorn?" asked Emily, with her black eyebrows bouncing up and down, blue-streaked crow's hair, and thick, black leather steel-toed boots.

"Is there a reward?" asked Felix.

"Yeah, minimum wage," said Emily.

"I was asking Chitchee. I mean, is there a reward for Chitchee?" asked Felix. "He's *wanted* all over town."

"Yeah, free ambulance ride," said Chitchee, "to the Hennepin County ER."

"I'll take a free ambulance ride to the ER," said Felix, biting his lip and then gurgling the leftover saliva in his water bottle. "That might come in handy someday."

Across the street, the neighborhood hangout, McDonald's, hummed, buzzed, and throbbed. Ironically, the multinational, faceless fast-food chain anchored the locals to *somewhere* instead of the "Great American Nowhere" as in Walker Percy's *The Moviegoer* or the authentic nowhere of John Kennedy Toole's actual *life*. In the 1980s on the family picnic tables of McDonald's once congregated the McPunks—nomads with pileated hair, safety pins through a hundred holes of flesh, chains for belts, and shredded bloody black jeans always ready to white-knuckle riot and be righteously and wrongfully trotted off to jail by the Minneapolis Police Department and its thumpers. Many of the locals looked back with nostalgia at this cultural flowering, which ended when rich people complained about it. McDonald's was forced to eliminate their funky patio and reggae-regaled picnic tables by order of the Uptown Association.

The BookSmart storefront sported plate-glass windows that looked out over Hennepin Avenue toward the McDonald's and reflected the top half of downtown Minneapolis, some twenty blocks away. Chitchee strode for the book store's front door.

"Spare change?" asked Owen "Hawk Eye" Rasmussen, wearing a surplus U. S. Army jacket, standard issue jeans, and a trounced Minnesota Twins baseball cap (the kind where the "C" is clamped to the "T"). Hawk Eye fanned himself with a pitiable, illegible, and tattered cardboard-box sign (Chitchee saw $$$ signs on it).

"Penny for your thoughts?" asked Chitchee who halted, curious to see whether a hard-bitten Vietnam War veteran had some *play* in him.

The July sunlight, reaching Earth after eight long minutes, of course, continued to illuminate Chitchee as he stood outside the eastern entrance to BookSmart. Hawk Eye made a face of ponderation, his forehead wrinkling like a waffle-iron and his jaw gesticulating unspoken thoughts, prepping the inner lining of his mouth with some spit to allow for freer speech.

"You're being followed," said Hawk Eye, frowning and activating his tongue sleeping at the bottom of his throat. "See that white Dodge van across the street?"

"Which one?" said Chitchee, spinning around slowly like the end of a merry-go-round ride. "There are two."

"The first one. Unless you are a National Security risk," said Hawk Eye. "It looks like people are taking pictures of you for no reason. Unless you are a celebrity. And you don't look like Prince."

"I know *that*," said Chitchee, "because Prince doesn't even look like Prince."

"These flyers of you are all over Uptown," said Hawk Eye, pulling out a samizdat of the same WANTED poster Chitchee had torn down. "It doesn't say anything about a reward though. Are you worth anything?"

"I don't know," said Chitchee. "I can call the FBI on my lunch break. What am I going to say? I want to report someone who has been reporting to the FBI about me?"

Hawk Eye goose-necked at the customers bellying out of Club Miami, the bar next to BookSmart. He looked past the interfering Chitchee and asked:

"Spare change, sir?"

Hawk Eye snatched the cigarette butt a customer shot into his face from off the hot sidewalk.

Chitchee fished up some small change for Hawk Eye, and Hawk Eye held out his hand for the six pennies, three nickels, and a dime. Hawk Eye blessed Chitchee as poor riches poured through his hand into his other hand. Chitchee wondered whether the Vietnam veteran had read Michael Herr's *Dispatches*—maybe he was *in Dispatches*.

"Hey, were you in Khe Sanh in '67?"

"Shit, never heard of that shit."

"I wish I had more to give. Veterans are heroes in my book. Especially snipers. Know any snipers?"

"One."

"You know what?" said Chitchee. "You should be my bodyguard. You ninja warriors always have special powers of some sort! Hey, here comes Randy Quaalude now!"

"Hey, I have to go potty," said Hawk Eye and strolled into BookSmart.

"Hey Chitchee, you're wanted, didja know," said Randy "Quaalude" Johnson toward Chitchee.

Randy held the wanted poster in his talons and leaned on his walking stick, his pale, cicatrized, blowtorched, and stitched-up body itself a warty shillelagh. Randy had so many tattoos on his hairless white body he could have been a sun-damaged Persian rug. Dripping wet, he weighed a hundred pounds, factoring in his jeans, T-shirt, shillelagh, and missing teeth.

"How was that Oxy I sold you?" asked Randy, folding the poster into four squares and handing it to Chitchee. "Wasn't that *you* I sold the Oxy to?"

Chitchee compressed his lips to say "no further," shrugged his shoulders, and with open palms waving about, said:

"Not me," said Chitchee. "I didn't buy OxyContin from you. I gave you money for benzos, wasn't it? I wanted them for job interviews. Maybe it was somebody who looked like me . . ."

Randy Quaalude patrolled Carousel Square—a rolled, tobacco stub behind his bullet-clipped ear. Before he himself died of an Oxycontin overdose, he used to sell prescription opioids, benzos, and painkillers from his fanny pack in front of Figlio's Restaurant, where even the security guards knew the man-shrew as "Randy Quaalude." Randy had shot and killed a security guard in Florida who had parked in his disabled parking space and had served 6 years for manslaughter in Broward County. Randy patrolled the Uptown neighborhood more than the 5th Precinct, who had all moved to the suburbs to get away from the crime.

In fact, whenever Chitchee dropped by the 5th precinct to say "Howdy, neighbor," Desk Sergeant Vlaisavljevich looked down and rearranged the blotter of pistachio shells.

"What's with all the pistachios?" asked Chitchee. "Is that some secret Fraternal Order of Police thing? Or the Illuminated Members of the Third Eye?"

"What's with all the flying monkeys?" said Desk Sergeant Vlaisavljevich.

"What does that mean? Are you alluding to the *Ramayana*?" asked Chitchee, feeling down. "I see you guys at Lunds Grocery store eating pistachios until your hands and necks turn red."

"Flying monkeys!" replied Desk Sergeant Vlaisavljevich and cracked another pistachio.

Chitchee had buzzed over to Randy's apartment on 31st Street South to help with Randy's twenty-year old desk top, which needed to be plugged in and powered on. That done, Chitchee could never figure out the connections amongst the junkie, his cats, and the kitty litter box overflowing onto the floor, the cat food smashed into the linoleum, the cat hair growing out of the flame-retardant cushions, and the cat shit in a litter box almost like a decoration, an ornament, or a juniper bonsai garden of fecal meditation, the opiated owner too trashed to do anything but contemplate the stillness of cat shit. Chitchee pictured the desperate Randy driving to pick up an eight ball and begging his dealer: "Come on man, could you throw in some Friskies with that, Classic Turkey with Giblets and Gravy, not the Salmon Pâté. Come on, man."

"Now Chitch! Why is your puss pinned to all the telephone poles from here to Liquor Lyles?" asked Randy. "Did you join the Siamese Twin Liberation Army or something?"

"With what money?" said Chitchee. "Randy, how long have you known me? Am I a terrorist because I almost learned Arabic? A suicide bomber because I read the *Qu'ran*? I've never killed a goldfish. I once shot a beehive by mistake. But that's it for my life in the martial arts."

Randy ignored this apology, beat his ribcage, coughed, and then mumbled a brisk "Up, gotta go!" when he saw two thumpers walk around the corner at Lagoon and Hennepin.

Chitchee thought back confuzzled: he made friends easily—too easily on reflection. Who was framing him? It was his ex. It was always the ex. And yet hadn't she drawn him out of his shell when he was a gawky, awkward Sindbad who had sailed off to the University of Minnesota and met the love of his life in a Middle Eastern history class? When Chitchee met her, she was Donna Jensen—that was before she had her name legally changed to LaDonna DeLaVelle D'Galactica.

He blessed her with sublimated pixie dust. Without her he was nothing, he exaggerated. Marriage would be nice—it was nice to have an Eternal Feminine around the house. She did save his life, especially the *one* time—at the U. of M. when he "flipped out." After an ill-advised, ill-prepared psychedelic shit from the bowels of madness, he was on his knees. He called out to God with a vow to liberate humanity if saved. If only Chitchee could please have the dorm room (Pioneer Hall, 615 Fulton Street) and the four walls of his freshman life back! When the froshy four walls did *not* pop back (with a nice floor and ceiling thrown in), he zigzagged for the Washington Avenue bridge and looked down. The Mississippi River. It looked like the end of a noose that hung from the overcast sky. He turned and jostled Donna.

"You're in my Middle Eastern Studies classes, aren't you?" she asked.

Leggy, thin, robin-haired, and hazel-eyed, Donna sported a white and black leather jacket with salmonberry slashings, striped pants of purple and white like the leaves of a Jack-in-the-Pulpit, earrings of tiny 45s, and 5-inch platforms. One ear's helix was malformed and bulged; her lips were Rubenesque but snarled when at rest.

"Sometimes," he said, his voice cracking like eggshells. "Who are you, pray tell the truth? Or we will both be in disguise."

"Who talks like that?" thought Donna, pulling him away from the brink of being dredged up by a river patrol.

"Are you ready for the Ottoman test?" she asked innocently. "Do you understand the millet system and tax farming?"

And her carmelized skin was honey-luminous, which gave him chills being near.

"No," said Chitchee, straining his neck to one side with disdain and disbelief. "I can't function in this vending machine of learning. My glasses don't fit my classes. I'm going to flunk out to the bottom of the Mississippi River. Like Raphaël de Valentin."

Donna walked him out of his river-leaping funk back and forth on Washington Avenue Bridge, not minding the strangely blank looks of the 50,000 fellow students shunting in and out of Coffman Union. In winter, the same 50,000 fellow snowflakes descended upon the drifts of snow banks and crawled up eroding stone steps into the mammoth brick monoliths of the mausoleums of learning on the Northrop Mall.

"With you by my side, everybody will think I'm a genius," said Chitchee naively, arm in arm with Donna, walking back to Pioneer Hall. "Not that I am a genius, but it would be nice if everyone thought I was."

"I can be your muse," said Donna. "How much does a muse make?"

Back to his carpentered world, Chitchee pumped out his guts to Donna. She smiled like someone who found an amethyst in the middle of the snow and wondered how it got there. He told her he had vowed that: "he would teach humanity," "he would help humanity," and "he would own a book store that would serve as Al-Ma'mun's *Bayt al-Hikmat*." When Donna returned Chitchee to his dorm room, they towelled the door, got high, talked the night away, and then quickly made love until dawn to make up for lost time. And they could not love each other fast enough to escape from the internal flames that both spurred and annihilated them, having lost interest in their Ottomans.

After this episode he lifted from *Le Peau de chagrin*, he plunged back into the book he had recently bought from Bert, a storied bibliophile himself, at the Book House in Dinkytown. Chitchee coughed up $2.35 in change mainly for its calligraphic cover: *Kitab al-Tawasin*.

"*The thought of the common people plunges into the sea of images and the thought of the elect into the sea of understanding. But these two seas dry up . . .*"

In Folwell Hall, he and LaDonna studied Arabic under Dr. Mohammad Sidow and the teacher's assistant Feras al Farsi. Shocked to discover that most Muslims dismissed "sufis" as loafers, fakes, and cheats, Chitchee persevered down his spiritual path; shocked again to discover that most of the classical "sufis" (a Western construction equivalent to "circus clown") didn't write in Arabic, but Persian, he continued with his Arabic, reckoning he could learn Persian from Dr. Iraj Bashiri (who had translated *The Blind Owl*)— then read and translate *The Conference of the Birds* by Farid ud-Din Attar, envisioning himself as a fully-funded eternal student of Middle Eastern studies living in Minneapolis forever. After making a killing in the field of translation, eventually, he would own his own book store, and there would be ma'rifa in the aloes and sandalwood-scented air, and a mynah bird in a bird cage recursively programmed as in Huxley's *Island* to screech at the brain-fogged browsers: the mantra: "Attention!"

Chitchee squatted like a squirrel at the register practising *dhikr*. That was what he wanted from himself and the life whose journey he had begun at the University of Minnesota.

Meanwhile, he journaled his ideas about a novel: a science fiction novel: *The Hell Hound Chip*.

The plot: What if Allah micro-chipped Mansur Al Hallaj, pieced him together, reincarnated him, and mailed him back to Earth, Al Hallaj knowing full well he would be crucified? But the only test of his virtue was to be accused of every vice, because it was more meaningful to die for the *summum bonum* than to live for the gross domestic product pointlessly.

I, Mansur al Hallaj, am being written down to record the incidents of my poor life, which I chose. So in effect I am two souls in one body. Even if everyone loved me, I would have to make them despise me out of love. Am I not the Truth? Are you not the *Tawhid*? Every path leads to the *Mi'raj*. Majnun loves Layla outside uncreated Creation. And who would ever suspect my soul living in the body of a book written in the middle of nowhere, in the middle of the Midwest, in a future replicant Minneapolis, circa 10,000 C. E. of the Spengler/Selden Plan? In my future of forked-over paths, the Great Ostrich Egg (who speaks through a L'eggs display stand of nylon pantyhose) rules over Earth, where everyone has Hell Hound-chipped brains that act as musical Antabuse. A couple bars of "Auld Lang Syne" and mad robo-dogs rip out your jugular. Music is outlawed and only available on the black market in powder form, which crypto-musicologists and closet descendants of Folkways Records cook in spoons and inject. These remnants of a dubious quantum catastrophe, who are straight out of a Stephen King novel, go straight back into a Stephen King novel and hide in underground cells (in the limestone caves pretty close to Pioneer Hall) where Stephen King cannot pursue and sue them. Led by the charismatic me, who can play the "twenty instruments of the God Marsyas," the underground rebels grok to the ancient Balinese gamelan, whose musical realization binds to the hip receptors in their hip-chips. They play music on their *trimbas* and go into shamanic trances. They dance backwards and forwards to the music of Harry Partch who they somehow conflated with Otzi, the 16,000 year old skeleton discovered in the Alps, who for some reason they think is also Ishi, the last of the Yahi. They think that Harry Partch/Otzi/Ishi was impaled on a giant cross-flute for his poor technique as a flautist. I am martyred by an International Police Force known as the Hegemons, none of whom got into the Berklee School of Music, although a few of them got as far as the U. of M.'s Ferguson Hall. The resentment-filled, sexually-frustrated Hegemons corner and flay me alive. They boil my back-up band, the High Notes, in castor oil and then drown them and their bickering wives in Lake Nokomis by the concession stand, which isn't open anymore because long ago nuclear winter shut down the beach, and the book concludes with "Sad. There will be no more flavored snow cones at the Lake Nokomis beach."

Of course it was a sandwich of balderdash, baloney, and fresh twaddle, topped with tangy dribble. Chitchee couldn't sustain the tightly-controlled narrative needed for a grocery list. Since he couldn't write a book, the next best thing would be to sell them.

Once *The Hell Hound Chip* had stacked up a word count of 300,000, he carefully pared it down, omitting every redundancy, superfluous comma, and long boring part, which then brought the word count down to absolute zero, without telling LaDonna.

Starting over years later, he once sat down to write a different novel. This time he had to abandon writing because when he wrote, for example, "a mouse swooped into a crack in the wall" he saw a mouse swoop into a crack in the wall! When he wrote: "Chitchee felt a mouse scamper up the length of his body towards his nose, forcing him to sleep with the lights on," that night Chitchee felt a mouse scamper up "the length of his body towards his nose, forcing him to sleep sitting up with the lights on" forcing him to sleep sitting up with the lights on, sweating dogs and fleas.

BOOKSMART

And what seemed an eternity later (and no closer to his dream) Chitchee approached the Yggdrasil building, which was across from McDonald's. He pushme-pullyoued (pulling a little Dr. Dolittle) the BookSmart plate glass door with its large, thick, bail-shaped handles. Half the customers pushed instead of pulled (right out of *The Design of Everyday Things*) the door. Inside BookSmart, his naso-receptors were fired by the redolent, white pine wood flooring, which drew him into a magical Arden of books (each book itself grown from a forest of books, seeded with symbols to grow another book).

Every time Chitchee strolled into BookSmart he began a new Dickens novel. When he skimmed over the book-crammed walls he was store-amazed by the Dickensian plateau. In a post-Windows world devoid of neighborhood, village, and vicinity, BookSmart opened up on a vast Neo-Victorian panorama, ensconced in a rational den of vitalist creativity.

"Hi, Aloysius, *the minstrel of the dawn is here!*" sang Chitchee with a light heart, spying around BookSmart for friendly signs of life or any McSapiens for that matter.

Chitchee had already befriended all the employees at BookSmart: 1) Noel Schoolcraft (manager), 2) Snorri Halversen (daytime assistant manager), and 3) Benjamin "Saami" Rolvaag (nighttime assistant manager). The managerial staff had convinced the owner of BookSmart, Aloysius Aalgaard, to hire at least one actual worker, Chitchee. Chitchee harmonized with the ever-feuding managers—and resonated with the bookworms on the counter side of the counter. Also, Chitchee had read at least 10,000 books and he knew a thing or two about nothing, and the owner hated interviewing complete strangers, whom he never trusted because they never knew anything. Aloysius Aalgaard hated doing things that ate up a lot of his life when he was better off doing nothing, which in his mind was close to the goal of Daoism, bringing him ever closer to a fishing trip on Jade Mountain with the Seven Heavenly Sages of the Bamboo Grove.

"Hello?" inquired Chitchee of the sudden vacuum.

A bulky, maroon linoleum-covered counter supported an old NCR cash register and next to that an alcove contained the book store's Dell computer enthroned (screen, keyboard, mouse) on the cheap computer desk. Facing the screen on the office swivel chair, swiveled Aloysius, criss-crossing the Internet for *kantele* tabs, swiveling back to the BookSmart inventory (HomeBase 2.3), then YouTube, then pivoting back to HomeBase 2.3.

"Haww-gghh—ello?" Chitchee heard. "Awwwughhk!"

"Is that your Joe Cocker?" joked Chitchee. "Little help?"

Chitchee's eyeglasses were black horn-rimmed monsters. They see-sawed awry on his pug nose. Demons on either side kept tilting the frames for laughs. He had a wide mouth and when he laughed his teeth jut out like a twisted dock on a frozen lake. It was: the wild laugh of a child about to be tickled, a beaming with galaxies-of-joy laugh, a laugh big enough to eat you whole in man-size chunks, and a horse's laugh chewing nettles through a picket fence. It was too much of a laugh for this existence. To those who knew him well it was almost infectious. To others, it was like: turn it off, bitch! It's too damn bright! What's in your toothpaste? Halogen?

What is he up to? In America, crime is either around the corner, next door, or on your TV. Chitchee's buck-toothed and equine grin, it threatened you—unless you happened to be doped up with Seroquel in the back room of a mental ward for stealing a burnt hot dog from a SuperAmerica, which was then mistaken for an AK-47 by the supervisor on duty, the Minneapolis thumpers, the prosecuting attorney, the news media, and the entire judicial system of Hennepin County. Whenever a beam of amusement split his sides he acquired the aura of a doofus, a doofus dogging you for being a fool. Was he a hipster who was really a geek posing as a nerd who might be an imposter because no one is that happy . . . not even Hegel's Absolute. Has any Western painter ever depicted the higher power as a holy fool? We're all imposters thought Chitchee, because we have to insist we are not.

"I'll be right there, buddy," muttered Aloysius. "Oh, goddamn it, not another goddamn *update*. What was wrong with the last update? I'll be right with you, buddy! Where's my cell-o-phone? Fucking computers! All they know how to do *is shit on you*. They are programmed to shit on you. That's all computers are good for. Shitting on average Joes like you and me. More digital shit."

"No problem, Aloysius!" called out Chitchee, picking up a stray *The Autobiography of John Stuart Mill* on the counter. He riffled through the pages. "Take your time! It's such a nice day outside! Oh here's my favorite part."

"I would embrace the computer revolution if someone could take the time to explain it to me," said Aloysius, casting the mouse aside.

"No explanations for anything anymore," said Chitchee cheerfully. "That's the latest revolution. It was a very subtle revolution. And nobody has an explanation for it."

"So you're here for first day training!" said Aloysius, lumbering up wearily. "I sure could use a nap! Don't grow old, buddy! Not after all the football I played!"

Aloysius, with his shoulder-length, thinning blond locks, blonde mustache, and graying Viking beard, wore loose-fitting blue jeans of a fatigued blue-jean blue (clean but fading into a bone-white, bleached blue) often matched with an equally baggy, blue jean jacket matching his blue jean blues. He wore a gray, very charcoal, over-washed T-shirt, with its "U of M" cracked, the collegiate letters peeling off like eczema. Sometimes Aloysius liked to wear a modest tie-dyed, white and purple T-shirt. That was when he felt up to making a larger fashion statement on Easter or something. In his white milky Adidas sneakers, he arched his back, pushed forward on his pelvis, yawned like a baby, and then looked more relaxed the farther away from the computer he strove to be.

"All three managers recommended you and we sure need a worker bee!" said Aloysius. "And thank you for all your volunteer work here. The guys all say you come in at night and alphabetize the store. I don't think we ever formally met though, for some reason, have we? It's Chi Chi? Like Chi Chi Rodriguez? Cheech? Like Cheech Marin?"

"Chitchee, like Itchy and Scratchy," said Chitchee. "I don't usually go out until after nightfall when I'm done thinking about nothing. I guess it was revolving doors between us!"

"What did you do before this?"

"Before Shakey's, where I got fired, I worked for Target."

"What did you do for Target?"

"As little as possible."

"What was your job title?"

"Operator."

"What did you operate?"

"Nothing really."

Aloysius's eyes were space staring into itself.

Chitchee's voice sounded anxious, nervous, and self-abnegating. He had slept in until the last minute, then he jumped up—rushing—he walked outside slovenly-looking, although he wore his last pair of matching clean white socks, so he was not *entirely* lacking in self-confidence. "Beauty is twice beauty," said Neruda on the *topos* of socks. Two socks are better than one.

"You're wanted by the FBI for conspiracy," said Aloysius. "Is that going to be an issue for scheduling?"

"No, because even if I'm convicted for sedition," said Chitchee cheerfully, "I can get in the Huber work release program and bus into town from Plymouth. Nobody is going to look for a radicalized terrorist in a leftist book store!"

Aloysius cast a glance at Chitchee who missed the meaningful glance.

"We used to riot in the Sixties. It was a riot to riot when a riot was going on. I guess my rioting days are over. But you were rioting recently?" asked Aloysius. "Where? Hidden Beach?"

"No," said Chitchee. "I'm being *framed* by a paid informant! I thought it was my literary agent from William Morris & Christie's, but it can't be her. I'm not really wanted anywhere except here! I don't know what's going on! Somebody wants me dead, but I can't imagine who. Like I'm in one of those dumb TV shows from the '60s: like *Run, Buddy, Run!*"

"*Run, Buddy, Run* was my favorite show," said Aloysius, his pupils dilating and his lips shrinking.

Chitchee's whole body cringed and his whole face clenched—showered by a bucket of ice cold Gatorade.

"Okay," said Chitchee. "Would you believe: it's like I'm in *Darkness at Noon*?"

"Ah!" said Aloysius. "I see! Was that on after *Gunsmoke*?"

Aloysius summoned up a supremely contented and forgiving smile on his crustacean, trammed-over, careworn, and kicked-to-the-curb limestone face.

"Wasn't everything on after *Gunsmoke*?" asked Chitchee, his wide eyes wide open and his hands waving about in nervous hand-chopping gestures, enumerating bullet points.

Chitchee thought about hanging himself from the track lighting.

"They say," said Aloysius, "you're the nicest guy in Uptown!"

"HAH!" shouted Chitchee. "That's debatable!"

"Why do you say that?"

"The nicest guy in Uptown," replied Chitchee, "is probably dead."

Crow's feet flexed themselves around Aloysius's darkening eyes, and Chitchee interpolated from them that the new boss had weathered many a Minnesota winter. Those infinite winters had skinned Aloysius dry, what with all the indoor salting and curing from bedroom blowers gushing hot air, and the heat on six months a year. Uptown locals loved Aloysius. He was a friendly bartender, a pastor of the put-out-to-pasture, and a good neighbor to the North. An actual human being for Christ's sake. He was so laid back that he got laid back pain from being so laid back. And Uptown locals gladly supported the Scandihoovian shopkeeper and his quirky book store on the Anishinaabe land of the spruce and fir, halfway between the equator and the North Pole. Aloysius Aalgaard had the long wavelength, radio voice of Eric Sevareid, Cedric Adams, Howard Viken, and Herb Carneal—indeed, Aloysius told Chitchee he regretted not becoming a successful Minnesotan radio announcer.

"You could think of me as a sort of frustrated Verne Lindquist," said Aloysius.

"Okay, okay," said Chitchee. "Keep it going! The mind of man is a maze with no entrance."

Who would have predicted that Aloysius Aalgaard would become the doomed proprietor of a used book store so badly in arrears, he couldn't remember the months or years? That he would be killed by the Kindle? Nullified by the Nook? And—at a time when illiteracy like measles was making a big comeback? Weighing him down were: his daughter's education, his employees' paychecks, the unpaid utilities, the neighborhood's need for neighborhood, and the dilations of the heart he felt for all his neighbors. Except one big one.

His US Bank loan officer, Fjard Gardet, had been stopping by more and more lately. Fjard truly wondered how Aloysius made ends meet. So too did Aloysius. *So it has come to this.* He existed in a singularity of debt that he could not communicate to his own mother.

All the while the daily chorus of "No Future in Books" was sung by local soothsayers walking up the center aisle of BookSmart into the bathroom and out the back door. The same customers who never read anything, unless it was *Wonder Wart-Hog* by Gilbert Shelton, an Aloysius all-time fave (and the FFF Bros.) he had decorated the BookSmart bathroom with.

Aloysius had to put his daughter Aubrey through college—St. Olaf's in Northfield, where she researched ecological substitutes for the bane of Bharat, the serial killer Roundup. At all costs, hell or high on water, his beloved Aubrey would get her diploma despite the Great Recession and unemployment at 10%. Every day, Aloysius steeled himself for indentured servitude to pay for Aubrey's higher education with his income-driven life of economic capture.

"Okay, are you ready for the football?" said Aloysius, game-face pasted on post haste. "Okay, buddy, any which way but loosey-goosey with Miss Lucy!"

"What football?" asked Chitchee, looking around. "I'm not much of a football fan. Although I might be, if they made all the players wear phalluses—then maybe they wouldn't be so cocky."

Aloysius (hack, hack, the second hack he caught in his hand): "I mean, we can start the training now. You can fill out the application later (uhhhwagh)."

Chitchee started coughing too (uhwagh).

"We'll hold off on the paperwork for now," said Aloysius. "For today, basic procedures! You'll be training later with Saami . . . and Snorri will be in at four . . . and Noel has the day off."

"I should be taking notes from an old pro like you!" said Chitchee, hitting a high sycophantic note and ever ready to suckle milk like a spotted fawn.

"Nah," said Aloysius. "Being able to own and run a book store? I think it's something you are born with. Like pole vaulting. Saami told me *you* are a writer, that's great! What kind of stuff do you write?"

"I was trying my hand at science fiction epics in sesqui-hexameter, randomly-enjambed Alexandrines," Chitchee said. "But I set the bar too high."

Out of the corner of his eye, Chitchee's ex-wife, LaDonna DeLaVelle D'Galactica, created a mercurial red streak that lasered across the sidewalks of Hennepin Avenue. A sinking feeling filled Chitchee's bowels with dread, chased by a shot of panic. He had to pee. He tried to squeeze that thought out of his mind, quash that sensation, and requash that sensation.

Chitchee used to wear a thin glove on his right hand because of an urge when over-excited to bite the spandrel between thumb and index. He bit his bare hand. Here she comes looking for the reward money too! Is everybody that broke?

"What's it like, writing a book?" asked Aloysius.

"It's a bit of a bear, you know, like building the Stone Arch Bridge with your bare hands," smiled Chitchee, removing his hand from his teeth.

"Cool, you're able to do that?" said Aloysius.

"Yes," said Chitchee. "I mean no! Hey, Aloysius, as long as you are standing there—"

Aloysius, not controlling the conversation, which had been like a curling stone that he had frantically swept ahead of with his mental broom-strokes, looked perturbed at Chitchee's peculiar hand-biting reflex.

"—I want to open my own book store someday. Ulysses & Sons. That's actually why I took the job! I figured the knowledge I gleaned here from a Ulysses like you, I could parlay into my own book store. And then we could compete like brother siblings hatched from the same nest! So, what's it take to open your own book store?"

"Oh, I don't know, buddy," said Aloysius. "Thirty thousand dollars down. And a rabbit's foot. Neither of which I have anymore."

A pained crucifixion resigned his face to that of a man of sorrows.

"Hey boss, your stigmata are showing," said Chitchee cheerily, looking out the window. "Thirty thousand dollars and a rabbit's foot. I better write that down somewhere. Got a magic marker on you, buddy?"

He sneezed and hooked a finger to his mouth like a hanging question mark. He heard Doris Day sing "Red, Red Robin Comes Bob Bob Bobbin' Along," which he hadn't heard since childhood—except when he sneezed.

Bobbing along with her red bobbed hair, the red red not well-read LaDonna DeLaVelle D'Galactica bobbed with her red, bobbed hair, the red red robin with her robin red snarling upper lip, her exposed belly button, and her red-tabbed jeans bounced angrily down the Lake Street sidewalk—a package under her arm. She crossed at the zebra at the intersection in her pink high-top sneakers. He felt euphoria and depression at once. She was going to make a scene, throw a "spaniard in the works," and require damage control.

"Gee, thirty g's and a rabbit's tootsie for good luck," repeated Chitchee, biting his hand with a slightly downward parabola at the corners of his mouth. "Sorry, Aloysius, you asked me about writing a book? I'm not writing much lately. The juices aren't flowing. There has to be juice! Juice! Or at least Gatorade. Money worries and whatnot. Lately, I can't focus, no juice and no Gatorade. I guess I need a lot of distractions around me to *really* focus. But when I do focus, I focus like a firehose. I guess I need to feel financially secure for once. But thanks to you, I do have job security, and I ought to be able to sock away a few thou every month and save up."

"Oh? And you know I can only pay you in books, for now?" asked Aloysius.

Chitchee's whole body cringed and his whole face clenched as if expecting to be showered by a bucket of ice cold Gatorade.

"The guys told you, right?" continued Aloysius. "We will get back on track when the economy recovers from those gorilla marketers at Goldman Sachs. Hang in there, sports fan! We'll get there! Before you leave tonight—remember to pay yourself out for your eight hours in books, using your company discount of 7½ percent."

"Paid in books?" asked Chitchee, recovering from the uppercut to the solar plexus. "Books! Right, okay. I love books! They're my best friends."

Chitchee didn't expect much more than $7.00 an hour.

He turned to roll his eyes but couldn't because they locked on LaDonna's hazels and then tumbled toward her.

"Oh, and there are a couple bites of some cheese in the fridge you can have, I couldn't finish it," offered Aloysius.

Chitchee didn't hear Aloysius. He heard Handel's "Arrival of the Queen of Sheba."

"Does Charles Chichester work here? Oh there you are!" said LaDonna, taking off her sunglasses. "Madison said you'd be here, and sure enough, I knew I'd find you in a can of bookworms! I found this the other day, in a box. Your science fiction upchuck. With the obligatory male-fantasy, teen-age goddess version of an airbrushed *me*. How much love did you ever really have for me?"

"Yes!" said Chitchee.

Sounding like a door-smacked jamb, LaDonna big-banged a fat, postmarked, opened, and ripped Manila envelope down on the maroon counter. The first three empty chapters of Chitchee's failed sci-fi masterpiece, *The Hell Hound Chip*, arrived DOA, ready for the entombment. When the package spilled out like an unglued phone book (although on Eaton 25% cotton typing paper), he experienced the aura of a seizure and danced through the rest of the interview.

He woke up on the redolent, white pine wood flooring, blank sheets of paper like Minnehaha Falls in full spate. His next memory was Aloysius kneeling over him holding his wrist and murmuring questions about his name, date of birth, and address.

"I thought we were going to fill out the application later," said Chitchee.

Could he be falling back in love so easily? He sizzled looking at the steak. Could he ever have loved her more?

"He always does that when he gets over excited," said LaDonna. "Read him some Dickens or James Joyce. He'll snap out of it."

Aloysius touched his own temples with thumb and pinky and looked away and then up at the ceiling while he watched Chitchee stand up and collate blank sheets of manuscript, even though Chitchee had stuffed other copies of this nothing in various crannies, crevices, and cavities of their old two-story, frame duplex. He didn't need more typing paper. He liked longhand and notebooks. What was she thinking? He had back-ups of the nothing on floppy disks, CDs, Microsoft hotmails to himself, and even postmarked manuscripts (sealed) to his own address as evidence of an intellectual copyright paranoia concerning the intellectual copyright violation of stealing nothing.

Maybe she wanted to hang out. She was lonely. She was *crowded* lonely. Maybe she needed money. Heroin ain't cheap, Chitchee thought . . . labor costs, production, and rents. But wait, the price should be going down. The black market is the one true free market. The black market was where Ayn Rand got all her speed to run off at the mouth, the cheap whore! Maybe LaDonna couldn't even afford the Mexican *black tar* going around. Maybe she got herself addicted to huffing Endust and needed another can, case, or 2200-gallon drum of it.

"LaDonna! Are you sozzled? We'll talk about this later!" said Chitchee quietly in her face. He picked up the "manuscript," stifled it from view, and guiltily stuffed it back into the Manila envelope, conscious of what an imposter and liar he looked like to Aloysius. "You'll have to leave the book store, LaDonna . . . it's my first day on the job . . . now go! Go! Go, go, go, goo, ga, ga . . . you didn't bring any snacks, did you? I'm hungry!"

"Same here!" she said, her hazels dreaming in his for a second then getting all soft and sugary and melting him. "I'm a server next door at Club Miami. Maybe they have pretzels."

"Let me know if they have pretzels," said Chitchee. "I wanted to say something. Something that's been on my mind all morning."

When she spoke, Chitchee noticed little cobweb lines of spit between her red lips. A couple red lines of hair caught in her lipstick, drawn into the cobwebs. He tracked a red hair stuck in her thick eyelashes and removed it.

"I hope they have *Old Dutch* pretzels," he continued. "No, really you have to go. Obviously, we're not good for each other. Did you report me to the federal authorities for attempting a *coup d'état* of the United States government?"

"No," said LaDonna. "I don't think so."

He unfolded the unwanted imposter poster of himself as a Muslim terrorist.

"Does this look familiar?" he asked.

"Is that you when you were a Muslim terrorist at Minnetonka High School?" asked LaDonna, adding a bending, dominant 7th. "Uuuh-oooo-unh. Maybe you're wanted for a high-school reunion and this was the only way they could get your attention."

LaDonna perused the wanted poster up and down and up. She tried not to laugh, but the effort of turning the corners of her mouth downward, backfired in an ambivalent melange of emotion—she might have bitten into an ebullient lemon. Laughing, she stamped her feet, and her whole body shook in a staccato reflex.

"Where's your hijab?" asked LaDonna.

She combusted a rib after saying the word "hijab," doubled over, crossed her thighs briefly as if to prevent a pee pee, and crowed with laughter.

"Whoever wrote that doesn't know what a hijab is!" exclaimed Chitchee.

"I got one too," said LaDonna, straightening her slumped shoulders.

"Hijab?" asked Chitchee.

"No," said LaDonna, reaching into her jean back pocket. "A wanted poster."

They had studied Arabic together, back when she was a twig and had the hips of a tornado—especially noticeable when for years they stayed in bed and conjugated verbs; back when she and he were proud of their sprightly, upright buttocks and vice versa because of all their dancing together. This dancing energy, from her sneaker heels up to her bare-shouldered neckline endowed her with "intrinsic spin." Her body was proud of her body. She looked like a work of moving art, which is why she had studied dance—not to become a student of the dance, but to enjoy dance for its own sake. To her mind, music without dance was the cart without the horse, and she was moving like a cart, since she didn't dance anymore—from drink, drugs, depression, or death, Chitchee didn't know which anymore. Her squint lines had fanned into deltas, which called for sunglassing from among her hundreds of sunglasses. Chitchee opined that the bar of her beauty standards had been set too high, conditioned by her working for Wilhelmina Models and other agencies and modeling for clients like Buffalo Wild Wings, Great Clips, The Gap, Heartbreaker, and Target—they were all casseroled together in his memory. Remittance kids, they wanted to disco dance forever and never grow up. How married they were, in heart and mind united, as LaDonna supported Chitchee's literary career, which came to nothing despite her working stints at Rudolph's Bar-B-Que, Hair Police, and Moxie. She was never happier than when she led Chitchee on a leash to a goth prom on the first Hard Monday at The Saloon. She dressed him. Or undressed him, and off they flew to drink, dance, and dally. The same vegan, gutter punk friends they had met at a storefront dance collective in Seward neighborhood might show up later at Glam Slam (when Prince held court) or Norma Jean's. They wheeled out of Freewheel Bike blazing, read zines at Arise!, picked up free clothes at worker-owned community centers, and attended meetings with remnants of the Revolutionary Anarchist Bowling League—without blinking, they also drank Wanderer's Punches at The Nankin Cafe and liked to wander over to First Avenue and 7th Street Entry to see their friends' bands. Friends seen earlier at Mayday on Chicago were the same friends who later played at The Hexagon or Palmer's, tattooed at the same tattoo parlors like Twin City Tattoo, spun through the same racks at The Electric Fetus, drew the same gremlins at Espresso Royale and Cafetto, protested apartheid at the U., marched against CIA involvement in Central America, and bought electronics at Best Buy—whose founder Richard Schulz boycotted Carousel Square out of pique when the Uptown Association boycotted him (they saw no future for a "Best Buy"). After a demonstration against military aid to Israel at the U., they discussed the Nakba and later the Intifada over drinks at Mr. Nibs, dinner at Matt's Bar, and nightcaps at First Avenue. Agreed that China and Israel practiced abhorrent foreign policies, summed up thus: "If you crush your enemy slowly enough, no one will notice and no one will stop you." Round and round they went in love at co-ops, cafes, collectives, and nightclubs. Mashed up in Chitchee's fond, confused, and sentimental memories were all the people's parties, concerts, trips, and blackouts—not to mention the myriad drug dealers coming and going like envoys from the Spice Islands. Until the day it seemed they were at least ten years older than their friends, they roamed freely, passionately adoring each other while circumnavigating the Twin Cities—their spiritual union two wings of a bird in flight, against the neon-colored pastels of a black-oil, white board Hennepin Avenue, which Chitchee's toothpick memory, attenuated over time, scratched alive.

Donna Jensen—mass, spin, and charge—enchanted Chitchee the moment she sauntered into the Middle Eastern Studies classroom (a thick red comb of curly hair) like a rainbow from another world looking for a chair (the first day sentenced you to that chair and no other according to whatever local custom demanded that in).

"Fuck," exclaimed Chitchee, although he meant "wow." "What are you, a rose garden?"

He thrust his face back in his book, pretending to have been looking at a map of Mecca. His teenage lust throbbed. He blushed dramatically, guiltily. Exposed! Giddy, wobbly, terrified, cringing, and mentally on all fours, he gave her an arresting look of languor that came off like an infatuated halo. He apologized for being so forward, but he had yet to say hello. Trying to open a pack of ten BIC pens proved impossible—teeth gnawing, mouth swallowing plastic—he took out his keys and stabbed for a breach in the plastic. He pulled the plastic apart again. Bursting open, the BIC pens rocketed all over the floor and into various hairstyles and the myriad, identical backpacks.

"Do you need a BIC?" he asked Donna. "First time, every time?"

"Wake up," she said, slapping him across the face and handing him this:

MISSING: HAVE YOU SEEN ME?
LaDonna DeLaVelle D'Galactica aka Donna Jensen aka slut.
Sex: whore. Color of Pubic Hair: red or shaved.
If you have any information concerning her
Don't Hesitate to Call 1-800-BIG-SLUT.

"Your missing poster is much more recent than my wanted poster, and I've never seen this picture of you," said Chitchee.

Chitchee gazed at her face and noticed the aging, and she noticed he noticed. He might have immersed himself in her, but he had to hide that feeling, douse that little flame, and prevent more emotional outbursts—or face the firing squad.

"Wow, you're still beautiful!" exclaimed Chitchee.

(With her thick, red, satin lip-stuck lips looking a smidgen smeary, she had shine.)

"What do you mean *still*?" she slurred and rolled up her lips like scarlet carpets, her hazels, taut and sweaty with determination. "I'm sorry, Ch-chee! I'm not drunk! It's something I swilled next door."

"Something you swilled . . ." said Aloysius, deadpan as a wrestling sportscaster.

"LaDonna, I'm in the middle of my training to be a book store owner. You know it's been my life's dream, if life really is a dream."

"I'm so sorry," said LaDonna, flattening him to her bosoms with a sloppy hug that drew Chitchee close enough to notice zygomatic peach fuzz on her cheeks.

LaDonna raised her hand over her face, flustered, and hid behind the blush she stole from MAC for kicks. LaDonna had been broke since her parents, Jennifer and Wirt Jensen, who had been and hadn't been financing her foibles and delusions of grandeur for years, died; in any case, they had always supported her through her arrests, detoxes, rehabs, relapses, and overdoses—they had tried everything including electroshock, and when that seemed to help, it shocked everyone.

LaDonna's adoptive mother Jen had been married twice before marrying Wirt Jensen. The first marriage ended in annulment; the second in divorce. Her first husband disappeared on her; her second she divorced after he had to serve out a sentence for manslaughter. Jennifer Jensen never talked about either husband—much less her kidnapped twins—with Donna. Jen couldn't understand why rebellious Donna never expressed much love toward her, even though the Jensens had given her a home, an education, and everything it seemed Donna didn't want.

"Chitchee," interposed Aloysius. "Training? Less talk?"

Chitchee's whole body cringed and his whole jaw clenched as if expecting to be showered by a bucket of ice cold lemon Gatorade.

The whole store stared at Chitchee. The prurient eyes of the community judged LaDonna as a prostitute as she backpedaled and turned to walk out the door.

"I will always love you, LaDonna!" he yelled.

Aloysius was startled and seemed to want to take off.

Chitchee released the test balloon of a slow lover's sigh.

Chitchee smiled possibly the fakest, most dentureless smile in *The Guinness Book of World Records*. Then he shrugged sheepishly while Aloysius hoisted the flag of one blond eyebrow expressing unbelief, disbelief, and astonishment. Aloysius didn't like to disrupt the daily schedule.

"That was my agent," Chitchee lied and then he couldn't stop lying. "That was the talk of agency. She also does copy editing. If you pay her enough she'll tell you where the comma goes when it has no place to go and all those technical matters. It goes everywhere, doesn't it? And up in the air after possessives. So who needs her? Ummm . . . am I fired?"

"No," said Aloysius. "You see, I need people in the store. So it looks normal. That's why you're here."

Chitchee blushed at the self-consciousness of his lie. It was the devil in him—the goblin who had a craving for chaos. Red prickly heat flushed his chest, neck, and head. He noticed that Aloysius had noticed the change in Chitchee's color, blushing himself in the cheeks—both trapped in a feedback of embarrassment of embarrassment until Aloysius stabilized his blush. Aloysius's skin renormalized to the texture of a sun-bleached sidewalk, pitted, cracked, and splotched with splotches as from a mulberry tree's fallen mulberries.

"Hey, you know what I thought of now, Aloysius?" asked Chitchee, giving Aloysius a brotherly slap on the back that scared him. "There aren't enough words for *love* in English. That is a niche for a real entrepreneurial wordsmith. By the way, I know my *Hell Hound Chip* isn't *A Canticle for Leibowitz*! Which is even more relevant today. There's this post-Post Toastied world where monks—"

"I don't want to hear about monks," said Aloysius. "Let's get back to training. More work, less talk. Okay, Chitchee?"

"Okay," said Chitchee. "Sorry. Hey, have you read *The Stars, My Destination*? That's a really good one—totally different—this guy Gully Foyle is like Edmond Dantès—"

Aloysius held his hands up like a conductor conducting *Eine Kleine Nachtmusik* with enough gesture to maintain a lively, Mozartean tempo at an outdoor Sommerfest.

Chitchee felt the sweat on his palms precipitate out; now his mind wandered like a break in billiards. The billiard balls skimmed rapidly over the felt pitch but refused to go in any of the six pockets. He wished life were a joke so he could sit there and wait for the punchline.

Aloysius looked helpless and hopeless too. Aloysius had already redirected his *qi* (气) toward the McDonald's on Lagoon Avenue, creatively visualizing a sort of mental mandala with a drive-thru menu on it.

"And everybody *jaunts*, or teleports, with the thought of their destination—"

"Okay," said Aloysius, exhausted. "Why don't we *jaunt* to a break?"

"I agree, it's already too much information, TMI," said Chitchee, giving Aloysius a side hug. "But whoady doady, I'm already learning a lot. I want to learn about marketing and business psychology too. When do we get to the part about supply chains and bitcoins? Is that tomorrow's tutorial? Is it on the syllabus, buddy?"

Okay, thought Chitchee—Aloysius (walking away, looking stunned)—give the Old Hippie a break! A lot on his mind, poor old rocker, never grew out of the '60s. Aloysius had the creaky aura of the Interstate 35W Bridge when its gusset plates groaned under the weight of the construction equipment moved in for the very repairs that destroyed it. And then the lives floated down the Mississippi River. I had better leave the Old Hippie alone! But what smells like French fries? Maybe I could offer to buy Aloysius some French fries . . . Chitchee considered . . . or bake him some cookies . . . I guess I could knit him a reindeer sweater if I knew how . . . maybe buy him a pair of socks. Socks! Remember to buy socks!

Kennedy Kimani, who was almost always downstairs in Self Help, had been reading *Do You! 12 Laws to Access the Power in You to Achieve Happiness and Success* by Russell Simmons when he woke up, overheard the *contretemps* upstairs and casually, or as if casually, padded up the redolent, white pine wood flooring staircase. In his square-shouldered, stiff print shirt Kennedy looked not a little bemused, having caught the tail end of LaDonna's lunar exit. Short black hair, chestnut brown eyes, and square glasses, Kennedy stood on the store's red runner, leaned over the maroon counter, looked over all the books behind the maroon counter, and grinned over the entire store.

"What was all that purported raucosity, Aloysius?" joshed Kennedy. "I bet you could have heard those perturbations in the upper status-sphere!"

"What, Kennedy? Oh that, that was a—a—a—," began Aloysius, pulling down on his blonde mustache with thumb and index.

"It was a nothing," interrupted Chitchee. "She was a little puffed out that we didn't have . . . the . . . the Bunny Yeager *Bettie Page Confidential*—she was looking for."

Kennedy emitted a laugh like an asthmatic walkie-talkie, but with a masking hand over his broad smile of white white big teeth and receding gums.

"Bunny Yeager? Who's that, a striptease test pilot? Single question: Is there any reward money for your capture?" said Kennedy. "I will split the dividends with you right now if there is real legal tinder involved. I mean if the totality of the Uptown vicinity hasn't called the Federal Bureau of Investigations about the reward remunerations already! If their website hasn't crashed!"

"Sir, I'm being stalked, trolled, doxxed, and cut in half. Those wanted posters are bogus! I don't know who is doing that! Hey, what's your name? You know mine," said Chitchee. "Hey, that's an awesome shirt! It's kind of like a batik billboard for can openers in the middle of the Sahara Desert."

"I didn't catch the classical allusions you were academizing and you are obviously cognizant of no little education but: can openers?" said Kennedy, looking surprised, offended, and flattered. "Those *are* East African hummingbirds that eat honey out of honeycombs. *If* you are interested, I can *get you* can openers, or hummingbirds, or honeycombs."

Kennedy grasped Chitchee's outstretched hand.

"Oh, I get it," said Chitchee. "The hummingbirds use the can openers to open up the honeycombs! Birds! So sweet and so clever!"

"Sure," said Kennedy, taken aback, but not *too* taken aback as to fall backward and jump back up, "and I am *going* back downstairs to resuscitate *my* research *into* the realms *of* motivational psychology in your *self*-help files!"

(Kennedy's sentences often had stresses on the unexpected off-beats.)

"Wow, Aloysius, how can you get anything done around here with all these great customers?" asked Chitchee, turning back to face the boss Aloysius.

Aloysius looked speechless. His forget-me-not blue eyes forgot themselves in clouds of blue in a blue sky.

"Eliot's: the very existence of a book store affords us hope, eh buddy?" said Chitchee to Aloysius. "Wow, what if it had been *Forty Four Quartets* instead of *Four*—that would have been stupendous. Like late Beethoven or the Bartok six. Hey, more quartets, Tommy! I'm sorry Aloysius. I'm wasting your time. Maybe I'm not the right guy for this job. Maybe you should hire a woman. A black woman. A black, non-gendered, trans-Jewish, aboriginal Muslim, one-eyed grandmother who likes old hippies and science fiction. Wait, that's almost me!"

He felt so absolutely hateful he considered turning himself in to the FBI for whatever crime they needed a criminal for. The square floor of his roundabout Self fell out from under his feet, and a rapidly spinning whirling vortex siphoned out his squelched spirit: "*Je suis le Ténébreux, le Veuf, l'Inconsolé.*"

"I let you down, Chief," cried Chitchee as if hanging from a barred window, pet lobster on a leash.

An ambivalent smiling frown wavered at the corners of his mouth. His whole nose stung inside and turned red. His eyes crimson were. Mucus dripped from his nostrils. The play of muscles on his face caused an avalanche of irresistible grief that resisting made worse. His event horizon of suicide pulled flesh and follicle toward his ultimate destruction and the erasure of all his information . . . as if he had any knowledge of anything! At the end of all the education, his mind was a blank slate.

"No, you're fine, we're fine, we have to stay on track," said Aloysius as if picking up the pieces of a dropped tip jar broken by a hard-tiled floor. "Okay, good job!"

"Oh, okay!" said Chitchee. "I should write a book about this place! And you'll be in it, buddy! And we will all be in it, which we are anyway, you know, like 'Penny Lane,' and I could even call it Penny Lane Books. A book store with nothing but Beatle books."

This remark brought the sky blue back into Aloysius's Arctic Circle sky eyes.

"*Penny Lane, Penny Lane* . . ." Aloysius hummed along. "Maybe we should listen to some Beatles."

"I would never argue with that," said Chitchee, completely back to high-octane normal—and so quickly!

Now he could appreciate Aloysius's outstanding qualities as a human being. He seemed as wise as Solomon or Shackleton. He thought he could worship him already.

"I remember when *Penny Lane* came out," said Aloysius with a note of melancholy. "Those were the days of honey, music, and sunshine. Oh, I miss my old reel-to-reel TEAC, Bose 901s, Kenwood receiver, Garrard turntable, Shure cartridge, and then the Pickering stylus. In those days you had to pick the Pickering. Then the Dolby. Not sure what that Dolbys did do. But Bose 901s went well with the Lebanese, Altec Lansings went with the Moroccan, and Klipsch woofers gelled well with the Afghan. Everything seemed so light and breezy and—"

"Go ahead and vent, old hippie," said Chitchee. "I'm here for you!"

"What? Oh, yeah," said Aloysius, second-looking at Chitchee. "Ah, and my old friends! You know, Chitchee, it's almost like the fading of our jeans the way our old friendships fade away."

"No, it isn't, what are you talking about?" asked Chitchee, surprised. "Once you know a person, feel free to call him up anytime at any period in your life! That's what I say. What's the worst that can happen? You get reported to the FBI?"

This mood swing scared Aloysius, and he suspected Chitchee of manic depression, his diagnosis based on "Manic Depression" by Jimi Hendrix. What else could wrench Chitchee so far out of joint and then wrench him back in a trice?

Aloysius staggered back to the CD player and internalized: "All three managers must really hate me. Are they, are they playing Merry Pranksters? This Chitchee *can't* be the guy they recommended. They are gaslighting me. Damn it, I love the guys. They know I'd give them all the T-shirts in my closet off my back, but you can't win, you can't whine, you can't unwind, you can't even break wind, what *can* you do but rack up more debt? And it has come to this?"

ALOYSIUS AALGAARD, BOOKSELLER

Chitchee decided to give his two week notice. It was time. There comes a time in a man's life when he realizes he must change. When is that time? Never. When Chitchee was down, he knew he wasn't ever going to be hired again anywhere, or if he was hired, he'd get fired, or if he didn't get fired, he'd get tired, and if he got too tired he wouldn't get paid, and if he didn't get paid, he'd get evicted, if evicted he'd be homeless, if homeless in Minnesota, EMTs would find him hugging his knees, frozen like Captain Scott as recorded by Cherry-Garrard (*The Worst Journey in the World*) . . . so bleak here too . . . so bleak . . . winters are beyond the woods of words . . . beyond screams . . . beyond the whisper of a tear. Maybe he could get a good recommendation from Aloysius for a job in the Department of Transportation driving stuff. One thing he could *not* do was: leave his good friends—Aloysius, Noel, Snorri, and Saami—in the lurch. Nor could Chitchee let down his whole friends' friends' network of friends, fractalizing like the branches of hundred year-old oak trees as they grew toward the Sun every Spring with more flowering buds—while Chitchee was carried off like pollen, flowing in the wind of a dream.

All his co-workers were geniuses, and he needed to support them. Saami was a pop culture, purple-socked wizard. He had heard of every comic book in the world. Snorri was the next John Keegan (*The Face of Battle*), because he had a unique grasp on military history, and he had the self-discipline to write volumes of Bancroft winners. Evidently he had chosen not to. Noel's IQ was up there where the crows fly. Witness his phenomenal zingers—his aphoristic put downs to all comers in the store for a political fray, e. g.: "Of course, man is a socialist animal. That's how we evolved. Cooperation, not corporation. I'd like to see a *libertarian* bring down a wooly mammoth all by himself without a rifle. And then eat it, all by himself, while the rest of his tribe sits hungrily saying, 'That's his! He earned it all by himself! It's his private property now.'"

Saami and Snorri butt heads like Jefferson and Hamilton. Noel was John Adams. Chitchee was the ambassadorial, beaver-brained Ben Franklin. Aloysius reminded Chitchee of George Washington. The Washington of Flexner's *The Indispensable Man*. Aloysius had crossed the Delaware of the used book trade; Aloysius inspired his staff through the winter doldrums of Valley Forge with Minnesota Iron Man patience.

Furthermore, Aloysius, *mutatis mutandis*, patronized the arts like a Barmecide and was as magnificent as Suleiman in rewarding Minneapolis with his cultural artifacts. Chitchee often compared Saami with H. P. Lovecraft, Snorri with Captain Sir Richard Burton, and Noel with Louis Pasteur.

"Hypothetically speaking, buddy," began Aloysius, having returned with an assertive manner, "what if . . . okay pop quiz time! Okay: A customer is offended by a book on the shelves he deems hurtful or harmful. What are you going to do?"

"Remove it from the shelves," said Chitchee excitedly, "wait until the customer leaves, then put it back in a different section! Aha!"

Aloysius slightly nodded in approval, reluctant to say aloud *anything* for fear of evidence against him.

"O," said Aloysius in a non-committal, nonchalant tenor, "kay."

"Yes, okay good job, I'm doing a good job, buddy, and you're doing a good job, buddy," whispered Chitchee to himself, imagining BookSmart morphed into a second Santa Fe Institute where physicists like Murray Gell-Mann rested their brains on chaise lounges by an aquamarine swimming pool of Tuscan sky, Mexican sun, and cold-blooded cacti, while they sipped sugar-saturated iced teas and dreamed up new quarks and jaguars.

"Hey Aloysius, pop quiz: aren't we going to train to music?" asked a re-inspired Chitchee, elated at how in tune he was with the new boss. "My agent kind of threw me for a loop and I sorta froze like a snowman! A 'snow-broth' filled my veins."

"Been there, buddy," said Aloysius.

"Frozen?" mused Chitchee, daydreaming off into space.

"Never been frozen," said Aloysius, his trusty *Magical Mystery Tour* in hand, which he set aside to forget about later.

This was a good chance for Aloysius to show his leadership, West Coast style, easygoing as flip flops, surfer shirts, and Orange Sunshine. Chitchee thought of Apple's Jobs.

"I've never been frozen, Chitchee. But I've been *buried* in snow. The other snow. Oh, for the good old high days. The sixties.

Followed by the seventies. I think it went in that order, hah! Yeah, ditching, dodging, dumping on the *draft*, getting showered with pepper spray by the *man*, and driving the old brown bomber, the o-o-o-old Econoline—the *fuck bus* all through the 70s. I went on the hippie trail. It wasn't a *Lonely Planet* back then! Istanbul to Bombay. What hospitality! So many great experiences! So many great people everywhere! Back when everybody loved Americans despite hundreds of CIA plots to cut their countries' throats. As Mary Hopkins once said: *those were the days my friend we thought*—"

"Cut," said Chitchee abruptly when he saw Aloysius mist over, "enough!"

Chitchee had welled up too, his eyes laughing tears. And he wiped the corners of his eyes with the heel of his right palm, bit its spandrel, and added lugubriously: "That's when you could buy cocaine with S & H Green Stamps."

"Seriously? I don't know about that," said Aloysius, muzzling a frown, his glabella ridged. "But I heard of a guy who bought ibogaine with Gold Bond stamps. Hold on while I go have a smoke. We sure had our dreams. Dreams I'll never see, I guess."

Chitchee grabbed Aloysius by the elbow and said face to face:

"Hey, bud: *you're* the dreamweaver! You're the one bud wiser!"

"Sure, Chitchee," said Aloysius, doing a ¾ double take. "Sure thing! That's what I tell myself every time I wake up in the middle of a dream. Like last night—I was driving naked on a snowmobile to Winnipeg to see Hot Tuna, chased through underground tunnels by Wonder Wart-Hog—and then I noticed I was pregnant in front of a draft board in Alberta. When I tried to explain—"

"Let me guess," interrupted Chitchee, "your teeth fell out."

"How did you know?" asked Aloysius, looking as if the steering wheel had just come off.

"Dreams are hackneyed like that," said Chitchee. "Dreams don't mean a thing! They never come true! Unless . . . unless it was a message from the future! Let me see your teeth!"

Aloysius, feeling cut off and sliced like a sausage, flinched.

"It's my guess, you've been flying too close to the sun," said Chitchee, "and that's why I'm here. To catch you when you fall."

Aloysius thought the new hire a bit contrarian for his first day on the job.

"Don't you wish," said Aloysius, himself sounding contrite, conciliatory, and benign with second chances, "you were 20 again?"

"Never!" said Chitchee with a bit of tap dance. "That was the old me. THIS IS THE NEW ME! I think you've got it backwards."

Aloysius looked offended, shocked, and as if a tiny green lizard landed on his shoulder then turned into nothing. He stepped outside to escape the book store's perplexing new hire. Zalar Gossick, looking as if he might parachute in behind the DMZ with a barrel roll, slipped in behind Aloysius.

"*The snows of yesteryear*," said Chitchee. "Whatever became of Fat Margot? I wonder if Francois Villon would have been a coke head if he were in the Allman Brothers. The Almond Brothers—what if all their eyes were almond-shaped? *Oh no, not you!*"

Zalar was blonde, crew-cut haired, and six-foot three. Muscular as a farmhand who hurled bales of hay all day into flatbeds, Zalar pulled a face with a screwed-up expression stamped into it like that of a bull's with a nose ring in a bull ring. He looked sketched by a pissed-off Picasso: two snort pits on his upturned nose, green eyes not the same or level, and the torso of a broad-chested auroch in a black, knit Lacoste shirt, tucked in tightly. Zalar wore a thick leather belt and its brass buckle was a tool-and-died, goblet skull of Satan. Girdling his flexed biceps, his votive tattoos of Baphomet's beheaded head proclaimed his allegiance to an incubus, a succubus, or some sort of bus full of Luciferian oafs hog-riding to Sturgis, South Dakota in a mythological, motorcycle facsimile of the *Rape of the Sabine Women*.

Chitchee had a history with Zalar, which Zalar acknowledged with a wry smirk wrapped around Chitchee's head like a boa constrictor hijab. Chitchee responded with a vacantly terse flat smile to suggest he didn't know Zalar from Zoot Sims. Zalar wandered around the store as if he knew where he was going, but not exactly; meanwhile, Chitchee, trapped behind the maroon counter, felt poisoned by Kremlin gremlins and thrown into a cauldron of boiling tar. His armpits were leaking.

Chitchee remembered the smell of Zalar's peculiar body odor like frying olives in olive oil.

Ten years ago or so, Zalar like a big, white-walled galoot boarded a #6 bus. It was a hot, humid, downtown, simmering, summer day on a #6 bus. A torrid, road-rage of a day on an overheating #6 bus moaned toward an oven-hot Uptown in the mirage ahead. Zalar sat down in the back next to Chitchee. Zalar had on a wet, white, slightly ribbed, spaghetti T-shirt. He flicked the sweat from his armpit hair into Chitchee's face.

"You know what, faggot? I was raped last night and it was a beautiful experience and now I'm in love with my attacker, and I'm going to meet him tonight and then bring him back and introduce him to you, his name is Jack . . . okaaay . . . faggot?"

He unctuously wiggled his tongue at Chitchee. He squeezed Chitchee's butt when Chitchee stood up. Chitchee stepped shakily off the bus humiliated. Humiliated for *not* confronting his attacker, because he had paved the way for even more bullying. Finkle was right! Finkle was street smart! Why wasn't Chitchee appreciative of his own father, who refused to talk to him now? His father had drilled him to face the bullies; indeed, Finkle drummed it into Chitchee's "weak, spineless head" the need to defend his "queer self" against the billions of bullies in the world. Return with relish a black eye for a black eye, because the world was full of billions of bullies lining up to clobber Chitchee into clabber. All the world could see Chitchee was a fearling, a sissy, and the most cowardly coward cowering in the closet who ever cowed. Although, at Finkle's invitation one more abusive day—bam— Chitchee *did* floor Finkle, a right jab to his father's captious mouth—Chitchee felt none the better for it. Despite the pain and surprise, Chitchee felt that his father truly loved him. Later, Chitchee regretted smashing his father's face in—he had let himself down and would pay the price forever in self-pity.

The whole sweltering bus observed Chitchee's abject cowardice with the broadening silence of disapproval. Maybe the hot, humid blanket of sweat draped over everything affected the bystanders' judgment, but it always rankled Chitchee that no one had intervened, not even Lily Holmgren the perennial flower of the #6.

Some years after that, Chitchee traipsed into the US Bank for the ATM in the after hours lobby. Zalar was in front of him in line, and when Zalar was done and walked away, Chitchee saw Zalar's ATM card in the machine; Chitchee pushed it back in and tried some pin numbers, seeking damages out of court for mental torment.

"Looking for something?" presumed Zalar over Chitchee's shoulder.

"Oh, is this yours?" asked Chitchee, handing the debit card to Zalar.

For some reason Zalar refrained from killing him with the nearest blunt instrument, which was a potted rabbit fern from Carousel Square. On yet another occasion, Chitchee witnessed Zalar shoplifting a book on Charles Manson at Odegaard's book store in Carousel Square. In a corner, Zalar removed the RF tag with some difficulty so that Zalar didn't see Chitchee. Zalar stuffed the book in the small of his back, between his blue jeans and his black, sleeveless torn Skullfuck Supreme Ugliness Tour T-shirt. By coincidence, no one paid attention because freshman Senator Paul Wellstone was in the store, which caused the clerks at the register to flop around like Muppets in the hopes of meeting him at point of purchase.

Strung out, Chitchee vibrated with fear, whispered nervously to himself, bit his hand, and stepped up to Odegaard's checkout counter:

"Hey, Mr. Ernie," said Chitchee, leaning forward toward the sales clerk whose name plate he focused on. "There's a guy in the store shoplifting. He's about six feet sixty. In jeans and black sleeveless T-shirt. Buff, biceps. Blonde, crew cut. Blue eyes, like Bud Grant's but with corkscrews of hate twirling out of them at you."

"Bud Grant is here too?" said Ernie. He bingoed. "Hey, you guys, Bud Grant is here too!"

"Wait, no," said Chitchee. "Start over. There's a shoplifter in the store who looks like a minotaur. His face has a smeared-around look—like his eyes are frying in a frying pan, off kilter. *And I just saw him stuff Helter Skelter by Vincent Lugosi in his pants! The mass market version!* He looks like a minotaur! That's what he looks like! How many fucking minotaurs can there be in Odegaard's at any given moment?"

"Do you mean the guy right behind you?" asked Ernie, looking over Chitchee's head.

Chitchee didn't even turn around. Then he did.

And faced Zalar, flicking more sweat from his armpit into Chitchee's face.

"No, it was some other minotaur, that's not the right minotaur," said Chitchee in a hurried voice, motioning to go. "*My* minotaur actually had red hair and freckles. Big box ears like Prince Charles—little guy—about three feet tall, yay high. What time is it? I have to see a man about a bull. There's my bus! The #6!"

"Are you looking for a book," asked Chitchee, "on minotaurs? This book store is a labyrinth. And all labyrinths are book stores."

Chitchee bit his hand like a bat, but remained poker-faced.

"Don't I know you from somewhere?" asked Zalar, daggers of irony flying through the air.

"My name is Mansur al-Hallaj," said Chitchee. "*Ana 'l-Haqq*. And your name?"

Zalar mocked grinningly with a smug, tacit conceit:

"My name is Farag the Pure One," said Zalar, dripping with irony. "My God is the Avenger, Allah, and I owe you one, you little snitch bitch."

"You don't owe me anything," said Chitchee. "Except maybe a big fat kiss, sexy fascist."

"Why do you need to know my name anyway?" said Zalar with a dying question mark.

"I don't!" said Chitchee sharply. "Because I already know it! It's Zalar the Minotaur! We met on the bus once, then at US Bank, and then again at Odegaard's. We've met so many times we must be relatives from parallel universes."

"I was wondering," said Zalar, looking a little skeptical concerning the ultimate sanity of his interlocutor, "if you bought and sold Family Photo Albums."

"No," said Chitchee, laughing at Zalar. "Aren't all the Family Photo Albums nowadays uploaded to MySpace, safely locked away for future generations?"

"MySpace can suck my dick! I think I see some albums over there by the planners and diaries," said Zalar. "Enough of the bullcrap. Have you bought any used Family Photo Albums recently? YES OR NO!"

"Zalar is *clue-less*," said Chitchee behind his hand to no one. "Pass it on!"

"A used photo album?" continued Chitchee, arching backward when Zalar filled Chitchee's field of vision with a pointing finger, a leer, and a flick of the tongue like a Peavey hook. "No, a used Family Photo Album would be like a used family condom! Try Magers & Quinn Booksellers for used family condoms! If that's your bag."

"Yeah, right, that's my bag, groover!" said Zalar, smirking. "Fuck you!"

Zalar pounded his right fist into the counter to smash it into toothpicks, cratering the cheap plywood, and he charged with his heart in his ruby red throat out the front door.

Chitchee's heart pounded like a giant tick.

"Why did I say that?" repented Chitchee, looking a fright and around for an *ifrit*. "And how can that big galoot know the first thing about the peaceful religion of Islam? He's got it all upside down. He must be getting it off the Internet. Isn't that where you get everything upside down?"

No worse timing could have unraveled Chitchee. Panic surrounded him with premonitions and possible false positives. Omens, portents, bad signs. Demons of anxiety triggered migraines in Chitchee, and the last migraine he sustained had thrown him off his high horse and nearly killed him with so much pain he froze. He heard the earwigs tunneling through his brain, humming to themselves the earwigs they heard in their brains. He sneezed and heard "On Top of Old Smoky." He was on top of Old Smoky, waiting for the hangman's hood over his eyes, seeing floaters, and feeling unready, unsteady, and gone when he blinked.

"Good job," a thankful Chitchee babbled aloud to himself with gratitude. "No Family Photo Albums! No! Okay, so I lied about LaDonna. Had to, frozen as a snowman, need a job. Okay, go ahead and kill me. You'll get the chair this time. And two freebies for *Black Swan* before you go. Bully beef! I better go back to my crib or shut my rat-trap's rap-trap. God, I have a mouth like the Mississippi River. And Old Moon River. *Ta* and *Sin* for *tawasin*. I keep on babbling like a spring brook . . . *fitrah* is my original nature . . . and *paid in books*?"

And *paid in books* wasn't on the *tabula rasa* thought Chitchee blankly watching Aloysius smoke outside in clouds of emphysema. All the profits are going into his Carousel cigarettes! Uhhhwagh. No one mentioned that. Snorri and Saami! You guys! Noel! Now what? What kind of friends are you guys? I've been duped by everybody! Oh, I get it, Lord Jim here with a checkered past—a marked man, doomed. Toss me a pace-maker, horseman, pass by! The heart surgeries at Abbott Northwestern: he saw the suspended, nitrile, electric blue gloves of Dr. Egbert Verbrugghen above him, above him like a Damoclean scalpel. Chitchee, desperate for fresh air, hawked up mucus he had to gargle back first, and then he remembered his debts, his bank account, and his bills. Calm down, friend, I can't quit, but I can commit suicide. He circled down on a stool, placed his head on the maroon counter, and cried the loneliest cry in existence. He had been alive for a million years in a cage and then was sentenced to another million.

He ransacked his black JanSport backpack to find his meds: vasodilators and beta blockers for consequent hypertension. He once could have begged LaDonna's parents, Wirt and Jen, for financial assistance. Wirt, despite looking like a mouse with mutton chops, was a decent and kindly diffident soul, whose milquetoast glasses belied the engineering genius of a true tinkerer like Claude Shannon. Wirt owned several patents (which had since expired), including the Weatherball for Northwestern National Bank (which burned down in 1982). That had been inspired by a drunken salesman Wirt met at the soda fountain of a roadside restaurant in Hibbing called The Lingonberry Inn. LaDonna's mother Jen had since died of a brain aneurysm, trowel in hand, planting a potpourri of wildflowers in her backyard garden. Wirt survived her by a year. Then he died penniless in their basement—tinkering with a battery-operated walleye that sang old Mississippi Delta blues songs—of an ischemic stroke and heart attack, surrounded by battery-operated walleyes singing Mississippi Delta blues songs.

Chitchee had so many medical bills from Fairview U. of M., he avoided his mailbox like the Black Death. Health and Human Services stuffed his mailbox slot with notices that enrolled him, disenrolled him, billed him, killed him, gave him life, and took it away depending on which letter he read first. When he did venture near his death box, he tapped it like a watermelon; a thud, and he knew something was in there (like the thirty notices for the monthly EBT food displacement); a hollow sound, and he laughed to open and see the empty death box, and he danced like an Aztec prince from the overly lived-in, livid lobby to the pre-Mercator-mapped, gloriously weatherless day of *no mail*.

Recently Chitchee warded off a slew of anxiety attacks, rashes, flu, migraines, impacted earwax, gum disease, nervous leg, vertigo, colitis, toothache that turned into a migraine and then back into a toothache, heart murmurs, and two impacted balls of earwax in the same ear—not to mention an ostinato drumming in the background of his forebrain like a tinnitus lowered three octaves. What gnawed like an old file the most was the uncertain financial future before him from which he had been mathematically eliminated. *He* was the unknown that dropped out of the equation. Then the equation dropped out of the equation. Helpless without a focused LaDonna's hand-tuning his dials, he had to learn to walk on both legs every day without her.

"'Poverty is my pride,' said Muhammad," announced Chitchee. "I deserve poverty for believing I was book smart enough to know anything! What do I know? How could I? Given the gravity of our situation, even Isa's message had to travel parabolically to reach us. Maybe ol' Shlomo can tell us. Peace be upon him too."

"Well, do you at least know how to find a book for me? Since you are working in a book store now?" asked Beda Holmgren. "Don't ask me to ask Saami! He broke his friendship contract with me, which he signed and notarized, when I heard he talked to a Republican! I think he is a mole for the Great Boyg! Now I have to cut him before he cuts me."

"What's the book about?" asked Chitchee.

"I've been looking all over for the book, but I can't remember the title!"

Beda used to work with Saami at Half Price Books on Miracle Mile in St. Louis Park and discoursed her "discoursees" at long length, at work, about neuro-programming, media mind control, celebrity covens who ate babies, and various cabals of the Illuminati who shanghaied runaways fresh off Sunset Strip, forwarded them to Luzon in the Philippines as tinned and canned corned beef, and all she got for it was being called a blabbermouth.

"It's out of the true-life story," said Beda, "of a Mind Control Slave named Cathy who was alternately raped by Senator Robert Byrd and Boxcar Willie—even though the CIA used to store lizards in her vagina. And then she finally healed herself of the PTSD by snorting coke with Manuel Noriega on his yacht. And then it starts . . . getting . . . really . . . w-*eird*."

"Oh, *Trance Formation in America*!" said Chitchee.

"That's it!" said Beda. "Thank you so much, believe me, you have saved my life! I love you!"

"All our books on the Deep State," said Chitchee, delighted that he could be of some use, "are in the back under the hidden cameras of the Deep State in the corner."

"Why would you say that? Why?" asked Beda, her eyes narrowing and joining in the middle to form one big eye. "Are you chipped and programmed to say hurtful things? I don't care about that book now, you evil slimeball!"

"Oh Venerable Beda," said Chitchee. "Is that any way to talk? It's my first day on the job. You're going to make me look like a 'sota jerk!"

Silenced, Beda Holmgren showed her lower teeth to the despondent Chitchee.

"The bathroom mirror better not be two-way!"

Beda stalked off and bumped into Aloysius, who had lingered outside to talk to Nancy Newman, a regular customer passing by on her way late to Orchestra Hall for another Finnish symphonic poem, Grieg's *Holberg Suite*, Dvorak's *Bagatelles*, and a *Firebird*, and then Aloyius pivoted toward the panhandling Hawk Eye. They reminisced in perfect echoes about the old Weatherball on Northwestern National Bank; that too had symbolized a Golden Age that would never return—no matter how much god-prospecting you did. That too meant the good times had rolled. We were entering the Age of Kali, they said. Without the Weatherball on Northwestern National Bank they agreed. Soon humankind, unable to forecast the weather, would drift into an age of evil so dark it would flicker out. Earth would be a giant Easter Island of cursed, clueless termites eating the entire planet down to the shambles of brambles and the gristle of thistle. Eco death. Sad as it was, they laughed. That's what we devils deserved! Disaster can be hilarious. God laughed.

"Aloysius, your new employee was quite rude to me!" said Beda.

"What did he say?" asked a concerned Aloysius.

"It's not what he said, it's how he said it in such a little mockingbird tone! I am going to take my or mine and Minerva's business to a real book store!"

"Is there one?" asked Aloysius, asking a shrugging Hawk Eye who avoided her eyes and triumphant swagger toward Magers & Quinn, Booksellers, one block south toward Lakewood Cemetery. "Aren't they all pretty much imaginary?"

"Aloysius," said Beda. "Being nice is not enough. It's all about community. Let that sink in, you class traitor. ABOLISH AUTHORITY NOW!"

"It sounds like she's bluffing," said Hawk Eye.

"She'll be back," said Aloysius. "They always come back and I always take them in."

"And I'm never coming back! Oh yeah, and call my mom back, dork!" yelled Beda over her shoulder. "She has a crush on your sorry ass!"

Chitchee would have to ask for Emergency Assistance to help with his rent. At this rate, Thanksgiving would be at Sharing is Caring with Mary Jo Kopechne and Christmas would be at St. Stephen's with Mary Magdalene. He'd be filmed by a Skip Skipperton News Crew and directed to sob into his sobby mashed potatoes, shower tears with heart-breaking tokens of pity over his peas, drop swelling tears of compassion over his turkey, and weep thanks to Jesus while crotching pecan pies to take back to the cold, isolated, and moldy floor of the downtown Salvation Army. If he couldn't swallow his pride, he sure could drink a helluva lot of humility. Aha! Better write that one down Chitchee thought then forgot about it.

After Aloysius smoked, he looked rejuvenated. Gung ho, ready to go, he returned juvenescently to rejuvenate the training session. Customers appeared in the store, jaunted in like Gully Foyles. Randy opened the front door.

"Hey, Aloysius, have you read all those books yet?" asked Randy.

Randy did a double take, punctuated the air with his walking stick, and gave Chitchee an air poke.

"Wha-a-a-h? You work here now?" asked Randy. "I thought you were writing some fucked-up book about some fucked-up squirrels who fucked up in outer space or something. Or was it an all-hamster musical about the Hormel Meat Strike? Shouldn't you be dodging the FBI by now? I couldn't get through to them this morning. I think their website crashed. What about you, did you have any luck with those fucking assholes? If there is any reward money, you can bet your bottom dollar they already embezzled it."

"I didn't call the FBI," said Chitchee, "because I'm not too excited at the thought of a life on the run, criss-crossing through underground networks and winding up in Morocco without the proper luggage or toothpaste."

Torg On shuffled in, legally blind, no bigger than a June bug. He wore Medical Assistance-sponsored, box-framed casements for eyeglasses.

"Oh! Well!" said Randy, high on something. "Then welcome to the Hotel Minnesota! Let me give you a piece of advice, Aloysius! Never give a Viking an axe!"

"Hi, Aloysius! How's tricks?" cut in Torg On.

The BookSmart staff had dubbed Torg On: "The Counter-Klingon."

The Counter Klingon was a retired Hennepin county clerk living on social security, who gleaned aluminum cans for resale, dragged them shop to shop in Carousel Square, bogarted the check-out lane with his Bogart cigar, and looked like a crushed can himself.

"You must be Torg the Counter Klingon," said Chitchee. "I've heard all about you! The guys make fun of you all the time! In a fun way."

"Yesterday, I found a lodestone of Big Band albums in Braille," said Torg to anybody who would listen. "It was at a lady's garage sale down the street," continued Torg, unbuttoning his thrifted, brown leather jacket and brown, floppy-eared, fur-lined, trapper's hat, "and there I was . . ."

"So . . ." said Chitchee. "There you were . . . standing there . . . go on . . ."

". . . standing there thinking, I've got to have the entire swing set. The entire swing set!"

Nothing.

"Look, kid," said Torg, "there are moments in life that make you savor the bad things with the good things."

"There are?" said Chitchee. "Like when?"

"Like when that lady at the garage sale," said Torg, "reminded me of a sweetheart I once had who didn't like my playing the Duke all hours of the night. So I got on the next train out of Kansas City so fast my suitcases were out of breath when we got to Cleveland."

Nothing.

Aloysius had greeted Torg so many times, the greeting had lost its meaning, and now it was understood. He'd heard all the Torg jokes before. But Aloysius hadn't the spite to say:

"Haven't we had this conversation before?"

"Why did you go to Cleveland? Family there?" asked Chitchee. "Let me guess! You had another broad there waiting for you, but when you found out the dame didn't like Benny Goodman, you hopped the next red ball to Detroit to play with your own licorice stick."

"Do you work here?" asked Torg.

Chitchee absorbed himself in the stench of Torg the Counter Klingon, who carried upon his person a wrapped turd of a cigar from Carousel Tobacco in Carousel Square. He sensed that Torg expected to be waited on.

"Let me guess! You crave recognition of some kind," said Chitchee.

"Oh, you sense that do you?" asked Torg. "It's all about respect!"

"What's that odor? Have you been tarring roofs in North Carolina all day?" asked Chitchee. "Oh, it's a cigar! I thought for a second you crapped in your pants. All about respect! What kind of a hand-rolled cigar is that? And where did you get all those crazy-cool, crushed aluminum cans? You should get a Great Dane to guard those! And ride a Shetland pony. Actually, what you need is *The Art and Science of Dumpster Diving*, a Great Dane, and a Shetland pony."

"Chitchee?" said Aloysius, realizing that Chitchee had an attention disorder. He flitted after whatever tinsel caught his eye. He had the focus of a minnow. "Chitchee? Training? Uhhhwagh? Over here?"

"Who is this new guy?" puzzled aloud Torg.

Torg looked surprised that someone like Chitchee might want to spark up a conversation on *anything* with *anybody* at *any* given drop of the hat—*especially Torg!*

Fjard Gardet, the loan officer from US Bank, nosed in the front door past Torg who saw only the smudges of Fjard's dyed-black short hair, black mustache, Aviator shades, cargo shorts, and black Polo shirt.

"Do you like Big Band music?" Torg asked Chitchee.

"Yeah, how many jazz musicians does it take to play 'Summertime?'" asked Chitchee.

"Evidently all of them!" riffed Torg.

"Everybody has heard my jokes! You know, we might have a Gershwin bio, and I know we have *Lush Life*, the Strayhorn book, used," said Chitchee to Torg. "We might have the new Van Morrison bio: *Lush for Life*."

" . . . uhh Chitchee . . . over here?" said Aloysius. "Always take the customer to the shelf! That's the cardinal's rule!"

"Aloysius?" asked Fjard Gardet. "W. E. B. Griffin?"

"Downstairs somewhere, Fjard," said Aloysius. "Where was I?"

"Always take the customer to the shelf," said Chitchee.

"*Always take the customer to the shelf.* Oh yeah! Maybe he'll buy something else he sees there, if we don't have the book he asked for," continued Aloysius, "even if (cough, cough hrrrgghhkk!) he doesn't want it or will never read it in a million years!"

"Whoazy doazy, that *is* gumption!" said Chitchee.

"Tricks o' the book trade, buddy, you pick them up over time. Don't rush in trying to learn all of them though. If you're too good, you'll gut the store. And we won't have anything to sell," continued Aloysius, asphyxiated to a whisper, to no longer breathing at all, and to turning a corpse-like shade of Nile green. "I'll be . . . right (aaaaggghkqkqkqk) . . . back!"

Chitchee didn't get the economic sense of not wanting to "gut the store." Wouldn't an increase in the velocity of book turnover increase the book sales volume? This was sort of the lesson Chitchee took away from *The General Theory of Employment, Interest and Money*.

"Have you read Keynes?" Chitchee asked Aloysius.

Aloysius grabbed the counter and tried to stop gagging, eyes gooping with water.

"Are you okay?" continued Chitchee, slapping his BookSmart boss smartly on the back. "Are you okay? Do you know where you are? What's your name? How many Presidents can you name in order? Who was the Secretary of the Treasury under John Quincy Adams? What was the historical relationship between the Revocation of the Edict of Nantes and the Peace of Westphalia, if any?"

"I'm okay, okay?" Aloysius said, looking terrified and double-crossed. "Uhhhwagh. No, never read Keynes. Did he write anything recently?"

"Well, no," said Chitchee coldly. "In the long run he died."

Speechless Aloysius seized up. He motioned toward the cash register. He clutched his throat. He wobbled as if rocking a 14-foot Alumacraft by standing up too fast. Chitchee flashed back to a Red Cross training class and drew a blank. How did he ever pass muster? True, he knew how to save the neck of a truncated plastic dummy. He would do his lamoid best with what skill sets he had. If Aloysius were to collapse like a cardboard box on Chitchee's first day, the result would be a catastrophic engram of survivor guilt.

"Don't worry, I can do a Heimlicher, buddy!" said Chitchee. "I read about it in an old *Merck Manual*."

Chitchee bear-hugged Aloysius from behind. Chitchee clasped his hands around the jean-jacketed sexagenarian and jerked upward in quick, short tugs, violently bruising several bones in the big kahuna's rib cage.

"Ah! Ah! AHHHH!" yelled Aloysius.

Out jumped a malformed Carousel cigarette from the gullet and gob of Aloysius, his *square* parachuting to the redolent, white pine wood flooring.

"Just in the nic-o-tine," said Chitchee, buoyantly looking around for a cheerful audience.

"I knew I was missing one," said Aloysius, picking up the remains of the fallen Carousel cigarette. He pocketed the mournful remainder (carefully so as not to break it) in his jean jacket pocket (on the left), then buttoned it with a firm hook.

"No use throwing away perfectly good tobacco. I'll dry it off and hand-roll it later."

"Yesirree, Boss," said Chitchee, "that ain't hay!"

The mere sight of a Carousel cigarette incited Aloysius to smoke a cigar store, so he excused himself from the training session for another smoke break, which caused him to cat-walk toward Torg the Counter Klingon. Aloysius's big Adidas, like cats' paws, deftly carried him eastward; his Carousel cigarette, he hoped, issued him a safe conduct and free pass through his own store.

"Excuse me, Torg," said Aloysius.

"You wanted to get by?" asked Torg.

"No," said Aloysius. "I wanted to see if you were listening."

"Listening to what?" asked Torg.

Fjard Gardet had ascended the staircase empty-handed and approached Chitchee behind the counter. He looked at Chitchee as if Chitchee had been painted on a museum wall.

"I couldn't find it," he said to Chitchee.

"Then we don't have it," said Aloysius over his shoulder.

"Is there anything else I can help you not find?" pleaded Chitchee.

"Do you have *The Secret*? I have to run to US Bank," said Fjard, questioning Chitchee's face when their eye-strings tangled up for a split second too long in a knot.

"Are you a bank robber?" asked Chitchee. "You look familiar! Is your face on a wanted poster by the FBI or something?" Chitchee saw an Alhambra of track-lighting blaring, brilliant, and blazing. The multitudinous rows of books resembled the canals of Venice. The narrow aisles' alleys of endless books were parti-colored, vertical brick facades—cobbled with intricate mosaics and arabesques. And where the sunlight had beamed into the store, the book spines had faded.

"Books on snowmobiles?" asked Kennedy, climbing half-way up the stairs. "KckckKkck."

"They are in Transportation," said Chitchee. "I'll be right with you when I complete my first training session on customer service. You'll have to wait for me in Transportation."

LaDonna's love for books died after her miscarriage, replaced by bouts of Bally pinball at Rifle Sport, roller derbies, heavy drinking, and hard drugs. *It was impossible* for LaDonna to read a whole book as it was for her to read Chitchee. Books were graveyards to her. Twenty years ago she started *And Then There Were None* by Agatha Christie but set it aside at a bus stop saying "and then there weren't even none." Meanwhile Chitchee had been increasing his injections of bibliophilia to blot out the past. Thinking over his book store *agape,* he vaporized when he sneezed and heard "The Old Gray Mare" sung in his head.

He often heard children's songs after he sneezed.

"Always take the customer to the shelf," he rehearsed mentally, "even if you have to strangle him," he added.

Matilda, Hermione, and Lisa Simpson? What if the three of them walked into BookSmart and asked for a book? He ran back to the young adult fiction (past heaps of *American Girls* and *McGuffey Readers*, DK Eyewitness books, David Macaulays) to affirm his idea for the Y + Y/A absolutes: Dr. Seusses, *The Very Hungry Caterpillar*, *The Little Prince*, *Where The Wild Things Are*, the *Ramona* series, Roald Dahls, *The Giver*, *The Boxcar Children*, and the variorum editions of the complete works of Shel Silverstein.

"Phew!" Then he ran back to the counter. "Oh, I forgot. Do we have *The Neverending Story*? Gary Paulsen? Sharon Creech? *Stellaluna?*"

"Not so good job!" yelled Chitchee and bit his hand when a couple heads turned. "Attention! To be clear, I meant to say 'I *have* a good job. I have a *good job.*'"

Wasn't Minneapolis aware by now that Chitchee was "on the spectrum?" Wasn't Minneapolis itself "on the spectrum?" Two spectrums implied he had to account for the relativistic effects of two spectrums traveling in space. He was on all the spectrums. But which wavelengths of the spectrum was he the strongest in? ADHD, autism, or Asperger's? Being a bookworm invited "spectrum" diagnoses from everybody, because in the United States reading itself could be on the spectrum for its anti-social, anti-Statist, reclining positions.

He felt peculiar. He emerged from the immaculate cocoon of his body. He looked down and saw his autoscopic self 90-years old—old, crooked-boned, mush-brained, and senile—outside Walker Public Library, panhandling to get his overdue fines under ten dollars. *Puer aeternus.* His dead sallow skin cells shrank inside his plaquing brain. His two glassy eyes detached from their retinas. He wore blue jean shorts, a regulation James Dean, white T-shirt, and a beanie with a propeller on top, twirling. "Hi everybody, I was 'book smart' once!"

"NO!" shouted Chitchee at his vision. The customers looked up and around. "No . . . no, no, no . . . *avocado!* I forgot my Swiss Army knife at home, so now I can't eat my Hass avocado! That's all that outburst was about! Hey, does anybody have a Bowie knife I can borrow? No? Then WHAT GOOD ARE YOU?"

Chitchee wanted to start a Pickwick Club 2.0 for books. How he anticipated hosting reading groups, book clubs, and televised interviews like Bob Chromie's *BookBeat* podcast from BookSmart! The classics needed to be digested and updated—Ovid, Tacitus, and Plutarch for starters. He chewed his plans slowly like the blue plate specials at the Best Steak House before Block E was razed to make room for a hole in the ground.

Really, Chitchee needed to get into the Carlson School of Management. Find a mentor, dig up a unicorn, then launch it into outer space. But first, a scalable prototype. Then the IPO thing. Or was it stock options and equity something or other? A business partner! That's what Chitchee needed! He imagined Bouvard and Pecuchet as web developers.

"Flaubert! Yes!" he yelled. "Wow, I have to shut up . . . yes, we have Flaubert! Is this Tourette's? But where's my fucking tic? Fucking lack of a tic, fuck!"

Chitchee trotted out the wanted poster from his back pocket, scribbled *$30,000 and a rabbit's foot* on it, and listed his ideas for Ulysses & Sons: ping pong and pool tables, a free Sioux quartzite and finnan haddie hot dish for every 50th customer, 2-for-1 coupons for Taste O'Dane, Little Meaty's Sweetmeat Treats To Eat Outlet, and Scandia's Famous Cabbage Roll Bar (*Stuff Your Face Here!*). For every purchase over $100, a raffle. Prize: a luxury pontoon excursion around Leech Lake for two, with two free Singapore Slings, and complementary lanyards in black or gray. A YouTube podcast, *Lost Volumes: The History of Lost Book Stores in the Twin Cities.* Knock on Larry Millet's lost door. Interview Fluffy at The Book Trader. Pay her in Stevie Ray Vaughan bootlegs (she would love that!). TV show on MTN: *BookTime.* Email Brian Lamb for advice. Torch résumé and watch it burn like a marshmallow. No more lunch pail jobs, no more temping at Dolphin Staffing, Pro Staff, and Manpower, and no more temping at Target.

Because, after the great divorce, Chitchee entered a coma for ten years: a coma of jobs. He scrambled. He worked at a Gedney's pickle factory bottling sauerkraut, then he was a machine operator for Northwestern Screw, then a friend shanghaied him into roofing asphalt shingles with a stapler gun for Kump & Kumpf Roofing, which led him into paint jobs—latexes, enamels, and varnishes. He worked at Bill Hook's Hardware in the main yard selling plywood, crated lumber, hardwood flooring, millwork, trim wood, cabinets, mantels, stairs, and common brick as well as face and fire bricks. Then he had a stint at Prudential Life Insurance performing secretarial chores, filling in business forms, typing, and filing. He volunteered at Lutheran Brotherhood answering phones. The temp agencies sent him to Target's print rooms under the Multifoods Tower in the City Center. He volunteered at the food shelf at Joyce Methodist Church, and it was while volunteering for the downtown Salvation Army on 4th Street that he discovered employees bought the donated books themselves and sold them on AbeBooks. His co-workers talked with book fever about their finds at the Goodwill on Highway 280. Chitchee became a book scout. He sold his first "scouted" book, *Guns, Germs, and Steel* for three dollars (he had paid one) to Noel Schoolcraft at BookSmart one night. It devolved into *un' ossessione*.

All the while he was closing in on his dream job—working in a book store. Ultimately he wanted to own a City Lights, and he would be the next Lawrence Ferlinghetti, and then the next Cosimo de' Medici, and then Pericles.

ONCE UPON A
SHAKEY'S PIZZA PARLOR

No more durned, darned, danged, and damned banjo jobs like the one he had at Shakey's Pizza Parlor on Highway 7—his last extensive gig. After Chitchee read *U.S.A.* by John Dos Passos, he, along with Sartre, deemed it "The Great American Novel." He read the last page with a sigh, closed the back cover, and said farewell friend. Then he read *Manufacturing Consent* and *Necessary Illusions*. Then he tackled the first volume of Marx's *Capital*. Made sense. Now the thing to do was act. In the beginning was the deed. Chitchee played to the Meister's baton on that score, because he loved *Conversations with Eckermann*.

So engaged by Goethe, Chitchee read MUSICIAN WANTED on Craigslist. Chitchee was unusually adept at musical instruments—and gifted with perfect pitch. Not a piece of music went by without Chitchee's body responding with transport like the string to the bow, urging him to dance. He killed the Shakey's audition, playing behind his back "Foggy Mountain Breakdown" and "Camptown Races" on his old Salvation Army banjo. The owner, Brock Throckmorton, hired him on the spot, although Chitchee took the job with the sole intention of unionizing the low paid workers in the kitchen: working over the hot ovens, washing the dishes, and mopping the floors at night by the sweat of their straw boaters.

Chitchee in his peppermint jacket and straw boater danced off the bus on Highway 7—big bright Gene Kelly smile, IWW literature in the banjo case, and membership card in his wallet.

Shakey's Pizza Parlor was branded for family fun, and it crawled with goofy stuffed animals named after the pizza toppings—the Canadian Bacon Bears, the Pepperoni Parakeets, and the Anchovy Aardvarks. Pinballs, games, toys. A small wooden-planked stage consisted of a stool and an upright, honky tonk piano (a bumper sticker on its side read: BURL IVES FOREVER) and bench, manned by Grover Gossick. Grover had written an arrangement of "The Ballad of the Green Berets," "My Country, Tis of Thee," and "My Way," which he demanded Chitchee play. Chitchee played along. For a while they chatted back and forth in a friendly manner over favorite folk songs. They agreed to start with "On Top of Old Smokey" and tested the crowd with it. Chitchee suggested: "Sixteen Tons," and medleys from the Kingsmen, the Weavers, and Leadbelly's "Goodnight, Irene." Grover shook his head, rolled his eyes, and frowned. Grover refused to share agency with regard to his playlist. It was his band. It was his American Songbag.

Grover retailed jokes to the Minnetonka T-ball teams. "What is brown and sticky, little boy?" "Your face!" "No, a stick!" "Oh. What's another one?" "Why did the belt go to jail?" "I dunno!" "It held up my pants." Grover serenaded the long picnic tables of little league teams yipping with wide-eyed wonder at the baseball cards from the Shinders in Hopkins. Grover: "Oh my, who'd ya got there, tiger? Harmon Killebrew? The Killer? Lemme see!"

Chitchee tiptoed past Grover and befriended the "phone girl," Courtney Kirkwood, a snarling growl of a woman with grit in her crop. He loved her blindly at first sight. Courtney took the reservations. She answered the phone and greeted the suburbanite families with her hostess-like attempts to not thwack the children running in circles around her, calling her "Weirdo Wanda."

"Hey Courtney, what's up with the piano player? Do you know this guy, Grover Gossick?"

Turns out, the "Asshole from El Paso," a former priest from the Chichesters' very parish in Deephaven and friend of Finkle, Grover Gossick had turned huckleberry in Texas—he adopted everything he thought was Texan. He bushwhacked a clear path to the nearest Welcome to Texas store and shook the clerk's carpel-crushing, knuckle-dusting, bone-twanging, thumbreaking, howdy-and-die handshake, followed by the clerk's twisting and thrusting Grover to the floor with a loud, distinctly Texan, "Welcome to Texas! Anything I can help you with?" Just like that, *floored* by Texas, the friendliest state in the Union, Grover bought the whole shebang: Tony Lamas, confederate kerchiefs, ten gallon hats, Ford pick-up trucks, and garage calendars with cowboy-booted girls in cut-offs chewing blades of straw, hunting rifles across their bare thighs dangling down off the backs of Ford pick-up trucks, month after month. He was an ambitious missionary wearing Tony Lamas for the Church of the Holy Uncircumcised Christ, a Christianity whose central teaching was that circumcision was the true Original Sin and the Fall. Circumcision was a necessary evil through which only the true redemption could take place; therefore he planned to circumcise mainland China, even its hinder parts, and then force them to repent. All of them right now. Chinese police followed him as far as Guangzhong where he got sick from intestinal parasites through fecal contamination, funny that. Deported to Minnesota, Grover logged in his seven years at a theological seminary and became a deacon at St Theresa's in Deephaven. Chased out of there for accusations of inappropriate touching of altar boys, he agreed to leave immediately under a cloud of suspicion. The shiny-faced Grover Gossick simply moved on and joined the Seventh Day Adventists, whose steeple was down the road from Shakey's Pizza Parlor. Able to maintain cordial relations with his previous Catholic parishioners, he continued to offer them spiritual guidance over games of golf at Wayzata Country Club and to preach the Gospel to the Adventists on Highway 7, whose congregation was happy as a clam at a clambake to receive Grover's "message of love," which he had brought along with him when he landed the job at Shakey's Pizza Parlor playing piano.

Back on stage, sandwiched between "Joe Hill" and "God Bless America," Chitchee editorialized to the Shakey's customers about the secret war in Guatemala, CIA involvement in El Salvador, and the covert support of Contras in Nicaragua. One night he dedicated the next song to "my high school gym teacher, Gene Debs." Grover glared over his shoulder from the piano; his lips curled up and disappeared as he ate them. He slammed the cover over the keyboard.

"Heads up," said Grover, grabbing the microphone, "the next song is not dedicated to Eugene Debs, the next song is dedicated to the great American hero and anti-communist Richard Nixon."

"Richard Nixon?" howled Courtney into the flexible microphone at her hostess's workstation. "Oh, kiss my pimpled ass muffins!"

"He got us into China, didn't he? Huh, Courtney? See, no answer!" said Grover. "And I suppose you're going to tell me Ronald Reagan wasn't the President of the American Dream?"

"No," said Courtney over the flexible microphone. "He was. He succeeded. America is a dream now."

Grover hunt-and-peck typoed a 30-page notarized letter to Brock. Courtney should resign or be fired because she was "an enemy of the children," "the whore of Guevara," and "the most dangerous woman in Minnetonka." Brock slapped her wrist with a written warning, which was also hunt-and-peck typoed. She photographed it, Facebooked it, and claimed it was another example of social control. Exhibit #117. 120 likes.

On another occasion, Chitchee performed "Union Maid." Unbeknownst to Chitchee, the generic-looking owner Brock Throckmorton was there, wearing large khaki shorts with zippered pockets, a button-down blue shirt, white sweat socks, and Birkenstocks buckled to his loafish, oafish feet.

Brock set down his frosty mug of Lowenbrau beer, looked aside, and asked the stage:

"Where did you get *that* song, Chitchee?"

"'Union Maid'? Right out of the American Songbag, sir . . . you haven't *heard* of the American Songbag? Burl Ives ring a bell?" asked Chitchee.

"Who? Burt Reynolds? Is that something he wrote?" asked Brock. "I don't understand."

"*Burl Ives* was a frickin' stool pigeon, you didn't know that?" said Chitchee, looking back at an incensed Grover's hideous smile. "He squealed like a canary! Who knows how many people he fingered for HUAC? Hundreds of political prisoners disappeared into the American Gulag for that American Scumbag!"

"He fingered who for what?" asked Brock, who shook his foamy, "fun face" sober, the beer's snow-foamed hops having bearded him. "Chitchee, this is a family restaurant. We don't need no Burl Ives fingering windbag songs, you guys. Let's get it together."

Grover glared at the string-tied Chitchee singing:

"*I'm stickin' with the union!*"

Grover grabbed the microphone:

"Don't listen to him, my little ones! That SHIT song is from The Little RED Songbook."

Brock talked Grover down into a compromise—each musician would play one song solo.

One night in the kitchen, waiting for his free dinner slice of Canadian Bacon Bear pizza, Chitchee talked to the happy-faced cooks in their straw boaters about the labor theory of value.

"You guys don't resent the fact that your consciousness is determined by your class? Well okay, something to think about—it never occurred to you that if we went on strike, we—"

"Chitchee," said Skylar Joyhouse, "you're great to work with, but really you don't have to start a GoFundMe to fly the entire

Shakey's staff to visit some guy named Bakunin's grave in Berne, Switzerland. Really man, we want to stay in the good old USA, you know, living the dream, bro, you know, bro, the dream, bro? Order U-U-U-P!"

A broom handle timbered over to the tile floor with a sharp report. Chitchee turned to see Grover walk away, granite-faced, hands in pockets, and with an air of sabotage.

Later that night Chitchee felt a note in his peppermint jacket pocket:

"*I know what you're up to. A hundred bucks says I won't tell anyone about your trying to overthrow the United States government and planting the black flag of anarchy on top of the Washington Monument.*"

Chitchee didn't have a hundred smackers to throw at a blackmailer. The show went on. But the "show" stood on tender, inflamed tenterhooks like something out of a Harold Pinter play: flows of negative emotion abounded silently and rubbed rawer the raw wounds with eye stabs. While joyously packed-together family-packs pie-holed pizza slices of family fun and children cheesed it all the way home betimes to bedtimes, their stomachs tight as ticks, on stage there was a darker scenario. Chitchee and Grover faced off like two Cold War chimeras of the deep, harboring poisonous political resentments. They thrashed inside with animalistic emotion that lurked beneath the surface tension of their onstage presence with seething resentments.

Every night the "band" played on, but the stress squeezed Chitchee's skull to the bursting point. He was stranded on top of Old Smoky, frying, steaming, coiling with rage, and playing the banjo. Chitchee rigged a pickup to connect his banjo to a small Fender practice amp to hear himself better because Grover pounded on the piano keys like Jerry Lee Lewis or Cecil Taylor or Cecil Taylor pounding on Jerry Lee Lewis. Grover installed his own microphone. Felix Weatherwax loaned Chitchee his wah-wah, his fuzz tone, his flanger, an array of other pedals, and a 85-Watt Fender Twin Reverb amplifier. Grover enjoined the patrons to partake of the Pledge of Allegiance (hands over hearts), facing Mecca-like the American flag and eagle-topped flagpole—one of ten Grover donated to Shakey's Pizza Parlor.

"There is one among us, boys and girls, who is a traitor!" said Grover. "Can you guess who it is?"

"You?" said Brock, pizza coursing through his digestive system like a rat made of cheese through a python's guts, hampering his critical faculties.

"No, not me," said Grover. "Let's say for now . . . someone with *red* stripes on."

Chitchee tuned his banjo. Grover launched into "God Bless the U.S.A.," sounding like a bullhorn with a frog in its throat. Chitchee didn't know the tune, so he transposed "For What It's Worth" into Grover's key of C major. He wove that melody in and around Grover's flag-wrapped squib. Then Chitchee sampled "The Internationale" at which point Grover segued into "America the Beautiful." Chitchee responded with "Ohio."

"This is our tribute to Charles Ives," apologized Chitchee, but no one got the Charles Ives joke (too soon?). "How about a tribute to Chet Atkins's 'Yankee Doodle Dixie?'"

When Chitchee drifted stonily into "Coming Into Los Angeles," Grover pulled out all the showstopping stops, threw off his peppermint jacket, rolled his sleeves up to the elbows, fisted his dukes and, lathered in a suit of sweat, shouted:

"Come on down off your high horse, punk! You're on the list for my fist! An uppercut, C. O. D!"

The din grew into a clamor, the clamor branched into rackets, and the rackets flowered into fracases. Grover fully throttled "P. T. 109." He followed that with the theme song from *Bonanza* and a ball-busted, head-banging version of "This is My Country." Chitchee countered with "This Land is Your Land" and "Wish You Were Here."

Grover cued Courtney to start his antique Kodak Carousel slide show portion of the concert, throwing images against a white bed sheet. Grover claimed he was not a Nazi in Stars and Stripes clothing, but he liked to shock his opponents with Nazi hints, suggestions, and implications. A more perfect America of perfected patriotism would bend more and more toward Third Reich ideals.

Panzer divisions, Luftwaffe, marauding German soldiers, and *Triumph of the Will* outtakes topped the tabletops' pizzas' toppings. Silhouettes of themselves walked through Poland, 1939. Death's headed divisions played across their peppermint stripes and straw boaters. Grover played an air from a Haydn string quartet, but no one recognized the melody except Chitchee who knobbed his Fender practice amp to 10. He left it feedbacking while he plugged in his pedals: wah wah, flanger, and distortion.

He hacked through "Machine Gun." Electric current sluiced through his synapses. Electrons sparked from his fingertips to the picked-up strings. The Fender Twin Reverb roared like a wounded Bengal tiger.

Chitchee chopped—chuck, chuck-a-chuck, chuck. His broken thumbnail comped the banjo strings to imitate M60 machine gun fire. "*Machine gun . . . machine g-u-u-u—n . . .*" The cooks craned out of the kitchen, potential customers lickety-split in a chaotic retreat, and the rafters, windows, and plaster walls trembled like gallows with prisoners sentenced to hang. A few blubbering tykes in baseball suits and soccer shorts ducked under the picnic tables. The suburban dads of Minnetonka didn't know what to do—except to call home.

Where is Brock? yelled the dads. Probably Lord Fletcher's on the Lake in his cabin cruiser getting his balls sucked, screamed Courtney. Brock yelled at Courtney that she was fired (she shouted back she didn't give a dead rat's ass-cheese that she was fired). The walls guffawed. The floor buckled. The ceiling cracked in half. Chitchee adjusted his whammy bar and re-tuned. A grease fire flared in the kitchen. The fire department was on its way.

"What are you doing, Chichester," broadcast Grover, "trying to start a riot? Exactly like I figured from the get go: you're an atheist, a liberal, and a hell-bent FDR supporter."

Grover rolled out a Keeler Polygraph Test on a castored table with an extendable bread cutting board. Grover held electrodes triumphantly in the air.

"Can you prove you're *not* a Communist?" said Grover, finding the wall socket.

"That's it," said Chitchee, "this little Simon and Garfunkel gig is over! Love ya man, but I'm going to pursue my own destiny. *Buddham saranam gacchami.* To paraphrase John Lennon, I've gotten nothing but subconscious sabotage from your reptilian brain stem and limbic system, *Paul!* But that's all right, 's all right. Fare thee well, Grover! Are we friends?"

Grover refused to shake hands. Chitchee hugged him and kissed him on both cheeks.

Brock fired Chitchee the next day for causing the kitchen's grease fire, which could have burned down nearly all of Deephaven as fast as matchsticks. Chitchee thanked Brock for firing him.

VIKTOR MARTENSEN

"So, what's your interest in snowmobiles?" asked Chitchee.

"Have you ever circumspected a black man from Kenya articulating about Lake Minnetonka on a snowmobile?" asked Kennedy.

"No," said Chitchee.

"Then that is your answer."

"Since you're from Kenya," asked the curious Chitchee. "I assume you've heard of the great Ngugi wa Thiong'o?"

Blank.

"Well, okay, but the world-renowned *Chinua Achebe* . . . Okonkwo?"

Another blank.

"Are those types of snowmobiles?" asked Kennedy.

"Fair enough," replied Chitchee. "There might be some books on snowmobiles on the Automotive shelf. Chiltons or Haynes for snowmobiles? I don't remember seeing anything. I have to man the register, but as soon as he gets back from wherever, I'll go downstairs."

"Aloysius is outside on the sidewalk, worrying up a storm," said Kennedy. "I'll tell him to stop his woolgathering, wake up, and commensurate some *real* matriculations for a change! I really think he needs to see a self-help specialist. You know, someone with business credentials like a sports psychologist—like Brent Mussburger, or a reality TV talk show doctor like Oprah. That's it! He could go on Oprah and *she'll* straighten his *Wonder Years* ass out."

"I don't think we even have a Self Help section," said Chitchee, looking at the titles in the holding area behind the counter. "It looks like someone put the entire section on hold."

Aloysius stood outside BookSmart, trying to forget how many months back rent he owed to Viktor Martensen. Maybe their New Deal wouldn't work. Aloysius smoked and swallowed a fresh roll of Rolaids whole. His peeling, eczematous eyes ran over the BookSmart display of books on white, wire stands in the front window facing Hennepin Avenue. The well-shaped, sexier books titillated like paper prostitutes, forcing pedestrian perspectives inside. Beyond the display of trade paperbacks, one saw directly through the store toward the back alley, the dumpster, Lunds's parking lot, and westward into the woods of the green-wooded lakes that stretched all the way to St. Bonifacius, the Badlands, Mount Rushmore, and Mount Powell's in Oregon.

Kennedy opened the front door. Who should show up but Lake Street Rodney! Kennedy about-faced mechanically.

"It's Lake Street Rodney! I suggest you run for your life," said Kennedy to Chitchee. "I'll be hiding downstairs."

"Aiya!" said Chitchee, unable to understand how Lake Street Rodney could be worse than any other book store regular in any other city in the world. "Weren't all men alike as squirrels?"

Chitchee pretended to browse in the Cookbooks and Crafts section as an escape route if an emergency arose.

"'allo! Aloysius!" announced Lake Street Rodney to Hennepin Avenue and strode up to Aloysius like a golfer eager to make a world-shaking putt on all the Comcast cable channels you never knew you were paying for. "Are you outside enjoying the weather because you're not inside enjoying the weather outside? But how *could* you be inside *and* outside enjoying the weather? Or are you smoking outside to enjoy the weather but not enjoying the weather at all?"

"Rodney?" said Aloysius, pacing, sweating, and fuming. "You should meet our new hire, Chitchee. You should like him better than me. Please! He's our new guy for customer service and he's heard all about you."

"New guy!" called out Lake Street Rodney, entering BookSmart. "*Gormenghast*! Is it still in my hold pile? HELLO?"

Torg swiveled his head, opened his mouth, and squinched his nose so that his glasses reflected nothing.

Chitchee and everybody else browsing wheeled around, jumped, or cursed the middle-aged Rodney. Curses on his plus fours, argyle socks, newsboy's cap, rubber lips, and bright brown eyes darting in an awakened REM dream state all day long! Rodney fidgeted and ticced for help. His facial muscles seemed to shimmer in expectation of rising, red velvet curtains revealing a Bolshoi performance of the *Firebird* at Northrop Auditorium.

Rodney's helplessness, which had perforated the social fabric of Uptown many times over, had been well self-advertised for years. And whenever Kennedy encountered Rodney, he reckoned it was time to conduct some business or other with his Self-Help book club, connections, and networked customers at the McDonald's board room across the street.

Rodney cornered the careless Kennedy.

Trembling like an aspen grove, Chitchee crouched in the Cookbooks and Crafts section. He hid behind two elderly grandmothers in shirt dresses, veiled hats, white gloves, and stuffed stiff purses, who had just stepped out of an 1960s issue of *Better Homes and Gardens* and into the latest editions of Julia Childs, Craig Claibornes, Jeff Smiths, Rachel Rays, and other chefs looking extremely pleased with new sources of sauces.

"Would it be all right if I hid behind your skirts?" asked Chitchee on all fours.

"Oh my goodness, are you all right?" said Kriemhilde, clutching at the tight collar around her neck with her white-gloved hands. "Mel, I knew there would be trouble if we came here. Let's go now. I don't want any trouble. If that man in the golf costume is that loud, who knows what terrorist act he is capable of?"

Kriemhilde fanned herself with a *Fannie Farmer* and became an instant fan.

"Where? Oh, that young plaid man!" said Melusina, looking like Betty Crocker's mother as she idled in the Cookbooks and Crafts section. "Hildy, he's a kook!"

"He is?" asked Chitchee, standing up in front of the crafts

"Mel, he must be from Southern California, dressed like that!" said Kriemhilde, her younger sister. "Oh no, oh my, he must be on something weirdo, Mel. Does he think he is in Walker Public Library or something? I think we should go, all the same. All the wackety-wackos crawl out of the carpentry in Uptown."

"Sister," said Melusina, "it hasn't been safe to go out ever since Hubert Humphrey took off for Washington. What can you do? We're safe here—as long as we watch each other's backs!"

"You two are sisters?" asked Chitchee. "No wonder you are so adorable!"

"Are you interested in books like this?" continued Chitchee, pulling down and handing Melusina *The Horizon Book of Needlepoint*.

A wheel of fire jumped off the page. Spaced between the chariot spokes, stitches of gold yellows, diamond blues, red rubies, and soft oranges illuminated the pattern on their faces.

"Hildy!" said Melusina. "A Carousel Square pattern!"

The pictured pillow case, a helm-shaped wheel encased in a square frame of yarn, was so bright it seemed to delight in its own existence.

"Where? Crochet too? Ooo!" said Kriemhilde, absorbed by the Carousel Square pattern.

"It looks like the Wheel of Dharma!" added Chitchee, absorbed by the splashes of fire on the eight-spoked wheel. "The Dharmachakra. Are you two on the Eightfold Path?"

"Oh, heavens no," said Kriemhilde. "We drink root beer."

"In *The Horizon Book of Needlepoint* from 1966!" said Melusina with tremulations of giggling excitement. "Gudrun will love this! Let's buy this for Gudrun!"

"Oh, this book store is magic! Thank you!" said Kriemhilde, soft as a pigeon billing and cooing with Chitchee in gratitude. "Well, it's about time *someone* sprang Gudrun out of her closet and let her breathe!"

"We have books on flower arranging, origami, woodcarving, calligraphy . . ."

"Yes, I see them, and books on magic!" said Kriemhilde.

"How do you like that?" asked Melusina, looking lovingly at her sister. "In this book store even the magic books appear like magic!"

Chitchee gave a sudden peck with his lips to Kriemhilde's white-gloved hand. She blushed and ignored him, not knowing what to think.

"Look at all these books on candle-making too," said Kriemhilde quickly. "I knew we should have come here! I . . . had . . . a . . . feeling. The Good Lord provides a silver lining for everything."

"Indeed he does, Lord Krishna provides for us all!" said Chitchee, pulling down a book at random, overcome by the sweet perfume of violets extending across the Cookbooks and Crafts section from the two darling doves.

"Lord who?" asked Kriemhilde, pulling back and tightening all her buttons.

"We should get going," said Melusina. "A-hem."

"We can't leave yet!" said Kriemhilde. "We might miss all the action!"

"Look at all the creative things you can do with *buttons*," said Chitchee, assimilating everything he could about buttons. "We should start a button club, ladies!"

"Why, yes," said Kriemhilde.

"Hello? Somebody? I wanted to check something in my hold pile," announced Lake Street Rodney. "For the fourth time. This week. I want to buy back the Scottish-Gaelic dictionary I sold you guys. And Mervyn Peake's *Gormenghast*. Four times. This week. Where are you? Hallo?"

"I'm over here!" said Chitchee. "In a magical book store in a magical world of buttons."

"Where is here? Because if you are really as there as I am here, your here is neither there to me and nor is my here, here to you, which doesn't help me locate my Scottish-Gaelic dictionary," said Rodney.

"Watch this, ladies," said Chitchee. "I can make the world stop with my own button."

Chitchee delved into his pocket for the acorn he had particularly fancied a couple hours ago and snapped up off the sidewalk under Jove's tree on Hennepin. He stood on one foot, raised his knee, and positioned the acorn cap between his fingers. He trumpeted hard through his thumbs into the acorn's cap. A blood-curdling, heart-stopping, high-pitched shriek that could have sliced a Concorde SST in half emerged.

Melusina and Kriemhilde heard nothing much above 15,000 Herz and continued to read in their "magic bookshop."

"Stop!" begged Lake Street Rodney, falling to his knees. A dog barked outside at a traffic accident. "I hear you! I'm right here! My ears are bleeding! Criminee!"

"I'll be right with you, sir!" chuckled Chitchee. "We are having some fun now! Par-tay! Lay-dees!"

Chitchee double-winked at Melusina and Kriemhilde, the features of their faces taking on the contours of raisin oatmeal cookies. Chitchee curved back behind the maroon front counter. Rooting around, he made a show of looking for the Scottish-Gaelic dictionary, but he did not know where Lake Street Rodney's "hold pile" was stored.

"Don't let me interrupt you, you book people!" announced Lake Street Rodney, unplugging his ears and lifting himself off the floor—plus fours and newsboy's cap realigned over his bald crown with its curly hair on the sides.

"Is this your *Mabinogion*?" offered Chitchee, getting no response. "The Charlotte Guest? Guest? I *Guest* not . . . and Mervyn Peake doesn't get asked for a lot. I *Guest* he *Peaked*!"

"Continue with your usual rig-a-ma-ro-lee!" said Rodney, addressing the store. "You two lovely old women in cookbooks, hallo, that means you too! Go back! Go back to what you were doing! Turn back! Go, now!"

The two sisters faced each other with unbelief as if ordered to pull apart two teams of fighting sled dogs. And the dozen or so customers went back to browsing and circling slowly around the New Arrivals on the shallow, sandbox-shaped, day-of-the-week tables.

"Beatific sheep are safely grazing," sang Chitchee.

The AT & T cordless phone bleated. Chitchee gripped the old model phone like an old phone hand and with a new sense of authority. It was an older woman than Aloysius for Aloysius. Chitchee peeped out the crash-barred, front plate-glass doors: Aloysius was talking to Larry Sangster, who wore a blue Macy's suit and a French's Mustard-yellow tie.

Larry Sangster from the Martensen People's Group held an iPhone 3, fret-tapped it, and talked into it. Aloysius turned his empty hands palms outward toward Larry.

"Looks like he is in a kind of a business meeting right now," said Chitchee, shifting his weight from foot to foot like a peacock.

"Is he get . . . ting evicted?" asked the breaking-up, garbled voice of an elderly woman, who sounded like a wild turkey gobbling her words and clucking her syllables while fleeing a tornado.

"Hold on, I'll ask," said Chitchee, waiting for the right moment.

He inferred from Larry's body language that Larry was the top money dog to Aloysius, who bowed his money dog's head downward.

"Do I have . . . right num . . .? This is his . . . [m]er speak call . . . [fr]om . . . hour ago . . . he . . . called me. Who is this?"

"Evicted? Hey lady, that can't be right," continued Chitchee, "the store is too much fun for us to be *evicted*. Everybody loves the store. Everybody hangs out here. We do not judge. Besides, I just got hired. Why would Aloysius hire me if he knew he were getting evicted? Hello?"

Thudding silence.

"Wello?" continued Chitchee, "if that is all you have to say, maybe you should go down to the nearest word shop and buy some more words. Ma'am? She hung up on me! Wild Turkey Woman, who do you think you are? I oughtta bitch slap you for that, you old floozy! Who made you Queen of the Underground?"

"Hello? I'm still here! This is Ariel," said Ariel. "Sorry I dropped the phone!"

"That's okay, Ariel, anytime you want to drop the phone, go right ahead! Nice to meet you!" said Chitchee, making a screaming face. "This is Chitchee. And how is your day? I believe Aloysius is tied up with his portfolio coach."

When Chitchee peered out the storefront window at Larry Sangster, Chitchee thought of dried apricots. Larry didn't have a nose. Maybe he had lost his nose. The Taliban or some rhinoclasts had swiped it, and now it sat in a Taliban Nose Museum in Kandahar, surrounded by fields of opium poppies. But Larry's nose retained tiny flaps of flesh hovering over the two viper pits. Especially marvelous to Chitchee was Larry's filigreed blonde, fluffy (possibly permed), definitely dyed, Golden Fleece-gold, all curled as curly fries in curlicues, super-silky, treacley-tressed, framing-his-cherubic-cheeks (though beady-eyed as a corn borer), flaxen, angel's, and musical *hair*.

"So Aloysius, I told the main office you're alive!" said Larry. "We were hoping maybe you weren't sick. I mean we thought you hadn't paid your phone bill and your phone was turned off. You haven't returned the Martensen main office calls for some time now."

"Larry," said Aloysius, "I had a month's rent, but I stashed it in a book one day and now I can't remember which book. It's around here somewhere. It's bound to turn up!"

Larry's iPhone 3 ring-toned like a smoke detector that couldn't quit smoke detecting. His boss Viktor Martensen barked (on speaker-phone) a string of obscenities that out-Scorsesied Scorsese. Larry looked alternately cashed, cowed, bullied, and gored. He looked at the sky for a reference point. The bright sky might include Viktor Martensen relaxing in his Laz-Y-Boy recliner. Larry nibbled his tiny lower lip.

"Hey, boss!" yelled Chitchee. "Are we getting evicted? Someone on the phone wanted to know!"

Aloysius cringed and word-mouthed the word "Quiet!" toward Chitchee.

"Hurry up, Larry!" said Viktor Martensen on speaker. "Get the fucking money! That idiot fuck *Zalar* you hired lost something valuable of mine. If he can't come up with the goods, he is going as far as his broken kneecaps will carry him. Teeheehee. And you, Larry, will have to do his dirty work. Because it's all your fault. Everything is all your fault, Larry, for having the fucking name Larry! I am leaving the Minneapolis airport now for downtown. But I could be in my *Lear Jet*, waiting for my *Bloody Mary* and a *blowjob* on my way to the tables at *Caesar's Palace*! Tee hee hee! (Snnnnnnnghghgh)!"

Viktor's high-pitched laugh always sounded like the shits and giggles of a boy pulling the legs off a dragonfly.

A bout of choking from a blocked air passage reminded Viktor of the pain he always paid back when he laughed too hard. Viktor had been snorting cocaine with a recidivist, deviated septum or a double deviation, caused by the inflow of cocaine since his Golden Gopher days fresh out of the University of Minnesota. He had made the easy transitions from tooting coke dealer to real estate agent to developer, laundering his proceeds by buying recently foreclosed houses and dilapidated apartments and applying his secret business trick: buy fixer-uppers, don't fix them, rent them, squeeze them, tease them, and always leave them.

"And I don't care, *Lare-ee*," continued Viktor, "if you take that old mutt out and shoot him in the back of the head. That whole block is going to be cheap podium condos soon. MAC, BookSmart, Sweet Jap Jeans, Vision Blurred, and the Uptown Movie Theater. Condos 29 stories high, Larry. Luxury, boutique apartments are the wave of the future, and I'll be surfing on that wave. In the Greater Achilles. The local sissy liberals won't like it, but fuck them if the idiot socialists don't like being kicked out of town. Why do you think I bought Carousel Square? It was to fuck *them* over!"

When Aloysius overheard Viktor, he retched up Egg McMuffin. He blocked that reflex, chewed on the reflux, and defluxed the reflux back down to his esophagus with a false sense of gusto, which might necessitate a tuba full of Tums. He dredged a large tablet of Tums antacids from his right blue jean pocket, and with only one left, he savored the sugary, Necco-tasting candy high. The fuss over the back rent made Aloysius feel about as low as a homeless carpenter ant. And made Viktor the ant lion. Pincers out, in Viktor's vise, doomed Aloysius sensed an infinite lack of movement and zero degrees of freedom.

"Larry!" begged off Aloysius. "I have to go back inside and check the spreadsheets for yesterday on the Excel PowerPoint website data inventory management program beta system development program."

"Just a second," choked Larry, getting off the horn with mounting heartburn. "We have to talk! You are a full two months in arrears now. Mr. Martensen says he is going to put a lien on all your assets or break your face, whichever is the most inconvenient for you. He says you're his bitch now."

"Yeah, let's hold off on that," said Aloysius. "Tell him our phone keeps falling off the hook because the hanger is broken, and the phone hasn't worked for days, but we're going to get Northwestern Ma Bell to come out and take a look! How do you get a hold of the phone company without a phone? You would need one of those bullroarers."

"Aloysius, the phone!" said Chitchee, having walked all the way outside with the phone. "It's Ariel! She says she's calling you back from an hour ago!"

"Tell her I'll be there in a second!" said Aloysius.

"Aloysius," said Rodney, en route to McDonald's, hand resting on his ear. "Phone."

Chitchee, guarding the cash register, anxiously watched Aloysius take his sweet time. Hurry up! What if this Ariel thought he had made it all up? She might drop the phone again. Aloysius exhaled residual smoke in Larry's face by accident. Residual, scarred lung smoke had crawled out of Aloysius's lungs like a ghost. Larry jerked his head back. He looked like an ostrich wearing a blond, curly Harpo Marx wig, which jiggled higgledy-piggledy angel locks.

Chitchee noted the frantic worry lines "W" across Aloysius's pate like the symbol for a resistor in an electronic schematic when Aloysius said:

"We will have to hold off on our training session—too much important business to attend to in the book trade, buddy! Good job. I think you pretty much got the basics down. Saami can train you later and we will pick up on the training tomorrow where we began today."

"Good!" said Chitchee, hugging a frozen Aloysius. "We're going to make it, boss! We'll get there! Now I don't have to take the civil service exam and become a mailman. Thank you. Thank you."

"Aloysius! You didn't answer our emails either," said Larry, dogging Aloysius's soft rubber heels into BookSmart. "Why is that? I want an answer!"

"Larry, Larry, Larry, Larry," said Chitchee, "the fastest means of communication will always be word of mouth."

When Larry looked around the store, Chitchee read his mind: Larry was thinking: who reads books? Losers. Who even *needs* literacy when we have iPhone 3s now? Only the losers. Chitchee mused: if no one reads books, there is no need to ban and burn books. *Johnny Doesn't Need to Read.* Why? Why has America turned its back on learning? Why the "I Hate Science" T-shirts and license plates? Larry looked at the new loser Chitchee: just like Aloysius! He missed the new wave of technology, and now he lies becalmed off shore with no tide. One more standing wave-form in a dirty, tie-dyed shirt, still revolting from the days of the Sixties!

"Hello," said Chitchee. "I'm Chitchee. So you must be Larry, the sex addict? I've heard so much about you! How are you?"

"Hi," said a purposely inattentive Larry.

"Then when are you going to come down?" asked Chitchee. "Got ya, Larry!"

Chitchee felt for his acorn cap, placed it between his thumb knuckles and, with the embouchure corrected, blew his ear-piercing whistle in Larry's face. Larry's arms and legs tingled, and his field of vision blurred with black snowflakes. He clamped his eyelids shut and saw flashing lights. When he stopped twitching, he gaped over the head of Torg, who clove to the counter like a large woodpecker.

"Are you sober now, Larry?" asked Chitchee.

All the BookSmart customers looked at Larry like hypnotized and unresponsive zombies, craning their pencil-necks. Larry looked over his shoulder and saw the bunch of them—absorbed in stupid conversations about stupid people who wrote stupid books about stupid people who whine about how stupid people are. What's wrong with being stupid? Stupid people have always run the world for the betterment of mankind. These "book people" think that CEOs walk around board rooms, quoting from *Julius Caesar.* "Friends, Romans, Countrymen—give me all your dough. And I'll toss you a Parkerhouse dinner roll." Larry felt ignored and marginalized by the entire book store for his almost expressing his private opinion that stupid people have the right to be stupid. Could BookSmart (might as well call it BookStupid, it would do more business) be anything but a joke? Little do these poindexters know of Viktor's plans to gut it, gill it, batter it, and deep fry it for an hors d'oeuvre.

Then Chitchee thought: Could Larry possibly want to buy Harvey Mackay's *Swim With The Sharks*? Maybe I should ask him if he'd be interested in some classic business books? Good stuff (although a yellowjacket could have written it on a picnic table in his spare time), eh Larry! Business books seem to be worth the sea shells to barracudas. There you go, Larry. You can proceed to power lunch wearing your bid-for-power tie and power down at Club Miami.

Chitchee walked over to shake hands and apologize to Larry when Ye Young Kim flagged Chitchee to ask him a question. Simultaneously her bored-by-the-books boyfriend, Cameron McCocky, dropped a Victoria's Secret shopping bag of Ye Young Kim's lingerie because a camisole and some hosiery weighed too much.

"Do you have *Siddhartha*?" Ye Young quietly inquired, parting the black velvet curtains of her hair over her face.

"Who? Sid Hartman?" wise-cracked Cameron McCocky, waiting for a late laugh that didn't show. He made a wry, whiskey and sour face and made to walk for the door, "Come on, Ye Young! There could be a happy hour at Figlio's!"

Chitchee watched her exasperation, her anguish, her wave-tossed eyebrows, and her looking like she might cry. She ran out after her boyfriend, clutched his sleeve, and they disappeared.

"I'm sorry, Larry," said Chitchee, "for giving you shit. By your aloof stance you seem to think you're better than all of us."

Larry inserted spy-like glances into the discourse here and there.

"And you think BookSmart is a looney bin, a scrap heap in the way of the bulldozer, and even a scrap heap in a trash bin inside a looney bin. But I can assure you we are all quite well within the margins of sanity."

"Hey, have you guys," asked Lake Street Rodney, throwing open the front doors, "seen Gollum here?"

Larry refused to comment on *Rodney*. Torg stared up at Larry, Torg's mouth open. Larry swam by like the giant remora in the aquarium at Como Park. Torg reached up with one index finger to touch Larry's butter-colored hair. Rodney plopped a blue and white composition book on the maroon counter.

"No? Yes? No? Maybe I *am* invisible!" said Rodney. "Can someone tell me if I am invisible?"

Silence.

Rodney jotted down some Elvish notes next to some Gaelic word lists. With an ordinary Ticonderoga pencil, he diarized in Westron: "Achieved invisibility today. Ring must be working. All is well."

"See this?" asked Rodney to Larry. "Each language requires a different magic marker: Purple is Elvish, Red is Gaelic, Orange for Manx, Blue for Cornish, Green for all the tree alphabets, and Glittery Sparkles for all the undeciphered languages of mountain trolls and the pidgin Creole of Middle-earth's cave fish."

"Here's the thing, Aloysius," said Larry. "I'll come back to the store when you are less busy! When's a good time?"

"How about the weekend of the Aquatennial?" suggested Aloysius, pretending to use the phone and looking at his wall calendar featuring birds unflipped since the wood duck of February, which he then flipped forward to the blue bird of June, although it was July. It didn't matter. Aloysius didn't know when the Aquatennial was either: he didn't even know what it was.

"Aloysius," said Chitchee. "I forgot about Kennedy. He wanted a book on snowmobiles. I think he has potential as a regular."

Chitchee's lack of social skills ironed out many an irony, but frankly his frankness served to make him silly in the world's eyes.

"Later," said Larry, drawing a long face shaped like a spent shell casing. "Look, I have to go and talk to Viktor about this whole fucked-up situation."

Viktor Martensen owned not only Carousel Square but the entire block from MAC, the make-up store on Lake Street, to the Uptown Theater on Lagoon Avenue. Viktor thrived rosily as a shareholder in a diverse portfolio of developers and realty organizations. Along with being a University of Minnesota Law School alumnus, Viktor plumed himself on being CEO and managing director of the Martensen Peoples Group, MPG, the MPG Financial Group of the Minnesota Foundation of Business in Minneapolis, and the Minneapolis People's Fiduciary, Inc., which had recently acquired Uptown's shopping mall, Carousel Square. Overseer to more than 350 employees he owned more than 4000 rental units in the Twin Cities alone and 1200 more in Florida. He recently had been awarded Business Leader of the Year by *Minnesota Business Monthly* and afterwards had been toasted in the Cavalier Room at the Minneapolis Athletic Club. Considered an outstanding leader, Martensen always out-generaled his competition. MPG was a business model as one of the top producing Minnesotan financial groups. His Orion rising, the gossip columnists for *The Downtown Daily Grackle* saw in him the next Minnesota miracle, business-wise. He was mentioned in the same breath as George Draper Dayton and Gino Paulucci. Martensen stood next in line for the Governor of Minnesota.

Recently a national publisher had approached him for a book deal. Immediately uninterested, Viktor demanded, on second thought, Aloysius ghostwrite the book, tentatively titled *Quantum Vision: Ten Keys to Success*, as partial payment of the back rent's going into the third month. Viktor envisioned a Presidential Medal of Freedom out of this bestseller.

Viktor, out of contempt for Aloysius's "Woodstock farm hogwash," enjoyed seeing the "flower child" Aloysius squirm helplessly. Viktor used the patsy Aloysius as window front cleaner. BookSmart was a window front, a screen for "gray area" business opportunities Viktor had invested in. Viktor used the BookSmart basement to warehouse "product." Nobody suspected the dupey dope or "world's nicest guy" Aloysius. Perfect book cover: a book store of mealy-mouthed simps cluelessly wasting their homo lives on the aesthetic nose-pickings of midgets. A perfect book cover is worth a thousand books.

"I bet if I get my dick wet every night," Viktor once dreamed at the wheel of his latest Porsche, driving around Lake Minnetonka shopping for lakefront castles, "somehow I'll wind up owning a castle in Germany! Or a fucking chateau in Scotland!"

Larry smirked at the slackers on welfare, whether they were smirking on welfare or not, slackers were slackers no matter what they smirked at or slacked about, he smirked deeply within his bowels, a place where no one could see him smirking: the book store workers all *qualified* for welfare. The mouthful of smirks would have sloped off Larry's face toward Figlio's Italian-American hamburgers, but Viktor hijacked Larry for lunch at Club Miami.

Larry exited, holding the door for the entering Courtney Kirkwood—nattering, grumbling, cursing streaks of blue (urethane-wheeled cart in front), and singing to herself in a hamster-wheeling harangue. Its bullet points were: everything has been fucked up ever since the Big Bang didn't happen . . . everything! And that sucks the wind right of a girl.

Chitchee ran downstairs to see whither Kennedy. Find the snowmobile section or anything on snowmobiles? Which Kennedy hadn't. Disappointed, Chitchee clambered back up the stairs. Courtney's creative medium was abstract, pre-rusted iron giraffes in pink diapers, installations of giant laundry baskets filled with cucumber people, and smeared oils of herself as a three-headed Mary Magdalene in barbed-wired, three-breasted bikinis at the Los Alamos test site. She shoved her broken folding cart forward, Bette Davis cigarette holder in her mouth. Then the one loose cotter pin on her cart with its tine stabbed into Larry's leg and drew out a dew drop of blood.

"You stabbed me with your cart!" cried Larry, grabbing his bloody shank.

"Better get your tetanus shot then, Sunshine!" said Courtney sideways, spitting out a chunk of something behind her.

"There's a hole in my pants!" said Larry, hiking up a trouser leg to reveal the incarnation of a red dot on his sickly shin.

"They were ugly anyway," said Courtney, "maybe you can make shorts of them."

"Sssssee-Ssswwoo!" whistled Chitchee at Larry's exposed bacon-fat white of a hairless limb. "Nice leg, Larry. *It's all about the leg*, Willoughby! Oh, Larry?"

"Yes?" asked Larry, compressing his lips like brick-and-mortar.

"Don't be a stranger!"

"Oh, hello handsome! You work here?" said Courtney to Chitchee. "I love this store! Especially after Dale the Raging Librarian kicked me out of Walker Public Library for smoking crack in the men's room. Where else was I going to smoke it? The women's bathroom was filled with valley girls from South smoking meth. I hate meth. Tastes funny. Like chicken. Crack is my caviar. Is Snorri working?"

Chitchee listened (Aloysius was on the phone with Mother Aalgaard) to Courtney explaining her preference for crinolines lately in various Victorian versions. Today was the day to wear her Etsy-bought, off-white, wedding hoop skirt, and to show off her dyed-black hair, dyed-again blonde (lime streaks and tangerine highlights added). Her folding cart contents: a set of steak knives, a pink Wilma Flintstone purse, a Cooties toy humping a Chatty Cathy nailed to a crucifix, green Wellingtons, Snoopy glasses, a bottle of hydrogen peroxide, a bag of mothballs, Fels Naptha, and the economy-sized box of 20 Mule Team Borax.

She vaguely apologized for something by blaming her foul mood on #6 MTC busdriver Lily Holmgren, that piece of garbage, whose big mouth always set Courtney's jaundiced teeth on edge with her "*Ja, ja, ja*," and her "Don't you know, that's Minneso-o-o-ta?" With that one dumb look of hers, Lily strangled Courtney's cheerful, chirpy soul and poisoned it.

Beside Courtney's #6 MTC bus transfers always expired too soon, too soon. Coincidence? Courtney thought not! And, jiminy crickets, the *hell* if Courtney was going to argue with another ass-hatted, bus fucking driver like Lily Holmgren on the #6—over whether her folding cart filled with Cooties, Chatty Cathys, and crucifixes was blocking the front butterfly doors—again, not anymore than the ripening elephant family in the front seat (probably only riding one block before getting off and tipping the bus over) with their shit-ton of cola-sucking, Botero blimps, with their dawning butt-cracks at the butt-crack of dawn, slamming pawwwps and co-las and Fantas from Minnesoo-oo-da.

"What an amazing crinoline! Is that taffeta, Courtney?" asked Melusina with an unaccustomed diffidence. "Did you get that from us at Treasures Await?"

"This? Thank you for the compliment, you sweet dearie," said Courtney. "This is just some crap I threw together. I found it at a vintage landfill."

"How have you been, Courtney?" asked Kriemhilde, half walking, half reading an old dog-eared copy of Adelle Davis's *Let's Get Well.*

"Execrable!" said Courtney with a screechy pitch. "On the 1 to 10 scale of execrability: PURE SHIT! Thanks for asking . . . that was very, very thoughtful of you."

"Oh, honey," said Kriemhilde. "You need a rooty-tooty root beer. A root beer So—Da from Minn-e-SOTA! Don-cha, ja?"

"Speaking of pure shit," said Courtney, cutting off all arguments with a large exhale. "No, I'm upset since I discovered Revlon's High Gloss Nail Hardener had been purposely designed so that the screw-top would detach itself from the applicator brush after approximately 5 milliliters have been used, forcing the consumer to buy more and more hardener until a poor girl like me drops dead of a stroke. The applicator brush itself ends up a centimeter above the bottom of the bottle! I'm trying to get a class-action suit, but Revlon won't answer my emails. I sent them twenty emails and they can't even answer one? Total incompetence I tell YOU!"

"I'm really sorry to hear that," said Chitchee. "Try the Volunteer Lawyers Network! Can Legal Aid do anything? I can call them for you right now! I'll call the State Attorney's office. Paging Alan Page. Aloysius! Can I use the phone? Who are you talking to, Chaucer's Wife of Bath? At this rate, we're going to have to surgically remove the phone from the side of your face!"

"Chitchee, I'm talking to my mother!" said Aloysius, making a stunned face of slack disbelief that Chitchee completely missed because he had bent down to diagnose Courtney's folding cart, which he might quick-fix with duct tape but probably needed a soldering gun kit, which he might find at Treasures Await or maybe The Axe Man in St. Paul next time he approached the end of his map over there in that terra incognita. And then he found a soldering gun kit in Courtney's folding cart.

"Hey look what I found in your cart that you own," said Chitchee. "Want me to fix your court, Cartney? I could probably figure it out."

"Blah!" said Courtney, waving Chitchee off and wheeling forward. "Does Snorri work today? I don't see him."

SAAMI ROLVAAG

Benjamin "Saami" Rolvaag sneaked into work like Harry the Dirty Dog only to slink downstairs and lock himself in his doghouse. Saami's parrot head shirt, shaved short brown baize fuzz in a flying Vee down the middle of his forehead, socially deviant grin, leprechaun green eyeballs, and tetchy skin created in Chitchee's mind a pubescent, middle-aged Mr. Mxyzptlk in 14 S Boys Wranglers. Hiding, Saami propped himself up on the downstairs counter—nursing a hangover, buzzing with busy boredom—thoughts like flies caught between windows. Saami fetched books, processed orders, and packaged the mail to go out, but every time he stripped the adhesive tape from its thick roll, it screamed bombs, and every thirty seconds another tape bomb exploded. A migratory migrainish deathbird with the face of Harlan Ellison hovered over his work station.

Saami wondered how many "likes" the BookSmart Facebook website had gotten since yesterday (around a fuzzy midnight). Had he posted one or one hundred store selfies, running around the store blacked-out? He couldn't remember. For about an hour, he worked downstairs hearing the voices upstairs banging around in his head like pots and pans in the back of a Depression-era soup kitchen attacked by desperately starving brown bears.

Saami tried to remember being at his last ComiCon many spiderwebs ago. He had a photo stored in the memory of the computer of himself: his arms are around all the other Spidermen in their fluctuating body shapes—some Spidermen were as large as President Tafts, polyester holding them in like Knox gelatin molds—some Spidermen had bodies as thin as syringes in loose tights. In *Saami's* too tightly-fitting Spiderman cosplay, he sat on Harlan Ellison's lap. And then he ran out to pick up Ellison, his sliders from White Castle. Or was he with Elvira in her black, spidery, full-bosomed gown at the White Castle? Didn't they win the prize together from the crane and claw machine? Wasn't it a rare Harlan Ellison Beanie Baby? Then Elvira autographed his face. Or was it the face of Harlan Ellison, the Beanie Baby? Oh no, it was Saami who was in the crane and claw machine, *which was his life.* Ellison and Elvira disappeared. He had gotten so fucked up, he couldn't remember what he had got fucked up on, pulled up into the air by a crane's claw in a White Castle—when he remembered the night before: he had been FacePlanted on FaceBook, DeathYelped on Yelp, and then Tweetfirestormed on Twitter by Beda Holmgren.

Chitchee watched Saami lug a mail bin of online-ordered books up the staircase and swing it down behind the front maroon counter. Ready to mail out, Aloysius would take the books to the post office by the 5th Precinct police station. Saami sat down on the ripped bar stool at the end of the maroon counter, onlined the second Dell computer, and mouse-clicked Firefox / Mozilla.

He smacked his head with an open palm. He had re-absorbed BookSmart's recent one-star customer review by Beda Holmgren, just as Minerva Singleton, Beda's partner, ventured up from the basement and saw Chitchee reading over Saami's shoulder:

Dear pasty white males at Bookmart: Benjamin Rollvague, please do not post updates that put down and shame people with regard to body weight and dead-naming, these insensitive attacks are indirected at me and My Facebook friends, there is no such thing as 'overweight,' weightism is racism, and when you post jokes addressing a person's body shape, intelligence, personality traits, or mention anything about the person's characteristics or existence, you are driving the train to MinneAuschwitz. Not so far fetched when I recall your micro-aggressions and micro-fascisms and even nano-anti semitisms which were detectable if you don't like Israel like I think I heard you tell Minerva a couple years ago. BookSmart is a patriarchal, rightwinged exclusively white male *old boys club* of little totalitarian jerks and fat ass-cheeses who would like nothing better than chip every objectified trans woman into nazi sex slavery and then turn them into wood chips. Obviously your insensitivity to persons of Other is also genetically-encoded in your barbaric posts with pictures of *big fat hamburgers* and *mounds of fattening French fries* and *white people eating pizza and other sickening caucasian occasions* and why don't you realize how offensively you sound to someone in transition?

"In transition? Huh? Beda isn't in transition. I've known her forever," said Saami. "In transition from what to what? From cheeseburgers to fish filets?"

Note: although I am not non-binary I am a spokespeople for all 64 biological genders on Twitter.

"Oh, Saami," said Chitchee. "You can't be insensitive to Beda, especially if she weighs in on Twitter. That makes you *the* very cis-sexist, transphobic architect of patriarchal power she loathes. Besides, Beda can kill you with one punch! Shoot her an apology for your abusive posts and buy her a Whitman's Sampler! Tell her you love her for who she is, not for what she tweets. And remember to keep your genders straight or not."

"Oh, Lord," said Saami, smacking his head. "I don't even know how to know I *know* any transes!"

"Typical phobism," said Minerva, reading over Saami's other shoulder, "but that's your male binary privileged narrative suppressing the narrative of the female underprivileged non binary experience. You have a very terminal case of gender-dysphoric, inflammatory, subconscious hate speech, which is icky-creepy, and an angry brand of radicalized male anti-feminism and a misogynistic, woman-hating adoration of female performers like Madonna. Like Courtney's feminism whenever her transfer expires or a painted turtle gets in her way. Have you written anything boycottable?"

"My name?" asked Saami.

Smack. Saami had a bad case of TMI and trembled, and shook, and grimaced, and he mowed with his mouth and he blushed like an apple. Then one more smack head down on the counter top like a self-flagellating follower of Husayn after the Battle of Karbala, and he felt fine.

"Hello, Saami, don't beat yourself up now, you should never internalize your own shortcomings, little guy," said Hjalmar Halversen, walking in and scoping out the BookSmart bookscape.

Hjalmar Halverson's gray rug-line rose up high on his head. He combed his hair from front to back. His black eyebrows, which were spread very far apart, climbed up his forehead, creating ridges with worry lines. The fine eyebrow hair, which grew thinly above his pale blue eyes, gave his blue eyes a distant quality. The frames of his silver, rimless eyeglasses didn't bring him any closer to you either. His eyes didn't seem to exist. Or he had simply never existed at all.

"Is my son Snorri working?" asked Hjalmar. "Hah! That sounded oxymoronic!"

"You got half of it right, the latter half that is," quipped Chitchee. "Snorri is always working, sir! He *works* and he even *sweats* like an ox."

"I'm his father, I believe I know him better than you!" said Hjalmar, pulling down his silver, rimless eyeglasses for a better view.

"He is an ox like St. Thomas Aquinas," said Chitchee. "Not to mention a genius like Chesterton!"

"Bup, bup, genius?" coughed Hjalmar Halversen, shaking his head, turning around, and bouncing on his feet a little.

Hjalmar had retired early as a top-rate Honeywell engineer, who then specialized in humidity and temperature measuring devices known as thermo-hygrometers, which he patented and sold for a tidy, ungodly sum. Then he bought and ran a printer's shop which did photo engraving, letterpress, lithography, bookbinding, and silk screen printing. After he had made that mint, maybe a double mint, he invested in Wendy's Company as soon as Dave Thomas went public. Hjalmar parlayed those capital gains to his stockbroker at Piper Jaffrey, and later at U. S. Bancorp, which moved the decimal point on his total assets to the right with steady regularity. Unfazed by the Black Monday Bubble, the DotCom Bubble, the Subprime Mortgage Bubble, and all the Mr. Bubbles, and all the Mr. Bubbles to be born, Hjalmar loved to show off his green thumb for investment, which he never failed to remind all his waiters, dentists, taxi cab drivers, and Sherman the Shoeshine Boy at the MSP airport, who had been shining Hjalmar's shoes going all the way back to Wold-Chamberlain Field. Hjalmar slowly closed his eyes to signify suspicion, examining Chitchee like a Shoeshine Boy. A sudden distancing of himself from Chitchee ensued. A hole in the spacetime continuum appeared in which Hjalmar drew an imaginary bead on the lung and heart region of a white-tailed deer.

"Smart aleck!" fired Hjalmar. "You must be Chitchee, the new guy. I heard about you. Snorri says you write science fiction. Of course, there's no future in that."

"No future in the future?" okayed Chitchee.

"*There aren't going* to be any books pretty soon," said Hjalmar, "if you haven't heard by now."

"Oh?" said Chitchee, "I know what you're saying. Eco-catastrophe is on the way. Corporate greedy cheeks, coal black clouds, widespread famine from political snowmen, mass extinctions like nothing on Earth, the entire planet denuded down to the last bucket of gray goo in a techno blackout!"

"*And* there's this brand new thing that came out," said Hjalmar, catting in closer to paw at a toy warbler on a string. "You can find out anything in the world by asking it a question. It's a little thing called the *Internet*—heard of it?"

"The Internet, not to be confused with the World Wide Web?" asked Chitchee. "Tim Berners-Lee—"

"*Every*thing is on the Internet now, where have you been, the *library?*" said Hjalmar with a snort, snort, and a chuckle held in escrow.

"Yes, sir," said Chitchee, "in a little thing called *Walker Public Library* much of the time."

"*And* there's this little thing called *Wikipedia,* on this little thing called the *computer,*" Hjalmer continued, "*heard of the little thing called the computer?* You can *already* download a little thing called software that will read all your e little thing books for you! Because there is another little thing that came out recently: it's called the Kindle, *heard of it?*"

"So in a little thing called the future, there will be all these little things called little things, which no one will have heard of because they were too busy waiting for the next little thing to come out, which would be *the wheel*. Heard of that little thing?"

Aloysius skewered his *Magical Mystery Tour* on the broken, one-speakered CD player, turned it down to virtual off, and walked over to shake Hjalmar's rectangular handshake. Chitchee walked over and turned it way up. His eyes rolled toward the back of his head. Chitchee's head spun like a kaleidoscope when he heard "I Am The Walrus." He danced wirily in an ectoplasmic trance. Aloysius, seeing Chitchee miming a walrus flapping his arms together, raced back to dim the volume down to nothing.

He darted an incandescent look at Chitchee and apologized to Hjalmar.

"If I were you, I'd fire him," whispered Hjalmar.

"Don't worry I will," said Aloysius, biting the spandrel between his thumb and forefinger.

UP NORTH FISHING

Often mountains of sadness buried Chitchee. Tears like common rain filled him to the gunnels. So many misunderstandings that could have been untangled and never were. He pictured his father: Finkle's Rushmore pose, face in a proud snarl, brows laced into knots, heart of corundum, and cloudy eyes squinting unable to see an inch in front of his face when it wasn't even raining. Chitchee looked back on his own failures, which all began with his father, who refused to talk to him—over two tiny folds of flesh!

Chitchee forgave his tormentor. He knew Finkle had burned himself out on the road *a la* Willy Lomax before he disowned Chitchee. For Finkle, sales was the answer after The Big One. Salesmen were the new soldiers after WWII. Peace was war in another key. Finkle went into advertising and canvassed the Twin Cities for Naegele's Outdoor Billboards. No sooner hitched to Paisley, Old Man Naegele laid off the loyal Finkle and half the staff a week before Christmas. Finkle reasoned that market forces were at work and who was he to judge a legendary tycoon like Old Man Naegele? He couldn't have made a fortune by being stupid, could he? Finkle stood in as much awe of millionaires as he did of Robert E. Lee, John Pershing, and Douglas MacArthur. By Easter, Finkle's Army buddy, Nils Nislander, nabbed Finkle a job working for an elevator company that specialized in oildraulic elevators, levelators, and levadocks. Then Finkle worked for H. J. C. Ganzer, selling Le Tourneau scrapers, traxcavators, air compressors, steam and drop hammers, and dragline and clam-shell shovels to construction companies.

Finkle peddled Keeler Polygraphs, working for Leonarde Keeler, the inventor of the lie detector. He cold-called the Keeler door to door. Then he came up with the idea of the "weatherball" and the "weatherball code." The towering metal ball had neon lights: white for getting colder, red for getting warmer, green for no change, and colors blinking for turbulence. Finkle claimed the "Weatherball" was stolen from him over drinks at The Lingonberry Inn, a roadside restaurant in Hibbing. In fact, Northwestern Bank erected the "Weatherball" superstructure whose giant blinking ball one day blinded Finkle driving into Minneapolis. He fishtailed in a raging snowstorm. He pulled over on Highway 12 to catch his breath. He could have been a millionaire! The rat face of humanity had stared him down and he blinked. Bitter, bitter resentment reshaped his circuitry. He blamed Paisley and all the women in the world—not to mention the patent thief. He asked himself: what do people on TV do in cases like this? They hire detectives. They always hire lots of detectives. Frustrated, Finkle visited the Hillswick Detective Agency, which had an office by Prospect Park. Finkle told Arthur Hillswick, the private investigator: "I don't remember the crook's name. I think he was a German Catholic Republican married to an Irish-Scottish Presbyterian Democrat. I could have taken out a patent on the Weatherball and never worked another day in my life. That Weatherball cost me a lost million dollars! I'll sue him and kill him!"

He sold one Keeler Polygraph. That was to Arthur Hillswick who found Finkle's "crook," LaDonna's father, Wirt Jensen. Hillswick could not *prove* Wirt was a crook, so he dropped the case. To the outrage of Finkle! Finkle accused Detective Hillswick of lying, conspiring, and covering up. In any case, after the red witch hunt of the McCarthy era subsided, the lie detector industry abated. Finkle cooled off. He spent the 1960s selling "food service contracts" for CRA, Corporate Retailers of America and raising young Charles, whom he constantly suspected of being born a fairy.

The long white road of winter led the black Falcon to Northfield, Winona, Duluth, Moorhead, Collegeville, St. Peter, Mankato, and especially Hibbing (and The Lingonberry Inn for unfinished business or pleasure) from which the road stretched out and out in ever expanding snow drifts of lost radio contact. And when CRA assigned Finkle its prison and correctional accounts, he found himself driving to Rush City, St. Cloud, Lino Lakes, Sandstone, Shakopee, Red Wing, and Stillwater, and hating it. After he complained about back pay on his commissions, CRA eliminated his position—and screwed him out of his pension. Finkle took this as a violation of the "American Dream," which in his mind loomed larger than the Bill of Rights. Life was a long cheat without the "American Dream."

"Paisley," announced Finkle over the dinner table, "I want to raise Chitchee up to be a professional forester. I think he would do well in the remote outdoors away from people. You know on account of his—his—queeriness."

"No!" cried Paisley. "He should be an Ambassador, an Ambassador to all the foreign countries. He wants to be friends with everybody as much as he wants everybody to be friends. He could be the Ambassador to all the United Nations!"

"When hell freezes over," Finkle retorted. "I will show *Charles* how real men do real men things—like war, slaughter, pillage, blow up bridges, and go fishing up north."

Hence the camping trips, the fishing expeditions, and the hints:

"Chitchee, do you think you could possibly get along with lots of different types of *trees*? And different-sized *lakes*? Come on, I'll take a week off, and we'll fly the Falcon up north and I'll show you how to blast a deer's head off. Does that sound good?"

Before flying off to the woods, Old Fink and Chitchee tried a pose of filial and paternal happiness with Chitchee's arm around Finkle's shoulders. Paisley was "tickled pink" that her "chilly-willy Charlie" had bonded with her "darling finnegan Finkie," and she twisted their arms, wringing from them a forced family photo for the forced Family Photo Album. She waved goodbye all the way to the end of the hot, asphalt driveway—waving to Chingachgook and Uncas on their way to Rainy Lake. From a long shot view, Chitchee felt the anguish of this "family" going through the motions of family motions without emotion. The Chichester family was dead. The whole fishing expedition—camping, hiking, fishing, hunting, killing, and slaughtering—served as a cut-price Outward Bound, which they could never afford. Meanwhile, Finkle dreamed that if Chitchee developed survival skills, he might even have a career in the Air Force as a test pilot. Obviously Chitchee wasn't cut out to be a foot soldier. He had even overheard Finkle tell Paisley: Chitchee could never survive going to the trenches of Vietnam, *because Chitchee could never even survive the Greyhound bus to Canada.*

Chitchee remembered how wreathed in smiles was Paisley snapshotting the Father and Son photos of the two glumly, morbidly bonding fishermen in front of the woods in the backyard. Paisley was so ecstatic over the fun-to-be-had by their hunkering down on the Canadian border, covering themselves with Cutter Anti-Mosquito Repellant, and doing "man things" like that. Finkle wondered whether she had a secret lover down the street. He ran over the unusual suspects but concluded none of the neighbors had his balls.

Finkle could never figure out the "genetics thing." So much so, Finkle discarded the science of biology as rubbish. Same with evolution, whatever that was. He suspected that God was punishing Finkle via Chitchee. In a dark and dreary closet, Finkle confessed formally his out-of-wedlock intercourse with the waitress at The Lingonberry Inn to a confessor in a different parish from his own. He had "sinned bad, although wasn't that excusable in a way? Father, the loneliness of the long white road of winter and the dark nights of the soul and all that—besides, I think she was two-timing me with the Weatherball Thief."

Finkle's Kodak Carousel Slide Projector revolved white, cardboard-framed memories of the Chichesters. Finkle (or the picture slide of Finkle) smoked his briar Dunhill and tilted his Sears canvas fishing hat. Relaxing on a La-Z-Boy rocker, he cheered at violent spurts of blood sports. He drank his "Irish whish-key like an Irish fish-key." He had a constitutional right to alcoholism. His WWII record was so impressive that no one knew what it was. The fray of civilian life frayed Finkle's nerves to a frazzle. He should have stayed in the Army where he could do no wrong. As the 1950s fear-mongered forward, Finkle dreaded "world overpopulation," "nuclear winter," and "weather seeding" as pretexts for a United Nations socialist putsch of Earth. When the 1960s exploded with anti-war, un-Minnesotan activities, which appalled him, Finkle traded in the Cold War for the Vietnam War. Protestors, protestors, and more protestors—he protested their protesting too much. He made a sign STOP PROTESTING and planted it proudly in his front yard. AND LOVE YOUR COUNTRY he added next to it, the next day. The traitors in his mind were always Henry Wallace, Adlai Stevenson, the "hydra-headed Kennedy clan," the Gene McCarthyites, the George McGovernites, and the Black Pantherites—referred to as "big black bucks," which precluded any usage of "big white bucks." A passable black woman was a "class act." "Now, Diahann Carrol, she's a class act." Or: "She *was* a class act until she married that big black buck." Finkle denied vehemently his racism by saying there was no such thing as racism anyway so he was not a racist. Being black was an advantage because of all the new opportunities. "Look at Sammy Davis, Jr. He works!" Finkle joined a "John Birch Society." Chitchee picked up its literature on Finkle's office work desk. Chitchee assumed the John Birch Society was The Society for the Preservation of Birch Trees. Then he quickly read the propaganda, shocked his father had an angry rage bottled up (from what provocation?) inside him. Could Finkle's bigotry have appeared like a genie, fully formed? Finkle believed in God and he believed in those who believed in God and only those who believed in God were to be trusted with the idea of God; however, Chitchee's maturing liberalism was the worship of Marduk.

A pristine, pure turquoise sky with azure-lined clouds was hovering over the fjords and fells of green pines when the traditional Father, Son, and Holy Ghost fishing trip re-enacted another D-Day. Their Boston Whaler skimmed onto the beachhead of sand, strafed by the krauts. Staff Sergeant Chichester never moved so fast as when he was barking orders, unloading coolers, throwing the fishing equipment on the beachhead, digging for the anchor a hole in the sand, and running in circles for the stringers, the tackle boxes, the fishing poles with their hooks flying, the provisions, the cigarettes, the chocolates for the villagers, and the Olympia beers. And . . . forward, forward. Never let your men see you *not* face the enemy unless you are surrounded, Chitchee, and then never then!

"Chitchee, set up the pup! Use a sailor's knot on that! That's not secure! Try the sailor's knot. Let me do that! Why are you always in the way? Where is the minnow bucket? Where did you put it? Did you pack the daredevils, those little red and white swively things? Forget it! Scrub the cast-iron skillets with sand and get a fire going with twigs and not those twigs! Don't you know your twigs? Where's the compass? Don't tell me it headed south, wiseacre! You packed the Ronson's lighter fuel, didn't you? Collect the dry wood. Where are my Snap-E-Toms? Smoke repels mosquitoes, so . . . I'm missing a beer, did you take one of my beers? I had a twelve-pack of Olympia. I only see five. Do you hear that? Owls!"

"Owls in the middle of the day?" asked Chitchee. "I think those are loons, dad. I think there are a lot of loons on this beachhead."

"Don't give me any of your sassy lip! Are you going to scrub the skillets or stand there with your mouth open to catch dragonflies? God damn it, how am I going to make Bloody Marys in this godforsaken wilderness? Look, owls are owls. I'll peel the spuds. See that? Lightning. South by southwest. The walleyes will be coming to the surface. They can smell lightning. They form perfect squares and swim away from its direction in strict formations. Old Indian lore. Get the bacon grease, and grease the skillet while I go fish my limit! Why isn't the fire going yet? That's not sumac, is it? Do you want to kill us with poison gas? Not with lighter fuel! That fire is going to burn down the entire Kabetogama Peninsula if you don't—watch it! Give me that can!"

Finkle grabbed Chitchee by the shoulders like an armoire and moved him aside.

"Why are you *still* always in the way?" added Finkle.

"I guess it depends on your perspective," said Chitchee.

"You see, son, that's how you get a fire started," said Finkle, standing back and watching the fire sputter out.

"If all else fails, burn the StarTribune at the stake!" continued Finkle. "Hateful, hateful stuff!"

The newspaper Finkle torched defiantly curled up black behind the line of fire that would not catch. The birch twigs did not catch.

Finkle, looking at the sky, lectured a dry and wooden Chitchee:

"You know when a storm is coming, son, because the gooseberries turn up their leaves to catch the rain."

"Where *are* the gooseberries?" asked Chitchee.

"It doesn't matter," said Finkle, savoring his tightly-clutched Olympia beer can. "Now chop down a couple birch trees. Here's an axe, Viking. I thought I gave you an axe for Christmas. I'm going to set up the snares and the traplines. Can't be too careful out here in the wild blue yonder, eh Chitchee! Isn't this great? Maybe catch some venison, your mom loves deer meat. Deer for a dear! Are those deer tracks? Which way is the wind? Don't move, Chitch! If it's down wind your body odor might be giving us away."

"So?"

"So? What if a 500-pound bear decides he likes your smell? What do you do?"

"I smear myself with my own feces?"

"No."

"Curl up into a fetal position?"

"No! Are you a coward?" asked Finkle with grim, challenging grit. "My son, the coward. A Chichester never gives up. A Chichester always ends where he starts. A Chichester never says uncle *even to his uncle*."

"So, a Chichester says mother's brother instead of uncle?" mumbled Chitchee.

"Hear that, smart mouth? Something rustling in the brush."

Finkle grabbed his shotgun and shot what he thought was a snake, but he was not so sure. There were no traces of anything but shredded alder leaves and gun smoke.

"I think it crawled over there," said Chitchee, pointing.

"If you know so much from reading books," his father's head pivoted, swiveled, and tilted. "Why don't *you* go finish it off with the .22?"

Finkle tossed the .22 crossways at Chitchee's chest, and it bounced off Chitchee like a football, and fumbling it, Chitchee dropped it. The .22 discharged.

The bullet struck the branch of a hollowed-out oak, alerting a wasp's nest to give marching orders.

"What was that for?" said Chitchee, practically crying. "I am fine with snakes. Probably a common garter snake."

"You don't know everything! There's nothing common about snakes. Could have been a water moccasin. Or a brown recluse. Or a red squirrel."

Finkle re-loaded the shotgun.

"Goddamn red squirrels—they're probably all communists too! And you didn't think I had a sense of humor?"

"You do when you're drunk," said Chitchee. "For an hour or so anyway."

"Now I have to find a trading post," said Finkle a little tipsy, "and pick up some more bear."

"I didn't know you could pick up a bear!" laughed Chitchee, spontaneously feeling like his young self again.

"Okay, Einstein," said Finkle, walking up to Chitchee and slapping him with the back of his hand. "You're grounded! I don't want you to leave the tent while I'm gone. Go ahead and sit in your tent and read books over your head! I'm going hunting."

Chitchee, shocked by his father's violence, tried to think: why? Chitchee had brought two books for the fishing trip: Che Guevara's *Guerilla Warfare* and Ezra Pound's *Guide to Kulchur*. When he grew tired of one, he switched to the other. He didn't feel like reading much. Chitchee collected litter and tidied up the woods, and grew bored.

Chitchee masturbated into a white sweat sock, and his foot, touching the tent, caused the tent to jiggle, rhythming out beats.

"What were you doing?" said Finkle, flinging back the flap of the tent. "What were you doing? Don't tell me! I know what you were doing."

Finkle made the sign of the cross.

"Nothing!"

"You'll have to confess that to a priest. Only a Man of God like a priest can absolve you for that. Or even thinking of that. Otherwise, you'll be damned in hell."

Father and son didn't speak to each other. Chitchee sulked in the tent, and Finkle resumed his mission of hunting for little birds, fishing for little fish, trapping little mammals, and taking target practice on a hollowed-out oak.

Bang. Bang. The forest echoed like the slight applause of an almost empty high school auditorium for a junior high performance of *The Crucible*.

A wasp ravened on Old Finkle like a wolf. The wasp adjusted its stance, thought for a second, then jabbed its stinger into Old Fink's neck. Then another wasp came down on Finkle's cheek. Finkle swatted and crushed the wasp into his cheek dead, but a rash spread from his neck downward and then back up like someone painting a barn door red. Finkle stumbled back to camp, tripped over the tent, and screamed. Chitchee jumped out of the tent. His father's face turned blue. Finkle's bulging lips protruded, and his eyes slammed shut puffed out like caramel apples. While his upper lip doubled in size, his tongue filled his entire mouth with a wad of blue flesh.

"Jesus Christ, Kristina," mumbled Finkle. "Right after Kristina, if God is listening right now."

"Kristina?" asked Chitchee. "Dad, you're delirious! There's no Jesus Christ or Kristina here."

"Last Rites, Chitch," muttered Fink, his face redder than beet soup. "Get a priest here. My will it's . . . there's a reason you aren't in it! Damn your eyes!"

"Dad, listen to me! Lie down, here's a pillow. Where's your medicine? Where is the medicine?" said Chitchee, sweating like a pickled plum. "Don't worry I won't let you down!"

Chitchee cried cry-eyed. He remembered that his father always carried a First Aid kit with medicine for his allergies. Chitchee scurried around and rifled through his father's duffle bag and found the epinephrine-type antidotes, syringes, and needles. He tweezered the stinger like a splinter out of his father's flesh. He jammed a Benadryl down his father's throat and rubbed Calamine lotion on the wound. A wasp tickled Chitchee's ears with its wings and the vibrations produced a note Chitchee guessed as middle C, but there was no way of testing his perfect pitch against the wood winds. Chitchee, feeling strangely calm and compassionate (even though more wasps zoomed in and hovered in holding patterns, attracted by the first sting of his father's venom), piggybacked his father, a feisty but tiny man, into the Boston Whaler. He calmly steered him to the trading post where the officials put in a few phone calls. A stranger volunteered to flatbed truck them to a local county hospital near Rainy Lake.

They never spoke of that camping trip again, nor did they go on another one. If anything their relationship almost ended then and there. Because Chitchee saved his father's life, his father felt humiliated and could never forgive him. It expressed a truncation of the dynamic that placed Chitchee, a Skeptic, on a higher moral ground than Finkle, a man as devout as a 17th century Jansenist, or a "man of one book." After the fishing trip, Paisley blabbed Chitchee's secret to Old Finkle that Chitchee was having a sexual relationship with a classmate at the time—a *boyfriend*—and then there was no end to his father's anger.

That abrogated the Chichester line of transmission. The last conversation approached a punctuated equilibrium that finally exploded when Finkle kicked Chitchee out of the house on Graduation Day. Chitchee climbed into his Volkswagen bug, window up. Father walked out of the garage (Paisley cried behind the screen door to the kitchen); Father stood on the driveway next to the rock garden, which they had once planned to cart off and replace with a real garden of real flowers, junipers, and geraniums, but never would. Chitchee drove to the room he had rented with friends in a dilapidated Cape Cod cottage, which had rotted like a two-story cheese along Highway 101 on the way toward Wayzata. Chitchee recited from Wordsworth's poem "Michael" and then burst out crying, sobbing, and runny-nosing.

The pity which was then in every heart
For the old Man—and 'tis believed by all
That many and many a day he thither went,
And never lifted up a single stone.

SNORRI HALVERSEN

Snorri Halversen, six feet tall and two hundred pounds of hangover, greeted his own father ambivalently with a reluctant smile. His upper torso rounded outward like a blast furnace actively smelting pig iron. His long black dreadlocks added to his air of noble weariness, mixing Stoic rectitude with a Confucian respect for learning. Snorri sweat pools through the already stained armpits of his Minnesota North Stars jersey (VASKO). He wore blue-jean cutoff shorts year round, and lumpy long underwear beneath the shorts when it dropped below zero. His thick buckled sandals greeted the store with his huge hairy summer sausage toes. Snorri never felt the cold. A genetic mutation had allowed Snorri to skinny dip in Lake Calhoun every winter without feeling the ice water.

Snorri surveyed the room for troublemakers. His eyes made dashed lines at every purse, back-purse, shopping bag, hidden pocket, baggy jacket, and all the possible endgames and exit moves from the building, down to a toilet paper roll absconding in a heartbeat out the back door. Snorri made his father prickle uncomfortably, because Snorri acted as if there were a dire, ongoing emergency at all times, and Snorri had mickle time to discuss family matters. The book store was in pieces. It wasn't a good time to shamble about the usual mandatory family plans to watch fireworks somewhere not on television for the Aquatennial, whenever that was.

"Snorri, your mother and I want to get you something for your birthday," said Hjalmar expansively. "How old are you? Mom thinks you might appreciate a Land Rover. But I reminded her how you totaled the last one. So I was thinking of something more stationary: an ice-fishing house. What do you think? You could live there—all winter in your shorts."

"Fine," said Snorri. "I could use an ice-fishing house. Fine. Chitchee, watch those two old ladies in Cooking and Crafts . . . their purses are rather large."

Snorri set in motion his thick neck, which rotated like a human panopticon and geared him into thought: Ugh! Not that guy! Or gal! Crazy Courtney? Let's say vagrant (gender neutral) or squatter (can be male or female): anyway that human being / cousin to the "bon-robos" never buys anything, never will. Because she can boost them, that's why! Trust no one, like Claudius played by Derek Jaccabees.

"Hi, Snorri, it's my first day!" said Chitchee. "And it's *crazy amazing*! It's like a Petersen *Guide to Book Store Geeks*. I've got some great ideas for the store too. We could have a whole section for books on empathy!"

"Hi, Snorri," said Courtney.

"We had an empathy shelf, where the compassion section used to be," said Snorri, "but everybody ripped on it, and so we had to tear it down and throw it out."

"Well, I'll bring it back!" said Chitchee. "We can work it out! I have some empathy books I can donate: *The Path of the Empath*, *The Empath Wears No Clothes*, and *To Dream The Empathable Dream*. You can't *not* have an empathy shelf!"

"Why not?" asked Snorri. "No other book store has an empathy shelf. Why should we have empathy for an empathy shelf?"

With a smirk, Snorri smirk-kicked Saami off the coveted bar stool. Snorri plumped down in front of the store's second Dell computer. Saami had dragged the tacky, ripped leather bar stool into the store as a real find only the day before yesterday, and it was already Snorri's catbird's seat. Saami frowned and slunk back downstairs.

"Chitchee, do you think I am emotionally numb?" Snorri asked, tossing back his dreads, his jaw the envy of every politician exuding overconfidence to get elected.

"Yeah," said Chitchee, "numb as petrified wood. Don't worry, Snorri. Inside every tortoise there is a hare struggling to get out. But you'd make a kind and decent husband. I mean for Madison, not for me. Hah! Cheers! Did I say I love my job? I could marry it. How many people can say that?"

"Not me," said Courtney.

"Chitchee, I thought this job, which I got you, not to be repetitive, would be your cup of tea! We definitely needed someone to help customers, and, well you can help me too," said Snorri, thumb-nailing the hamburger fat gristled between his molars. "Checking bags for me is a full time job not to mention the foot patrols for suspicious types. Wait, I smell diesel. Yep, Blue Diesel."

Snorri sniffed around with his nose in the air.

"I think it's hey . . . check out the two suspicious elderly ladies with pearl earrings in Cooking and Crafts. Go over there and stand next to them! See if you can smell Blue Diesel on them!"

"Excuse me, ladies," said Chitchee, "while I smell for Blue Diesel on you."

Melusina and Kriemhilde lifted up their arms for some reason.

"Hey, Snorri, they're clean!" yelled Chitchee. "I think the Blue Diesel is you!"

"God damn it, you're right," muttered Snorri, padding himself down. "Never mind!"

Saami announced on the stairs a smoke break for himself, walked out the door, and returned with the wanted poster.

"Hey Chitchee, you're wanted by the FBI? The Federal Bureau of Investigation? Wow!"

Hjalmar dealt Chitchee a double take. Torg stiffened. Courtney filed it away. Melusina and Kriemhilde cocked their ears, leaning out of Cooking and Crafts. Aloysius snored.

"So?" said Chitchee.

"Do you think there is a reward?" asked Saami.

"Go ahead, use my name, and shoot the FBI an email," said Chitchee.

Snorri handed the keyboard to Saami without standing up.

"How do you spell it?" asked Saami, clutching the keyboard awkwardly.

"'F' as in Foucault," said Chitchee. "'B' as in the 'b' in Habermas, and 'I' as in the penultimate letter in the French word, *trompe l'oeil*."

"I guess there isn't really a reward," said Saami, walking away. "Forget it."

"I didn't think so," concluded Chitchee.

"Father," said Snorri, standing up, "you will have to excuse me. It's extremely busy right now, and it looks like I'm the only one working at the moment. As per usual."

"Okay, Snorri, I'll let you get back to *work*," laughed Hjalmer, making to leave. "Don't *work* too hard, Snorri. Maybe we can go shopping for ice-fishing houses tomorrow. If it's not too much *work*. I love you, son!"

"Can I bring Madison?" called out Snorri, inflected with a rising tone of hopeless doubt.

Courtney groaned.

"No," said Hjalmar peremptorily disgusted.

"Good," said Courtney.

"Oh," said Hjalmar, "and thanks for the inspiring biography you gave me! I really liked that Bull Meechum. What character! Unfortunately I left it at O'Hare airport and never finished it. Some hobo probably grabbed it."

"That *novel* was a signed first edition, presentation copy, inscribed *Great Santini* by Pat Conroy," said a disgruntled Snorri.

"Oh!" said Hjalmar, leaving. "It was fiction. I read the first three pages. Then it wasn't worth anything anyway."

Everyone who knew Snorri eventually discovered Snorri's hobbyhorse: the Civil War.

His distant relative, Harald "Hal" Halversen, was in the Minnesota Regiment, which turned the tide of the Civil War by its crucial self-slaughter and sacrifice in a reverse Pickett's charge at Gettysburg, throwing themselves in front of the Confederates who had almost breached the Union lines. The Minnesota Regiment at Gettysburg (as related in James McPherson's *Battle Cry of Freedom*—a Gustavus Adolphus alum Snorri reminded everyone) conducted a brilliant blocking maneuver that allowed reinforcements the sacred time to save the Union.

The State of Minnesota thus preserved democracy, the rule of law, and the peaceful transition of power.

"Yes," Chitchee agreed once, "credit where credit is due rests squarely on the shoulders of those happy few, those happy dead of the Minnesota Regiment on a day similar to—if not more memorable than—St. Crispian Crispin Crispo Day Crisco Cisco Kid Crispy Critter and Rice Crispy Day. What was it called?"

"Are you giving me shit?" said Snorri.

"No, Captain, no Captain," said Chitchee. "Where did you get that paranoid streak, homeslice, your mother or your father? I agree with you! Okay, I won't talk from now on. You're *mean* today, *toro*!"

Snorri cherished home, hearth, and high school. His territorial allegiance extended his Norwegian roots into obscure Norwegian branches of Norwegian woods. Snorri supported everything around him in fiercely loyal, logarithmic circles starting from the house he grew up in, to the suburb, the county, the state, the neighboring states, and thence to Canada. His allegiances died out ripple-wise quickly in the states that had no ice hockey, "the wretched states that don't know how to skate on ice."

"You *don't* want to work here?" asked Snorri. "I got you this job. You can't quit on me. You don't like *books* all of a sudden? Well, I'll be jiggered."

"No, this is my home!" continued Chitchee. "But, uh Snorri, one thing, I didn't know I was going to be *paid* in books. Books . . . forever? Or as long as the world lasts? That's not even minimum wage, that's minimum book!"

"We figured you wouldn't mind being paid in books for a while anyway," said Snorri. "Most start-ups take a couple years to turn a profit."

"Sure, Snorri . . . but I won't make rent for August, unless I go back to dealing. I might have to give notice in a couple minutes. Look, we had a good run."

"You volunteered for free before! What's the dangle-berried difference?" said Snorri, sorting a few books as he warmed toward the daily chores and looked at the new arrivals and hummed. "Sorry if I'm a little edgy. Haven't you heard about all the robberies in Uptown? Dunn Brothers got robbed."

"I'm back!" said Lake Street Rodney, presenting himself to the book store in an encore begun when the audience was leaving.

"No! Did anybody get hurt?" Chitchee asked plaintively, choking on a tear drop. "Or was somebody *killed?*"

"Killed?" said a shocked Rodney. "Somebody actually died around here?"

"Somebody was murdered?" Courtney froze. "Where? Dunn Brothers by Lunds?"

Rodney feared for his life and promptly ran out the back door and ran around Lake Street like a miniature poodle that wanted to jump over its own shadow.

"I don't know if anyone was actually *killed,*" said Snorri. "And anyway isn't death as inevitable as the sun that sets and the moon that shines?"

"Eh?" said Torg, cupping his right ear and pushing it forward from behind.

Torg's right ear had one long gray, stray hair growing from its lobe. The ear hair, the long gray one that is, came alive like a snake when Torg pulled the ear hair out between his fingers.

Melusina looked at Snorri. Kriemhilde poked her noggin out of the aisle.

"As far as death goes," said Snorri, "the Earth is always turning and sloughing off lives—a hundred thousand dead bodies every day. Death is nothing new; it is a part of life. It is a teacher and sage."

"Gag me," said Chitchee.

"Excuse me?" asked Snorri.

When Kennedy overheard "robberies," he strode up the staircase two stairs at a time, fearful of Rodney's magic markers, private language games, and cobwebbed speeches. Eager to catch the scuttlebutt though, Kennedy feinted a move at the maroon counter to buy a book, which was really a glance to see where Rodney was on the Uptown chessboard. Then Rodney flew up into Kennedy's face like a flushed game bird.

"Hold pile?" asked Snorri.

"You know," said Kennedy, "all of a sudden I feel so fecklessly peckish I better exiguate the premises. I'm going to Mickey D's for a conference call."

"You sure you want to risk abrogating the hold your hold pile holds on *you?*" asked Chitchee.

Exitus Kimanus stage left to McDonald's.

"Wouldn't murder make the news?" asked Chitchee. "I'll look! Are there any Cheez-Its around? I read the other day that Cheez-it poultices are a golden cure for scabies, and I've got a weird rash from some books on empathy I pulled out of a dumpster the other day."

Chitchee reached for the *Minneapolis Star Tribune*, itched his armpit quickly, and discovered a green pebble of Mennen's Speed Stick antiperspirant there. He removed the *Minneapolis Star Tribune*'s sports section, rife with heartbreaking losses to home teams, which he placed, careful not to wrinkle it, in the wastebasket. Why couldn't both sides win one for a change?

"Honestly, Snorri, I'm sorry," said Chitchee, accidentally thumb-flicking the pebble of Mennen's Speed Stick off Snorri's nose, which they both ignored.

"Please forgive me!" continued Chitchee, a tremulous shake to his voice because he wanted to please Snorri, who had heartily put his own head on the railroad tracks to recommend Chitchee for the job. "I'm grateful! I've been out of the job loop. The divorce dogged me and prevented me from looking for a job."

Snorri estimated the distance from himself to the ears of Aloysius, who was looking for the sports section and fruitlessly floundering through the Rainbow Grocery coupons in the wastebasket.

Aloysius sighed. He scooped up the obituaries and sighed a little softer.

"The divorce?" asked Snorri, repeating the word without moving his lips. "Chitchee, I love you man, but the divorce was years and years ago . . . sorry for your loss, but . . . you have to, don't be offended—be a man! Okay, don't cry! Gut it out, endurance at any task is commendable! Frankly, Chitchee—you should tell Aloysius that you're always willing to stay late . . . so I can get off work early. My rotator cuff is killing me again . . . flares up around high school hockey pre-season time . . . probably nothing I can't cure at the Bryant Lake Bowl with a couple Summit Ales! They are saying Josh Hartnett goes there. And he's dating Scarlett Johannsen and people have sighted her around Uptown. Don't tell Madison, but I'd give my eye-teeth to meet Scarlett Johannson."

"You better get going then, Big Dog," said Chitchee.

"And between you and me," continued Snorri, lowering his head, his jawbone frozen with liquid nitrogen. "Aloysius is full-tilt, bull goose loony. Nothing he says flies anymore. And it was that damned Ray Bradbury who shot him down."

"Dandelion Wine guy?" asked Chitchee as he walked over to Aloysius and looked at his sleeping face for any telling clues of an incipient psychotic break.

"He doesn't look mad as a March hare," continued Chitchee.

"That's because he keeps his madness bottled-up inside. Don't we all? Anyhoo, ever since he read 'A Sound of Thunder,'" murmured Snorri, lowering his head, "Aloysius has been terrified of the 'butterfly effect.' He told me himself that that story terrified him. And now he can't stand any change. Ray Bradbury personally sauteed the boss's brains with onions in olive oil. Why can't the store turn a profit? Why do we never invest in the book store? Come on, Chitchee! Do you really think the boss isn't bats? Come on, man!"

Snorri heard a squeak. He mean-mugged Courtney.

"Excuse me, Sir? Mam? Sir? Ma'a'am? Ma'amsir, you'll have to check in your cart!" said Snorri, walking kind of bow-legged with oak trunk thighs (he unstuck his jammed underwear from the crease between thigh and pelvic area and knocked his balls back into place). He carried half an Ace playing card and thrust the red card into Courtney's hand.

Snorri gripped the handle on the cart.

Snorri affixed the other half Ace of Spades to Courtney's folding cart with a wooden laundry clothes-pin—the clothes-pin type that looks like a fish with huge silver eyes in the middle. Chitchee marveled at its perfect design as if it were from Angkor Wat.

"All strollers go behind the counter!" declared Snorri to the whole store, scaring everyone and causing browsers to pat themselves down and declare, "No stroller on me!"

When Snorri walked away from Courtney she had a sob on her face, mulling over the love requited with amnesiac aggression. Aloysius snored himself awake, snorted, and asked Snorri for the Minneapolis Star Tribune sports page. He had fallen asleep because he had exhausted the obituaries and no one good had died there or no one of interest that he knew. And dead 100-year olds weren't very good at team sports.

"I was going to buy The Junie B. Jones Coloring Book but the deal is off, asshole!" said Courtney, throwing the half Ace playing card on the floor.

She limped with a crimp in her crinoline. She put on a lace, bridal headdress then spit out her Skol wad, missing the redolent, white pine wood flooring, because the wad splat like Basho's frog on an upper of Torg's brown leather Thom McAn shoes—the kind with breathing pin-holes—the stiff and ugly dress shoes men wore when they had jobs in the 1950s. Torg heard the sputum launch. He stayed at the maroon counter like a swimmer in the shallow end who won't let go of the tiled pool wall for fear of a pool of nasal mucus.

"Aloysius!" exclaimed Snorri. "Did you see that? We're going to have to trespass Crazy Courtney. She spit on Torg the Counter Klingon! How insulting!"

"What happened?" asked Torg. "Someone got spit on? A clinker clung to what?"

"Okay, okay, Snorri," said Aloysius. "Does anybody know where you can buy used *kantele* strings around here? B Sharp Music open tonight? Anyone know? Maybe I can run down to Knut-Koupee when I get a second to breathe."

"I wonder who invented the wooden laundry clothes-pin?" replied Chitchee, looking at Snorri.

Snorri stared at Chitchee and returned to him a rolling-eye look without even rolling his eyes.

"Are you guys listening?" asked Snorri. "What about these Lunds bags of books? Is this guy coming back? Aloysius? He's asleep!"

Snorri kicked one of the seven Lunds bags packed with mint-condition trade paperbacks.

"Aloysius, hello, we cannot have bags of books obstructing the entrance/exit behind the counter salient," said Snorri. "Give me a hand, Chitchee! We gotta move these bags of books somewhere or price them out. This isn't Bennett Lumber yard! Whose are these?"

"I'm here! Sommelguise," Aloysius gargled out, guttering an ice cube from his Jumbo Coca Cola.

The online *StarTrib* ordered Aloysius to subscribe, froze his online sports page, and shook him down for the fee.

"Some old guy's," Aloysius continued. "Old British grouchy gaucho guy in a paunchy pampas pompous poncho dealy-bob dealio. He was here a while back. A week, a month. He looked familiar. Like Charlie Weaver or Marcus Welby. He said he would come back later but never did. Go ahead and price out his books. If he comes back, you can pay him out forty bucks. Most of his books we already had, tell him. It was all stuff we've already sold a lot of and don't need anymore. And then the rest was a lot of horsefeathers by local poets. Ten cents a pop for those. Tell him you can't give poetry away. A lot of that Chilcote Carrothers kind of crap Yardley Singleton buys. There should be a couple twenties in the register. Yeah, cranky old British white guy who talks like Michael Caine or that Alexander Scourby on *Family Affair*. Like a British Mr. French from Spain."

Aloysius slammed his fist down next to his Coca Cola, launching lid, straw, brown fluid, and crystal cubes.

"Look at this shit! My screen is totally frozen!" continued Aloysius, frozen to his screen. "Only a computer can understand a computer! Now it wants the password to my password! Jesus! Where does it end?"

"It ends in your amygdala," said Chitchee, closely examining the clothespin, which he turned over and over in his hands, careful not to drop it.

Aloysius knotted his hands, seized up, and cried tears of cyber rage. Aloysius thrust his office chair backward. It sailed into the run-to-fat bookshelf of jerry-rigged shelves, wobbly already with double-shelved books. He wiped his face like a man waking up over a washbasin. Recovering his composure, he walked away from the screen. Then he walked back and gave the screen the finger. And then he meditated on the creative visualization of shoving his foot up Bill Gates's Microsoft ass.

In times of stress, Aloysius cradled the Aalgaard family heirloom, stroked the five strings lightly, and used his fingers as feathers to make nice, bland sounds.

"What *is* that? A winged instrument?" asked Chitchee. "Can I hold it? It looks like a ring dove in flight!"

"Sure! Be careful, it's cracked. Has anyone seen my *Barre Chords for Rock Kantele*?" Aloysius asked plaintively, excavating a wall of books for a second.

"It's tuned to open D major," said Chitchee, plucking it. "So . . . you know Epimanondas was a great guitar player in his time, but Thucydides never learned. He shunned music, and so Thucydides was despised by the Athenians. Let's try 'Little Martha' by Duane Allman."

Chitchee touched the strings and they rang harmonious bells. The crack mended itself. It was sorcery plain and simple. Two minutes of music changed the entire tenor of the book store for two minutes.

"This sounds bright like Ali Farka Touré," said Chitchee. "Do you have a *kora* too?"

Aloysius could have wept for both the beauty of the song and the nostalgia it evoked within his ice-bound soul for a childhood after so many winters lost and for the childhood past when Aubrey was but a giant broken thumb in swaddling clothes. He couldn't speak, overwhelmed with the music that had flooded and drowned him. He had gooseflesh getting up off the floor of gooseflesh and he resolved vaguely to stand behind Chitchee no matter how weirdly oddly Chitchee twitched, gaped, and gutturalized.

Mudslides of sludge and gloom returned to the foreground.

"Am I gaining weight? Do I have a big butt? Or is it my bones getting thinner?" asked Snorri, who stooped down at an awkward, back-breaking angle over the Lunds bags of left behinds and commandeered the desktop to look up resale values on Amazon. "Jung, *Synchronicity*? Hmmm . . . Campbell, Hillman, von France, Rainey Rilkey. Annie Dillyard, hmmm . . ."

"I smell vanilla," said Chitchee, returning the birchwood *kantele* to its pride of place, returning to the clothespin, and returning to the rush caused by a sudden absence of pain. "It must be one of those Doubleday/Anchor books. Penguins smell more like chocolate. Dovers are aloes. Need some help finding that *kantele* book, Aloysius? What did it smell like? Cloves, lemons, coconuts, or eucalyptus?"

Getting no answer, Chitchee pretended to have never said a thing. He toe-thrust a book-stuffed Lunds grocery bag about six inches over.

"There, in case we need to make a quick exit," said Chitchee and sang "*It was the last train to Clark's Bar/waiting for a train/On the double Es/Oh no, how long does this song go?*"

Snorri, sliding off the computer, bowed in a sarcastic, supercilious sweep toward Saami, who hopped back on the merry-go-round painted pony of the Internet. Snorri directed Chitchee to move the Lunds bags of books while Snorri patrolled the store for incidents to report. He had already informed Chitchee that the number one shoplifter profile was from the Minneapolis College of Art & Design. The "spoiled rich kid" in the Alfa Romeo with PICASSO license plates, who couldn't spell W-O-R-K and the dad was "another big prick from Edina." And the big prick shelled out the moolah like toilet paper for "little junior prick" with his: tattoos, piercings, half a dozen or so sex re-assignment surgeries, and round trips to Bangkok to do research on "Transgender Buddhism and Twitter."

"Growing up spoiled like that," said Snorri, "how could one know the true value of hard W-O-R-K? Or the history of labor?"

"Who is this guy that doesn't double-bag his books?" Chitchee asked the Lunds grocery bags.

"He's not a guy. He's a left behind grocery bag of a guy. That reminds me, Aloysius, we need to hire *professional* security. We can't be expected to do two jobs at once," said Snorri, his arms splayed out and then folded. "Bookselling *and* security? I mean, that's really going above and beyond the call of duty and even, well, liberty."

"It's a full time job," said Saami, "*not* answering the phone around here!"

Saami licked his lips, plucked the salt line off his mouth, and announced his break because his intestines had squirmed a half-inch from his butt and he had to stuff them back in surreptitiously.

"And," continued Snorri, "with all the robberies going on in Uptown maybe we *should*, you know, call in the Marines so to speak, for us. Look, I'm only saying we have to hire Securitas. They have Tasers. They might even have lasers by now."

"Someday," added Saami over his shoulder and trotting downstairs, "Securitas will have phasers, tractor beams, and death stars!"

"*Incense and peppermints*," sang Chitchee, "*and mairzy doats on ivy, yee, yee!*"

"Otherwise, Aloysius," said Snorri, masking over Chitchee. "I think the staff might risk getting heat exhaustion from the overwork of doubling up on duties. You know what Napoleon said about an army marching on its stomach?"

"It's better to stand up and march on your legs," said Aloysius, not looking at Snorri, who was on patrol, descending the stairs with a clutch of incident reports in his back cut-off jean pocket.

When Chitchee heard the word "stomach," he looked up at the castled battlements of books propped up by adjacent towering, undulating, and precipitously stacked ramparts of books and he tasted LaDonna's vulva. A booming, buzzing, budding cherry-tree-in-full-flower pink. LaDonna's vulva popped like a popover in his molded-tin mind. Memories flooded back against the shore of his will power. He used to get over her by saying her name, sniffing chloroform, saying her name, and as soon as he smoked a little weed he was a little snail blowing its own horn, diametrically reversing his mood and life was wonderful as ever . . . Popover, sniff chloroform, repeat. Love, rejection, love again, re-rejection. Popover, chloroform, headache. Time to get high. She had secreted herself in his fatty tissues and the heavy lifting of books metabolized her thought-forms out of his liver. *Kaya* now!

"Should we move the register away from the door?" asked Snorri, ascending the stairs breathing like an elephant with rings of sweat under his eyes. "Look what we're accomplishing, Aloysius, eh? What about it, Chief, move the register today? Chitchee can do the heavy lifting!"

"No!" yelled Chitchee. "I'll get aroused!"

LaDonna had reached into Chitchee's rib cage and wrenched out his heart again. He backstoried himself with her, lying *Olympian* in bed in the off moment of a morning romp.

"Chitchee!" she said.

"What?" said Chitchee, looking around for the voice.

"Chitchee," said Snorri. "Could you pop over here and give me a hand?"

"Pop over?" asked Chitchee. "Why did you say that?"

"Hold off, you guys," said Aloysius. "Slow down! Let me catch my breath! I appreciate the fact that you're thinking of the store, but honestly, where can the register possibly go? A yard sale? No one is going to boost the register out the front door like a Dunn Brothers tip jar! Are they, Snorri? I appreciate the irrational exuberance though. Snorri?"

"Maybe we could glue the vulva down to the counter," said Chitchee, nobody noticing anything. "Then it would never walk off anywhere. And then we glue the counter to the floor so the counter can't pop out the door either."

"My dad has power tools," said Snorri, looking askance with a short snort to prevent Chitchee's words entering his bloodstream. "I could call him right now. He's probably working in the garage anyway. He could round up what we need and pop over."

"Hold up on the pop overs!" said Aloysius.

"Didn't Pops just pop over?" asked Chitchee excitedly. "He must be out of pop overs by now!"

"Hold up you guys, you guys no," said Aloysius cautiously. "Slow down and hold-pile those pop overs. Whoa. Wait. Let's hold off on the pop overs for now. Trying to turn the world upside down only turns it all the way around. Maybe we should listen to *Layla* real low and lay low with Lowla?"

"Can we forget the pop overs?" asked Chitchee. "They make me see pubes!"

"Suit yourself," Snorri conceded, although hurt and feeling ganged up on.

"We need some glue," said Chitchee, moving with unusual gracility, a smiling swallow on the fly, swooping on a fly—looking under the counter for supplies. "Epoxy! Super glue! Wood glue! Where's the good stuff?"

"Wait, Chitchee," said Aloysius. "Don't move all those pencils around! I liked the pencils the way I had them! And let's ease off on the glue scene. We don't want to waste the good stuff. I'm afraid all that random gluing might spill over and have unforeseen consequences. By gluing the register to the counter, we might trigger someone's allergic response to glue and then the legal implications could be enormous. We'd better not affect the delicate inner workings of the register itself. It's a Venus fly trap in there. We might regret it later if we moved the book store to a bigger location, say Iceland, where we'd be forced to buy a bigger, more expensive register and probably get ripped off by a gang of roaming shepherds."

Snorri reached under the counter, moved a box of rock-hard erasers aside, and fingered a virgin pint of Phillips vodka in a brown bag. Snorri's back to Aloysius, he unscrewed the pint, squeezed some old super glue tube into the cap, and screwed the cap back on. Trying to make it look untampered with, he taped the seal back down with a micro-strip of 3M adhesive tape and discreetly placed the pint bottle of Phillips vodka in its brown bag and behind the box of rock-hard erasers.

Snorri tugged on Chitchee's forearm and elbowed him into an aisle.

"Now do you believe me?" asked Snorri without moving his jaw and bending toward Chitchee's ear to eat it. "Bradbury's 'A Sound of Thunder' paralyzed Aloysius for life. All change must stop for him to think. Even the *thought* of butterflies gives him butterflies. He refuses all change. Watch this!"

They returned to the front counter, the register, and the Dell desktop, where Aloysius was sleeping as a MPD squad car flew by the window in a mad pursuit of nothing visible.

"Aloysius," said Snorri, "you heard about the robbery at the Dunn Brothers on Lake Street this morning, correct?"

"Robbery?" asked Aloysius, waking up in a strange woods in somebody else's sleeping bag. "Really? What happened?"

"Tip jar was smashed for one!" said Snorri. "I'm sorry it might sound trivial, but that is real money. The fake, hidden camera wasn't on. Go figure."

"Wolp, oh," said Aloysius in a relaxed posture. "If you're angling for a security camera again, we can't afford one right yet . . . maybe hold off on that for right now. Hold off on everything for right now! Let's keep that on the back burner until . . . until . . . until we can afford a brand new, imaginary back burner. That can't cost anything!"

"Off topic, how did the tip jar get smashed?" asked Chitchee. "Why did they have to smash the tip jar? Was it the Mason jar with the clamped lid? Don't tell me it was the fancy Italianate Fido candy jar with the—don't tell me it was—my favorite tip jar at Dunn Brothers!"

Chitchee fell silent. He brightened like a blinking quasar.

"—I loved that jar!"

Snorri shot Chitchee a menacing blank look. Then Chitchee had a cinder in his eye.

"No, Chitchee, it's not about the jar, forget the jar," said Snorri. "Hello? What planet are you tripping on today? After the perpetrator couldn't find the safe, he tied the barista to the roaster, then he threw the tip jar on the floor and broke it."

"Wait!" said Chitchee. "You can't break a floor with a tip jar! Hey, I know someone who works there. In fact, I know everybody who works there."

"Everybody?" asked Snorri, and there was a moment's glitch in his eyes before one eyebrow registered a trepidation. "I don't know about your knowing *absolutely* everybody who works at the Dunn Brothers on Lake Street. I find it a little hard to believe myself."

"You had better believe yourself," quipped Chitchee, "who else do you have?"

Kennedy returned from McDonald's. He gaped at Chitchee and Snorri.

"I can't imagine what it's like to be you, believe me," muttered Snorri, disgusted

"Well, imagine that!" said Chitchee. "I can't imagine that either, although I'm imagining it right now!"

"So you're imagining yourself as real right now?" asked Snorri.

"Well, nothing really exists," said Chitchee, "does it? Hegel said that, so why not just read Hegel and disappear?"

"Is it safe to pop in?" snickered Kennedy, dropping off his backpack with a quick toss. "Am I imaginationing this book store? Or is this very book store set in a parallel universe next to another book store in its universe, and once in a while the two meet, when one pops over to the other?"

Chitchee blushed. His sphincter contracted as his glabella tightened.

"Where were we?" asked Snorri.

Snorri hiked up his cut-off jeans and tightened his tribal leather belt (brass buckle like a padlock).

"To tell you the truth," said Chitchee, "I wasn't listening."

Snorri shook his dreads and restarted his train of thought, which had vanished in a tunnel. Oh Saami, he remembered while forgetting the register. Oh yes, Saami's own good. For the good of Saami, the good of the world's best book store, and by extensions, the good of the world as a whole unit. This was empathy. Saving his colleague and coworker Saami from himself, who had to quit drinking even if it meant the shakes, seizures, and comas. For Saami. Yes, even if it meant Saami had to sweat needles and imagine rats for breakfast, Snorri would perform this good Christian deed for chum like Saami. If Saami was airlifted to the Sonoran desert, left to dry out by exposure, and stayed in isolation for a couple months without food, water, and *Mortal Kombat: Armageddon*, Snorri would support Saami in the collective labor to improve the humanity of humanity. "Saami, mad props," said Snorri once to himself on the way to the liquor store. Compassionate Snorri had seen the Phillips bottle and the damage done: the switched-off eyes for brains, the ranting repetitions, and the bloodshot jags of weeping over the dying cadence of a song, probably written by some knockabout kid who probably got kicked out of MCAD. And that was just from Snorri's looking in the bathroom mirror. Saami, on the other hand, who he loved like a brother, *he* was a different kettle of fish exactly like all the other different kettles of fish, who needed interventions to ever stop bending the elbow. Between the two of them, there was no comparison; because they were exactly alike. One was a *classic* alcoholic; and so was the other one! Of course everybody is either an alcoholic or an alcoholic. What miffed Snorri was the *unprofessional* alcoholism of Saami. He didn't know how to manage and hide his alcoholism. Although they had known each other for years, Snorri had yet to tackle Saami with an actual intervention for his *unprofessional* alcoholism. Maybe he could throw a party for Saami's intervention. Then he might trap the mouse for its own good death. Meanwhile, if Snorri glued shut Saami's vodka bottles, maybe Saami would get the hint that Korsakoff syndrome was only one small step for Saami, one giant leap for Snorri.

"Why did you glue Saami's Phillips vodka bottle shut?" asked Chitchee. "Oh I get it, it's that tough love stuffed with rough love stuffing dealie type bob cure. That always works!"

"I do it out of empathy," said Snorri. "I do everything completely out of empathy for my fellow human beings. That is my religion, Chitchee. And those without empathy? What can I say, but those zombies have no empathy and belong in a space station."

Hjalmar Halversen, having incorporated all the father-to-son beatings from the Vikings' invasion of Lindisfarne to the Vikings' invasion of Green Bay, Wisconsin, nevertheless instilled Snorri with the virtues of professional, military discipline. Snorri appreciated that gift from his father no matter how much he wanted to kill him. Inadvertently, his stern father had inspired him with an inner strength and a Hemingwayesqueish grace under his father's thumb. Snorri loved Saami as Saami's father, not as his brother, Snorri realized. In that way and so *then* he could dash Saami's brains out if need be.

"So, Saami is going to train you in?" asked snorting Snorri to Chitchee: "Good luck with that. Phew! I have to break pretty soon. Thirsty as all get out!"

Chitchee was being looked at, he was. The circumspect brass wire-rims pulled down on Saami's nose revealed Saami's drooping eyelids, draped over his blue windows and bloodshot window panes, which were loudly thrust open.

"Oh, that's right!" said Saami, appearing in his own Dark Horse comic and jumping off the page. "We hired two people! Chitchee! Awesome! And who else—I thought I saw—another."

"Saami!" said Chitchee, hugging Saami and whiffing the vodka that constantly bubbled from the pores in his armpit.

"Now I've got someone to suck my scriggly-scroggly!" joked Saami.

"I didn't know you had one!" said Chitchee.

"Bitch!" said Saami. "Yokay, no end of work to be done in today's modern book store. First order of business, let's see . . . Chitchee, could you run to the Henn-Lake Liquor store for me? How's that for training you into the book store trade?"

"Saami," whispered Chitchee, leaning forward. "*Paid in books?* You didn't mention that!"

"What? We can't all be rock stars," shrugged Saami. "We can't all be in Rush! There'd be no Rush! Anyway, we decided you wanted to work for us for free—that *free* was the one thing you insisted on for the job. Otherwise, you could have kept working for us for free, and it wouldn't have made any difference."

"Okay," said Chitchee. "Let's do the training so that one day I will own my own book store, and the wheel of death and rebirth will stop for me, and make the world's suffering, at least, meaningful."

Saami made the imaginary motions of a man shoveling imaginary manure over his shoulder.

Fjard Gardet from US Bank wandered back in, his knees like elbows, and Saami discreetly pointed with his thumb at Fjard. Saami mouthed the words "V. I. P. from the Bank" to Chitchee who asked himself: Could I sell the books I'm paid with, back to the store for cash? And pay my rent to the slaves of progress, who labor without birth, in kind? Where could I pay my rent in books?"

"R. I. P. THE BANK?" yelled Chitchee. "WHAT DOES THAT EVEN MEAN? IS IT A MESSAGE FROM THE FUTURE?"

Saami lowered his forehead for a smack, but he skipped it when he heard Chitchee say:

"Hey, R. I. P. over there!"

"Can I help you?" asked Fjard.

"As a fatter of mact, yes," said Chitchee, sweating bead thumbtacks on his upper lip. "I'm looking for a big loan. I don't have enough savings to start up a birdcage, much less a book store, but if I came to you at US Bank and took out a 30,000-dollar loan and got a stack of credit cards to go with it, would you fund my venture capital ideas to open my book store? It should be as easy as one, two, three, infinity! If you fly me to Silicon Valley, I'll talk to the Google Head there about doing all the fancy-schmancy paperwork. Then, once I learn how to run a small LSC, you'll be a shareholder with your own office as the CTO Loan Officer, with your feet up on your desk reading W. E. B. Griffin. We launch onto the Big Board and look for other start-ups—like, is there a new way to market ice cream? And then we recruit heavily from the MIT Media Lab to make sure there is."

"Chitch, training over here!" said Saami, feeling cut in two. "Here is the front counter, as you know! That's the broken register, and this is the back-up frozen computer for looking up all the books we don't have on the database, which we call HomeBase. I never knew why."

"Because that's what it's called?"

"I'm not into conspiracy theories, " said Saami, stroking the little beard he did not have, "but you might be right there!"

"I get that," said Chitchee. "*But where do you hide your weed?*"

"Shhh . . ." said Saami, reaching under the counter, feeling around, and answering the question with a confirmatory, prescient look. "Back there. Shhh. Don't tell. The Bank is here."

At the drop of the word "weed," Fjard's back bristled with prickly quills. Fjard returned to browsing, or pretending to be browsing, although alarms had jarred him off his game. Was Fjard required to report that information to a certain agency? Even if it were only NASA, someone in Big Government should know BookSmart was rife with illegal drug activity, narcotics trafficking, and money laundering. But how to trap them? These savvy dope fiends were street savvy if nothing else. And it might take super-subtle lines of questioning to incriminate them out of their over-savvified selves.

"So, do you have *The Secret* now?" asked Fjard.

"Yeah," said Chitchee. "The weed goes under the counter behind the office supplies."

"Okay-ay-ay . . ." said Fjard, looking for the fire alarm to match the fire alarm in his eyes.

In shock, a shock mitigated only by the fact that it wasn't shock at all but first-order glee, Fjard thought: "Another reason to throw the bums out on the street."

A copy of *The Secret* materialized by his thinking about it. And in his overjoyment Fjard forgot himself and embraced the "law of attraction." He plumped down on the torn, black leather couch and visualised himself speaking like the Great Communicator. He wanted to boost morale in his department, inspire his children to follow their dreams, and raise his vibrations so that he could market himself better. It was already working its magic!

"Here is where," continued Saami, looking popover-eyed, "here is where you price new arrivals, sort out books, here is where you put the books on hold for a week, or as long as the world lasts, there's the phone we don't answer. Book stands, plastic baggies, mylar, Brodart, U Line catalog, price gun. Baa, blah, blech. Goo Gone bottle. Obviously. Vintage, expensive, and rare books you give to Snorri, and the bastard takes them home and puts them in his closet, on hold for a week, or as long as the world lasts, until he totally forgets that he brought them home, and dies with his grow lights on. Then there is an estate sale, and the buyer cycles them back here. That's how it works, going around and coming back, and all that good karma shit. "

"That is absolutely not true! Damn your eyes, libeler, slanderer, little drummer boy," exclaimed Snorri, jumping off the second Internet bar stool and grabbing his back with a wince. "Aloysius! Did you just hear what you did not just hear? I don't have *any* of the store's books or borrowed books at home awaiting my death or the death of Earth from poorly digested junk food or whatever. Go figure! It's the same false narrative Saami spins all the time to get me fired! If anything is missing, well, it's not because of me, it's our sense of false security in general! The store is wide open to looting in the next well-educated riot! Security is non-existent here. Half the missing books pop out the back door every day and pop back in the front door every night and are sold back to Saami, who is too blind-drunk, bird-bombed deaf to see he is operating as a fence to himself!"

"Jesus, Snorri, what is it now?" asked Aloysius. "As far as I know, we don't have any missing books that I can find. The book thieves steal their good books from the Walker Art Center, Barnes & Noble, or James R. Lurie's art book store on Nicollet and . . . That's what all the emails from Denny's Majors are fluttering about. Somebody stole a *Minnesota Barefoot* by Lute Korngold once and then returned it. We don't have any books that are that good. If the thieves bring them here, I can't afford to buy them. So Saami buys them. I keep telling him not to! Or any stolen library books from Undone Buttons. He's 86ed times 86 already. Who would steal a book from a library? Why? That's lower than a snake's asshole half-underground! Speaking of snakes, I can't find the power cord strip thing. Seen the adapter?"

Snorri's grunt implied a reconciliation.

"It's that gray thing, covered in our loss of hair, in the corner," said Saami.

"Okay," said Aloysius, examining the power strip, which was covered in hair, grime, and mouse droppings, which weren't exactly raisins. "It seems okay."

"Hey, Chitchee, over here!" said Saami. "We have to talk about Snorri."

"What about him?" asked Chitchee, following Saami into the epicenter of the store.

"Ignore the half-baked bastard! He's," whispered Saami, twirling his finger at the side of his head, "zoinks. "

"Why do you say that?" asked Chitchee, who saw Snorri reading their lips with his mouth.

"He wants us to wear Civil War uniforms," said Saami, "of the Minnesota Regiment *on the job* and re-enact the role of the Minnesota Regiment at Gettysburg to draw in foot traffic off Hennepin & Lake."

"I'll wear one," hiccuped Chitchee.

Saami gulped. Snorri wondered why the Civil War was mentioned, unless it was about him.

"Oh Lordy, Lordy, Mama," said Saami, praying with his eyes toward the acoustic tiles. "I guess I am the only sane one working here now. How about if you price books Chitchee with the price gun while I go to the bathroom and whack off?"

"That sounds wacky," Chitchee agreed and gazed at the stacks and stacks of books leaning into each other like drunks. "You're the boss, Man of Onan!"

"Here," said Saami petulantly, grabbing Chitchee's wrist and slamming the Monarch price gun into Chitchee's palm, cutting Chitchee's hand by his thumb. "Price books! It's your hand job now!"

More stacks appeared everywhere the more you looked—unpriced, forgotten, and to be boxed. The stacks worked their way like hundred year-old oak trees through the ceiling to the sky.

"Aloysius, I'm afraid I'm going to have to go home early," said Snorri to Aloysius, hibernating at the second Dell's frozen screen.

"Kidney stones again, there Snorri? Watch your diet and cut out the sugar," said Aloysius, half awake. "Yeah, sure, okay, go home and rest. We've got Chitchee now, but first let me run to McDonald's and grab a Jumbo Coke."

"Aloysius," grimaced Snorri. "It's not kidney stones. The stones have rolled. I'm afraid I re-injured my back, the same ligaments I tore playing football in the conference championships, which I re-tore playing rugby and re-re-tore playing hockey and then ripped wide open yesterday moving a kitty litter box to get to a bag of peanut M & Ms that fell on the floor."

Aloysius hand-signaled a gesture that meant: first things first. He darted out the front door and decked Lake Street Rodney, who had only recently recovered from his fear of being murdered in the book store.

"Hi, Aloysius, where are you going?" asked Rodney flat on his back. "McDonald's? You must be, and that must mean Kennedy isn't there, because if you were there, he'd be here, and I'd go over there with you, waiting for him to leave here, or there, so we can both win by being there. Let us go, you and I, to the McDonald's in the sky together, and come back quickly so Kennedy can run over there, knowing we're here, safe at home."

"Rodney, let's hold off on that! I have to fly this mission solo! You know, like a kamikaze—it's gut bomb and run for daylight, I was thinking for today! It's so busy," said Aloysius, crab-walking backwards and talking to Rodney but with a diminishing volume to give the effect of attenuating distancing toward the vanishing point. "And Snorri has to go home early after stopping at the liquor store, I guess. Man!"

"Hello, book-loving world!" said Rodney, entering BookSmart instead. "Excuse me, physically-disabled guy always blocking the door, yes you Rocky the Squirrel from Frostbite Falls. Gee, Rocky, that's a cute hat!"

Customers like a flock of starlings blasted by gales of wind turned in murmuration. Torg turned around too, looked up at Rodney, and said from a gravelly crop:

"Are you *trying* to choke a cat with cream?"

"Did I say something wrong?" asked Rodney. "There's nothing wrong with being physically disabled, I'm mentally disabled myself, and there's nothing wrong with *me*! Is there? Do I look like a terrorist or something? Actually, I think of myself as a social butterfly."

The flock of starlings nodded in sync, looking over Lake Street Rodney for a possible firearms violation.

"Oh dear," said Melusina to Kriemhilde.

"Oh dear, you can say that again, dear," said Kriemhilde, "sister."

Kriemhilde added as a coda: the rising tone: "Mmmm . . . hMMM!"

The two loving sisters re-inserted themselves into Cookbooks and Crafts like bustling partridges in a stand of shrubs.

"We'll be safer back here in the shrubs," said Melusina. "Did you bring the butter knife that cousin Viktor gave you? The butter knife Frank Sinatra gave to Marlene Dietrich who gave it to Viktor when Viktor turned ten? That butter knife in your purse? In case of . . ."

The sisters exchanged looks alike as Mendel's smooth and wrinkled peas.

"This book store is a Marx Brothers movie in a madhouse," smiled Fjard to the two sisters, who softly screamed. He scared them with his grin and stare. He had addressed them from their behinds. "Isn't it? But a butter knife isn't going to save you from any real danger, ladies. You need to manifest the Law of Attraction."

"Stand back! You're too close!" said Kriemhilde, standing back. "I've got a butter knife in my purse. Don't you believe it!"

Kriemhilde opened her big white boxy purse. Beads of sweat flew off her tortoiseshell neck, and she produced a brush-comb combination switchblade.

"Jesus, that's a butterfly knife, not a butter knife!" said Fjard. "Allow me to help you with that. I know all about knives. I was on the Hamline University fencing team and quite a hit with the ladies."

"It won't open," said Kriemhilde.

She handed Fjard the butterfly brush-comb switchblade.

The blade would not switch. Any real threat dissolved like monarch butterflies in autumn. Then the knife flew open and sliced

Fjard's hand open at the spandrel. Sucking the blood down like a bat, the bleeding Fjard walked toward the counter, stopped, and walked back *The Secret* to where it had materialized by his desire for it. He was not going to buy it now. There was blood all over it. He sucked his spandrel, buried *The Secret* in a heap of books, and warned Aloysius he would be back later, depending on how fast things went at Tires Plus.

"We have Band-Aids," said Chitchee.

"Those aren't for sale," footnoted Aloysius.

"Thanks, Rodney," said Snorri, footing into his vintage RollerBlades and placing his street sandals in his backpack. "You lost us *another* customer! And of all people, our US bank loan officer, Ford Guardette! Congratulations, Rodney, your 'social butterfly' speech set in motion BookSmart's bankruptcy proceedings! You've never read Bradbury? You've never heard of Ray Bradbury? *Martian Dandelions* ring any bells?"

Rodney looked blank. Was Rodney supposed to apologize for being Rodney?

Kennedy ascended the staircase square by square, entered the arena, looked askance at Lake Street Rodney, and pondered an avoidance strategy. Was Lake Street Rodney coming or going?

"Everybody here, attention!" announced Rodney. "Attention! Please continue with your usual rigoletto! Sorry to interrupt! Carry on!"

"*La Donna Reeda snow mobile*," sang Chitchee to himself quietly in the corner—he licked the itchy cut near his thumb—too shy to reach out for a Band Aid as he was further distressed by the rainbows buzzing around his head like the winged foreshadows of a migraine, an ischemic attack, or a schizophrenogenic break with reality.

"Excuse me, Torgo," said Snorri. "Mind if I—can I—"

"I believe the word you seek so adventitiously is 'rig-a-ma-rollee!'" said Kennedy, grinning an all-knowing, skullish grin with a semi-smile. "And it's Italian for rigamarole. Rigamarole is Italian for rigamarole. We call it a *cheese stick*. The proper pronunciation is r-r-r-r-r-igamar-r-r-r-r-r-r-ole-e-e-e-e-e."

"Excuse me, Kennedy, Torg, Rodney," said Snorri. "Jesus! Can I get the cheese sticks out of here? This is a fire exit, Torg! Move away from the door! This path must be kept clear in case of another tornado of 1965."

"What's the hurry, Snorrio?" asked Torg. "Do you have diarrhea too? I've had the Mexican Two Step all day. I can't get rid of the Trotskys myself!"

"Apology accepted," said Snorri, picking up Torg and throwing him onto the upholstered but withered, licorice-black couch, warm from the US Bank loan officer's ass. "I'll see you guys on the backside of tomorrow!"

"*Bowling Alone?*" asked a customer *in potentia*, halting and pigeonholing Snorri.

"That's kind of a strange question to ask," said Snorri.

"No, it's the title of a book," said the incoming customer.

"That's kind of a strange title for a book to be asked for by a complete stranger," said Snorri. "Is there something else I can help you with? Look, I'm actually off the clock right now, so if you will allow me to scootchy-scooch by you? I have diarrhea!"

"I thought that since you worked in a book store, you could say something about books a bit more helpful than 'I have diarrhea!' I thought since this was a book store, there would be books in it that were all in a database— inventoried by professionals with Library Science degrees from St. Kate's, Macalester, or the University of Chicago."

"Boy," said Snorri, "were you off! That's like saying anybody who lives in a windmill can fly. Now if you will excuse me. I have to fly."

"What about *The Help?*" asked the customer. "Do you have any?"

"You'll have to ask them," said Snorri with an air of finality. "Good day, sir."

MELVIN "BOOKSELLER" MCCOSH OF DINKYTOWN

Blocking Snorri's exit from the front door, the new customer barred himself: the ancient mariner was an old white, white-haired man in spats, homburg, and a long black overcoat. A large white awning of a mustache with fringes blew around his mouth when he spoke, accompanied by his timid, cookie-crumbling mannerisms. His white moustache was an abridged version of his joined white shaggy eyebrows. His face froze like an old clock no longer ticking, the mainspring mainly sprung. His petrified hands, incapable of articulated movement, had sprouted liver spots that resembled unknown, potentially fatal fungi.

"Hello? Do you buy books? Hello?" asked the old white, white-haired man.

"Yes," said Snorri, unable to abandon the old man stranded.

"Well, what kind?"

"Classics."

"What?"

"All kinds."

"Do you buy everything?"

"No."

"Do I bring them here? Is this Melvin McCosh's book store?"

"Who?" asked Snorri, feeling trapped and regretting he hadn't skated for daylight.

"You're talking about the legendary Melvin 'Bookseller' McCosh?" asked Chitchee, setting down the Monarch price gun whose roll of stickers had gotten jammed in a plastic sprocket.

Snorri vamoosed right through this door in the conversation onto Hennepin, narrowly missing Aloysius's return from McDonald's, Jumbo Coke and Golden French fries grasped in his right hand, Carousel cigarette in his left.

"McCosh?" asked the old white, white-haired man of the entering Aloysius.

"Oh yeah," said Aloysius wistfully. "Old Bookseller McCosh! Wasn't he a character in a book about a legendary book store in Dinkytown? You asked him for a book, and he picked the book out of a room full of books like a needle from a haystack, even while he was blindfolded. The Amazing Kreskin of finding books. I read that book."

"*That's* the guy!" said the old white, white-haired man, excited in a wheezy, pitiful way. "He sure could saw the forest for the trees. Is McCosh here?"

"No," said Chitchee. "I'm sorry to say the Wizard of 4th Street died a couple years ago. Larry McMurtry from *Lonesome Dove,* Texas rode up here and rustled up a lot of his stock. But McCosh's Book Store lives on in local book store legend! He was a real character!"

"The old Minneapolis that I grew up with and loved like my mother? That, she is dead," said the old white, white-haired man, well to the brim with tears. "The Ten O'Clock Scholar, Bridgeman's, Perine's, the Podium, even Gray's Drugstore is gone. Dinkytown is developers' dust. Detritus. Everything's been stolen. GONE! I don't live here. Minneapolis is no more! The IDS killed it, stabbed it to death with steel and glass swords. When I went to the *ne-e-e-w* Guthrie to see the *o-o-o-old A Christmas Carol* I had to use the men's room and—up and down I went on impossible escalators, on Möbius strips of futility—and I crossed a dark lobby and took a wrong turn. I stumbled into a dark, dead hole. Suddenly I'm face to face with the ghost of Ralph Rapson, the architect of the OLD Guthrie! The REAL Guthrie that isn't there anymore!"

"No!" said Chitchee with ovals shocked into ellipses surfacing his face. "I bet he was livid! They scuppered his masterpiece! Did he look mad? What was he wearing? Anything? Don't tell me he couldn't find the bathroom either! Or that he had diarrhea!"

"Same clothes as me," said the old white, white-haired man. "Spats, homburg, and a long black overcoat."

Saami, bladder emptied out, returned, resolved to oversee Chitchee's training with even more oversight. A skyey look of nostalgia overcoming Aloysius distracted Saami. Then Snorri RollerBladed into BookSmart, catching an edge on the threshold, which tipped him forward over the red carpet hurling him on his knee-padded knees.

"Thank God my knees are still good!" said Snorri apologetically to himself. "Or I would have to have my dad pop over and pick me up!"

Snorri picked up on the nostalgia for the Old Minneapolis in the air too, having forgotten his backpack with the aromatic Blue Diesel in it. It might have been ransacked by Saami in revenge for revenge. Snorri double-checked for tampering and sabotage. This was the New Minneapolis. Every man for himself. Every Minneapolitan had a killer inside him, waiting to be let out, and unleashed on the Mall of America.

"*And*, sir," continued Chitchee, helping the breathless Snorri to his circular and plastic feet, "local legend has it that the ghost of Melvin McCosh haunts all the book stores in the Twin Cities. And if he thinks you are a fool, he shows up like an elf and plays tricks with your book store. He was spotted at James Laurie, Booksellers on Nicollet by Orchestra Hall. When he asked for a book on elves by elves, the owner told him to go to hell. Later, McCosh made a bunch of Abrams art books on Bruegel and Bosch disappear, and then he flooded the book store's basement. Then McCosh came back the next night and told Laurie that his prices were astronomical. Laurie escorted him to the door and kicked him out. He kicks everybody out. Or so this has been related to me by local booksellers who wish to remain anonymous. After that Laurie's stock slowly disappeared and he didn't even notice; then the books re-appeared at LeLand Lien's Book Shop, and *Lien* didn't even notice."

"Hah, Laurie, that asshole! His prices *are* too high! So nothing circulates," said the old white, white-haired man, his face clenched in an actor's pain. "I plan to be a regular here at this book store from now on! Yes! I feel comfortable here! It's like the old Minneapolis in this little circle. The old Minneapolis is back! Am I right? And kicking! The composer Dvořák, *he* was from Minnesota. Did you know *that*?"

"No, sir," said Snorri. "Actually, he was from Iowa. Spittleville or something? *Nevertheless*, he is still regarded as a native son of Minnesota."

"That's what I thought," said the old white, white-haired man. "Good to know! And . . . mmm . . . I guess I'll head back to Dinkytown. If it's still there!"

"You are certainly welcome to come back," said Snorri. "And let us know next time if there is anything in particular you are looking for."

"Okay," said the old white, white-haired man. "Now that I know you have a door."

"Yes," said Snorri. "We have two doors. Actually, the building is in the Tu-dor style (if you're in the mood for a joke at your age). And you have a good door day, now, sir, while I Splitsville."

"Point me in the direction of the Red Barn!" said the old white, white-haired man.

"The Red Barn?" asked Aloysius, salting his French fries and creating little ketchup puddles on his McDonald's bag, the red puddles ringed with toruses of grease. "We burned the Red Barn down after Kent State, Big Barneys and all. Me and my buddies, we took on all the military-industrial corporations: Honeywell, DuPont, Sperry Rand, IBM, Red Barn, Moloch."

Aloysius nursed contentedly from the straw nipple of his McDonald's Jumbo Coca-Cola. Then he pounced on his Big Mac sandwich like a feral cat playing with a dead mouse. He garfed it down so quickly he passed out for a second. His stomach distended with air into a balloon-sized comma.

"We sure showed corporate America, oh yeah baby, let's listen to The Doors," continued Aloysius, eyelids fluttering, falling into sleep, a tiny smile on his lips above his stuffed gills. Burrrrp!

Snorri balanced on his Rollerblades and wobbled in a muck sweat emptying his backpack in a frantic search for the Blue Diesel through every zippered pocket. Anxious at the thought of thinking about anything at all, much less taking Madison out for happy hour appetizers and drinks someplace decent for once, he ruminated Rudolph's Bar-B-Que, then walking over to the Red Dragon, then back to Rudolph's, then bouncing over to Mortimer's, and then crawling to Liquor Lyle's for a night cap. He had crammed his weed into his front jean pocket, relieved.

"Saami," said Snorri. "Can I talk to you in private before I go? It's about Chitchee. And since he's standing in front of us, I don't want him to hear us. Let's go into Cookbooks and Crafts. We can talk in private. Excuse us ladies, could you leave us in private for a few business minutes? It's business."

Melusina and Kriemhild sidestepped into the Home Repair section, whose books for them held no interest at first, but gradually took hold and possessed them.

"What!" said the overworked Saami. "I don't have time for privates. Especially yours."

"Yeah, hilarious, Saami. Mitch Hedberg, you're not! How's Chitchee doing?" asked Snorri in a collusive tone.

Chitchee couldn't thread the stickers through the price gun. The whole project before Chitchee looked like a map from Strabo.

"You know he's going to quit on us?" asked Snorri. "Who else can we gull into working here for nothing?"

"Nobody I know is as gullible as Chitchee," said Saami, exasperating and aspirating puffs of doubt. "Except us. We work for chicken feed, but we're different."

"You mean we're different because we don't like the customers?" asked Snorri with encouragement.

"Exactly!" said Saami.

"And Chitchee likes the regulars! That will wear off, of course, working here. He has always been like that," said Snorri quietly and thoughtfully. "Obviously he is sociopathic. He doesn't care if the customers find him rude. He continues to befriend anybody! If left untreated, that could grow into full-blown psychosis. He obviously has an undiagnosed condition of some sort. OCD something. It's disrespectful trying to help everybody. The customers don't want our help. They want to be left alone with their feelings of isolation. Who walks into a book store to make friends? Chitchee feels the need to befriend everyone—even the assholes."

"Assholes like you and me?" said Saami. "Or the assholes in the store?"

"I mean the assholes in the store, you asshole," said Snorri eye to eye. "He talks to the customers as if they had been friends for life and he jumps into their lives and starts talking books. In a book store? Come on! Isn't that the choir preaching to the choir? He editorializes on the purchases and has to add his own commentary—like a frustrated Verne Lindquist."

"Yeah, what an asshole," said Saami without any interest, scratching his scruffy neck so that his lips pouted when he added: "Weren't you going to Bryant Lake Bowl?"

"Did I say that he always checks out the chicks too? Like that hottie over there?" asked Snorri, trying for Saami's lost attention.

Scarlett Johannson overheard this.

"Why is there fresh blood on this book?" asked Scarlett Johannson, throwing *The Secret* on a table.

Disgust, disbelief, and destruction combined in her conflicted expressions.

"Take the dust jacket off," said Snorri. "And I'll sell it to you for half the sticker price. That's a sweet deal. Because that's a real HOT book."

Scarlett Johannson strode outside and walked down to Bryant Lake Bowl to have lunch with Josh Hartnett, where Snorri was to just miss them by the time he eventually started out the door and skated down Lake Street.

"Well, can't win 'em all, hothead," said Snorri. "Noel summed it up pretty well. Chitchee is a latent asshole compensating for it by projecting his asshole upon the world, which is really the asshole he himself denies that he is, and then he compensates for that with its opposite. So these opposites connect, being the same opposites."

"What's the point!" sobbed Chitchee. "I heard everything you said, and I don't understand why you're dissatisfied with my work. I thought you guys were my friends! I'm going to end up in a looney bin if I don't have any friends."

Saami reached out to give Chitchee a hug, but Chitchee thrust him back.

"Don't touch me!" yelled Chitchee.

"Well, I already can imagine one complaint from Beda," said Snorri philosophically, "about your Reeboks being too loud. And Minerva is bound to complain about your overbearing patronizing arrogance, snarky remarks, and insensitivity to the pain and suffering of those without enough to eat. [Snorri burped.] She'll say we can't have that kind of crypto-facist insensitivity in our store! Keep an eye on him, Saami, and don't let him sit around and get fat and too comfortable. The point is pro-rated compassion. You have to understand that the customers need their space! It's not all about you, Chitchee! It's about *us* and we have to give the customer his or her or their space or spaces! Okay, end of pep talk. I hope that helped."

On the way out, Snorri blindly hip-checked the old white, white-haired man into the maroon counter, picked him up off the red-runnered, redolent, white, pine wood flooring, dusted him off, and threw him on the black leather couch. The self-induced guilt from this action caused such an ocean of sweat, he needed cold splashes from the bathroom faucet to bring his fever down before he RollerBladed down Lake Street toward Bryant Lake Bowl to meet his belle Madison *before* her shift at the New World Sunrise Massage And Spa began.

The old white, white-haired man staggered out the front door.

"Is this the Red Barn?" asked the old white, white-haired man, turning around and re-entering BookSmart.

Saami gently prodded the man in the direction of the intersection where a blue-striped Hennepin EMS vehicle hot-rodded through the lights.

KENNEDY KIMANI AND LAKE STREET RODNEY

"Customer assistance!" announced Lake Street Rodney.

Rodney pulled out a St. Mary's Basilica-shaped call bell, which he set on the maroon counter and pounded, but he was unable to rouse Aloysius from his golden French-fried slumber.

"Chitchee?" asked Rodney. "Okay, newby booby! I wanted to check something in my hold pile. For the fifth time. This week. So I'm thinking of buying back the Scottish-Gaelic dictionary I sold to you guys ten times. This year. Or last year. That book is a very-hard-to-find book! But like I said, I don't really *have to have it*. Right now. Or even this year! I need to know the precise location—where it is, so I can find it again and again precisely. Catch my drift? Do you . . . catch . . . my . . ."

"You're drifting all right . . ." said Chitchee. "How much Ecstasy have you done? I bet you were a one-man rave-pack in the good old days."

"Indubitably!" said Rodney. "Until my partner tested HIV positive and died in my arms with Karposi's sarcoma. And I miss him every day! Every day!"

Chitchee groaned like a man dancing on air when the trap door flings open. He realized that Rodney had spoken with perfect clarity. Rodney was a time traveller trapped in his past. A tear droplet suspended in his eye suspended him from talking, suspended

"That's why I talk like this," said Rodney. "I threw myself off a roof when I was drunk."

"Oh, Lake Street Rodney, I am so sorry! Uggghh! My eyes are raining . . . sorry for the tearful outburst . . . ug . . ."

"What are you two tribulating about now?" broke in Kennedy to Chitchee. "Can I put this book on hold? I have to have this. *To Dream the Empathable Dream*. The author is a professional empathologist and personal friend of Steve Harvey."

Kennedy had not resigned himself to the ineluctable modality of Lake Street Rodney, even as Rodney felt great social anxiety at being formally introduced himself. Close friendships implied a possible crimp in Kennedy's matriculations, since he had been brutalized by something or someone. A war? A woman? A whiskey? He had encrypted himself in himself, living the life of a tear, suspended between two worlds.

"Have you two *amazing* pilgrims on life's way met formally?" asked an over-smiling Chitchee.

Introductions were Chitchee's specialty. Everybody hated him for it. Out of nervous tension, Kennedy cringed and laughed like static electricity and Rodney shrank from the sparks. Torg sensed an awkward argument, announced his swift departure, stood by the register, and surveyed the book store like an elegant sunset.

"Welp, time to go home!" Torg kept saying. "Welp, welp, welp . . ."

Torg dimly saw Rodney and Kennedy both approaching Chitchee from opposite vectors, both with hold pile issues. The BookSmart AT & T cordless phone rang. Chitchee shuttled over to answer it (Aloysius dozed off into a well-deserved siesta after the morning's catnap).

The store phone twitched when a housefly landed on it. It noisily changed gears from talk to talk-message mode. A voice box speaker-phoned aloud:

"Hello? Hello? I'm looking for *The Massage Book*, I forgot to put it back last night or was it [sinus congestion?] Sunday? *The Massage Book*, it has to be there. Hello? Cocoa, cookie, bus."

"Bobblehead," awoke Aloysius from sawing zizzes out of wood. He waved his hand at a housefly that landed on his hand. "Fffff . . . Is that Bobblehead? Actually, we're related though cousins of some sort. And he's been saying 'cocoa, cookie, bus' for years. It's a tic. Tell Bobblehead his book is behind the counter."

Rodney and Kennedy faced face to face, creating a feeling of drying cement. Chitchee assumed that all human beings were the molecules of one human being, which acted in concert toward teleological perfection. Kennedy and Rodney both looked checked. Both men coveted their hold piles with greedy fingers, and were unwilling to back down from double checking them.

"Chitchee, please DON'T introduce me to that guy . . ." whispered both at the same time . . . to each other when Chitchee stood between them and then stepped back to assess the situation.

"Are we all not companions—in the way of books, I mean?" asked Chitchee. "Since both you guys are constantly examining your own piles, maybe you could buddy up and each buddy could cover the other guy's ass by checking out the other guy's piles for him!"

Rodney looked at Kennedy. Kennedy looked at Chitchee. Chitchee looked at Rodney. Rodney looked at Chitchee. Chitchee looked at Kennedy. Melusina and Kriemhilde looked at Rodney, Kennedy, and Chitchee. Rodney, Kennedy, and Chitchee looked at Melusina and Kriemhilde.

"It might be a little tricky at first," continued Chitchee, "but I think you guys can each eventually nail it in the end."

The three of them looked at the two of them. The two of them looked at the five of them. The two sisters touched each other's noses and declared:

"Pea pods."

Then the three of them looked at one another and concurred without enthusiasm at the same time:

"Pea pods."

LARRY SANGSTER

Kennedy hightailed to McDonald's and Rodney invalided out, nosing south, holding on to his plaid cap lest his shiny pate glow in the blue sunshine, blister, and peel like leprous snowflakes. Tartan plus fours flailed toward Comic Book College for a *Little Dot in Dotland*.

When, guess what happened?

Larry Sangster re-appeared, and Chitchee fumbled the Monarch price gun, which flew out of his hands, landed on the floor, and knapped off a plastic shard. He picked up the price gun and then dropped it on the maroon counter—and the gun completely shattered. Larry dragged himself to the counter haggardly like chewed-up, spit-out hungry fat on two legs, and covered in the slobber of his boss's beluga maw. Viktor had threatened to waterboard Larry. Viktor had threatened to have Larry's jugular ripped out and have Larry hanged by piano wires from a meat hook. Viktor, laughing through his nose like a rusty faucet if a rusty faucet could laugh at all, told Larry that he knew three different guys, all named Kevin, who enjoyed this line of butchery. Larry suffered because he had to suffer. Larry figured that out for himself very vaguely. Larry had a wife, Kulap, and three kids, Laurel, Stevie Scott, and Seela. Larry was far behind in Bryn Mawr house payments, while also setting aside sinking funds toward three college degrees at the Carlson School of Management in case Viktor's pledge to foot the bills fell through, again.

The price gun whorled out of Chitchee's hands onto the maroon counter. Chitchee stood looking at the broken price gun, the exploded view, the sprawl of gadget parts, and the little balls of rolled up, misfired stickers gummed together. The thought of Aloysius having to buy a whole new Monarch price gun overwhelmed Chitchee with the guilt of Dostoyevsky's Stavrogin.

"Everything costs too much," said Chitchee and heaved a sigh and sobbed barely controllably.

Larry's blue eyes, bluer now that they popped wide open, iced white at Chitchee's self-pitying, maudlin, whining melt down. Larry quickly looked away.

"What's wrong Chitchee? It will be all right. We'll start that button club and you'll be the top button," said Melusina, using her empathy to sneak up on Larry to sneak looks at Larry's head to see whether Larry was wearing his real hair or were his follicles dead as nails.

While Chitchee bit his hand and accepted a hug from Melusina, Melusina stored the virtual JPEG images of Larry's face in her short term memory and then deleted them. Yes, the hair was fake like a "hair falsie." Kriemhilde shared the same thought at the same time. They did not have to voice their conclusions aloud. Smiles and nods communicated their signals without anything audible, because as close sisters they thought alike as glass grapes on the same coffee table.

"It's not that," said Chitchee, his chest heaving in sobbing waves. "I realized I will never love anyone like I loved LaDonna, and I never even loved her!"

He teared up, feeling the evanescence of time against a background of the pity of time lost.

"I failed as a husband to LaDonna! And what else is there to win at?" he asked the track lighting.

"Isn't LaDonna that slut on all those posters around town?" asked Melusina. "We called that number, but we only got a recording of some weirdo musical noise. And then a nasty man says, 'See? You're an idiot!'"

Melusina and Kriemhilde looked on with an inchoate but motherly affection. And as Chitchee pieced together the Monarch price gun with a mournful slowness, he pieced himself together. Suddenly he thread the price tags so that they were fed in correctly! Shocked, he squeezed off price tags like it was the End of Days.

"SNAZZY!" yelped Chitchee, his eyebrows double-bumping.

Elated that something *so* simple could make him *so* happy, he bounced up and down:

"Hey, the infinite universe is working for once!"

Clogging heel to toe and toe to heel, he shot price tags at the ceiling's track lights.

"Good job, Chitchee!" said Saami.

Saami gave his friend an encouraging pat on the back.

"But it's hard for me to wrap my mind around an infinite universe unless it's all porn," Saami added.

"The computer is down again!" announced Aloysius, waking up startled and brushing off deep-fried crumbs of potato and delicious salt grains from his pigeon-chested front.

Aloysius shook off Larry like a bad dream.

"What's wrong with the computer?" asked Larry, looking away to spare himself of having to feel *anything kindly* for burn-outs, miscreant misfits, and glorified hobos.

Somebody bumped Larry and he turned around to strike.

"Hey, Larry," said Chitchee, having shot Larry with the Monarch price gun, "you're 5.99 now without tax."

"Yep, the computer is down Larry," concluded Aloysius. "It's got something called a McAfee virus, so when you click on all the pop ups, the screen freezes."

"What happens to the screen when you reset the router?" asked Larry.

"It turns blue."

"What happens when you empty out the cache?"

"I turn blue."

Larry looked at the high ceiling.

"Anyway, there is no cash!" said Aloysius, anxiously trying to make headway toward the phone while it rang. "Could you get that, Chitchee? That's the problem with the whole world, Larry! There isn't enough cash to buy all the things we need!"

Chitchee picked up the AT & T cordless and an old woman asked for Aloysius.

"Aloysius, I think it's your mother," interrupted Chitchee. "Ariel? And how is your day developing? Hello?"

"Did you check the drivers?" asked Larry, thinking he might for an instant sound like that one oily Best Buy salesman Cameron McCocky he loathed, the computerese-speaking cock who sounded like a golf ball if a golf ball could think. "The hard drive space, Aloysius? And you've done your updates?"

"Are updates like upgrades? You mean like do the defragmentations? Hang on, Larry! Slow down, we're all getting older now. We're not Millenials anymore."

Larry rolled the blue marbles in his eye sockets and tapped his manicured fingers on the counter.

"Let me look at it," said Larry. "First let me see your email."

Chitchee handed Aloysius the dead phone and said:

"I'm sorry Aloysius, this is my two weeks notice."

"What?" asked Aloysius, beckoning Larry to go behind the counter and sit in the BookSmart swivel chair.

Aloysius rooted for the sports section in the wastebasket under the register. Larry clicked on Aloysius's personal email (Yahoo) from MPG. Larry opened an attachment that looked like a business letter. Larry closed it, smiled, and walked back to the other side of the maroon counter and called his boss—a busy signal. Then the BookSmart phone rang.

"Hi, mom," whispered Aloysius, "sorry about the bad connection. I know what you're going to say, but I can't talk. I'm in another dumb business meeting. I'm dealing with life-sucking vampire landlords mom, but we can go shopping tomorrow at Sealy's for a new posturepedic mattress with the whaddayacallit—memory foam!"

"Aloysius, hah, memory foam got you," boomed the earpiece. "This is Viktor Martensen, asshole, so you can cut the fucking dog and pony shit!"

Aloysius stared at the mouthpiece and saw a homunculus Viktor in there.

"You squatting piece of pig shit!" said Viktor. "Get me my money or I will fuck you up so bad your hippie ass will be hippie grass pushing up 'flower power' at Lakewood."

"That was a nice way of putting it," said Aloysius. "It sounded eco-friendly."

"Another thing," said Viktor. "Fjard says it's the same regulars in the store every day. And they look like beatniks playing bongos from the '60s. Get some fucking normal-looking people in the store! It has to look like a real book store! Don't you get it, 8-track head? I want BookSmart to look like a real book store! Like a book store in a book! With real people, not book people!"

"Okay, Viktor, calm down!" said Aloysius. "I've got the perfect guy for you! You'll love him. He's the perfect people person. He's like a big friendly squirrel. He's going to draw in tons of normal throngs. He's perfect for the job—"

"Aloysius," asked Chitchee, "did you catch that? I quit."

"And he's already given his two weeks' notice," continued Aloysius with a smile in mid air as fake as a set of false teeth on a bathroom soapdish. "His standards were that high! At least, I know how to pick 'em. You watch, Viktor. Give it time. And I have the cash for one month's rent somewhere, but I seem to have misplaced it in a book somewhere."

"If I don't get my money soon, I'll break your face!" said Viktor. "And throw you off a bridge! I'm sick of your shit! It's always the same runaround with your shit. Shit!"

"I can't hear you, Viktor!" said Aloysius, holding the phone at a distance. "Your phone must be dying! Did you check your drivers?"

Aloysius clicked off the phone with one hand under the counter while he held the receiver to his ear.

"Chitchee," said Aloysius. "You quit?"

"Hell no!" said Chitchee. "I was pulling your leg! This is too much fun!"

Larry's phone rang. The phone was Viktor.

Two boys, Carlos and Cesar Leon, walked up to Larry and stared at his hair while Larry waited uncomfortably for Aloysius to conclude the "phone call from Viktor."

"Oh, there you are Viktor," said Aloysius, raising his voice for his faked conversation.

"Larry," said Viktor, "the rat bastard hung up on me! Where is he now?"

Larry observed Aloysius's performance.

"I can hear you now, Viktor!" said Aloysius, acting stiffly. "The check will arrive at the end of the week! In full. Yes, twelve thousand and some odd dollars and some odd cents. You know me, Viktor, I'm good for it! Who do I make the check out to again? Do you know how much stamps are nowadays? Ok, good talking to you. Thanks for reaching out! Larry is here, but he's on the phone with someone else—probably one of his female admirers. Larry? Do you want to talk to Larry? Larry?"

"Wait a second, Aloysius," said Larry, annoyed. "I'm *talking* to Viktor Martensen."

Aloysius looked askance. Then he smiled a smile without any teeth in it, looking down at the floor as if the missing smile might be there. Where is that sports section?

While Chitchee sticker-priced the trade paperbacks from the cumbersome Lunds bags, he watched the two boys, Carlos and Cesar Leon, who Aloysius had taken in and paid them in Y/As to shelve a few books so their mother Katreena Polk could work without hiring a babysitter.

"Can we touch your hair, mister?" asked Carlos, looking up at Larry. "Is it sticky like peanut brickle!"

"It's *brittle*!" said Larry and returned to his iPhone 3.

"It's brittle?" asked Cesar Leon.

"You mean 'cause you're so ancient, and old peoples' hair fall out when they get all ancient?" asked Carlos.

"What are you kids *doing* in a book store?" asked Larry loudly, glancing at his Viktor-filled phone. "Aren't you supposed to be in school not learning anything? Or do you plan to skip school and go directly to Stillwater State Prison with the rest of your people?"

Chitchee arched an eye-ridge. Saami formed a "well-what-was-that" grimace. The kids looked puzzled. They had heard wrong but weren't quite sure.

"Mister," said Cesar Leon, "you're kind of stuff and nonsense cannot arise if someday we forbid this kind of stuff and nonsense from arising."

"Stuff and nonsense?" asked Larry. "I don't have a single drop of racism in my blood."

"How many drops *do* you have?" asked Cesar Leon.

"They work here," said Saami. "They're shelvers. They used to shelve books for Uncle Hugo's, but when the manager died, it was too sad for them to go there, so they shelve books here for books."

"You owe them an apology!" said Chitchee. "*Lar-ree*! Just because you can afford to walk around like a stiff duck in a stiff ducky suit, it doesn't mean you can grind your bootheel into everyone you step on."

After swiping the price gun out of Chitchee's lax hand, Saami sticker-priced Larry with a new price tag over the old price tag, and Saami said:

"Now you're going for 2.49 plus tax."

"I hope you die of rabies, Saami," said Larry, looking down at Saami, "bat face!"

"Please love me," said Saami, pressing his lips together for a kiss.

"Did you hear that, Viktor?" asked Larry, pretending he had not hung up on Viktor by pressing his cheek too close to the screen. In anger he snatched the price gun out of Saami's paw. "Look, I'm a businessman and businessmen are never nice. They never hedge about their hedge funds, derive apologies from derivatives, or thrive under too many government regulations. Too bad: that's the golden rule. That's how you know they are businessmen. They never look back. Nice guys die in seconds flat. Never tell a businessman what to do—that's his business. Are you running a touchy-feely charity drive for homeless crack babies or is this a serious American business? Because this poor excuse for a lemonade stand is squatting on the most primal real estate in Minneapolis. It's a complete waste of space. We could be building condos to the sky here with barbershops, beauty salons, and liquor stores on the ground floor."

Larry's inflammable complexion vacillated between red and white roses. Ire inflamed the marrow in his bones the more he felt threatened by his own inflamed responses.

"Larry, don't get your nuts up in a bunch!" said Aloysius. "I can give you one month's back rent tomorrow and we can work out the other months later. It's all good! After I repair this cash register, I will run to the bank and withdraw one month's rent in cash, as you like it, and place it in a nice safe, sealed envelope and you can pick it up tomorrow."

Aloysius produced an oxyacetylene torch, goggles, a welder's helmet, and an oxygen tank, which he lighted with a striker. Flame leapt out in a blue jet, singeing Larry's hairpiece.

"Aloysius! Jesus, you fucking idiot!" said Larry, dancing around on fire. "I'm not a flame-broiled Whopper!"

"Would you be quiet, Larry?" asked a muffled Aloysius like a cast bronze warrior. "I'm trying to concentrate! Quit moving around!"

Chitchee saw the store's Black and Decker cordless vacuum cleaner under the counter. He plugged it into the hair-encrusted power strip.

"This is a *definite* violation of the lease," said Larry, shaking and fuming like an underwater white smoker. "And a fire hazard! And a health and safety violation. I'm personally going to see to it that you vacate the premises! I'll be back tomorrow with the Notice to Quit!"

"Wait, Larry, we can fix that hairpiece!" said Chitchee, switching on the Black and Decker cordless vacuum cleaner. "Can't we all get along with or without PCP? Kidding! Hold still! I need to get the *char* off that bad boy!"

The Black and Decker sucked the toupee off Larry's head. Larry reached for his missing mane as he pushed the crash bar. He tumbled like an ostrich in a log-rolling competition. He sprawled onto Hennepin Avenue face down. The sewered hot air on the sidewalk rushed into BookSmart for a book on sewers, but they didn't have it, and Chitchee sighted a motorized LaDonna on her "vintage" motorbike, the model T. E. Lawrence probably died on. Was that a Triumph? Chitchee abhorred any machine louder than a vacuum cleaner.

"Turn it down!" yelled Chitchee from the front door.

He walked over and collected Larry whose position was prostrate on the sidewalk.

"Don't touch me," said Larry, standing up. "Stand back!"

He felt for the top of his head with two fingers.

"You don't look half as bad as half bald as you do not half bald, Larry," said Chitchee, making a sucking sound.

Chitchee watched Nestor Martensen back-hugging LaDonna on her motorcycle. Larry frantically looked around for his ringing cell phone. The no-helmeted Nestor flaunted his shaggy black hair, just like Elvis Presley's hair but de-greased and sent through a car wash. Nestor looked so in love. So in love with his own hair, that is (he twirled it into curls between his first two fingers), while it hung down around his ears and flowed past his shoulders. Of course, Chitchee speculated, when Nestor made love to LaDonna he entered her with as much love as when he entered a bathroom stall. Didn't she look back vaguely toward the BookSmart front window, the engine roaring—as if she were Jean Seberg in *Paris Match*. LaDonna narrowly missed a blue jaywalking Kennedy who flew out of the way thankful that his life had been spared.

Nestor, stiff as a peacock socially, but who thought *thought* itself was the world's greatest pleasure. E. g., he liked drinking orange juice only to guess its PH. And then he would litmus test it to corroborate his hypothesis—he was always right and then he would then tell everybody he knew he was always right about the PH of any brand of orange juice. He yelled at LaDonna:

"Did you see that idiot?"

Nestor justified all his judgment, because he had been IQ boosted by ten years of shipments from Bulk Nutrition of GABA, piracetam, aniracetam, phenylpiracetam, choline, hydergine, and any nootropic that buzzed across the Internet or any smart drug worth the old college try.

"Chitchee! Who is this bald-ass flamingo dancer?" asked Kennedy, having concluded his conference at McDonald's with a certain man, code-named "Frenchy," a fence in stolen goods, phones, DVDs, and orchids.

"That is our friend and landlord, Larry," said Chitchee, snapping out of his cloud.

"All he needs is the cucarachas," said Kennedy, "and he can go on *American Idolatry*."

Larry re-entered BookSmart, but his iPhone 3 stopped him, and he about-faced, allowing Chichee and Kennedy to walk into BookSmart.

"What is *this*, Chitchee?" asked Saami, setting aside his corn broom.

Saami examined Larry's hair ball in the vacuum cleaner's see-through, replaceable container like a newly-discovered species of vole. Carlos, Cesar Leon, Melusina, Kriemhilde, Kennedy, and Torg treated the vole as a newly-discovered species. A crowd formed at this zoo. Randy, walking stick held out like a sabre, stopped to see what this hub of a bub was about. But when Randy poked his head in the door, behind him three incoming customers collided together like a standing waveform. So Kennedy descended the stairs to avoid the noise and people, while Randy retreated to his listening post outside the entrance to Carousel Square, greeting the suburban shoppers with inquiries as to whether anybody needed any Oxys, Percocets, or Vicodins.

THE THREE GRASSHOPPERS AND YARDLEY SINGLETON

Chitchee clapped his hands with childlike delight when he saw Dougal Murchison, Mjollnir "the Hammer of the North" Rurik, and little Nicky Fingers, his old Uptown friends from way back or so they all imagined, there being no reliable narrator of "way back" amongst the entire coterie. Chitchee greeted Dougal, Mjollnir, and Nicky with great acclaim and waved them into the store as if to introduce them to a diorama at a World's Fair.

Dougal Murchison had lost his house on Bryant Avenue South in an assets seizure by the Metro Drug Task Force, even though it was the wrong address. Although Dougal lost his homegrown business, he had his SSI and his SSDI. After being released from jail, Dougal dyed his hair, beard, and eyebrows purple in the Walker Library bathroom, the Carousel Square bathroom, the Lunds bathroom, and the Cheapo bathroom. With mixed reviews. Then he thought he should read the directions on the box, which he never did. Then he remembered he was married, but didn't have any way of contacting his wife. So he bought a stolen phone from Randy, went to Walker Library, and checked the inmate rosters of every prison in the tri-state area for her.

Mjollnir Rurik, 6'8", harked back to the Nicollet Ball Park (shoveled under for Interstate 35W) where he went with his father to see the Minneapolis Millers play the St. Paul Saints. He dreamed of being a professional golfer, because "they get all the women." He toured in tournaments from tee to tee until tea time took over his tee times and he traded in his Titleists for a tea shop called the Tea Trader until the Uptown Trade traitors tossed him out so they could erect Carousel Square over his Tea Trader like a giant Tombstone. Ever since the good old days, Mjollnir wandered around both twin towns like a dreaming giant who appeared every time you looked out a bus window.

Nicky Fingers, much younger, tagged along the two elder statesmen of vagabondage like a pack animal. He had been seized at Miami International airport because his father was caught with an ounce of Jamaican in Nicky's milk bottle. His father almost disowned him. Nicky grew up to be a fine, young thief who stole everything not glued down. His pickpocketed Evangelical parents kicked him out of the house when he was fifteen for being a devil worshipper, because he was addicted to playing *Magic: The Gathering*. Nicky carried Mjollnir's old backpack, which replaced the old backpack from Midwest Mountaineering that Mjollnir gave Nicky, which a jailbird friend stole when his back was turned, which Nicky stole back from the backstabbing friend but lost when he walked into the Target on Minnehaha, stuffed that backpack with perfumes for his future girlfriends, and got caught on camera.

The manager pressed charges. When the thumpers from 3rd Precinct threw Nicky to the sidewalk they smashed his glasses in half, broke his nose, and permanently damaged both eardrums. Nicky's wallet was in his stolen backpack with his ID, which was stolen, and he got out three days later owning nothing except a blur, a broken nose, and no couch to crash on. After running into Dougal and Mjollnir getting high by a Lake Calhoun sunset, Mjollnir gave Nicky his second backpack, because Mjollnir felt confined by backpacks, which were always too small. Besides Mjollnir wore a bullet-proof vest, because he had nightmares from the RNC protests a year ago when a MPD thumper, Sergeant Robert Bob "BB" Robbins, broke Mjollnir's nose, fractured his jaw, concussively brained him with a flashlight into a pool of blood, and kneed him in the back.

Mjollnir gave Sergeant Bob "BB" Robbins the finger, who applied a chokehold and replied:

"This is the land of free speech and what you are saying is not free speech."

Six MPD thumpers in the "circle of silence" watched, saw nothing, and absorbed the object lesson as a "training exercise." Then Sergeant Bob "BB" Robbins let Mjollnir off his leash. Later that year, Sergeant Bob "BB" Robbins had so many complaints against him that he received a ceremonious Merit Award for "good numbers." Further upping the ladder, Sergeant Bob "BB" Robbins was rewarded with a transfer to MPD's counterterrorism unit and more recently to MPD's sex crimes unit, along with moonlighting as a bouncer at a cantina on Lake Street.

Chitchee flattered himself that he had lots of friends and that *everybody in Uptown* had heard that *Chitchee Chichester* worked at BookSmart by late afternoon, because even "The Three Grasshoppers" penciled in BookSmart on their slacker itinerary and schlumped over to test the BookSmart couch.

Courtney Kirkwood re-entered (to wait on the same couch for Lily's Excedrin headache #6 bus), pretending not to look for Snorri. Her hoop-skirted crinoline walled off the doorway when her lame folding cart tripped on the threshold. A chunk of solder splintered off and bounced. She stooped to find it.

"Hey, Chitchee man!" said Dougal from the couch. "Are you still working at Shakey's?"

"Hey Dougal man, no," said Chitchee, "I work here now! It's great! The people are great!"

"I'm all trained out, Chitchee," said Saami. "After the boss leaves, we can sit around and get high. Got anything? I'm almost out. Should I call Raven to front us a blueberry nugget?"

Saami walked downstairs when he saw the grasshoppers schlumping toward the couch, resentful because Chitchee looked at him and only shrugged helplessly: "Aren't grasshoppers people too?"

"Please don't block the entry way, Courtney!" said Aloysius in a delayed reaction, while he stood behind the NCR cash register, opening and shutting the till, which had come off the runners—it wouldn't shut flush—it wouldn't run true.

Bald as a steel ball bearing, Larry set his iPhone 3 on the counter—i-vibrating . . . nnnnnnnn . . . nnnnnnn . . .

"That's mine!" shouted Larry, locating his migratory wig in the Black and Decker.

He pointed his finger at Chitchee:

"What's your name?"

"Chitchee Chichester, sir! No relation to Sir Francis! If that's where you were going."

"You'll pay for what you just did, Francis Chichester, so help me God," said Larry, staring straight into Chitchee's eyes with a skull-fucking glare from the depths of hell. With icy menace Larry repeated: "So help me God!"

"What?" asked Chitchee, his attention shrinking in direct proportion to his decreasing glucose. "I didn't catch that. Books on God? Theology is next to Philosophy and Godliness is next to Cleanliness. Aisle One. Larry, do you think the Universe had a beginning?"

"I *said*—" began Larry.

"Hold on, is anybody else hungry?" shouted Chitchee over Larry. "Maybe we should order pizza from Pizza Luce! If we all chip in, we can get more. Social facilitation, it's called."

When Aloysius slammed the till into the housing of the register, the armature for the roll of thermal paper printed off the BookSmart receipts for the day in undeciphered computer languages. Lunging, Larry snatched the vacuum cleaner out of Chitchee's hands, which surrendered it easily. Larry disappeared into the bathroom and emerged with his hairpiece fitted back on. Chitchee was delighted:

"Well, look at you! Strutting like the only cock in the yard!"

"Excuse me?" asked Larry. "Excuse me?"

"Sorry, Larry," said Chitchee, moving towards Larry. "But your rug looks so good now—here give me a hug—a hug for a rug!"

"Get away from me, fucktard!" said Larry, vibrating like his vibrating iPhone 3. "Viktor? You there? The jerk off here said his computer is down. When are you going to get your computer fixed, Aloysius? *Viktor* wants to know!"

"Hold on, I'll call the Goon Squad right now," said Aloysius.

"Aloysius, I need another self-help book," said Kennedy, emerging from the basement.

Kennedy stood on the red runner and leaned over the maroon counter.

"Another one?" asked Aloysius. "You're getting addicted to those. They are self-enabling you. You need a self-help book to get you off self-help books, Kennedy! Damn, I need the cash register manual. Saami! Saami! Where are you? Could you come upstairs and boot the computer?"

Saami screamed himself into ululations.

"Boot the computer? Huh?" yelled Saami upstairs. "What's wrong with it? It was getting Porn Hub fine last night!"

Larry's face spoiled like a bowl of month-old Land O'Lakes cream. The iPhone 3 barked a string of obscenities, and Larry looked at the jeweled Piaget watch that Viktor had rewarded him once in lieu of cash.

"I'll be back later, Aloysius," said Larry and presented Aloysius with a face of month-old Land O'Lakes cream.

"What am I going to do?" asked Aloysius to Saami. "Geez, I can't remember anything anymore! I put a large amount of cash,

6,000 dollars, in a book somewhere. Did I tell you that already? Did I call my mother? Did Aubrey call? Do you remember *Dialing for Dollars* with Jim Hutton? What was I going to do? Oh yeah, bye Larry! Thanks for going, I mean stopping . . . stopping!"

Larry headed upstairs in the Yggdrasil building to discuss with Corky Skogentaub at MPG whether the virus Larry planted had infected the BookSmart computer yet.

"Is it working, Corky?" asked Larry.

"It's the only thing in the dumb store that is!" laughed Corky, who rippled over his dinosaur hips with his obesity, jellification of adipose, and grocery bags of fat for gluteal buttocks.

Corky blamed his sedentary lifestyle on long hours at the MPG cube farm.

Larry and Corky decided on Bloody Marys at Club Miami.

Chitchee thought Jason Unterguggenberger looked familiar when Jason sallied into BookSmart, JVC headphones clamped over his ears like Mickey Mouse muffs and long unwashed black hair to his shoulders. Jason had no lips, giving him a flat-ironed mouth (his "smile" revealed a graveyard of dead teeth). His bulbous forehead bulged so it made you wonder whether he was a genius or a big frog.

"Can I help you?" asked Chitchee.

Jason's thin black eyebrows looked penciled-in over his tiny raisin-brown eyes.

"Has Grant Hart been in?" asked Jason.

"Who?" said Chitchee. "I don't know."

"Anyway, I'm not looking for a book, I'm looking for a couch," said Jason.

"Couches are downstairs," said Chitchee, watching Jason descend the stairs. "They're kind of old though. Not exactly up to Crate & Barrel standards. Don't expect Gabberts! Nevertheless, *Marhaba*!"

Chitchee bowed a pretentious bow.

"Chitchee, what are you doing?" asked Saami. "You're encouraging all the hoi pollois to hang their hats here!"

Saami saw something and slammed his head on the counter.

"Oh no! *This* guy!" cried Saami. "The world's worst customer! Shoot me! Whatever you do, don't engage *him* in conversation!"

"Okay," said Chitchee. "I promise."

Libor Biskop flew like a broken-winged sparrow into BookSmart. Libor had black hair shaped like question marks behind his oily ears, and his black-holed, super elliptical eyes received phobia after phobia in photon packets of ego-tectonic, quaking fear. Libor—looked—at—Chitchee, he—looked to see if Chitchee would maybe hassle him—Libor—froze. Libor saw that Chitchee had a machete and planned to roast him sacramentally. Chitchee had already met Libor through Randy Quaalude's girlfriend Susquehanna, which Libor always forgot.

"Hi, Libor," said Chitchee, "how's that squaring-the-circle machine coming along? Did you win the $15,000 yet?"

"What does that mean?" asked Libor Biskop with a voice that seemed to come out of a cracked teapot. "How did you know I was going for the Fields Medal? How do I know you? It's all too epistemologically non-modal in here."

Everybody knew but did not want to know Libor Biskop, drowning in his oversized, out-of-season, pea green winter parka, its funnel hood trimmed with fake fur so that upon looking into it, one saw a scared, treed, and trapped human rodent wearing duct-taped, tortoiseshell glasses. All the local shop owners from Prospect Park to Powderhorn and from Kenwood to Kenny dreaded Libor Biskop. Once Libor Biskop entered your store, he discovered electromagnetic radiation everywhere. He measured it on a device he ordered from *Boy's Life*. Whenever he was not allergic to eye contact, chem trails, fresh produce, electronic scanners, Northern Lights, kangaroo dander, zeta functions, clam chowder, the tritone, spider mites, and the letter "Q" when not followed by a "u," he labored perpetually on his squaring-the-circle machine, which he needed to prove Einstein's General Relativity wrong. He reasoned that if he could take down Einstein, then the rest of them—Bohr, Heisenberg, Schrodinger, Pauli, Fermi, Dirac, Planck, Maxwell, Faraday, Newton, Archimedes, and Ahmes—would fall like dominoes in reverse motion and Libor would re-establish a primordial, ordered universe of humanism.

Libor, a promising theoretical physicist in the 1960s, was picked up one day on the West Bank for wearing only a loin cloth and a crown of thorns made of MOSFET transistors.

"I am Shiva," Libor told the West Bank thumpers around Cedar/Riverside. "Crucify me. Nail me to a transformer."

"Can I help you, Libor?" asked Chitchee, smiling and almost pleading.

"Chitchee," said Saami. "What did I just tell you?"

"Allergies!" yelled Libor.

"Allergies are downstairs," said Chitchee.

"Then I can't go down there," said Libor.

"I'll go down there for you," said Chitchee.

"Then I'll be allergic to you," said Libor.

"We'll be fine," sneezed Chitchee with a shout. "Here, give me a hug. And *we'll frolic in the autumn mist in a land called Honah Lee.*"

Libor Biskop, experiencing a short circuit, misheard the previous statement, which reverberated in his brain, sounding more or less like:

"Here, here, my love duck, how about a nice fuck?"

Chitchee appeared leering with a lustful satyr's sadistic smirk, flicking his tongue, and rolling up the tip of it like a birthday party favor.

"Rodney the Rodent!" shouted Libor.

Libor hallucinated Chitchee's words solidifying. Each letter turned into an arrow, and all the arrows pierced the flesh of Libor Biskop like Saint Sebastian the Martyr as cosplayed by Yukio Mishima.

"I'm not that way!" said Libor, shaking with fear.

"No, you're *in* the way, duckie," said Saami.

Libor extracted from his inner pocket an inflated Ziploc baggie, which he opened and sucked the air out of, breathing from it like an inhaler. He hyperventilated, dry heaved, and fled.

Did Chitchee say something out of line to Libor?

Chitchee stared out the window and the dumbfounded window stared back.

"Have a nice allergy!" said Chitchee.

Libor chased the #6 Metro Transit bus like a wounded timberwolf after a nimble white-tailed deer.

"Oh Lord, what a looney" said Saami, speechless and shaking his head. "I'm going downstairs to pack up some orders."

"Saami," said Chitchee. "Libor has a disability. He has 'squaring circle disease' times two. It all started when—"

"Not interested," said Saami, "everybody has a disability of some sort. Get over it."

"What's wrong with everybody today?" asked Chitchee.

Melancholic humor (Burton's *The Anatomy of Melancholy*) undermined Chitchee's previous mood of joy. It was that type of uneasiness John Locke (*Essay Concerning Human Understanding*) claimed led to migraines. Social vertigo snapped those delicate possible friendships like dental floss. One misguided word and poof!

"Libor! That poor guy, Libor," said Chitchee to Aloysius, "he's probably suffering from prophylactic shock."

Aloysius turned away from Chitchee, leaving behind their cone of silence. Chitchee—only barely listening to his thoughts—felt betrayed. Aloysius had a Jumbo Coke headache and dreaded diabetes—he had read a factoid that told him diabetes triggered erectile dysfunction, not that he was hooking up with Lily Holmgren anytime soon. But the very idea—Aloysius felt dizzy. Vertigo was it, could it be a mini Coke-stroke? Is there such a thing? He didn't want to talk about it with anybody because it would make him look like a Coward-in-Chief.

"Are you okay, boss?" asked Chitchee.

"Uggghhhwaah, never felt better."

"You mean you *don't* have diabetes?" asked Chitchee.

"Like I said, whatever I just said."

"Maybe you should go out more?"

"Did I say I didn't? I go out plenty—I walk to the mailbox, I walk back—"

"No, go out! Socialize! You know, online dating. You're never too old to be a Romeo, hey ninny nonny no, eh Romeo?"

"Yeah," said Aloysius, dreamily. "You stick it in once and then you got 'em. But it's been awhile since I hauled my ashes."

"Sounds like it!" said Chitchee, making a wry face and looking away in embarrassment. "Hauling ashes? What's next? Graphic use of the word 'poontang?'"

Aloysius shook off the oncoming headache, the migraine, the concussion—whatever it was, he was Quarterback Joe Kapp, fourth and goal to go, nothing to lose; however, instead of the end zone, Aloysius fixated on the redolent, white pine wood flooring.

"I have to make a run to US Bank," said Aloysius.

Then Aloysius stood up too fast, so that the whole trek to the end of the counter dusted up variegated stars, floaters, purple algae, blood-colored and skewbald clouds, and intimations of mortality in every swimming phosphene. He palped each cheek with his fingertips to see if either cheek had started drooping down to the redolent, white pine wood flooring. Wasn't that a sign of stroking and tinnitus? (He heard faint bells when his spare change jingled). Wasn't that a supposed warning sign, according to a Dr. Phil video he had seen on strokes on YouTube, but how would Dr. Phil know that without stroking himself? Or asking a lot of guests who had stroked it?

"Saami, could you—could you come back upstairs—and look for the cash register manual? I have to jaunt down to US Bank!"

Saami pretended he didn't hear that, because how many times did he have to climb those stairs in one day?

"Hey Saami!" yelled Chitchee down the stairs.

Saami didn't hear that either.

Chitchee extracted his acorn cap and whistled its siren scream.

"I'm coming! I heard you! For Christ's sake, stop!" Saami shrieked, buried his *Bone,* placed a cap on his BIC, and quickly organized the mailers for the books at his dingy workstation, surrounded by scissors, tape, magic markers, empty pints of Phillips vodka, and dozens of empty Altoid breath spearmint tins.

"God, I forgot to hide those Altoid tins," continued Saami to himself, satisfied his traces had been erased when he finally shoved the Altoid tins into a 13-gallon diaphanous trash bag where everyone could see them.

Saami charged up the staircase.

"Hey, Saami, I committed a terrific mistake the other day!" piped up Kennedy at the maroon counter, with a stentorian British East African Upper Class roar able to mow down whole aisles in the Old Vic. In a slow crescendo towards fortissimo, Kennedy proclaimed: "By mistake, the other day, I purchased this self-said volume, *Mindfulness: from Serenity to Success in Thirty Four Easy Investment Strategies.* Now I have the receipt presently upon my person. And I'd like to persevere this receipt, to refund this book of a mistaken occlusion, because *that's what it was.* An occlusion! I didn't realize the whole thing was an ONTOLOGY! I THOUGHT IT WAS A COMPLETE BOX SET. Help me out, my friend."

"You mean," said Chitchee, backing up a little for more breathing room, "you'd like to parallelize that item for a particulate volume on your wish list."

"Exactly! You should be teaching anthroposophy at Harvard, you learn fast!" said Kennedy. "But *first* I want to pursue the new arrivals for something better. What I'm really excruciating for is *The Memory Book* by Lainie Kazan and Ben Bradlee."

"Oh, *The Memory Book!*" said Aloysius over Saami's scrounging head. "I saw that around here somewhere the other day. It might have gotten re-shelved."

When Saami saw Hawk Eye coming, he announced his failure to find the NCR manual and walked back downstairs, where Kennedy, standing in front of the Self Help section repeated to himself "Kazan, Shazan, Shazam," amid BookSmart's other eighty thousand books. If Kennedy could not find *The Memory Book* he planned to peruse and ponder and to otherwise while away the wee hours of his SSI life plan and to sit there in the BookSmart basement like a book, wool-gathering entrepreneurial schemes that would make Warren Buffet blow his own brains out for not thinking of. Kennedy found a copy of *The Memory Book,* which he opened. A stuffed, sealed envelope landed on the floor.

Chitchee saluted Hawk Eye's entering and said:

"Thank you for your service, sir! And I guess if you're panhandling you might as well bring a book along. I'll be right with you after I help a gentleman downstairs."

"Don't worry about it," said Hawk Eye with a half-raspberry cheer, his lips sputtering out half curses.

Hawk Eye, sporting a surplus, faded U. S. Army jacket and unshaven beard of crawling uneven hairs that had sprouted in a few hours, slumped up to the counter with an exhausted posture. He had a punched-out look to his face as if he had been reared in Naples, adopted by the Cosa Nostra, and rope-a-doped by Oscar de la Hoya on an HBO special.

"Hey, Aloysius!" said Hawk Eye. "I have to use your potty."

The dark orbits around Hawk Eye's saturnine eyes looked like the catacombs of Rome as he walked weakly to the back of the store toward the bathroom. Kennedy pocketed the envelope to open later, re-shelved the book, and ascended the stairs.

"Can I look at the book, *How to Stop Worrying*, in my hold pile?" asked Kennedy. "And negotiate on the way out? Which should be about twelve hours from now. You'll be here later? Right? I have to have that book too. You won't lose it? Because *I have to have it*! For my collection of have-to-have books."

"Quit worrying, Kennedy!" said Chitchee.

"Thanks, I needed to hear that," said Kennedy, cupping his chin with his hand and double checking his shaving that morning. He looked upward, fishing for something in the ceiling. "You know, maybe, you know—I don't think I really *do* need the book. You can toss it back into my hold pile for now, thanks. But I definitely plan to buy all the others—don't ask me how! If something by way of dividends occurs!"

"Kennedy, we should write a book together," said Chitchee. "*How to Stop Worrying About Your Hold Pile and Take Your Life Back!*"

Saami clumped back up the stairs and told Chitchee to spray the maroon counter with a little Lysol Lemon Breeze All-Purpose Cleaner and squeegee it off. Saami looked at the NCR cash register again and thought he saw a Cray Supercomputer mainframe. So he declared it officially dead and clambered back downstairs, hoping Kennedy would leave him alone, even though Kennedy always did. Chitchee sprayed, admired, scrubbed the maroon counter as bright as California Bing Cherries, and sponged the counter with renewed elbow grease.

"Easy on the nozzle there, buddy, they break easily," said Aloysius. "Oh, and Chitchee, try not to leave scratches on the linoleum, that's the good stuff. Okay, I have to make a US Bank run."

"Right-o!" said Chitchee. "You know, Aloysius, I want to own BookSmart! Let me know when you want to sell it. And I'll buy it for thirty thousand dollars and a rabbit's foot."

The check-out area sparkled like a commercial for disinfectants.

Aloysius's eyes curdled like milk scudding in coffee. He sat back down on the swivel chair, worried, and fell into golden slumbers.

"Chitchee," said Aloysius in his sleep, already dreaming, "could you watch the register, buddy?"

"Could I get some cardboard and a magic marker for another sign?" asked Hawk Eye, returning unrefreshed from the bathroom.

Chitchee handed over cardboard and a box of magic markers with undue haste. Panhandling was a kind of stock car race and Chitchee was in Hawk Eye's pit crew at Elko Speedway.

In the course of Hawk Eye's creation of a pitiful sign, Chitchee looked at his discharge papers, which Hawk Eye showed to everyone proudly although the certificate was almost confetti from normal wear and tear.

"Hey, Hawk Eye, we both went to the same high school," said Chitchee, realizing they probably shared a few acquaintances with families in and around Excelsior. "You went to Minnetonka Senior High? Me too! What a coincidence! Hello, Skipper! Now I see why you—"

Hawk Eye wasn't responding.

"Aloe-wissius!" interrupted Yardley Singleton, sporting a stern, well-manicured beard, hairdresser's haircut, witty mustache, well-trimmed eyebrows, and pedicured nails. "Singleton HAS returned!"

"Hooray!" Chitchee clapped his hands. "Welcome to BookSmart, Baron de Dandy!"

Aloysius awoke and with one eye peeked at a three-piece tweed suit and tie: Uh oh it was Yardley. Aloysius faked a snore, pleased that Chitchee fielded these human fungoes like sandlot baseballs.

Yardley's Victorian vest was invested with a stemwinder and a fob. A throwback to the day of *belles lettres,* Aloysius would throw his back out to stay thrown back to Dickens's or Huysmans's revisited Dickens's London in Huysmans's *Against the Grain.* Chichee saw in Yardley an American gentleman resembling an English gentleman who simulated an age-progressed, back-of-the-carton Chad Newcome from *The Ambassadors* combined with a character from Woolf or Forster, who could have frolicked with Harry Crosby and other Lost Generation types out of *Black Sun.* Yardley wished he could have been perfectly fictional. He was the aesthetic scion of Walter Pater, burning with the "hard, gemlike flame," of poetry; he loved poetry of refined and exquisite tastes; he measured every vowel for value and every consonant for consonance. He surfaced the globe for rare books. He collected antiques, time-pieces, pens, quills, nibs, inks, inkstands, ink-stones, book store paraphernalia, and book store women, who were attracted to his fastidious style, his red lacquered lips of vermillion flesh, his absurdist montage of mustaches, and his eyefull for the damsely damoiselle on the Isle of Style.

Home slumming in his backyard, Minneapolis, Yardley rubbed shoulders with fellow veterans like Hawk Eye, who was designing a beggarly, "homeless guy" sign as pitifully as possible. He observed Hawk Eye trace in purple magic marker: PURPLE HEARTS: $20/each. Yardley sniffed an essential oil of lavender from a minuscule phial. Yardley filed past Hawk Eye and saw Aloysius zonked out with his Dell computer screen frozen and his golden French fries unfinished. Aloysius slept like a potato dreaming of a solanaceous slumber of potato fields in the Peruvian cloud-hatted highlands. Aloysius swiveled 90 degrees due east, golden French fries in a pectoral display over his T-shirt, facing the Hennepin Avenue sidewalk. Randy, making his scrambled deliveries, stalked past and whipped BookSmart's front window with a warty thwack from his walking stick. Startled, Aloysius quickly fastened himself to the frozen Dell screen like a mountain climber falling off the Peruvian highlands and holding on by *quipus.*

"Yardley Singleton has returned," repeated Yardley, "for his books on hold and especially any new books by Chilcote Carrothers. Any new book of his poems *shall* be welcomed heartily. Strangely I only find them here, Aloe-wissius!"

"Let's play the 'Royal Fireworks Suite' to swell your progress!" said Chitchee.

Aloysius sighed over the cash register. It wouldn't open except in a statistically random distribution.

"Aloe-wissius! Yardley Singleton always—"

"I know, Yardley, Yardley Singleton always returns for his books, and it's *Aloysius,*" said Aloysius. "You'll have to ask Chitchee here for help. I'd love to render you some assistance, but I'm fixing a hole in the cash register."

"Why? Is the twittering machine recalcitrant?" asked Yardley with an air of being on stage at the Chanhassen Dinner Theater. "Is it br-r-r-roken again?"

"No, it's not broken *again,*" said Aloysius, looking directly at Yardley. "I'm taking a course in cash register repair at Dunwoody Institute and this is my homework for tomorrow."

"Good for you!" said Yardley, clasping his hands together. "Who says when you're over the hill you're merely a coat upon a stick—merely a hunk of rotting meat?"

"Yeah, who says?" said Hawk Eye, looking like a coat upon a stick, a hunk of rotting meat.

"Hel-low, new employee!" Yardley said to Chitchee. "May I introduce myself, Archie? For Archibald? I am Yardley Singleton and Yardley Singleton always comes back for his books on hold. That's the first thing you need to know about Yardley Singleton!"

"What's the second thing?" said Chitchee.

"He never buys them!" said Saami, crawling up the stairs.

"Of course, Mr. Rolvaag, you know I despise your type—you little . . . popster . . . pipster hipster pop culture gremlin," said Yardley, licking the acid on his burning lips. "The powers that be have two concessions for all you Saamis, the candy bars of music and the popcorn of movies."

"Then let me rectify the situation," farted Saami with elfin ears and pointed chin.

Cloacal statement flushed down, all customers made shift at the warning except Yardley, who stood at the counter coughing his brains out in a line of drool.

"Disgusting," said Yardley. "Saami? Could you run down a book for me outside in the middle of the intersection of Lake & Hennepin?"

"Oh, come on book people, kiss and make up, and shake hands," said Chitchee.

"Not with this little yawp!" burst Yardley. "He's not a genuine bibliophile. He's not even a book person! He's a movie person! It doesn't take a Marxist like myself to realize the entire entertainment industry is like pizza: it's all about the dough. Only poetry is pure. Like a child. And I *will* buy a book as soon as I go to the ATM at Lunds, if I can remember my pin number. I shall have to pick up a small bag of FunYuns! The which I am quite fond of as of late. Then I shall return for any books you might have on non-Tagalog languages of the Philippines or any of the languages of New Guinea. But I shall settle for any textbooks on Linear A *in* Linear A. I have never abandoned a book! Be it in Bombay, Bangkok, or Burnsville! Let it be known, Yardley Singleton *always* RETURNS FOR HIS BOOKS! I will never let my books down."

"You don't have anything on hold, Captain Shackleton," said Aloysius dryly, sucking on his forgotten Jumbo Coke, slurping it dry, and jangling the ice. "Nothing to 'shall return' for!"

Saami stood idly by, shaking his head.

"Nothing," said Saami, having secretly reshelved Yardley's hold pile out of spite. "Nothing on hold for your royally pompous, pimpled, rash-bitten butt, sir, not even one book of rancid poetry."

"You see the treatment I receive in your establishment, Aloe-wissiussius? Is it anxiety of influence? Is it because I always maintain the highest browest, the highbrowiest, the most highbrow, the best taste, the best tastiest, the most *Racine* standards for literature," said Yardley, poking his right index upward and gyring in a rotary motion.

"Oooh," said Saami, wiggling his fingers. "Racine, Wisconsin. I'm *scared*!"

"Why you mewling, puking donkey's ass," said Yardley, moving forward in sabot-shaped slippers, his hands outstretched to break the chicken's neck. He looked to have swallowed an apricot pit giving intense pain. "Ah! My back went out! Oh, I'm down! Singleton down! I have to lie down. Oh God, I think my knee popped too!"

The Three Grasshoppers on the couch sat stoned with a folio reprint of Audubon's *The Birds of America* propped across their laps, the book open to a watercolor of a passenger pigeon, and they didn't hear a thing.

"Could someone get up for this old bird?" said Saami. "Someone? Hey, you janky-assed jerkwads, rise and shine! No sleeping in the store this early! Hey Chitchee, come here and I'll show you how to do this. You have to kick the bottoms of the bums' boots, 'cause if they're vets they might wake up and kill you with their headbutts like giant nutcrackers."

"Um, Saami? These guys aren't vets . . . I know these guys . . ." said Chitchee.

"Oh no, oh no, it's incoming," said Saami exasperated, looking out the front window. "No, no, no, God damn it! The Indestructible Book Jesus is coming in with another ton of worthless books."

"The Indestructible Book Jesus?" asked Chitchee. "Is that his name? I have to meet this guy! Sock it to me, mama!"

"I think I'm dying in Egypt," said Yardley.

Yardley asked Chitchee to make the proper funeral arrangements at Washburn-McReavy. Yardley had given his daughter Minerva the coupon for his funeral. He had instructed Minerva: "I want Chilcote Carrothers's poems read at my funeral—no matter how long it takes, and the music of Lully, truffles for the peanut gallery, my nominal ashes sent to the Pere-Lachaise cemetery in Paris and placed in limbo between the graves of Abelard and Heloise."

"Chitchee, give me a hand!" said Saami. "We'll lift up this old spunk-smelling couch, hunky dory, and dump these dumb stoners like a Van Camper can full of pork and beans."

"I've got a better idea," said Chitchee. "Hey Saami, I've got black Afghani hash!"

The Three Grasshoppers' eyes popped like open poppies on the playing fields of Kandahar. They sniffed traces of reality.

"Hey Chitchee, man!" said Dougal. "We were waiting for you! You work here now? That's why we came here, *I remember now*."

They looked stoned to Yardley, whose monogrammed handkerchief flitted out of Yardley's pocket. Yardley hovered, mopping his sweaty brow, pat pat pat.

Yardley, unable to stand up any longer, threw himself across the couch, and The Three Grasshoppers sprang up, quickly sliding the Audubon *Birds of America* to the floor and sliding off the couch themselves.

"That's so much better," decided Yardley. "Ah! Collagen might have helped the joints but . . . Chitchee, could you fetch me a La Croix Sparkling Water? I . . . I . . . am parched . . . I'm so parched I'm bleached . . . my malaria from Chiang Mai is recrudescing. I'm so cold, I'm hot, and so hot I'm cold!"

"What should I do?" asked Chitchee. "Run down to CVS for artemisinin? They're not gonna have it. How can I help you?"

"Water!"

"Malaria!" said Chitchee. "Wow! I'll go wash out someone's Solo cup and be right back. Malaria, wow, like Alfred Russell Wallace! How exotic!"

"Carlos!" said Aloysius. "Cesar Leon! Your mom's here to pick you up! Thanks much, fellas! Don't forget your books! Saami! Can you get our young scholars their . . . Bertrand Russells and *The World of Mathematics*? So you didn't want the *Gooseberries*? Whatever. Okay, I'm going to run a beeline to US Bank now. Ufff."

Aloysius smoked his way down to US Bank, withdrew six thousand dollars from Aubrey's sinking college fund, and sealed it tight in a #10 envelope.

The Three Grasshoppers pushed themselves off the floor, rolling papers and orange prescription bottles tumbling across the redolent, white pine wood flooring, clanking like croquet mallets in front of Carlos and Cesar Leon—absorbed by their books on chess, puzzles, knots, string, origami, and kite-flying. Saami escorted them out to their mother Katreena, who was in a hurry to catch a #6 bus arriving at McDonald's.

"You folks interested in some *Gooseberries?*" asked Chitchee, holding the books the two kids had grown out of.

"Do you want to smoke some weed, Chitchee?" asked Dougal.

"Sure Dougal, but by the same toking . . . you know . . . I can't be . . . *one toke over the line.*"

"Why? You always were at your other jobs," said Dougal.

"What other jobs?" asked Chitchee, keeping his voice down.

"Yeah, Dougal," said Mjollnir. "You must be thinking of you."

"Oh yeah," said Dougal. "It was me I was thinking of. That was me at all my jobs."

"What do you mean, Mjollnir?" asked Nicky Fingers. "Dougal hasn't done a stroke of work in his entire life except deal."

"You mean dealing *isn't* a job?" objected Dougal.

"Not the way you do it," said Nicky Fingers.

"You guys, I have to get back to *my* job!" pleaded Chitchee.

"Oh," said Dougal. "Where do you work?"

"Here, Dougal, here," said Chitchee. "Remember?"

"Oh, yeah," grinned Dougal. "We'll have to come by some time and say hi!"

"Yes, do! Thanks for stopping!" said Chitchee holding the door, which he held like a doorman.

Dougal and Mjollnir helped Nicky repack Nicky's shabby backpack, securing all possibly lost paraphernalia. They scuffled out of BookSmart. Nomads in their own neighborhood, they sallied down to Lake Calhoun to rest, relax, regroup, and reminisce about the last ten minutes for ten minutes and then spend the next ten minutes looking for Dougal's weed, which must have fallen out of Nicky's backpack on the way there, or it lay sleeping under the cushions of the BookSmart couch, or Dougal forgot it at Raven's apartment after buying it, or none of this happened at all and Dougal hallucinated it.

THE INDESTRUCTIBLE BOOK JESUS

Chitchee ran a cup of water and a blanket from the utility closet to suffering Yardley, shaking, sweating, and imagining bats hovering over the black, leather couch that was a giant bat itself eating him, while an unmufflered, down-at-the-wheel, camshackle '65 Chevy Bel Air Station Wagon with rack and ruin steering, double parked in front of the #6 bus stop—boxes of books packed to the Chevy's hood.

Chitchee ran outside and greeted the book lover.

"Afternoon, boss!" said The Indestructible Book Jesus, unloading boxes in the front door. "Aloysius, I got some books for ya! Hopefully there's a Gutenberg in there!"

"I'd settle for a Bay Psalm book or a Mainz psalter!" said Chitchee with the cheerfulness of a mouthful of halved peaches as he hauled boxes, which he always found arousing. "Do you have any incunabula?"

"Not since I discovered Preparation H," said The Indestructible Book Jesus, with his peregrine profile of sprinkled dirt, paint, and cinder dust, with his plump pack of Carousel cigarettes in the front pocket of his Oshkosh bib overalls, which an old gallon bucket of Sherwin Williams latex, abandoned in a tool shed, had drooled down dry in rivulets down his coughing chest.

The Indestructible Book Jesus in the local ecosystem of the book trade nose-dived for books in the bowels of every dumpster in Minneapolis. In effect, you couldn't trash a book in Minneapolis without his digging it out. His initials on sign-out sheets (for tax purposes) were "I," "B," and "J," so BookSmart knew him as The Indestructible Book Jesus. Chitchee felt a kinship with this old man and wanted to plot the trajectory of this odd creature's life history immediately.

Was The Indestructible Book Jesus really a toothless prairie gopher up from the tunnels of the Badlands? In stages, he lurched forward, layered into a whole system of ropes and cables tying him down to shopping carts, dollies, hand carts, full boxes, and Lunds grocery bags (filled with *Field & Streams*, *Look*, and *Wonder Wart-Hog*) on toboggans like the man in Luis Bunuel's *Un Chien Andalou*, towing grand pianos, dead donkeys, Catholic priests, and pumpkins.

"Looks like an old cash register," said The Indestructible Book Jesus to Aloysius, returning from US Bank. "I've pulled *newer* ones than *that* out of the dumpster, boss! Golly, hyuck!"

"Uhhhwagh," Aloysius cleared his throat of residual Carousel tobacco, choked guiltily, and blushed.

He set the envelope aside in a safe place under the counter directly below the NCR register as he heard:

"I can help you with the register, Aloysius!"

"That's okay, Chitchee, I'd rather break it myself," said Aloysius on all fours and looking for the NCR cash register manual in the trash and snuffing around the wastebasket; of course before he stood up without thinking, the till popped open.

He banged the top of his thinly blonde-haired head on the bottom of the outstretched metal cash drawer. Gash, cut, blood. Aloysius winced so firmly that his face disappeared into a little button.

"Do you need a Band-Aid for that, buddy?" asked Chitchee. "You need to clean and dress that wound before there is a bacterial infection and the entire book store smells like green pus! SAAMI! WHERE DO WE KEEP THE MERCUROCHROME?"

Chitchee grabbed a nearby spray bottle of Lysol Lemon Breeze All-Purpose Cleaner, tore off a sheet of Bounty paper towel, squirted the bleeding cut with Lysol, and wiped it clean with a single sheet of Bounty paper towel. Saami opened the tin of Band-Aids, which was empty. Saami clutched a small brown jug of hydrogen peroxide and read the Walgreen's label with sudden interest.

"Hold off on that guys!" said Aloysius. "You're wasting paper towels. That's the Bounty, the good stuff. Don't use whole sheets!"

Aloysius lifted himself from the ground, fought gravity, groaned, and staggered upright.

"Chitchee," asked Aloysius, "can you look around for the little NCR cash register manual, white thing? It's around here somewhere!"

"You're interrupting me! Everything is around here somewhere!" said Chitchee. "That's a tautology! I want to help this guy bring in his books! Isn't that more important? Gee Zeus!"

Aloysius stood staggered. Chitchee offered his hand to The Indestructible Book Jesus.

The Indestructible Book Jesus unloaded two loaded dollies of roped-in, shattered boxes of books from the back of his friend Skooge's '65 Chevy Bel Air station wagon, with its red, blue and brown rusted paint job and its muffler attached by jump ropes. Chitchee swore it was the same model his family had owned and used for his lost paper routes. It looked to have travelled around the Straits of Magellan and the Spice Islands to get to where it was parked now.

"Where did you dive for all these old books?" asked Chitchee. "The caves of Lascaux?"

Saami walked outside to count how many boxes he would have to break his back for—all to find the latest edition of *What To Do When You Are Expecting* at best.

"I'm not sayin' boss, you'll go there!" The Indestructible Book Jesus replied.

"Shrewd, shrewd," said Chitchee. "You know your trade all right, Indestructible Book Jesus."

"Chitchee!" said Saami. "We only call him that name behind his back!"

"Right!" said Chitchee, snapping two fingers once. "Otherwise he might assume we're bad mouthing him all the time!"

"Heck, I ain't no Jesus," said The Indestructible Book Jesus to the returning Chitchee.

The blood-rust, dirt, grime, plaster, egg shells, tobacco stains, and coffee grounds that coated the face of The Indestructible Book Jesus shifted around a little and flaked off onto Chitchee.

"Whe-e-el, your *books* arose from their graves," said Chitchee. "Huh, Jesus?"

"Well, there is a Second Coming for everything," he said, munching on a sunflower seed whose shell he spit out and placed in a pocket.

"No offense! Hey, were you in the Armed Services? Were you in Vietnam? Everybody around here who looks like you was in Vietnam," said Chitchee.

"Nope," said The Indestructible Book Jesus.

"You would have made a great tunnel rat in Cu Chi, I'm telling ya! You should meet Hawk Eye, he's as down and out as you are!"

"Nah, I never served," said The Indestructible Book Jesus. "My dad always said we're farmers, we've always been farmers, and the farmers of the world ain't got no beefs with the other farmers of the world."

"Fair enough!" said Chitchee. "There it is! You're *interesting*! You should write a book!"

"I wanted to write a book about my ancestors, the Parsis, but I'm illiterate," said The Indestructible Book Jesus. "I can't read or write."

"Well, that never stopped *The Art of the Deal* guy or his ghost writer, who also needed a ghost writer," said Chitchee, "to write the epitaph for his stillborn, deadbeat book." "At least Joan Collins had style."

"Son, my pappy boiled it down to three things: Good Thoughts, Good Words, Good Deeds. He was Zoroastrian, born in Samarkand. We're Uzbeki. Pappy built a fire temple on the U. P. right outside of Sault Ste. Marie. Later we added a gas station to it."

Yardley yelled from the couch:

"Can someone put some *civilized* music on? Please stop this insane mediocrity!"

"No," Saami countered at the counter.

"Chitchee! Friend!" said Yardley. "Something civilized! A mass of Palestrina perhaps? Or on a more secular note—a sonata from Scarlatti, the Kirkpatrick 380."

Chitchee, muttered "380" in his iconic memory, ran over to the CD player, and rummaged for the Scarlatti, "380, 380, 380, 420, 380, 380, 420, 420."

Aloysius, off to the side, made the hand motion across his throat to "cut it" to Chitchee.

"Goodness, don't you have any Beatles?" asked Melusina, stalled in Cookbooks and Crafts and unable to decide which books to buy.

"But not the *White Album*," said Kriemhilde. "That's the one when they were all on pot and a lot of other koo-kee drugs."

Saami clenched his fists. Then he stomped around and around, elbows at right angles with fists so clenched they caused his shoulders to bunch up, forcing his neck to run parallel with the floor so that his eyes were like wormholes looking down at actual wormholes.

"No, Mel," insisted Saami, "the dream is over. The CD player broke yesterday. Are you going to stay here all night? How long have you been here?"

"Since *Yesterday* . . ." hummed Melusina. "*All my troubles . . . seemed so wonderful . . .*" and then Kriemhilde whistled and hummed and threw in a few words like "*singing in the dead of night . . . la la la.* It was working earlier!"

"*Yestiddy, yesta . . .*" Melusina with Kriemhilde chimed in.

"That's okay, we know all the words . . . even when they are out of order," said Saami.

"*Know the words . . . and we'll be free!*" sang Chitchee, sifting the BookSmart CD collection. "I guess Aloysius you have an inordinate fondness for the Beatles. God, you even have *Yellow Submarine*! I don't know anybody who bought that one!"

Chitchee and The Indestructible Book Jesus dragged, lugged, and travoised on tarp an exhaustive and exhausting stream of boxes of books to the maroon linoleum counter. Saami's drill for The Indestructible Book Jesus was: buy *something* so the coot could afford ratty mittens (come winter) at Treasures Await or an already opened, half-full pack of expired CONTACTs to fight off the colds he caught like a sheet of human flypaper from all the world's rhinoviruses five times a year. Saami flipped through the pages of a Family Photo Album at the bottom of one of the cat-tattered, Henn-Lake liquor store Phillips vodka boxes that IBJ dragged through the BookSmart keyhole. Chitchee sidled over to see. He screamed. At the sight of blood, he always fainted. Saami had witnessed often compromising photos of nudies, naked girls in showers, girlfriends lying on beds showing off their private parts, coupling couples, bare crotches, and all-too-human sad penises falling out of forgotten books.

"Shut up, Chitchee!" said Saami, kicking the floored Chitchee in the shins.

"Family Photo Album?" asked Chitchee, looking at the embossed gold lettering on the fat, calf-leather front cover.

Rubbing his shin, he peered at the pen-and-ink dated Polaroids (month date year) and other photographs showing a succession of rapes, acts of rape, and possible murders. Girls were passed out on crummy mattresses in abandoned, post-eviction apartments. The plaster walls were stained, the closets filled with kitchen garbage. Chitchee's eyebrows tied themselves into a Welsh knot, which he could not untie. Saami moot the idea that the scenes had been staged. They looked like a pair of spectroscopists decoding helium in the spectra of a galaxy light years away.

"My lord," said Saami.

"What is *that*? What's that guy doing?" asked Chitchee and selected a #10 sealed envelope nearby. "Let's bookmark *that* page."

Saami bookmarked *that* page with the #10 envelope. He looked perplexed, and he scratched his chin with a light bulb, which was not turning on. He swiped the light bulb across his rusty chin of stubble. If only to repress the distraction, he shoved the Family Photo Album under the counter.

"That does it," said Saami, lifting a dead brown mouse by its striated tail from another box.

The mouse had been flattened into a dried-out coaster. The eye-watering stench from it could have felled the entire Buckingham Palace Guard.

Chitchee pinched his nostrils together. He quickly turned and motioned to play a knocked-off Beatles *Greatest Hits* CD, which Saami intercepted, saying "Skips!" He Frisbeed it over the tops of the book shelves like ducks and drakes. "See? It skips."

"I didn't see any Palestrina, Yardley. No Scarlatti either. What about the Manhattan Transfer version of *Pelleas et Melisande*?" asked Chitchee.

"No," said Saami flatly.

"How about the Billy Squier version of 'Hot Cross Buns?'"

"We don't have it."

"But maybe we can order it, can't we Saami?" asked Chitchee excitedly.

"Not if he never recorded it, Chitchee, for fuck's sakes!"

"Can't we order Billy Squier to record it, and then order it from him? We're a book store, aren't we?" asked Chitchee, looking over at Aloysius. "Who are you calling, boss man? Dialing the number for *Dialing for Dollars* with Jim Hutton? Ha, ha. But this book store sure could use the money! Right boss? Let me tell you!"

"Awwwwgghgkkk," said Aloysius into his AT & T cordless receiver, swiveling his high-backed office chair and clearing his throat when the receiver picked up.

"Who is this?" said Noel Schoolcraft, hearing a cement mixer outside his window.

"Noel, it's Aloysius at BookSmart," said Aloysius, his body conforming to the comfortable foam covered in bonded leather.

"I'm having problems with the cash register again. Do you know where the instruction manual is?"

Aloysius experienced, in the pigments of his imagination, Noel's slow interface.

Noel waited while Aloysius coughed with enough violence to bruise an elephant's rib.

"Is the drawer coming off the runners?" asked Noel, quickly, peevishly, and matter-of-factly. "It's probably that the rubber band I jerry-rigged dried out and snapped. You need to get a new rubber band. And then hook it around the back castor wheels inside the register. Hello? Are you there?"

Aloysius looked up at Chitchee worried. You might have thought the entire universe was held together with *that* rubber band in *that* old cash register.

"How much is a new one?" asked Aloysius.

"Cash register?" asked Noel.

"No. Rubber band."

"I can bring a fresh one in from home."

"Phew," replied Aloysius, blowing out a sigh, "okay partner, rock 'n' roll. Oh, Noel, is there any way we can order the Billy Squier version of 'Hot Cross Buns?' Hello? You guys, the cash register will have to be down until Noel comes in to fix it."

"No register!" Saami threw up histrionic hands in a disingenuous show of despair.

He quickly created an "OUT OF ODOR" sign and Scotch-taped it to the NCR so that it hung at a desolate angle as from an old Pogo comic strip.

"I can go 5.50 for these," said Saami to The Indestructible Book Jesus, Saami placing a benedictory hand over a mound of kid's math books, *The Voyage of the Beagle*, and some Jules Vernes.

"Thank you, boss man, God bless you," said The Indestructible Book Jesus, kowtowing.

The Indestructible Book Jesus initialed the payout sheet with a circle like the signature of Lu Xun's Ah Q, his hands so mud-caked his fingerprints had been wiped clean. Signing a circle in the square forced him to squint strabismically while he mulled over the room with good thoughts.

"Ah, the sweet smell of success!" said Chitchee, chirping in late. "Maybe now you can save up for some choppers to keep your mouth from caving in like a Kentucky coal mine."

The Indestructible Book Jesus double-looked at Chitchee, eye-frisked him for insincerity, found nothing sarcastic, packed up all his rejected boxes, and schlepped them to the curb.

"5.50 in credit, IBJ," said Saami. "The cash register is jammed again."

"Will you have the money tomorrow?" asked The Indestructible Book Jesus with his sad eyebrows drawn upward.

They planned to meet in the middle of his forehead but had to cancel.

"If business picks up tonight around here (here (here))," said Saami, hearing an echo, "we'll have some cash (ash)."

The Zoroastrian had promised to split the capital gains with his chauffeur Skooge. A crestfallen Indestructible Book Jesus momentarily lost all zest for survival.

"Indestructible Book Jesus, if it's any consolation, here's a story," said Chitchee. "About a thousand years ago in Kashmir a destitute mother told her son, Kanishka, 'you must have a trade. Visakila lends money to the poor. Ask him for a small loan!' Kanishka found Visakila. He was yelling at a merchant's son, 'You fool, you have nothing. You should be able with that dead mouse in the corner to create wealth.' Kanishka said, 'Let me try, Visakila.' Kanishka took the dead mouse, signed a receipt, and sold the dead mouse as cat's meat for two handfuls of chickpeas. Then Kanishka stood at the crossroads and traded the chickpeas for some wood from passing wood carriers. Kanishka sold the wood in the market, bought more chickpeas, went back, and got more wood. Kanishka did this every day until the monsoons came, which wiped out the local wood supply—except Kanishka's. Kanishka set up a shop and became a wealthy man. Then he had a mouse of gold made for him, and he returned to Visakila, and he paid him back. And Visakila gave Kanishka his daughter's hand in marriage."

"And here is your starter mouse!" said Saami, holding his nose and handing back the dead mouse.

"Thanks, boss," said The Indestructible Book Jesus, pocketing the dead mouse with the sunflower seed shells.

He rambled outside and flagged the coasting Skooge's '65 Chevy Bel Air station wagon. It coasted around again, and they reloaded the rejected boxes and packed them off to Half Price Books, St. Louis Park. Half Price bought all the boxes for $5.50, tossed them, and locked them in their dumpster.

Gloria Ganyea Skogentaub almost tore the front door handle off.

"Phew!" said Gloria, looking around for an open manhole.

Gloria looked like Barbara Taylor Bradford on a bad hair day that turned into a bad hair week. Her skin was white as Noxzema cold cream, but her face had little bumps all over it like stucco. Nattily dressed in a navy blue business skirt, large light gray pullover, and a sparkly silver and dark gray scarf (the dark gray to pop the shade of the light gray), the dull silver popping the light gray of the pullover, the grays cut from the same cloth as an overcast Minnesota sky.

"Hi! My name is Gloria Skogentaub. Do you have planners? I'm in a bit of a hurry, I work for MPG upstairs in the law office with my husband Corky Skogentaub. You might have heard of MPG? Your landlord? Martensen People's Group? Martensen People's Fiduciary? They own Carousel Square! Have you heard of Carousel Square?"

"What's a planner?" asked Chitchee. "Is that like a Glam Doll donut? No, that's a sculler."

"You've . . . never . . . heard . . . of . . . a . . . *planner* . . ." she said. "O . . . kay . . . I'm on my break and I don't—"

"Well, we can order some planners," offered Chitchee. "Can't we? Let's write that down, Saami!"

"On what?" said Saami. "A planner? We don't have any planners because we don't have any plans."

"So you don't have any plan-ner-zzz . . .? O . . . kay . . ." Gloria slowly wagged her head from side to side with condescending disbelief.

"O-kaaaaay . . ." she added, making sure they knew it was not okay.

"Lady, they don't make planners anymore, they're all on the Internet," said Saami, who immediately hated this woman and all she stood for, and all who looked like her—shallow, mean, petty, never read a single Robert Bloch, Robert E. Howard, or Richard Matheson novel, and unable to identify a single Japanese anime action figure. He felt like Rodan and wanted to wipe out her Tokyo. "Why not live your life spontaneously? Instead of flying around like a hopped-up hippogriff, trying to *plan* everything?"

"Ma'am," said Aloysius, half paying attention, "try Chester E. Groth for diamond needles. Don't go to Torp's."

"What decade are *you* in?" asked Gloria, addressing Aloysius briefly and then boring down on Saami. "And did *you* call ME a hippo? You? That's 'discrimination,' Pee Wee, and—that's unacceptable in the business world. But then how would you know anything about the business world where there are standards of politeness? How would you like it if I called you a midget from Mars?"

"No ma'am, Saami didn't call you a hippopotamus," advocated Chitchee. "It sounded like 'hippo,' but it was really 'dipso.' He called you an alcoholic, which really isn't that bad at all. It's normal! I mean we're all alcoholics or recovering alcoholics in the Twin Cities, aren't we? One . . . big . . . happy . . . family . . . of dried-out, old wet brains?"

"WhatttT?" she stated, leaning on the dental, very staccato last letter.

Chitchee, stung by the "T," cringed as if avoiding the inflected "T" wounding him from a quiver of more "T" arrows.

"I said '*hippogriff.*' It's from *Harry Potter*," said Saami. "Okay, I apologize! I'm SORRY! Shake on it!"

"You could try the Jolly Troll Smorgasbord on Wayzata Boulevard if you're looking for a good place to eat," Aloysius continued and tinkered with the cash register.

When Saami approached Gloria to shake hands, she stepped backward clumsily—she broke a high heel, landed on her buttocks with her legs in the air.

"Unless you're ready for me to check you out?" said Aloysius, standing up straight, seeing that Gloria saw him accidentally glimpse her gray underwear shielding the circumflex of her crotch revealing her Tigris-Euphrates by accident.

"I can see your home plate," said Chitchee.

"I'm never stepping foot in this hovel again!" said Gloria.

Gloria crawled to her knees, stood up, straightened her gray wardrobe, readjusted her frozen hair style, and looked at Chitchee like a bull's eye.

"What's your name?"

"Chitchee Chichester, ma'am," said Chitchee.

"On his majesty's secret cervix," said Saami.

"You'll pay for that laugh, Chichester, so help me God," said Gloria.

She stared a double-barreled shotgun straight into Chitchee's eyes.

She added a skull-fucking glare summoned from hell to go with it. Her evil eyes turned red and burned with flames and then with icy menace. Gloria repeated: "So help me God!"

"What?" asked Chitchee. "Could you repeat that? I wasn't paying attention. I'm not processing theology at the moment. Are you as hungry for pizza as I am, G-L-O-R-I-A? Do they call you Glore? I bet the kids used to call you Glory Hole."

Chitchee's nervous laugh escaped like a parakeet from its cage.

Gloria tramped out the door furiously chewing the bone of contention and spitting out fuming splinters.

"Philistine!" yelled Saami, twerking toward her and walking back to the cash register. "Go back to Philly!"

"Oh, that was awkward! Why did she have to come here?" asked Chitchee, tears like lighted matches lighting up his eyes. "That did not go well. Why was she so mean? I think I know her from somewhere. I'm sorry about that Aloysius. I bollixed that relationship as usual. What am I doing wrong? I should have taken Gloria to the shelf and gotten her to buy something like *The Thorn Birds* or *Minnesota Barefoot* by Lute Korngold."

"Meh, it happens," said Aloysius. "She sounded maybe a little looney."

"Poor looney," said Chitchee. "I think capitalism drove her to the outer edges of schizophrenia. Gloria's compulsive planning is the sickness of our times."

"I'm looking for book," said a Chinese man shyly and not wanting to approach too quickly after Chitchee's Dust Bowl-sized dust up with a classic American businesswoman.

Li Fan wore a blazer, dress shirt, and Dockers. Shuwen Qu wore a churchy, but sheer silk dress depicting cameos of crows kowtowing on power lines as a thousand gongs of geese sounded overhead. Pendant loopholing onyx earrings and a brooch of honeybees to boot completed her attractiveness.

Chitchee thought: Oh, I want these customers!

"Let me guess!" said Chitchee. "*The Giving Tree? Inside the Third Reich? The Kama Sutra? Soul On Ice? Go Ask Alice? Kids Say the Darnedest Things? This Band Could Be Your Life?*"

"No, it's two monks who are brothers," said Li Fan.

"*Narcissus and Goldmund* by Hermann Hesse," said Chitchee. "Except they're not brothers, they're gay!"

"That it!" Li Fan smiled at Chitchee.

Li Fan, smiling ear to ear, held Shuwen's limp, almost wilted hand. She smiled toward him. Chitchee escorted the couple-in-love to a bookcase of shoddy mass-market sized books. He pressed into Li Fan's open hand a copy of *Narcissus and Goldmund*, sticker-priced for 2.99 but the purple "2" had faded.

"99 cents? It says 99."

"*Yi, er, san, that's an er*," said Chitchee, pointing at the "2." "Come to think of it? *All Men Are Brothers*, the *Water Margin*. Have you read *Shui Hu Zhuan*? By Shi Nai'an? You know, the really big *shu*?"

"Ah! *Shui Hu Zhuan*! Do you speak Chinese?" asked Shuwen Qu with anticipation.

Chitchee racked his brain for a few more words in pidgin Chinglish, a language for which he had an unrequited love. The musicality of Mandarin's four tones drew him in—only to drown him in a flash flood of unmanageable characters.

"Try! No *yuan*! Couldn't afford it! Not good time for *renminbi*! Year of Being Broke Animal. But I try speak Chinese," Chitchee unconsciously almost lalling like a baby.

"Oh, I am proud of you!" said Shuwen.

"*Eh!*" he remembered the word for "hungry," clutching his stomach.

Li Fan reached out his hand to shake.

"Your name is '*hungry?*'" asked Li Fan.

Chitchee escorted Li Fan and Shuwen toward Saami, also tinkering with the cash register.

"Come again!" said Chitchee, bowing. "*Xie xie!*"

"I'm sorry the cash register is down," said Saami to the disappointed couple. "Our credit card machine is up and running though."

Then Saami looked at the sticker price: 2.99. He added:

"*But* we have a three dollar minimum on credit card purchases. Sorry!"

"*Dui bu qi!*" said Chitchee.

Li Fan and Shuwen held hands, acknowledged defeat, and walked out.

"We can waive that rule for today!" said Aloysius. "Chitchee, go ask them if they have plastic."

Chitchee trooped outside and asked.

"Plastic? No we are real," Li Fan told Chitchee, who felt unreal after that remark.

Chitchee thrust three dollars in Li Fan's hand and convinced him to go back and buy the book. Li Fan said he would pay him back someday.

"Okay, buddy," said Aloysius, after putting the three dollars in his wallet. "Good job! You studied Chinese? You *must* be *kind* of smart! At least you will be prepared when the Chinese take over the world!"

Aloysius paused. He dreamed football even while awake.

"And that will be the end of the Golden Gopher football program, sports fans."

"I'll be downstairs," said Saami with a trace of curt disgust crossing his lips as he returned downstairs and shook his head at Aloysius whose eyes misted over with unremembered touchdowns gone by.

"And nothing but *Tai Chi* everywhere!" said Chitchee, excitedly anticipating the event, agreeing that *Tai Chi* would be a *great improvement* over the Big Ten football program, and dancing a bizarre version of the Shake. "Far out! A little 'Eight Pieces of Brocade' action!"

Chitchee day-dreamed out the front window, staring at the intersection of Lake & Hennepin, a business quadrant whose direction had recently changed more often than a busted Mall of America Tilt-a-Whirl.

Beyond that lay Carousel Square, a 1980s populuxe, once franchise-filled mall of flowing water fountains, flourishing vendors, and hanging gardens. Carousel Square had already been raided and gutted like the Alamo in 2004 by the New York-based BlackRock, Inc., which sold it for an undisclosed amount to Marten Martensen's investment group, Minneapolis People's Fiduciary, Inc, based in Florida. Carousel Square's small businesses were further trampled underfoot by MPF rent hikes, lack of investment, and dearth of repairs. While the guttered mall lingered on like Baudelaire's swan at the Place du Carrousel, Chitchee speculated that some day Chinese investors would buy it. Someday it would all be pagodas . . . Chinese music twanging on *qin* and *pipa*. . . the traffic lights at Lake & Hennepin paper lanterns (with hidden facial recognition cameras for framing Uighurs) . . . ten thousand millions of Chinese bicyclists yelling: "Critical Mass! Critical Mass!" Millions of Chinese hookers behind *them* on bicycles! Tens of million millions of Chinese police on bicycles, each one blowing a shrill whistle and a pocket trumpet.

"Someday, I'll own my own book store, Ulysses," said Chitchee.

"Ulysses? Chitchee! Hello?" said Aloysius. "It's Aloysius! I forgot to tell you, as far as making book buys, *that* will take some time to learn. And to be an old pro like (awwwgghkkekkkkekek) yours truly, *that* could take years. But here's a list of books we DO NOT want (cough, cough, cough) to (cough, cough) to buy into the store (cough)."

Aloysius handed Chitchee a Xeroxed photocopy of a sheet of spiral notebook paper with a list of books on it. Aloysius gaveled up some phantom phlegm. Chitchee crumpled the list like a dollar bill into his back pocket. Aloysius itched a nodule on the side of his white-as-a-dried-bean-curd nose and watched Chitchee to make sure Chitchee didn't treat *that* list on *that* piece of spiral notebook paper like *just another piece of spiral notebook paper.*

"Yeah-uh," said Aloysius, hesitating to broach a difficult topic, "um, Chitchee, don't lose that piece of paper! That's actually the master copy. Maybe someone could run over to Kinko's later and run off a copy. How much are copies nowadays? Maybe they'd be cheaper at the Five & Dime. If that's still there!"

Chitchee felt guilty for touching the spiral notebook paper. He hadn't realized how strapped BookSmart was! What if this incident were to force his boss to write out a whole 'nother list, wasting energy on a second piece of spiral notebook paper? Another list—possibly as labor-intensive and costly as the original! Aloysius determined himself to sweat out the paper shortage for the nonce and focus on the grime-smudged cash register he wanted to sledgehammer. He foresaw the 20s locked in the till. He scratched his Adam's apple and blew a kiss at the moon. He rubbed the back of his wrinkled, moley, and warty neck. A crawling rash broke out on the nape, burnished by his itching, which made it burn like nettles. Hives, considered Aloysius. What are hives? Why are they always in the plural? Can't you have one big hive? Wouldn't that be cheaper?

"Say Chitchee, why don't you give me that Xerox copy of the piece of spiral notebook paper back for now. Well, no wait, I'll get it before I go home. Hold off on that and hold onto it for now."

"Sure, Aloysius," said Chitchee. "I had a bad feeling about taking that Xeroxed sheet of spiral notebook paper from you, knowing you didn't have a master copy. It was too much responsibility for anybody on his first day."

Aloysius key-punched and key-punched the register, sat down on the computer chair, and stared out the front window, flummoxed, and exhausted, his eyes like soaped windows. If Aloysius's most gorgeous dream dates of all time walked by naked he wouldn't have noticed a nipple. Aloysius's dream dates walked by naked: Barbara Eden, Barbara Feldon, Barbara Ella.

"Where was I?" he said, getting up slowly out of nowhere. "Oh yeah, the Chinese are taking over the world. Someday the entire Golden Gopher football team will be Chinese! Well, so be it. Ninja ho! They're my team. *Golden Gophers hats off to thee!*"

"No, that was where you were a while back!" said Saami, trudging upstairs and transferring his packaged packages to the mail bins for shipping. "You were thinking about investing in a brand new spiral notebook."

"Oh yeah, yeah, yeah—how much are spiral notebooks these days?" asked Aloysius, sitting up, sitting down, and feeling exhausted with an exasperated groan. "What is it, Mead Spiral Notebooks, they're pricey, aren't they? We don't have to go for top of the line stuff all the time. We can afford to be frugal paper gourmets. What about the kind with the plastic coil? Are they any cheaper, Saami?"

"The Spiralastic?" answered Saami efficiently. "I think it depends on the number of loops you want in your coil. We could go generic and buy loose-leaf—in bulk. Maybe we can call the Weyerhaeuser Main Office and get some free samples sent out to us for free."

"For free?" said Aloysius, sitting up. "You can't argue with *free*! The price is right! Give them a call, Saami! Explain our situation to them and see what they say! Tell them we'll give them a sweetheart deal on blank books!"

Aloysius flailed at the pile of work orders, slumped, and dry-wiped his face. He stared out the window, waiting for Chitchee's Chinese to take over the world.

THE RETURN OF SAUSAGE MAN

Chitchee heard a familiar voice.

"*Ja, ja, ja, oink, hee haw, I'm the Sausage Man, I've got a Vienna tan.*"

Sausage Man wore his faded, shapeless Oshkosh overalls and his checker-boardish, black-on-white plaid flannel shirt, the top button tightly buttoned—a sausagey wrappage to Sausage Man and his sausage body. His red swollen nose had grown since the morning and resembled a newborn piglet with scarlet fever. He clasped a fishing pole in one hand and in the other a minnow bucket, which sloshed with water and clanked with galvanized chain links.

Sausage Man had become an Uptown regular not that long ago, standing in front of McDonald's every day, not asking for anything, and giving back spare change, incorruptible as Andre Breton. He had no past. He had no historical consciousness and thus would not be reading Gyorgy Lukacs soon. Sausage Man had dropped out of the sky from the giant eagle talons of an Arabian-taled Roc. What was on his bedside reading table? *Clarissa? Xaviera?*

Sausage Man on fine summer days sported a canvas, floppy fishing hat (shiny Daredevils hanging off it) from which grew upward a coat hanger and a ten-pound test line, knotted at the end to a tied-up, vermiform Vienna sausage. The sausage swung in front of his face. The sausage was a substitute for the horse's carrot of "carrot and stick" fame. Sometimes he fished in Lake Calhoun. Sometimes he stood around Lake & Hennepin watching the pedestrians and reading them poems while a sausage swung in front of his face.

Chitchee picked up the skinny on Sausagey from the steamed punks panhandling outside McDonald's, next to Snuffy the Cop's old graffiti-covered cop shop. On the subject of the dangling Vienna sausage act itself, *that* was an ironic critique of the bougie world of obsessive money monomania, asserted the grunge band of sidewalk punks. Sausage Man was "outsider performance art" and possibly an example of Artaud's Theater of Cruelty. He's "another Darger." He could be explained through Lacanian analysis. They all agreed: "Sausage Man knows what's up. He knows *exactly* what he is doing. He's *parroting* the Man. True dat. He's a *neuromancer* in disguise!"

"No! Sausage Man!" said Aloysius. "I told you last week you can't come in here anymore. We don't give poetry readings. And that is final."

Saami crossed his arms and puffed his chest like a spring chickadee.

"Out!" he chirped firmly. "Sausage Man! You heard the pit boss!"

"But I have a new poem, Aloysius," said Sausage Man. "It's a poem about the spirituality of sausages. Spirituals and sausages—like guns and butter. You can have both. *Ja?* And the despair over buttered guns? Well, that's a poem for another day. Dark Night of the Sausage."

"Hey, Sausage Man," asked Chitchee. "How did my picture turn out? The one you took this morning? Can I see what I look like? I don't think you captured my frontality. Can I see? Can I see? Maybe we should do it over."

"I gave it to the FBI," said Sausage Man. "I'm waiting for my reward."

"Are they going to pay you in sausages?" asked Chitchee.

Aloysius shook his head. He didn't have the heart to throw out anyone who had the pluck to call himself a poet. Aloysius pigeon-holed Chitchee.

"Don't tell Saami, but I actually let Sausage Man take naps downstairs in the morning," said Aloysius. "Saami hates the guy!"

Aloysius saw his life pass before his eyes:

"Skip Skipperton. *Good Morning, Minnesota.* I am standing outside BookSmart at Lake and Hennepin where a local poet *with a Minnesota connection*, which means he has been to Minnesota at least once, has been thrown out of BookSmart, a local book store, for allegedly reciting bad poetry. But who is to say what is bad? It's poetry! It's all bad! Some say. Others claim Minneapolis is a cultural hub of poetry. Even members of the Amalgamated Meat Cutters and Butcher's Union have voiced concern over the incident today at BookSmart. Charges of sausagism have been expressed by offended parties and neighborhood vigilantes have charged the owner Aloysius Aalgaard with appropriation and the weaponizing of sausages."

Sausage Man, his blue eyes shining into song, danced like crab legs on crab grass:

Rattle his bones
over the stones
man ain't but
a lying porpoise
don't you know
ja ja ja
hee haw
oink oink oink
hee haw!

Some of the customers clapped, but all grinned at one another in acknowledgement of their grinning at one another. It was an *uff da* of some significance. It was a Minnesota moment.

Chitchee imagined every decent bodhisattva worth his weight in salt looking down at Lake & Hennepin from cloud-high heavens. Hearts and heart chakras opened like pure white lotuses on Lake of the Isles. Warblers warbled the air, lacing it with sweetness, kindness, and gentleness. Octaves of pure light flew all the way back to the Sun with gratitude.

Chitchee nodded in agreement with the steam punks. They were right! They were always right! Street smart, those punks across the street.

"Awwww . . . " lowed Linda Rolvaag, dottily-dressed, beribboned, and weighed down with too many packages to pass the Rosenhan test of institutionalization.

"Thanksh for sharing Shausage Man . . . encore?" Linda asked Sausage Man.

"No encore, Linda! Encore, no! Sausage Man, no, we don't give encores here," said Aloysius, waving his hands. "Store policy! And that is final."

"Hi, Aloyshiush," said Linda, pineapple-blonde Linda, who had sauntered in, possibly psychically attracted by the troubadour's raw energy.

Linda ambled to Sausage Man and kissed his hand.

"Thank him for sharing, Saami," said Linda to Saami, "for reaching out . . . awwww . . . oh that was sho beautiful. Encore!"

"Linda!" said Saami. "How many times . . ." he smacked his head. "God, I need a drink."

"You shouldn't pray to God for drinksh, Saami," said Linda. "You know alcohol shrinks your hard little liver into a little hard turd. Why don't you switch to meth? Can't you get any more crystal?"

"Can I get some of yours?" said Saami.

"I'm all out," said Linda. "Cashed. Oh, Saami ba'e, I brought you some food in case you want some actual food."

"*I will go / whichever way the wind blow / hope it don't snow*," sang Sausage Man as he stepped outside. "*Oh to cut a lot of sausages / with one hand waving free . . .*"

"*O Sausage Man*," sang Linda. "*You're the sausage in my heart!*"

Linda joined her hands in the shape of a callipygian rump.

"Saami," continued Linda, "I bet Sausage Man knows Dylan. Or at least Dave Von Rock. Willie Murphy or Shangoya or Shpider John Glover Somebody from the West Bank. Do you think he might have met Prinsh on his way up the local ladder? Brainwave in a brainmaze! He might have known Kirby Puckett!"

"I'm going out for a smoke. Watch the register, Chitchee!" said Aloysius, smiling a tired smile, which progressively flattened into an old Dunlop bicycle tire.

Saami followed Aloysius outside with Linda in tow.

"Saami, your dinner!"

"What is it?"

"Vienna shausages," said Linda. "This whole bag was on shale at Dollar General!"

"Oh."

"Across from Franklin-Nicollet liquor."

"Oh."

"Isn't that what they call 'shinchronicity?' When you go to buy food and thersh a liquor shtore right there!"

"Yeah," said Saami, "that's what they always call a bag of expired frozen Vienna sausages from any dollar store. *Synchronicity.*"

Linda looked at Saami with such a look of love—dingy, dotty, flaky, wigged out, and twice-his-age—of unconditional love that Saami's heart thawed as usual.

For the sausages he kissed her lips, which tasted like sausages.

Linda had worked a lot of jobs: 1) chairwoman of the Horticultural Society in Eveleth 2) publisher, editor, and printer of *The Triweekly Trillium* in Wilmar and 3) founder of the Society for the Preservation of Salvia in Cloquet. It was not until she moved to Minneapolis that she became 4) procuress of endangered/protected orchids for the underground, black market orchid trade who dealt with notorious criminal fences such as the mysterious "Frenchy" alleged to run an ongoing criminal enterprise from here to the Rockies via 89 cell phones that worked off and on.

Aloysius, Saami, and Linda watched Sausage Man cavort down Hennepin Avenue like Howdy Doody. He danced, stopped, and picked up a hundred-dollar bill. Hawk Eye had missed it. Where was the Hawk? That hundred-dollar bill had sat on the pavement outside Club Miami next to a parked BMW of five guys with their windows down for how long?

"Go back to the Sixties, grandpa, you burn-out!" said Cameron McCocky to Sausage Man.

"Cameron, where is the fucking hundred I gave you?" asked Towey Levins.

"Go to hell, you custard pie-faced prom queens!" yelled Sausage Man, his head in the passenger front window as he waved a hundred-dollar bill under Cameron's nose.

"Hey, that's my hundred!" shouted Cameron.

"Duh!" said Towey. "How are we going to pick up for the house, bro? What do I tell the bros? How long has Nestor been waiting, you idiot!"

The three giggling high bros in the back bust their guts and split their sides laughing.

Insulted by his friends, Cameron jumped out to fight Sausage Man. As Cameron punched at him, Sausage Man kick-boxed Cameron's jaw, turned, and then kicked Cameron with the other foot on the chest, turned again, and kicked Cameron square in the groin. Cameron shrank back into the BMW angrily. His fraternity brothers mocked him, ribbed him—the "dum muh fuk"—and Cameron was in no mood for Ye Young's calling him out for his being so angry at being called out for his being so angry, which made Cameron angry.

Sausage Man fastballed a sealed package of Ball Park Franks at the departing BMW, turned, and waved the hundred-dollar bill at Aloysius and Saami.

"I didn't know the ol' Sausage had that much spunk in him!" said Aloysius, padding back inside BookSmart, his eyes looking into a wilderness of debt. How in the scheme of things did Sausage Man "deserve" that hundred-dollar bill? Maybe if Aloysius had gone outside earlier, the wind could have blown it into Aloysius's hand.

"You can't win," said Saami, looking at Aloysius. "Yep, like that old hobo said, Jack Black, Jack White, Jack Black White, Black Jack White, whoever the fucking guy Burroughs dated *was* before that other guy who went out with that other guy."

"Could you show me to the poetry section again?" said the upright Yardley to Saami. "Why is it that the poetry shelf moves around the store like Saint Brendan's Isle? You're not hiding it from me, are you? Keebler Cookie Elfman from the Firth of Filth?"

Saami suppressed the hidden smile of an invisible assassin.

"Yeah," said Saami. "Poetry is now in the back by the stuffed shirts and animals. Are you looking for the poetry of Ron Jeremy or something? That's on Porn Hub nowadays."

"Why would I be looking for Ron Gemini on Porn Hub?" quizzed Yardley, crinkle cuts at his eye-corners. "I have no idea what you are talking about!"

"I meant to say Jenna Jameson," said Saami, scratching his onion-bulb navel. "Porn rules."

"I forgot, Slimy," said Yardley, "you always take the obscenic route."

"Saami!" said Aloysius, flicking his head.

Saami groaned and strolled to the sidelines.

"You're being a little confrontational, Saami . . ." said Aloysius. "Chitchee? Can you help Yardley while I talk to Saami?"

Yardley, from atop his thin-stemmed white gizzard, slowly examined Chitchee. Yardley held the blue scalpel of an icy stare over Chitchee, suddenly anesthetized.

"I need someone to come to my apartment and organize my books," said Yardley. "I can't do it. It's bibliomania, and it's a debilitating disease. I read all about it, and then I couldn't stop buying books about it—and then reading about it. I called Book Control, but they were booked. Can you come over and sort things out? I can pay you in *Golden Boughs*."

"Okay," said Chitchee. "When?"

"What? Okay? Just like that?"

"Sure, why not?" said Chitchee. "What else am I *supposed* to say?"

Yardley's eyes moved closer together to hide something. Yardley and Chitchee exchanged phone numbers.

"Oh my," said Yardley and pulled down a volume of *The Dream Songs*.

"Aloysius! Yardley is in here all the time and he doesn't buy anything," said Saami. "He's only looking for a book by some wanker of a salami stroker, Coldcut Fabio Caruso, or some other poetically-inclined, cum-frosted cornflake like that, who likes to shag sheep."

"I know, I know, but we're more than a book store!" said Aloysius, his hands gently pushing back the air in front of him. "We are also a community with a social conscience, and we don't put a dollar value on that. Accept him! He's harmless, he's human. There are people in this world who 'go' with book stores like mustard on hot dogs. Hey Chitchee, can you come over here? I'm going home as soon as Noel gets here to fix the register, so it will be you and Saami for tonight."

Chitchee helped Aloysius organize his Manila bubble wraps and USPS boxes in two large beige U.S. MAIL bins.

"Thanks Chitchee for helping with Yardley, he can be difficult," said Aloysius. "So for tonight (aaaaaghghghghaaaa), Chitch, help customers! Postpone the training until tomorrow if you get swamped. Have Saami show you the employee's break room in the basement. Saami! Pay yourself out of the till tonight! There should be some twenties in there for you, if you can find a way to open the register, 'k? Another slow business day in the subprime mortgage rate recession brought to you by Wall Street's War Machine. Well, you know the drill—dull as it is. Good game, Saami, good show, good job, it's all good, whatever it is. It is what it is, and it is all probably good! Cross your fingers, we'll get there. What's taking Noel so long in rush hour?"

NOEL SCHOOLCRAFT

Noel Schoolcraft differentiated customers like polynomials and tallied the head count subliminally as soon as he entered BookSmart hurriedly; he wore a cotton, short-sleeved, buttoned, checked shirt, white T-shirt, immaculate blue jeans, and heavy-heeled sandals that pounded on the floor from a gait hitch. He wore the air of the eternal schoolboy. Although that changed when, in September, 2008, a week before the Republican National Convention in St. Paul, Sheriff Bob Robinson caught Noel exuding bravado on YouTube with his "Anarchy and the Coming Revolution." Robinson and his Ramsey County thumpers from St. Paul, granted a no-knock warrant, smashed the bolts and hinges off Noel's apartment door in Lowertown, St. Paul.

"Protesting scum like you are trespassing wherever you go," said Robinson, hurling Noel to the floor. "Get on the fucking ground!"

Noel was arrested at dawn for "conspiracy to riot." As evidence, the St. Paul thumpers pissed in a bucket and claimed they found a bucket of urine (which could have been weaponized and thrown into Sheriff Bob Robinson's Ramsey County face). They obliterated, destroyed, and looted (down to his Eagle Scout badge) his apartment for anarchist literature, finding nothing, because they didn't (or couldn't) read and had no definition of "anarchy" beyond "things not worth the piss in a bucket." When Noel recited passages from the Bill of Rights, the U. S. Constitution, and Supreme Court decisions, St. Paul's Sergeant Bob Robinson pulled a spit hood over Noel's head and handcuffed Noel's hands behind his twisting back. When Noel said, "This is Abu Ghraib all over again," the thumper called in a K9 unit specifically asking for "Sarge." Faced with a furiously barking hell hound, Noel surrendered. When the thumpers checked Noel into a detention cell in Regions Hospital, the thumpers chained Noel to a hospital bed, twisted his ankles in broken circles, and, applying pressure to the pressure points in his neck, laughed, and sang with a cruelish smile: "*When the red, red robin comes bob, bob, bobbin' along, along.*" Although Noel pursued the matter, he was stonewalled. "The use of force by police is embedded in the City Charter." Reprimand in the offing, Sergeant Bob Robinson was put on paid leave, flew to Miami for a vacation with his friend Viktor, bobbed back for his reinstatement, and created the Minnesota Fugitive Anarchists Mobile Force Field & Emergency Strike Unit. Noel walked home with a broken left ankle from Regions Hospital and moved from Lowertown, St. Paul to Powderhorn Park, Minneapolis, appalled, embittered, and "fucked for life" by memories of the Republican National Convention and the corrective shoes—like he was a Byronic clubfoot with the mark of Cain on his foot.

Noel tore down Saami's handwritten, misspelled sign. He blew the hair out of his eyes, not that it was in his eyes, but the gesture symbolized: problem-solving time.

Noel pondered the niceties and velleities of book placement in relation to optimal book sales. He skillfully jostled the National Cash register open to attach a fresh red rubber band to the back of the castors. He had shown Aloysius this before, but Aloysius had evinced no more interest in it than a comb jellyfish in phenomenology. Noel's first rubber band broke. He pulled out another back-up rubber band.

"Oh good, hey Noel, thanks for coming in on your day off again!" said Aloysius, getting up to go again.

Chitchee felt a surge of gratitude towards Aloysius—impelled to give him a hug, although Aloysius held two U. S. MAIL bins. Chitchee hugged him awkwardly over the bins with Aloysius protesting and backing out of the store.

"Thanks for hiring me, Aloysius," said Chitchee sincerely, "and giving me a chance!"

"Cool," said Aloysius. "I'm going to skip the post office and go straight home so rush hour won't be so long."

Aloysius wondered what the "chance" was and he wondered whether he had hired the right "people person" to draw other "people persons" into BookSmart. God is the new guy squirrely—is he nutso too? Understandably, the other guys worked like dull safety razors scraping along, and how much longer would *they* last, pretending to work? Hiring Chitchee should please Viktor, who must be planning something big. Why else would Viktor commandeer the basement and blackmail me into keeping the store open? I can't even talk about it and I want to scream.

"Well, sell some books!" said Aloysius, crashing through the front door crash bars. He paused: "Good job, every buddy! See you hep cats on the B-side of the A train! I'm going on home and will see you in the morning. I keep thinking I was supposed to do something though. I was going to go to The Wax Museum one of these days . . . then hit Circus Maximus or The Optic Nerve.

Whatever it was, it will have to wait. So long!"

"When John Berryman showed up to teach English," said Yardley, immediately pigeonholing Chitchee, "he rushed into the classroom at Andersen Hall like a King Lear who has read Shakespeare—smoking, drinking, swearing—a magnificent Scotch and soda in one hand and in the other hand—"

"—a bazooka?" asked Chitchee.

"No, another Scotch and soda!"

"A two-fisted drinker was Henry?" said Chitchee. "*Life is boring/* we must say so. Who are we looking for again?"

"The poet, Chilcote Carrothers," said Yardley, sighing. "I've only ever found his books in this store! Believe me, I've been to Wales and beyond, looking for Chilcote Carrothers. I abhor the internet. I'm not going to ABE Books or Bookfinder. I enjoy the hunt! I don't know who Carrothers was, but I believe he was the last great unsung, great Cubist poet of the Great War. Possibly Russian. In the circle of Akhmatova perhaps? His poems are sometimes absurd or surreal, sometimes sublime. Always ahead of their time. Uncanny and sublime."

"I am sometimes slime," said Saami, pulling up his jeans and toddling up to Yardley. "Why don't we look for me?"

Chitchee also wondered about the poet Chilcote Carrothers. Strange he had never heard of him. Was he someone like Rupert Brooke, but more obscure? Like Wilfred Owen but never saw action? Like Robert Graves but died young? Like Siegfried Sassoon? Carrothers? What? Chilcote Carrothers died *on the way over* to World War I? Or he missed the boat and fell into the English Channel? Or stumbled onto pruning shears by tripping over the dahlias when mowed down by a passing fox hunt?

"Who *was* Chilcote Carrothers?" asked Chitchee, looking over the Poetry section.

"No one knows for sure," said Yardley, also gazing at the shelves of poetry. "One thing Chilcote Carothers was *not*, he was *not* anything like a 'slam' poet! I don't want to know anything about him, but I think he died serving his country. He exists only in vanity press reprints. But I wouldn't be surprised if he knew Pound, Ford, and F. O. Mathiessen. I do know he had a love of poesy. You can see it in his *love of craft*."

"His love of Kraft?" said Saami, wincing. "You mean their macaroni and cheese?"

"I think I fixed it," barked Noel. "It needed a good rubber band. Chitchee! Saami! Be careful with the register. Try not to shake it too much. And a corollary to that: don't push the till too hard either or it will get unhinged and get stuck. Careful with the 'NO SALE' button! I'll see you tomorrow, if there is one."

Shrugged Chitchee, "*Inshallah*."

Chitchee and Saami abandoned Yardley in the Poetry section.

"Saami, *if there is a tomorrow?*" Chitchee scratched his head.

"Don't listen to Noel, he thinks too much!" said Saami. "He hasn't gotten over the death of Che Guevara yet."

Saami stalked behind the counter on a sneaky feline prowl for something. He screwed up his nose and set out little boxes of dessicated Sharpie pens and never-used colored pencils on the counter. Then he found the "something." Saami bit his lower lip with two yellow front teeth.

"Oh my my my . . . God damn it," said Saami with a palsy and a dropsy, unable to open the pint of Phillips vodka Snorri had glued shut.

"What should we listen to now that the cat's away?" asked Chitchee, trying not to see the Associate Night Manager drink on the job. "You know I love music! Sabbath? Maiden, Metallica, Motorhead, AC/DC, Rush, Queen, Slayer, Tool, Queen, Leppard, Scorps? Huh? Heavy metal? Saami? We can listen to: death metal, crunch metal, grind metal, thrash metal, speed metal, comic book metal, graphic metal, action figure metal, beer metal, pot metal, bronze metal, serial killer metal, blood metal, dirty sex metal, copro-phagilistic metal, bloody stool metal, or snuff cannibal black magic disemboweled clown human lampshade metal. Which do you prefer?"

"So what was your book about again?" asked Saami, twisting without torque the cap to the nectareous Phillips vodka, which caused his face to burn kandy korn orange and yellow.

"My book! Thanks for asking! A true friend! I love talking about my book," said Chitchee.

"As a writer, I make sentences. That's what I do. What's the point? The point is to *enrich* the dialect of the tribe. As such I am *une étoile* for repolarizing Eliot's elitist dictum, derived from Mallarmé; fair enough *en Français*, but "purity" doesn't jibe well with English."

Molecules of joy flattered through Chitchee's bloodstream and suffused his blood-brain barrier, so glad *someone* took an interest in his putative *pustak*, his dystopian novel, *The Hell Hound Chip*. Dystopian novels, so Chitchee averred, were hotter than hotcakes, hot off the griddle in 2009. *Utopia, Looking Backward, News From Nowhere, The World Set Free,* they were positive, progressive visions of humanity; then along came World War I and there followed nothing but dystopias: *We, Brave New World, 1984, The Man in the High Castle, The Moon is a Harsh Mistress.*

The sheer act of describing a dystopia had caused Chitchee his own writer's dystopia and talking about dystopias had mired him in a quaggy bog of book sand. He had forgotten already how he had been sucked under into a dysthymic silence, a writer's silence. How his writer's oblivion had triggered his writer's rage, which caused him to destroy all his worthless work. Frankly, there was no book. It was like something out of Zola.

"It's a dystopia, Saami, called *The Hell Hound Chip*," chattered on Chitchee. "It's about a future totalitarian state on Earth where music is outlawed and sold on the black market as a powdered drug, which is injected. But everyone is 'chipped' so that if you do hear music, you see a snarling, three-headed rabid German Shepherd, which multiplies itself into a hundred German Shepherds all in a row, and then they chase you everywhere. And the hell hound's bite carries a virus that causes the unfortunate music lover to throw up for days—it's like Antabuse—until his ears bleed and fall off like potato chips. But without music, society breaks down. And then you know what happens? Underground cells of unemployed musicians hack the hell out of the hell hound chip, but they break out in a dancing sickness when they inadvertently hear "God Bless the U.S.A" by Greed Leanwood and are destroyed by the melody-detecting German Shepherds, leaving behind a remnant. Mansur Al Hallaj is sent by Allah to organize the remnant of rebels—"

"—I'm sorry, I wasn't listening," said Saami. "I was thinking about masturbating."

"O . . ." said Chitchee without enthusiasm. "Ummm . . ."

"Are you into meditation?" said Saami, stymied by the sealed pint of Phillips vodka. "What's with all the Ummms . . ."

"Meditation? I can meditate for about as long as I can hold my breath! Watch me," said Chitchee, holding his breath and passing out onto the floor. He jumped up and looked at the store's CD shelf again. "Well, we should play some music. I hope you like Flagitious Idiosyncrasy in the Dilapidation! Or here, I'll try this one, Pizzicato Five!"

"What the fuck is wrong with my Phillips vodka bottle?" cried Saami, as he watched his hand tremble and he felt a fever flame in his brain that scorched his tongue. "I can't open this. I Hate HATE HATE Pizzicato Five! Don't even play it when I'm dead! I hate that band so much I hate all bands with the number 'five' in them: the Dave Clark Five, the We Five, the Jackson 5, the Marooned 5, and the Five Little Rubber Raincoats."

"*What's* your book about?" asked Saami, flushed with the unslakable thirst.

"It's a cystopia, Saami. The future is a giant cyst. When the cyst explodes, a remnant from Earth travels into a key lime pie, and they establish a laboratory of genius kittens who have received Fulbright scholarships to develop a nuclear reactor from the cans of tuna fish they found in the United Nations parking lot. An evil badger named Stite, made of dense neutron star matter, is sent from Earth to the key lime pie to see if the Earthlings are enriching photosynthetic Cheerios with magnesium and phosphorus, which he planned to lace with viruses cultured in prussic acid—"

"Hey, will you be okay running the store for a bit?" interrupted Saami, who licked his white lips with his cotton-mouthed tongue, his innards coated with limestone dust and salt-lines around his alkaline mouth.

"Yes . . . ," sang Chitchee, . . . *terday.*"

"*All my troubles seemed to go away . . .* " echoed the aisles, Melusina and Kriemhilde being the owners of those dulcet tones.

They hummed merrily over their disinterred WWII cookbooks and larked about now that all the excitement had settled into dust.

"Shut up!" yelled Saami toward the cookbooks. "This isn't Let It Be Records! Put on some of that complicated Bach shit, Chitchee! Fuckin' Bach shit that shuts them fuckers the fuck up. Look Chitchee, first thing you gotta know about this store, if you put the Beatles on, and this only applies to the Beatles, the customers will start singing along. And I can't stand listening to an entire store singing *Eleanor Rigby*!"

Saami bounced back to the glued pint bottle of Phillips vodka. He wrestled the bottle to the floor WWF-style over the cap. He twisted his face and his face twisted him back. Lips corkscrewed. The more he twisted to torque the twist-off cap off— going nowhere—the more he swore. With each new obscenity, he contorted his body into a new topological wonder. His teeth tightened. He gripped a claw hammer. He propped the bottle between the cash register and the National Bankcard side-swiping credit card machine. He raised the claw hammer into thin air (he looked like the papier-mâché face of a Noh horned demon), missed the pint, hit his thumb, and nearly shattered the screen of the credit card machine.

"*I said something wrong, now she's leaving home*," sang Melusina.

Saami looked over the top of his glasses at Mel:

"Mel, you are out of here!"

"Saami! You can't kick me out of here for that!"

"Okay Mel, you *might* be out of here!"

"Can I make a suggestion?" said Kriemhilde

"Metallica," said Saami.

"Can you play some music to calm yourself, Saami?" she asked. "*Dialogue of the Carmelites*? Swingles version preferred."

"Poulenc," said Chitchee. "As soon as I check out this *Secret Diary of Adrian Mole* and compare it with *Diary of a Wimpy Kid*."

"Oh thank you, young man!" said Kriemhilde. "But we're going home to try out this new Liberty chipped beef and baked potato entree, topped with our own Kemp's sour cream and Bac-O-Bits family recipe, which goes back to the old country. Pennsylvania."

"Wait, can you watch the register, Linda?" asked Saami, looking disturbed.

"Why? I don't think it's going anywhere, Shaami."

"I have to show Chitchee the downstairs areas for tonight's 'official' training session."

"But I've been invited to these good ladies' homes for Liberty shipped beef," said Linda. "So some other day."

THE BOOKSMART BASEMENT

Chitchee followed Saami down the staircase via the landing (overhead from a string dangled a large arrow pointing downward). The plastic, potted Ur plant from Gondwanaland signaled the half-way point on the staircase, and the steps of the wooden stairs led downward until—creak! creak!—the stairs stepped into the darkness of history itself. There, besides history, followed the underground Ultima Thule of genres, occult, true crime, abnormal psychology, drugs, *Star Trek*, *Star Wars*, *Warhammer*, *Forgotten Realms*, *Dragonlance*, *Dragonriders of Pern*, *Flowers in the Attic*, Kings, Gabaldons, Auels, Rices, Charlaine Harrises, *Calvin and Hobbes*, *The Far Side*, *Garfield*, *Nancy and Sluggo*, *Wonder Wart-Hog*, *Doc Savage*, comic books, comics, and comix.

With *The DaVinci Code* retreated into the background, a passel of requests for *The Hunger Games* had been blitzing the maroon front counter like an attack of Crowingjays while a going strong *Twilight* series, and an even stronger going Harry Potter series with installment 7, *The Deathly Hollows* maintained their upstairs status as quick sells.

Chitchee read Winsor McKay's *Dream of a Rarebit Fiend*, distractedly overbiting it. He shuffled toward a couch.

"Oh yeah, let's make this quick," said Saami. "Books on the Middle East are next to the books on Middle-earth—Hitler and Holocaust books are in the middle of the two—and then you got your Churchills and Fibromyalgias over there, and your shit-*Shacks* and *Left Behinds* UP THE BEE-HIVE in the corner over there, with the rest of the Christian gangrene."

"Hey, Saami? " asked Chitchee, unconsciously aligning stacks of *Men Are From Mars*, *Tuesdays with Morrie*, and *Marley and Me*. "What if Marley and Morrie were from Mars, which is where *The Celestine Prophecy* was found? Saami, when do you think I'll start getting paid *real* money? Are there stock options?"

"Soon, I hope! We need you here. I'll talk to Aloysius," said Saami. "You heard about his condition though? Butterfly effect phobia syndrome thing? The slightest change can cause a seizure of grand mal epilepsy in him. And then you have to grab his tongue and roll him around like a Tootsie Roll."

"But there are always people in the store. It's a beehive sometimes. So where does all the honey go?" asked Chitchee. "Everybody in the neighborhood loves this store. This book store is a community, while the powers that be keep planning in their insidious planners more Playsets for the upper brackets. Which destroys any sensibility of *place*. Developers will pave over our *place cells*, build a parking ramp on top of us, and reduce us to parking lot attendants for their condominium paradise. Can't Noel figure out how to push the store into the black? I mean he's not a genius, he's a *fucking* genius; so why can't we all put our heads together? What's wrong with everybody?"

"Between you and me," said Saami, "Aloysius is really concerned about Noel."

"Noel?"

"Aloysius is convinced Noel has lost his fucking mind."

"Why?"

"Lately, Noel has been calling for a revolution."

"What's wrong with that?"

"Over the phone?"

"Okay, maybe he's that shy?" asked Chitchee with a rising tone.

"Well, between you and me and the Moon," said Saami, leaning in toward Chitchee with a whisper in his cupped hand. "Aloysius thinks Noel has lost all grasp on reality. I mean actually lost all reality. Whenever Aloysius sets anything down, Noel comes along and moves it somewhere where Aloysius can't find it. Aloysius thinks it's, it's—*on porpoise*."

"What?" said Chitchee, looking around for eavesdroppers. "Noel is gaslighting Aloysius with Ebbinghaus-type memory tests? Or do you mean like those developmental tests Piaget used on children? Does Noel throw tennis balls behind the couch to see if Aloysius knows the tennis ball is behind the couch? That's so cruel!"

Chitchee surveyed the BookSmart basement with a quick once-over for spies and listening devices. He saw nobody and nothing but the stone-floored, damp, cool, moldy, and cobwebbed basement.

"Yep," said Saami. "And ever notice how Noel keeps to himself? That tells you a lot!"

"It sure does," said Chitchee. "What?"

"It tells you Noel is planning a lot," said Saami.

"That's where all the planners went!" said Chitchee. "Oh, I see now, this book store is like something out of the T'ang Dynasty!"

The basement was dotted with cheap, leaning-tower floor lamps with directional, gooseneck-cones spotlighting the black flyspecks that peppered the putrid wall stains, which resembled old mattress splotches. Aloysius and Saami had interior-decorated the basement with dumpster finds, overstuffed gutted couches (on one Jason sat looking and looking at pictures of Patti Smith), and measley, mushy-cushioned, stuffed chairs. In the dark recessive corners Chitchee witnessed a mouse scamper by, a bat circle around and fly into a dark corner, and a couple gay guys, who had been making out, separate like strands of DNA.

"Aloysius fears a major book store coup, because Noel has been awful quiet lately," continued Saami, in a darkening Y/A Phillip Pullmanesque tone. "Awful quiet."

"But," said Chitchee, "when I am with Noel he keeps saying the book store is doing well, turning a profit, catching up to its bills, and that soon we will open a second store in Juneau, Alaska and if that fails, on to an annex in Iceland."

"The second store is the first store without Aloysius," said Saami. "Don't you get it? Noel is waiting to make his move on the throne—waiting for Aloysius to show signs of dementia, of schizophrenia, and of losing all his cookies. I think Aloysius is already hallucinating that he is the owner of a used book store and we are working for his hallucinations. That's why Aloysius wants Noel to see a psychiatrist and stop interfering with his own ongoing hallucinations. Or see a therapist. Or at least talk to a bartender. Or talk to a fucking chick once a month on Dial-a-Chick."

Saami stopped. He looked Chitchee eye to eye. With a leering smirk that could have felled Dr. Strange, Saami's voice dropped a perfect fourth:

"He's not one of us. Noel doesn't drink."

"That could be a social inhibitor right there," said Chitchee.

"*And Noel doesn't even do drugs,*" said Saami. "HE DOESN'T DO ANYTHING!"

"Shhh . . ." said Chitchee. "He does math problems."

"Aloysius thinks that Noel is immune to relationships, that he has never loved, that he can't love, because he never partied in high school, never went to the high school prom, never fell in love, never dated, never even got divorced, and now he is paying the price for all those years never doing drugs, by becoming the complete nebbish," said Saami with a rare rarefied air, "that he is. Probably a virgin."

"So?" said Chitchee. "So he's a virgin? You mean we should spread that rumor before we ask him if it's true, in case it isn't?"

"No! Don't you get it? You don't get it! Revolution? He's reading *Revolutionary Road*. He is not planning to take over the country, he's planning to take over BookSmart and replace us with clones of himself! Although he said he might keep *me* on because of my extensive knowledge of Batman's enemies. But as for you, you would have to sell vacuum cleaners."

Sausage Man, clutching the complete one-volume Plato (Edith Hamilton translation) in one hand, pillowed by the two-volume Aristotle (Richard McKeon translation) behind his head, started up with a big snore that he ate with a big lip-smacking sound followed by digesting, swallowing, and humming emissions.

"Who else is down here?" asked Chitchee, whirling around. "I'm getting scared. Let's go back upstairs. The basement is giving me the creeps."

"Sausage Man must have entered through the back door," said Saami, walking around a corner with Chitchee behind him.

Saami pulled out a hand mirror from behind a bookshelf, the mirror's customary hiding spot, and he placed it under the old man's giant, black-headed, pitted red nose and hairy nostrils.

"Sausage Man is harmless," said Saami, "but don't tell Aloysius I let him sleep on the couch down here at night!"

The hairs reached out like rotifers and crawled down the side of the couch. His eyebrows, like overgrown paths, had old hairs that had grown thick enough to grow bark.

Sausage Man slowly woke up like a log.

"*Ja*, Saami! Didja know that if you pick up a wooly bear caterpillar and it tastes crunchy it means we are in for a long winter? All men by their nature seem to know this!"

"Look, here's the deal, Sausage Man," said Saami, "you can stay here as long as you don't pester the customers with your high falutin' drivel about Plato and Aristotle. And don't tell Aloysius I let you stay here at night!"

"'So above, so below,' said Hermes Trismegistus!" said Sausage Man.

Saami and Chitchee walked into rueful rooms like roaming ruminators followed by rheumier rooms following them. They entered two linked storage rooms even Saami didn't know about. The basement was a superannuated Bastille of horrors that never ended and never began, encompassing humanity's poisoned hopes and murdered aspirations.

Saami unlocked a door that opened to an overstocked, overstock backroom, where Aloysius kept the safety deposit box safely hidden from himself and all BookSmart's business records in loose-leaf folders labeled either "POOP SHEETS" or "MORE POOP SHEETS." And then there were 10,000 or so saved pieces of paper and receipts pooped all over the floor.

"This is where we keep the good stuff," said Saami, directing Chitchee's gaze toward one whole wall dedicated to hundreds of *The Kite Runners*.

"God, we have so many *Kite Runners*," said Chitchee, "I don't even want to read it now. A single, naked woman is sexy. But a million of them is biology."

"That's the stupidest thing I've ever heard!" exclaimed Saami, his tongue white with saliva and face purple. "It's never about biology, it's about sex! Okay? You're working in a book store, now, so you have to consider the customer's desires . . . which is always for more and more sex, drugs, and rock 'n' roll."

"Sorry I'm just an ethical slut," rejoindered Chitchee, "but how many *Angela's Ashes* do we need? Twenty? She isn't going to make a comeback! And do we have *The Joy of Sex, Our Bodies Ourselves, Masters and Johnson*—"

"Look in Biology, how should I know? I only work in a book store," said Saami, sweating and shaking. "Do I look like Dr. Ruth? Aloysius wants us to clear this area because the landlord wants to use it for his own storage space."

"Move all this?" asked Chitchee. "One question: How? And why?"

There were Oprah books, book-club books of yester-reads, oddball books the size of matchboxes or packs of firecrackers, other books the size of Dutch doors, yard-sale oddities, pack-ratted zines, *Field & Stream*s, stacked and overflowing boxes of *Dakota Tawaxitku Kin*, and random out of order tabs and sheet music on cluttered shelves in unorganized, obese, weighty, bulky, and demented bookcases. The aisles of bookcases that went on forever like infinities had hopelessly out-of-date post-it notes tagged to them, the stickum strips with dirty, wispy beards. A cornucopia of bills with cartouche-shaped address windows and radish-colored Final Notices on them carpeted the cement floor with an intricate pattern of tessellation.

"Watch your step," said Saami. "This is Accounting."

Chitchee looked down at Accounting. He tried not to step in it. The Accounting department also *accounted* for a couch covered with fake wood-looking, cardboard file cabinets containing expired coupons, menus, and more guitar tabs. Another departmental couch was covered with old pagers, mix tapes, overhead projectors, Sony VCRs, Sony Walkmans, and floppy disks of 1.2 megabytes tied together by twine in bundles of SuperAmerica gas station torn plastic bags.

Continuing the tour, Saami walked Chitchee into another corner where a mouse swooped into a crack in the wall.

"And here's the kitchen," said Saami, salivating and rubbing his belly.

Chitchee cracked open the creaky gate to the inside of the vintage microwave oven, which had one dial and one switch for a control panel, its walls cholerically crusted with refried, fly-blown bean paste and fried-brown house flies underneath the revolving platter.

Chitchee sneaked a sneak peak inside the fridge: six crumpled Aquafinas each finished but for the last drops, a centimeter high inside, on the door rack. And on the single refrigerator shelf was nothing but a chunk of unwrapped blue cheese to greet his nose and some empty ice cube trays in the little crisper.

Saami placed his hands on his hips and tapped a foot impatiently when Chitchee noticed one corner of the break room stacked with gallon jugs. Brand new boxes had been stacked up there recently.

"Hey that's not ours," said Saami, upset. "Don't touch that! Boss's orders!"

Chitchee pulled his nose out of a gym bag and then held the iron padlock of a padlocked, heavily-bolted iron door.

"Okay, but what is behind this iron door?" Chitchee asked. "A U-boat?"

He felt the warning stickers and ribbons in loquat yellow with KEEP OUT stencils between his fingers.

"You ask too many questions," said Saami.

"I bet you," said Chitchee, "there is gold beyond imagining and diamonds beyond even the most illuminating descriptions in

The Arabian Nights behind that iron door!"

"Who cares?" said Saami. "I gotta get to HennLake liquor store before it closes."

"Holy shit!" yelled Chitchee. "This is the tunnel system I heard about from Felix!"

"Your friend who works at the theater?" asked Saami. "Can he get me and Linda in to see midnight movies for free?"

"Of course," said Chitchee.

He followed Saami out of the mazey underground jungle of printed matter, kicking the detritus of obsolete innovations out of the way to make room for more obsolete innovations on their way.

"Okay, now you know everything I know, which is nothing, congratulations," said Saami. "I gotta get to the 'lick' before it closes! I'll be right back! If Aloysius calls, don't answer!"

Saami scampered up the stairs on which he had a seizure, dreamed a dream of consciousness, awoke trembling, and bounded upward, seeing the Henn-Lake liquor store clock tick like an Olympic stopwatch.

"Take your time with that, buddy!" yelled Chitchee after him. "I got this job down flat! And I'll be upstairs in seconds flat!"

Chitchee knew that behind the basement's giant submarine bulkheads lurked an underground tunnel system that somehow snaked its way south to Lakewood Cemetery and somehow east to the Mississippi River, where in the days of Prohibition underground speakeasies existed. You bought your poison in the Gateway District, not from a gangster with only his eyes showing from behind a slotted door, but from a guy looking up at you from a sewer grate.

"Find everything okay?" asked Chitchee as he approached the slouched, couched Jason.

Chitchee introduced himself while the introduced Jason Unterguggenberger picked up off the floor the latest oral history of Joe Meek, *Joe Meek: Satellite of Rock* with a New Afterword). Jason—shoes off, rolled little worms of dirt found between his toes.

"Hey, man," said Chitchee, wanting to impress Jason, "I found the door that leads to where the mythical tunnel system starts! And it leads underground all under Minneapolis!"

"What?" Jason tore off his headphones, shrugged his shoulders, and stopped logrolling the dirt in between his toes. "Can't you see I'm reading this garbage?"

Chitchee dismissed the banging sounds of something on the counter upstairs.

"Are you homeless?" asked Chitchee.

"No," said Jason. "I sleep in a storage locker."

"Doesn't that count?" asked Chitchee.

"Who's counting?" asked Jason. "Sometimes I sleep in a garage."

"The owner know?"

"The owner was my mom. But she is dead."

"No further questions."

"When she died, I couldn't make the house payments," said Jason, his tongue released from its fetters. "The sheriff threw me out. So I moved back into our old garage. Nobody was looking. I was going to leave the new owner some Fudge Stripe cookies when I left."

"Fudge Stripes?" asked Chitchee, hearing a metallic thud. "What if the owner is allergic to Fudge Stripes? Maybe you should ask."

"That's okay, I won't have time," said Jason. "I got a new job. With MPG. Breaking up concrete floors. In abandoned apartment buildings. Ingersoll rock drills. I'm working for some millionaire guy. He buys up distressed apartment buildings and flies back to Miami. I'm thinking I could use them for squats."

"That could be a healthy alternative to a storage locker," speculated Chitchee. "And you could save up rent money, first and last month's rent. Hey, I have some spare space on my kitchen floor, if you're really strapped!"

"Thanks! But I'm going to get 200 dollars emergency assistance tomorrow. Then I'll be able to afford my 60 a month storage locker. And I can sleep in there for the winter. As long as I leave by five every morning. Then I'll save up. To bury my mother."

"She's not buried?" asked Chitchee, his head jerking forward a notch.

"What am I supposed to do? At least I got all her . . . in boxes."

Pondering this, Chitchee trudged upstairs to see if the cash register was there.

Which it was not.

"Oh my God!" yelled Chitchee. "Somebody stole the cash register!"

Chitchee's heart-strings tightened. Pinching himself awake from a dream, he tried to dream that he was dreaming, but he could not. Phone. Call. 911. And.

MELCHIZEDEK

Standing next to the counter, marooned Kanishka Amma fondled *Vikram and the Vampire* face out. He looked a bit upside down and bewildered.

"Can I buy a book?" asked Kanishka. "Is there a cash register?"

"I don't know!" said Chitchee, scampering for the BookSmart phone, but someone had left it off the hanger. "Can you?"

It was out of charge when he dialed.

"Hello?" asked Chitchee of the entire store. "This is an emergency. Emergency! Does anyone in the store have a cell-phone, a mobile phone, a satellite phone, a smartphone, a flip phone, a slide-out phone with a keyboard, or a very long landline?"

"I'd like to purchase this book," said Kanishka with a mellifluous Indian chit chat, unconcerned with cash registers, robberies, and emergencies as he admired the old, dog-toothed book. "I had a different version of this when I was growing up in Kerala. I used to own it, but I loaned it to a friend, who died of rabies. He barked himself to death. I never got it back."

"Wait, what book is that?" said Chitchee, looking over the customer's shoulder. "You have the Burton version. I have it in the Tawney *Kathasaritsagara*! I've read it. Have you?"

"No, because I keep lending it out, but never get it back. I bought another *Baital Pachisi* and loaned that out," said Kanishka.

"Why would you do that?" cried Chitchee.

"I thought I'd get it back!" said Kanishka. "I better read it now that I've gotten the book back in a sort of myth of the eternally returning book."

"You can't a lender be with a rare book, man," said Chitchee. "Gee, it's not another stick of butter!"

"Ha ha, well do I know!" said Kanishka. "By the time my friend gets around to reading it, years if not centuries will have passed. Even though I put a bookplate on the inside cover: 'Whosoever defames, defaces, or destroys this text, so shall he be defamed, defaced, or destroyed.' I know it's sitting on my friend's book shelf forgotten . . . like the book fiend himself, who has been forgotten by all his friends, because of his obsession with books."

"You know, the vampires of Bharat," said Chitchee, "are different from our feeble-minded Draculas and LeStats. South Asian vampires are fond of riddles and have been to college. They're like logicians. Wait, did you say 'pachisi'? Like the human board game? Parcheesi? Are they cognate? Crosses and circles?"

Chitchee looked at the BookSmart phone. Another dead phone for the dead phone graveyard. Would Aloysius ever invest in a new phone? Couldn't he write it off on his taxes? Not that it mattered, because Chitchee was fired for sure. His head spun on his neck.

Kanishka grew up Christian, converted to Communism, became an expert on B. R. Ambedkhar, converted to Buddhism, married a Muslim, and taught Hinduism in Northfield. He knew Gujarati, Bengali, and Hindi-Urdu. In fact, he had written a book on Primordialism and Savarkar, with an introduction by Romula Thapur. Chitchee might have launched into a discussion of the *Ramayana*, the *Mahabharata*, but he only had seconds to save the store.

"By the by . . . Kanishka," said Chitchee, "have you read Desani's *All About H. Hatterr?*"

"Yes!" said Kanishka.

"That makes you a credible witness!" said Chitchee. "So did you happen to see someone walk out the door with a cash register that was here a minute ago?"

"I did hear a *kind* of commotion, some *bits* of swearing, and the *fall* of a hammer!" said Kanishka. "But I thought it was a Bugs Bunny cartoon."

Chitchee accepted five dollars for the tattered book, although reluctant to cut off such an interesting fellow. They exchanged numbers and Chitchee suggested they should get together for Thanksgiving dinner and discuss Kabir and Mirabai. They shook hands and parted.

"Paging Jason Unterguggenberger, could you come upstairs and watch the counter?" yelled Chitchee down the stairs. "I have to run an errand, Jason. Someone stole our cash register! The Dunn Brothers robber kidnapped Saami for ransom money!

Ransom with what money? All the ransom money is in the till."

Chitchee paced, thinking, they've got Saami. Chitchee saw before his mind's eye: Saami holding up a *StarTribune* with the dated headline: ROLVAAG KIDNAPPED FROM BOOKSMART HELD FOR RANSOM NO TAKERS.

"It *must* be the Dunn Brothers guy. Snorri was spot on as per usual. That's why he keeps both ears close to the ground! Wait— no, first—I've got to find a phone!"

Chitchee yelled downstairs.

"Jason! Can you watch the counter? Jason!"

Jason staggered up the staircase. Time was flowing backwards and he was a tired, spavined dray horse with glaucoma. Once arrived, Jason lay across the maroon linoleum check-out counter like a dead sturgeon caught in seaweed.

"Is this 'watching' the counter?" muttered Jason, his lips not even moving. His straight and thin lips (with a small oval opening) were a potato peeler for words: "Can I wear my headphones?"

"For sure," said Chitchee. "And I can pay you in bars of soap from the bathroom."

"I already took those," muttered Jason, "unless you have some better ones stashed. Do you have Castile? Or Neem? Preferably Neem."

Melchizedek looked like a famished and sick stork with a rosewood cane.

"Sir, do you have a cell phone?" asked Chitchee.

"I don't own a phone, never have," said Melchizedek, raising his hands. "I never needed one because I never communicated anything the Earthlings wanted to hear."

Bald with moles on top, Melchizedek had a white beard tied in little braids through tiny beads from Bobby Beads down his brillo-haired chest. His frozenly astonished eyeballs were blue, and his face was without cheeks and weathered. His yellowed, wallpapery skin was framed by greasy gray hair, which curled behind his ears and then reached his shoulders in two plats like goby fish fins. He gripped his lacquered rosewood cane (the finger bone of a Nephilim), which kept his skeleton on its feet. He looked made of wickerwork in his rattan sandals and too weak to skin an egg.

"Do you have the book *Why We Know the Ramans are Here*? Or do you have *The YETI Are From SETI*?" asked Melchizedek.

He scratched the sun-damaged scabs off his upper pate and offered them to Chitchee, who then looked at Jason, who rolled off the counter and stood up.

"I don't want them," said Chitchee looking at the scabs like Ants on a Log at a picnic. "Do you? Jason?"

But Chitchee was supposed to be panicking. So he hustled outside, hared down Hennepin, and yelled:

"Fire! Fire!"

Almost immediately a bystander assumed Chitchee had been shot, filmed Chitchee, and hashtagged him with #manshotcallingforhelp #highspeedchasedownonmainstreetmanonfire #bookstoreburningcityinflames #minneapolisdestroyed-bydemocratscityclowncil #whereisnationalguard #obamaworstpresidentever #theregoestheuptownartfair

"Isn't that little elf guy working tonight?" stammered Melchizedek, astonished that Saami was not working the night shift for the first time ever.

"Where did they get this?" butt in a scavenging Jason to himself, looking over a Family Photo Album. "I thought I threw this Family Photo Album out. After I cleaned up my building, somebody pulled it out of the unlocked dumpster. Who the hell is crawling in the dumpsters over there?"

Jason had cleaned up that mess. Photo albums, polaroids, plastic jugs, ropes, chains, tools, and gym bags were all over the evicted tenants apartment. He didn't really look at it. He threw it in Lunds bags and threw the Lunds bags in the dumpster.

"Do you have any of David Icke's conspiracy books?" asked Melchizedek.

"No. A bunch of lizard people bought them all," said Jason, placing the Family Photo Album back under the counter.

"Oh," Melchizedek whispered, his eyes thyroidal orbits around planets of doom, "no."

"And I'm a lizard too!" said Jason, his eyes clicking. "Hurroo!"

Jason monkeyed with his JVC headphones, an interrupted look bothering his face. He returned, rolled over, gorbellied on the maroon linoleum counter, and showed off three inches of butt crack.

Melchizedek backpedaled, quietly shaken and puzzled at the sour eye candy.

"Hey wait, you can't leave me here, alien guy!" said Jason, jumping off the counter. "I have to catch a bus to Central. Can you watch the counter? Just lie down here so nobody buys anything. There, thanks."

Jason re-muffed his ears with headphones blasting Hüsker Dü's *Zen Arcade*.

"What?" said Melchizedek. "Just lie there? Across the counter? Well, I guess. Can I pick out a book?"

"Of course," said Jason, lifting up one headphone, skyjacking his neck for the #6 bus at Hennepin and Lagoon. "Have a good one."

Melchizedek snatched a book off the new arrivals table. The crash barred front doors crashed, Jason thrusting aside a ski-masked man, a killer whale of a man, who looked around BookSmart and adjusted his ill-fitting, woolen, black ski mask over his white skin.

"All right," said the masked man, nervously looking over his shoulder, "empty out the register! This is a stick up! Give me all the money now! Or I'm going to cut you up like a box of of . . . oh I don't what—like a box of Cheez-Its! Where *is* the register? Who are you?"

The robber flashed a box cutter at Melchizedek, who looked up from his book, *You Are All Sanpaku*, peeved, and folded an ancient bookmark into the book.

"I am Melchizedek. And I am telling you, Earthling, there is no register!" said Melchizedek as if announcing a new Apple product to no response. "And I fear no Earth Man who says it isn't so, for I am two hundred years old. And I think I look pretty good for two hundred."

"But I was here earlier," said the dejected ski-masked robber with his rejected box cutter. "Did you see any suspicious looking art school students from MCAD casing the store for a heist?"

"When I landed here, somebody had already stolen the register, Earth Man," said Melchizedek. "Or somebody had it teleported through a quantum hole more likely—that's the usual method."

THE THUMPERS ARE ALL SANPAKU

"I guess I should call Aloysius with more bad news," said the ski-masked robber, turning toward the door. "Can you hand me the phone, Melchizedek?"

A MPD squad car squealed to the curb, spinning its harsh beacons from the light bar—red, white, and blue like a screaming Fourth of July popsicle.

"What can a mere priest from the Pleiades *do* against the malevolent forces of the Nephilim?" asked Melchizedek, his drawn face gaunt, glaciated, and wrinkled as a chain-linked fence.

The police vehicle, idling, attracted a small crowd of bar goers (Club Miami), who attracted a larger crowd of moviegoers (Uptown Theater) outside BookSmart.

The ski-masked robber addressed the entering two thumpers, Officer Lowry and Officer Weatherwax, who stood aloof as bald eagles with their blue blouses, nightsticks, handcuffs, Berettas in their chained holsters, pouches, Tasers, and lapel microphones.

"There's been a burglary," said the robber through his ski-mask. "Can you cops call the cops?"

"Hands up!" yelled both thumpers, outstretched hands gripping Berettas. "Drop the knife! Show me your hands!"

"I work here," said the ski-masked perpetrator, dropping the box-cutter. "I'm the box cutter."

"Is that you Snorri?" asked an exhausted Saami from behind the two thumpers.

Saami cantilevered the beat up old NCR cash register in front of him.

"What are you doing here?" asked Saami.

"I am testing our security," said Snorri, muffled through his ski-mask. "It's for the good of the store. In lieu of real security or off-duty bouncers . . . hey, are you thumpers for hire?"

Officer Lowry and Officer Weatherwax examined every micro and milli-movement of molecules and sniffed for marijuana so they could unload if needed.

"Snorri, can you tell the thumpers I work here?" asked Saami, unable to hold the cash register much longer, which fell from his hands like a cherry bomb, and still didn't open.

"If you tell them I work here first," said Snorri.

"I asked you first," said Saami. "Dibsed."

Officer Weatherwax tore off Snorri's ski-mask in the most painful way possible, with the twist of a garrote to half-strangle him and choke him to his knees.

"Officers, like I said, the register is jammed," pleaded Saami. "I couldn't fix it so I thought Tammy and the gals at Henn-Lake Liquor might have a crowbar, if I could get in there before closing. That's why I was running. I was paying myself out. The store owes me. That's why I was running. So that I could grab a pint of vodka for after work, for when I run home, for when I need a drink, for tonight, after I run home to watch *Akira* for the fourth time running—"

"Yeah, you said that already," said Officer Lowry.

"Chitchee? Chitchee? Where's Chitchee?" asked Saami.

"He went to catch a bus to Central! You missed him," said Melchizedek. "But, what I was wondering was, do you have an MK-Ultra Section? I'm looking for books on the sudden disappearance of the Hale-Bopp comet."

"He quit on his first day?" said Saami, plugging the register back in. "I guess it was too boring."

Saami rubbed his eyes to rub Melchizedek out of them.

"Fire! Fire!" said Chitchee, running inside the store and waving his hands above his head. "Who has a phone I can borrow? I promise I'll give it right back!"

Officer Weatherwax and Officer Lowry snicked the safeties on their triggers. Each thumper aimed dead straight at a dead Chitchee in three seconds. Two in the chest, one in the head. Firing pins cocked.

"Who ordered the thumpers?" asked Chitchee, belly-flopped to the floor.

Saami and Snorri followed suit.

Melchizedek crouched behind the front counter like an alien fetus. His pucker lost, his sphincter opened audibly. Sausage Man peeped up the stairs, wrote something on a memo pad, and softly tiptoed down the stairs. Anyone texting downstairs continued texting. The gay couple that had parted re-united and continued having sex obliviously humping—until a mouse ran under their four feet and they screamed and ran up the stairs and out the back door into the alley, leading Officer Weatherwax on a merry chase. Chitchee, Saami, and Snorri lay like three pigs in a blanket.

"Don't shoot, I work here!" said Chitchee to the redolent, white pine wood flooring. "American!"

"He works here too!" yelled Saami, face forward into the redolent, white pine wood flooring.

"Let's sort this out fellas," said Officer Lowry. "Get up!"

Chitchee, Saami, and Snorri stood up at attention, unhandcuffed after the police officers pulled them off the floor by their wrists.

"Hey, we're all law-abiding citizens," said Chitchee.

"As long as you guys aren't black, you are!" said Officer Weatherwax, returning from chasing the gay couple out the the back door.

"We're not even African American!" said Saami.

"But *you* are black!" said Chitchee to Officer Lowry.

"You got a problem with that? You get back down on the floor! *You're* black now!" said Officer Weatherwax, shoving Chitchee back down and handcuffing him.

"I could use a snack right now," said Chitchee. "Did you guys bring any snacks? Snacks for blacks?"

"We'd take you downtown right now," said Officer Lowry, "but we know Aloysius, and everybody in the neighborhood knows who he is."

"Why? Is he a registered sex offender?" asked Melchizedek, poking up from his hiding spot.

"Who are *you*?" asked Officer Weatherwax, close-upping on trembling Melchizedek's face.

"Let's see some ID, Van Winkle."

"I am the priest called Melchizedek, and I am from the planet Arcturus, Altair, or Atari, wherever, doesn't matter," said Melchizedek, "and I've never heard of Aloysius, and I know all the registered sex offenders in this neighborhood."

"Melchizedek is a customer," said Saami. "He comes in once in a blue moon for David Icicle books. And he came all that way for nothing because we don't have any."

"Do you need validation?" asked Chitchee from the floor.

"No, I accept the fact that I come from an alternate universe," said Melchizedek.

"I meant for parking," said Chitchee.

"I didn't drive," said Melchizedek, "I flew."

"Then you can take off," said Officer Lowry.

Melchizedek benumbed and disconsolate almost collapsed. The collapsar looked sadly at *You Are All Sanpaku*.

"You break it, you buy it," said Snorri to Melchizedek, plucking the book out of Melchizedek's hand and breaking the book's spine in two.

"Can I put the book on hold?" asked Melchizedek.

"We can hold your book for a week or as long as the world lasts, whichever comes first," said Chitchee.

"Cocoa, cookie, bus," said a customer timidly from outside. "I called earlier about *The Massage Book*? Are you open?"

Bobblehead sniffed his way past Melchizedek and looked around confused.

"Can't you see we're busy getting arrested?" asked Chitchee.

Bobblehead had a nose like a putty pyramid plastered to his puss. Referred to as "Bobblehead" by staff for his monstrous head on his relatively tiny body, his legs thinner than dodder stems. He always wore a blue windbreaker, blue work pants, and a button-down, white shirt, the standard security guard threads from Uniforms Unlimited on Lyndale. He always combed his thinning hair from one side of his head over to the other, never washing it—his own sebaceous oil always placked it down better than Brylcreem. Drooping inward, Bobblehead scooted by the dust-up to the top of the downstairs, avoiding eye contact with every man, woman, and mouse.

"*The Massage Book* by George Downing!" said Bobblehead. "Or someone will buy it!"

"Hey, you thumpers uncuff me, I'm on the clock!" said Chitchee. "And don't touch my penis this time!"

"Yeah, he can't very well work with his hands tied behind his back," said Snorri, "but, hah, lord knows that's the way it really is around here. When I first started here it was great—Aloysius—don't get me wrong, I love the guy to death—but now we are literally working in straitjackets. We are simply hamstrung by a complete lack of entre-peneurial imagination, spirit. *I* was the one who set up the computer with Homebase Inventory, and I entered the data. I was in charge of data management until Saami got a virus clicking on Russian and Nigerian porn, neither of which, if you like porn, is the best porn out there, and that lack of technical—"

Officer Weatherwax threw Snorri to the ground and ground his knee into Snorri's back.

"Shut the fuck up, asshole!" said Officer Weatherwax. "We don't give a fuck about your imagination. We have families, wives, lives, TVs, not like this fuckin' candy-assed Kandyland store for faggoty eggheads!"

"Yes sir, I understand sir," said Snorri. "But I think I'm having an appendicitis attack. I had my appendix removed, but it keeps growing back. Officer, please I have to go to urgent care immediately!"

Officer Weatherwax picked Snorri off the ground by his wrists and uncuffed him.

Then Officer Lowry uncuffed Chitchee.

"I don't want to fill out another incident report tonight," said Officer Weatherwax to Officer Lowry.

"Creative writing isn't your style?" asked Chitchee. "I can help you write it. I'm a writer."

"You think this is an episode of *Law & Order* or something?" asked Officer Lowry.

"No, but it could be," said Chitchee. "Would you guys be interested in collaborating on a TV script for *Law & Order*? Is *L. A Law* still on?"

"We don't collaborate," said Officer Weatherwax.

"So I've heard," said Chitchee.

The thumpers agreed to let the whole matter drop for the sake of Aloysius and for the sake of Viktor Martensen, who they had known longer than Aloysius. Snorri immediately felt good, having tested security for loopholes. Officer Lowry fetched a crowbar from the trunk, pried open the cash register, out sprang rubber bands, and magic money appeared. After Saami begged the thumpers for pliers to open the Phillips vodka bottle, the thumpers watched Saami twist the bottle open and winced when Saami swigged it, because they heard Saami's liver sop up the Phillipa vodka and slurp like a hungry loofah sponge.

The thumpers, radios squawking static voices, turned their spare tires and heavy hips toward the front door.

"Thank you so much officers, I'd give you a hug but I know you'd shoot me in the back seventy times!" said Chitchee. "But even the thumpers deserve love, right? I mean your suicide rates are sky high!"

Officer Lowry and Officer Weatherwax stood, hands on holsters, not reacting, looking like two blue eagles.

"Have you ever tried mindfulness?" asked Chitchee.

"Mindfulness!" said Officer Weatherwax. "You've got a big mouth."

"At least I don't go around torturing anarchists," said Chitchee with an innocent look on his face, "like it's a game show!"

Officer Weatherwax removed his family heirloom knuckle dusters to consider braining Chitchee.

Snorri tagged a post-it note for Melchizedek's "hold pile," observed by Melchizedek, who watched Snorri packing-tape the broken *You Are All Sanpaku* back together. Once satisfied that his book was a book, Melchizedek stilted out the front door with *You Are All Sanpaku*.

"Hey, thumpers!" said Chitchee, rubbing the back of his head. "What do you make of this? Let me show you something! This came in today! This could be big!"

The thumpers politely paged over the Family Photo Album spread-eagled on the maroon counter.

"It looks like an album of dated pics that show the same man raping passed-out young women in abandoned buildings," said Saami.

"Yeah and a dumpster diver brought it in with a bunch of boxes of books," chipped in Chitchee. "I think we have a case on our hands, gentlemen, of a serial rapist."

Melchizedek tender-footed into the store, said nothing, departed, walked back, and finally walked away, unable to remember what he wanted to say or do or feel or live for.

"Did I leave my book here? Oh, it's in my hand! And away we go! Vroooo-o-o-mmm!"

Snorri puzzled another look at the album but could not see from his angle. When Snorri took a stance for a closer look, he took purchase of the book's boards, and prompted a brief tug of war with the gendarmes, which he lost.

"This will go straight into the evidence locker tonight, and we'll bring it to the state attorney's office in the morning, thanks, you guys," said Officer Weatherwax. "Good job!"

"Hey wait," said Chitchee to the departing thumpers at the threshold. "Do you guys like old *Field and Streams*? We got a bunch in the basement you could just have, you know, for when you are sitting around on horseback in grocery store parking lots, waiting to punch out or falsify time cards or whatever. Whaddya say, a bunch of old *Field and Streams*? Do you remember Gadabout Gaddis?"

"Nope," said Officer Lowry.

"Let them go," said Saami to their backs, watching the thumpers drive off. "Why do you say such random things like that Chitchee? You're going to get us into trouble with the law someday. Be Minnesota nice for once!"

"You can't Minneapolize the police," said Chitchee, "they're not from around here. And YOU brought them here, what are you talking about? You're the one trotting down Lake Street like Curious George with a stolen cash register. It's not like I shouted 'fire' in a crowded theater!"

A giant cherry red, cherry red cherry red red red red truck with giant ladders and giant lights parked outside BookSmart like a Bristle Block fire engine. The lights and sirens blinded the entire store, deafening the mice in the walls.

Firemen in yellow helmets and yellow-banded black suits jumped off the fire truck.

Paramedics shook themselves out of a white box ambulance like a salt shaker.

Then the firemen, black and yellow rubber clad, ran in the front door in a flurry, blurry hurry.

"We got a call for a fire! Did you call 911?" barked out Fireman 1.

"Not us," said Chitchee. "But I did yell fire earlier! But that was for a burglary."

"So what do you shout for a fire? Burglary?" said Fireman 2, turning around and motioning the others with a wave-off: false alarm.

"No, I don't shout anything, that would be impolite," said Chitchee. "Wouldn't it?"

The firemen, in their black and yellow rubbers and yellow helmets, about-faced.

"WAIT!" Chitchee shouted. "We have the complete *Field and Streams* in our overstock. You guys can have them as a sort of consolation prize. Like on game shows when you lose. TELL YOUR BUDDIES!"

Bobblehead scrambled up the stairs. He looked around. Sausage Man minced out the back door into the alley.

"I can't find *The Massage Book*. I left it out last night," said Bobblehead.

"This book?" said Saami, producing *The Massage Book* from beneath the checkout counter.

Bobblehead's eyes widened like a pink-eyed rabbit pulled up from a high-crowned top hat. His lips twitched, and his nose hardened into a nasal erection.

"Yes!" he said, rubbing his nose and making slightly orgasmic groans. "Cocoa, cookie, bus!"

Staff had joked with Chitchee that Bobblehead jerked off with his nose—he played with it, made weird sounds with it, and exited BookSmart in a cold sweat having deflated it. Off hours, Bobblehead wore his blue windbreaker inside out, the word SECURITY backwards right to left, exposing his shoulders when he drew the pockets in around his stomach.

"Okay, Bobblehead," said Saami. "Don't take it into the bathroom."

"Cocoa," said Bobblehead, "cookie, bus."

"And there he goes with his promiscuous proboscis!" yelled Chitchee.

"All right, Chitchee, clean up this mess," said Snorri. "I'm going home."

"All right," said Chitchee, grabbing a corn broom with no intention of sweeping. "Have a beautiful night, Snorri! Saami, why would you risk running down Lake Street with a cash register for *Phillips* vodka?"

"Vodka!" cried Saami. "It's in my backpack!"

Saami remembered that Linda had placed a 1.75 liter of vodka in a brown bag in his backpack. He opened it and chugged it, gulp, gulp, gulp. He stopped shaking.

Chitchee tossed the corn broom at Saami, who caught the javelin throw dexterously with a javelin catch.

"Have you ever heard of self-medication, homeslice?" asked Saami. "Aloysius doesn't pay us enough, nupe! Not for all we have to deal with. Not for eight dollars an hour. Not for a perfect yam, not for another shot glass collection, or a rice farm called Krunk! Nupe. And certainly *not for all the loonies out there*!" said Saami, looking a little looney.

"What am I doing?" Saami asked the corn broom when he realized he was sweeping the floor.

Saami looked at the corn broom. It was a gruesome artifact from Tenochtitlan. He threw it to the floor.

"We close," shouted Saami with a wounded, non-human wail, "SOON! If you want to purchase a book, please check out your reading material NOW!"

He removed two ones from the open till. He hugged the register, and kissed it.

"One, two."

"Should I be doing something to help close, Saami?" asked Chitchee.

"Damn it!" said Saami, slamming his fists down on the counter. "Now I have to start over! Where was I?"

"You were on two," said Chitchee.

Saami looked at the till. The till looked at Saami. With one look, Saami knew the till could not be counted on.

"Okay, one till," said Saami. "I'm on a roll. Of one. I think I'm ready for two."

Over and over, unable to get the cash reckoning right, he needed another drink. The till never came out the same. First it was off by 20 dollars. Then it was 200. Each time he counted the till for the daily reckoning, the total increased by powers of ten. Flustered by the till, Saami himself did not come out the same Saami each time he counted.

"It's off by 2,000 dollars? I want my mother!" cried the little boy in a nursery rhyme gone wrong. "Nobody understands me! Nobody listens to me! Nobody ever asks me: 'How are you doing?'"

Chitchee grabbed him, shook him up, and looked in his bleary eyeballs, turgid and blue.

"Saami, buddy, you're my friend, and I love you," said Chitchee, crying dry tears. "I can't watch you like this, all reason spent, come on, get it together! I can't stand to see artists suffer!"

"What is your problem? Jesus, you're weird!" said Saami, shrugging off Chitchee's hug like an actor with Kapgas syndrome. Saami looked up and inside the register's cavity. "I think there is a mousey in the register. I think a mousey ate some of the twenties. A mousey. Do you have any cheese, Chitchee?"

"There's that blue cheese in the breakroom fridge," said Chitchee, sensing he could eat a little something after midnight.

"Blue?" said Saami. "That was Monterey Jack cheese a week ago. What is going on around here? It's like a Stephen King novel. . . there *is* a ghost in the book store, ghosts . . . that's what they do when you're not around. First they start misfiling your Stephen Kings under King Stephens and then they switch the colors of your goddamned cheeses on you! What a looney bin! Chitchee? Are we all going to end up in a looney bin?"

Saami welled up like one big tear about to drop a little tear.

Saami shoved the till back into the register and it jammed shut.

"Why did I do that?" mumbled Saami. "Me, heap big idiot!"

Chitchee read Aloysius's "Don't Buy These Books" list to pass the time while Saami continued to jam the till back and forth until Saami pulled the plug and dropped the cash register on the floor. The till jumped out of the cash register.

"Asshole!" said Saami. "What was I going to do? Wasn't I looking for something?"

Saami looked behind the corn broom in the corner for something he heard, while holding the till like an open box. He nudged the broom, turned, and then stumbled over the broom, falling face forward onto the floor, and landed on his knees and elbows.

"We are officially closed, Chitchee," said Saami, getting up and holding the till intact. "A mousey ate the money, the money in the tilly. Oh no, here comes a customer! Lock the door! Lock the door! The EDPs are coming! It's past midnight."

Chitchee heard something crash. Saami plugged in the cash register. Chitchee looked up at a leaping Saami. Saami had climbed over the counter with an Allen wrench in one hand.

Toby Pfeiffer, who lived in a nursing home on 31st and Lyndale, liked to swallow a few schooners of Hamm's at the Uptown Bar every night, cap them off by looking through the CDs at Cheapo Records, and pass out in a pool of his own urine—wherever he and it might land. A man of simple tastes you had to admit. Toby had turned the corner, walked straight into the locked BookSmart glass doors without looking up, bounced off the glass, and pratfell on the pavement.

"Ow, when did this get here?" asked Toby.

"You mean the Earth?" said Chitchee through the locked door. "It's been billions of years, Toby."

"Naw! You know what I mean!" said Toby, scratching the slight beard on his chin, which matched the slight scratch he gave to the top of his matched head.

"BookSmart has been at this location for five years," said Chitchee through the plate-glass. "If that is what you mean?"

"What is a Book Smart?" whined Toby.

"BookSmart is a book store," said Chitchee. "A *mart* for books. It's a pun!"

"Book-a-Whirl? What kind of pun is that? For a book store?" yelled Toby hurtfully.

He twisted and pushed down on his stained, fleece gym pants's crotch when he weebled to his feet.

"BookSmart, not Book-a-Whirl! We sell books!" said Chitchee.

"Not to me you don't!" said Toby, pulling on the handle and banging his head on the door over and over. "Let me in! I have to go to the little boy's room."

Round as a wrecking ball with a small lawn of well-clipped black hair on the top of his medically-shaved head that veered down to his eyes and joined there with his eyebrows, Toby never looked up. He never made eye contact even with himself in a mirror: he bounced off objects in his way and figured out what those objects were later in incremental moments of loneliness.

"*To-by?* What kind of name is that? Is that a pun on 'Toby or not Toby?'"

"What do you mean? That's a real name! Hey, didn't you used to be over *there?*" Toby asked, his voicebox squeaking like a rusty tricycle. "Was that either Orr Books or Not Orr Books? Or what book store is this?"

Toby looked at Lagoon & Hennepin where Cheapo Records and BookSmart once shared the same building—the old Schlammp's fur store. Toby scratched his unsheared beaver-haired neck, tugged at the hem of his over-size purple Minnesota Viking jersey (PETERSON on his shoulders), touched his dick, and grabbed for it like a snaking garden hose.

"Can I come in? I NEED A CAN!" screamed Toby.

"Okay," said Chitchee, searching for the Allen wrench.

"Hey! Where's the old furniture store? They keep moving everything around in Carousel Square! It's like a merry-go-round in a mega-mall!" cried out Toby from his tortured heart. "Geez, when they gonna stop moving everything around for no reason! There's no neighborhood! Where is everything *going*? MAKE IT STOP! How am I supposed to find my way home? THEY'RE GOING TO MOVE MY HOME BEFORE I CAN GET BACK TONIGHT!"

"The developments never stop, Toby," said Chitchee. "It's like the developers are trying to square the circle by approximating their idea of a neighborhood with no idea of a neighborhood. And then everyone forgets everything. Then they blame Derrida and post-modernism."

"The furniture store moved years ago, Toby," said Raven Ilmarinen.

Chitchee heard Raven's familiar voice behind Toby:

"Remember, there was a fire at the Stems and Seeds furniture store? They moved out to Woodbury, or Wisconsin, or somewhere out there in the boonies."

"Ooohhhhh," said Toby with a goose egg-and-dart-shaped mouth. "Post-mortemism, I don't like it. It sounds mean. I'll *go* next door!"

Toby, stunned, downcast, and devastated that post-mortem city planners had played hopscotch with him, dreideled down the block.

RAVEN ILMARINEN

Raven Ilmarinen importuned the glass doors jauntily with his short red curly hair and black eyes like two whole notes. He stood straight as a ridgepole and stroked his shovel-shaped red beard, which reached his chest. Dressed in black jeans, red doo rag and white kerchief (one for the head, one for the neck), a checked, untucked red plaid shirt, and Eddie Bauer boots with ratty cat's cradle lacing, Raven blinked at Saami. Saami reeled back from all the strange numbers when the numbers changed into spiders, snakes, and bats from a stock nightmare in the public domain. Saami pounded his head on the maroon counter and watched his own head fall off his neck and bounce across the redolent, white pine wood flooring.

"It's past closing time, Raven!" simpered Saami toward the door. "Go away, you old crow!"

"Can't you guys let me in? I have something for you! What's wrong, Saami?" yelled Raven apologetically. "Are you closed already? It's only closing time. There should be a few seconds left on the clock."

"Raven! Why are you always here at closing?" whimpered Saami, his eyes blinking and sometimes fully closed. "It's time to go *home*, we *close* at midnight, we don't *open* at midnight! After midnight, you're messin' with my time! Oh, I'll let him in."

Saami plucked the Allen wrench from his back pocket and gave the crash bar a twist. Chitchee moved to the crash bar and opened the door for Raven. Toby heard this and cannonballed back. Squeezing into the entrance, Toby attached Raven and himself at the hips like Chang and Eng. Toby wobbled past and ran for the bathroom, urine squirting down his running legs. Raven spied around suspiciously for suspicious cameras—in the ceiling, outside the door on utility poles, and possibly behind the bird calendar? Raven held on display a nugget of the same Blue Diesel Snorri smelled on Melusina and Kriemhilde. Chitchee's palm closed like a Venus flytrap around the nug. Raven looked in opposite directions on purpose to throw off any impending no-knock SWAT platoons.

"Chitch," asked Raven, cheerfully wide awake. "Are you still writing that science fiction thingamabob? How's it going?"

"No, it's not, no," said Chitchee. "I'm still getting through the divorce grieving period."

"Well, you better hurry up!" said Raven. "You've been framed all over town with wanted posters. Either the FBI or a FBI front is railroading you into taking the fall for one of their covert political operations from the Fusion center. That's the way they do things. If I were you, I would find a good cheap plastic surgeon, tuck in your eyes, get a big nose, gain some weight, get rid of your hijab, flee to Helsinki, and melt into the night like Sausage Man. I have a cousin there who can get you a job as a lifeguard for an underground swimming pool. Start a family there for cover. I'm telling you, this is good advice."

"I tried to start a family," said Chitchee. "Remember? It didn't work? Now I'm on the path of blame for life."

"What," said Raven, "what is LaDonna's face doing on all those wanted posters I see up and down Hennepin?"

"Some jilted, jealous beau brummel went berserk, same old bunch of bananas," said Chitchee.

"Sure," said Raven. "You should have never married her. I told you back then. That's why I objected to your wedding at the reception. You should have dumped her after her third DUI and first DUH. Are you still taking Arabic?"

"No," corrected Chitchee, "that was thirty years ago."

"It doesn't matter," said Raven, taking a pull off his brass one-hitter. "You're on a terrorism watch list obviously. Maybe just for taking Arabic at the U. Same with LaDonna. And you know all those language professors at the U. are CIA. The Russian, Chinese, and Iranian ones anyway. What did you see in her? She was using you, for what I don't know. Born again one year, and the next year the proverbial bomb-throwing Jain! Now you're being tracked to be chipped! It's a set-up to make both of you Manchurian candidates. Those fake wanted posters came out on the same day. Come on! Coincidences don't happen for no reason. For sure, why wouldn't they program an Arabic-speaking couple like you two? Then fly you undercover to Iraq or Iran? The CIA thinks they are so clever, but actually I see right through their false disguises and smiley faces. Take my advice! I had a prophetic dream that ISIS would change its name someday and they did within months!"

Raven drilled the pipe into the stash, smoked, and exhaled successively shrinking cumuli.

"You know Muslims are taking over the world," added Raven.

"And that will be the end of the Golden Gophers' football program, I know," said Chitchee, sucking on the one-hitter and handing it back. "Somebody else was saying that today."

"And you'll be able to get a job as an interpreter," said Raven. "Get a job as an interpreter at the United Nations. Work for the NSA! Work your way up to the Deep State and beyond to Wikileaks!"

"Translating from English to English for Muslims?" asked Chitchee.

"You should look into it. I'm telling you. This book store will never make it, but that's great you're working here now!" said Raven expansively. "Now I can come by after close and hang out with you guys all night long! Hey Saami, have you seen any books by David Icke teleport in? Or how about: *Why We Know the Ramans are Here* or *The YETI Are From SETI?* Can you look up some books for me on your ultra cool and groovy com-PUTER?"

A tap on the door reminded Chitchee of the prison code in *Darkness At Noon*, and outside stood a man made of cardboard, a two-dimensional man talking through the window:

"Do you have books on Flat Earth theory?" asked a monotone man with a claymation mouth.

"No," gulped Saami. "Fuck me running. We're closed!"

Saami started running in place, "We're closed! WE'RE FUCKING CLOSED!"

"What's wrong, Saami? Is it . . ." snickered Raven, smirking behind his red beard, "*irregularity?*"

Raven escorted Chitchee out of Saami's sight. Raven discreetly hand gestured the International Drinking Sign to Chitchee: hand above head tipping bottle into open gullet like a Nordic skier with a reindeer-skin flask. Raven walked the one hitter and dugout over to Saami, who silently smoked it like a baby nursing on an erect brown teat.

"Well, how have *you* been?" Chitchee asked Raven.

"Oh, depressed," said Raven, his aura going from saffron to ashes. "No one takes my advice! A musician friend of mine is missing. I know she didn't commit suicide."

"What?" asked Chitchee with a head cock.

"I think it was the thumpers."

"What? The thumpers killed her?"

"They're always going around killing musicians."

"What? Why?"

"They don't like us musicians. We're a threat. Especially attractive young girl musicians or strippers."

"Oh, brother!"

"They drug them, rape them, and throw them off the Hennepin Avenue Bridge. You don't believe me? Minneapolis thumpers going back to Stenvig are all corrupt—they get thousands and thousands of complaints and no consequences. You can get a bad cop with a hundred incidents piled against him."

"And then what?" asked Chitchee.

"And then he runs for office," said Raven, "and gets elected."

Chitchee recalled news about missing University of Minnesota students—a jilted sorority girl was dredged up downstream. The U. was that depressing, Chitchee knew firsthand. And then there was a young woman who was drunk and tried to swim across the Mississippi River and drowned. Another missing girl was last seen dancing at Ground Zero and was later found downstream with no explanation. The Mississippi River carried off so many missing women that you never heard about them later. The thumpers routinely altered the cause of death for the altered autopsy in the Hennepin County examiner's office, especially if the family requested silence.

Although everyone *did* hear about the distraught mother who threw her unwanted child off the Hennepin Avenue Bridge when the local news teams needed an arresting, lead-off story.

Saami calmed down wonderfully, turned off the lights, and set the alarm. He jaunted toward the front door (they had one minute). Chitchee reminded Saami that Toby was in the bathroom. Toby had passed out on the throne. Saami ran back and yelled through the bathroom door at Toby. Toby thought the entire 5th Precinct was on its way. He aborted his evacuation—pants around his ankles like a gunny sack. The burglar alarm sounded. Toby sprinted for his life in a gunny sack marathon. The alarm sounded again and again.

Saami sweat globules of vodka. The deactivation code was wrong. On the second try, he cracked the purple code and the alarm deactivated. Saami's affrighted white and exhausted flesh no longer trembled, but his heart zoomed around his rib cage like a long-horned bee.

Chitchee had forgotten to pay himself out the equivalent of 8 hours x $6.50 = $52.00 worth of books. He looked at the space needles of book towers, and he noticed a little white pamphlet underneath one—*the National Cash Register manual*! Chitchee, to prove himself to Aloysius, thought: if I apply a quick but decisive force, eliminating as much as possible the μ of friction, I'll get the manual. As soon as Chitchee yanked the pamphlet stock footage re-reeled through his mind: Zanclean floods, volcanoes, avalanches, himself buried in books, trapped for months, drawing lots like Josephus with survivors, reduced to cannibalism with three guys, kuru, death, pink pools of vomited brains, and teeth-marks on pocked bones everywhere.

A book Watts tower crashed over Saami, flabbergasted as to how an earthquake could have reached Minnesota. Saami staggered out of the store and joined Chitchee, Raven, and Toby, gathering their lost wits on the sidewalk as they watched a few, last books topple from their perches.

"I got the NCR register manual anyway," said Chitchee. "Saami."

"What manual? I don't know what Aloysius was thinking," said Saami. "There's no manual. I got that register at a rummage sale at Minnehaha Academy. What did *you* get?"

"*Pull My Daisy?*" Chitchee read aloud, shaking his head at the pamphlet. "Huh?"

"We've been looking for that forever!" said Saami.

Pull My Daisy was a screenplay by Jack Kerouac and Robert Frank, first edition, and this one was inscribed to Neal Casady by Kerouac, Frank, and Ginsberg.

"It's probably worth more," said Saami, "now that it's been missing for so long."

"What if it had been lost forever?" asked Chitchee, thirsting for stores of book store knowledge.

"Then it would be priceless," said Saami.

Sirens sang from the 5th Precinct's direction, their distant moans rising to shrieks. Since the Boss Man would hear about this and Saami would have to answer to the Boss Man for the alarm the next day, he ran down to the Uptown Bar and treated himself to a night cap for another job not only well done, but burned to a crisp too! Raven and Toby quick-stepped homeward conspicuously zigzagging, Toby running into Raven, Raven ignoring Toby, Raven ditching Toby, and Raven running into Carousel Square and popping out the back . . . into Toby. Chitchee read:

MPG PROPERTY MANAGEMENT COMPANY
MPG APARTMENTS VIRTUAL TOURS BY APPT.
EVERY NEW DAY IS HISTORY IN THE MAKING
RESTRICTIONS APPLY YOU WILL LOVE US

On Chitchee's way to the Rainbow Grocery store on Lake Street, Chitchee read another billboard on the Cheapo Records front wall—where Hawk Eye had hunkered under it.

FOR LEASE BY MARTENSEN PEOPLES GROUP
FOR RENT RETAIL RESTAURANT SPACE
BUILT BY CONTRACTORS WE BUILD DREAMS
GREAT LOCATION BY OUR OTHER LOCATIONS

A thousand-yard stare beamed across Lake Street. Back up against the wall, Hawk Eye, makeshift crummy corrugated cardboard sign of scrawls on his lap, the wind blowing, nodded off.

Vietnam Purple Heart Vet Needs $$$ for Room

Chitchee gave Hawk Eye his pocket change.

"God bless you, sir," said Hawk Eye.

"Hawk Eye!" said Chitchee. "Are you going to spend the night out here? You'll get mugged! How can Minneapolis allow a Vietnam War veteran to go homeless? Don't veterans get benefits? Don't you have a family? Doesn't everybody have a "phantom family" as a man without an arm or leg has his phantom limbs? Do you need a place to stay for the night? You can sleep on the floor in my kitchen. There's room. I'll be your family."

Hawk Eye said no. He slept *next* to Lake Calhoun. Hawk Eye was as adamant on that as if he slept *with* Lake Calhoun, so Chitchee backed off and asked Hawk Eye about the winter. Answer: Hawk Eye slept in the Porta Potty by the beach on the north side by Calhoun Beach Club. Chitchee redoubled his offer:

"We're practically classmates of a different class from the same and different high school."

"Okay, I'll go with you," said Hawk Eye. "But I owe you a favor, because you're a good guy. Anybody gives you a hard time. Tell me. I'll come running. My vision is 20/10 and I almost went to the Olympics for trapshooting, but that was the year President Carter pulled us out of the Olympics to protest the Soviet invasion of Afghanistan."

"Jesus, Mary, and Joseph," said Chitchee, lifting Hawk Eye off the ground.

They picked up milk, bread, peanut butter, and Old Dutch tortilla chips at Rainbow Grocery store, and then they stuffed themselves into Chitchee's stuffed studio and stuffed themselves. A little kitchenette floor space for Hawk Eye was the back forty. Hawk Eye repeated things he had already said, making Chitchee feel a bit unremarkable, but that was okay because he was unremarkable. Three purple hearts, a silver star, and a Navy cross, blah, blah, blah. Hawk Eye rambled about all the countries he had been to and not as a tourist, but in another capacity as what? As CIA? Picking up languages and gathering information. He demanded Chitchee raise his right hand and swear secrecy to never reveal what state secret he was going to reveal.

"Here," he said, "this is to prove I served. DD214."

Right there on the shredded government form Chitchee had already seen.

"I believe you man," said Chitchee. "Don't you have veterans' benefits?"

"I'm not going to no more fucking government agencies for any more motherkillin' favors from Uncle Sam!"

"So I suppose you were drafted?" asked Chitchee.

"I *had* to go to Vietnam," said Hawk Eye.

"You wanted to see the beautiful sand beaches and picturesque redoubts?"

"I lost a bet," said Hawk Eye.

"Hey, thank you for putting your life on the front line for me, while I was busy chasing squirrels up oak trees. Thanks, because you lost a bet!"

"And I lost my girlfriend," said Hawk Eye, one eye on the past (car-dating A & W car hops, Chuck Berry on the AM, and driving the automobile toward the DQ for a dipped cone). He continued, "I lost her in a snowmobile race down Water Street in Excelsior. Jenny Van Roo was the god damndest cutest girl in Minnetonka and the World. And all the boys fought to take her bra off. God, the fun I had when I was young! I had the bastard beat, but when I looked back, something hit me in the face. I lost control and fell off the snowmobile. I couldn't figure why until much later I realized—an iceball ambush. I had been set up by The Groover. Grandma Groovy in cahoots with his buddies, the shit-assed bastards."

"Nobody said anything? Not even the cutest girl in Minnetonka and the World?" asked Chitchee.

"No," said Hawk Eye, squinting a thousand yards through the apartment walls into the cold past. And then he resumed slowly, "because I had a lot of scores to settle. I was a scrappy fighter in high school and most of those guys wanted me out of the picture, because I could whup 'em. And Jenny went along with whatever wind blew her breeze. I enlisted the next day. For her."

"That is such a sad story, Hawk Eye," said Chitchee. "So that was it, the last goodbye, and you never saw the love of your life, your high school sweetheart Jenny O, again?"

"Oh, I saw her again," said Hawk Eye. "I married her."

They smoked some old weed in a crusty, glass pipe and arranged their sleeping spaces on the floor so that they didn't actually share the same North-South orientation. Then Chitchee took a prescription Ambien, saw a mouse, and conked out. Hawk Eye let himself out in the early morning and walked back dejectedly head down and mouth open to his favorite spot for panhandling by Club Miami.

"Did we lock Bobblehead in the book store?" thought Chitchee when he awoke on his floor the next day.

A FIRE HAZARD IN
CHITCHEE'S APARTMENT

Chitchee had sandbagged the walls of his garden level studio at 2825 Fremont Avenue South with a Maginot Line of dictionaries, encyclopedias, and reference books. He had to fortify his walls—shelled by the neighbors' unneighborly loud parties. The loud fire doors slammed like loud gates from an ironclad hell. With the usual thieves, robbers, and burglars in the neighborhood, he kept his windows locked and blinds drawn. In America, crime is always around the corner, next door, or on TV. He couldn't move out because he couldn't move his books; he couldn't move his books because there were too many books to move. Trapped by his own books, he suffered from book paralysis. He had dug his own pharaonic tomb and gilded his own grave, the visible shelves displayed thus: *A Study of History, The Decline of the West, The Decline and Fall of the Roman Empire, Civilization and Capitalism, The Histories, The Peloponnesian War, The Rise of the Roman Empire, The Jewish War, The History of Rome, The Art of War, The Histories by Tacitus, The Lives of Plutarch, The Alexiad, The New Science, The Prince, The Autobiography of Benvenuto Cellini, The Civilization of the Renaissance in Italy, The Spirit of Laws, The Wealth of Nations, Democracy in America, Capital, Strategy, The Gulag Archipelago,* and *The Story of Civilization.*

He needed more than Sunzi or Basil Liddell Hart to strategize his defenses against the attack of the neighbors, much less could he *by indirections find directions out* and pull off a surprise attack to make the great generals weep with envy. Now that his marriage had failed, he was broke, if not broken. If attacked all he could do was warn the other squirrels.

"Hey, I can't find my Sima Qian's *Records of the Grand Historian*! Hey! Whatever happened to my Ibn Khaldun's *Muqaddima,*" said Chitchee, going through his boxes. "Somebody stole those? Who? Dan the Maintenance Man?"

Such a plethora and plenum of books he lost track of plenty of them in the past. He bought a book, read it, and shelved it next to the copy he forgot he had bought. Then he would forget where those books were. He would ransack his Jack-in-the-Box, box-shaped studio with its double book-shelves, bags of books, and plank shelves built of books. He'd find it mis-boxed inside a handled, file-type cardboard box he had color-coded by subject matter. Green, books on nature, music, relationships, and cooking. Red, books on war, poetry, humor, and sex. Blue, books on physics, memoirs, Buddhism, and Shakespeare.

He sighed and fell back to sleep on the floor in the front room (the only room). A bed took up too much footage and shelvage. So did actual furniture. "Furniture belongs in a furniture store where it can be with the other furniture," he announced to Dan the Maintenance Man.

Chitchee dwelt by the old railroad and trolley tracks. At night, he heard trails from old ghost trains at night—no, actually it was the roar of alcoholic college students on rooftop bars resounding over the neighborhood that filled the arenas of his ears like the Roman Colosseum. Here and there older factories remained, but the ever-present future had razed the past for an evanescent Uptown of fly-by-night bars attracting fly-by-night co-eds. Signposts marked Minneapolis's buried past like quack grass. An old skating rink from the 1930s was supplanted by the Rainbow Grocery store, next door to an old greeting card factory called Buzza's, and that was an MPG building, slated for unaffordable, gentrified lofts to attract the fly-by-nights with the collegiate perk of not having to crawl far for a bar. Every summer cardboard developments and giant blocks of housing assembled themselves like von Neumann machines. Piledrivers bore down to the very foundations of his eardrums. Excavators hovered over bare lots. Then up shot a condo not even a termite developer could be proud of. With the charm and personality of stacks of old boxes from Domino's Pizza, the developers themselves duplicated their boring selves through this repetition. The repetition created the air of a simulacrum of repetition.

At the heart of the Uptown Minneapolis neighborhood pulsed Carousel Square, a 1980s three-story structure with gothic windows niched like a Gorey-designed columbarium. Arching dark entrances were crowned with a sunburst of advertising that radiated an ad for Famous Dave's Ribs.

MPG BOUTIQUE APARTMENTS WITH SOUL
THE BEST PLACE POSSIBLE TO CALL HOME
UPTOWN, MIDTOWN, DOWNTOWN NEARBY
PROFESSIONALLY MANAGED TAKE A TOUR!

Uptown jumbled together different styles like jelly beans—Moderne, Classical, Renaissance, Islamic, Romanesque, Bauhaus, and Mission. The old Milwaukee road ran East-West straight through the neighborhoods. Sometimes coyotes wandered up the old railroad corridor and howled at the residential Queen Annes with their wild grapevined verandahs, rose-bunched pergolas, and flower-coated yards leafed out with lilacs in late April. White-tailed deer used to stray through the red maples around Lake Calhoun, surprising morning joggers, but recently taller and rent-higher apartments reached the upper canopy, overshadowing the lanes, back alleys, and garages.

Chitchee woke up looking like a witch doctor in a village of ants, because that morning revealed to Chitchee a dawn of a hundred ants. They were at a picnic Chitchee had created from a bag of Old Dutch tortilla chips eaten when he was half-asleep. Chitchee's body itself felt like a chip, stiff, and stale. In the middle of the night he dumped the bag of Old Dutch tortilla chips upside down on the floor and on himself sprawled on his sleeping bag. There were so many ants in an anthill on top of the Old Dutch tortilla chips the ants had already formed a colony and elected a governor.

"Landlord!" heard Chitchee.

The heart-shaped brass knocker knocked on his door three-and-a-half knuckle knocks.

Looking through his peephole, Chitchee absorbed twin amoebas looking back at his disembodied eye-ball looking at them. One amoeba was Gloria Skogentaub.

"Could you come back in ten minutes?" begged Chitchee. "Don't come in, you might see my sausage."

Chitchee seized the green Eureka electric broom with the motorized brush roll (and he loved motorized brush rolls). Planner Woman is my landlady? Since when? I'm doomed! Vacuum cleaners had a soothing effect on his live-wired nerves, so he often vacuumed for no reason at all. He did not abhor a vacuum cleaner, especially the one he bought at Target with LaDonna. Their buying a Eureka electric broom bettered playing beach ball on a trampoline. The Eureka needed a friend so they brought home a Dyson vacuum cleaner they found by a dumpster. Then they vacuumed together in perfect fifths.

Chitchee grabbed the bag of Old Dutch tortilla chips to finish off the last of the chipped chips for breakfast, crumbs flying everywhere again. He re-vacuumed. Chitchee prepared a half pot of Hills Brothers coffee—half pot because he had filled the Fresh Cup filter too full and the basket-hole clogged. Coffee overflowed the basket. Grounds floated in the brew. It tasted wonderful. Chitchee celebrated his cup of coffee with half a Carousel cigarette (to get himself going) rediscovered in his glass ashtray leftovers.

Too pooped to pop, Chitchee lay back on his sleeping bag, his body sprawled like an ink stain. He scooped up a *Discover* magazine off the floor and perused an article that said depression could be lifted by a very blue light. How blue can you get? Cobalt blue pigment in a Giotto sky? He tried to get out of bed again, but it was a no go . . . ugh . . . blech . . . yuck . . . coffee . . . mud . . . email . . . mail . . . people . . . ugh . . . blech . . . phone . . . nothing . . . bladder . . . coffee . . . sky . . . yuck . . . Gloria . . . not . . . void . . . cancel . . . blank . . . up . . . walk . . . go . . . may I help you . . . Dan . . . people . . . nothing . . . what was the point of this juggernaut . . . rent . . . noise . . . no . . . not a thing . . . what's the point . . . and what if there isn't one? . . . make one up?

Something beeped Chitchee like a sonalert. He looked out the window of his garden level studio and saw a very gray light. He looked at the stubble of rooftops and the rows of white, gray, and black cars on Fremont Avenue. The lawn squad of the Delta Force had gathered outside his window carrying air bazookas backed up by wide-track lawnmowers engaged in a platoon-sized firefight with a few dead leaves creating a raging inferno on a tiny manicured lawn. The soldiers fired away with Sears leaf blowers. A Mexican American grandfather on a sit-down John Deere lawn mower a Stoic like Seneca stared ahead, protective ear muffs on. Chitchee considered complaining to Gloria about all that noise at 11:59 in the morning, but he had already complained about Washington Spelz (so his #106 mailbox read) and his crack gang broadcasting enormous ear-splitting beats before and after hours. And even louder than a meteor shower were Towey Levins (read off from his #110 mailbox) and his coke gang of fraternity brother-bro-bruh brouhahas in feed caps, baggy shorts, and X-tra large jerseys on the opposite side shouting grunts until four in the morning about their creatine muscles, tattooed with Greek letters, gaudy flames, fiery pick-up trucks, snake pits of fire, golf clubs on fire, and demons from hot sauce bottles.

The Delta Force broke off their engagement, moving on for corn husk-wrapped tamales under an idyllic catalpa tree.

From his hole in the ground, Chitchee looked up at the sky, which was mottled like a smoked kielbasa. There was no very blue light, there was no very cobalt blue sky. It was always a very gray Minneapolis sky like the giant brain case of a skink. Chitchee had gotten up too early to be awake, so he lurched around for a candy bar then hotfooted it back to "bed," back to a delicious sleep and the tenderness of his dreams, hoping to wake up happier on the second try.

High-pitched beeping of F#s began . . . oh no, not another Amber Alert at the antipodes. Where's the LG Optimus? He checked it for nothing. Was he getting Facebook-spammed by Facebook text girls who had no profiles, no friends, and five photos each one the same? Beep, beep. Had he been microwaving oatmeal? A garbage truck on 28th Street was backing up like a sick, iron rhinoceros? A car alarm was howling "Banzai!" on Girard? His dusty Sony CFS-204 ghetto blaster was gasping in an electronic death rattle? Was it his hacked Dell Inspiron 3's distress signal before it exploded into zeta bits? An NSA drone thumb drive? A fire alarm in an unmarked Blackhawk whose cockpit burst into flames over Fremont Terrace Apartments?

He squinted through his broken-screened window and saw a black-capped chickadee. He couldn't recognize bird songs anymore. He had lost touch with nature. How urbanly depressing. He lost his sense of taste, his ability to dance, and his capacity for bliss. He verged on a crying fit.

His LG Optimus ring-toned. He picked up, still sweating from the black-capped chickadee.

"Awwkkkkghghgh?" asked Aloysius.

"Hello?" asked Chitchee. "Aloysius?"

His apartment door knocker tippy-tapped three times.

"Maintenance!"

"Saami hasn't shown up for his shift," said Aloysius. "He's sick I guess. And he forgot to lock the front door. So when I got here, there were already customers in the store browsing. It's okay, because Torg was here to guard the store."

Tap, tap, tap.

"Maintenance!"

"So I was wondering, can you come in early?" asked Aloysius.

"Come in!" yelled Chitchee.

"Yes, come in. If you're busy sleeping," said Aloysius shocked, "I can get Torg to stand here all day but—"

"Come in?" asked Dan the Maintenance Man.

"Yes! Come in!" said Chitchee.

"Okay that's great buddy," said Aloysius. "See you in a bit."

"As soon as I get some clean socks!" said Chitchee too late.

The key turned in the lock. The door opened and shut respectfully.

Chitchee like a stage magician threw open his door to #108 and saw Dan (something wrong with his nose—Band-Aid taped over it) and the property manager Gloria, like a bewitched and mediocre 1960s talk show host, dressed in a dated, glittering, nouveau riche style seen in *Vogues*, terraced on glass coffee tables decades ago.

"Come in?" asked Gloria.

"Sure! I haven't done laundry in months, so I stink," said Chitchee.

Gloria marched in, wrist on hips, her hair blazing from a sharp dyed-black bun.

Saami had loused up any cordial relationship with Gloria Chitchee might have enjoyed after Saami's infamously misquoted "hippopotamus" remark.

"You know, Gloria," said Chitchee, "even if Saami *did* say hippopotamus, hippos aren't really fat to other hippos. Do you know what I mean? Moomins love Moomins! And hippos abound because of our overuse of antibiotics. But I'm really sorry about my colleague's outrageous *aperçu*. Give us a hug and that will make it all better. Everybody needs a body to hug. It's what makes us human."

Gloria blocked Chitchee like an offensive tackle with her elbows out and teeth locked as Dan the Maintenance Man walked straight for Chitchee's bathroom. Since he had a bandaged nose, maybe he went to check the dressing. He stepped back out and told Gloria that Chitchee's bathroom was unaffected by the ongoing local plumbing disasters. In a silence that created its own hostility, Gloria scowled at Chitchee's books, pinned her eyes to each spine, and ticked her tongue nervously: *The Upanishads, The Analects, The Tao Te Ching, The Republic, The Ethics, The Four Gospels, The Crest Jewel of Discrimination, The Fundamental Wisdom of the Middle Way, The City of God, The Sixth Platform Sutra of Huineng, Summa Theologica, The Mathnawi, The Hundred Thousand Songs of Milarepa, The Divine Comedy, The Essays of Montaigne, Discourse on Method, Pensées, A Treatise on Human Nature, Critique of Pure Reason, Parerga and Paralipomena, The Phenomenology of Mind, Either/Or, Beyond Good and Evil, Human Knowledge, Philosophical Investigations, Mysterium Coniunctionis, The Masks of God.*

"Weird religious stuff," she said. "Are you in a cult?"

"I've always had an affinity for Zoroastrianism," said Chitchee.

"Sauro-astrianism? It sounds familiar. I don't care if you worship at the toes of pygmies, this is a fire hazard," said Gloria. "If you don't get these books off the floor, I'll call the fire marshal!"

"To go back and unpack your question as regards cults, religions are cults with forty divisions."

"You're stalling!" said Gloria, swallowing her plastic Halloween smile and frowning stiffly as if a brooch unclasped and jabbed her breast.

"I've never been called Stalin before!" said Chitchee. "Rand-om!"

Side to side Gloria's head oscillated like that of a pitcher negating his catcher's signs. And yet this motion did not change one plastic hair of her hair-do, shellacked with so much Aqua-Net she must have bought stock in it.

"All these strange books have to get off the floor by the end of the week," said Gloria. "What's this?"

Gloria had focused on the half-open linen closet. She high-heeled over to the linen closet and thrust aside the folding door. Her jaw dropped automatically, and she kept it dropped willingly when she saw and oversaw: *The Notebooks of Leonardo da Vinci, The Origin of Species, On Growth and Form, General Chemistry, The Principle of Relativity, Sociobiology, Critical Path, A History of Western Music, The Art of Color, The Book about Books, A History of English Prosody,* shelf after shelf of science textbooks, Dover books on mathematics, and Schaum's Outlines on every branch of mathematics ever invented, discovered, or revealed.

Dan peeked under the kitchen sink and shuddered: *The Odyssey, The Odes of Pindar, Sophocles's Plays, Metamorphoses, Dialogues by Lucian, The Arabian Nights translated by Richard Burton, The Canterbury Tales, The Tale of Genji, Gargantua and Pantagruel, Don Quixote, Orlando Furioso, Shakespeare's Plays, The Anatomy of Melancholy, Journey to the West, Strange Stories from a Chinese Studio, Moliere's Plays, Tom Jones.*

"Gloria," said Dan, opening all the kitchen cupboards, and unable to cope with the sight of the inhumanity of Chitchee's abusing a garden-level studio with such recklessness. "Get a load of this."

The kitchen cupboards bulged: *Gulliver's Travels, The Life of Johnson, Candide, Tristram Shandy, Faust I & II, The Story of the Stone, The Red and the Black, Hölderlin's Poems and Plays, Old Goriot, Les Misérables, Flowers of Evil, A Season in Hell, Moby Dick, Great Expectations, The Possessed, The Brothers Karamazov, Bouvard and Pecuchet, The Stories by Maupassant, War and Peace, The Stories by Chekhov, Ibsen's Plays, Strindberg's Plays, Man and Superman, The Golden Bowl, The Journals of Gide, In Search of Lost Time, Ulysses, The Castle, Good Soldier Švejk, The Man Without Qualities, The Sleepwalkers, finnegans wake, The Trilogy, The Stories of Borges, The Recognitions, Gravity's Rainbow, Infinite Jest.*

"And you don't have a TV? O-k-k-k-ay-ay," said Gloria, disgusted. "This is called 'hoarding.'"

"Too many books I know . . . I guess if they reach a critical mass," said Chitchee, "a chain reaction will result, incinerating us all into radioactive dust. Of course that's the power of magical thinking. Gloria! You have to read *The Making of the Atomic Bomb* by Richard Rhodes. Dan, you too! I have a second copy somewhere—but you'll have to buy it yourself with your pin money. I don't like to lend out my books without a written contract. You know of course what Samuel Johnson said about lending books—"

"Look, Chitchee," interrupted Dan, "couldn't you put up *bookcase-wallpaper* instead?"

Chitchee heard Samuel Johnson talking. Aloysius had forgotten to hang up the phone, so Chitchee, Gloria, and Dan clearly heard Aloysius's private thoughts aloud:

"Fuck! Where did I put the fucking rent? Where is the money? If I don't have the rent, Viktor said he'd cut my nuts off. I can't remember anything anymore! What happened yesterday? Oh yeah, that *bitch* Gloria wanted a planner and—"

"—Aloysius! Shut the fuck up! Hang up the phone! Aloysius! You're going to run out of battery charge!" yelled Chitchee.

Dan the Maintenance Man maintained a mountainous silence, making a huge production out of blocking his arms like a mountain pass.

"Tell me, Gloria, are you disgusted by life itself like Sartre's Roquentin?" asked Chitchee with sincerely large eyes. "Is that why we are here?"

Resigned to a long day, Dan followed his insulted, crabbed boss out the door when she turned on her Gucci high heels and pumped toward the higher moral ground in her MPG office.

"Well, I guess you can't really call yourself a true bookworm until you've been turfed out as a fire hazard!" said Chitchee down the hall after them. "Thanks, you guys! I can't wait to introduce you to Leo Szilard!"

"It always helps to bring humor into the situation," continued Chitchee, chuckling aloud to himself. "If a used *The Making of the Atomic Bomb* comes into the store, I'll buy it for Gloria and Dan and gift wrap it with some used gift wrap and they can hotbox it." Aloysius hung up the phone.

Chitchee hopped on his Huffy mountain bike and pedaled to Treasures Await for used, clean socks.

TREASURES AWAIT YOU AT LYNDALE AND FRANKLIN

Musty, dusty, rusty, fusty, and crusty Treasures Await thrift store had dodged the wrecking balls of developers, bankers, council members, and the city's usual enemies—thank God, thought Chitchee because most everything Chitchee wore had trickled through that dear dilapidated, dollhouse of donations. After his divorce, Chitchee no longer styled himself stylish. His bluntly bland, dumbed-down shopping list consisted of blue or black jeans: $5.00. Long sleeved or T-shirts: $3.00. Athletic socks ankle high: 25 cents/pair. Worn running shoes: $2.00. Winter accessories: two pair gloves, three knitted wool caps, and four mad long scarves: less than $10 combined. When Chitchee bought clothes he thought: How would this look on me at a food shelf? What about a catwalk for the apocalypse? Are jeans appropriate for Laurie Garrett's *The Coming Plague*? He wanted to look inconspicuous as hell if all hell broke loose. Would contact lenses be okay if Nightmarica's anti-intellectuals sparked off a second Killing Field and massacred all the University professors at the State Fairgrounds?

Melusina, Kriemhilde and the other senior citizen volunteers skippered a slow boat at Treasures Await. It was a haunted, roadside museum off off Route 66. The square, brick building at Lyndale & Franklin itself existed as a half-remembered radioactive memory decaying in half-lives. Every time Chitchee walked into Treasures Await, time slowed. Then it elongated in slow-motion backwards. It was like Z-folding, twisting magnetic tape aborting GPS programs. Chitchee had a deja vu feeling from the last time he walked into the store with a deja vu feeling, and he waved to Melusina and Kriemhilde, who themselves exhibited an eerie, unreal feeling and looked at each other saying: "He looks familiar! Are we dreaming this? Who is he? Is he us? Or are we all not ourselves? No, it's the guy with the acorns!"

"Hello, you wonderful ladies," said Chitchee, dispelling the phantoms with a broad smile. "Is there a sale on pine wood coffins today? It always helps to bring a sense of humor to awkward social situations like this one!"

Chitchee plowed ahead straight to the books, the steel gondola racks displaying stacks of plates, cups, kitchenware, appliances of the most outlandish variety, and ingenious combinations: toaster/radios, telephone/hairdryers, printer/ovens, suitcase/bar/mousetraps, and no pine wood coffins. What was he going to buy here? He forgot.

Shabby, drabby, crabby, flabby, blabby books! Chitchee loved churchy, effete, out-dated, and all-too human and all-too animal books; also books that had no purpose, use, or hope. You found millions of them at Goodwills, Salvation Armys, and St. Vincents. Chitchee inferred the average age of the thrift store employees from the books they set on wire-stands: Herman Wouk, Robert Ruark, Irving Wallace, Ernest K. Gann—the Book-of-the-Month club relics lovingly alphabetized by precious-as-their-pearls mothers of the Church of Luther. These lovable ladies in their cotton floral print dresses religiously manicured their Caldwell, Costain, Cozzens, and Cronin . . . inevitably ending with Frank Yerby (*The Foxes of Yarrow*). When Frank Yerby had his own entire section, Chitchee's skin crawled, his flesh crept, and he writhed like a snake, knowing he was in the Eisenhower administration. Lately, to catch up to the Internet, Treasures Await had gone from the old school half-the-cover-price pricing system to a more global paradigm of pricing-to-the-world-market on the Amazon Stock Exchange. Chitchee bemoaned this progress. Knowledge should be getting cheaper according to Adam Smith and R. Buckminster Fuller (in his book *The Grunch*).

Chitchee scooped through the book section and scoped out potential competition from local book dealers, scouts, and Internet scavengers.

Dagny Knutsen, with her back turned, perused titles a little too slowly to be a buyer of significance. Real buyers had a methodical nervous aura and nervous hands. They browsed in straight lines without browsing. On the display stands: *Reader's Digest Guide to Breakfast*: $6. *Time-Life: The Photographer's Tools*: $10. *Napoleon* by Emil Ludwig, with a broken cover: $4. A biography of Kitty Carlisle: $5. Paperbacks used to be four for a dollar. But overnight, every dog-eared mule of a book was revalorized into a virtual show dog of a collectible. On the shelves since the Stone Age, many of the books could have been bronzed and sold as commemorative sets. Ten-year old travel books to countries that no longer existed were "classics," complete with rated hotels that had burned down, maps of streets that had moved during earthquakes, and landmarks that had been eradicated by revolutions. James Michener's *Hawaii* was displayed like a Byzantine Madonna and Child behind glass. *Hawaii* held their pride of place—though this hardbound, dust-jacketed behemoth had frays, rips, and small tears; and its paper was ugly and thick as crepe de chine. Yet compared to this much loved book, most of the other books looked like bums with missing teeth in a soup-line that itself looked like missing teeth. *Hawaii* was yours for the low, low-down price of seven dollars and fifty cents, friends!

Once upon a time, Americans believed that education was its own reward and so Chitchee time-travelled to the 1950s' Book-of-the-Month Club Era when half a loaf of Wonderbread was better than none and the middle class felt obligated to read books like Will Durant's *The Story of Civilization* and the Great Books series of Hutchins and Adler. Bennett Cerf, the Glass family on *The Quiz Bowl Kids*, and the huge, informationally rich BOMC sagas oriented suburbia toward the global American Century, because the United States was a neophyte civilization thrust into alpha dominance, and its beta citizenry thought Malaysia was something that could be treated with the Milk of Magnesia.

Chitchee espied a hardcover *Duino Elegies* by Rainer Maria Rilke lying on the floor, mint condition, "50 cents." He looked at the back of Dagny Knutsen, who was looking at the bookshelves. She grew younger all of a sudden when she actually moved. To be able to move—that's always a good sign. It symbolized movement.

"Is this your Rilke?" asked Chitchee. "Who doesn't love Rilke? *Who—if I called out*—doesn't love Rilke?"

"No," said Dagny petulantly.

She did not turn around—not wanting to be addressed, grabbed, knifed, and dismembered that day.

"Excuse me, is that your Robert Bly book on the couch?" asked Chitchee.

Chitchee pointed to a copy of Robert Bly's *The Man in the Black Coat Turns* on the used, plastic-covered, ruffle-skirted couch for sale. Dagny glanced at her interlocutor in the murky cathedral beams of the religiously moldy light and stale air of the secondhand store's wooden mallards, pewter plates on ten-ton hutches, and gold-lipped tea cups on dining room tables—set for bereaved Victorians eager to communicate with anyone who can speak through ectoplasm.

"Hell, no!" was Dagny's comeback.

"Hell no?" asked Chitchee. "But Bly's a great poet, isn't he? I'd like to meet him someday! The Minnesota Maybe Mandelstam! Why 'hell no'? Why not the milder 'heavens no'? Why such anger? That's a sign of imbalance."

Dagny Knutsen, in a seriously low husky voice, informed Chitchee she had heard from her best friend, Astrid Eskola, how Minnesota's Poet Laureate had gone to Lunds grocery store in Uptown last winter, caused a scene in the bakery section, and humiliated his wife at the bakery counter where Astrid waited on and served him reluctantly.

"Everybody gets hot under the collar," said Chitchee. "It's a sign of *projection*! That's where your shadow lies, according to Jung."

Chitchee fingered the books on the display stands above the bookcases. Euphoric and feeling sweet, he nonchalantly penciled in new prices in the right hand corners of the books for sale. *Napoleon:* $40; the mass market biography of Kitty Carlisle: $55; the *Time-Life: The Photographer's Tools:* $210; and James Michener's *Hawaii* a whopping Sotheby's: $7,500.00. He also inscribed *Hawaii's* frontispiece: *For Treasures Await, See You in Hawaii! Love, Jimbo.* He reset *Hawaii* on its bookstand on top of the bookcase facing Dagny.

"You should stop by BookSmart, I work there, Lake & Hennepin, if you want to find a good book," Chitchee said. "We have a better selection than these bench-sitters. I can hook you up!"

Which wasn't completely true—because it wasn't true at all. But he could offer to buy Dagny a book with his own money and she was sure to appreciate the gift of a book she had never heard of from a complete stranger.

"Yeah, if I'm extremely depressed but not so depressed that I can't get out the door," said Dagny, trying to sound more depressed than usual.

"I'm always depressed too," said Chitchee, "but I don't let that stand in the way of my getting out the door and getting more depressed."

Chitchee bombarded Dagny with questions about Robert Bly. What was he wearing? What time was it? What did he order? Where was Astrid? Wasn't Neal working? You mean it was last winter? Any other witnesses? Humiliated her? A tantrum? Maybe Astrid is a thin-skinned snowflake and she was having organ failure and she gets delirious when serving genius? After all, wasn't Robert Bly Iron Johning around because he *is* THE Iron John? Who am I compared with a man whose first name is "Iron?"

Chitchee remembered he had to work.

"What am I doing here? Looking for a soldering iron? I forgot what I was going to buy . . . so where do you work?" Chitchee asked Dagny.

"I don't want to say," said Dagny.

"It's not as if I'll go to your workplace and ask you out for coffee," declared Chitchee, shaking his head that she automatically assumed that all men aggressively sought a woman's company for coffee all the time. "Besides, I can do all that right here. Well, do you want to go out for coffee?"

Chitchee approached Dagny to give her a hug. She pushed him away like a corpse and touched the pepper spray in her handbag.

"But I really like talking to you," said Chitchee.

"Yeah, but," she said, completely disappointed. "But you're too friendly. Go away."

"Yes, as far as hanging out goes, it's always a fine line you walk between ecstasy and agony," said Chitchee. "What if we dance, like a slow waltz, one foot apart as a boundary condition, but hold hands? *Some enchanted evening . . . Rodgers and Hammerstein wrote this song . . .*"

Dagny thought him absurd, but she indulged his whimsy with a for-a-second waltzetto, even though Chitchee had a body like a dilapidated mattress from living so long in a garden-level basement.

"Awww," said Melusina, turning the corner.

She clasped her hands, knotted her fingers together, beckoned Kriemhilde, and wiped a tear on her arm so that the water dried.

"Such a cute couple," said Melusina. "I'm so happy for you, Dagny! I didn't know you were even seeing anyone, Dagny. How long have you two been in love?"

"We don't know each other," said Chitchee.

"Oh, you don't *say*," said Kriemhilde, her voice cracking. "Mel? Are Tom and Bruce here? In case someone gets butterfly-knifed?"

"Butterfly-knifed?" said Dagny, pushing Chitchee against an unstable bookcase.

Hawaii fell off its display stand, beaned Chitchee's head, flew to the floor, ripped, and bounced on the floor.

"Hildy," said Melusina, "*that* is the fellow, the nice young man who works at that nice young store, where he works for our nice young nephew, *Aloysius*. So we don't need to call the nice young men from security, Tom and Bruce."

"Tom and Bruce hopped a bus to the Burger King in Stadium Village because they say the whoppers taste more char-broiled on that side of town," said Kriemhilde.

"Shhh! Do you want the whole store to know we have no security?" asked Melusina, toe-thrusting Kriemhilde in the ankle.

"Well, it's true," said Kriemhilde.

"Ladies, ladies," said Chitchee. "We should all get together and play cribbage! The four of us! A cribbage clubbage. Should we have a round-robin cribbage tournament?"

"Piff—!" spit out Melusina. "I mean, why yes . . . cribbage would be interesting . . . and different . . . and possibly even interestingly different. Maybe we could do that when Kriemhilde and I return from our trip to Pennsylvania to tour the Hires Root Beer factory."

"Who are you anyway?" asked Kriemhilde, suddenly suspicious and coiled like a cobra and looking through two slits at Chitchee.

"I'm the button guy with the magical acorn," said Chitchee. "Why? Hey! You know me! Why the cold shoulders? I'll be your Securitas! I'll go get the Whoppers! All right. I'm going."

Chitchee, inspired by his love for the muse and goddess squinting inside Dagny, bought the Rilke for fifty cents and the Bly for two bucks.

Chitchee raced home on a sudden flat tire, bending his rim. He dashed off a quick homage to Robert Bly. Chitchee titled his heartfelt tribute: "The Wild Man at Lunds."

"It's not Shelley or Schiller, but it's the best I can do. And I think Bobbie Bly will dig it. If I could knock on his door, assuming he would open the door, and *assuming he has a door*, then: magic!"

Chitchee printed the homage to Bly on his rattletrap Hewlett-Packard Inkjet 3-in-1 Cartridge Eater, Paper Jammer, and Scanner. He could proofread it on his break, *if he ever took a break—he was having so much fun at the book store*. He took a resin hit of the leftover weed from the night before, caked in his glass pipe's bowl . . . Mr. Coffee machine purring in the background . . .

hello Toni Morrison . . . go ahead you can feed the exotic roosters . . . and help yourself to caffeine-driven mental stimulation . . . sure we'll give your work in progress a listen . . . next up . . . what might have been David Foster Wallace debating Bret Easton Ellis . . . then in August we have Thomas Pynchon on tablas . . . Alice Walker is showing off some quilts . . . Jonathan Franzen has cancelled . . . that's okay, maybe we can entice Zadie Smith, Joyce Carol Oates, and Denis Johnson. This book store thing might work. Did The Hungry Mind's Dave Unowski bring all those authors with him to Magers & Quinn book store? Okay, so we're not in their league—*yet*. We get a bunch of animals to come to Book Smart instead—armadillos, boa constrictors, gazelles, flying fish, koala bears, and Lipizaner stallions with Habsburg lips. Buy ten books, get a free condor.

He walked hurriedly to work, on the fly, dreaming in the clouds: you walk into BookSmart and cozy up in an easy chair, take your slippers off, and you're reading *Geek Love,* and a tabby cat crawls in your lap, and in walks Katherine Dunn out of the blue, and it's no big deal. You throw another log on the fire, popping popcorn with a long handled, old-fashioned, mailbox popper. Care for some popcorn, Katarina? What's that heavenly smell, she asks. Oh no, you say, I forgot to buy socks at Treasures Await.

Chitchee, stinking like tarragon vinegar from his toes to his nose, bumped into Lake Street Rodney ("Top of the Morning," said he), who tipped his plaid, peaked cap and strode from BookSmart. Kennedy approached BookSmart from the McDonald's direction and planned to use Chitchee as a human shield to screen Lake Street Rodney.

Aloysius gave Chitchee, upon entering, the most desultory and half-hearted test pilot's thumbs up Chitchee had ever seen. It looked like the old "hit the road, piker" gesture, but the Boss Man gleamed beams of satisfaction when Chitchee rounded the counter past Kennedy on the other side with Torg clinging to the maroon counter next to the NCR register.

"Welp, I will be leaving soon," said Torg.

"Said the barnacle to the swart ship," added Chitchee. "'*Ate atque vale*,' as Catullus said to Lesbia."

"Oh, so I'm a lesbian now!" said Torg. "What would my mother think?"

"Oh Chitchee, damn," said Aloysius. "I forgot to call you. I read the schedule wrong. Snorri opened, not Saami. You didn't have to come in early after all. You can go back home."

"I'm here, I'll work for free until it's time to work for books," said Chitchee. "Is there any cheese left in the fridge? I hope not."

"Chitchee," said Aloysius close up. "Did you happen to see any envelopes lying around the other night?"

"You mean last night?" asked Chitchee, showing off his scrupulous attention to the obvious.

Chitchee replied no. He was afraid to say yes. One more mistake would cost him his job and his future.

So for the first hour, Aloysius trained Chitchee to buy books, which was pretty simple: just gyp the guy.

"Wait, whose books *are* these? They've been here forever!" Chitchee asked, reading the side of a Lunds grocery bag.

Chitchee noticed for the first time "BLY" written in magic marker down the sides of each Lunds bag. Chitchee's heart syncopated. He smiled widely and with great pleasure. Dopamine, serotonin, phenylalanine, epinephrine: he was hitting on all four pistons at once. Chitchee's big break. Ahura Mazda had handed down to him from high heaven on a silver platter: the poet laureate of Minnesota. Tradition continued down through these lines of local transmission. Chitchee was Robert Bly's disciple.

"Those books are some old guy's," said Snorri. "Aloysius said you should put his books out. If he comes back, tell him we priced them at fifty, no, forty bucks. They're taking up space, and they look like they've been abandoned. Let's get them out for sale. As long as he abandoned them, they're becoming a fire hazard. We'd better get them out of here as fast as we can!"

Chitchee gripped the Monarch gun and sticker-priced most of Robert Bly's trade paperbacks at half the cover price. Snorri moved the books off the new arrivals table for Saami to shelve later, and Chitchee carried two tall columns of newly-priced trade paperbacks and flung them down in perfect order for the day's new arrivals. He mixed and stirred in a bunch of recently bought books from the day before. He sprinkled two more bags of trade paperbacks wherever there was room on the day tables that weren't full and on display stands, end caps, and front window perches. More valuable books he set aside for Snorri to price. Chitchee rummaged through the Lunds grocery bags and found all sorts of documents with Robert Bly's name on them.

"You guys," said Chitchee, "*don't* you *know* whose books these are? Haven't you heard of Robert Bly? He's the unacknowledged poet-legislator of Minnesota! The very literate state of Minnesota, Snorri. The author of *The Tomcat of a Tan Man Turned Black*. Whatever it was. You guys, he has won an award! An *award*."

Snorri and Saami rolled their eyes in opposite directions.

"He had a British accent," said Saami. "I know that much!"

"So?" asked Snorri.

"So he was kind of a cock!" said Saami.

"Well, what if he had a French accent?" asked Snorri.

"Then he'd be a *real* cock!" replied Saami.

When Chitchee rooted through the Lunds grocery bags of books, he found a *Pilgrim at Tinker Creek* dedicated to Robert Bly from Annie Dillard. Not only that but a nice little note from Annie Dillard, a sort of "Nice to See You" card in a cute envelope wedged inside a copy of *Synchronicity* in a stack of Carl Jungs (Bollingen editions), Eranos yearbooks, von Franzs, and Hillmans. Bly had also left behind a personal note from Annie Dillard—he didn't go through his own books? He was in that much of a rush for money? This most spiritual of American poets had a vision of Dollar ign? Was he in the grips of his *Shadow*? It can only be that he needed the space, because writers don't sell their books. Do painters pawn their brushes?

Aloysius signaled for a huddle, gesturing staff to bow down low so the rival book store down the street with all the PEN PAL authors could not steal Aloysius's plans like they stole every famous author in America away from Aloysius, who couldn't name one off hand anyway, so it didn't really matter what the plans were.

"Briefly, all right you guys, I . . ." Aloysius coughed. "I (hhhuuuuaaawwwgggghhhhh). Uff. Pardon me, the store is not doing well, and you know I can't pay you that well, but, so, from now on, we'll need to do *more with less*. That's all I'm saying. If you can figure out how to do *more with nothing*—that would be even better. We'll get there, that's all there is to it. Sell more books. Good (aaawwagh) job, everyone (awawawawgghhh)! Get all those books priced out and on the floor. My book intuition tells me that old British guy abandoned his books here on purpose as donations. He never intended to come back, but he couldn't admit it. I could sort of tell by the distant look in his eye. I got the impression he might also be Native American or Tibetan and was preparing for his own death—preparing to go off into the woods to die of exposure. Anyway, we're not a storage locker! Remember: *more with nothing!*"

"We have *nothing* for toilet paper," said Saami. "Nothing!"

"I'll run over to Lunds and buy a 96-roll economy pack," said Snorri, thrilled at the thought of his potential usefulness by running an errand and showing off the taut muscles of his legs, which often made him consider wearing a kilt of skulls.

"Snorri," said Aloysius uneasily with a pickerel glance, "wait, let's wait. We'll hold off on the economy packs for now. Why don't you buy a single roll for now of that single roll tissue, the one that is usually 89 cents? Unless they have half-rolls . . ."

Aloysius peeked cautiously with a quick dread into his authentic, ranch cowboy-style, leather wallet. He caught Snorri peeking into his cash compartment. Or was he thinking Snorri was peeking, when he wasn't? So what if he was? When Aloysius looked up, Snorri looked down; when Aloysius looked to the left, Snorri looked to the right, and vice versa. Snorri might have looked away too quickly, whose guilt he failed to cover up with a tone of innocently lost innocence.

"Uhhhh . . . can I get paid today for all those good books I brought to the store last week?"

"Pay yourself out from the till, Snorri," said Aloysius. "And make a note of it on the pay-out sheet."

"We're out of pay-out sheets," said Snorri.

"We might be out of pay-out sheets," said Aloysius, hearing but not hearing Snorri. "And we're running out of ink, so go easy on the ink cartridge today. You might need to shake the ink cartridge around. Sometimes smashing it into the floor works."

Snorri spit out splinters of nervous air, feeling like that ink cartridge, smashed on the redolent, white pine wood flooring.

Aloysius rubbed his dry face with his dry hand, creating the sound of Rice Krispies and milk. He wanted to say something important. How could he? It wasn't like he was in a book and all he had to do was read the lines aloud!

"There was something I wanted to tell you guys," faltered Aloysius ". . . but I . . . I . . . uuuggghwaaggh . . ."

"You don't have to say anything," said Chitchee. "We know what you are going to say. And we love you too."

"No, that's not what I was . . . oh well," said Aloysius, "later . . . see you tomorrow . . . I'm not feeling good . . . migraines . . . probably from not drinking eight gallons of water every day. So go ahead and finish off that chunk of cheese in the fridge whoever wants it."

Aloysius cranked the engine of his old smile like a Model T, carried off three U. S. Mail tubs piled with packages for their Amazon customers, and tottered toward the parking lot for his behind-on-the-payments Chevrolet Trailblazer. He'd skip The Wax Museum for today again and blaze a trail to the nearby post office on 31st Street by K-Mart first or second thing in the morning, whichever came first.

"Did you hear that?" asked Snorri, having watched Aloysius walk on a heron's legs toward his white Chevrolet Trailblazer. "Chitchee? Did you hear how Aloysius blew me off for wanting to save the store *some money*? Come on! I love the guy, but Aloysius is a miser—I've seen him lowball a guy for a bag of books for a price so low, the seller refuses to sell them. Then the seller decides to trash the books because he doesn't want to take them back to his car. Then Aloysius charges the guy five dollars for a 'bag removal fee.' Once paid, Aloysius pretends to take the bags to the dumpster, but really he prices them in the back for the next day's new arrivals. *The customer pays us to take his books.* Neat, huh? Again, I love him a lot, but *man*, he won't invest in the store one penny! Why? It's like he's being held hostage by fear . . . some fear of the unknown . . . it's like he's in the grips of a diabolical secret, which, if unleashed, would destroy him, his family, his friends, and well, possibly Minnesota, and the rest of the civilized world. It's like he's in a cheap mystery where no one dies and that's the mystery! Well, it's the fear of 'The Butterfly Effect.' That much we do know. He will never be the same man again after reading Ray Bradbury. That's a given. Bradbury destroyed Aloysius's ego. His sense-of-self bolts have all come loose. I hate to say it, but the poor guy has been obliterated! He's finished! He's a walking ghost, not even of himself; he's the walking ghost of somebody else."

"Bradbury did that to him? Snorri," said Chitchee, looking in the Lunds bags of Bly's books, "I'll ask you too: where *does* all the money *go*? How come BookSmart *can't* turn a profit? Does that imply that no used book store *can* turn a profit?"

"If I had an ounce of dank for every time I asked myself that question," said Snorri, placing a brotherly hand on Chitchee's shoulder, "I'd light up the Minneapolis skyline *every time I toked*."

When Chitchee placed his hand on top of Snorri's hand, Snorri withdrew his hand like lightning. And then Chitchee and Saami shelved the day's books in alphabetical order in all their appropriate sections ranging over the entire two stories of Book Smart, while Snorri straightened out the book stands in the window a little bit more to the left and yawned like a bull moose on its hind legs. Snorri leaned over the counter, checked a bag (his own), and rang up a payout (his own) on the Texas Instruments hand calculator (his own) that replaced the NCR cash register until they could take the NCR register into a shop, if there was a cash register shop in North America that wasn't up on blocks itself.

"Torg!" said Snorri. "Do you have to stand so close to the hand calculator? Sorry, man—but you're blocking my light."

Torg snorted the grunt humans produce when rolling their eyes isn't stinging enough, and the sound of a grunting pig better expresses the complete exasperation of the stung listener.

"Other than that, it looks like everything is under control," said Snorri casually. "So I can go home a little early and relax. Wow, Madison! Good timing!"

Snorri hastened and bustled to hold the front door for his approaching girlfriend Madison and *her* girlfriend.

"I thought I would surprise you at work, Snorri, and take my man out for lunch," said Madison.

Madison Winterfoot and Madison's older friend Katreena Polk swirled their pink umbrellas, camped it up like unconvincing Broadway hookers acting in a Broadway farce, and strutted around BookSmart, leading with their homely kneecaps.

"Snorri," said Madison. "We found these summer umbrellas at Treasures Await! Aren't they dope?"

When Madison introduced Katreena to Chitchee, Katreena said "Trouble" was her middle name—Chitchee said what a coincidence, "Trouble" was *his* middle name.

He added they were "double trouble" and should get married and have twins.

"Mitch?" asked Katreena.

"Chitch like Rich."

"Wretch?"

"No, not Wretch, Katreena, Rich! As in Richie Rich!"

"Who? Wretchie Wretch?"

"Yes!"

"Do you have *Wretch Dad, Poor Dad*, Wretch?"

"I can't think, you're making me retch!"

"But you *are* a retch. What is this, a library?" paused Katreena. "So this is where my sons work? They sure love your store, Mister Rich."

"Oh, I'm not the owner," said Chitchee.

"Actually—" interposed Snorri. "Torg is—"

"Oh, Torg!" said Katreena. "*You're* the owner of this big ass book store? I know Saami, Snorri, Wretchie Wretch, and the stuck up frozen guy with glasses who stares frozenly at my tits, but I don't remember *you*, cutie pie!"

Although Katreena's cleavage divided Torg's attention in two unequal halves, Torg acted as if he didn't see Katreena's lacy *embonpoint* because he didn't. He did smell the vague outline of her milk cartons, which sent a shiver of theoretical pleasure up Torg's spine like the option of whipped cream on New York cheesecake.

"Torg is always in the d—" said Snorri.

"—store!" said Torg, with mosquito-sized hearts humming around his head, "so I can personally welcome the customer to my magical book store!"

Torg flicked his unlighted Carousel cigar, which slingshot out of his nervous hand, nervously adjusted his trapper hat flaps, and plucked another Carousel cigar from his inner jacket pocket.

"Actually, that was a magic trick gone wrong," said Torg. "My show is a little rusty."

"Actually, this is Torg," said Snorri, who was getting signs from Madison to shut up.

Madison once complained in a letter to Cosmopolitan that Cupid really couldn't hit the broad side of the Schmitt Music Wall and, since Torg was as susceptible to such projectiles as anyone who has ever had their heart cut out of their chest and flung down the steps of a church, Madison found it so amusing *and* so worth 50 bucks to hook Katreena up with Torg . . . but, but that was much later—sorry, you will have to wait until we get there!

Madison and Katreena slipped away to the Children's and Y/A shelves.

"Did I ever tell you, Chitchee," perked up Torg, hoping to be overheard, "about the time I was with my Calvinist jazz band on a Reformed Lutheran Church group goodwill tour of Egypt? On a two-week expedition to the Great Pyramid of Giza for postcards? I made the mistake of drinking the water. Suddenly the train from Cairo took off like a greased pig. There I was, you see. The bathroom was far in the back, and I could barely walk, let alone see. When I got inside the bathroom, there was no toilet. Only a hole where the railroad tracks ran underneath. I had no choice but to brave it, Lion King that I am. There I was, braving the windswept Arabian sands, with no Arabic, playing God with Kings, bare white hamburger buns on the line—I—anybody listening? I have the postmarked postcards to myself to prove it!"

Chitchee glimpsed a mint-shiny, obsidian Porsche 977 swimming into view, its design drawing nods of unbelief from wealthy-shoed consumers as if a bald eagle perched on a flagpole and saluted with one wing each American.

"Chitchee," said Torg. "You there? Wait until I tell that dame I'm personal friends with Leigh Kammen. She won't believe it!"

A bald eagle with its wide plumage winged across the sky and with a proud gaze looked over its right shoulder at the city's piles of garbage.

The Club Miami valet car parkers all said:

"Who gets to drive the Batmobile?"

Viktor Martensen unfolded his bat wings from his Porsche 977. Wearing a chinchilla coat, he handed the lucky valet parker a hundred-dollar bill between two fingers.

"Hello, Mr. Martensen!" said another valet parker, holding the front door to Club Miami for his Boss Man.

"I'm not going into the Club," said Viktor.

Viktor lighted his Sherman cigarette and positioned the brown filter between his cold-sored lips.

Viktor's tongue was black and long as a fruit bat's drooping before nectar.

He looked weak and trapped while he puffed rapidly, not exhaling, wrapped in thought and second thoughts. Viktor high-stepped past Hawk Eye.

"I don't know how all you people live in poverty," said Viktor to the squatting Hawk Eye. "How can you bums live like that?"

Viktor said "bums" without thinking, and he flicked his long, thin Sherman butt off the wall over Hawk Eye's head. Dressed in full Twins fatigues and a bucket hat, Hawk Eye fielded the butt like a fungo.

"I've met Louis, and I've met Duke," said Torg, "through Leigh Kammen. Hello? Operator? Bigelow Five-O Five-O?"

SPARTAK BOK

Viktor in a chinchilla (silver-and-black sheening in a standing waveform) coat burst in the front door of BookSmart.

"Is Aloysius in today?" asked Viktor.

"Did you get your rabies shot?" asked Chitchee.

"For what?" said Viktor. "Who the fuck are you, fucking Blackwell?"

Besides the out-of-season chinchilla coat, Viktor wore a stoutly-fitting Brooks Brothers blue suit, which caused a Chi-square crease across it. Viktor's chops and jowls revealed the gleam of white teeth like the white teeth of the Crest 3D White Whitestrips ads but whiter. His skin had been tanned "to a turn" and the tone of the tan said "wealthy man." Something in the way he tanned also caused his tan to say: "This tan is from Palm Beach, not Planet Tan."

Viktor's high hairline had two widow's peaks. His Grecian black hair shocked up straight like black corn, black corn that rolled backwards in black, corrugated furrows.

"Two widow's peaks! That must be a record of some kind . . ." continued Chitchee, leaning forward to examine Viktor's hairline as Viktor was leaning backward to avoid punching him. "Aloysius left his office for the day. Leave a little love note?"

"Yeah, ask the fucker," said Viktor, leaning forward, "where is my book? *Quantum Vision*? Isn't it done by now? What's it take to write a fucking book? If you can talk, you can write like a fucking book!"

"Biscuits!" said Chitchee when he thought he heard a golden retriever.

And he loved golden retrievers. He wanted to *be* a golden retriever. "Do we have biscuits here for dogs?"

Chitchee looked around for the woof on the leash and saw Beda Holmgren on the sidewalk. He barreled outside.

"The fuck?" asked Viktor of himself, shaking his head, transforming his smile into a gremlin's thin grin.

"When did you pick up a pooch, Beda? What's its or possibly their name?" asked Chitchee, rolling on the pavement and tickling its underside.

A jet-eyed woman, six-feet four, her black hair docked into bangs, with the delicate, veined skin of a Ming vase, pigeon-toed toward Beda. Bare-thighed, lazy-eyed, togged in a *seifuku* uniform—knee high socks, pleated skirt, and middy blouse, Minerva Singleton had been lying in bed all day narrating the possible disasters that might befall her if she twitched. Minerva plagued herself with an unnatural fear of natural disasters that included drought, tsunami, hurricanes, earthquakes, sun-spot driven crop failure, and being called a "Skinny Minnie."

Whoever called Minerva a "Skinny Minnie" would be shot through the throat.

"LGBTQ! Beda! Wait up!" said Minerva. "It's so early. I'm not used to getting up in broad daylight! Ugh, look at all the peoplification going on. People are so predictable, peopling themselves. That's all they seem to do."

Minerva's countenance changed. She had left her car keys in the ignition, her house keys in the front door, and all her passwords on local billboards, not.

"I pictured there being more dogs out today actually," said Minerva, half sobbing to herself and half to Beda. "Is LGBTQ okay with a *man*?"

"Cu-u-u-ute," said Chitchee, gurgling and slobbering his dog's drool, pooling on the pavement. "Cu-u-u-ute! What kind of dog is it?"

"It's a pit bull," said Beda, struggling with the leash. "Can't you tell?"

"*It's a pit bull*, the ducky," said Chitchee. "I wish we had some Milk Bone Biscuits for LGBTQ," said Chitchee. "We should keep Milk Bone Biscuits behind the counter and allow dogs like LGBTQ in the book store for biscuits and gravy trains."

"No," said Minerva, her chrome red lips full and naturally blossoming into a joker's smile, "not good. LGBTQ hates men because the male previous owner got her addicted to cocaine, and we had to get her into treatment to get her off coke. She has panic attacks at the sight of snow. She refuses to go outside in winter. So we will stay inside all winter long this winter and cuddle by the fire. The three of us. We can read Jane Austen aloud together."

"And the pit bull?" asked Chitchee.

"LGBTQ has ADHD, but she *loves* JA," said Minerva. "I mean anybody who *doesn't* love P & P or *Clueless* must be filled with hate and cannot be our friend without signing a friendship contract, which of course Saami broke, as everybody knows by now. That's why Saami cannot join our Agoraphobic Horror Book Club for shut-ins, which only meets by handwritten mail—except on Halloween, when we meet at Lakewood Cemetery, sponsored by Walker Library."

Chitchee, Beda, and Minerva heard a squeal and a crunch. They paused to watch a white Dodge van's wheels squeal and crunch over the curb, parallel park clumsily in front of McDonald's, back out, try again, and again. Park. Then no one got out of the van.

"We've been taking the darling 'dog' to empathy classes in Bryn Mawr," said Beda, feeling LGBTQ's distraction in the air. "So that she can spare the men who happen to have empathy (like there are any) and then go ahead and kill the others who do not, which is all of them."

"What?" asked Viktor, scowling at Chitchee on the sidewalk. "I was talking to you, you dumb fucking squirrel! Get up off the fucking sidewalk! Don't tell me you're Aloysius's '*people*' person!"

LGBTQ growled—leaping toward Viktor's obese throat, and the pit bull's teeth chomped at Viktor's chinchilla-sleeved forearm. Beda and Minerva squeezed the leash like bad water skiers.

"What are you doing," continued Viktor to Chitchee, "in the middle of a conversation with me, you run out to talk to a dumb dog and her dumb mutt? And what have we here? Are *you* with *her*?"

"Oh, I'm sorry sir, I'll be right in," apologized Chitchee, "and we can talk about your dumb book, *Quantum Biscuits*, as much as you want."

"It's *Quantum Biscuits*," misspoke Viktor, "not *Quantum Visions* . . . who are *you*?"

"That's what I said," said Chitchee, "a dumb book."

Viktor looked over Minerva. Viktor weakly whistled something a waxwing might try.

"Are you looking for work?" Viktor asked Minerva, oozing over her. "Work for me, and you'll make four or five hundred bucks a night! Oh, honey, you ooze sex. You have a great portfolio right between your thighs."

Beda and Minerva walked downtown to apply for a restraining order on all of Minneapolis. Viktor watched them walk.

Chitchee strode inside and stood sentinel next to Snorri behind the maroon counter, and Snorri hurried to the Children's Books section and stood sentinel next to Madison and Katreena to protect something—his instincts told him to—he wasn't sure why. Saami crouched in the basement to hide from Snorri.

And Viktor, noticing the white Dodge van across the street, pretended not to notice the white Dodge van across the street. He walked back inside BookSmart to observe the white Dodge van across the street from behind the store front's plate-glass window, at the same time grabbing tall, skinny Minerva's crotch, which was lodged in his mind's eye like an eyelash.

On the driver's side of the van fidgeted Spartak Bok—his clothes not only made of bedbugs but *tailored* by bedbugs. The prickling was feverish. Spartak's recently-scratched back begged to be itched. The bugs bugging him themselves itched and they scratched themselves continually too. Meanwhile, a bug crawled into Spartak's brain although his brain was another bug in his skull. A giant hypodermic needle squirted a brain-liquefying poison into his right parietal lobe then sucked his dissolved brains back out. Every bug disrespected Spartak and owed Spartak money. Spartak's crow's black hair had been cut under a pudding bowl! The handle of his large shovel nose ended in a flat square blade. His lanky body was all polygons, taut with enormous tensile strength. He changed postures uncomfortably. He unbuttoned the second button on his Hart Schaffner Marx shirt then loosened his red and white peppermint-striped tie and threw it at the trash in the back seat. Mosquito bites ran up and down his back, which he reached creating the pools of sweat he swam in. He felt under the driver's seat the submachine gun that was snuggling with its sweetheart 9mm Glock.

When Willibald "Willis" and Iona "Io" Bok retired in Hibbing, they signed over the Hibbing Lingonberry Inn and its branches—Detroit Lakes, Pequot Lakes, Thief River Falls, Blue Earth, Circle Pines, and Worthington—to their only son Spartak.

Spartak, in a manically, maniacal cloud of celebratory coke, con men, and hookers from Kansas City, changed the name of "The Lingonberry Inn" to "Rancho Calypso World." Every Rancho Calypso World was a hot chili parlor in the summer and an ice cream shop in the winter. Each edifice complex resembled a giant Conestoga wagon; the servers dressed as reptilians, the placemats depicted Area 51, and a replica of the Kensington Runestone stood in the middle of the dining area. With his parents' leverage, Spartak borrowed to the hilt. Then he took his line of credit and line of hookers to Mystic Lake casino. What had been a traditional, home-style family restaurant with fieldstone fireplaces, wood paneling, hand-hewn pegged chairs, and leaded windows with rosemaling stained glass, Spartak junked. He refurbished each Rancho Calypso World with art deco aluminum walls, checkered floors, purple tablecloths, blow, and more blow, until one afternoon he woke up to find himself engaged to a woman named Crystal with diseased and tingling gums and eyes burning white hot in outer space.

Spartak reached for the bulb-shaped crack pipe in his glove compartment, plucked out the M9 Beretta, lighted his pipe, and threw the pipe in the back, lighted.

Next to Spartak breathed Yakov "Yakky" Vorchenko, a .40-caliber high powered rifle on his lap. He wore a Brooklyn Cyclones baseball cap, Nike Swoosh T-shirt, 100% polyester snakeskin shorts, and saffron slip-ons. Yakky's neck swallowed his chin when he swallowed, and when he swallowed, his chin disappeared like a fly into his own mouth. His chin on his fat neck was almost flush with his face when he swung a look over his shoulder at the back seat and saw where Spartak's crack pipe landed: between two bulky Graco baby chairs containing a digital scale, a box of diabetic needles, 1.2 pounds of Ecstasy in powder form, and 5.6 pounds of meth.

"Do you know who I am?" asked Viktor, picking his teeth with a gold-plated toothpick, which matched the gold fillings backing up his piano-wide set of denture-perfect ivory elephantine teeth.

"Oh, enough about you," said Chitchee, turning the pages of the Borde and Malovany-Chevallier translation of *The Second Sex*. "No, seriously: You're the guy who just asked, 'Do you know who I am?' Which means you'd probably steal the crucifix off your mother's neck and pawn it for five bucks."

Viktor looked as if a dead seagull landed on his head and Brylcreemed down his shoulders.

"You're Robert Bly, aren't you? Those are your books over there by my hold pile, aren't they?" asked Kennedy, having eavesdropped, thinking he might have contacted the founder of the Men's Movement, one of Kennedy's favorite all-time men's movements besides football.

"Who? No! I own MPG! I own Carousel Square and every building on this block, I probably own *you*," Viktor said to Kennedy and then turned to Chitchee. "I'm Martensen. *Martensen.*"

"Nice to meet you, Marty," said Chitchee. "We met in a past life. You look familiar. Were you ever in a Disney book?"

"Yeah, *Run, Bambi, Run*," said Viktor. "Now shut the fuck up, Snow White! Are you listening to me! Stop reading!"

"But *The Second Sex* is a textbook on women, man," said Chitchee. "You should read it! Man, it's really cool. See, right there! How embedded sexism is in the language! Wouldn't it sound odd to say: '*Woman*, this book is really cool,' or 'This book is really cool, *woman*!'"

"If you called me a woman, I'd punch your lights out," said Viktor. "You tell your fucking asshole hippie burn-out boss, I want my rent money! I'll be next door at Club Miami, which I own too, teeheehee, having lunch. And then I have my G5 to catch—to Egypt! But I don't suppose you women could ever afford to go *there*."

"Egypt?" butt in Torg. "I had diarrhea all over Egypt! We were *just* talking about Egypt. Diarrhea by degrees all over the step pyramids and the real pyramids! Diarrhea all over the Sphinx—where is that woman, woman, woman?"

"Katreena!" shouted Chitchee. "There is someone here to see you! What was I writing? Tell . . . boss . . . *asshole . . . has plane to catch . . . to Egypt . . . diarrhea all over the pyramids, where is book Quantum Biscuits . . .* I will relay this message to El Jefe. And you are?"

"I just told you! Are you de-e-ef?" said Viktor. "I just fucking told you, you fucking *people person* moron!"

"How should I know the name of Vincent Mortensen? Are you related to Vinny the Chin? I'm sorry," cried Chitchee, sadness and tears swelling his cheeks. "I didn't mean to lean into ego. I have a disability and to me you might as well be a baby cyclops or a lobster who grew up in a Neapolitan grotto and lived off the yolk of sea dragon eggs until a princess fairy kissed you and you turned into a flaxen bag of wind, which is what you are now to me. Hugs?"

Viktor Martensen's jawbone crashed through the floor and feverish blood pinched the inflamed black sore on his liverish lower lip as he watched Chitchee extend arms, round the maroon counter, and step toward him with tears of love overflowing his eyeglasses.

"I'm *Viktor Martensen*! Who do you think, ya fuckin Hoosier, not no fuckin'. . ." said Viktor, inserting his thumb behind his unshaven knuckles.

His closed fist rocketed into Chitchee's nose, flattening the nasal bridge and cutting a clot of blood from his philtrum. Chitchee screamed, reeling backward holding his nose. Had he not flinched like a spider speeding up a line of suspended silk, he would have had a broken nose on his hands and bankruptcy proceedings after the million-dollar, spider ambulance ride. Instead he gladly accepted a merely bloody nose. While Chitchee excused himself to go to the bathroom, Viktor's thoughts ran together like an open tin of Goya black beans.

Viktor's iPhone rattled him with rocket-fueled ringtones.

"Yeah, Sangster?" said Viktor, snorting from his runny nose a grayish effluvium left and right. "Did you get a table? Sangster, you chinless tortoise! Get the fucking spare rib plate with extra sauce! Do you need an invitation to work before I fire your flaming ass? There's no sign of my book. No rent money. I got an idea. Make Aloysius my personal slave! He can work it off or the cops can pay him a house call. Still there? Did you get the ribs?"

"Hey you!" said Katreena, seeing Viktor. "What are you doing in a Books Mart?"

"Get the fuck out of my store, trash!" said Viktor, phone to his ear.

Katreena, her phone slammed to her ear, looked at Torg.

"You heard the lady!" said Torg. "Are you deaf?"

Katreena resumed dinner plans with Carlos and Cesar Leon, covered the mouthpiece, and turned toward Viktor:

"Who you callin' trash, you fucking fat rat! I guess you thinks you gotta big cock to go with your big mouth—so suck on it, bitch!"

Chitchee returned with toilet paper scrunched up his nostrils, his head held back so that his eyes slanted downward at the cash register when Madison came up to the counter holding *The Wind in the Willows*.

"I'll deal with you later, whore!" said Viktor. "You gave me herpes, bitch!"

Viktor extracted a monogrammed cigarette case of Sherman cigarettes from an inner pocket and put it back. He lightly touched the black sore on his lip.

"Say what?" said Katreena. "Get the fuck out of here! I didn't give you no herpes, because I don't have no herpes! Fuck outta here! 'sides no woman want your ugly hairy mean ol' ass, when they could have an adorable storytellin' real man like the owner of a BookSmart like this guy."

When Katreena lifted Torg off the floor by his slack armpits, smacked his mouth with a big red kiss on his virgin kisser, and landed him gently on his toes, Viktor growled and kicked his canine feet backward covering dirt with dirt—and the wings on Torg's trapper's hat flew up like Pippi Longstocking's braids.

After Madison deposited her Pocket Book *The Wind in the Willows* in her Kate Spade bag, she kissed Snorri goodbye.

Viktor's iPhone hook-wormed into his ear and Madison and Katreena gladly strolled off with Carlos and Cesar Leon for Krispy Kreme donuts on Lyndale.

"Larry!" said Viktor. "You know that Katreen bitch who used to work at Sunrise Spa And Massage? I want her legs broken. You don't like hearing that? I know you liked her, because you're weak! You are so weak you *like* being called 'weak.'"

Kennedy, sitting on the couch, quietly skimming stacks of computer manuals on computer manuals—although Kennedy didn't know a MacBook from a Big Mac—jumped up. And then grabbed his back.

"What's wrong with your back?" asked Chitchee.

"It's a bifurcation in the upper dorsals, my guess!" said Kennedy.

Kennedy was bowled over by Katreena. He was dying to know who the dynamic, vivacious hell was she? If Torg was as low as she would go, Kennedy was definitely above that level as a catch. Even if Katreena married Torg tomorrow, she would get sick of him in ten years, and then *you know who* would be around? High, wide, and handsome as ever, with his sparker in flames: THE Kennedy that's who. Conceivably he could take her for a spin on his brand new Arctic Cat as soon as it snowed.

"Hey, Richard Speck over there," said Viktor, half-talking, half-snorting to Chitchee. "Tell your boss, the loser, to call his owner, unless he likes having his legs broken and getting fucked up the ass through prison bars!"

Through the front window, Viktor watched Spartak *door* a #6 MTC bus, jump from the van, and shout profanities at Lily Holmgren (the bus driver) for trying to kill him.

Spartak smoldered with an incendiary air that either exploded into violence or diffused into merely cruel laughter. There was a crazy confidence in his intensity—threatening, probing, and mocking. He thrived on reckless brinkmanship, seeking it especially if it caused pain that he could watch and deride. All elbows and knees (at acute angles) Spartak spidered through spacetime bare-ankled. No socks in his split-toed, lizard-skinned slip-ons, he bell-bottom trousered toward Club Miami, but when he felt Viktor's stare shining his way, he re-angled toward BookSmart.

"*Marhaba,*" said Chitchee, greeting Spartak at the door. "Hey you look like the kind of guy who likes to read Gunter Grass, *and* we have *The Tin Drum.*"

Spartak recoiled and slinkied backward (one eyeball looked painted dead) one step.

"Sir," said Chitchee, pinched his nose, and removed the toilet paper's two blood-stained polyp-shaped pillars, products of Viktor's closed fist.

"You have an interesting, arresting face," continued Chitchee, examining Spartak's black hair combed forward in curls like Greek key ornamentation, his bracketing eyebrows, and the deep scar crawling upwards from his nose to halfway up his forehead. "You wouldn't want to buff it out. Like William Vollman's, it's like one of those faces where the pieces don't jigsaw. Your nose is too big and flat and slants. The wrinkles and the scars mesh together like quilty pieces, but there are sloppy overlaps and loose threads. Interesting. Scars and tattoos engross me. But unlike Vollman's, *your* eyes reveal nothing. Did you train your eyes like Dobermans to play dead? We have some William Vollman over here if—"

"Get off my face, loser," said Spartak, boxing Chitchee's nose with a force that spiralled Chitchee to his knees.

Chitchee, feverish and seizurish, tried not to think of the pain, because he feared the pain's pain feeding itself with more pain, throwing him into shock.

"Mercy! Scratch the Gunter Grass," said Chitchee, holding his nose, scrutinizing his T-shirt for rips, and feeling his back for twisted muscles. "You're more like the jerk Elfriede Jellinek writes *about.*"

"Hello, Viktor," said Spartak. "Do you have anything for me today?"

"Like what?" said Viktor, laughing at Chitchee.

"Like money for your gambling debts."

"Oh, *that,*" said Viktor with nervous gold-toothed smiles, looking around for an easy exit and blowing his nose left and right to clear his sinuses. "I can pay you back with—I've got that Viper, you can have that."

Spartak held up to the track lighting (like Bordeaux in a wine glass) a M9A1 Beretta.

Viktor back-pedaled a few steps and held out admonitory palms.

Chitchee had never seen anyone pull a gun on anyone—except the thumpers on COPS and now at BookSmart. Besides Finkle's home arsenal and militia-supporting gun rack, he had never seen a live hand gun in such an Ingmar Bergman close up—loaded, and in the wild. Spartak's handgun pointed toyingly at Viktor's hollow-pointed, bullet-shaped chest.

When Yakky Vorchenko bobbed into BookSmart—surprised or lost—Chitchee had never seen a human body so covered with human hair—hairy neck, hairy upper arms, hairy back, hairy waist, and legs so hairy you couldn't see where the hair was coming from—hair on knuckles, hair on toes, hair probably on his tongue and bodily organs—even his palms had a few stray hairs from all the hairs falling out and sprouting back. And yet Yakky was bald as an ostrich egg on top with his bushy side hair clumped, clownishly sideways.

"What stinks?" asked Saami, who dropped a stack of *Akiras* on the maroon counter and skedaddled back to the basement.

"Me!" said Yakky.

Yakky cultivated repugnance. After a good workout at the Calhoun Beach Club bench pressing a Minneapolis-Moline G series tractor, Yakky loved drinking asafoetida iced tea in the steam room. He never once in his life brushed his teeth; he paid dental hygienists to scrape the lichen off his teeth; he never flushed his own toilet, because he tipped the Calhoun Beach Club house cleaners to do that.

"We have books for body odor," said Chitchee, shielding himself behind a copy of *Body Odor Blues* by J. J.

Viktor moved forward as Spartak glanced at *Body Odor Blues*.

"You stink, you say?" asked Chitchee. "There is a book for everything!"

"Huh?" asked Yakky, reading the back cover of *Body Odor Blues* with his lips. "I might want to read this. Do you have anything on yeast infections? 'cause that's what I *really* want to smell like."

"Excuse me, sir," said Chitchee to Spartak. "Is that an actual *gun?* Like in Godard's *À bout de souffle?*"

Yakky tossed Chitchee aside, landing like a cat falling off a roof.

Yakky clamped Viktor from behind, popping his mouth open.

Spartak shoved the Beretta into Viktor's open mouth.

"300,000," said Spartak.

"I'll pay you," slurred Viktor, a barrel cigarred in his black-sored mouth. "I have a Prestige cigarette boat on the St. Croix and a cabin on Gull Lake, and the Viper. The Viper, that's yours, Spartak!"

"He don't want your fucking Viper, or your cabins, or your cigarettes!" said Yakky, spitting out recently-eaten cheeseburger chad from Mickey D's.

"Wait, take my Armani," said Viktor.

Spartak slipped the Armani watch off Viktor's wrist, dropped it on the redolent, white pine flooring, stepped on it, and, under his lizard-skinned bootheel, crushed it.

"I'm going to pay you back, Spartak! Buddy!" continued Viktor. "I can get you the 14k gold, 1 carat troy weight dragon earrings that Nancy Reagan wore to a royal breakfast in Luxembourg, a Marine Band harmonica once owned by the King Of Thailand's foot valet, Steve Madden sandals that retail for a lot, and cases of Lancome vanilla-bean perfume! Vanilla from Mad-Dass-a-Car!"

For good luck, Viktor wore the Armani watch at Mystic Lake and his Michael Kors watch at Canterbury Downs.

"Geez, Spar-tack," said Chitchee, picking up the dropped Armani and looking at it, "you killed it! Can I have it?"

Chitchee stood up, faced Viktor, and proclaimed:

"For a guy who looks like his Mongol bloodline leads back through high-priced, genealogical websites to Genghis Khan, you sure caved fast!"

Then Spartak removed two inches of the black snout from Viktor's mouth and rammed it back down Viktor's throat.

"Don't make me pull the trigger," said Spartak Bok. "Don't make me do it. Please don't make me do it."

"Okay, okay," sweated Viktor, his eyes bright and wide with sweat.

"And 10% of everything you are involved in, Porky Pig!" said Spartak, removing the Beretta from Viktor's mouth.

"Okay," said Viktor, exhausted having planned a hundred schemes at the same time.

In front of Viktor's mind's eye rolled images of the tortures perpetrated on the Other's flesh. When Chitchee handed Viktor the broken Armani watch, Viktor gripped it with prehensile talons until he bled himself.

"Do you still want it?" asked Chitchee. "I'll take it if you don't!"

Yakky smiled at the cowering store, his teeth spread far apart like a manure fork encrusted with manure, the fork left in a cowshed to rust. The asafoetida reeked and overwhelmed BookSmart in Yakky's wake, following Spartak out to the sidewalk.

"Hey, you guys," said Chitchee, following them out the door, "are you into Scandinavian mystery writers? Because we have *plenty* of Stieg Larrson, Henning Mankell, and some other good ones. OR YOU COULD READ STRINDBERG! Hey, you guys."

CLUB MIAMI

Viktor lighted a Sherman cigarette, decided against it, flicked it away, and walked shakily into the Club Miami restaurant lobby where he wanted the bare-shouldered hostess, Dagny Knutsen.

He squeezed one buttock through her knee length, black slit-skirt.

"Hi Dagny, have you seen my slave lately?" asked Viktor.

"Hello, Viktor," growled Dagny, pushing his hand away and sneezing molecules of Yakky's body odor in Viktor's face. "He is at the bar, having a drink with one of your lawyer friends."

"Ever seen one of these?" said Viktor, holding out a hundred dollar bill that was wet.

A guttural escaped from Dagny, but she stifled herself. She cemented her face and was waiting for it to harden.

"It's all yours, cuzz," Viktor continued, "it's on me!"

He stuffed the banknote in Dagny's bralette with a quick squeeze and sauntered into Club Miami.

"I can't live in this hell," said Dagny shakily. "I hate this life! Corporate Asshole Penis Tart!"

Misery welled up in Dagny and her throat closed down so she couldn't talk. As she tried to not start crying, she felt the tears dripping in her nose. From her eyes (turned away from the door to recover) two rivulets created black clots in her mascara. She dried her eyes with a Club Miami napkin, having to keep the hundred-dollar bill to pay for her captivity.

Viktor licked his sensual Capone lips with a look happily vicious. He scanned Club Miami for the bastard Larry. Opalescent lamps shone a light from oyster shells over the pink and blue booths, purple mushroom tables, horseshoe bars, and high-backed chairs with stemmy legs. Eiffel towers of iridescent and phosphorescent liquors lined up in front of a pond-sized, pier glass mirror, covering a carpeted wall. The mirror reflected the geometric repetition of hexagonal designs from the checkered dance floor. The pop of the op art continued into the lounge area where a chair, shaped like a vulva, wrapped around an MPG employee, resting his yarbles, nursing his tropical cocktail, and watching the candle wax cry dry, wax tears. Pretty women? Two lookers, with legs crossed, sat on the sofas. One was Julia Roberts, but shaped like two large lumps from a burning lava lamp. Then she stood up with hips like a Coleman lantern. Viktor spit her out. And there was *another* Julia Roberts lunching with a loser by those couches that looked squeezed out of a couch-paste tube. Viktor considered offering her a server job. Instead, he blew a snot rocket to the floor. Insipid office workers on cushions in dark corners, chinless as sharks, sipped in cocktails over their lunch plates. Other corners looked like zebra mussels with hair-thin purple stripes from the black lights' refractions, black, white, and purple. To Viktor's annoyance, Club Miami attracted street people and low-class locals from the old Rainbow Bar like Mad Jack Apple Jack the ancient sot, his eyes blinking like cuts of red knackwurst.

Club Miami simulated a sexual, kitschual, posh, lustful beach. Here and there neoclassical, Corinthian pillars with gilded columns and pediments led to the bathrooms—marked off by stylized, geometrical male and female genitalia.

"I want to expand my portfolio, Corky, but Viktor, well you know Viktor—kind of hard to deal with sometimes," said Larry Sangster. "Now he is demanding my wife be his silent partner."

"Viktor has to vacate his properties one way or another," said Corky Skogentaub, adjusting his svelte, leather belt, a buckled notch allowing for the flow of his waist, which was a flesh barrel (the kind of barrel pictured in cartoons going over Niagara Falls). Corky sat in his flesh barrel, created by salty pork rinds and other snacks, all thin above the chest. When Larry looked at the trapped Corky in his barrel of pork rinds, going over Niagara Falls, the circular girth disturbed Larry. He found disturbing most of all Corky's flatulence—bubbling up from his chair like a third unintroduced person at the table.

"With three Delaware shell corporations," said Corky, loosening his canary Hubert White tie, the front of the tie loosely reaching between his knees, the back as short as his tongue, "we can maintain our portfolios and keep stuff nicely hidden."

Viktor sneaked up behind Larry and fastened on his shoulder with two claws. Larry turned around startled and clapped his cringing eyes on Viktor.

"Oh, there you are Viktor," said Corky, "ready for some home-cooked ribs? Look-see, we got your favorite table in the back."

"You mean so no one can see you guys drinking yourselves to death back here?" asked Viktor. "It's 80/20, Larry. I built this empire. You're just a manager. A stooge."

"Let's get another drink and talk," said Larry, wearily Larrily.

The bartender, Nestor Martensen, cleaned a glass with a towel and stroked his thick shaggy black hair with all his fingers twisting. He mirrored his aquiline profile in the mirror, walked grinning at his father's table grinning at him, and landed two Bloody Marys and for his father the usual Tanqueray gin gimlet, no almonds.

"Hi Dad! Get you guys something?" asked Nestor.

"You can get me out of town," joshed Viktor, his twinkling eyes twinkling stars. "Youououou keeping out of trouble, Nestor?"

"No," said Nestor. "Are you?"

"Not since I married the old lady," said Viktor.

It wasn't much of a joke, but then most jokes aren't much of a joke, and everybody laughed for lack of something to laugh about. What a joke, thought Nestor. Nestor grinned, tilting his head to one side briefly. Nestor thought he realized something peculiar in his father's fMRI. The "stupid" areas in his father's brain lighted up whenever his father said anything.

"How's your 'group?'" asked Viktor, saying "group" ironically.

"Oh, the usual," said Nestor. "I'm playing music with a bunch of idiots to a bunch of idiots, and it's like talking to a bunch of idiots. Just like my girlfriend, who is nowhere to be found. I'll go find your server."

The business trio adjusted their chairs and elbowed down.

"We've got the City Council by their balls, sure as eggs *are* eggs," said Corky. "They can't afford to turn all your tenants out on the street. How many apartment buildings, 100, 120—?"

"I'm sick of this whiny little town of liberal Minneapolis and the Minnesota welfare whiners. I could be on my G5, first class, if you guys weren't so incompetent," said Viktor adjusting his prosthetic septum, which kept slipping. "I could have a young gorgeous chick licking my balls, but no, I'm in strange-weather Minnesota again with all the cornfed Norwegian scuzzies!"

Viktor had evoked "licking my balls" as a joke so many times, Viktor didn't expect much of a laugh. No one chuckled—not a signifying snort through a nostril—not an eyebrow a-flicker. Viktor demanded people be as polite to him as he was never courteous to them. He fawned upon unjustified praise by constantly claiming his prestige and his status as a near-celebrity: Viktor went to nursery school with Prince, the Trashmen played at his wedding, Vanity Six all gave him a blow job in First Avenue's VIP lounge, Leo Kottke gave him a Martin guitar and an iguana for Christmas, and Viktor gave the Replacements the helicopter he won from Iggy Pop in a game of pool at The Viper the night Joaquin Phoenix died.

Viktor effused with a borrowed glory that made Larry wince. Larry ground his clenched teeth and smiled at the same time, ending with a burp of heartburn. Corky battled ulcerative colitis, which nevertheless hadn't deterred him from fiery spices and hot green sauces.

"Corky, I got pull inside the State Attorney General's office," grinned Viktor grimly. "I'm racquetball partners with the vice president of the policemen's union. I'm in 1% of all the motorcycle clubs around here. Angels, Outlaws, independents. All the thumpers in this town are on my side! Of course you didn't hear all that or I'll rip the hairs out of your asshole. The problem is I'm getting too high profile. Whiny little journalists from Shitty Pages are making it sound like I am a bad landlord by providing affordable housing to scum. They're all welfare moms, and their sons are all drug dealers anyway. You get what you pay for."

Viktor cackled broadly. Corky giggled one giggle from a possible gaggle. Larry smiled at his Cobb salad, reached for his Bloody Mary's celery stick, and nibbled on the leafy crown.

"To sell your units to me, Viktor," said Larry, not hungry, "Corky will draw up the contracts for deed, but since the buildings will still have cockroaches, I want 40%."

"Okay, 40%! Doesn't every apartment building in Minneapolis have cockroaches? It doesn't matter," said Viktor. "The tenants bring the cockroaches in with them from Mexico. Any case against me I can get dropped. America is a free country, everyone is free until they get caught."

"Pretty much," said Corky, distracted by the anticipation of his barbecued beef ribs, his low glucose level causing him to see 'B-B-Q' written in excited neon gas across his forebrain.

"Did you fuck up the BookSmart computer, Larry?" asked Viktor.

"Yeah, the fucker's about as dumb as a cake mix," replied Larry poker-faced, covering his face with a Bloody Mary gulp. "We can remote view everything he does, read his email, and drain his accounts."

"Excellent," said Viktor. "I can't wait to get to the home office in Fort Lauderdale and see what my techie geekie geniuses can do with that."

"Why do you hate this guy Aloysius so much?" asked Corky.

"Aloysius is a hippie! I hate hippies," said Viktor. "They fucked up the Sixties, and they are all Commies, and they should all be shot and ground into wood chips. Wood chips. Speaking of wood chips, you guys seen the new squirrely guy they got next door at BookShit? Is he from around here? Can't be. People don't walk around Minneapolis grinning normally unless maybe they are morons from St. Paul. He reminds me of John Wayne Macys—that McDonald's killer clown. We should give him the bridge treatment for shits and giggles. Suspend him by the thumbs over the Mississippi, after we drop Aloysius into the drink when we no longer need his hippie ass as a front."

"Suspend them all! And Squirrely Guy better be hiding his acorns for the coming winter," said Larry, shaken up recalling his anger. "Not that I give a fuck about his Down's syndrome medical condition like—it's time to kick them all out. Shake 'em out like a pillar of salt. That's all."

"Like because they're all psycho stupid fuckin' morons over there?" asked Viktor.

"We all have *something* wrong with us . . ." trailed off Corky.

"Yeah, well there is nothing wrong with me! Except I got herpes from that Katreena bitch," said Viktor. "Ever had herpes, Corky? What am I saying? You're too fat to fuck! With your medical condition! Which is being a fat fuck!"

"Okay, gentlemen," said LaDonna, smiling.

Her dimples had dimples and yet sensed the table's hostility toward her as a hateful love object. Someone said she could have been "an actress or a model." Ironically, LaDonna did think she should have been "an actress or a model" because she had the wits and smarts to do so, unlike the successful actresses and models she envied, rivaled, and accused silently for their having no empathy and being bad listeners.

"Who had the slab of beef ribs and who had the slab of pork ribs?"

"Me," said Corky.

"Where's mine?" fleered Viktor. "You served that fat slob first?"

"It was the first order up," commented LaDonna. "Is there a problem?"

"I oughtta fire you for that!" said Viktor, rising from his chair. "Get out of here, bitch face!"

LaDonna's hazels emptied like two hourglasses of their color. She turned her addled brain around and immediately walked back to Nestor, who ignored her although he had spied on the interaction as best he could. Nestor had gotten LaDonna the job there with his recommendation, which indebted her, like chattel, to her owner. Nestor would be to blame in his father's eyes if LaDonna caused problems—shapeshifting into a maenad or Medea. For the moment LaDonna was perplexed, an ambivalent dusk with a sun not ready to set.

Her thoughts were clouds plashed with bug-bite reds and implacable bruises, her face as inanimate as the bluffs along the Mississippi.

Viktor's iPhone ring-toned an explosion.

"Fuck you," Viktor said with blackening eyes and squashed END to the breaking point. "Another mortgage lender making idle threats! There should be a law against obnoxious bounty hunters like that."

"Viktor," ventured Corky, "the city wants to revoke all your rental licenses and blacklist you for five years from owning rental properties. Remember?"

"I want to fuck that bad waitress bad," said Viktor, implying there had been an air of stagnation to the discussion so far. "I thought you fixed all the Yelp and Google reviews?"

"City regulators," said Corky, "can't control the city they are *supposed* to regulate. They don't have the resources. So they go on the honor system of 'Minnesota Nice.'"

"I go on the honor system too," said Viktor, "when I see a chickiepoo like that: I get *on her* and stay *on her*. That's how I honor *pussy*."

"Look, Viktor," continued Corky, "you have to testify that you have already sold 45 rental properties to Sangster & Associates. And you will lie under oath, no big deal; thumpers do it all the time around here. And then you claim you have no interest in renewing any licenses. We're done!"

"Spartak Bok is done," said Viktor. "That's who's done. Done like a spare rib, which is all that's going to be left of him—soon."

"We wait 30 days, then the hearing officer gives his recommendation to the City Council. The City Council—" began Corky.

"—the City Council," interrupted Viktor, blowing a nostril to the side, "or is it the Metro Council? It's one of those. I'm on their Board of Directors. They know better than to vote against me as a successful millionaire! And they know I'm a nice guy. Sometimes I think I'm the only nice guy in Minnesota. Who else is providing so much affordable housing? And there will be even more affordable housing once Zalar and his little butt-buddies spread more mice around like I paid them to! Fuckin' assholes. Then, we infest the buildings with bats and raise the rents after each move out! What's wrong, you guys? Wimping out on me? I can't wait to see the looks on those dumb wetbacks' faces, who can't even speak English and can't even complain!"

Corky's place setting included a contemplative napkin, two spoons in a trance, two knives in mindfulness, and a placid fork.

"Fortunately they don't know the meaning of unlawful detainer," said Larry, "so they . . ."

"You're not listening to me," interrupted Viktor. "Don't waste my time! I'm a legendary philanthropist around here. Someday they will have a statue of me on Nicollet Avenue to replace that fake Minnesotan cunt who's not from around here, eh Corky? Eh, Larry? Or maybe name a whole mall after me—like Krollwood Plaza—or like a museum—the Martensen Institute of Art—or a baseball team—the Minnesota Martens! Except I hate the whole fucking state down to the last liberal gopher hole and the last Communist corn cob! I'm a fucking genius! The cops, the council, the judges . . . I've got them all. And I'm playing Minneapolis like a violin!"

Viktor looked like Baba Yaga when he smiled with rictus teeth over a danse macabre on his invisible violin.

"Minneapolis is a slumlord's paradise," continued Viktor. "Fucking farmers! No class."

"Speaking of farmers . . ." said Corky.

Sausage Man, in his Oshkosh overalls and top-buttoned, plaid flannel shirt, carried a fishing rod with a barbed #14 fishhook flying loose, stumbled into Club Miami past Dagny, waved at Nestor, and walked toward the bathroom. He stopped at Viktor's table and recited:

> The geese have come to Watkins
> If only to rhyme with the catkins
> There, they, the geese, that is
> Should wear crew-necked sweaters
> When they dance around in Vs by night
> To look a little dressed up
> When they go HONK HONK
> Or when the geese make love
> By the moonlight of a summer's day
> So much grace and excretion

Viktor pinned Sausage Man from behind and jack-knifed him over.

With a red silk handkerchief, he strangled Sausage Man, who spit out lines of drool and foamed with a froth like a cyanide-poisoned spittlebug. From behind, with his forged and customized Alpha Kappa Psi fraternity ring, Viktor pounded Sausage Man in the face and drew blood over his left eye. He half-nelsoned Sausage Man to the floor and kicked him in the head.

Sausage Man gripped Viktor's dinner table to steady himself when allowed up.

"Get the fuck out of my restaurant, you fucking wet brain!" said Viktor, sitting back down. "That's it! I'm hiring bouncers. I have a lot of cop friends like BB who would love to pound the shit out of losers like that."

"What happened?" asked LaDonna and asked Sausage Man if he was okay.

"Hey, when you get tired of my talentless fuck of a son," said Viktor, writing on a napkin his latest iPhone number. "Try calling me and we can make *real* beautiful music together."

"Who had the pork spare rib plate with extra sauce?" asked LaDonna, presenting Larry his plate of ribs.

Sausage Man staggered past Dagny and he recovered himself on Hennepin Avenue. Hawk Eye hunkered on his heels like a Vietnamese farmer. He exhaled over his lip blister smoke from a Sherman cigarette stub Viktor had "donated" on his way in. Hawk Eye watched Sausage Man jaywalk in the middle of Hennepin Avenue toward a white Dodge van that looked like all the other white Dodge vans, one of which had parked in front of the other white Dodge van, because a white Dodge van is so obviously obvious and undercover, it's obviously not what it is, nor what is not—that was dazzlingly obvious too.

Awakened from a nap, the first white Dodge van sped off, honking its goose horn through a red light.

The parked second white Dodge van's door flew open and closed behind Sausage Man.

"Here, sexy," smiled Viktor, laying his hands on one of the dinner plates. "That's mine."

"What isn't?" asked LaDonna, fumbling the large plate of pork spare ribs, baked beans, and coleslaw. "Ah!"

Baked beans and coleslaw covered Viktor's head and shoulders with a hood of food.

"I'm so sorry!" said LaDonna. "It slipped! I'll get you another plate!"

When Larry and Corky instinctively pushed their chairs away from the table, the table reared up and revealed a black lump.

"Where did *that* come from?" asked Viktor, immediately recognizing the particular model, make, and price of the brand. "That's a listening device. I've seen this type before too. Nestor told her to plant that there, because Nestor was jealous of me! That little shit! Traitor!"

Viktor's eyes clouded over and flashed retribution, retaliation, and revenge at both Larry and Corky, the sitting wooden ducks before the hailstorm. Viktor removed his suit jacket and tie, stripped to his shirt sleeves. Dumbfounded, humiliated, and hungry, his neck grew thick as beeswax while he ate from Larry's and Corky's plates. Swallowing, he held his head up stiffly with a narrow candle flame of consciousness flickering inside it. Viktor rolled up his sleeves, baring his bare arms and wiggling their muscles. He tore at the ribs between his gold teeth and he ate with his mouth open so that he amplified his chewing the saucy, slurpy pink pork.

"Who's following me?" asked Viktor, cracking his knuckles and splicing together sentences. "You two numskulls?"

"Viktor," said Larry, flexing his hand to avoid its cramping from dehydration. "Don't you remember? You put that listening device there! You are following you!"

"Oh yeaaaaaahhhhhh," said Corky as a singer ends a song, waiting for the band to stop. "I remember. I was there that day."

"That's impossible," Viktor snorted.

Hawk Eye, smelling of stale chew, smoked Sherman butts, and campfire ashes padded with splayed feet into BookSmart and asked Chitchee for a magic marker and a hunk of cardboard. He looked sleep-deprived and draggle-tailed.

"Having a good day, Hawk Eye?" asked Torg.

"Nope," said Hawk Eye, scrawling his message with a weary disdain for the world he found himself in: VEtEran needs $$$ Cash for hotEl.

"Why not?" asked Kennedy radiantly and expansively, sitting alone on the torn black couch.

Kennedy looked for anyone looking over his shoulder. He watched the nonsense of the world with wry amusement, crossed his legs, and contemplated his good fortune.

"That same asshole outside Club Miami flicked his cig in my face and called me a bum," said Hawk Eye.

"What did you do with that provocation?" asked Kennedy with supreme confidence.

"I smoked it," said Hawk Eye.

Peeking inside BookSmart, Courtney Kirkwood searched for a sign, tilting her head up, down, left, and right. Chitchee motioned to her that the coast was clear. When the front door opened, a shivaree of searing, soaring sound of squad cars passed overhead.

"Chitch, can I use your potty?" asked Hawk Eye.

"It's your potty and you can cry if you want to," said Chitchee. "Where else do you go?"

"I'm used to sleeping in Porta-Pottys around Lake Calhoun after dark," said Hawk Eye.

"Isn't that dangerous?" asked Chitchee.

"I've got something on me for that," said Hawk Eye over his shoulder.

Customers scattered and returned—except Torg—flinchless and magnificent. A war hero in his own mind's eye movie, Torg of the Nile, Explorer, Tomb Raider, puffed up with a puppy love that melted himself into Katreena's infinite ocean, an ocean of fantastic, unconditional love.

Courtney swept in and thrust a numbly dumb Torg into Kennedy, advancing toward the maroon counter to re-confirm the status of his hold pile.

Torg, hearing only a confabulation of Katreena's conversations of love whispered across a pillow, bounced off Kennedy. Torg thought about calling his lady love. He pictured himself flying on a Turkish carpet, whisking Katreena off her stilettos, and fighting dragons derived from unwatchable Rudolph Valentino potboilers from Hollywood's collective unconscious of kitsch.

"Man," said Kennedy to Chitchee avoiding his name, "can you quote me a price for this Fossil watch? A very expensive time-piece?

"Did you ever find *The Memory Book?*" asked Chitchee.

"What is memory anyway? It's over-valorized."

Chitchee handed Kennedy his hold pile and then examined the Fossil for a sign of the time.

Hawk Eye strolled outside, squatted on the sidewalk, and copy-edited his cardboard sign with a few superfluous and ornamental apostrophes.

"I brought these up from the overstock area for you, Kennedy," said Chitchee and grinned at the embarrassment (for BookSmart) of having twenty copies of *The Memory Book.* "They've probably been down in the basement since before the first writing system sprang up in the cedar groves of Lebanon."

Chitchee expected by a quick x-ray of Kennedy's wide grin that Kennedy had expected Chitchee to do BookSmart a whale of a favor by unloading a discounted *The Memory Book* on Kennedy. Kennedy pushed the piles of *The Memory Book* away.

"No thank you," said Kennedy. "Memory interferes with my thought processes. I am no longer preoccupied by memory and its triflications. Now, it's snowmobiles!"

"All right, but if you change your mind . . ." said Chitchee. "I'll shelve these in the Self-Help shelf for future reference."

Hawk Eye squatted on his heels between BookSmart and Club Miami. When he saw Lake Street Rodney windmilling toward BookSmart, Hawk Eye placed his Twins cap back on his head and his eye-bags darkened with ink.

Rodney carried a briefcase—but he never *dressed* like a briefcase—he wore a mesh soccer shirt and kelly green pants, but a briefcase locked to his wrist? Plaid cap, white sneakers, secret languages.

"Hello, book-loving world!" announced Rodney, ignoring the Fossil fascinating the others. "So glad you are here, and not *not* here and not in the condo complex someday going in everywhere until the here is not co-hering anymore. And *then* we lose all co-here-ence. Someday this will all be gone. And we'll all be dust, hah, ha! There will be fast-food drive-ins called Bin Laden's with Al Qaeda burgers, Taliban fries, and Suicide Bomber cherry cokes. Tragedy will be monetized into a brand!"

"What's wrong with you, man?" asked Kennedy, shaking his head. "Homebrand Security can arrest you for traitorous speech like that and incarnate you in Guadalupe Bay."

"Rodney," said Chitchee, "I think you have neighborhood separation anxiety disorder, complicated with extreme condophobia and a poverty of ideation due to a fixation on *Lord of the Rings*. I think you should renounce the world and become a Benedictine monk."

"Yeah, that occurred to me too," said Rodney. "But I don't think that's the thing. Here's the new thing—"

Recently Rodney had been banned from a local biscotti bistro for soliciting threesomes, or even fivesomes, by dropping fortune cookie slips on their tables that suggested that the polyamorous group could encounter in their near future a "super fun roll in the hay, not in real hay, which would itch, unless the hay were made of silk and it would not itch as much as hay itches because silken hay hasn't been invented yet."

"It's super hot in here," said Rodney, completely forgetting what the "new thing" was.

"Maybe it's because of the hot weather," said Torg. "Even the pigeons are slapping on the Coppertone. I saw a mosquito with a can of OFF!"

"I need a ride to Big Brain Comics," said Rodney. "The answer lies there. I better check the bus schedules again. I will be right back."

"I need to buy the books in my hold pile," said Kennedy, "before they warp speed into lumberous dead wood and attract fungi to their spines. So why not give this extraordinary Fossil watch a proper home before fungi eat my hold pile?"

The proper home? Chitchee didn't enjoy the proposition. He feared Kennedy would be a stray cat led to milk with his endless dickering—first the milk, then the soy milk, then the almond milk, then straight out breastfeeding from Chitchee's nipples.

"Your hold pile for this Fossil watch that doesn't work?" asked Chitchee. "I can't be bartering with BookSmart property. Unless I paid for the books then bartered for the watch. Don't you ever have any money for books?"

"That old Fossil watch only needs a battery," countered Kennedy. "Do you think I'm holding back on you? I'm doing my norms. Nothing's changed, right? Nothing's new in the store?"

"Do you have anything else I might want to buy from you outright?" queried Chitchee. "You know, something that works, or fits, or a dented can of kidney beans that doesn't need to be Carbon-12 dated?"

"My friend," said Kennedy, "I have just the ticket for an outwardly mobile young man on the make like yourself! While doing my usual machinations on the circum-ambulances of my daily matriculations. Then . . . and suddenly in my own back alley, I spotted out of the corner of my field of vision . . . WHAT DO YOU THINK I SAW?"

"Venus?" asked Chitchee.

"Nope! There across my horizon like a Spanish galleon," said Kennedy, "was a MINT futon! And it was a *Coyote* original. Made in Japan. Japan! Coyote, Japan. Seeing that was like a vision! Promise not to tell anyone about this? Let's keep it strictly in confidentiality mode for now."

Kennedy had nabbed a perfectly good futon by a dumpster outside his rented room. He appraised the futon's resale value at two thousand dollars; meanwhile, he had been sleeping on it, but it was lumpy and lumpy bounced him awake, injuring his back. He dreaded lying down on the original Coyote from Japan, because the thought of staying up all night kept him up all night.

"The frame and the cushion were in factory condition," bellowed Kennedy. "But there was a PROTUBERANCE in it, and it was goring my BACK! Don't interlocute anyone about my score! Word MIGHT get out at MICKEY D's!"

"Shhh . . ." said Chitchee. "I bet they heard that at Mickey D's."

"I want to list it on Craigslist," said Kennedy ambitiously, "but how do you get on his list? Can you call this guy Craig? Maybe you can show me how to program the computer to get on his guest list? I'll never learn how to compute those programs everyone's jaw-blocking about: Twixter, Weezly, Hooters . . ."

Chitchee watched a Lincoln Town Car wheel to the curb.

"Is it prom week?" Chitchee asked Kennedy.

Chitchee handed the Fossil back to Kennedy and expected an ireful rebuff. In fact, Kennedy without so much as a worry line, serenely sat on the black leather couch and dreamed himself out the window.

The Lincoln Town Car did not have an ending or it was a space-time dilation of a Volkswagen black bug tripping on itself. The satin-black finished chassis and the iodine-tinted windows elongated like a stick of black gum. Bomb bay doors opened: The Indestructible Book Jesus spread-eagled out of the prom car: parachuting without a ripcord. The Indestructible Book Jesus was dressed in second-hand, baggy, charcoal swallowtails, a studded, piqued shirtfront, a white bowtie, and a black cummerbund. Once landed like a warbling, red-eyed vireo, he slicked his hair back, his comb filled with Crisco shortening.

"Books to sell, boss!" said The Indestructible Book Jesus. "That last step was a doozy, hyuck!"

Sergei Vorchenko, the chauffeur, had double-parked, engine idling. He offloaded the boxes of books. Duct tape, bungee cords, carabiners, and climbing ropes spraddled over the curb. Sergei shoved the ratty boxes of books (this batch donated from seven churches of seven different denominations) onto a dolly and wheeled the books into the store.

Ionized into action, because The Indestructible Book Jesus threatened his link in the food chain, Kennedy snapped out of his couch fog. The store's ability to pay out used book sellers fluctuated wildly, and the bread in the rusty till might be bread crusts.

"Wait, my friend," said Kennedy. "I have other things for sale too. I have a gym bag filled with gym bags for you: Land's End, L. L. Bean, Lululemon—look at this, a Giorgio Armani fanny pack—top of the line designer *brand* new *brand* gym bags and these Luxottica *brand* glasses. Without their lenses *alone*, these Luxottica frames are worth 200 dollars. Can you look these up on your computer programmer?"

"Kennedy," said Chitchee, "this isn't Pawn America! Are we done wheezing and deezing, theeing and thouing and—?"

"—and this Borax," said Kennedy, "wait! I'm not finished! I found it in my futon. I was sleeping on this lump of BO-RAX! Until it punched my back out of joint! I crowbarred it out of there!"

A sealed two-pound Ziploc baggie of white powder kerplopped on the BookSmart counter. A plastic sticker of an alligator with a trapped squirrel in its mouth, soon to be swallowed and digested, clung to the Ziploc baggie.

"Good old Borax!" said Chitchee. "Thanks for reminding me! I have to do my laundry because I don't have any fresh socks. That ain't Tide, that's not even Gain, so how much do you want for that crap? A couple bucks for the Borax? Will that satisfy your desire to be a millionaire?"

Kennedy squinted and raised his thumb to say "higher, higher."

"Make it five," said Kennedy. "I had to spend a lot of money this morning for something I had to have and my cash liquidity is on zero. Make it five bucks. Help me out."

"Deal."

They high-fived, missing each other, so they "high-foured."

Chitchee left the baggie of laundry detergent on the counter.

"Howdy, homesteaders!" yahooed The Indestructible Book Jesus like a rootin' tootin' Chill Wills cowboy.

The gussied-up Indestructible Book Jesus doled out Corona cigars to whoever: Torg, Courtney, his chauffeur Sergei, Randy Quaalude (pushing his girlfriend, the wheelchaired Susquehanna), Felix Weatherwax (who couldn't find his glasses whoa! he was wearing them) on his way to the Uptown Theater, the macquillage artistes Sarah, Olivia, and Nikki inside the MAC makeup store, Sho "Sweet Jap" Nokaido from Everyday People, the Club Miami valet parkers, Pat, Jarod, Ryan, and Tyler, and the maverick Sausage Man, who stood continually at the Club Miami valet parking stand and gave his poetry readings. Sky blue clouds of cigar smoke mushroomed above Hennepin Avenue. The smokers smoked themselves into smoky, grinning silhouettes outlined against the brood of cloudy office towers in the distance. They coughed their lungs to shreds. They needed iron lungs and without medical insurance some would have to share.

"What's the occasion, Indestructible Book Jesus?" asked Chitchee, choking outside BookSmart. "Did you give birth to a son?"

"Wouldn't you like to know?" chortled The Indestructible Book Jesus, walking inside.

Chitchee spread-eagled on the sidewalk, crying unable to breathe:

"Oh, God, what is *in* these things? Couldn't you have celebrated with Thai Stick instead?"

The party osmosed back to their respective positions of employment.

Sergei laughed out smoke like a bell-rung bell boy, hair punk-cut like a half-eaten cake, earrings in his nose, plumber's fittings in his lobes, tattoos crawling over his clavicles, and a shadowy beard composed of black ants. His dark eyes roved. Sergei unloaded the twenty-five boxes. With little crying boy eyelashes, entranced by the slow ladies entering Club Miami and the fast women coming out, Sergei Vorchenko lost all direction, watching a swinging skirt waving from Rubenesque hips—into the Club Miami he disappeared for a quick Fat Tire or any Bruges style-beer and maybe an appetizer of deep-fried wild shrimp for the proverbial "one beer."

The Indestructible Book Jesus was a religious man. And Chitchee guessed correctly that the religious man was selling boxes of religious books by televangelists who were the religious men who wrote the religious books religious people swore on. The televangelists were all religious men. They spoke to God. When He spoke to them, He spoke to them in a foreign language, which they countered with body English, ululations in strange tongues, and collection baskets.

"Look at you, Indestructible Book Jesus! Aren't you the cat's meow!" said Chitchee, hands on hips like a sassy woman. "Hey Saami, look what the cat drugged in!"

"Yeah, I can see it's the cat's meow, great," said a disgruntled Saami as he mentally foraged through the arriving cargo and rejected it in its totality. "Meow."

"Hey, you!" said Lily Holmgren from her bus driver's perch to Rodney, who was returning to BookSmart, "that limousine cannot be there! Move your car before I call Bobby and Steve's, the thumpers, and the Fire Department. DO YOU UNDERSTAND?"

"Okay!" said Rodney. "Okay! Can't we all be as affable and charming as me sometimes?"

In Chitchee's back pocket itched Aloysius's guide to buying used books. The list had been handwritten in felt-tip pen and Xeroxed. One by one Chitchee checked off each line with the matching unwanted item in the torn boxes of The Indestructible Book Jesus's books for sale.

BOOKS WE DON'T BUY FROM
THE INDESTRUCTIBLE BOOK JESUS

Books held together with masking and / or duct tape

Books with pages missing / falling out / chewed / broken spines

Books with mildew, mold, fungi, dry rot, worms, parasites, centipedes, snakes

Books by Televangelists (except Schuler and Swindall)

Books with underlining / highlighting / magic markering / tomato soup—crayons OK

Books of fiction without dust jackets unless Brautigan or Shakespeare or Richard Brautigan

Books on war before World War I–Civil War no dust jacket

No books on economics, political science, or crime extreme right or left

Mass Market romance more than two years old and / or less than $1.95

Hardbacked romance / big outdated fat books on diet

Travel books and cookbooks that are more than ten years old and / or no pictures

"Yep," said Chitchee, checkmark by checkmark, "they're all there. All the books we don't want, or need, or even want to look at, Boss Man!"

"Oh, don't say that, Boss Man!" said The Indestructible Book Jesus. "I'm usually broke!"

"Where did you get the money for a limousine?" asked Chitchee.

"I came into a little inheritance this morning, you could say," said The Indestructible Book Jesus. "Hyuck, hyuck."

"You're really an inspiration to all of us experiencing adversity," said Chitchee. "Your Epictetian perseverance against impossible odds after life gave you a lemon—it's pretty damn refreshing. A weaker man would have seppukued his sanpaku."

"The wisest man needs the wisest advice," said The Indestructible Book Jesus.

"Hey, wise man, do we really need *used* Q Tips? They're not *completely* yellow!" said Saami, twirling them in his ears and looking at the goo. "But now they are! What is this thing, looks familiar . . . a planner? Hey, Chitchee, look! It's a giant *planner!*"

"No, it's the Family Photo Album!" said Chitchee. "The exact *same* Family Photo Album I gave to the thumpers! The one I put the rent in by mistake! Where's the envelope though?"

"Finders keepers?" said The Indestructible Book Jesus whose crest looked ready to fall.

"The cash you found in our trash was our stash?" moaned Chitchee.

"Ain't that some shit, boss?" crowed The Indestructible Book Jesus, admiring his work like a brick-mason at the bottom of the Tower of Babel.

"Oh, that is definitely some shit!" said Chitchee. "No two shits about that shit!"

"Boss, I can't give it back," said The Indestructible Book Jesus, crow's feet disappearing into other more interesting wrinkles forming a graveyard of Celtic cross-wrinkles with tombstones.

"I used it to make a payment on my sister's medical bills this morning. Hennepin County Medical threatened to take her house to pay for the operation for her breast cancer."

"You had to save her house or she would be in a home, and you had to follow your *dharma*? That's right out of *The Mahabharata*. I'll tell Aloysius the good news, that you are an avatar of Vishnu and Krishna!"

Saami, at sea, felt torn apart. His head swam like a swan. Saami looked at the ceiling for his mother. Chitchee phone-called Aloysius, who was taking a nap.

Chitchee told him what had happened to the rent money:

"So the rent money went to a great cause after all," said Chitchee. "Hyuck, hyuck, hyuck."

"Okay, okay," said Aloysius. "Let me think."

"Hello?" snorted Chitchee, rolling his eyes to fill in the dead air of silence, awkwardly expanding outward. "Still there?"

"Nothing we can do," concluded Aloysius, coughing aggressively, a Saturn coughing up a hairball. "I guess in the future: don't use envelopes stuffed with thousands of dollars in them as book-markers again. And—we'll think of something—I think—

something—oh this is terrible news damn—hey—did I leave my *Lovin' Spoonful Songbook* there? Oh, don't worry about it. It's only money (*groan*). Good job, buddy. I'll be in tomorrow morning, bright and early, around opening time. We're going to turn this thing around. Don't worry, we've got this (*groan*). And Chitchee, thanks for sharing the truth. Good job, buddy."

"Good job, buddy?" Chitchee asked himself, hanging up, stupefied by the *sans souci* of Aloysius. "I'm not fired? Saami! Why doesn't Aloysius seem to care about anything? Does this job make any sense at all? Is this it: Aloysius fears BookSmart's rent taking off because the land values will go up and then we won't be able to afford the rent?"

"Eh?" said Saami. "My God, questions, questions, questions, where do you get all these questions?"

"What questions?" asked Chitchee. "Was I asking too many questions? What exactly are too many questions? Where do you draw the line? What kind of line? From where does one derive the authority to determine how many questions are too many? I'm not *not* doing a good job? Is that what the Boss Man thinks?"

"You won't get fired for doing a fucking *terrible* job," said Saami unphilosophically, kettling all the televangelists (including Schuler and Swindall) in their own quarantine, "unless you somehow failed to flunk the drug test. Noel the goody two-shoes somehow passed. He bribed his way in here I bet with his goody two-shoes."

"Sure, but how are we going to pay the rent?" said Chitchee. "I feel really bad about giving away our rent money outright. How could there have been six thousand dollars in there? I guess in thousand dollar denominations. I owe the store six thousand dollars. How am I going to come up with six thousand dollars? Organ donation? What if we each chipped in a kidney?"

"I don't think," said Saami, "all our kidneys equal one kidney. Hey Chitch, can you take over? I got mental carpal tunnels. I can't do this shit anymore. What's the point? I'll be downstairs dying, the sooner the better. Fuck, sick of everything."

"Okay, skipper!" said Chitchee. "I will take over the steering wheel. Hugs? No? Why don't you go look at some porn and make yourself feel better?"

"So much porn," muttered Saami, accelerating down the steps for a pull, "and so little time to take it all in. Sad."

Chitchee chilled when looking at books. He rooted through every box carted in by The Indestructible Book Jesus, who packed them as quickly as they were rejected. Like a tag team, Chitchee took them out, and The Indestructible Book Jesus put them back in. Questioning and resenting nothing, The Indestructible Book Jesus simply put his hand to the plow. Usually sellers felt shorted, cheated, and outraged—even if the offer had been given a fair price in good faith at 20%.

Chitchee examined: *The Calling of Dan Mathews* by H. B. Wright, 1909, pub. by The Book Supply; *Hal Keen: The Hermit of Gordon's Creek* by Hugh Lloyd; *Time for Living* by George Soule, 1955 (its lone blurb: "Are we entering a new instar?"); *Donna Parker at Cherrydale* by Marcia Martin, 1957 (Chitchee opened it and read the title: Chapter 18: A Rosebud Opens); and *Two Flutes Playing: Spiritual Love / Sacred Sex* by Andrew Rammer, 1990, spiral-bound.

Chitchee appreciated how much time, effort, and skill it took to write a horrible book and submit it to an even more horrible publisher, but he shook his head at the books on his plate and said:

"Oh how I pity mankind for the dreck it produces, oh look, more dreck, *Being and A Waste of Time*," said Chitchee. "Wait! Wow! The complete Müller *Rig-Veda* in reprint from the Sacred Books series!"

Jorma Ringquist led with his crew cut of blonde Astro Turf when he entered Book Smart on the balls of his feet like a kangaroo with plantar fasciitis, tilting him forward, with his sunny gray irises, quick with flecks of blue, behind purple-tinted sewing glasses.

Jorma had jacked abs to have such a spring-loaded body.

"Do you have books on mushrooms?" asked Jorma, leaning over the maroon counter.

"Yeah," said Chitchee. "The *Rig Veda* (according to *Soma* anyway). It was written on mushrooms!"

"Do you have books on ayahuasca?"

"Hold on, I'll be with you in one second," said Chitchee, sneezing after which he heard the children's song "High Hopes."

Chitchee set aside the returned Family Photo Album from the boxes of The Indestructible Book Jesus and shoved it under the counter, "Evidence for the FBI."

"Where did you get these books, Indestructible Book Jesus?" asked Chitchee, wiping his itchy nose clean. "I promise I won't go there! I swear on a biblical jawbone of wooly mammoth proportions."

"Outside abandoned buildings, boss!" replied The Indestructible Book Jesus. "A lot of them from them run-down MPG apartments on Hennepin or Lake or in Northeast off Central."

"But where did you get *this* Family Photo Album?" pressed Chitchee.

"Right outside *your* building, boss!" said The Indestructible Book Jesus. "Hyuck!"

Illiterate as The Indestructible Book Jesus was, he maintained the manners of a bindle-stiffed Thomas Merton with the spine of a Martin Luther, stiffened by year after year of his pushing around grocery carts all day filled with books for ten bucks and smokes, thanking everyone profusely for his martyrdom and the pay-dirt for every abuse he suffered like Mansur al-Hallaj.

"Thanks for having the car parked, man," said Sergei, bouncing in tardy to BookSmart. "Are you ready to pack up the 25 boxes?"

"I didn't park the car," said The Indestructible Book Jesus. "I thought you parked the car."

Sergei turned around and around.

"The keys were in the ignition," he said. "Oh, shit. My goose is cooked."

Lake Street Rodney drove east on Hennepin Avenue, Torg riding shotgun, Courtney Kirkwood, Randy Quaalude, Susquehanna, and Sausage Man in the back of the Lincoln Town Car. Corks ricocheted like rabbits. Champagne bottles foamed.

"Big Brain Comics here we come," sang Rodney at the wheel of the Lincoln Town Car. "Anybody remember where it is?"

"No," said Courtney, "cause it sucks! Those guys are assholes! Let's go to the Book Trader and see whether Fluffy has gotten in any new stuffed Pee Wee Herman dolls for my playhouse. Make a U-ey and get back on Lake Street so we can avoid the highway."

"Okey dokey, Captain!" said Rodney and U-turned on Hennepin.

When he drove over two curbs, he added:

"*The Streets of San Francisco*! I feel just like Karl Malden!"

His passengers sandwiched to the right side of the Lincoln Town Car's interior when he took a sharp left.

"Ow, I hate Rice-a-Roni," squawked Courtney. "What are you doing? You gave me a concussion! My skull might be fractured. Take me to Hennepin County! I need to go to Urgent Care!"

Rodney saw flashing lights in his rear view. He slammed on the brakes, pulled over, figured it must be a mistake, and sped off accelerating as if to elude pursuit.

"The ayahuasca is downstairs," Chitchee yelled across the room to Jorma.

Customers looked up, minced downstairs, and searched for ayahuasca, looking to see vines from the Upper Amazon entwined around the bookcases.

"Saami, can you cover the register?" Chitchee yelled down the stairwell.

"Why?" Saami yelled upstairs, tossed aside his empty half-pint of Phillips Vodka, and trudged grumpily upstairs to mind the store. "Lord!"

Downstairs, Jorma openly explained to Chitchee that he imported "research chemicals" in hollowed-out, electronics catalogs from Taoist alchemists in China, which he bought with electronic gold. They discussed the Silk Road, bitcoin, Erowid, and trips.

They stood before the Drugs and Narcotics shelf.

"Richard Schultes here?" asked Jorma.

"Like you're going to find Schultes anywhere," said Chitchee with an upwardly rising tone and it wasn't a question. "So you know all about entheogens?"

"I used to sell Erowid Kid T-shirts at South High School at our high school football games," said Jorma, "but I don't pretend to be a *Sasha*."

"Well, if you need a front man, let me know," said Chitchee. "I lost BookSmart six thousand dollars today. That's a bad omen. I might be a 'cooler' of bad luck for the store, and the store is doomed because of me."

Walking up the stairs, they exchanged email addresses and agreed to get together for caffeine, nicotine, and possibly DMT, DIPT, or MIPT. And Chitchee would keep an eye out for: Alexander Shulgin (THIKAL and PHIKAL), Albert Hofmann, Peter Stafford, William Emboden, anything from Loompanics, and the *nom de guerre* pamphlets you used to see on the wire racks at Shinders.

Jorma on the way out the front door halted.

"What is *that*? Do you always leave your cocaine out?" he said, pointing at the laundry detergent.

"Cocaine?" whispered Kennedy, looking up from his books on snowmobiles. "What?"

"CO-caine?" whispered Chitchee. "As in co-CAINE? Co-ca-EE-na?"

"Cocaine," declared Jorma, dipped his index into the powder, and licked his finger.

"Wait one half second," said Kennedy in a crescendo. "I would like to put a court order on that item, *in vitro*. I was under duress at the time of the contractual term, so I hereby revoke and anNUL the orAL agrEEment A-FORE-SAID."

"Wait," said Chitchee, taking the bag in hand. "Why don't we split it three ways, if Jorma can sell it for—ten grand?—or—"

"At least 6,000," said Jorma.

"6,000 dollars worth?" said Saami. "That wouldn't have gotten Rick James through an intersection."

"Maybe 10,000," said Jorma. "I'd have to weigh it."

"But who is this gentleman?" asked Kennedy.

"This is Jorma, Kennedy," said Chitchee. "He knows everything about this subject and probably can sell tons of anything off the Silk Road for us. We have to do *something* to pay the rent. Or the store dies. And then we die. Everything will die. Civilization. Period . . . end of sentence . . . end of period . . ."

"Is that the end of your sentence? Question mark?" asked Kennedy.

"Yes! Exclamation point!" said Chitchee. "Wait, I was thinking of beginning a new sentence. I sure could use a semicolon right about now."

"Let's pool our heads together and the universe will float us the answer!" exclaimed Kennedy. "Isn't that what all the good books say?"

"Aha! Aha! Aha! The universe has answered for free!" said Chitchee. "Here's the answer: by whatever means necessary we must love what we can love until we have loved all that we can love because it's all we can do to love everyone we can love in the hopes of promoting local book stores like this so we can get paid."

"No wonder the universe didn't charge you! You are expostulating the premise that we donate to a complete unknown this unknown amount of *product*? And we expect that a COMPLETE STRANGER—" said Kennedy to Chitchee, cutting himself off in mid sentence—out of words completely.

"He's not a *complete* stranger," said Chitchee. "I've known him forever since I met him."

When Kennedy reached for the Ziploc, Chitchee wouldn't let go.

"I'll sell it," said Saami, jumping. "To *me*. For free."

Seeing Saami lick his finger and plunge for the Ziploc, Chitchee and Kennedy grappled for possession of the cocaine with intensity.

"Kennedy, you sold the bag to *me*, and a deal's a deal," said Chitchee. "We high-fived on it. I will donate the proceeds to BookSmart, so we can all have a community center for alternative medicine."

"But, officially speaking," objected Kennedy, "you missed my whole hand by the nature of not including all five digits. Why should we bother, we HAVE a community center for alternative medicine. It's called McDonald's."

"Yeah," said Chitchee, "but if you want to sit around McDonald's all day, you have to buy something. That's a whole different ball game across the street."

Jorma claimed he could sell the Ziploc to his friends, but Kennedy counter-claimed he himself had partners, partners with real prison records—*guys who knew what they were doing*.

Thus ensued the struggle for the Ziploc, and it turned into a row with Jorma trying to make peace and Saami trying to disturb it.

In a three-way tug of war, the Ziploc plastic sheared. Kennedy and Chitchee stretched the bag and held it high. Saami clawed at it. The Ziploc tore open. Blizzards flew upward. Puffs of crystal particles in a white ermine cloud cloaked Noel Schoolcraft sallying into BookSmart. The ranking night manager, Noel immediately calculated the verified purchaser/free rider ratio, resisted a roll to his eyes, walked behind the counter to start his shift, rolled his eyes, and found himself covered with cocaine hydrochloride.

"What's with all the baby powder?" asked Noel, brushing a little space free for his pens and notebooks. "Did somebody have a baby?"

"You know how the regulars are, always having babies," said Chitchee. "Yep, quite the baby-powderized situation. Why don't we sell diapers by the gross?"

"I never know when you are kidding, Chitchee," said Noel.

"Neither do I," said Chitchee, giving Noel a thwarted hug (who thrust him back). "Are you kidding? You didn't have to call in a SWAT team."

"Look," said Noel. "I wanted to officially welcome you to BookSmart. I hope you enjoy your term of employment here. Other than that . . ."

Kennedy, Saami, and Jorma scuttled like one giant robber crab across the redolent, white pine flooring, salvaging what hadn't blown down the aisles. Noel threw open the front door, allowing the wind to disperse the powder. He wiped the powder off his glasses (actually he had shed a little tear but had to delete it) like a dentist reviewing his instruments.

"Lord, we almost had a month's rent!" exclaimed Saami, licking the redolent, white pine wood flooring.

Noel drilled his eyes into the back of Saami's shaved head (was Saami in another crapulent state?). Noel felt pappy and maternalistic: like he was Saami's grandmother when Saami was in kindergarten, and Noel checked to see whether Saami wore clean underwear and didn't have any fruit in his loom. Owlish Noel's eyeglasses glowed fowlishly at Saami. Who was Saami anyway? How did a Saami persuade himself, with what philosophical underpinnings, to exist every eternally-recurring morning? Noel wondered whether Saami had any class consciousness at all. Behind that leprechaun face, was there a brain exhibiting functionality, or a dead *E coli* at the bottom of an empty stairwell? Noel felt contempt for Saami. Saami had transmogrified his brain into scrotal tissue and didn't care like an ignoble runt!

"Saami," said Noel, bending his back over an Amway ring binder, which contained the store's accounts, Noel's script so small an ant with contact lenses could not tell what language it was.

"Noel."

"Why are you licking the floor?" asked Noel.

"I'm dreaming I'm a corn broom," responded Saami.

"Can you clean up the place?" requested Noel, brushing the cocaine off the counter. "And get this stuff off the counter, whatever it is."

BookSmart's customers always said that Noel had the warmth of a Mars rover collecting soil samples, but Chitchee admired Noel's self-control. Cold Noel was always: I can educate you all, down there in your sty of self-ignorance. Noel had really put his heart behind the Enlightenment of Diderot, Locke, Hume, and Mill, and on through to Russell. He pushed the Enlightenment ahead, micron by micron, with dogged, idealistic optimism. Hegel, Husserl, Derrida—he thought obscure at best and at worst deliberately obscure. Noel believed in incremental perfection, equality, progress, and dignity, but with an almost misanthropic, lordly hauteur. He had no use for non-utilitarians. He hated people out of a love for abstract humanity.

Noel had sacrificed a doctorate in political science from Columbia University to partly own a half, belly-up book store. Not a day went by, he did not regret it. He once imagined himself as a civic leader and City Council Member fighting corruption. Canvasser, census taker, get-out-the-vote volunteer making phone calls, staunch Progressive, and La Follette follower, he was a self-described neo-Chomskyologist, post anarcho-syndicalist, syndicated techno-anarchicalist, and synarcho-analist.

"Okay, Chitchee," said Noel, "if you haven't noticed, I love to split categories into sub- and sub-sub-categories. Our sociology section is not clear enough. It has to be divided and clarified until each book has its own section and label. That's how we achieve inclusivity and at the same time diversity. We need to create sections tonight. For Social Justice. Work ennobles, *real* work! Let's go downstairs and take some measurements. Saami can watch the register."

"Moving books around is work?" asked Chitchee, following Noel downstairs. "When I think of moving books around, I think of moving books around."

Noel didn't process it as a question. His brain went: legitimate question? Yes/no? If no, don't answer. If yes, file under: Trivia, Bourgeois Thought, World Religions. Noel's mind was all BookSmart. Now, the store needed to rethink its book shelves, *vis a vis* Urban Studies, Labor Studies, Gender Studies, Trans and Cis Studies, Trans-Gender Philosophy and Non-Binary Algebra . . . No joking around (he reminded himself) when it comes to touchy private parts round these parts—so BookSmart needed to differentiate GLBTQ studies, Women's Studies versus Women's Global Studies, Straight Women Who Are Studying Lesbians' Lesbian Studies, Women in Labor Studies, Laborious Women's Studies, Superfluous Men's Studies, the Iron John Studies shelf, and bell hooksiana. Noel wanted a Mary Daly label beneath the no Mary Daly books (just in case) section. He shook his head at the slow-selling *Women Who Run With Wolves*, *Women Who Can't Keep Up With Wolves*, Camille Paglia, Susan Faludi's *Backlash* backstocked in stacks, and multiple remaindered copies of: *When I Grow Old I Shall Turn Purple*.

"Chitchee, where is the Aging Section? Let's put Aging on the bottom shelf."

"But that's ageist!" said Chitchee.

"You're right,"said Noel. "*Anything* on the bottom shelf would be discrimination. But how do we get around not having a bottom shelf on a bookcase?"

"We might have to call the whole social justice project off," said Chitchee sadly, "in the interests of social justice."

"Chitchee, do you think we should move," said Noel, measuring the available shelf space with his forearm like a cubit, "the chick lit next to the feminist section or as far away from it as possible? I'm uncommitted about *The Devil Wears Pravda* and all that fluff."

"Excuse me, excuse me, Noel," said Minerva, reading her *Little Lulu.*

BookSmart basement was one of the few places in Minneapolis Minerva felt safe, because no one ever went down there except to hide. She also liked to cake on the white pancake make-up to look like an anime version of Kate Moss with crossed eyes and osteoporotic postures. She was at the ready for alpha werewolf repulsion. Black-jeaned, rip-sleeved, Morphine-shirted, Goth-mascaraed for Gothmas, nose-pierced, kohl-eyed, and sandalwood-soaked, Minerva stood up and wilted like a stick of uncrisp celery.

"Hi Chitchee, how are you?"

"Oh hi, Minerva! Good, thanks. I didn't see you hiding there. How are you?"

"I—I—I—"

"Are you okay? What's wrong?"

"I'm having an anxiety attack. It's that question again!"

"What question?"

"How are you? It follows me everywhere!"

"Chitchee," said Noel, surprised with no joy. "Let's hold off on this project."

"Noel, did I hear you use the word 'chick?' What's with a 'chick lit' section?" asked Minerva, following Noel and Chitchee to the top of the stairs.

"Are you guys serious?" she continued as if standing in her own front door. "You don't ever have any female employees here either, I've noticed. Why is that?"

"We could have hired a chick, but we hired a dick," said Saami, stepping downstairs in passing.

"I'm not talking to you, you prick!" said Minerva to Saami.

"Why?" asked Saami.

"You're mean, insulting, and hate me!" replied Minerva.

Saami stared at the stairs, blew out a pouch of air, and shruffed her off with a glance.

"Well," continued Minerva, "aren't you mean?"

"I never really noticed it," said Saami over his shoulder.

"I hate you sometimes," added Minerva. "Beda hates you more than me!"

"Saami isn't rude. He's an unorthodox businessman," said Chitchee, "whose American vision embodies free market competition, the labor theory of value, and the American Maverick."

"Oh, the American Maverick," said Minerva, fingering her key-chains of pepper sprays, one of which looked like red lipstick, one like a BIC lighter. "Maybe I'm a little wrong . . ."

Another pepper spray was strictly for brown bears, another had a range of a hundred yards. She wore two easy-to-grab, illegal, cyanide-spray canister earrings for hand-to-hand combat.

"Minerva, would you like to work *here?*" asked Chitchee at the maroon counter. "I can get you an application and put in a good word."

"Hell no, work here with a bunch of chick-lit bigots like Noel?" asked Minerva, seeing the arrival of Beda Holmgren. "I'll ask Beda."

Beda approached her partner and they kissed immediately and without drawing blood—difficult because the silver daggers in Beda's eyebrows and the caltrops in her ears made love-making dicey.

"Beda, do you think I should get a job here?" asked Minerva.

Beda's stomach proudly rolled out of various black garments hanging on her like pirate flags, her flesh shot through with skull jewelry.

"Yes, for you, Minnie," said Beda. "A book store job would be ideal! You could finish your Halloween novel *Lakewood Underground* in the basement! The workload is slight, and you'll get a discount on the graphic novels and comics. Besides Saami, the libtard staff is generally friendly and courteous."

Beda handed Noel five beat-up mass market mysteries to sell: Grisham, Grisham, Clancy, Clancy, and Patterson.

"These five books look like a dead man's hand," commented Chitchee. "How about Louis L'Amour? Go back and swipe some of those from a free shelf! The sundowners love Louis L'Amour! Keith Richards's favorite author. Just in case Keith Richards walks in the store, we'll be ready as daggers drawn with cocked triggers to take him to the shelf of our cool Westerns section."

"I'm sorry we can't use these, Beda," said Noel.

"WHAT! I knew it! That's what you always say. YOU ARE SO EVIL!" screamed Beda Holmgren. "I HATE YOU! You're the type that ends up guilty of war crimes! Maybe you should be brought before a White Man's War Crimes Tribunal and hanged for subalternity! Those are damn good books."

"Beda," said Noel, "I've seen you at Dunn Bros, grabbing their free books. In fact all five of these paperbacks have Dunn Brothers's bookplates on their flyleaves in them. You stole these."

"That doesn't mean they're bad books," countered Beda, backing up and holding hands with her partner, "unless you're going to pass judgement on them just because they are mine."

Noel's book radar sensed another book buy oscillating his way.

"Do you still want an application, Minerva?" asked Chitchee.

"Work in this sweatshop?" asked Beda. "No medical, no child care, poverty wages, and demeaning, inhumane working conditions? No way!"

"Yah way," said Chitchee although no one heard him.

Kennedy, distracted by the unprofessional commotion, stepped downstairs to get away from all the "hullabaloney" of the "confrontationalist artist types."

No longer the famous tattoo artist he once was, due to his disability, Brady "Skooge" Skogentaub had a complexion like deviled meat petrified, thick straight-up gray hair uniform as magnetized needles, and a curly gray beard of coconut shreds. Carrying a load of books on a japanned tea tray, he smiled his way in the door with a smile that accelerated into nervous jitters and twitches. As a Hawaiian-shirted sparrow in loose-fitting trousers and green flip flops, Skooge nervously glanced at the front door, at the floor, and then at an invisible mirror that made him self-conscious of his Hawaiian shirt because the shirt itself covered him with killer whales and Portuguese men-of-war, which might affect the amount of money he could wring from Noel, who already didn't like him, and drat! Skooge felt Noel's sting and stinger.

"Chill out, Beda," said Chitchee. "We can't sell these books, Beda. Look, they're water damaged too! They're in ruins. *Someone left the cake out in the rain!*"

Minerva and Beda looked at each other like: what do you think?

They stepped aside for Skooge.

"We're leaving," said Beda, frowning incisors visible.

"And," added Minerva, "we're never coming back until tomorrow! But we might be back tonight after the movie."

Chitchee indulged Minerva's genius, because she really *was* a genius—unlike all the other geniuses who gifted themselves with their own absent presents—Minerva graduated from The Juilliard School after her recital of the Berg *Violin Concerto*. She went on to write the world's first atonal novel, in which the twelve characters spoke only after each of the twelve had a chance to say something about graduating from Juilliard. The money from her novel *Jumping Over Juilliard* was swindled out of her by a holy shaman, Torsten Tripspittle, a Sioux of some sort, who she met at the Walker Art Center bar at a minimalist opening, which closed early that day because of a blizzard and white-out conditions. She fell in love with the medicine man, whose spirit animal, the jackalope, promised to cure her of her abusive past. She moved in with Torsten the Oglala. He persuaded her to invest in a fictitious company whose brand of spiritual lake water he called "The Essence of the Great Spirit Charged 'Sota Water." It was a soda water made from "non-molecular" water, holy sage, gold made of silver, the Acropolis, "essential hormones," and ingredients whose emanations he could not reveal. After Torsten frittered Minerva's royalties from *Jumping Over Juilliard*, his attempted invention of a smartphone/OhMibod-type vibrator fell through. When Torsten suggested Minerva sell her body for staged sex on their bedroom bed, surrounded by Thai businessmen with jeweled front teeth in town for Timberwolves games, Minerva took a sledgehammer to the roadman's Volvo, ending her faith in male transcendence, and he raped her.

Beda Holmgren frequented Oar Folkjokeopus and she was telling the manager, Mono Boondalicks, how much he sucked just because he sucked for no particular reason, when Minerva walked in looking for "healing music." The manager smirked, "Oh, you mean like Whitney Houston? How about her ripping off Dolly Parton? Whitney sucks." Mono looked offended. "Does she write songs? Does she play an instrument? It is all done in the studio for her—and all she does is chirp."

"You know what, Minerva? This dump's a dump! Let's go to Cheapo!" said Beda.

Eventually Beda becalmed Skinny Minnnie's anxiety attacks, and Skinny Minnnie homed in on the silence of dark rooms or the reading of innocent comic books like *Little Lulu* in the BookSmart basement.

"Hey, am I next?" asked Skooge shakily. "I have some books to sell. They were my grandfather's. Sigurd 'Slow Siggy' Skogentaub. Heard of him? He bought John Dillinger a whisky and root beer at the White Swan. That was in the Thirties when Dillinger was living around the corner on Girard."

"I'm sure Dillinger was delighted," said Noel, glazed over with a sarcastic mask. "And that was pure cocaine."

Noel looked down at the books: *Reader's Digest Guide to Breakfast*, *Time-Life: The Photographer's Tools*, *Napoleon* by Emil Ludwig, *Kitty Carlisle*, James Michener's *Hawaii* (signed by someone).

"A friend of mine found these ones in a dumpster," said Skooge. "I left the good stuff in the car. Do you want me to go get them? I have tons of Michael Crik-Tons."

Noel pushed the japanned tea tray back in Skooge's face without looking outright at Skooge's face.

"Poor condition," sniffed Noel. "They're shot."

"Shot like Dillinger, huh. I have more in the car," said Skooge. "Check this out!"

Skooge unbuttoned his Hawaiian shirt from the bottom, lifted up the tails, and showed off a sepia tattoo of Frank Sinatra in a brown fedora and brown jacket. A body suit of Frank Sinatra covered Skooge's shoulders, back, and buttocks.

"Oh my God!" said Chitchee, placing his hands over his cheeks in surprise. "Everybody! Check out this masterpiece of pop art! Andy Warhol, move over! Norman Rockwell, eat your heart out!"

"Howayah!" said Skooge, "I won't say another word. Ol' Blue Eyes, huh? I thought I'd get a response, huh? Like it, everybody?"

Something in the way Skooge moved was like an after-image of himself—shaky, sketchy, nervous, and skoogey. A single memory's effort shook him like a leaf.

His shaky confidence in his leafy memory itself shook him like a hickory tree, fully foliated until a sudden loud sound. And then the starlings startled, started off, and stripped the hickory tree bare.

"Did I already introduce myself?" asked Skooge. "Skooge. Howayah!"

His aura of being wired together by a thin broad smile derived from too many dehydrating raves where he molly-danced himself to death in an ecstasy of enough sweat to rehydrate himself if he could only capture it or drink his own urine to keep dancing.

He shook hands again and again with Chitchee.

"Hey, did you eat too much Ecstasy at First Avenue?" asked Chitchee. "Yes or no?"

"Can't remember," said Skooge. "You see, I think I have 55 personalities at last count."

"Are there that many human personalities *in total*?" asked Chitchee.

"Ah," said Skooge. "That's where I got lucky. 45 of them are zombies, 5 are chauffeurs, 3 are homeless like me—"

"So all of them don't have to agree on something for a memory to be recalled?"

"No, no, no," said Skooge, holding the japanned tea tray, trembling outwardly. "And two of them are dolphin personalities I acquired swimming through the interstellar matrix on the way back from First Avenue one night after a Prince concert. And those memories don't have hands. But I'm being followed, follow me? See, I used to chauffeur Mr. Martensen. Mr. Biggie Upstairs. Bib, big, bigtime guy. Gangster. He loved my tattoo and wanted one just like it. I suggested Marilyn Monroe. He said no, because when Sam Giancana's goons pinned her down with a poisoned enema they killed her, stuffing downers down her throat. I wanted Frank for myself. I says how about Dean Martin? He says great, how about Jerry Lewis? I thought he was serious. He fired me for knowing who killed—oooh I almost did it again! I don't want to bad mouth the Martensen People's Gang at all or their involvement on the dark web with hit men, because Mr. Martensen made me what I am today! And he is a good man at heart. He does a lot of charity work for biker gangs, supports their day-care centers, and funds their community centers, like a lot of narco-traffickers in Mexico. Besides, BookSmart is bugged. Ooops! Nobody heard that."

Skooge glued himself together—tessellated like a glass and marble mosaic but with pieces chipped off—and he loaded the rejected books onto a japanned tea tray that looked pilfered from Whistler's *Peacock Room*.

"Did I already say how Mr. Martensen knew I was on hard times after the concussion he gave me from a tire iron and continued to pay my wages with five pounds of MDMA? That's the kind of em-em-empath he is! He's always looked out for me—even after I went on disability because of him. My uncle too. Loyal to my uncle, yeah."

"Have you thought of getting an fMRI?" asked Chitchee.

"No, because I'm living in my car," said Skooge, "and it only gets AM radio."

Among the paperbacks on Alvin Karpis, Bonnie and Clyde, and Pretty Boy Floyd was *Trance Formation in America*, which Chitchee pulled for Noel to purchase in order to sell to Beda Holmgren.

"But that's all I need, oooh," continued Skooge, "and Alex Jones, because he shoots from the hip with the plain truth or he wouldn't be on the radio speaking about 9/11 and that it was all a hoax. I know all this because Mr. Martensen gives me his Infowar brain pills. I'll be right back with more of the good stuff."

"That wasn't cocaine, obviously that's impossible because it is impossible," said Noel, brushing the cocaine aside, hunching over the BookSmart ledger, and sniffing at the numbers, which did not add up. "I always wanted to try cocaine once, because it is really caviar for the few and therefore unethical for the many. Anyway, cocaine isn't around anymore. Cocaine was a very 80s drug, and it defined the Reagan era, right? Chitchee? Over here!"

"Cocaine defined Reagan? Morning again in America," said Chitchee, "defined it pretty well because of all the all-night coke parties ending in the morning again."

"What was it like, back then with all that cocaine in the air? Nobody does cocaine anymore, because it is so hard to get, right?" asked Noel. "People never see it anymore."

Chitchee studied his gangsters.

"Oooh, I'm back with more goodies," interrupted Skooge—no longer trembling like a foal in a wolf's den. "I've got a matchbook signed by Machine Gun Kelly, a placemat signed by the famous fanny dancer Aynie Rand, Clark Gable's honorary membership card at the Green Lantern, the autograph of Ferris 'The Wheel' Alexander, the Prom Ballroom's coasters, (oooh, I have a baseball bat signed by Morganna in the car, Morganna!), Irish Mob shot glass collections from St. Paul, newspaper clippings of unsolved murders, I might want to keep those. Here's some of Uncle Corky's stuff in here too. You know he works upstairs. He's the little big man upstairs. Ha, ha, get it? Hey look, it's pictures of you guys!"

Chitchee wry-necked his head at the photo prints, dish-plate pupils wide open.

Printed-off headshots showed: Noel examining the Dixie Chicks live, Snorri emailing Madison dick pics, Chitchee Facebook-stalking LaDonna, Saami on PornHub searching for Jenna Jameson frantically, and Aloysius on a dating site, clicking on ads, cascading through false warnings, and calling a pseudo-Trojan scam line in Irkutsk, his hands up in despair at the receding prospects of any meaningful relationship or date before death and liquidation.

"Noel, we're under surveillance," said Chitchee. "There's a hidden camera somewhere."

"Oh, sure we are *that* important!" said Noel. "And that white Dodge van parked across the street is the FBI, and Sausage Man is in there with Koss headphones and a Nagra tape recorder like Gene Hackman in *The Conversation*."

"So when *is* the store closing?" asked Lake Street Rodney, walking in the front door.

Curious heads sprouted from their books like a field of sunflower Rodneys.

Kennedy stepped upstairs, gathering one thought on each stair-thought. (What could he salvage from his lost drug empire?) He looked at the torn Ziploc and groaned, a betrayed Shakespearean king who blamed the sky for his own madness.

"Rodney! Where did you hear that?" asked Noel, looking up from the legerdemain of his tatterdemalion ledger, his cheeks ochre anger.

Noel looked inside-out at Rodney.

"I heard it from Kaylee, the counter girl at McDonald's," said Rodney, his white cheeks blushing red Lincoln roses. "And she heard it from Aloysius."

Noel scratched a hitch in his throat. He coughed into his elbow's crook and planned to wash his hands soon, as part of his ongoing hygienic regimen. His numb leg was asleep as the grass.

"The store is on a sound business footing," said Noel. "Trust me. And I don't chew my cabbage twice!"

"I did not accuse you, sir," said Rodney, offended, "of chewing your cabbage even once! Much less twice, unless you meant two separate cabbages, two unrelated cabbage events, which implies two separate cabbage chews twice each and two cabbage hands, which, frankly, um, does not seem possible even for you, sir."

Off the stool (ankle buckling), Noel collapsed to the floor. He stood up. The "five second rule" applied to him, and he turned to Chitchee:

"Chitchee, are you old enough to remember Jimmy Carter delivering his notorious 'Malaise speech?'"

"Noel," said Chitchee, "yes, of course I remember the 'Malaise' speech. If only because I was in the living room with Burger King wrappers cheesed between my toes, empty Frito bags everywhere, Budweiser cans crushed around me like cockroaches, and dirty carburetor bongs covered inside with tarry black mold. I was sitting in my favorite pair of old boxers, I was so demoralized by the President's message that I couldn't even scrape myself off the cushion-missing couch to turn Carter's face off. I had a Willie Nelson cassette in hand. I was trying to play it on my baby boomer box when I woke up the next day."

"Don't make friends with this guy coming up the stairs!" nudged Noel.

"Who?" asked Chitchee.

"His name is Kennedy . . ."

"Okay, but—"

"Hey!" said Kennedy, walking ponderously up the stairs. "We have to restructure our business partnership."

Noel slapped his hand down on the counter and looked aside with disbelief as if he swallowed too much ice cream.

"Good friend," said Kennedy, "now that we're back to square one, could I induce you to allow me a quick gander at the volumes I set aside over the last few days—"

"—weeks!" interjected Noel.

"Yes, weeks," said Kennedy, "and we'll forget all about the *laundry detergent* and baby powder hullabalonification—and admittedly, that whole humonguloidal ball of confusion. I would like to add a couple books to my hold pile, and I'd like to request and petition to take one of those books back in an act of subtraction in an exchange of cultural relationship, benefitting both of us, because I can appropriate a whole motherlode of motherlodes of self-help books and popular business books for your establishment—to thereby replenish your business shelves, *especially after I put back all the ones you have on hold for me*."

"OK, Kennedy," said Chitchee. "You have to give us some time to figure out what you said."

"If you need time to consider my machinations, I have time, and I can go about my business and matriculate about the store and come back for the end result of your jurisprudence in a couple minutes."

"Okay," said Chitchee.

"Investment is what I'm talking about," said Kennedy resentfully. "Which is what I will do with the 30,000 dollars you owe me now!"

"You really owe Kennedy 30,000 dollars?" asked Noel.

"Yeah, if you round up to $25,000 from $6,000," said Chitchee. "But I can pay him off in book installments amortized over time. And: *Everybody gotta fight about that spoonful.* Willie Dixon was right, eh Skooge?"

"How did you know my name?" asked Skooge.

"It's BookSmart," said Chitchee. "You are under our surveillance now. Smile, you're on *Hidden Camera*."

Torrents of perspiration pooled around Skooge's green flip flops. Dark turmoil muddied Skooge's face. His arms and legs jitterbugged out of their sockets and he said a Lord's prayer to calm his nerves. Then he said meekly:

"Did I mention my Uncle?"

"Corky?" asked Chitchee.

Skooge's eyeballs burst like water balloons.

"Oh my God! Did I really mention Uncle Corky? Did I spill the beans on Uncle Corky?"

"Yeah, Skooge," said Chitchee, "you didn't *spill* the beans, you flooded the entire Mississippi Delta down to New Orleans with beans. But I don't get how your Uncle Corky had snapshots of us! I want to know where those particular beans are coming from?"

"Oooh," said Skooge. "Uncle Corky works upstairs, you know. There must be a hole in the ceiling or something. I wasn't supposed to talk about him! He made me promise! But he's a bigtime fixer in real estate, and he's got bigtime connections like Mr. Martensen. Oooh yeah, bigtime! And you're not supposed to know that, bigtime!"

Noel offered Skooge a fair market price for his books, and Skooge daintily carried the japanned tea tray of rejected books away like a geisha. He said he had even more gems so Chitchee threw on his black wool beanie and geisha-walked with him to look at the other gems stored in the back of Skooge's '65 Chevy Bel Air station wagon, parked in the Cheapo Records parking lot. Skooge lived in his '65 station wagon outside a Bloomington Wal-Mart—and now he had the gas money to drive back to his drive-in sleeping space in the Wal-Mart parking lot.

"You can't park here," said Chitchee. "Cheapo Records posts spies in Amarillo Slim's across the street to watch who goes into Cheapo and who doesn't. They call Bobby & Steve's."

"It won't happen," said Skooge. "There should be oodles of great mysteries back there: Grishams, Clancys, Pattersons, Criktons, tons of them, huh—everybody loves a good mystery, huh? Except all the corpses littering every page, huh?"

Skooge's station wagon sat drooping, crammed, stuffed, and trashed with hopeless laundry, red Totino's boxes, used suits from Justers for bedding, an AC Gilbert Erector Set with everything missing, a patched inflatable Dolores Del Rio, a broken air conditioner, watermelon rinds, a hoe, potting soil, larvae, Solo cups, and assorted crime-ridden paperbacks.

Chitchee reached for Raymond Chandler's *The Long Goodbye* and squeezed a dead man's wooden leg. It felt like the fallen tree branch of an oak.

"Don't tell anyone this," said Skooge, "but—"

"—whose leg is this?" asked Chitchee. "Oh my God, you killed a guy! We don't buy *used* people! Skooge!"

"If you do tell anyone what I'm about to tell you, they will come around and slice your nose off or cut off both your hands, huh?" whispered Skooge, his breath like tuna fish so close to Chitchee's face Chitchee could read the ingredients on the tin can. "I mean they will kill you, if word gets out. Viktor Martensen told me. Dose guys don't fool around."

Nicky Fingers sat upright, pushing away a Justers overcoat.

"Are we there yet?" asked Nicky. "Chitchee? What? We're still at McDonald's? Oh, let me sleep!"

"Hey, Dougal, stop kicking me with those Red Wings," said Mjollnir, waking up next to Dougal. "Why don't you roll another one just like the other one with that indica, Dougal?"

"Uggh," said Dougal, waking up next to Mjollnir, who uncurled himself so that his feet stuck out the back of the station wagon when he yawned. "What time is it?"

"Go back to sleep!" said Skooge. "We're still in Uptown. Get your legs in! I'm locking up, we're almost done here!"

"Oooh, Chitchee," said Skooge. "I'm letting these guys sleep in my car because they're homeless. But let me finish. Here's the deal. Like I was saying, Viktor Martensen doesn't own Club Miami. It's under his wife's name. And she doesn't have one! Shhh . . ."

"So what?" asked Chitchee, making to walk back to BookSmart. "That's it?"

"Okay, okay," said Skooge, following Chitchee. "I've been a little jumpy since Viktor told me he wanted to have Spartak Bok killed with a car bomb. And it's that white Dodge van right there in front of McDonald's! I get so shaky—just spreading the rumor. That's why I'm so shaky. When I heard that secret, I knew I couldn't keep a secret like that. But you can, can't you? Can you keep a secret for me, Chitchee?"

Chitchee held his chin, pushed out his lips, and looked up at the sky for a sign.

"Yeah, I can keep a secret," said Chitchee.

"Oh, thanks," said Skooge. "I'll let Corky know you are the only one I blabbed to—"

"—for about a day anyway," said Chitchee, over his shoulder walking away.

"Brady?" asked Corky Skogentaub, cradling two extra large red boxes of French fries, having been standing near Skooge and Chitchee.

"—and you won't rat me out, Chitchee?" shouted Skooge into vehicular traffic.

"Brady!"

"Uncle Corky!" said Skooge.

Skooge's heart fluttered and fibrillated. His blood pressure reached 200/120, and his heart rate 240 beats per minute.

"Worrrrr-king late?" gasped Skooge. "Un-cle Cor-ky?"

"Brady!" said Corky. "I thought you were homeless! What are you doing out here on the street?"

"Skooge!" said Chitchee, who turned around, walked back, and stood next to Skooge and Corky. "I get it! I GET THE WHOLE PLOT! It's like a book. Viktor Martensen is going to kill Spartak Bok because Spartak Bok is in that white Dodge van waiting to kill Viktor Martensen, who owes him hundreds of thousands of dollars, which Spartak Bok already spent when he bought a Pyramid scheme from Egypt for his Rancho Calypso World."

Corky halted to a standstill, still as livestock. He warbled something wooden. He looked nauseated. Curtains of perspiration flowed over his forehead. The temperature outside McDonald's was suddenly 104 degrees. Corky skulked toward the Yggdrasil building like a poisoned rat, a rat too bloated to squeeze into its dying hole and die.

With a fluttering heart, with rising blood pressure, and with the heart beats of a ruby-throated hummingbird, a stunned Corky ballooned across Hennepin at Lagoon.

"Wait! What's wrong, Uncle Corky?" asked Skooge, calling out.

"I don't think he heard you," said Chitchee. "Do you need to borrow five bucks for gas money?"

"Okay," said Skooge, his anxiety mounting at Uncle Corky's frozen behavior—his uncle iced him, cold-shouldered him, snubbed him, and disowned him. Skooge was a kitten in a box left on the side of Highway 7: "FREE KITTEN."

Chitchee insisted he walk the collapsing Skooge around the block. Skooge couldn't even walk, but Chitchee embraced Skooge around the shoulders and restored Skooge's breathing by pacing him slowly step by step. Chitchee allayed Skooge's terrified state—at the risk of getting fired for "coming back from break too late"—and returned Skooge to Hennepin and Lagoon, where they saw that Bobby and Steve's white tow truck had latched onto the '65 Chevy Bel Air station wagon. The white tow truck drove Skooge's station wagon toward the impound lot on Colfax Avenue, and Skooge chased after it on clumsy feet, his head filling up with too many questions: What if Chitchee knew too much? What if Corky tattled? What if Spartak heard about their plans? What if Viktor overheard Spartak overhearing Corky overhearing Skooge overhearing Chitchee?

If only Chitchee could jaunt back to his childhood and re-experience the *qualia* of reading a Little Golden Book. But now his Little Golden Book was a Little *Bloody* Golden Book with pictures of gangland slayings and pools of gangster blood on the redolent, white pine flooring with its yellow cautionary CAREFUL FRESH BLOOD signs . . . police photographers behind Officers Lowry and Weatherwax . . . detectives dusting for fingerprints . . . drug *deal* gone wrong . . . or drug *bust* gone wrong? Chitchee's predicament overwhelmed him with danger, adventure, hare-brained heroics and—or the subject of a worthless, dime-store, airport novel or the next Academy Award-winning cinematic masterpiece based on squirrels.

Either way, a hit man could be anyone, anywhere, at any time. Chitchee, looking up for invisible Blackhawk helicopters in the gray, polluted, black sky—dashed to the parked white Dodge van. He peered in its window for answers.

With his large knuckles he rapped hard on the glass.

"Window down! Window down!" said Chitchee, trying to see inside a black box.

Felix, burning popcorn at the Uptown Theater, wondered why Chitchee pounded on the van's windows. Leaving the doors on the popcorn machine open, Felix drowned in a sludgy drowsiness for lack of Benzos. He wanted to ask Chitchee if he had seen Randy Quaalude lately, who had sold Felix the wrong drug again. He wanted Benzos, not Molly; he wanted to refund the Molly, which either drove him mad or did nothing at all. Felix sluggishly walked outside.

"Chitchee! Chitchee!"

Chitchee feared all the off-duty MPD thumpers, who moonlighted as hitmen, and they already knew his name?

"MURDER! MURDER WILL OUT!" yelled Chitchee, running back to the cross walk at the intersection.

A window above BookSmart in the Yggdrasil building opened and Corky leaned out in shirtsleeves and watched Felix shag Chitchee into BookSmart.

"Noel, throw me the Allen wrench, I'm locking the crash doors," said Chitchee, soaring into BookSmart, his plaid flannel shirt and black beanie cap wet as a mop with sweat and fear.

He reached over the counter and probed for the Allen wrench. He locked the crash doors.

"Hey, Chitchee, it's me," said Felix, locked out, babying his water bottle. "Can I come in?"

Having eaten nothing but very heavily salted popcorn from candy-striped boxes, Felix twitched and cramped (with hypertensive button eyes and jumpy eyebrows). He unscrewed his water bottle and swigged in a sideways fashion, maintaining eye contact while slaking his thirst. Parched and sweating, he looked straight ahead with half-closed his eyes.

Noel wrestled the Allen wrench out of Chitchee's paw and admitted Felix into the store.

"So," asked Noel, dismissing Kennedy with a busy look. "Did *everyone* in the '80s shovel pounds of coke up their noses?"

"Oh yeah," replied Chitchee. "Except me of course. In the '80s, I was always reading books about the '80s as soon as they came out. Maybe it was a coincidence. But I do recall there were trains of cocaine rocks in coal-cars pulling into Tooterville all day long. In the '80s we had drive-thru deviated septum clinics. Fleetwood Mac album covers were whited out permanently. You brushed the coke off Alexander Hamilton's face to make sure you actually *had* twenties for the next eight balls. So much blow in the air you couldn't even SEE the '80s for about a decade. It *sounded* like Reagan was in charge, but since he couldn't complete a sentence without his drawstring being pulled, we figured he was fucked up on coke too. The country was really being run by scrawny, chicken-necked Nancy Pants with her court of royal astrologers and celebrity wizards. But through the rolling fog banks of coke everywhere, how could you tell, why should you care? You couldn't drive anywhere without hearing 'Hotel California' and without smacking into the coke dealer driving in front of you, also listening to 'Hotel California,' and then that coke dealer was usually an off-duty cop, coked to his gills on the blow he stole from the drug dealer he had smacked into, who had been listening to 'Hotel California' too."

"Okay, forget it," said Noel. "Do you take anything seriously?"

"Love, and—let's see—um—I guess that's it! Huh! I thought there was more to life than that. But no. It's either *Romeo and Juliet* or *Robinson Crusoe*. More serious things . . . let me see. I'm blank-slating."

Noel rounded his fists on the maroon counter instead of Chitchee's shoulders, fuming at Chitchee for his taking Noel's innocent inquiry and turning it upside down, *reductio ad absurdum*, into a wastebasket joke. And Noel hated the Kierkegaardian absurd with an absurd Kierkegaardian passion. Jung would have said: As a man walks into his shadow, he makes the mistake that no shadows exist. Noel wanted facts; therefore Chitchee must want facts too. Noel wanted rational history. What is the point of history? Why does it have to have a point to even be history? Why is man capable of evil? Without evil, would there be a history? Can there be an equitable, democratic world order? Who did coke and when?

"Chitchee, it connects," whispered Felix, approaching the counter. "It connects."

Chitchee nodded an all-knowing nod to hide his ignorance. Felix inferred a profound thought noodling around in Chitchee's bowl of basal ganglia.

"Really?" asked Chitchee.

"Yes, really; and I've got the right tools," continued Felix. "I can pick the lock downstairs from the tools I ordered off the Internet. I bought a bolt cutter and Freon too. Do you want to go down to you-know-where tonight?"

"I don't know about you-know-where tonight, besides I'm working with," Chitchee flicked his head to one side in the direction of Noel, "you know who."

"Why are you twitching in the direction of Noel?" asked Felix.

"Do you have book: *Synchronicity*?" asked a young woman, Ye Young Kim, who had been waiting dutifully behind Felix. She had entered holding hands with her older "sister" (her roommate) Jungsun Um, a fellow Korean, who Ye Young spun off, once achieving the social velocity she needed—a U. of M. Global Studies major, applying for jobs at the United Nations Human Rights Council (as regards Pyongyang's use of medieval torture)—to approach the maroon counter.

Felix noticed Jungsun slowly and jumped back at the first sight of her warm smile and friendly face. He dropped his water bottle. When it hit the floor, the floor detonated. Chitchee leapt like a depth charge of water. While Felix spread the spilled water around with his toe to phase change it to a higher rate of evaporation, he remembered he needed to ask Randy for benzos as he gazed at Jungsun's sitting down on the crummy couch so sweetly.

"It came in, ma'am," said Chitchee. "It's around here somewhere."

"No," she said.

"Do *you*," continued Ye Young, directed specifically at Noel, "have *Synchronicity*?"

Noel gazed like a raptor that pushed its glasses down its beak to get a better look, looked right and left, and then pushed its glasses back up its beak.

Ye Young in her late twenties enjoyed long black hair, which swayed like a lithe willow tree in the wind with black leaves.

Chitchee plucked the Robert Bly copy of *Synchronicity* from the stacks and stacks of new arrivals, and Noel extended his talons and swooped down, seizing Chitchee's wrist under the counter. They hand-wrestled. Noel's pinching fingernails forced

Chitchee to release the *Synchronicity* and Noel said: "She was asking *me*, not you."

"Okay, Noel," said Chitchee, "who am I to stand in the way of evolution?"

Noel stood up straight, sternum out. Chitchee grabbed at his own sore wrist and bit his hand between thumb and index.

"*Synchronicity*? Jung? The *occult* is downstairs by Folklore and Mythology," said Noel like an honorable Boy Scout. "Follow me. I will lead the way."

"My hero!" said Chitchee.

Leading Ye Young down the stairs, Noel appeared jaunty, too jaunty—he was sweating jaunty. His latent stutter started to stutter up again, "C-c-c-an you watch the c-c-c-ounter, Ch-ch-chitchee? And don't m-m-m-make any new friends I wouldn't make."

"And Noel," said Chitchee, "don't stare at her cleavage."

Noel gave him the finger.

Jungsun, studying to be a registered nurse, sat on the couch and worked on the homework she brought along.

Chitchee walked to the banister, saw that Noel was out of earshot, and looked down the staircase at Ye Young's cleavage.

"Oh no, Felix," said Chitchee. "I glanced at her cleavage or I looked for her cleavage. But I'm leaving off cleaving to her cleavage by my own leavage."

"Do you want to go down into the tunnel tonight?" asked Felix. "I discovered how to get to the tunnel system that connects the Uptown Theater to both Hennepin Avenue Bridge and Lakewood Cemetery."

"How do we get to the Mississippi? Does it involve underground dynamite?" asked Chitchee. "*Dy-no-mite!*"

A customer in a wide-lapeled, wide gray suit with a fat planarian-shaped, red tie trundled out of the Science section. His stiff gray hairline was so low it squashed his face into a square: his eyes, nose, and his non-elastic smile covered a space no bigger than his fist.

"Well, well, well, if it isn't the old bomb-throwing anarchist talking about dynamiting dams and bridges!" said Grover Gossick.

"Hello, Grover," joked Chitchee cheerily. "Still tickling the ivories? Heard any of them *laugh* yet?"

"Why don't you," asked Grover, "have *any* books on Intelligent Design? Where's *Darwin's Black Box*? I see plenty of *pro*-Darwin books, but that is only *one* belief system. Darwin's 'science' is only another belief system. How come you are not representing the other side of that belief system?"

Ye Young walked upstairs ahead of Noel by two steps.

"Sir," said Noel, trying with one eye to pin a fly to a pin-wheel. "What *is* the other side of that belief system? There hasn't been another side since the dawn of Darwin."

"Yes," said Chitchee, "because imbibing the Bible with the imbibition of a bibulous all-night Bibleing party is NOT my idea of Fun."

"Oh, come on!" said Grover, tensely cracking an imaginary peppercorn on his back teeth with a distinctive click. "Are you going to believe scientists? That's not science. Like their cockamamie global warming theories? Or their vaccines, really? Vaccines kill. Where's the evidence otherwise?"

"Scientific theories are falsifiable as Karl Popper in *The Logic of Scientific Discovery* says is the true test of empiricism," said Noel looking at Ye Young. "David Deutsch asserts in *The Fabric of Reality* that theories, to be true, must have explanatory power, which your pet 'design' theory lacks. We have both books on our shelves if you would like to understand the *other side*. Not bad, eh Yay Young? See, he doesn't know what to say! He doesn't have a single fact!"

She smiled and briefly held Noel's cold hand. She had a smile that curved at the corners of her mouth both up and down, both amused and disappointed.

"Facts?" asked Grover Gossick with a defective smile devolving to a frown shaped like a fence around his property. "Thank God I'm a dumb ass, because I can't stand smart asses like you!"

"You shouldn't be so hard on yourself," said Chitchee.

"My faith in Jesus Christ the Savior is good enough for me," continued Grover with a solemnity that belied his contempt for Chitchee.

"Grover, everyone worships the One God," said Chitchee, "who is different from all the other One Gods. If you could show

how all the world's religions were topologically One Gods, you'd be murdered for trying to mix various customs and traditions. Yes, Jesus is love. He's a lot of things. Life is a miracle, but is it a good miracle? Here, give me a hug, all men are brothers, assuming they don't have the flu."

"Over my dead, cold spiritual body," said Grover. "Get away, don't touch me! This is an atheist, communist book store right in the heart of Minneapolis, which is *my town*! And *you* are going to 'h' . . . 'e' . . . double hockey sticks with your plots to overthrow the United States government! And I am going to Heaven, where I will spend eternity looking down at you in your 'h' . . . 'e' . . . double hockey sticks eternity! Aw, phooey on you!"

"Watching hockey is hell on ice for sure," said Chitchee. "The puck is the size of a grain of pollen. Can't they make it bigger with flashing, blinding lights?"

"You Reds don't belong in Minnesota!" said Grover on the boil, his round head red as a bucket of rock crabs. "I'll be back someday with the Truth and I'll prove y'all wrong, you brainwashed scum!"

Inflamed Grover flew the coop like a jail bird on a jailbreak.

"Right! We are brainwashing Minnesota to right-think like me, right Chitchee?" continued Noel, forcing *Manufacturing Consent* into Ye Young's suddenly cold hand. Followed by: *Hegemony or Survival* and *Failed States*. And then Michel Foucault's *Madness and Civilization*, *Discipline and Punish*, and *The History of Sexuality* (heavily highlighted), volume 1. He topped that off with Richard Dawkins's *The Selfish Gene*. And for dessert: *Capitalism and Schizophrenia* by Gilles Deleuze and Felix Guattari (two volumes, University of Minnesota Press).

Chitchee added *Synchronicity* to the top, but Noel removed it.

"Ugh," said Noel. "No occult!"

"You have to strike when the iron is hot I guess," said Chitchee.

"What?" asked Ye Young, annoyed at Chitchee's distracting behavior.

Ye Young sorted through the books Noel had recommended while Noel ran around to find more and ran back. She had pre-selected *The Selfish Gene*.

"Iron's hot?" said Ye Young, parting her hair from her eyes to read the back blurbs.

"What's playing at the theater, Felix?" asked Chitchee because he knew, with Felix hanging out, Noel would admonish Chitchee about having too many friends in the store.

Snorri had told Chitchee that at the last company meeting, Noel had expressed reservations about hiring Chitchee. "He attracted too many people."

"We can't have too many people in the store," agreed Aloysius.

The meeting adjourned having made no sense of anything.

Chitchee wished Felix would say something sensible about politics, which was theoretically possible—to legitimize Felix's presence before Noel. Noel championed the highest, unrealistic intellectual standards of conversation in *any* book store. BookSmart provided his Chautauqua lecture hall. And *now* he had an actual woman in his audience, close enough to smell. There she was dreaming in his bedroom eyes. This could be real love, not fool's love, she's the one. Chitchee and Felix were a crowd.

"What's new, Felix?" Noel asked mechanically by way of politeness, demonstrating to Ye Young his debonair Cary Grantitude with the *plein air* of a *citoyen*, a Daniel Cohn-Bendit.

"What's new?" said Felix, stumped. "I don't know. I'll have to check my notes."

Felix reached in his back pocket for a folded-up piece of paper and read aloud:

"Nothing," said Felix.

He laughed to start a laugh, but it was catching a rainbow in a soup tureen.

Noel looked at Felix. This caused Felix's forehead to worry itself into steep monoclines of doubt.

"What's new? Hmmm . . . the other night," stammered a desperate Felix, "I was working at the Lagoon Theater and Toby Pfeiffer came in and loudly demanded to see an R-rated movie. We were having a Rosanna Arquette Film Fest and Retrospective; so to get rid of Toby, Emily said we didn't have any R-rated movies. They were all PG. Toby asked for the cardboard stand-up, life-size, cut-out of Rosanna Arquette in the lobby. When Emily said no, Toby carried it off into the bathroom, jacked off on it, and then he left the cut-out in the bathroom and bounced."

"Like we needed to hear that?" said Noel with feigned and unfeigned horror.

"Hah!" laughed Chitchee. "I can picture Toby leaving the Uptown Theater like an Airedale terrier blowing dirt out of his nose, snorting away. Nothing had happened: 'Rose Anna Danna? What kind of a name is that?'"

"Chitchee," said Noel, "do you always have to tear people down? Are people a joke to you? That story was offensive to me, to Yay Young, to Rosanna Arquette, to Gilda Radner, possibly even to Bill Murray . . ."

"One man's gravity is another man's acceleration," offered Chitchee.

Chitchee examined his conscience. Do I treat people like jokes? Noel would never let an argument go. It would come back fifty years later and he would win that argument on his deathbed, dead or out of bed.

"I treat people as jokes?" asked Chitchee. "Is that true, Felix? Do I do that?"

Felix cleared his throat and sipped two water drops from a near empty water bottle.

"What? I didn't know having a conversation in a book store could be this awkward . . ." said Felix, who then turned to Jungsun. "Do you like Rosanna Arquette . . . movie actress . . . she was in *Crash* . . ."

"She was in the Clash?" asked Jungsun.

Felix looked at Noel for permission to laugh while Noel rang up *The Selfish Gene* and Ye Young paid for it. After Ye Young waved good-bye to Noel, her hand fluttering like a landing dove's wings, so Jungsun waved at Felix, and Noel told Chitchee and Felix "in confidence" (everything was in confidence with Noel unless he said "spread the word" in which case the word was not worth spreading): Ye Young had given him her phone number.

Her phone number galvanized Noel down to his nerve ends with no end to the giddy limit.

"You know what they say about Korean women!" said Felix, drawing in his upper lip, biting it, and pouting with his lower lip.

"What?" asked Noel.

"When Korean women go on a man hunt, they don't come back empty-handed."

"They don't say that," said Noel.

"Yeah, I know," said Felix. "Kidding . . . I guess . . . I guess not . . . besides you can't listen to what they say, they'll say anything . . . for a laugh . . . and not get it . . ."

"I don't know about Yay Young," said Noel. "She likes ghost stories. That's pretty morbid. Moribund? Plays into the hands of the Right Wing like opium. Chitchee, don't you have books to shelve? Let's get back to work."

"Does LaDonna still work at Club Miami?" interrupted Felix. "Somebody said she's been smoking crack, hanging out with crackheads, cracking for weeks at a time, and fighting with lap dancers outside Schiek's over crack. She was thrown out of the Gasthof for accusing the server of goose-stepping. Stand Up Frank's cut her off at the knees for being sloppy drunk. The 400 Club wouldn't serve her after she complained that the bartender tried to poison her with date rape drug."

"How do you know all this?" asked Chitchee.

"My ex-roommate's ex was ex-roommates with her ex-roommate's ex's ex-roommate," said Felix. "And boy can she talk!"

"Felix," said Emily at the front door, "are you coming back to work? You left the popcorn doors open. There is a ton of popcorn on the floor."

"After all the cockswallop you hear about LaDonna," continued Chitchee, "well, don't worry about her! She's a big girl—she carries a .45 caliber in her purse and wouldn't hesitate to pump lead into some bimbo's testicular tabernacle or slice off his dick with a buck knife and toss his red wiener into someone's vegetable garden. In that regard, she is a strong role model for young women."

"Felix!" said Emily.

"LaDonna is . . . your ex? Right?" asked Noel. "Is that who we are talking about?"

"Felix," said Emily, not mad yet, but not amused, not even entertained, but a little concerned, "are you coming back to work or not? The movie is getting out now."

"The movie?" asked Felix, recalling where he had heard that word "movie" before. Word association aroused a vague soundtrack and the soundtrack brought back memories, sensations, and perceptions.

"Whoa! I forgot! The *movie*! *Black Swan* with Natasha the Night Porter!"

When Felix ran out the door, he sneezed on an elderly, distinguished silver-haired man with flowing silver hair. Shaped like a stuffed grouse in a Peruvian serape, he bellied up to the counter. Was he the *habitué* of every Loft Literary reading ever lofted? A jewelry designer from Taos, New Mexico in town for the Uptown Art Fair with its wagon trains of booths—booths of bangles of brass, booths of baubles of glass . . . exotic greasy snacks, phalanxes of pale green satellites . . . and silver-haired jewelers in turquoise?

"I've come back for my books, I'm sure you've looked at them! I was in Paris," he said and pregnantly paused.

He looked piercingly at Chitchee.

"France," he added with mysteriously poor enunciation.

"And your first name is—?" asked Chitchee. "France? As in Anatole? *Penguin Island* guy?"

"No, Bly."

"You like to rhyme, Bly Guy! Are you related to THE Robert Bly?" asked Chitchee. "If you are, can you tell him he left his books here too long?"

"Oh, you're the Bly!" said Noel. "We didn't know if you *were ever* coming back! So we priced out your books and put them out on the floor. And we owe you, what is it? Forty bucks? Twenty bucks? Does anyone know? Saami! Could you come upstairs, please?"

"Then I want them back," demanded Bly. "Get them *off* the floor."

"We can't get them off the floor, Bly," said Noel ingenuously.

"They're stuck to the floor, Bly," said Chitchee. "Except the ones we sold that went out the door. From floor to door!"

"Yes? You had better give me all my books back," said Bly, older than his thumb-nailed, back-cover photograph portrayed him to be.

Chitchee age-progressed Bly and heard opportunity knocking. Bly paced in front of the maroon counter like a caged panther unable to obtain service at the zoo.

"I left my books in your care," said Bly, "and now you are telling me you don't have my books? What are you going to do about it? What *are* you going to do about it? What are YOU going to DO about IT?"

"It is you! This is great!" said Chitchee. "Finally, my big break is here! Thank you, God! Noel, this guy *Bly* isn't some nobody like us! He's the brain behind all those copies of Iron John we have in overstock."

"What are WE going to do about it, Chitchee?" asked Noel, nervously drumming a Sharpie on the counter and looking over at Chitchee.

"I'm a poet too," said Chitchee, ignoring Noel. "And I'm itching to get a great poet's autograph and opinions on my poetry. We could do linked-verse readings of Japanese renga together! Renga? What am I going to do about what? What's your problem, Noel? Can't you see we're having an intellectual conversation?"

"This gentleman, whoever he is, wants and deserves his books back," said Noel. "Did you set them out? Do you know where? Did you shelve them all?"

"I set most of the gentleman's books out," said Chitchee. "I could try to remember which ones were this gentleman's. This gentleman had a lot of mostly unread, brand new books of poetry like the kind book reviewers sell to us for booze money."

"Who are *you*?" asked Saami of Bly. "Juan Valdez or Pepe Le Pew?"

"What are YOU going to do about MY books?" demanded Bly, pointing his finger at Saami. Then he turned the anger knob on his face up a notch. "You're the one I left them with! What are you going to DO about my books?"

Saami imagined he was a chorus line of twenty Saamis kicking up his legs at Radio City Music Hall. All the Saamis in knickers sang:

"What are we? What are we? What are we? GOING TO DOO DOO DOO ABOUT . . . it?"

Saami danced and showed off his French can-can from *Orphée aux enfers*:

Ta Ra Ra Boom Dee Ay
There is no school today
Our teacher ran away
While she was standing there
We took her underwear
Now she's in the C-I-A

"Sir, you abandoned your books," continued Saami. "They have been here for more than two weeks. The store policy is two weeks as plainly stated on that index card by the cash register in thick green magic marker. That is a common policy in all used book stores. I am sorry, but the rule is: any person who leaves their books in the hands of the store for more than two weeks can consider those aforesaid books to have been abandoned, and the rightful ownership of those books is in effect terminated."

"What's going on, Saami?" asked Chitchee. "Are you sober all of a sudden?"

"There is one bag of books," answered Saami, "back here not yet set out, right Chitchee? Could you give the gentleman his bag?"

"I want to *know*," said Bly, "WHAT YOU ARE GOING TO DO ABOUT MY BOOKS!"

"Okey-dokey, donkey doo," said Chitchee, dropping a Lunds bag of books on the maroon front counter. "I didn't put *this* bag of books out, Mr. Bly, because I so enjoyed reading all your personal mail. And I am a great fan of your poetry too."

"I was in Paris for two weeks!" said Bly.

"Did you go to Sylvia's beach?" asked Chitchee. "Hyuck, hyuck."

Bly puffed up his chest and took up a more leonine stance, the tail brushing off Chitchee with a flick.

"I come back to this? This is an outrage!" said Bly.

"You know, Annie Dillard sounds really nice, Mr. Bly. May I call you Bobby or Roberto? I read the letter Dillard wrote to you . . ." said Chitchee.

At the end of a coat hanger, a Kielbasa dangled in BookSmart's front window.

Chitchee retrieved his "Homage to Robert Bly" from his backpack.

"Could I read you my poem, Mr. Bly?" asked Chitchee. "I dedicated it to you, because I've always been a great admirer of your work and your stand on Vietnam."

When the dangling banger, fresh from Kramarczuk's, then the hanger, and then the headcheese face of Sausage Man spread across the front window, Noel's eyes popped out like Keck telescopes.

Sausage Man's poxed, black-headed nose jiggled like meat jelly. The chin-strapped fishing hat anchoring the hanger's banger declared his lunacy, and the hooked fishing pole and the slimy fish smell from the minnow bucket would drive away customers, Noel thought.

Noel wiped his glasses clean on his dirty shirt tail. Saami locked arms. Chitchee felt a jealous rage toward Sausage Man who, as a published poet, might steal Robert Bly from him—those two would link up and fly off like two loons in love and launch a literary journal for the Upper Midwest, calling it something like *The Wild Mother's Oven Explodes* or *The Caribou Shouts Out Some Shit Review*.

"Who are you?" asked Sausage Man to Robert Bly. "Juan Valdez?"

"No, I'm Pepe Le Pew! Doesn't anyone in this book store know who I am? I am Robert Bly! The poet!"

"The poet? I'm a poet too!" said Sausage Man, standing at BookSmart's front entrance, blocking it with his meaty, feety, rotten salami odor, and causing sneezes to bounce around the store faster than a racquet ball.

Bly, without saying a word, sneezed. He thundered a look at the lowly book store clerks. Shouldn't they be cowering? They're just standing there like a tornado-torn cornfield. Spiritual idiots who had never even heard of him? Never?

Although Chitchee sensed Bly was in a Wotan phase and would give him battlespace, he wavered on Bly's "Man Theory," that all men should not be pandas but heroes, and heroes should express their maleism by engaging in WWW battle royales over Lunds bags of used paperbacks. Maybe flying off the handle like a big baby *was* justified by something Carl Jung had footnoted about big babies in his *Psychological Types*. Chitchee simply did not know. He would go home and forget to check.

Grunting, snorting, and cavorting, Bly pawed at his last bag of books (for the first time). Chitchee stood by with eager anticipation, waiting for the ice-breaking moment when the elder statesman would pick up Kafka's "axe" and discover Chitchee like Dr. Frankenstein's monster in a frozen sea.

"I'm sorry about your ah ah lost ah books," said Noel, measuring his words with word spoons. He started to stutter a string of iterating sticky vowels sounding as from *Bhārat* (भारत): "To ah make things up ah ah ah we'll ah give you ah ah ah a 20-dollar ah ah ah gift ah certificate."

The phone rang once. It died before Noel could get to it. Seeing Lake Street Rodney dripping down the sidewalk in the heat, Noel rummaged around for the old Kleenex box of carbon-backed gift certificates, buried under all the kipple and caboodle.

"Chitchee, can you look for the gift certificates?" asked Noel, begging with a weakening will.

"A gift certificate?" asked Bly, his eyes two unbelieving sand dollars. "To buy my own books back?"

"What's wrong with that?" declared Lake Street Rodney, entering in a cloud of broiling mosquitoes while swatting strikes at them. "For me, that's as common as eating breakfast if I ate breakfast, but I usually don't, because it means getting up extra early for something I don't even want to eat. I like to eat all at once and pass out late at night watching *Mayberry R. F. D.*"

"I don't have time for this," Bly growled.

"Wait! Mr. Bly!" said Chitchee, reminded of the Greek word *kairos*, καιρός, the perfect timing for the right moment. "I've read all your poems. Can you read one of mine? I dedicated it to you after reading your *Abraham Talks to the Stars*!"

"Okay," said Bly, snatching it out of Chitchee's hand.

Typewritten sheet in hand, adjusting the focal length for proper optics, Bly seemed to be lip-reading the white, inkjet paper impossibly fast.

His quivering eyes rolled like breakers on Gitche Gumee's high tide.

Noel took the pulse of the store. It was already a public relations disaster not even Edward Bernays could bulldozer into the ground. For Noel this was another Chitchee-induced, damage-way-out-of-control situation, and Noel saw his BookSmart dreams go up in smoke and ridicule.

Bly cleared his dramaturgic throat and intoned with a bard's recitative:

THE WILD MAN AT LUNDS
(for Robert Bly)

Waking up in the snow I long to go grocery shopping
My wife dresses me in the darkness so that my poncho
Is on backwards, but I am hungry and do not mind.

We drive through pastures to get to Lunds
Over the homeless, the leaping geese, and the pine stumps
My belly rolling behind the wheel, I do not care
I see the dying moon and blame the State Department
Underneath all the snow are thousands of dead Egyptians
We listen to a hockey game on the radio,
The sons who have not read my books score and die.

The parking lot is empty, the checkout lane girls remember us.

I stand before the bakery counter and see the baguettes
My wife deserts me when I whistle for service and seeing
Me stand like an oak, even the manager fetches me the wrong coffee
And disappears. In touch with my solitude, I prophesy fewer turkeys
For Lunds. Waiting for my honey, walnut-covered, sugar breakfast rolls
I visualize biting the face off
The counter girl, Astrid, who is not there, not responding to
My shouts. This is what caused Vietnam.

Standing forever in my long johns, waiting for my long johns, paid for
By my Iron Johns, I grieve at the lack of service. Where's Astrid?

Hard to imagine Machado without a scone
Or Rilke without an apple crispy. I could be
Skiing in my flowered down vest, or tuning my
Dulcimer for the first time. Some fathers long for bear hugs,
Others bags of doughnuts, some both at the same time.
I long for a long john, at least a cranberry
Muffin, or a simple cinnamon twist. But no one sees my angry jowls
And baby face, shaped like a sugar pine cone.

The way the snow melts from a Lake of the Isles mansion
I leave through the automatic sliding glass doors,
Cursing those vultures from Europe who eat our souls—
My car is gone. Stolen. A sorrowful man with a snow blower
Turns to look, but does not recognize me, raging.

    Chitchee Chichester, 2009

Bly squinted at Chitchee.

"What garbage! How ridiculous!" said Bly. "Tripe! Have you tried submitting it to *The New Yorker?*"

Bly thrust the poem at Chitchee—an uppercut to the solar plexus would have been more pleasant. Chitchee couldn't breathe. The room darkened. The stars grew back.

There was no way Bly could not accept Chitchee's tribute. Chitchee had crafted it specifically for Robert Bly, the father he never had. Now he would never have the father he never had. Downcast, Chitchee curtained off his cloying tears.

Chitchee threw himself at Bly's feet, hugged his ankles, and sobbed.

"I know who you are," cried Chitchee. "*I* know your name!"

"This is the WORST BOOK STORE I HAVE EVER BEEN IN!" said Bly, leaving one sandal behind in Chitchee's hands as he walked half-barefoot toward the door.

"Oh ja, sorry you're not one to like the wurst here," said Sausage Man.

"We'll find your paperbacks, Mr. Bly," called out Chitchee, drying his tears and sniffling. "Don't leave us in the darkness of the dark night of the soul! "

"Sausage Man," said Noel. "You have to go!"

Sausage Man about-faced, gave Noel the Hitler salute (saying "Hey you, Hitler!"), and goose-stepped out the door.

The BookSmart phone rang. Noel picked up the receiver. Nobody there.

Sausage Man marched back into BookSmart, and the Kielbasa sausage at the end of the hanger gob-smacked Bly in a frenzied snarl of waving arms, constricted by the stiffness of his poncho as he reeled backward.

"Where is my other sandal? God damn it!" said Bly, looking down at Chitchee who had not recovered from the sniffles. "I want my shoe back!"

"O Poet! O Singer of Tales! Don't you want to hear my *Ode to Potato Salad?*" asked Sausage Man, his eyes gray cataracts of crestfallen ice. Sausage Man looked at Bly and sang:

Oh you chunks of potato salad I sing
A life is like a potato salad, too too ta roo!
Blow the horns for pickled peppers, you!
Ain't nothin' here but a picnic a-mixing, ja ja ja
Mayo, mustard, egg, and onion—yummmm—onions ring out!
Camerado, will you join my song and sing my tune

My friend, and join the potato salad too?

"NO!" said Bly, huffing and puffing out the door. "I will not join the potato salad! Go away! I'm leaving! Keep my books, you bastards! Sonsabitches!"

"Yes, go away, and you too Sausage Man!" said Saami firmly and pointedly like a pet owner to a pet rock. "You are bothering the customers."

"What customers?" muttered Sausage Man and marched out the door.

"Who was that, Chitchee?" asked Kennedy, shanking up the stairs, looking concerned, and strolling to the maroon counter, which he leaned over.

Kennedy's hold pile was still there after a whole hour had passed.

"*Kennedy*, that was Robert Bly, the poet," said Chitchee admiringly. "I wish I had his chutzpah. What verve! Behold the Man! He goes around yelling and everyone gets out of his way. He's awesome. He's a man's man's man. Authoritarian, domineering, hierarchical—but he manages to pull it off! How? Genius! That's how! The noblest Minnesotan of them all."

"*That* was Robert Bly?" asked Kennedy of Chitchee, beginning in a whisper that crescendoed into a shout. "The Men's Movement MENTOR? King Viagra-memnon of the Midwestern Literarian Sphere? *The author of books that sell? The* ROBERT BLY was HERE and you didn't tell ME? This is like a betrayal of our friendship, a betrayal of human decency."

"Well, yes . . ." said Chitchee. "So? What's your point?"

"Wait, one second," said Kennedy. "Are you supplying me with the valuable and vital information that *Iron John, the* Iron John, is currently matriculating around Uptown Minneapolis out in the open like a sitting duck? Matriculating around Uptown and no one even knows what he looks like?"

"Yes," said Chitchee, "that is precisely the point of my previous sentence."

"Stupendously strange for such a reputatiously, high-built parsonage to grace our presence in a book store! Is he . . . mad?" asked Kennedy, laughing, hoping Bly *was* completely mad—so Kennedy could tell all his mad friends at McDonald's that he had met a famous author who was more bonkers and off his chump than they were.

"No, he's not mad, he's famous . . ." said Chitchee. "You can be both, but it is better to be famous first; otherwise it's pointless."

Kennedy asked for and received a pen and a piece of scratch paper, and flew like a cormorant out the door and down Lake Street to wring an autograph out of Bly's clenched fist.

Meanwhile, Chitchee gnashed his teeth and bit his hand. If he had wings himself, Bly had clipped them with his judgment. Why did that whole pizza of events taste so bad? It could only be that Chitchee's writing was no damn good. That explained the four walls of silence every time Chitchee read aloud his works. But "tripe?"

The Great Poet had judged, making Chitchee a self-consumer of his woes, and he accepted the judgment.

"Jesus, Kennedy is riding a lightning bolt," said Felix.

Cut early from his shift, Felix asked Chitchee about their exploring the city's underground tunnels when Kennedy flew back to his nest at BookSmart.

"I got me a Robert Bly autograph!" said Kennedy, overjoyed, beaming at his score, and slap happy as hell. "This could be worth a couple cheeseburgers at McDonald's—if Kaylee is working."

"Cool, Kennedy," said Chitchee. "Let's see Iron John's signature. I bet it is big and bold and heroic like—well, like John Hancock's own Iron Johnlike John Hancock."

Chitchee's eyes froze. He turned to Kennedy:

"*Sausage Man,*" said Chitchee out of breath and frosted with fear. "You got Sausage Man's autograph, Kennedy."

Kennedy bit his lip, and it looked like a gashed, white bloodless worm.

"So, I don't have Iron John's Ironlike John Hancock?"

"Kennedy," said Saami, shaking his head and reading over Chitchee's shoulder. "Dude, what you have isn't worth Iron John's Iron Hand around Iron John's Iron Cock!"

"Nuts," said Kennedy, heartbroken. "The proverbial Cat has got my Tongue! Do you think Sausage Man's signature might be abscessed at *half an apple pie* across the street? I mean I know Kaylee at the counter very well . . . she always helps me out. Sausage Man could be famous someday—and I oh—feel so damn old and inconsequential."

"Me too—I wish I were Robert Bly!" said Chitchee with a dreaming aloud sound. "Now I'm a Chitchee Chichester! What a ridiculous name. Who's going to read a book by some guy named Chitchee Chichester?"

"Maybe Chilcote Carrothers would read it?" suggested Saami. "You almost have the same name as him!"

"Maybe," agreed Kennedy from the couch. "Or you could write Hallmark greeting cards and then no one would even *want* to know your name."

Officers Weatherwax and Lowry turned around the corner lock-stepping Torg On into BookSmart:

"Is this one of yours?" asked Officer Lowry, his face flat as a slab of marbled meat.

"Yes," replied Chitchee before Noel and Saami responded. "He works here. Was he bothering you?"

"He says he's blind," said Officer Weatherwax, glancing over at Kennedy on the couch reading (it looked like *Chicken Soup for the Soul Man*) superstitiously and suspiciously suspecting Kennedy of being some other suspect they were looking for.

"Torg is our accountant," said Chitchee. "Because he can *account* up to a hundred!"

"We picked him up," said Officer Weatherwax, heaving his butterball belly forward and drawing in a big breath, "driving a Lincoln Town Car down the center stripe on Hennepin Avenue."

"Was he swerving or something?" asked Chitchee. "What seems to be the problem?"

Officer Weatherwax pointed a double-barreled stare at Chitchee, the stare of tiny gray beads close-set as birdshot. Chitchee seemed to Officer Weatherwax to be at Woodstock dancing topless to pure feedback. Officer Weatherwax's frown simulated a parabaloid undergoing the method of slicing.

"I'm legally blind," said Torg, "not totally blind. It wasn't me, I told you. It was that guy from Middle-earth. He made me switch seats and he ran off with all the other trolls. They left me holding the bag. Those dirty rats. See? They double-crossed me. See? They played me for a sucker. Which is what I am. See?"

Rodney's Scotch plaid-capped head popped out of an aisle, his plaid cap slipping off his fringed baldness, his face expanding to include his forehead too.

"Do you mean that guy running out the back door?" asked Noel.

"Rodney!" shouted Torg. "You no-good, double-crossin' bum! Go take a long walk on a short dock! Can you hear me? 'Cause I'm singing like a canary to the coppers about you . . ."

He ended with a sigh, sobbed, and coughed; and then Torg let out a wild moan:

"Katreena!"

"The limousine," said Officer Lowry to Chitchee though looking at Torg instead, "is in the impound lot. 51 Colfax. Do you know Sergei Vorchenko?"

"Is he soft-spoken, reserved, and nonchalant like Torg, our accountant?" asked Chitchee.

The thumpers looked at each other.

"Oh, forget it," said Officer Lowry.

"No, really, you guys must be doing a great job," said Chitchee. "You can tell by the way you receive an award every time you get up to ten complaints."

The blue jay-blue shirts walked back to their wheels (immediately a shivaree of sirens jarred Chitchee's perfect pitch). Officer Weatherwax limped from a pinched nerve in his back, pinching his eyes together.

Torg, alone in a cloud of despair, condensed into water droplets. He leaned against the maroon counter and sobbed and cried and wailed that he was still a virgin.

"I don't have any friends, that's the problem," said Torg.

"Everyone always says that," said Chitchee, "so it can't be true."

"Yeah, but I'm so depressed."

"Why?"

"I told you, I have no friends."

"I'll be your friend," said Chitchee.

"No thanks," said Torg.

"Okay," said Chitchee. "Check."

"I'm going to take the long way home," said Torg, "and blow my brains out."

"I'll join you," said Chitchee eagerly. "Can I go?"

"Katreena!" moaned Torg. "God that woman is a woman. When she enters a room, everyone can feel the electricity."

"Because she turned on the lights?" asked Chitchee.

"No," said Torg, deframing himself and squeezing his eyes into one. "Because she is a heavenly black angel!"

Torg departed. He lost himself in one thought, walked to the bus stop, and stood directly under the #6 street sign, without a hope of caressing her breasts or licking her ears.

Chitchee's own deepening depression crept back and clutched his throat. *Night Falls Fast.* Jealousy of Torg's passion for Katreena clutched his entire body. He excused himself from Noel and Saami to go to the bathroom, because he ran off in a flurry of tears and massive alienation. Did he have one friend, without including the long gone LaDonna? Unable to finish his shift from a loss of confidence in life itself, he splashed cold water on his face and looked in the bathroom mirror.

"Wait a second," he soliloquized. "I don't have to kill myself. I have the green, green grass of home."

He stood on the toilet seat, reached into the acoustic tiles, touched a tiny baggie of Blue Diesel Raven had set there for him days ago, and placed a twenty in its place. He took one hit, felt fine, couldn't remember what all the fuss was about, and hopped back to work, only to have the hidden depressions of his friends cross his mind and haunt him—the friends he did nothing for, the friends he never loved, the friends who thought they would become great artists who became great addicts and greater and greater alcoholics instead, who, if not brain dead already, had died in the alleys of the dumpsters, died with hard-rock livers, arrested hearts, and last looks up at the satellites through the light pollution of Minneapolis, having suffered the privations of loneliness most of their guttered lives anyway.

Stars in her own eyes, LaDonna grew bored with Chitchee's preoccupation with literary fame and his slovenly attitude toward his disability, which he dismissed as a unique advantage, although Chitchee could provide LaDonnas with neither a roof, nor babies. Her miscarriage was the loss of twins and the mandate between them. They never talked about it, although they thought about it every day. LaDonna complained to her motorcycle club friends at Dulono's Pizza that Chitchee was "a Beanie Baby with baby fat who had to be babysat." She had become his "convenience store that had to stay open for him 24/7." He had reverted to a "permanent fetal position on the couch." She confided this to Madison (who confided it to Snorri who confided it to Chitchee) because Madison, methed out, had gradually slipped into a delusional state in which she had been the secret mistress of David Bowie, posed for Robert Mapplethorpe, and had long imaginary conversations with Princess Leia, in which Steve Martin was Darth Vader, and little blue-faced gremlins followed her everywhere asking her out.

Chitchee and LaDonna often recalled their favorite parlor game of bibliomancy when all their doomed friends in the good old days would come over for a black-out party before and after the Longhorn, Zoogie's, First Avenue, or the CC Club. One player opened a page in the DSM-III, read the symptoms aloud, and the other players had to "Guess the Insanity."

"I can't find you in here, Chitchee," said LaDonna. "But you have to have Anti-Autistic Syndrome. You want to be friends with everybody and you talk to complete strangers like they were your relatives! It's embarrassing! You're too nice! I hate that!"

Uncannily enough, the random diagnosis jingled a small bell with all their increasingly gothic, as the night wore on, friends.

"Sorry!" smiled Chitchee. "That's not me! I'm rather cold, have no friends, and exist in complete isolation! I'm *not* hypersensitive to criticism—*no matter what you say*! Most people cross the street when they see me coming—to avoid a lecture on the world's sacred texts and the perfect human, *al-insan al kamil*."

"The perfect human! Hah!" scoffed his wife. "Look at you, you look like a drug addict!"

"Well, that's what I am," said Chitchee. "Something wrong with being who I am?"

He searched under the cushions for his little glass pipe, found it, and declared:

"You're the one who shoots up while I'm cooking brown rice and tofu."

"You have tons of friends," said LaDonna as the entire party followed her into Chitchee's bathroom to get away from Chitchee so they could do lines of coke without Chitchee's knowing it, because there was only so much coke to go around anyway.

"What about your morbid fear of the dark?" continued LaDonna, stepping from the bathroom. "And you need a night-light? And you have no sense of direction, can't read a map, completing a jigsaw is impossible, and you get lost at night going out for cigarettes, and our furniture has to be arranged in alphabetical order? It has to be OCD of some sort. And yet you won't see a doctor."

"And what about *you*, LaDonna," continued Chitchee, "the love of the so-called 'dark side' meaning sexual arousal dependent upon danger, sexual attraction to alpha males with felonies, fascination with violent—"

"I don't have that!" said LaDonna.

"No? Then why do we have a poster of Richard Ramirez over our headboard?"

"It's camp punk," said LaDonna. "It's punk or something equally meaningless."

"Is your favorite movie *Bonnie and Clyde*? Didn't you start an Ann B. Rule book club for 'people who hate people'? Look at your bookshelf! All bodice rippers!"

"So?"

"Non-fiction bodice rippers?" asked Chitchee. "Look at your bookshelf: let's see, what else, *Faces of Death 3*, *Dating Serial Killers*, *Funny Russian Prison Stories*, *The Satanic Torturer's Guide to Safe Sex*—you're like a man!"

"You're like a woman!" she said.

"Then we get along fine!" he said.

"That's not true, not at all!" she said. "You don't know what you're talking about. It's exactly the opposite! In fact, men and women only get together to mate. And even then they seem clueless like horses being broken in. My best friends are women because women make the best friends."

"And Nestor? According to Nestor, the history of music is the long history of the decline of Nestor. Don't ask me why his music always comes out brown! Nestor—who always says a friend to everybody is a friend to nobody. Platitudes like that are only platitudes like this one. Make no rules? You just did."

"I love Nestor, God bless him, because he knows everything," she said. "It's all wrong of course."

"A friend to everybody is a friend to nobody!" he said. "Is that a confession of vapidity or what? Let's agree to put the DSM-III away."

"It's so outdated anyway," said LaDonna.

"Yes," agreed Chitchee, "there have been so many advances in madness lately, the doctors can't keep up."

"Where did everybody go?" asked LaDonna, opening the bathroom door.

LaDonna was unable to open the Carling Black Label beer bottle with her worn-out Surdyk's bottle opener. She chipped the bottle's rim and the bottle dropped on the floor and she lost a beer. She blamed Chitchee, because he was always "rushing her." Worse than that and more incriminating, Chitchee threw her timing off because he had deliberately double-bagged their groceries, and LaDonna had been forced to lose time debagging the double bags for garbage bags—and that separating the double bags flustered her because she couldn't figure how to do it without tearing the paper handles off.

"Okay, do you love me? I don't love myself anymore, I know that!" he said, looking up from his book shield of *Ulysses*. "How's that for a loophole? And you? You don't like *any* of my friends! I'm going out for Carousels."

When Chitchee donned his Gogol's overcoat, he noticed that his overcoat had gone to the dogs, charred by cigarettes and stained by sour mash. To get away Chitchee wanted to make a pilgrimage around the corner to an all night grocery store. He sat back down fully winter-clothed on the leather-fatigued couch and poured sweat.

"Get real, Chitchee, I'm real," said LaDonna, using another can opener and opening the bottle, which shot its beer out in the form of foam, leaving a few sips behind. She finished the bottle. She belched in a belching contest. "I like real people. My friends are real people. They like loud motorcycles and roller derby and gun ranges and monster trucks and Patsy Cline. Your friends all have problems and then you have to babysit them, and I have to babysit you, because your friends are your problems. And I can't babysit you and your friends anymore!"

"Is my timing that Bird's Eye frozen?" asked Chitchee.

Where had he lost her? Supported by his wife, who had once thought he was "really onto something," he was later revised to "going nowhere." He had wasted her life in middle-class boredom, giving her a "mediocrity complex" and holding her back from her career as a dancer, artist, and famous personality.

"We used to be so happy, and now we're so bored," said LaDonna, looking at her six-pack of Carling Black Label on the kitchen table.

"That's life, isn't it?" said Chitchee, tending the primitive VCR.

The magnetic tape of Ingmar Bergman's *Scenes From a Marriage* stuck between the heads and the rollers so that Liv Ullmann's prepossessing, emotional palette of a face was a large onion and Erland Josephson's beard wavered like seaweed breaking on the beach. Johan and Marianne were in bed chatting in a frozen pause that would soon time out.

LaDonna interrupted the spewing, crunching machine:

"Poor you! You don't deserve to be happy. For you it's half nightmare, half vacation. I'm persecuting you with your own boredom and then forget it—oh, I'm disappearing!"

"Yes," said Chitchee, "you're disappearing into a searing analysis of nothing. Where are you going?"

"The CC Club!" she said over her shoulder swaggering out the door as CC Club's Woman of the Year.

"Who will be there? Nestor? You know his biggest mistake is that he believes the stupid are always wrong."

"Maybe. I'm going to go out dancing with the girls, girls night out I guess!" she said, her swagger in the frame of the door. "I'm going to Nestor's music camp this weekend, is that the poisoned apple you are referring to? There's nothing there! Get real! You're being childish again!"

"I'm sorry that I hurt you by causing you to feel guilty after hurting me, which was as beneath you as far as I am beneath you for making it my fault that you stooped to my level, when you should have held the high ground, which you have now lost!"

His condescending, childish grin triggered her to throw the green Eureka electric broom at the wall above his head where the broom burst into fireworks.

"I want a divorce!" she said. "I divorce you. I divorce you. I divorce you. You didn't tell me that you erased *The Hell Hound Chip!* You were faking writing it with typed-over George R. R. Martin pages! The hell hounds will bite you in the ass someday."

Chitchee sighed, and the door slammed. Numb, he thought of tearing his eyes out or sticking forks in the sockets—so as to never see the worlds of hell hounds spinning around his head. Slowly he repaired the vacuum and replaced the motorized brush roll in its place.

Musical retreat weekend at Interlachen? He confiscated her suitcase for something and discovered unopened SexWorld packages: latex skirts, mesh bras, crops, spike heels, hot pink lace lingeries, thongs, edible crotchless panties, strap-on, spiked choker, and leather cuffs—none of which he had ever seen her wear. There must have been a sale at SexWorld. Half off on everybody.

Chitchee came to, startled out of a dream, heard:

"Do you think it might be worth at least *half* an apple pie?" asked Kennedy, his hand on the crash bar.

"What? What's worth a pack of edible crotchless panties? Is that what you're asking me?" asked Chitchee. "I don't know, go ask Kaylee! She knows everything!"

After his shift for *Black Swan* at the Uptown Theater, Felix, a one-man Ace Hardware Store, clanked into BookSmart. Felix wore a heavy black duster, its inner pockets loaded down with tools, a large bolt cutter, a canister of Freon, and his trusty water bottle. In a hopeless and nervous attempt to not appear like a high school hit man, Felix browsed over the new arrivals and idled, his eyelids fluttering over his pinpointed pupils from the dehydration of the over-salted popcorn dinner he had eaten all the livelong night, causing him to break in and out of cold fevers and repeatedly slam water from his water bottle, while Chitchee cleared the store of customers, homeless, and stowaways.

Chitchee punched a few buttons on the TI calculator, a few more on the credit card machine, and then he tabulated those totals on a recon sheet. The closing took five minutes and all the arithmetic added up.

Noel had been so elated by Ye Young, he bounded like a hare for home (although completely puzzled by his attraction to and the attraction of Ye Young to him—was it a set up?).

"I'm turning off the lights, but I'm not setting the alarm, Felix," said Chitchee. "Remind me to set the alarm back when we get back."

They heard a thunder clap and they jumped in harmony. A lumberjack's red beard and sideburns nested on his large cliff face with his two dilated eyes shining in the night. When Chitchee let Raven in, Toby Pfeiffer, like a purple puppy in his Vikings' blouse, in yet another nocturnal mission, turned the corner and jammed his body into Raven's body so they were double-jammed into the door jambs again.

"Mercury in retrograde," said Raven, stroking his mercurial beard.

"Hey," said Chitchee, "do you guys want to go down into the tunnel system with us?"

"Tunnels?" demurred Toby. "What if there are dead bodies down there?"

"The more, the merrier," said Chitchee. "Come on, Toby, do something dangerous for once in your life! Man or mouse?"

"Dangerous?" asked Toby. "You mean like in the movies?"

Chitchee closed the store. He led Felix, Toby, and Raven into the basement of BookSmart and into the Employees Only area where Felix tripped over twelve sets of the complete works of Rebecca Wells (*Divine Ya-Yas* author), fifteen *Girl with the Pearl Earrings*, four Jan Karon's *The Deluxe Illustrated Mitford Companion*, Garrison Keillors by the gross, Jane Hamilton, Jane Smiley, Jane Pauley, *Peter Lawford: Friend of the Jack Kennedys*, and *The Rat Pack Singalong Scrapbook with foreword by Dick Shawn* tossed together in a sea of books on the cement floor, which Felix dog-paddled through with apologies.

"This goes to Lakewood *Cemetery*?" asked Chitchee, helping Felix off the cement floor and looking at the bolted and padlocked submarine door, crossed with electric yellow ribbons (KEEP OUT).

"Yeah, I'm pretty sure it curves around," said Felix, brandishing his bolt-cutter.

Felix popped the vaulted door of *Das Boot*.

The foursome stumbled forward into the abyss.

"We're going south, right?" asked Raven. "To Lakewood Cemetery, right? Are you sure?"

And the darkness was like no other darkness Chitchee had experienced, and he felt the darkness with his hands as his eyes adjusted to the vertigo of universal black. Toby turned around and whammed into Raven, who groaned like an elephant with a toothache.

"Toby in retrograde," joked Felix. "Zinger? Guess not. Whoa."

A glimmer of light in the shape of a fluttering sphinx moth offered the only shimmer of illumination to Chitchee. Glimpsing a chink, refracted where the onyx walls glowed, they resembled upright walking bats with only the slightest sensation of gravity beneath their feet. They were only the sounds of their own disembodied voices floating transversely through the subterranean air, dark as bitumen, pitch as night. Chitchee experienced the final darkness of death. He feared the complete and permanent dissolution of his inked-out ego. He was salt in a jet black manifold. He dissolved into only heartbeats.

"Hey!" Chitchee called out. "Where are you guys?"

With his fingers he forcepped the acorn cap from his fob jean pocket and blew a shriek to touch the skies.

"What are you doing?" asked Felix. "What is that? Stop! I know where you are now!"

Raven plugged his ears, quietly investigating his surroundings, and responded:

"Out of sight, dynamite!"

"Yeeooowwwww! Knock it off! Hey Felix, who are dose guys? Are they alive? What kind of Lakewood Cemetery buries people sitting up?" asked Toby, kneeling on a stool, sticking his head through a transom, and viewing a room full of strangely-staring stiffs sitting stock still, eviscerated by a taxidermic procedure.

The life-sized stiffs gazed upward with half-slit eyeballs.

"Whoa, this isn't Lakewood Cemetery, this is the midnight movie, *Crash*," Felix realized aloud. "Wrong turn! Sorry, guys! *Crash*! Boom. Bah."

Chitchee looked from a proscenium through a transom.

"Talk about *The Drowned World*!" muttered Chitchee to Toby underneath him.

Bobblehead sat entranced with a saddle-shaped grin and touched his nose, his legs far apart, in the first row. In the back row LaDonna kissed Sergei Vorchenko. The middle seats included Minerva and Beda Holmgren, who looked bored and held their holding hands upward to corroborate their fingers were interwoven. Beda broke off and knit with a ball of yarn and two knitting needles, which was a constant in her bag, with winter around the corner and three months away. Off to the side and closer to the screen sat Henry "Heinie" Heinemann, looking *absolutely* fascinated, and that was by his box of popcorn. Who invented the popcorn box? Could it be another inventive Minnesotan? Was it something to be researched at the Minneapolis downtown library next week, using the entire library staff on all floors for assistance?

Heinie loved local history and the Minnesota Historical Society. In fact Heinie had found a nook there between two couches and had himself locked in overnight so he could crawl out after closing and read up on local geological formations in Minnesota. He would lie on the floor for weeks like an emaciated Casey Jones in his engineer's overalls and engineer's cap from the decade of the refrigerator cars. With a magnifying glass from an old OED, he would shine a flashlight and suck up useless knowledge.

"Let's get out of here," cried Toby, peeing. "I want to get out of here! I want to go to Lakewood Cemetery! This theater is creepy!"

"We just got here," said Raven. "Perfect place to get high during *Crash!*"

"I don't want to get high! I'm afraid of heights!" said Toby. "*Crash?* What kind of name is that for a movie? *Forrest Gump*—now that's a name for a movie."

The audience, cradled in theatrical-red velour and folding auditorium seats—the kind that go bang when they fold up—was no longer hypnotized by the silver screen, the moving images of a lost eternity having moved on. Light no longer lambent on their eyeglasses—the audience sensed something awry and anomalously disruptive. Shaking them by the shoulder as it were, they heard a referee's or a traffic policeman's whistle.

It was Toby's head pumpkined over a three-foot drop. He looked to be a giant spiny anteater, his head and arms stuck in the transom, unable to go forward or backward.

"Hey! Manager! Emily!" chortled Heinie, popcorn interrupted, annoyed he might miss even one frame out of twenty four per second. "There are *live people* beneath the stage! Blowing whistles! Stop the movie!"

Heinie, so ancient legend had it, had been created in La Crosse in a geological era even the fossil record forgot. Heinie, with his ice-cream white, vanilla Van Dyke wizening on his thin chin, glasses thick as rock salt, and old-fashioned hearing aid leapt up. He waved his engineer's cap.

"The show must NOT go on!" yelled Heinie. "There are live *people* below the stage!"

"No, there isn't!" said Toby, sticking his head out of the transom. "It's only me! Right guys?"

"Yeah," said Felix, poking his head out of the transom, "he's not making it up!"

"Hold your horses—it smells like they are smoking pot!" declared Heinie. "It looks like they're catching a buzz down there. And it smells like the Blue Diesel going around!"

"Wait," whispered Felix. "Where's my phone? I can't find my wallet either."

The house lights flickered like *Le Sacre du Printemps*.

"Chitchee, go back!" yelled Felix, handing Raven's glass pipe back to Raven. "Here comes my manager, Emily! God! I am so busted."

"I'm stuck!" squealed Toby, thrusting forward. "I have to piddle!"

Toby had pushed his podgy arms through the transom to prop himself up. His plan was to somersault downwards to the proscenium before the first row, but his jacket zipper (somehow he had zipped his jacket zipper into his pants zipper) constrained his muscular flow—he couldn't see what he was doing—although the entire auditorium watched open-mouthed amazed.

"Help, I'm trapped," yelled Toby. "Someone film this!"

"Shut up!" said the crowd, debating in a lively caucus. "Refund!"

While Emily strobed the house lights, Heinie turned around and asked for a show of hands.

"Who is *for* continuing the film? And who is *against* continuing the film?"

"Gatecrashers," said Beda with disgusto. She sprang up with her pepper spray. "I loathe loafers who can't even pay their own ways. Free riders! The cheating *balls* of those bastards! I hate them all! I'm going to tell Felix as soon as I see him we won't be accepting his free tickets anymore—unless they clean up their act."

"If you want," shouted Heinie slowly in a staccato, "to start the film over, raise one hand! If you want to keep the movie going raise both hands—high above your heads so I can see them! Now, does anyone have a pen and paper?"

Minerva fingered the pepper spray for brown bears from her own arsenal of mace because Toby most resembled a brown bear cub to her, a very round brown bear cub—with a very disgusting moon-white, pie-of-hair face.

"The trouble with Tribbles," quipped Minerva.

Beda looked over and nodded her tacit approval.

"You, girl, go grrrrrrgirl, get him, girl, go!"

Minerva fixed her emotional state between a laugh and a frown securely on her face and said nothing about how hackneyed "go girl" sounded. And yet, bursting with pride, Beda, not without amused detachment, watched her heartbeat, her Minerva, walk pigeon-toed down the Uptown Theater aisle.

"Asshole, you wrecked the movie on our only night out!" said Minerva.

Minerva pressed the nozzle. Toby screamed. Blowback immediately diffused down everyone's throats. Heinie fled backwards, crying, tearing himself from the screen and leaving a piece of his heart behind.

The audience evacuated under the direction of Emily, the manager, onto Hennepin Avenue to breathe. Paramedics, firemen, and police rolled in.

Officers Weatherwax and Lowry drove a tearful, brimming-over Toby Pfeiffer to the door of his nursing home, where he was questioned, scolded, and grounded. Toby turned on the waterworks for the head nurse, peed himself, and reluctantly lay in bed. They allowed him to go only as far as Carousel Square for a month under a curfew that required him to be in bed (lights out) by ten o'clock sharp.

MEMORY LANES

Two weeks later, Spartak Bok was charged with driving the wrong way up an exit ramp onto I-94. He was also in possession of meth, Ecstasy, rifles (with altered serial numbers), ice picks, open cases of Moët & Chandon Ice Impérial champagne, a year's worth of *Outlaw Biker*, and a man's finger. Spartak pleaded not guilty, deporting himself with indignant, outraged looks, gestures, and a bout of frenetic phonetics. Released on a non-cash, surety bond of $40,000 bail, Spartak blamed all his problems on Yakov Vorchenko. Spartak accused Yakky of secretly working for Viktor Martensen. This eventually came down to an ultimatum: Viktor or Spartak. Not only *that* (as a show of loyalty), Spartak demanded that he and Yakky play Croatian roulette. Spartak would point the revolver at Yakky and he would also pull the trigger for Yakky. That way Spartak really wasn't risking much. Yakky had second thoughts about any ideas of fidelity.

And it wasn't a good sign when Spartak's employees at Bok Properties on Miracle Mile arrived at the office in the morning and found Spartak's spermatozoa crawling all over their computer screens. Whoever complained about it was blamed, tamed, and flamed. Prostitutes flew in and out of the main office, coke dealers held conventions in the break room, and meth bugs crawled out of the woodwork whenever Spartak showed up for work.

Enter Viktor Martensen to meet Yakky Vorchenko at Memory Lanes bowling alley on 26th Avenue South. Yakky sat under his Brooklyn Cyclones cap, which he took off to inspect for drops of dried blood. Yakky was bald but a few hairs stood on top of his head like alfalfa sprouts, which he yanked out periodically. He looked good for the interview. His clothes were his usual out-of-style glitzkrieg of late 1970s flashy/blingy wear from a kind of *Soul Trainwreck* wardrobe spatchcocked together with random athletic gear. At his breast he nurtured his .45 caliber like a baby vervet monkey. The crash of bowling balls punctuated the dining area like thunder in an electrical storm after heat lightning strikes.

"That fucker wants me dead!" was the second thing out of Yakky's rotten mouth.

The first were some pubic hairs that he had acquired from a girl at New World Sunrise Massage And Spa.

"Yakky," said Viktor apprehensively. "I want Spartak Bok out of my hair too. He's too dangerous. He's going to blow the lid off everything. He has to go."

"Yeah, sure," said Yakky, looking at the dessert menu. "How do you want it done?"

"I don't care," Viktor tee-heed, "as long as it's done well."

"Oh yeah," said Yakky, "of course, only the most professional."

Yakky liked to hang out at DreamGirls, Deja Vu, and the Skyway Lounge, or anywhere female flesh exposed itself like the Moon to the multitudes of moon men in strip bars along Hennepin Avenue. And Yakky loved taking offense at last call over nothing and then taking a whining frat boy from the whining frat boy store out to the whining frat boy parking lot and cold-cocking the jock with the pistol-grip of a Colt .45 until the whining frat boy puked. On his quiet nights, Yakky passed out at Mousey's Bar not in a dark corner, but in all the dark corners, which wasn't too hard because all the corners were dark even with the lights up.

"Ready to order?" asked Dagny, suppressing the agony she felt seeing Viktor in her booth.

"Hello, Dagny," said Viktor. "You're looking good, cuzz."

"Why don't we—I'll have—" said Yakky, "cake. One quart of ice cream on it—and we blow the lid off that asshole—a plate of chocolate marshmallow cookies on the side."

"We don't have cakes or cookies—only what's on the menu," said Dagny, her husky voice stayed emotionless so as not to engage.

"Root beer floats—what kind of root beer? A & W? Oh that motherfucker! He'll be swimming with the sturgeons," said Yakky.

"Barq's," said Dagny. "No sturgeons."

"Shoo-oore," said Yakky.

"Dessert for you?" Dagny asked her old boss without looking up.

"I'll have a gin gimlet, no almomd," said Viktor. "Your guy is late. I'll have a steak sandwich."

"How do you want it done?" asked Dagny.

"I don't care," said Viktor, making eye contact with Yakky across the table.

"As long as it's done well," chuckled Yakky.

"Nice and dead," giggled Viktor lovey-dovey eyed.

"Curly fries?" asked Dagny.

"Do you have short and curlys?" asked Yakky, his eyes two center-holed kroners.

Dagny's eyelids lowered and her eyes slowly rolled in their gutters.

"I'll be back," is all she muttered.

"The waitress was fucking weird, like we was harassing her?" questioned Yakky. "Hey, she didn't get my steak sandwich! I'll go hunt her down."

When Yakky worked for Spartak (when he was a wee little hit man) he got the call and order from the debtee Spartak Bok. Having stalked the debtor for the debtee, Yakky chopped off the debtor's fingers and toes, wrapped them in dollar-store Christmas wrapping paper, tied him up with a red ribbon, and stuffed the body parts in the debtor's mouth. Then he and his helpers, Dicky Joe Griesedieck and Joey Van Pee in cheap track-suits, driving gloves, and Adidas shoved the gagged debtor in a bed of cement. When the debtor dried in the cement, the debtees stood the debtor upright like a giant cinder block and immured him behind the drywall in his own house's basement. And then in the dead of night, the debtees drove away to the accompaniment of the debtor's muzzled screams.

Croffut Gleet clacked on cleats into Memory Lanes, clop, clop, clop. Croffut wore a tear-drop black helmet (covered with skull stickers), a Spandex jersey for an Italian racing team, and scrotum-tight lycra shorts, showing off cable-tight muscular calves and thighs although his shortness canceled out any impression of buff.

"What do you know about explosive devices, Croffut?" asked Yakky.

"Everything I know is from an old *Anarchist's Cookbook*," said Croffut, licking his lips and shaking his thinning, glistening, disappearing, marcelled, and dyed-black curls.

"Hey waitress, classy chassis!" continued Croffut, looking crazy when his earthworm tongue crawled out. He wiggled his worm at Dagny.

When Croffut removed his helmet, his forehead was square as a meat-hammer. Out of that meat-hammer, a storm of hair gathered behind his double widow's peaks. Hair blew every which way toward the sky like black fire. Croffut always looked surprised. He had been arrested for arson so many times in the 3rd Precinct he had his own corner on their bulletin board.

After Yakky and Croffut worked out details, Viktor tossed his gin gimlet and ice cubes across the floor and excused himself for an appointment in Uptown. Croffut bike-raced to Lunds Uptown, swiped all their free coffee cakes and spare bread parts on their sample trays, wheeled over to The Sick Joke Cafe, bagged all their free samples of day olds, spun by Ragnarok's Choklit Stoppe in Carousel Square, and hogged all the free chocolate turtles. He threw it all into a dumpster, lighted the dumpster on fire, and sped home. Yakky beefed with bowlers until he was bounced out by two bouncers, whereupon he bounced downtown as the crow flies, drunk to the closest strip bar.

YARDLEY'S LIBRARY

Chitchee woke up again looking like the village witch doctor and it was late. Depressed, lonely, and exhausted (the cicadas grinding like power drills in his ears) in a hot, humid, soupy August sweat—he felt swamped, backstroking in a bog, and unable to sleep or rest or think. Ragweed pollen saturated the air that morning, sneezing him into song. And although his air conditioner worked, Chitchee feared running up a tab of ten thousand dollars with Xcel Energy. He taped aluminum foil over his windows, placed pre-frozen metal bowls of ice water in front of floor fans, took a cold shower standing in his bathtub filled with ice at his feet, kept the lights off, sat in the dark, ate Kemps orange sherbet, wore a floppy hat with an ice pack stapled to the inside crown, removed the fridge racks, sprinkled cornstarch on his white bed sheets and pillow cases, then stuffed the pillow in the freezer, and then the bed sheets in the empty fridge. He lay on the floor, wearing only his ice pack hat, with the fans blowing over the ice cubes in the metal bowls—in the dark by a low-heat reading light. Then he wrapped himself in cool, white bed sheets and lay his head down on the frozen, corn-starched pillow fresh out of the freezer. He chewed mint leaves—a slice of cool cucumber stuck to the middle of his forehead. He shaved off all his body hair and watched Youtubes of Emperor penguins jump from calving ice shelves into the icy Antarctic drink.

Jolted off the floor by the memory that he had told Yardley Singleton he would bike over to Yardley's apartment that day and help sort out his library, Chitchee gripped his mountain bike, then noticed the rear tire had gone flat overnight, needing a new tube from Flanders Bicycle on Lyndale Avenue South. He walked.

The surface of the Earth inflamed Chitchee like a magnifying glass on the burning sidewalks and soft blacktops outside A & J Chicken. He crawled through a chain-link fence and sumac down the embankment of shattered McCormick's Vanilla bottles and flittering cabbage butterflies to the railroad tracks. The dandelions had sprouted into death. The tulips, the lilacs, the daffodils— all dead. Drooping power lines were perched with swallows discussing uncertain futures, pondering the day's events and future migrations.

Chitchee followed the railroad tracks, the same railroad tracks that ran past Lake Calhoun, which once (he had read) served as an ice farm with outlying ice warehouses, lumber yards, coal warehouses, brickyards, silos, and chimneys. It was only the sumac sweating it out now. Sumac perched on sweltering retaining walls, overlooking the old Milwaukee Road line and hobo jungles. A dying sunflower himself, he walked on the gravelly tracks, dirt bike trails, and goat paths while loosestrife in purple patches thrived. A bald-faced hornet stared at Chitchee's sweaty neck. He waved it off, feeling miserable.

Chitchee scrutinized Yardley's street address, which Chitchee had written on an old grocery store receipt from Morris and Christie's grocery store on the corner. Yardley lived behind the facade of another MPG building, a towering, expensive, skyward apartment building. His condo gazed over Lake Harriet. It faced the Lake Harriet Bandshell by the Rose Garden, where sometimes Hawk Eye slept, assuming he reserved his perennials in advance, because homeless people planted themselves in and around Lake Harriet all night long. Even with Airbnb reservations, raccoons attacked the homeless in the middle of the night for trespassing.

Whistling "Country Gardens," Chitchee glowed with rapture at the sage, bellflower, and blazing star in the simple garden of a flower box, also enraptured. Well-tended planter boxes of dahlias, geraniums, and zinnias sat outside the bluestone entrance. A Vietnamese gardener tended to the chrysanthemums, lining the limestone and granite-faced building. Firebirds of clamoring daylilies burst above a galliard's brilliancy in a rhodopsin rich infinitude.

Fancy pants Yardley Singleton had money all right. He frittered it on a fruitless, worldwide dragnet for first editions/first printings of Chilcote Carrothers at book fairs in Portugal, Wales, Argentina, and Lebanon.

Might Chitchee make some extra cash for a house call? Or turn this into a sideline? All of which evaporated when, buzzed in, he tapped his two bits and a shave on the door and heard Yardley say something into a shoe.

Slowly Chitchee pushed the unlocked door open and flinched at the contours of a winged shadow.

A big brown bat grazed Chitchee's black-capped head.

Screaming, Chitchee's eyeballs started backwards in swirls swallowing themselves like holes.

The big brown bat disappeared down the alabaster hallway like a dot of India ink in a glass of water. Like a boomerang, the bat came back. At the end of the hall, Larry Sangster opened his apartment door and screamed. Chitchee lunged into Yardley's apartment, slammed the door behind him, and heard crickety crickets playing cricket.

He felt a mildewed mist creeping through the buggy dark. He smelled the plastic-covered furniture, covered with hardcovers. Silverfish left off and ran. Chitchee cocked an ear. Was that a natural gas leak from an archaic gas stove? He checked for salamanders. Brown recluse spiders reclined on spider chairs. He saw a gecko stain on the concrete ceiling. The thermostat registered 111 degrees Fahrenheit and the needle pointed toward New Delhi.

"Hello?" asked Chitchee, his voice as cracked as the crack in the door he spied through.

Yardley might, like a Tonton Macoute, kill him with the fell stroke of a machete, chop him up, toss him in a gunny sack, and trade him for a tin of eucalyptus snus.

"Yardley? It's Chitchee!" continued Chitchee. "Don't shoot! Where are you?"

"In here!" said a muted, muffled Yardley. "Singleton down! Singleton down! You won't believe what happened!"

"I'll believe anything that happened," said Chitchee. "And more!"

"I pulled down my *Vikram and the Vampire* to see if it was a limited edition so I could sell it to you at BookSmart, but I couldn't remember buying it. Did someone give it to me? And then I opened the book. AND A GODDAMNED BAT ATTACKED ME! It flew out of nowhere!"

"I know! I let it out of your apartment. It's probably pretty thirsty," said Chitchee. "Wait, this seems all too familiar . . . it's like I have read this somewhere—*deja lu*."

At first glance, Chitchee surveyed the book hoarder's paradise; at second, he thought of those English eccentrics whose collections collapsed whole buildings and trapped ground floor dwellers in blazing infernos like the night of the Fall of Constantinople.

"Do you have any IEDs?" inquired Chitchee.

"No—only punji pits and tripwired grenades by the medicine cabinet in the bathroom—near the empty prescription bottles of Oxycontin," said Yardley from the other room. "Do you know that veteran, Randy Johnson? I swear he sold me the wrong prescription."

"Nice place, Yardley," said Chitchee as if looking through a *Good Housekeeping*. "It reminds me of Derek Bickerton's description of the lifestyle of *Homo erectus*: 'they sat for 0.3 million years in the drafty, smoky caves of Zhoukoudian, cooking bats over smoldering embers and waiting for the caves to fill up with their own garbage.' Where are you? Yardley?"

"Underneath this bookcase," said Yardley. "It fell on top of me. My back! Singleton down!"

Yardley, already thin as a crack in a door and with a full bookcase on top of his back, lay buried in books like a sun god in a cold tomb. He was paralyzed. Shut-in Yardley's locked-in library of papers, letters, mail, magazines, books, pamphlets, parking tickets, and ephemera of ephemera was out to get him. His library had erased him.

When Chitchee lifted up the bookcase, Yardley squirmed out and breathed again. Chitchee examined framed photos of Yardley in Vietnam at a landing zone next to a Huey helicopter.

"Hey, you have a young Vietnamese girl in your arms—like in *A Bright and Shining Lie*! Did you pal around with John Paul Vann?"

Yardley had walls of foreign language dictionaries—every Cassell and Larousse dictionary Chitchee dreamed of coveting: a Hans Wehr Arabic dictionary, a Liddell and Hart Greek dictionary, Hippocrenes, Tuttles, Collinses, Kodanshas, and Oxfords.

"You were a helicopter pilot in Vietnam? You never know with some people. I pegged you for the Archdeacon of Barsetshire," said Chitchee, slapping his thigh and laughing. "First off, soldier, no *Final Exits*! We will get you back on your feet, Yardo. And we'll start by getting rid of your ten copies of *Final Exit*."

"My name is Yardley," said Yardley. "Not Yardo."

"It must be near *Fahrenheit 451* in here," said Chitchee, throwing Yardley's suicide manuals onto a pile of books, which sent them rolling back down to Chitchee's feet.

"Can we open a window?" asked Chitchee.

"No," said Yardley. "The flies will get in."

"How about sunlight?"

"No," said Yardley. "The migraines will get in."

Yardley looked himself over in a hall mirror: ax-faced, hatchet-nosed, ice-cube eyes gouged out, blue dress shirt with cranapple juice stains, greasy dark slacks scuffed at the knee, and a thin shredded leather belt that had missed half the loops on his slacks.

"Well, at least I don't *look* depressed," he said.

"No," said Chitchee, slapping Yardley on the back. "You don't look depressed. You look more like a guy who moved on to the actively planning stages and fell asleep."

"I need a friend—"

"—you've got a friend in *me*—"

"No—a real friend! Let me finish! Someone has to help me organize my life. I really appreciate your coming over, because no one has ever been in my apartment heretofore, except Minerva to drop off a box of chocolates and run."

"How long have you lived here?" asked Chitchee.

"I don't know," said Yardley. "Twenty, thirty years."

"You don't even know the years?" asked Chitchee, taking off his shirt and then using it as a bandanna to keep the sweat out of his eyes. "This is fucking pitiful."

"Does it matter? Look, I can pay you," said Yardley, his shoulders the bent corners of a book, "in books."

"In books!" said Chitchee, already spitting out perspiration from off the top of his lip. "But could you also reciprocate by coming over to my place and lifting bookcases off my back? This book thing gets out of hand, but *your* insect-like activity to inter yourself in vaults of paper— gentle madness gone mad."

"If you're hungry," said Yardley, not listening, falling asleep on the plastic-covered, book-covered couch, and plucking at a tuft of actual couch grass, "help yourself to a tangelo or mangosteenogranate in the back of the fridge by the expired onions. And there is some wild rice from Leech Lake in the defrosted freezer if you like fresh rice. I can make Grape Nuts Jello, if you really want to make me work! I've been too swamped to cook a baby pea. I have as many books as far as the eye can see, as you can see, and—I'm overwhelmed with this deluge of books. I don't even remember buying half of them! I'll do the bedroom and you clear the front room."

Yardley wobbled back to his bedroom. Chitchee on all fours in the living room sorted books into meaningful piles, but his sweat caused water damage to Yardley's leather bounds. The Deluxe Limited Edition *Leatherstocking Tales* unboxed set bubbled up with blisters. A gold-inlaid, gilt-edged *Atlas Shrugged* slipped out of his paws when he pulled it out from the box, and it whoopsed into a kitty litter box. Chitchee yanked down a Franklin Library hub-spined, full leather, sewn *Mr. Sammler's Planet* while his brain boiled and his body stood in a shower of greasy ooze, getting his fingerprints all over the acid-papers. When he held it by its satin, ribbon bookmark, it snapped. Sweating like a little bug swimming around in a swimming pool of sweat, Chitchee perched on a hairy chair for a break. When he stood up greasily in a muck, he found cat hairs clinging to his arms and legs. He looked like a furry Maine Coon, but he felt like a wool carpet that had been beaten by beaten Russian serfs.

"How's it going in there?" called out Yardley from the other room. "It's not too hot, is it? The air conditioner has black mold and I'd open a window, but I caulked all the windows shut after Dan the Maintenance Man broke in. I broke his nose. I'll see if I can break open my bedroom window."

Yardley turned around and walked straight into a stack of travel books, then caromed into a bookcase, which he grabbed off balance, dehydrated, drawing the bookcase towards himself as he clove to its sides. The bookcase smushed him like an overripe Hostess Twinkie. The complete *Golden Bough* knocked him unconscious.

"Do you have any coffee? No? Any luck with that window yet?" asked Chitchee, sorting through the other room. "Does the spigot contain water?"

The minutes passed by like any Wagnerian opera. Chitchee looked at all the unpacked boxes of poetry marked CHILCOTE CARROTHERS blocking the kitchen whose miasma stagnated with rotten chicken skins, ancient Chiquita peels, unfinished tins of reeking sardines, and the sour run-off of rennet from standing month-old milk—all of which stuck to Chitchee's sebaceous pores when he opened the refrigerator door.

"Yardley?"

The light fixtures were at the melting point of a brass ring. The couch steamed like a giant dead mouse, and the humidity bedewed the cat hairs that flourished in every available cranny—even though Yardley's cats were nowhere to be seen. Chitchee triaged: Rossetti, Swinburne, Browning, and Tennyson. Distracted, he paged through Hazlitt and Coleridge. Byron's *Don Juan* made him laugh unromantically. When he read Wordsworth's "Michael," he harked back to high school. He recalled his ill-natured, solitary adolescence. Bored, distracted, irritated, and thirsty as parchment, he sobbed feeling sorry for himself with tears of emotional sweat. To splash his face with cold water, he shuffled into the bathroom, which looked like the Lost and Found at Sexworld. He turned back and opened the Venetian blinds.

Looking down from the fourth floor, he jumped out of the planes of his skin.

He wiped his flanged hands on his jeans. He saw that Yardley had placed a pair of Bushnell binoculars on the windowsill. Magnified giants outdoors bounded from Yardley's building and into Chitchee's field of vision like billboards. VIKTOR MARTENSEN and LARRY SANGSTER. He lowered the Bushnells for a second look. Yes, in front of the building, Viktor Martensen and Larry Sangster were conferring under the green canvas awning by the planter boxes. Larry clutched, rubbed, and itched the back of his neck. He winced in great pain. He steadied himself like a child learning to walk. A giant WALLET flitted upward from Martensen's giant BACK POCKET. Giant GREENBACKS fanned out and fanned back into Viktor's wallet and back pocket. Chitchee pounded on the window that Yardley had caulked to deter flies and spies.

"Hey, Yardley," said Chitchee. "Larry Sangster is outside! He must live here."

"Yes, Lawrence has an apartment at the end of the hall for—well, his girls," said Yardley, returning to consciousness, a consciousness brimming with hot shame when he boiled over with the memory of his eviction notice. "He's a sex addict, and *he* is evicting *me* for having too many books. Dan the Maintenance Man squealed. That's why you're here (to tell you the truth). I'm going to be homeless and sleeping in the rose bushes down there pretty soon. And I hear the raccoons don't take too kindly to strangers."

"That's nice," said Chitchee, "but I'm going to see if I can catch a ride with Larry the Sex Addict to the Yggdrasil building! I can't be late for work! I can't let down the dear team at BookSmart."

"What dear team?" asked Yardley, blushing to his ears and crawling out from under the bookcase that had wounded his pride.

The bookcase filled with anthropological and mythological tomes of 19th century British expeditions had ripped a tiny tear in his rotator cuff, crucifying him. Exhausted Yardley came to rest like a Sikorsky rotor on his delirious couch. The room was spinning around him like a malarial backflash of the sunny, dungy dikes of southern Vietnamese villages.

"Wait," said Yardley, "I have to pay you. I don't have any cash. But can I pay you in *Golden Boughs*?"

"*Golden Boughs* are too bulky," protested Chitchee, "how can I lug them to work? I don't have room. That's okay, don't pay me in anything, Yardley. We are brothers in books."

"How about a Kindle?" said Yardley. "I never use it. It was a Christmas gift from a friend of mine in the Hemlock Society. He doesn't need it anymore. But it will put BookSmart out of business."

"BookSmart is already out of business," said Chitchee.

Yardley dusted off his Kindle and handed it to Chitchee, who turned it around and around.

"How do you turn it on?" puzzled Chitchee.

"I don't know," said Yardley, slightly abashed. "I never found the ON button."

"Okay, thanks! I'll take it."

Chitchee hugged Yardley, grabbed him at the elbows, and said, "You'll be okay, but I gotta run or I'll be late!"

Chitchee threw the black thin sleek Kindle into his JanSport polyester backpack. He squirreled down the stairs and popped out under the green canvas awning of Yardley's high rise by Lake Harriet.

"Larry, you douchebag," said Viktor to Yakky. "Larry, how did you get bit by a fucking bat? That's hilarious! Now you're going to have to get those fifteen shots! I should call Animal Control and have you put down!"

The sun brightened the Wedgewood porcelain blue sky. Oceanic light waves threw Chitchee into a sneezing fit and he heard a song off his Wurlitzer: "Nobody Likes Me." He blamed the rose petals at Lake Harriet's Rose Garden. Standing up, he felt seizurish. He hated being late for anything because he was always late for everything; and now he was going to be late again. He selected an acorn from the sidewalk. He placed the cap between his thumbs, his two fists pressed together. His thumbs pressed the cap against his index fingers, bent over his thumbs, and he blew a shriek that froze all action and all traffic, and all spacetime froze like an ice cube.

"Hey, you guys! Can I get a lift to the Yggdrasil building? Are you going to Lake & Hennepin?" asked Chitchee.

He ran to and jumped into the back seat of a white Dodge van. A half-case or so of plastic milk jugs with built-in handles cluttered the van.

"Hey, who's GAB?" asked Chitchee. "Gabby Hayes? His initials are all over these gallon jugs of water. He must be one thirsty fellow! Gabs too much, hyuck, hyuck!"

"What the fuck is that dweeb doing in there?" asked Viktor, blowing his nose into the planter boxes. "Zalar, get him the fuck out of there! Now we gotta get 'Batman' to the fucking Animal Hospital in St. Paul! Did you got that bat, *Batman*? Aren't you going to kill it? We'll need it to scare the *Robins* with. Let me see it!"

Walking up to the white Dodge van and carrying plastic gallon jugs, Zalar Gossick looked lanky, wiry, and muscular. Zalar grasped Chitchee like a bale of hay by the T-shirt.

Zalar hurled Chitchee into the gutter at the feet of Viktor, Yakky, Larry, the Vietnamese gardener, and several with the nescience of ineffectual bystanders who jaywalked to get away.

Zalar laughed uncontrollably like a gang of hyenas on poppers.

"What are you laughing at?" asked Yakky, who Tasered Zalar. "You fucked up, you fuck up!"

Zalar didn't seem shocked when he quietly dropped to the cement, as if poured out of a pitcher.

"Stealing? You know what I should do with you?" asked Viktor.

"I didn't steal your product, Viktor," said Zalar submissively. "I hid it in a futon and your guy Jason Undergreasyburger threw the futon out when I wasn't there. Somebody came along and took the futon home."

"Yeah, you took it home," said Viktor.

Viktor gripped a rusty tire iron from the bottom of the passenger seat. He brought it down on Zalar's head. (Chitchee heard something snap like a peanut shell).

Zalar tried to get to his knees, to pray to the intensely blue sky for help, but he slumped to the gutter.

"Stop! Please, please, please, sir," shouted Chitchee. "What are you doing?"

Chitchee's flesh melted in puddles of sobs.

"Please don't tell me you killed a bat! That's illegal in the state of Minnesota," continued Chitchee. "You should have called Animal Control. They have regular hours nine to five on weekdays. Or you could have donated it to the Goodwill in Hopkins. I'm going to tattle on you, Rat Finkenstein!"

"Let's go, Viktor," said Larry, placing a friendly hand on Viktor's shoulder. "I'm starting to feel sick."

"Get your hand off me," said Viktor. "You're not sick! Bats don't have rabies anymore. That's an old wive's myth. Ozzy told me that personally. He's a personal friend of mine. He sends me bats all the time. In the mail. Give me that box!"

Viktor seized the box, opened it, pulled out the stunned bat, and bit its head off. He spewed out the chewed furry ball of blood into Larry's face. He placed the winged torso back in the box and slammed the box into Larry's stomach.

"Fuck rabies!" said Viktor.

Larry gazed at the imperfectly-bladed lawn. The eavesdropping Vietnamese gardener dragged out a bag of seed and threw a handful onto the grass. He looked busier and busier until rock doves blew him backward, not because they surprised him but because they outweighed him, and the doves pecked up all the seeds of grass.

"And you? Do you want a taste of this tire iron, geek?" asked Viktor of Chitchee.

"Does it taste like chicken?" asked Chitchee.

Viktor, tire iron clamped in his viselike fist, dilated, walking toward Chitchee who backpedaled—his hands up to the sky.

"If you say anything about what you saw, Dorkenheimer," said Viktor, "I'll throw you off the Hennepin Avenue Bridge myself."

"Dorkenheimer?" asked Chitchee. "You have me confused with somebody else. Remember me? I'm Chichester, the guy who just witnessed in broad daylight your attempted murder of Zalar Gossick. Like anyone could keep their trap shut after that?"

"Hey buddy, need a lift?" Chitchee heard.

He looked at the wall of Yardley's apartment. The echo originated there and then tunneled into Chitchee's soft-shelled ears.

"Over here! Chitchee!"

Chitchee looked around. He peered into the portable cave of a Ford Escort. Jorma Ringquist cradled the wheel, leaned over it, and threw open the passenger side door.

"Hop in," said Jorma. "I've got some new E too. These are the Blue Dolphins. Do you want to check out any molly? And I'm down to the last of the research chemicals that I got from China."

"Sure, Jorma," said Chitchee. "But I'm broke and I have to go to work just in order to stay broke. Sorry, I'm a little shaky. I saw a man almost die. *Me*. Then there was that other guy, Zalar, the guy lying in the gutter. He'll snap out of it. He's a starship trooper."

"That's not good," said Jorma. "Anyway, I'm going to a rave tonight. EDM. Let you off here?"

"Hey Jorma, do you know of any drug called GBB, GFB, GAP?" asked Chitchee.

"Is it an entheogen?" asked Jorma, his face brightening as he said: "Unless you mean *GHB*? Gamma hydroxybutyric acid?"

"Maybe, I don't know, I never heard of it," said Chitchee, getting out of the Escort.

Jorma drove to a semi-secret warehouse off University Avenue where he gave out free chemiluminescent glow sticks, sold molly rolls, and mingled with the magic of the houseband, Pepsi Beaucoup, who were almost as big as Atmosphere, Doomtree, and Solid Gold rolled into one, at least according to the critical thinking of local record store manager, rock critic, band member/ manager, and impresario for himself, Mono Boondalicks, writing stringers for *The Daily Beehive*.

SOLOMON DERESSA

"Hey, Chitchee," said Nestor when he saw Chitchee draggle through the door. "Have you heard from LaDonna, the *slut*? She said she was coming here to talk to you. Coming off your abusive treatment of her for twenty years. The years and years of degradation while you stifled her creativity and held her back from becoming as smart as I am. You ruined her life, and now she is brain damaged and says stupid things—like everyone else around here."

"I," said Chitchee at the door.

"Don't let the air conditioning out, Chitchee!" said Snorri, looking a spot-of-bothered. "Your friend Nestor *here* has been waiting for you *here* for quite a while *here*."

This amounted to a public avowal of war between Snorri and Nestor. Snorri hated Nestor through Madison who leaked LaDonna's confidence.

Aloysius peeled himself off the Dell screen like a plastic protective coating, packed up his tablatures, and emptied the till before preparing to go home.

"Aloysius, did you get my note?" asked Chitchee like a cocker spaniel waiting to be petted behind its runny ears.

"About Viktor's *Quantum Biscuits*? Yeah, I saw it," said Aloysius, looking depressed and anxious. "Good job . . . bud . . . dy . . ."

Aloysius opened the till again, couldn't remember why he was interested in it, and slipped two twenties back into the twenties slot.

"Is *Quantum Biscuits* a book Viktor ordered from us?" asked Chitchee. "I've never heard of *Quantum Biscuits*. What the hell is a quantum biscuit? Has it been detected at FermiLab?"

"No, sort of," said Aloysius. "A bigtime publishing house out East—Arthur's OutHouse or something with a house in it, offered Viktor a sweetheart book deal. Or so he claimed they out-bid Simon & Schuster and Penguin. Viktor commissioned me to ghostwhite his shady self-help book, ghost write I meant, but I couldn't get started on that whitewash job. I've never been a writer. I don't have the quantum biscuit vibe. So Aubrey is working on it—based on notes Viktor made for me. The proceeds are supposed to go toward Aubrey's college education. Fat chance."

"When pork chops get off the ground, eh?" said Chitchee eagerly, grinning, beaming, and shining. "Can I help? I'll write it! I'm a writer. I tell ya, that Viktor is a character right out of Black Sabbath's worst nightmare. I'm almost proof positive that he is guilty of murdering a bat. He incriminated himself to my face an hour ago. I have witnesses. He must have gotten the idea from Ozzy when they were roommates at the Chelsea Hotel in Des Moines living on cockroach soup and snake's piss lemonade."

"Cool," said Aloysius, his cheeks bloating from stomach pain. "So do you want to write *Quantum Rickshaw*? I'll let you work here for free, if you can write that book for me."

"I'll start work on it tonight, boss, when I'm doing nothing," said Chitchee. "As per the usual. As soon as I finish *Buddenbrooks*."

"Talk to Aubrey," added Aloysius, brightening as he packed his books and things to drive to the post office at the Lake Street station on East 31st Street, chat with his old buddy Senior Postal Counter Clerk Fred, and pilot home to his Pleasant Valley hell. "That might work, self-help, you know self-help books . . . reading them is like spreading cream cheese on a bagel and you eat it and can't remember it the next day, or what day it was you ate it. I don't have a creative bone in my body. I'm all gloop inside."

"Yeah, I know," said Chitchee. "But maybe that has something to do with your irrational fear of Ray Bradbury."

"Irrational fear of Ray Bradbury?" asked Aloysius.

Aloysius's windpipe was cut off. He stared death down. He breathed again but his disquieted eyebrows concerned themselves busily with stitching together the meanings of this implication (—he smiled in expectation of an explanation—) and the implications that possible rumors were running wild inside BookSmart and down the street as regards Bradbury and himself.

"The Butterfly Effect touch a chord with you?" asked Chitchee. "Death by butterfly? I thought I heard you were terrified of butterflies. If even *I* heard you were terrified of butterflies, everybody from here to the Rockies knows you're afraid of butterflies. That short story infected you with an irrational phobia of Ray Bradbury's short stories and an hysterical fear of *anything* that suggested the tiniest change resulting in chaotic perturbations across the globe."

"What?" asked Aloysius. "Chitchee, could you concentrate on ghostwriting *Quantum Butterflies* for a second? I read *Dandelion Wine* and *Martian Chronicles* in high school . . . good stuff . . . good job, good guys! We got this! I'm going now, as soon as I stand up."

"Did you mean *Quantum Biscuits?*" asked Chitchee, leaning forward and moving his ears around like a TV antenna. "Is your memory on the fritz too?"

Aloysius smiled, glowing brightly as a freshwater stream in Winona County where the trout nibble your pooling waders. He received a mild shock from the red runner when he touched the crash bar. He jumped back and dropped two U. S. Mail bins filled with Amazon orders on his left foot's big toe, cracking the white of the fungoid nail. So he had to make forward progress quickly, renew his goodbyes, take on the full frontal furnace of hot air outside, and escape before the Yggdrasil building melted like a square plat of butter on a skillet. The way things were going—maybe Bradbury was spot on to predict the end of the world someday in the far-off future when things might get bad. Aloysius reached his car safely. He drove off happily to the Lake Street station on East 31st Street, where he could chat with his old buddy Senior Postal Counter Clerk Fred something. He wanted to ask Fred whether he had heard anything about some weird butterflies going around town creating chaos.

Chitchee wondered whether Snorri invented the Generalized Chaos Theory of Butterflies. Maybe Snorri mentioned his theory to Noel, who crunched the statistics, went over the Bayesian equations, and came up with a more elegant equation of probability. Maybe Saami saw the equation and mistook it for a verification. Maybe Saami told Snorri that Noel had confirmed their suspicions, which in itself was a valuable piece of intel for Snorri, Saami well knew.

What if Ray Bradbury himself was an unintended consequence whose birth brought together Chitchee's parents and Aloysius's parents so that eventually Chitchee and Aloysius would meet and look at each with complete incomprehension on that particular day, resulting in the static electricity whose spark electrocuted Aloysius, causing him to drop the U. S. Mail bins? And that information was now on the surface of the nearest black hole and could not be checked out.

Nestor resumed nervous isometric piano exercises. He drummed his fingers into the maroon counter and intuited his dopamine and serotonin levels' effects on his musical IQ of 180. He looked eager to find an entry point into the flow of conversation, found none, then announced:

"You know, I feel sorry for the ignoramuses, idiots, and musical midgets who give ABBA videos a 'dislike' on YouTube. ABBA was better than the Beatles! Most people in Minneapolis hate ABBA because they are idiots, see, and they don't know they're idiots, see, until you call them an idiot. And then they get mad at you! And then you know they're an idiot, and then they call you an idiot, out of idiocy, but you can't be an idiot if you're the first person to call out an idiot as an idiot, follow me?"

"Do I have to? You're not *not* an idiot, Not-Tor!" said Chitchee.

"Thank you!" said Nestor.

"No, you know I love you man," said Chitchee. "I've always loved you. How long have I known you, twenty, thirty years?"

"Something pitiful like that," said Nestor, his teeth girning in disapproval. "I haven't had water today. That's why I am fidgeting so slowly and cannot communicate my thoughts as well as I should."

Checking his Fitbit, Nestor looked around for LaDonna.

Nestor would settle for an argument with an imbecile. He longed to puncture a brain dead douchebag with a mental razor. When his eyes alighted on Chitchee, Nestor dismissed the cuckold as cuckold from a transcendent point in space; and yet Nestor thought that in some sense Chitchee had cuckolded *him*; Nestor hated his friend Chitchee for FOI. When Chitchee looked at his rival—intense eyebrows, dramatically hurt eyes, open mouth, and head always slightly pulled back in ironic mockery—Chitchee admired Nestor, who had not the patience to finish his musical education or the humility to accept instruction and yet Nestor beat on, against the current, borne ceaselessly back into mediocrity, beat, beaten, beating. He used to bitch about Perpich, rail at MacPhail, and couldn't rally at McNally. Humiliated by even a pinch of failure, Nestor failed at every job, every career, and every relationship and blamed his father for all his flaws, *almost in order to become his own father!* Indeed Viktor Martensen had been a poor student when he married Nestor's mother. With Nestor in the picture the whole family lived on stolen packages of sausages, tins of Spam, and expired hamburger from a dumpster behind The Triangle Bar on the West Bank. It scarred Viktor's pride and created cravings for arrogant comforts. He had married the wrong woman who had borne him the wrong son, a son who disobeyed his every command.

"Why are you punishing me?" asked Nestor. "It's because I'm smarter than you!"

Smack across Nestor's jaw! Nestor's teeth stayed crooked after the bargain basement student dentist on the 8th floor of Moos Tower botched his first surgical procedure. The student dentist claimed he had been distracted by the grad students observing him. Nestor's teeth had a passing resemblance to David Bowie's teeth, but Nestor refused to see ever again a dentist so the resemblance passed.

Viktor harked back to the love he had for his own father, Marten.

"Starvation maketh the man, boy," Marten Martensen always said. "Anyway, besides giving you the gift of life, what have I to do with you? I clawed my way through life, now you claw yours."

Marten had scolded Viktor for spoiling Nestor.

"You're feeding Nestor *sausages*?" asked Marten. "I was never allowed to eat sausages. Once a year on Christmas I was allowed one single slice of salami with my lard and herring."

Viktor, in order to teach Nestor the dangers of Communism, brought him up on bread, water, rice, frozen beans, *and* sausages. Marten considered sausages too much and never tired of admonishing Viktor that his grandson was growing up soft as a sausage.

Nestor's birthday was never celebrated so that Nestor would know what it was like to grow up under Communism where all the days were equal. And yet Viktor loved his son, even though he admitted "Nestor was a mistake." Christmases, Nestor received typically: a kiddy duty belt, plastic handguns, rifles, and machine guns from Clancy's basement in Edina. As a teenager, Nestor had to prove his birthright with a .22 and a .38 by shattering jackdaws in the cornfields of Eden Prairie. And then he would be allowed to take the driver's license test in Chaska.

"How come you guys don't have any books by Republicans?" asked Nestor.

Snorri, overhearing Nestor, had become agitated, like a jazz anglo-saxophonist who was about to overblow his reeds.

"We have *My Life* by Bill Clinton," said Snorri. "I assume you weren't old enough to have the privilege of going to Vietnam. I suppose we could always go back to Hanoi and try bigger and better bombing. For some privileged people a war of aggression is never enough."

Chitchee hated to see these two hate each other and fight openly, so his heart melted for Nestor when Nestor backed off for once out of common decency.

"Chitchee, have you read See-oran?" asked Nestor, wryly smiling but really looking around for LaDonna. "He's like a weak Nee-chee. How do you say it? Leftists like you are bereft of all reason like children. They can only baa baa black sheep at the smart conservatives."

"Man," said Chitchee, "you jump around like Mad Jack Flash. Did your dad used to beat you with a razor strop across your back in a crossfire hurricane too?"

"Excuse me," said Beda Holmgen. "Excuse me, Chitchee, this book you are selling in your store is anti-semitic! I WANT IT OFF THE SHELVES NOW! I'm going to report you to the Anti-Defamation League if you continue to ignore me. Hello? Excuse me! I'm calling the ACLU right now! Can I use your phone?"

"Here, Beda," said Chitchee, handing her the phone. "Is it Martin Luther's?"

"It's by Lewis—"

"Wyndham Lewis? *Tarr?*"

Beda looked at Nestor.

"No," said Beda. "Busy signal? No, it's Lewis Ferdinando See Lee Nee."

"Excuse me for a second," said Snorri. "Could you watch the register, Chitchee?"

Chitchee hoped they all might have a civilized political debate on civilization. Something like William F. Buckley's *Firing Line* or *The McLaughlin Group*. An image of Mortimer Adler arose like Hamlet's father in Chitchee's mind (he had written a fan letter to Adler, to which his daughter wrote back that he was dead).

Snorri bristled at any imaginary slurs cast upon the manhood of Minnesota, which explained why Snorri returned from the bathroom dressed in a blue Union uniform (authenticated replica), the jacket covered in white lint from his mother's washing it together with a white fleece that their pet Angora liked to sleep on.

Snorri loved a good uniform, his dreadlocks a-flutter over the chest of a frigate bird.

"Straight outta *Tristram Shandy*!" said Chitchee. "Or Flannery O' Connor."

Snorri was a Colonial town crier in early Philadelphia—Snorri presented Nestor an article from the *Minneapolis Star Tribune*, taken from *USA Today* (he kept it handy in his wallet), stating that Minneapolis had been rated the most literate city in the Union and the United States.

"What do you make of that? Hmmmmmmmmmmmm? It's all Minnesota's book stores. Specifically *this* store, *this* BookSmart. We are educating the world. Contrary to what you might think!"

"Where are all these literate people?" said Nestor. "Shouldn't they be here buying books? No, because everybody here in the Midwest is an idiot who doesn't read books. Other than wheat and corn. The socialists surround the genius and smother him with pillows of 'nice' until he is mutely methylated into a deep slumber. Minnesotans don't know what to make of the exceptionally bright. They resent the original. They can't measure creativity, which comes from the soul. The socialists gather their forces. Their art is a sickly, consensual hallucination, arising from their long winters of isolation. Of dissociation, yeah. They feel the need to herd together because of scarcity. Minnesota is a socialist hallucination rising to the level of a mediocre daydream. It's all leveling leveled toward the already-leveled playing field. Everyone's IQ is exactly 100. Because nothing is based on merit and IQ is anathema to liberals like you, because you say: it's discrimination. Look, I can't get a good band started in Minneapolis. I'm called *weird* in Minneapolis, so all the idiots in town put me down. I can't get shows. I need a big city—like Cleveland—to recognize me as the next Prince or even to pretend to be the next Prince."

Snorri gulped down Nestor's words like a mouthful of rice covered in Louisiana hot sauce, which cut off his oxygen and forced him to regurgitate the mouthful. His teeth grew sabres. His jaw became a piece of earth-moving equipment. He seemed ready to charge on his giddy feet into the rough waves off the port bow toward shore. Instead he gripped the maroon counter with newfound eagle claws. Snorri wanted to "level" Nestor with the swoop of a sword and then run both halves through—with a Horatio Hornblower-style bravado.

Nestor sucked on his tongue like a truffle in the back of his mouth now that he had his sacrificial imbecile on the altar.

"Minneapolis is a fake Chicago," continued Nestor. "Here the big lie is that everyone is equal. It's a progressive, liberal city where everyone vies to be more self-loathing than his neighbor. Weaklings who worship weaklings—like Che Guevara; instead of strong-minded, courageous men—like Newt Gingrich."

Chitchee split his sides laughing—each side saw in the other the absolute negation of the other, and each one had the other's heart turning on a spit.

The heated air from the volcano of a molten Minneapolis so hot you could smell the sulphur rising from the sidewalks, whisked into the cold, air-conditioned BookSmart—Solomon Deressa on the red runner, where he gave a possibly ironic bow toward Chitchee.

Chitchee threw himself at Solomon's feet, prostrate, stretched out with Albrecht Dürer hands clasped in gnarled prayer. He stood up and said: "Solomon's here."

Solomon sweated from the heat, fanned himself, and emanated the Lion of Judah. Solomon was the scion of a noble Oromo family. His sister had been a nurse to Hailie Selassie; and his brother had been mayor of Addis Ababa. Translator at the United Nations, Amharic poet, Peace Corps/Vista teacher, enemy of the Communist revolution in the land where Aesop was born, and pupil of Tarthang Tulku, Solomon had spent many a long winter's night at BookSmart comfortably reading, sanguine, *sans souci*, and sans everything.

"Solomon," said Chitchee. "What is wisdom?"

"History is wisdom," responded Solomon. "Wisdom is history. Your own redemption, you have to work out for yourself, because humanity can fathom the universe, but not time."

He paused:

"Now reverse everything I said," he laughed. "And keep reversing the reversal of the reversals until there are no more . . . words about wisdom!"

"You sound knowledgeable," Nestor said to Solomon, who favored one side as he traipsed toward his comfort zone and stopped.

"What's so great about Minneapolis?" asked Nestor.

"Weren't you looking for LaDonna?" asked Chitchee, embarrassed by Nestor's always measuring strangers with old school IQ tests. "Hey, time for *Live at the Village Vanguard*. Solomon's favorite. He's on it or in it, because he was there that night."

"LaDonna can wait," said Nestor, annoyed at being both interrupted and talked over when he was talking over his own interruptions. "She's pretty smart, but a couple vodka martinis and she's an idiot getting older. She'll never learn to play an instrument, that's for sure. I tried to teach her drums. She played without feeling. Her music needed a pacemaker. No heart. No soul. Sort of like you, Chitchee. You're sort of randomly smart, but you've been kicked to the curb emotionally. And you don't know how to love."

"I have no soul," said Chitchee, cocking his head to one side, unheard and drowned out by talk over. "So I could have been aborted and avoided all this fuss?"

"But *you* look like someone who has been around the world! You *look smart*," Nestor prodded Solomon. "Do *you* think Minneapolis is on the world map? No, Chitchee let me talk!"

"Nestor, really?" asked Chitchee, thinking he might have to kill Nestor out of respect for respect. "You never met Solomon? He is a retired professor from the General College at the University—before they leveled it for the funds to field a lacrosse team's trip to Serbia. I'm sure he doesn't want to be bothered by a bunch of dumb geniuses when he's trying to read Buddhism."

"There is no Solomon in Solomon," said Solomon. "Your friend sounds like a contentious Athenian. He imagines American cities contending for the gold medal in the Most Smartypants on Every Block event."

"No question, he is a gadfly," said Chitchee. "He always asks the big questions like: BookSmart? What kind of name is that for a book store? What's the BookSmartest American City? Besides Cambridge or Berkeley? Minneapolis, right Solomon? We're on 'the map,' aren't we? Aren't we anywhere by now?"

"It depends," said Solomon. "Which map? Mercator's?"

"A good old American Rand McNally map," said Nestor. "Because that's American! Isn't it? Rand McNally? Anybody know for sure?"

"Rand McNally," commented Solomon. "It's based on Mercator, a Belgian!"

"Belgians are smart!" said Nestor. "Smart enough to be smart Americans! So you're not a Muslim, I take it? And not a Communist? We're exactly the same!"

"Yaa-a-a-sss!" said Solomon. "Except totally different. When I was growing up in Addis they religioned me with religions. Christians, Muslims, Marxists, Hindus, Fascists—judgment after judgment by the believers was harsh and overweening. Organizations gave me a feeling of *contraction*. I craved a feeling of *expansion*. After Robespierre was the Counter Enlightenment, which was more of a revelation that humanity cannot cure itself of humanity than it was a romantic embrace of 'darkness.' Existence is absurd and so is its technology. So we have returned to the ages before science happened."

Normally, Solomon would have secluded himself by the Sagans, Hawkings, and Kuhns, but he lingered at the maroon counter.

Beda didn't get through to Keith Ellison, Alan Page, R. T. Rybak, or Al Franken, but she swore up and down that if Paul Wellstone were alive, "he would have picked her up."

"Hello," said Lake Street Rodney, saluting Snorri, "book-loving world! Wait, did I already say what I said when I said it? We're wearing uniforms now? I want to be the sailor in a sailor's suit and cap!"

"Of course Minneapolis is on the map," said Heinie, rubbing his eyes together, his Ben Franklins lightly resting on top of his fingers. "It's a fantastic city!"

"Yes!" said Chitchee. "I love it here! So nice and green! And the lakes!"

Heinie had been fatiguing the couch but when he stood up (he stowed away his glasses in a case that contained four more pairs of National Health spectacles) he created a Heinemannian force field, which destroyed any nearby molecular structures involved in original thought or creativity. And there was no known antidote. "There is an enormous amount of Minnesota history pertaining to the spot we are standing on right now! I could go on for days about this one store! Starting here as we go from when this used to be a furniture store backward in time to when the Earth first formed its crust. Sticks 'n' Stones was here, the furniture store, that's why you have the pine-wood parquetry. And before that it was Pam Sherman's Bakery. Before that it was Annie's Parlor, I think, and before that . . ."

"Before that, nobody knows," said Chitchee. "There was no language!"

"Who cares?" said Saami, walking downstairs to avoid the congregation. "Before that it was a glacier. I'll be downstairs watching the rubble flow. I lead a sedimentary lifestyle."

"Pam Sherman's bakery! That's what was here! I knew it!" said Rodney, snapping his fingers. "Why are you talking about the old neighborhood? Are you guys moving? Or going out of business as usual? Because if you guys are flying the coop—or moving the coop to a different neighborhood—"

"No," said Snorri, crossing his arms. "Why?"

"Well," said Rodney, "you guys are nice guys and Comic Book College has a For Lease sign out front and that means if you're not here and they're not there we won't be here or there if they go and you go because if you go then that leaves only the Magyars and Queequeg book store peeps who would be there even if we weren't here or there and they aren't going anywhere but if you do move then my hold pile has to move too to there and then I will have to double check on it there, but you guys are nicer guys and I'll miss you guys when I'm over there, knowing that you were once here in Minneapolis, the literatist city there is I know of. Right? Did I say something out of line?"

"I have no idea what you are talking about, Rodney," said Snorri, using American football's somersaulting hand signal for a "false start."

"Minneapolis," said Nestor, "is a depression in the fabric of spacetime, warping the contours of what keeps us here in a warped state."

"Nestor," said Chitchee. "Don't pester!"

"Don't listen to Chitchee," said Nestor to Solomon. "He's wanted by the FBI for anti-American activities. What do you really think of Minneapolis?"

"I was framed!" protested Chitchee. "I never distributed subversive literature!"

"Oh, really?" asked Nestor. "Where's your anarchy section?"

"There isn't one," said Chitchee, "it's all over the place."

"Is Minneapolis really a *polis*?" asked Solomon. "A *polis* is more than a city-state in a federated union of states. Socrates, Plato, and Aristotle—could not live in Athens. So what's so great about Athens? Or anywhere? I happen to be here. Or I could be with any depersonalized population on the planet. Minneapolis is nice—quaint, even cozy. Especially if you are an Oromo escaping from a war-torn Ethiopia and fleeing from Mengistu's Communist takeover and you have a bounty around your neck. So ya-a—a-as, Minneapolis was on my map as an exile. For refugees fleeing Mengistu's Communist takeover it was a safe island on my odyssey."

"Yeah, Nestor," said Chitchee, "Solomon lived in Paris. His friend, Skunder Boghossian used to take him around and introduce him to people like James Baldwin, Richard Wright, and Chester Himes. And Sartre was always sitting at a coffee table on the street looking up into space, taking dictation from transcendance or waiting for Beauvoir."

"Ya-a-a-assss, my friend," said Solomon slowly, "a *polis* must have a *Gefühl* to be authentic, an *asabiyyah* as ibn Khaldun coined it."

"Ibn Muldoon?" asked Nestor. "Was he a famous globalist or something?"

"No," said Beda Holmgren, "I've heard that name! Ibn Muldoon was a racist. I know he was."

"Ya-a-a-asss Khaldun was a Muslim, who was a racist and the father of sociology," said Solomon. "Tunisian. A polymath. His social coherence theory predates Victor Turner's *communitas*. His map of the world was not on the map—and yet his grandsons were Max Weber, Durkheim, and Marx—and they begot our *polis*, where Socrates here works in a used book store."

"Until he has to go home for dinner," offered Chitchee. "If he has a home for dinner!"

"Ya-a-a-sss," said Solomon. "Maybe the entire history of western philosophy is beholden to the untamed shrew who drove Socrates to the marketplace to pick up a few arguments for dinner."

"I love a good shrew," said Chitchee. "They make death bearable. Did Socrates knock her up and have to marry her? He couldn't afford a black market abortion? What did he see in her? What was he to Xanthippe, or Xanthippe to him?"

"What? Today," said Solomon, grimacing from a pain in his leg that he grabbed, "we would substitute individuated Self for Socrates's soul or *psyche*. And spirit for *pneuma*. All free men in the *polis* desire television over individuation. Do you have *Synchronicity*? That's what I came here for. I honestly don't have an opinion about Minneapolis. It's been good to me. I don't even believe in *soul* or *souls*. That's all Platonism to me. *Spirit* or *spirits*—that's more of the ether of lies people breathe to exist, which doesn't exist—except in Cuckoo Land. Chitchee, I have to sit down, my feet are so sore, but I *will* buy this Cantor before I go back to my lair."

Chitchee curved around under the maroon counter for the copy of *Synchronicity* that Noel forced out of Chitchee's hand.

Chitchee plucked the book off a pile of books and placed it in Solomon's surprised old hand.

"Chitchee," said Solomon, "I doubt there *are* meaningful coincidences—except in Dickens."

Solomon placed Cantor on the counter and cantered at a hobble slowly toward his favorite armchair, a friendly but broken down, wicker-work quadruped next to Science. Solomon opened Gleick's biography of Feynman. Chitchee noted a little sweet smile in the middle of Solomon's gaunt, gray beard.

"Hey, Solomon," said Chitchee, talking past Nestor. "Isn't this almost like that scene in *Ulysses* where Stephen Daedalus is at the public library theorizing about *Hamlet* and then Leopold Bloom walks in because he is avoiding his wife Molly's tryst, and so Bloom becomes the real father of Stephen, who is fathering a discussion on *Hamlet*, which Stephen thinks hints at 'Father' William Shakespeare's own hints at his cuckolding by his wife Ann ('incestuous sheets' and 'second-hand bed') and wishes his own real son Hamnet had the incentive to 'revenge foul and most unnatural murder'? So Solomon, now you're my father, and I have to avenge your honor, as Joyce imagined Shakespeare to be his real father and Leopold Bloom his new son. Stephen then becomes Joyce's grandson. Kinship, not kingship."

"Ya-a-a-a-sss," said Solomon, bowing with Tibetan hands clasped toward Chitchee. "I don't know how to respond to that. I feel like the Ethiopian Navy, which in the face of the wake of a single American aircraft carrier, capsized, and sank to the bottom of the Red Sea."

"Which parted at that very moment in gratitude," added Chitchee, drawing in his lips like a prim schoolmarm. "Ummmm . . . hnh!"

Clucking female vocalizations and the chutterings of a wild turkey directed at thunderclouds perfused the premises. "Gobbgobblegobbgobble . . ."

"Minneapolis is *definitely* a community," said Snorri. "It has its own culture. The people here are world renowned for the kindnesses of their civilization. They welcome and tolerate everyone. Absolutely. It's our Norwegian hospitality. It's in our blood lines. You know, 'the binds that wound,' or whatever that saying is. Kind of trite but—there it is—go figure."

"'The fellowship of kindred minds / Is like to that above,' yeah, that's in *Our Town*," said Chitchee. "But I think that alludes to the Hebrew thing you tie around your head that has the box thingamajig like a little BookSmart on your face."

"What? Listen here, Chitchee," said Snorri, almost commanding Chitchee to fly across the room by orientalist magic and bend his ear.

"See these pages, these are *foxed*," continued Snorri. "Aloysius used to care, but now he turns a blind eye toward *condition*. At least Noel cares about *condition*. And Saami? Well, he cared once, but Aloysius stifled him too. All our ideas have gone down a golden gopher hole. And frankly, Chitchee, you *were* our last idea. Because the four of us are exhausted! We've run around in circles like squirrels chasing the tails in front of us for the sake of a . . . well frankly . . . a dungeon. Where was I? Anyway the red is iron rust from fungi. Are you listening? That's called 'foxing' from of course the Reynard the Fox cycle. Which you already knew, I hope. Are you listening?"

"Not really," said Chitchee crying. "It's such a sad story."

"What? What is?" said Snorri, looking sadly at his old tools. "*What* is a sad story?"

"You! Life! Everything!" Chitchee started crying, but seeing no hugs forthcoming bucked himself up and held back his tears like a gregarious dancer without a partner.

Snorri opened his solander box of book repairing materials—everything neat as the honeycomb hexagons in a hive of bees.

After Madison, Snorri loved his books. All the minutiae of the book collector's trade had captivated him since he first read *Ferdinand the Bull* when he was four. He mended the pages of his *Ferdinand the Bull* with Japanese tissue when he was five. At ten his father bought him a used *Iliad* and *Odyssey* set, which had underlining. Snorri with a surgical touch attacked the inked pages with a little steel scraper and filled up the worm holes with a paste created from the pulp of shaved-off paper stock. Aloysius hired him on the spot when Snorri showed him how a chunk of day-old bread could clean paper. Snorri's medicine bag on his first day included stain removers, benzene, toluene, ethyl alcohol, and acetone for the care of the collectibles. When the country recessed in 2008 and BookSmart fell on hard times, Snorri's morale plummeted. The lack of encouragement from Aloysius also trapped Snorri in his own self-described "dungeon of debt."

Snorri figured Aloysius's debt would pass on to Aubrey and would never end for her either, and her professional dream would be cut short at the 101 level, and this would ghost Aloysius, the new McCosh haunting his own book store. Anxiety, crippling depression, or failure of nerve—Aloysius never rose up against Viktor, who swindled him out of his power of attorney under duress when he signed over his townhouse in Pleasant Valley to pay the rent on BookSmart. Soon Aloysius would be renting a studio for $1500 from MPG—and he could not tell anyone for shame, especially Snorri, but really Snorri didn't even care anymore about the store as the weight of years weighed them all down with a collective depression. All Snorri hoped for now was that Chitchee would learn to shut the fuck up—he was always way off topic. If the topic was North versus South, somehow Chitchee catapulted the topic into the White Sea, the Red Sea, and the Black Sea all at once, and some see and some saw, but all must fall would be something he would say.

"I should play *Our Town*, do we have it? Every book store should have *that* one, because that is what a book store *is*. Found it!" said Chitchee.

He spun the disc, fell into an *Our Town* trance, slow-danced a mazurka, and cried.

"WHAT *Our Town?*" said Chitchee to the store.

Conflicting emotions stabbed him. He cringed, thinking he might break down. There was no *Our Town*. It was *Their Town* now.

DO YOU REMEMBER?

"Copland?" said Nestor. "Copland was a Commie, a Homo, and a Jew!"

"I heard that," said a customer, a nomad, forty or so, having roamed through fire and water into BookSmart from the back door.

The customer's greasy, shambling work pants and torn, disorderly blue scrub shirt were covered with burs, prickles, and teazles (had he walked along the railroad tracks to get there?). Axle grease splotched his hands and face. Bandages wrapped themselves around the middle of his arm—his life's blood sold to the Red Cross on River Parkway for twenty bucks? He had shoulder-length, straight black hair, parted mostly in the middle, sketchy facial hair on an unshaven neck, boyishly red lips, and brightly dark eyes or darkly bright eyes.

"But he was *our* Commie, Homo, and Jew," said the customer.

"What's your IQ?" asked Nestor.

"Oh, brother, I Quit," said Saami, stumbling up the stairs. "Not this again! I'll be downstairs getting hammered."

"Yeah yeah yeah is my IQ," the customer said to Nestor. "Hey guy, I'm looking for a Chilton or Haynes car guide. I'm changing spark plugs. I need to see the exploded power train illustrations. Can you help me?"

"Nestor doesn't work here," intervened Snorri. "He thinks he works here, but he only passes out IQ tests here on the backs of flyers for his shows at Memory Lanes."

This jab struck Nestor deeply and he recovered by sitting on the torn, black leather couch, fiddling with his phone, and watching YouTubes of himself.

"I'll help," said Chitchee. "I'll be your guide. I'll be your friend, I'll be anybody's friend! Chiltons and Haynes are downstairs in Transportation by all the railroad books. All the old dudes—they don't care about planes, ships, and cars. They care about railroads! The Double Es!"

"And could I get a copy of *Foucault's Pendulum*?" asked the customer, his black, fascinating, eight-ball eye-balls glazed at Chitchee. "By Umberto Eco."

"Are you an Ecologist?"

Chitchee sniffed out the Eco under the counter, plucked it out of the recently-priced arrivals, and said, "One Eco, coming up. Here you go, Eco!"

"And Snorri," said the customer with a definite familiarity, "nice Union uniform by the way—could I see that *Pull My Daisy* first edition, collectible again?"

"Sure, but it can't ever leave the counter area, it's *that* valuable," said Snorri, who always had second thoughts all of a sudden about anyone's intention to buy *Pull My Daisy* and only smirch it.

In its protective baggie, *Pull My Daisy* touched the customer's hand. The customer tugged. Snorri held it tighter and tighter. A tug of war ensued, back and forth—an even match as far as Chitchee was concerned.

"Valuable? I thought you lost it," said the customer.

"I thought we did too," said Snorri. "Lucky for us, because it has probably gone up in value."

"Snorri," said Chitchee.

"I'm sorry," said Snorri. "But I have to protect the collectibles. You never know who might have smallpox."

"Where are the Chiltons again?" asked the customer, releasing his grip on the book in the baggie.

"Downstairs," said Chitchee. "I'll show you."

Snorri sighed with relief, removed the book from the baggie, dropped it, wiped it off on his sleeve, opened it, and read.

"Are *all* your customers resentful of wealth and power—like that guy?" asked Nestor from the couch. "Why *should* the wealthy pay taxes for the underclass? Why penalize the hard-working, successful healthy-minded types?"

"How much do you pay in taxes?" asked Snorri, placing *Pull My Daisy* in the baggie.

"How much of what you make is due to a socialist government that provided the foundation for your having anything at all?"

"I don't pay any taxes, because that's socialism," said Nestor.

Chitchee escorted the customer to the shelf of automotive books.

"*Now* I remember the shelf," said the customer. "I was living in Kansas. Uptown sure has gone down hill!"

The customer said that when he walked past The Gap, Victoria's Secret, North Face, Columbia, and LA Fitness . . . he knew Uptown was slated for the dumpsters. The Uptown Association and the City Council must have handed down the *ukase*: *If all politics are local—eliminate locality!* It was planned as any planned economy. Minneapolis's erasure of old buildings also erased social memory, social capital, and socialism itself. Landmarks deleted from the customer's growing up presented themselves as plaques for tourists. The longest standing building in the neighborhood was Arby's. Would there be a commemorative plaque for the old Arby's too? Cheapo Records and its sister store BookSmart would be replaced by Target, Inc. and deluxe apartments with outdoor swimming pools, saunas, gyms, and private puppy parks for Fifi's poo poo.

"Mexico City is digging up the past, while Minneapolis is busy burying it," shrugged Chitchee.

A few minutes later the customer returned upstairs with a Chilton manual.

Uptown's Carousel Square had gotten facelifts, implants, and botox shots creating eyes like water rings on a wooden table. Goorin, Fluevog, Fjallraven, Puustelli, Arc'teryx, H&M, CB2—were enigmatic, cryptic, and acted as exotics. Practical stores like Snyder's Drug Store were homely, gawky relics from the Depression. Where once you could buy toothpaste, toilet paper, and soap MPG had constructed a design store named DeZign (by appointment only), boasting a showroom of three hundred-dollar Italian conceptual footstools, five thousand-dollar Bavarian ottomans, and ten thousand dollar ambulance rides to HCMC's ER at the sticker shock.

A police siren down the avenue roared like God in the whirlwind.

"It's one universal mind," said Chitchee, head rocking and listening to the unsung gospel in his head. "Maybe we should all hold hands and pray without hope!"

"I saw so many pizza delivery cars on the way here, they might as well turn the bike lanes into pizza delivery lanes," said the customer at the maroon counter. "What's with all the ultra-luxe towers of swinging singles, saunas, and hot tubs? Do we need more Class-A office space to raise the tax base for the revitalization projects?"

Snorri gave the customer half off on the Chilton as a "good customer discount" but charged him the full $3.49 for *Foucault's Pendulum*.

It was meant as a peace offering, but the customer had a haunted look in his eyes. He would not see his old haunts again. He said he wouldn't be around Uptown much anymore, because he had to move back to West St. Paul, where he had to take care of his mother, and his mother was dying.

The customer, with some nostalgia, thanked Snorri by name. On the way back to his beater in the new Potemkin village of bistros and boutiques, the customer boiled over when he read billboards like: "Follow Your Bliss, Rent With Us," "Life is a Swimming Pool Two Stories Up," and "Your Narrative Begins Here, Namaste!"

Three teenage girls, Laurel, Stevie Scott, and Seela Sangster, smooching with their kissy-faced iPhones, having gone to MAC (and left with baby spider eyelashes, caked-on foundation, and cheeks confected with blush) in their father Larry's vintage AMC Gremlin, SWERVing . . . shot over the crosswalk at Lake & Hennepin and almost bumped into the Uptown-piqued BookSmart customer. They laughed and shouted at him.

"Asshole!" yelled Seela. "Are you trying to commit suicide?"

The customer gaveled his tightly-closed fist down into the car hood and dented it. In doing so, the loosened Red Cross bandage around his arm fell off. The uncoagulated clot in the crook of his elbow flew off like a beetle. Spurting blood arced from his arm (his surprised jaw dropped) onto the Gremlin's windshield.

The kids screamed like brakes as the strong red spurt stuck to the plexiglass.

"Jesus! I'm so sorry," said the customer, "but watch where you are going! Squirt some windshield wiper fluid on that, and you can wipe off the blood with your wipers. Otherwise hydrogen peroxide will do THE JOB!"

Everyone in the un-buildings of the un-city in the new Un-town had been annexed by the encroachment of the Greater Carousel Square. And there was nothing in Carousel Square, because everything *there* could be gotten *elsewhere*. Only the locals were unique, and they were irrelevant. Chitchee lost himself in thought, thinking over the logic of what the previous customer had said.

"Chitchee, come over here!" said Snorri. "Watch this!"

Snorri mixed Gold Medal flour with boric acid in a Tupperware bowl as a solution to the silverfish he had seen licking the glue from the binding of a banged-up copy of *Hawaii*.

"And then you sprinkle that on all the shelves," said Snorri, bored and exhausted.

"Right now?" asked Chitchee avidly.

"Fuck it," said Snorri. "I need you up here. Do it tomorrow. What were we talking about? I feel a migraine coming on. *The Population Explosion* by Paul Ehrlichman? Whatever happened to the population explosion?"

Cluck. Cluck. Cluck.

"Everybody said fuck it," said Chitchee.

Chitchee opened the front door for a customer entering.

"Do you have *My Sister's Keeper* by Jodi Picoult?" asked the woman wearing a straw hat as large as an albatross.

She ignored Chitchee like a bad servant and solicited Snorri's solicitude instead.

"You do have two legs, don't you?" replied Snorri, one eyebrow up, keeping the other eye perfectly round. "Well? The ball is in your court now."

"The last time I checked," she said, her crest falling—annihilated by one short, curt quip.

"Fiction is directly opposite the cookbooks, facing us, on the north far wall, facing the south far wall. No, stand in between poetry in the back and the DVDs in the front, you'll be in the middle of the room. Now walk face forward into the wall. You're there! And I'm guessing you could use a little exercise," concluded Snorri, feeling faint on his favorite bar stool.

"Well, Snorri, that wasn't very nice," said Chitchee, watching the clucking woman's odd gait as she clucked off like a dumb cluck. "You do know that the ego is an illusion, don't you?"

Snorri made the face of someone recognizing someone from somewhere. He froze that person's face in a screenshot but no bell sang.

"Anyhoo," continued Snorri, talking to himself. "It's the *tradition* of socialist government that is progressive and that inspired Floyd B. Olson's Democratic Farmer Labor party. *Custom* is the backbone of good government. Right?"

"You old hen!" said Chitchee. "Are you going on and on about that? Wait here! Ma'am! Picoult is in Fiction, not Astronomy."

Chitchee intercepted the vocalizing elderly woman who was on a constipated trajectory that really needed assistance.

"Where?" asked the clucking woman, twirling around like a lonely, lost creature in the woods, looking at the sky for the North Star.

"Under P," said Chitchee.

"How is P arranged?"

"Alphabetically."

"How do you *know* P is arranged—alphabetically?"

"I peed it myself."

"Oh, on my word," she said, hand fluttering over her heart.

"You're not having a coronary, are you?" asked Chitchee. "Or maybe it's Parkinson's? If it is Parkinson's, we have good books by Oliver Sacks you might want to check out. His books are something to actually cluck about."

She looked up at the overgrown squirrel awkwardly.

Her gaze stamped on his face like a bird that stamps the earth for earthworms. As Chitchee smiled, she smiled. She looked at Snorri, who frowned at every smile—even photographed smiles—smiles, he once told Chitchee, were the attempted charms of emotional swindlers to get you to sign away your power of attorney. Snorri referred to one of the BookSmart regulars, John O' Donoghue, who explained this phenomena as: The Theory of Punitive Inclusion. Armed with the dynamics of this theory, Snorri defended himself against a lot of friends. You are befriended now in order to be defriended later. But as Chitchee laughed like a turkey, she laughed like a turkey, and when Chitchee laughed like a louder turkey, she busted a gut until she saw Snorri freeze a frown at her, and she turned into a frozen turkey.

Snorri sized up the large shopping bag she had slung over her shoulder and did not appreciate the incriminating frown that she threw back at his neck like a horseshoe. Snorri observed her whole body getting bent out of shape by the force of his cast-iron frown thrown back at her frown, which instead landed near her spavined pony ankles.

With his suspicious, cynical detective's intuition Snorri pegged her for a jewel thief like Murph the Surf, killing time and planning to knock off Thurston Jewelers on Lyndale & Lake.

"Hey, you old turkey," said Chitchee, "your face right now is reminiscent of the Greek letter 'Omega.' Don't worry! We have that Picoult book up the wazoo."

Chitchee all but took her hand to "P."

"We have enough Pekoe to black out China," continued Chitchee. "And we need to unload them all before they become *My Widow's Keepers*."

"Ma'am," said Snorri, walking with determination in his large jaw, "you'll have to check in that oversize shopping bag on your shoulder up front first before you go to 'P.'"

"But, my son—"

"Ma'am, I'm sorry," Snorri said in short, clipped words, "but that is store policy, as stated by the owner, under whom I am contracted to enforce security regulations. Oral agreements are legally binding in the State of Minnesota. In their courts of legal law, they bind them. So if you'll hand over the bag, I can either check you in or ask you to leave."

"Then I'll leave," she said.

With her shocked mouth propped open, a quivering pink blush bristled over her perfumed and powdered cheeks. Then her already porcelain face turned whiter than a Tappan stove.

"Have a good night," said Snorri, mechanically sweeping her like dust out the front door.

"So Solomon! Do you agree that there is no stronger sense of community than that of the one in Minneapolis?" asked Snorri, walking over to Solomon's chair. "Haven't we welcomed all the world's refugees with open arms? Like the Hmong for example. We let them have St. Paul, didn't we? Not that we ever wanted it that bad!"

Solomon shrugged.

"Excuse me, do you have *The Latehomecomer*?" asked Kao Kalia Yang to Snorri.

"Never even heard of it," said Snorri, returning to the front counter. "You could try Dick's Sporting Goods for homecoming equipment. You guys, I have to pack it in! I'm bushed from helping customers all day long. Oof Dah!"

"Have a seat," said Chitchee, offering Snorri the bar stool.

"With the Internet . . ." paused Solomon, "the days of polises might be over. The power of the Internet empowers anyone to fly anywhere. Internet Man always thinks he has the right-of-way on the Information Skyway. Under his rule, we will have assassinations of causation, left and right. Civilization becomes meaningless. Anyone not on the Internet, how would you say, will be left behind to forage."

"Life in the past lane!" barked Chitchee.

"Thank you, Solomon," paused Snorri, "that's what *I* was trying to say. As I was saying to your friend here, Minnesota *is* a bastion of liberality and literacy. Our educational scores are the highest in the nation. The South has nothing in its schools. No respect for learning. You hand the kid a pencil, he breaks it. Nothing. Look at their writers! Who do you have? One. William Faulkner. Black strap molasses that won't come out of the bottle, that guy. Frankly, he's unreadable. It's like he never took a course in creative writing—too busy chopping wood and getting hammered in the backwoods. Was he building a log cabin back there or what? Hiding his corn-likker? Pretty strange guy even for a Southerner. He could have come up here and taken a class in creative writing at the U. from Garrison Keillor or somebody half-way sane. I reckon Faulkner would have been too proud. Pride is a big deal down South—like 'down here in the bayou we's proud of our mint juleps, proud of our bourbon, proud of this, proud of that, we got cicadas as big as your fists and grasshoppers that could eat your granny.' Or the opposite is true too: 'My granny likes to crawl up live oaks and toss alligators at them Nutheners when they fly overhead in their po-lice heli-chopters. Ain't no SWAT team ever catch *my* granny. We's proud of our grannys! You know their drill. It gets so tiresome how they go on and on about their goddamn grannys, doesn't it?"

Nestor had wasted the evening fiddling with his phone watching YouTubes of himself.

He had spent valuable practice time looking for LaDonna at BookSmart. She was with some other guy. She had tricked him. Nestor dragged himself from BookSmart, bumped into Jason Unterguggenberger (entering with headphones full-tilt boogie), apologized, walked next door to Club Miami, and looked for LaDonna with a military-grade insect net.

Vacantly disheveled, shlubby, muscle-shirted, baggy-blue chinoed, boom-boxed, gym-bagged, basketballed, and cell-phoned,

Jason might have been a roadie for a roadie lost at the MSP International Airport looking for the baggage claim area. His thin lips parted for a re-usable straw. Jason flicked his mulleted hair backwards so that it flowed behind his ears (modeled after his idol), underwent a bodily rearrangement of belongings, and relocated his Borkum Riff, his wallet, his knife, and the key to his storage locker. He carefully unzipped his broken-zippered, off-brand gym bag and offered to the maroon counter a shrink-wrapped, University press, *Immigration Medicine*, without saying anything.

"Has Grant Hart been in?" asked Jason, lifting up one headphone briefly.

"Yeah," said Snorri. "He just left."

Jason left his stuff unguarded, turned around, walked out, and squinted at the boulevard.

"Who?" asked Chitchee.

"Eco," said Snorri, giving Chitchee a look of utter disbelief. "You were just talking to him!"

"Eco guy?" said Chitchee. "Echo of an Eco . . . echo . . . echo . . ."

The phone rang. Chitchee hoped it was Robert Bly. Big Break Bly. Bigtime.

He rehearsed his little speech:

"Hello, Mr. Big, Mr. Robert Pie, I mean Mr. Blah, hello Mr. Bland Blue Bobby, oh by the Bly, I guess you didn't like my poem, the poe-emm? The way Keillor pronounces it. Poe-Mmm. I have more Po-iiims. I can send you a bushel of Puh-Oh-EMMMS. With your backing, I half-expect my POE-EM-AN-EMS to be read at the White House by Ed Asner or Danny DeVito for that matter. Who knows? Maybe Burt Reynolds would recite them. Is Professor Irwin Corey still available?"

"Hello, BookSmart? This is Linda," heard Chitchee. "You know me as Saami's wife!"

Linda was drunk.

"Chitchee?" said Linda. "I wanted to know if you had a book on baseball. I want a book on baseball that will explain why the Twins one day will lose 9-1 and then the next day lose 2-1. Why is there such a big difference?"

"Oh, of course I know you as the lovely Linda," said Chitchee. "I think you will have to walk to the store if you can and look at the shelves for a *Bill James Abstract*. You will need a book on statistical analysis and have to take night classes in mathematics at MCTC."

"But I can't do all that," sobbed Linda. "I love that Kirby Puckett. Goodbye."

"He's dead, Linda! I fluffed that one," said Chitchee and put the phone down, but it jumped back into his hand.

"Chitchee? It's Aloysius," said Aloysius. "How is it going, buddy? I forgot to tell you guys. My mother is stopping by the store to pick up a book for her book club. *My Sister's Keeper*. Just let her have it."

"Snorri already let her have it," said Chitchee. "Do you want to talk to Snorri?"

"Sure, put him on the line, uuuggghhhawwwaghhh," said Aloysius.

Lake Street Rodney, Saami, and Chitchee all at once grew restless at this announcement.

Chitchee had scooted onto Snorri's bar stool when Snorri leapt up to seize the BookSmart phone. Snorri listened and jammed the pencil eraser into his other ear. Snorri held the phone in such a way as to twist its windpipe and kill off its oxygen. His grip looked painful while Chitchee sat behind the counter dumb as a picket fence. Snorri expressed a nervous smile like a stitch of loose thread and a sickly white dew coated his anxious brow.

"Minnesota history is so fascinating! Did you know," continued Heinie, pointing his finger at the track lighting, which sparkled like fireflies, "that the first French entrepreneurs, seeking Kublai Khan for silkworms, canoed around Lake Superior and got lost? That's why there are all these French names like: Radisson, du Luth, La Salle, and Le Sueur. Pere Louis Hennepin came to baptize beaver for their pelts, wait let me finish, Saami—where are you going?"

Saami, nauseated and headachey, teetered at the top of the stairs, inhaling what Heinie was expatiating to the room of customers like an anesthetic nerve gas. He stood stock still but for his vibrating skull.

"After Radisson brought back furs to the King of France in 1660, France poured into Minnesota with its voyageurs, birch bark canoes, portageurs, trading posts, stockades, and forts around which the settlers settled."

"Heinie—" said Saami, his eyelids fluttering over his eyes blank as zygotes.

"Wait, let me finish, have a seat, Saami sit down," insisted Heinie. "Then began the broken Indian treaties, the land grabs, and the swindles. After tampering with and defrauding the already corrupted Office of Indian Affairs, the developers despoiled the land they bought."

"It's the Heinemannian Force Field of Boredom," said Saami, trying to escape an imaginary Faraday cage, silently screaming like Marcel Marceau with ambulatory locked-in syndrome, on all fours.

Lake Street Rodney slipped out the door. Everyone in the store struggled against a reverse dark energy to leave. Tidal waves of boredom drew them backward and forward. The "Heinemannian Force Field of Boredom" as Saami had dubbed it, was a gravity independent of the two masses, but was inversely proportional to the square of their distances, so Saami crawled on all fours toward the front door slowly for a glass of air.

"Wait, Saami!" said Heinie. "Where are you going?"

"I'm going where I always go," said Saami meekly. "To the corner of Emerson, Lake, and Palmer's."

Solomon too looked wearily tired of life. He massaged his left foot, numbed the itching, removed his glasses, speculated at the lenses closely because their optics had lied to him, stroked his graying beard, stood up, stretched, and walked *Synchronicity* to the maroon counter where Chitchee amazed at him said:

"Solomon, are you in another dimension where the 'Heinemannian Force Field of Boredom' can't bore you to death?"

"I gue-e-e-esss," said Solomon.

Solomon skimmed *Modern Concepts of Mathematics* by Ian Stewart, and he placed it on top of *Contributions to the Founding of the Theory of Transfinite Numbers* by Georg Cantor.

"I'll buy these three books, Chitchee," said Solomon. "And do you have a pen? I like to write my name in the fly leaves of my books. If they are stolen, I can get them back. Even if it's in another lifetime."

"In another lifetime I will have my own book store, Solomon," said Chitchee. "And you'll be there at Ulysses & Sons with all our book store friends! Remember that! Aloysius said all I needed was thirty thousand dollars and a rabbit's foot."

"Bless you, son," laughed Solomon. "I'll see what I can do about the rabbit's foot."

"Thirty thousand dollars," said Chitchee. "It might as well be a transfinite number! But some infinities are bigger than other infinities!"

"The polymath Maimonides," said Solomon, "also said that. 700 years before Cantor!"

"Hey Solomon, stick around!" called out Heinie. "I was getting close to the end of the Minneapolis story. It wasn't infinite!"

Solomon turned round, bowed, said: "Good night, gentlemen," and vanished.

The open door was a night sky. The Milky Way streamed with stars running through fields of frozen space.

"Sibley, Ramsey, and their gangster friends," continued Heinie, "faked Chippewa bloodlines! Anyway, so let me finish—"

"—how can we not?" asked Snorri, staggering toward the bar stool.

"—backed by bankers, investors, and land speculators, the wealthy with fictitious powers of attorney—stole fifty million acres of Chippewa/Ojibwe land! *They stole the land we're standing on! We are standing on the land we stole!*"

"That's no story," said Snorri, propping himself with his elbows on the maroon counter. "That's a book! Are you done, please?"

"Heinie?" asked Chitchee, sweating, the conversation lasting two hours or two days without him getting in a syllable, a nap, or a bathroom break. He would have to stand there and pee in his jeans and wait for the men in rubber coats.

"What?" asked Heinie. "'What?' is always a good question! I'm glad you asked. *We stole the floor we're standing on!* There used to be tons of forests around Minneapolis. Norway, white, and jack pines grew interspersed with birch, spruce, balsam, ash, and maple trees—all turned into lumber, corded up, and floated down the river on barges. We absolutely destroyed everything for a goddamned buck! I was trying to say: like today! EVERYTHING IS FOR A GODDAMNED BUCK!"

"BUNCH OF LOONIES OUT THERE!" yelled back Chitchee.

Snorri's brain's articulations were like gears in Heinie's gears, locking his mind in step with Heinie's mind, cog by cog.

"You see," said Heinie, "whole deciduous and hardwood forests floated down the Mississippi River to St. Anthony Falls. Did you know it's 1600 miles to the Gulf of Mexico from here? Whole forests also bobbed down the St. Croix River to Stillwater where, let me finish—"

"Heinie," said Snorri. "It's time to close. "

"Wait," said Heinie. "I wasn't going to narrate the whole 1600 miles! So, in *1849*, a den of robber barons, or *drunken thieves*, or *founding fathers* came up with the whole idea of a 'Minnesota Territory.' 1849, the year Henry Sibley went to Congress disguised as a representative of the 'Wisconsin Territory—'"

"Heinie . . . it's time to close . . . your mouth . . . that is it, please!" said Snorri, falling to his knees. "Shut up! Shut the fuck up! I can't think! You're frying my brain like a grilled Swiss cheese on rye!"

"Do you know the history of the grilled cheese sandwich, Snorri? It's really fascinating stuff! But—where was I? Oh yeah, 1849 . . . and *then* after the usual shenanigans, Sibley got President *Zachary Taylor* to appoint *Alexander Ramsey* to be the Governor of Minnesota, which was a complete fiction! *Minnesota* was a complete fiction, ha ha ha, with a Territorial Legislature and a capital, St. Paul, which was *ceded* by the Dakota. Minnesota is a lie based on a swindle!"

"Look, Heinie," said Snorri, struggling to his feet, "in 1858 Minnesota was admitted to the Union. In time for the Civil War! Of course you know how Minnesota's Regiment at Gettysburg turned back the rebel tide and thus saved the entire Union from the hands of Johnny Reb?"

"Which provided the world with all those Bruce Cattons," added Chitchee. "Bruce Catton must have been a millionaire a million times over after investing in Antietam."

"Wait, I haven't finished," said Heinie. "It's only *1858*!"

"Attention! Attention! BookSmart will be closing in four and a half minutes!" said Snorri. "I'll close up, Chitchee. You and Saami can go home early."

Heinie wondered why BookSmart was closing early.

"We're having a company party, employees only," lied Snorri.

"Employees only?" laughed Heinie. "Why do you need a party for that? Whenever I come here, it's 'employees only' anyway!"

Reluctantly Heinie mounted his two-wheeled Rosinante. Loaded down with milk crates, ropes, baskets, and bags, Heinie ruminated over 1858 until he arrived at Lake & Hennepin like the Kon-Tiki at Easter Island and collared Dagny Knutsen.

"Excuse me, Miss, do you know what happened in Minnesota history in 1859?"

"It turned into 1860?" said Dagny, crushing her Carousel cigarette on a lamp post and blowing her smoke at his old wizened hollow face, thin as a hickory switch.

Saami jumped up, "Is he gone?"

Snorri ran to the front window.

Saami walked outside and screamed:

"Y-e-e-e-e-ssss!"

His tonsils wrapped Dagny Knutsen around a lamppost.

"He's GOOOOOOO-O-O-N-E!" said Saami and hightailed it back to the "Employees Only" party.

Heinie cycled through cycles of history down Hennepin Avenue South and wheeled into his graveyard shift at Lakewood Cemetery.

DAGNY DIGS MINGUS

"Are you open?" asked Dagny, opening the door, her voice husky from her fresh smoke, the smoke that enveloped her, the smoke on her shirt, and the smoke that feathered her hair.

Her collarbone-length, shaggy brunette hair had some threads of gray beneath the red silk, grosgrain headband. She wore actually-torn jeans from a garage sale, embroidered sneakers from a church rummage sale, and a Hendrix black T-shirt from Treasures Await.

Screeching blues and screaming reds and stolen cars with stolen catalytic converters flocked by and shotspotters swiveled when Dagny opened the door, which had overtones of violence.

"Open till midnight! Like it says on the sandwich-board sign in front of the store," said Saami with mechanical pride, pointing toward nothing. "What happened to the sign?"

"Maybe it booked," said Dagny, who blushed because she hated jokes for being stupid representations of reality.

"You forgot to put the sign out, Saami," said Snorri, another strike against Saami.

Puns, riddles, all that *Alice in Wonderland* bullshit—and Dagny had compromised herself out of existence for trying to be funny in an unfunny world. So when Dagny saw Chitchee, she felt guilty and depressed. Overwhelmed with boredom, she asked Chitchee for a "really good depressing book."

He saw that her teeth were bad, so bad she censored her mouth-parts. The main thing to Chitchee was that she *had* her teeth, or at least most of them. At least the crooked ones in the front had sprung from the original data set, thought Chitchee as his heart leapt up to his throat, because he was overjoyed to help anyone find a "really good depressing book." That was his mission in life.

"I'm only happy when I'm miserable," said Dagny.

"Ye-e-e-ss," said Chitchee. "You know your own mind (not everybody does) and you recognize the fact you're miserable all the time. But you're looking great tonight, how does that work?"

"Are you joking? I don't take jokes seriously. Why should I?" asked Dagny. "I expect everyone to be polite and not stoop to narcissistic harassment."

Chitchee thought: she must be attracted to me. Why else would the universe force her in the door? She is making her moves. If I play my cards right, we'll be making love in a fortnight. Three dates, and then the first long kiss. The kiss was the trap door she would fall through, and he would catch her in his arms and cover her with kisses and she would fall upon his neck and then her eyes would sparkle.

While he made notes in the margin of this woman, she felt and thought she had made a mistake. He would give her the hours and days he worked, act like her servant, give her his phone number like it was a hot tip, get too close, and talk about love like it was something he had read about in a novel, where the woman "is covered with kisses," "she falls upon his neck," and then, miraculously and metaphysically, "her eyes sparkle."

He breathed in four counts, held five, and exhaled eight—then choked on a random, tiny piece of grit in his crop.

"Swallowed a bit of papyrus!" he coughed. "It goes with the territory. Occupational hazard! So what brings you to my book store?"

"*Your* book store?" she asked Chitchee, lowering her eyes at him.

He feared she might be a hen—ready to peck, peck, peck the hair from his head and feather her own hair with his.

"I *know* the owner, " said Dagny, twirling nervously the very hair in twisted locks he had admired.

"It's not *my* book store," said Chitchee (oh no, she thinks I'm a liar!), "but someday soon I'll open my own book store. Did I already tell you this? With spiral staircases that lead to rooftop gardens with live bluegrass, 100,000 square feet, three floors, quiet rooms for ping pong, free food on Fridays donated by local Sikhs, fishing demonstrations, and a tetherball court in the back sandlot. Wait, we will grow our own coffee on the roof too. Speaking of which, we should meet for coffee some day, like tomorrow?"

"I don't want a man," said Dagny. "I want a book."

"I'm sorry," said Chitchee. "I didn't mean to pop the coffee question. So what kind of man are you looking for? I mean book! (Oh no, she thinks I'm a joker.) Why do you remind me of Bertolt Brecht? Because you remind me of Ute Lemper *singing* the songs of Bertolt Brecht. You remind me of a moon over Alabama. Anyway, what do you like to read? I assume that you, like most Americans, think in movies. American Hollywood movies that is. Give me the title of a recent movie you saw and loved, and I will reconstruct your entire bookshelf."

"Okay," she said, but her chest constricted, caged—regretting she had walked through the door to be a token in a board game. "*Requiem for a Dream.*"

"Selby, huh?" said Chitchee. "You prefer being more of a sparrow (Piaf) than a swan (Callas); and more of a Miller than a Musil. Genet. Cult classics. Amiri Baraka. White-knuckled pulp. James Cain. MAUS. Iceberg Slim. Jim Thompson, Ellroy? Not *Ironweed*; you wouldn't sink that low, to the level of the ordinary, would you? If you liked *Ironweed*, I'm *out* lickety-split. No Proust. You like Bukowski. Maybe you like Kafka. For sure you have popped your Beat pills, were not too impressed, but they influenced you. Not Auden. Not Gaddis, ha,ha,ha. I bet you are a Black Sparrow girl. On your shelves I see: *RE/search. City of Night. The Baffler. Basketball Diaries. Billie's Blues. Horses. Princess Noire.* Alternative medicine tomes in translation. *The Secret of the Golden Flower.* Herbal encyclopedias. Grove Press. No science, no math, no chess books. Mythology yes, but dogeared where you stopped bored. Books written in prison. *Frances.* Anti-enlightenment zines and screeds. *Trainspotting.* Linda Barry. Toni Morrison. Jim Morrison. *Cain's Book.* Cindy Sherman. Sherman Alexie. *The Power of Crystals. How to Buy a Geode.* Poppy Z. Brite. Pushcart Prize anthologies. *The Book of Rabbit Ferns.* Am I close?"

"Yeah, kind of, not really," said Dagny, "but so what? Anybody who knows books could have figured that out."

"Like who?"

"Like my best friend Astrid, she's read everything," said Dagny.

"By the time you've read everything," said Chitchee, "you've forgotten everything."

Astrid had applied for a government job, working in an office. The problem for Astrid was the DEA-inspired, drug-testing craze, which was the latest government fad in social control. Dagny gave Astrid her own "straight" urine. Dagny didn't like pot. It made her "paranoid." Astrid microwaved Dagny's urine, wrapped it in duct tape, and stuffed it in her bra. When Astrid took the test, urine warm, she alone in the bathroom poured Dagny's urine in the Dixie cup. She passed. Then she told Dagny she was already bored at her new job. Mundane jobs always bored her. She wanted to go back to school for drug counseling and get a degree in ethnobotany.

"But you're supposed to feel paranoid, Dagny," said Chitchee. "Especially if you *are always* paranoid."

Keeping Dagny on her heels, Chitchee reminded himself to stay on his corn-fed toes.

Don't talk about *yourself* or *pot*. She hates pot, therefore she likes to drink. Don't sing: *everything gonna be all right.* Don't insert *Catch A Fire* into the conversation and start something. Don't self-promote. Don't depress her.

"Do you have any depressing novels?" she asked, her voice scraping along gravelly and pitched low—it sounded like his old red plastic sled dragged across a macadam driveway.

"Yeah, mine," said Chitchee. "*The Hell Hound Chip.* I need a copy editor, a continuity editor, and a copy editor for the continuity editor. Do you have time to proofread 500 pages? No, I take that back. I forgot I erased it. We don't have to smoke pot to be friends! I was trying *not* to talk about myself— to impress you! It's all in my head though. Maybe I could dictate 400 pages off the top of my head spread out over the next eighteen years. And you write it all down like Henry James's secretary. Sorry! You wanted depressing novels? *The Book of Disquiet, The Blind Owl, Of Human Bondage, Dopefiend, Disgrace, Lust, Extinction, Oscar Wao, Money, Oblivion, Blood Meridian,* and almost all of Graham Greene—God, I didn't realize reading was always so depressing! Ugh, why bother? Are you sure you want a book?"

"How about books on persecuted jazz musicians?" asked Dagny, looking at the exit.

"Let me think," said Chitchee, striding into and out of the stacks. "Quincy Troupe's *Miles, Really the Blues* by Mezz Mezzrow, which has a lot about Louis Armstrong, or *Beneath the Underdog* by Charles Mingus? We have that one! Have it! Have it! In fact, we have two copies! I'm so glad, I'm so glad—we found a depressing book for your depression. I haven't read it, so I can't guarantee it's depressing. But, hey it's Mingus! It will be great!"

His smile was as wide as Meade Lux Lewis's octaves on a grand piano.

"I've read it," drawled Dagny. "It's not depressing, it's weird. It's sort of . . . disembodied, but salty. It used to be my favorite book. But it's weird."

"Weird!" said Chitchee. "*Weird* is what everyone calls me. What a coincidence! Do you believe in synchronicity?"

No answer.

Maybe she has an ear infection in both ears. Since he had retrieved two copies of the book from the Music shelf for her, he expected to be petted or maybe scratched behind his ear.

He profiled his profile over his shoulder. He cast his sheep's eyes at her.

"I'll buy it anyway," she said. "Anything, so I can forget having to work for Corporate Asshole Penis Tarts."

Dagny looked happily depressed, glanced at the door, and avoided eye contact with Chitchee for the sheep's eyes he cast her way.

"Do you want your receipt?" asked Chitchee. "It's blank because the ink ran out, but you could use it as a bookmark until it gets ripped to shit."

Chitchee needed flirt time. Humiliated, he danced like a Phillips vodka-soaked Russian bear in front of Stalin. Do men in their fifties "date?" Dating dated him. "Everyone is so young nowadays." He was fifty, and it was not the new forty. If forty was the new thirty, it was all relative anyway and the new forty would not be sleeping with the new fifty. Do the Lorentz equations! Wasn't everything within the margin of error? Chitchee braced himself.

He was about to ask her out on a first "date:" windsurfing around the shores of Lake Calhoun, paddle-boating down Minnehaha Creek, or climbing cottonwoods down by the Mississippi.

ZALAR WANTS MORE MANSON BOOKS

Zalar Gossick shambled in the front door. Squalls of thought wrinkled his shrinking face and Phillips vodka broke from his mouth. Chitchee's irises shrank to little bats. Zalar looked somehow different. It had something to do with Viktor crushing Zalar's skull in half with a tire iron. Zalar had washed the blood off his face, but not his T-shirt. When he walked his knees buckled half-seas over. Zalar glowered and towered over Chitchee, who crouched behind the NCR cash register and busied himself with self-mutilation.

Zalar had always thought himself a smart cookie, because he had an education from St. Cloud State. St. Cloud State *Prison* that is. One night after getting tanked at Club Miami, Zalar ran all the red lights and led a pack of local barking, thirsty thumpers on a bloodshot, high-speed chase through Theodore Wirth Park. Zalar mowed down a water pump, patched out on the rolled-up sod of the 9th hole, and surrendered to a thrashing from the thumpers. A concussion, a separated shoulder, loss of vision in one eye, Taser burns like a roped steer, and threats to blow his head off were par for Zalar's course. Zalar took his lumps, served his time, and said he deserved his time. He decided to become a thumper himself, because they had all the fun.

"You're looking good, tonight," said Zalar to Dagny.

"*That,*" said Chitchee, popping up from behind the maroon counter, "is simply disgusting! Can I help you find an appalling book you repulsive, predatory scumbag?"

Zalar swiveled his screwy head toward Chitchee. Chitchee screwed up his eyes at Zalar.

"*Ma'am*, is he bothering you?" a stiffened, prickled Chitchee asked Dagny.

Chitchee not taking his eyes off Zalar asked:

"Notice my scowl? Pretty good scowl, huh?"

Chitchee watched Zalar sneer at him and watched Zalar smirk at him and he watched Zalar sneer, smirk, sneer, and smirk. Zalar turned to Dagny.

Zalar eye-of-desired Dagny—a long few seconds. His tongue peeped in and out. And while his wolf-whistling eyes went "va-va-va—voom," wolves sprang out of his eyes on eye-stalks, and those wolves had tongues rolling in and out. Zalar shopped over her body with a shopping cart—at the same time, he erased Chitchee with a disarmingly punchy glance. Zalar produced a pair of Harley Davidson glasses, transforming himself into a well-read English professor from St. Cloud State.

"Would you like to meet for coffee?" asked Zalar, super-sweetly, softly, gently, and even intellectually.

"Thanks, but I have a boyfriend," said Dagny so quickly that Zalar felt a cut, rubbed his neck to feel the cut there, and looked at his fingertips for blood.

He wanted to cut himself.

"Who?" asked Zalar, taking off his glasses and blinking he had been lied to.

"This guy," said Dagny, her lazy thumb tossed at Chitchee.

"And he calls you *ma'am*?" asked Zalar, his color changing. "Aw, you're full of yourself! It's *me*, not *him* you want. He's *old*. Old! Since you can't understand that, woman, you are a fucking bitch, a whore, and a cunt! I should eat your face off."

He thrust the owl's glasses back in their case, along with the professor's face.

"Sir," said Chitchee, "I call her *ma'am* to disguise the fact that we have secretly eloped to avoid blackmail, and because we want to live in a Jane Austen novel. If she's booked, we will settle for Beatrix Potter."

Zalar confounded his eyebrows. He formed mental punches in his frontal lobes. He stepped down the stairs to cool off and scream.

Chitchee and Dagny reviewed possible halfway points to meet (The Sick Joke Cafe was the closest midpoint).

"Oh, by the way, I said all that to ditch him," she said, looking for her Carousel cigarettes. "I guess we could meet anyway."

When Dagny walked out the front door, Chitchee's heart sank like a scuttled boat.

An hour later, Zalar, not firmly fixed on his feet, grabbed the hand-rail for support and looked upstairs through the leopard's spots in front of his eyes. He carried three books on Charles Manson. He slammed them on the counter; he wanted them to speak volumes. He thrust them down hard again and again, each time more ticked off than the other. Zalar was ticked off, ticking off like a ticked off time-bomb.

"Does anybody work here?" asked Zalar.

"Depends," said Saami, popping up from beneath the counter.

"Do you have any more books on Manson?"

"All our Manson books are out on the shelf," said Saami.

"When are you going to get *more* in?" asked Zalar, shifting his weight, stamping his feet, and looking at Chitchee who looked away.

"Chitchee, do you know when we are getting another shipment of Manson books? Okay it comes to $31.68," said Saami, ignoring whatever Chitchee's answer was before he answered "no."

Zalar handed Saami a hundred dollar bill. It was a delicate parchment, a Delft sugar bowl, or a precious locket from the head of Manson. Saami shook his shaved head.

"Nope, can't break that," said Saami.

Zalar, regrouping (plenty of cash loose and crunched up in his pockets), handed Saami two 20s and a 10. Then Saami handed back the 10.

"It's only $31.68," said Saami, continuing a hot, rare streak of mathematical confidence.

Zalar handed the ten dollar bill back to Saami. Saami gave him his change: the superfluous ten, a five, three ones, three dimes.

As Saami reached for the two pennies, Zalar reached into his front pocket.

"Oh, here, wait, I have a quarter!" said Zalar.

"It's too late! Oh no!" said Saami, slamming the cash register drawer and slamming the two pennies on the linoleum counter. "I can't take your quarter now, or it will look like a separate transaction. The boss man will notice and wonder why I opened the till so many times: no sale, no sale, no sale."

"What!" said Zalar, itchy with little red chiggers, lice, or a repressed sexual urge to rape all of Manson's women. "How much is the tax on books?"

"7 1/2 percent in Minnesota," said Saami impatiently.

"Well, *I'm* from Minnesota! And *I've* never heard of that tax! Anyway, I'm against taxes!"

Zalar examined his receipt. The ink incensed him the more it faded the more he looked at it. There was a malign purpose behind every event. A swirling cloud of conspiracy enveloped his brain: BookSmart had run out of ink on purpose.

"Taxes, taxes, taxes," said Chitchee. "They're grout. They keep together the political infrastructure like the elastic band on your diapers."

Zalar quivered like a rattlesnake on the Discovery Channel—a rattlesnake that would never stand for the highway robbery of a *book* tax. A pissed off, astonished, perplexed, betrayed, condescended to, stepped on, and run-over rattlesnake on the Discovery Channel. His eyes narrowed into tunnels as he shook his head no, no, no. Nonononononono.

"You guys overcharged me," said Zalar, flipping his books and looking at the sticker price tags on the back. Referring to the receipt he added, "I can't read this shit!"

A spark of paranoid lightning set on fire Zalar's brain.

"Taxes are welfare and welfare is for blacks," said Zalar. "And all their hands are outstretched for government handouts. The fuckin' n—"

"Halt!" commanded Chitchee. "What do you think this is, San Quentin? We don't need to hear that. We don't need you and your fractured skull concussions—stop whining and get a metal plate. When are you going to grow up and die? Pay the man and leave like a tree! Cut to the chase, she's mine! I saw her first. Let me see that, Saami!"

Chitchee looked at Zalar's receipt.

"Saami, you forgot to *add* the sales tax!" said Chitchee. "We didn't *charge* you the sales tax, Zalar."

"Are you calling me a liar?" said Zalar.

"Yes and no," said Chitchee. "I'm saying you have a tendency to nullify the reality principle whenever it conflicts with your wishy-washy wishes."

Zalar jumped over the counter, grabbed a box-cutter, and slashed open a corrugated cardboard box like a book clerk's throat.

"Dude!" said Saami. "Get out of here!"

"Don't call me dude!" said Zalar, walking back to the point of purchase.

"What about I call you a crab?" said Saami with a look of feigned shock that was real shock.

"Yeah, what's the fascination with Charles Manson anyway?" jumped up Chitchee. "He didn't even kill anyone!"

"He was against taxes," replied Saami. "That's why he never worked."

"Saami, you'd think a murderer could at least kill someone!" said Chitchee.

"He was more into his harem and couldn't get out of bed," said Saami.

"He's probably reading *Bridget Jones's Diary* right now," said Chitchee.

"Yeah, wankin' off to it," said Saami, aping a wildly masturbatory male.

"*Fuck* you guys!" said Zalar. "How *bougie* to think that to murder someone you really had to murder someone! Assholes!"

"He wasn't out there," said Jason, entering BookSmart, headphones jamming his ears with *Zen Arcade*. "Looks like there was a hit and run though."

With a not-looking-where-I-am-going look, Jason recognized Zalar Gossick as an immediate confrontation. Jason's face and ears blushed pale white as smeared cream cheese. He turned on a dime, carted himself back to the sidewalk, and faked a cell phone call. Then he crossed the street. This too dissed Zalar, who had an epiphany that that was meant for him somehow.

"Hey!" said Zalar. "You're the guy that stole Viktor's coke! He's avoiding me!"

Zalar grabbed his Manson trilogy, ran outside, and looked around.

Once outside, Zalar pounded on the BookSmart front window and kept shoving the finger at Saami and Chitchee, who mirrored each other and shrugged like bookends—and once Zalar disappeared, Jason returned from McDonald's with a surprised but not too concerned look.

Under his headphones, which his long, black mullet hair had gotten in the way of, he flicked his hair nonchalantly.

"Hey, Hüsker Düde, turn down your music!" said Saami. "This is a book store, not Seventh Street Entry!"

"Goddamn mullet!" said Jason, turning off his discus-shaped, silver Sony CD player. "So hard to maintain! Has Grant Hart been back since I left?"

"No, haven't seen him," said Saami, "in a while."

"Okay, Saami," said Jason, "wanna buy a really good book?"

"How did you read it through the shrink wrap?" asked Saami, holding up *Immigration Medicine*.

"It wasn't easy," swore Jason. "I had to wear shrink-wrapped glasses."

"Ten bucks," said Saami, drumming his fingers and looking like he needed a shot of Phillips vodka quickly.

"I'm finding all sorts of good shit like this at my new job," explained Jason, "clearing out evictions and abandoned apartments for MPG."

"Who was that guy that was here?" asked Saami. "Do you know him?"

"Zalar," said Jason. A slight shudder twitched his baggy eyelids. "He's a caretaker for some of the buildings I'm working on. I seen him around 'cause he works for MPG too. And the Boss Man upstairs."

Jason's phone popped off.

"Is ten bucks enough for diapers, baby? No? Yes, ba'e, yes, sure, whatever you say," said Jason, hanging up and giving his phone the finger. "I'm done with her!"

Zalar filled the front window and watched Jason pocket the ten bucks.

Then he waved *the* finger in the air again, shouted "Fuck you!" through the front window, and looking with bruised eyes to get drunk somewhere.

The used book store was more than used books—it was a concert of Beethoven in Chicago conducted by Sir George Solti every night.

"Bitch!" yelled Jason.

"What?" said the phone.

"No, by bitch I meant ba'e, you fine ba'e," said Jason, "fine like a mutha fucka, ba'e, you know I love you ba'e! I didn't know 'it' was on! Yes, I'm coming home now, do you want any Gummi bears, the kind with the liquid gooey centers?"

"Well, Jason," said Chitchee, "glad to see you got a job and you are back on your feet, and you're obviously in a relationship. Sounds like you found your dream."

"It's like a dream," agreed Jason, leaving the dream, "yes. But it sucks."

Chitchee suggested to Saami that he go to Health and Human Services for food stamps, or EBT, or SNAP—or whatever Keynesian tokens they needed to keep the economy going, provide jobs, and put food on the table for the employees who accepted them at the Rainbow Grocery store cash registers.

What could he do to give Dagny bliss? Was everybody depressed in Minneapolis? Then who are making babies? Or who are making all the *sad* babies?

#6 BUS STOP BY MCDONALD'S

That morning, Minneapolis smelled like dogshit, but the stink came from fertilizer in the cornfields of countryside farms thawing after a cold snap, but everyone blamed the gingko tree. The males blamed the female gingko tree and the females blamed the male gingko tree. And every year everyone turned up their heels to check for dogshit or rotten gingko; in any case it was a damp squib on everyone's spirits and Saami Rolvaag *was* truly a sad baby that morning. Under the depressed, olive-gray cloud cover, he had a scrunched-up face like a bloody, irregular skin mole. Saami was feeling like the last leftover wiener at the last local Episcopalian wienerfest on the hottest day of summer. But Chitchee smiled when he saw Saami slumped like a bad mattress by the drab, depressing McDonald's lusterless gray arches. Under the crossed dull crucifixes, both were under the depressed gaze of Hawk Eye, scrounging for stubbed, dull, depressed cigarettes like a depressed, scavenging crayfish on a post-apocalyptic, depressing beach. Hawk Eye collided with the depressed transient wayfarers on a depressed Midwest Coast, black hoods drawn over their tribal tattooed profiles, sitting in heaps of depressed duffle bags, occasionally letting out a cheerful bark, but mostly fizzling into a collective depression—made more depressing by the awareness of time wasted thinking about the depression itself. Street urchins, street limpets, and street barnacles sat backed up against the stores from Mickey D's down to Carousel Square, observing the play of pages in the book of life. Hawk Eye jaywalked to his listening post between BookSmart and Club Miami and thought: damn, Minneapolis is as gray as Gruyère cheese and cratered as the Moon looking down at me right now with its hollow eyes.

The oak trees fired their acorns like tiny cannonballs. Chitchee picked one cap from the sidewalk of caps.

"Hey Saami, there's Torg! Hi Torg!" Chitchee waved to Torg, sitting next to his bags of aluminum cans on the bus bench across the street.

Chitchee placed the miniature dome in between his thumbs and blew Triton's horn so loudly that traffic pulled over for its sirening.

"Hey, Torg!" yelled Chitchee. "There's someone pissing on you!"

"Fuck you, you're a peon!" yelled back Undone Buttons. "Eur-o-pee-on!"

"What's all that yay-hooing about?" asked Sausage Man when he emerged with his fishing pole from McDonald's.

Sausage Man licked his finger for the wind's direction. Hawk Eye noticed Sausage Man talking to an imaginary friend like Elwood P. Dowd. Sausage Man tilted his fish-hooked, teal fishing hat toward the gray sky for a sign, only to see The Indestructible Book Jesus (his ears pierced by acorn shrieks) push a shopping cart full of discarded library books (he had found in the Walker Library dumpster) into Undone Buttons, rammed by the maverick shopping cart in his back. Shamelessly Undone Buttons had peed on the back of the bus bench. Torg had edged forward, hands between his knees and bags of cans splashed with the urine, which interrupted his fantasy of boinging and boffing Katreena missionary style. Torg had been thinking what if she spanked me, what if I spanked her—when a tang of vinegar, smoky must, sugar cane sugar, and a salty sneeze inundated Torg.

"See that, Sausage Man?" asked Chitchee. "When I blew my acorn whistle, Undone Buttons stopped pissing on Torg."

"Randy!" shouted Susquehanna Stanton, standing up from her wheelchair, a folklorist and photographer of no note.

Whenever her wheelchair broke and she had a doctor's appointment, for which she had planners full of appointments, she called on Randy to meet her at McDonald's.

"Get a job, brother," said The Indestructible Book Jesus to Undone Buttons who strangely didn't object to being run over by a maverick shopping cart.

"Why are you always so violent, brother?" asked The Indestructible Book Jesus.

"What can we do to make more money for the book store?" asked Chitchee, turning to Saami.

Saami's eyes whited out with disgust.

"I will open my own book store someday!" claimed Chitchee.

Egrets taking off against a white paper sky . . .

"Plasma," said glumly Saami. "Plasma."

"There's a great future in plasma?" asked Chitchee.

"I can't help it," said Undone Buttons, zipping up. "It's in my genes."

"Well, keep it in your jeans," said The Indestructible Book Jesus, giving Undone Buttons five bucks. "Take care, brother. You know we love you, and you can always come home. We're not going to lose the house now. Ahura Mazda gave us a gift."

"Fuck that," said Undone Buttons. "You fuck me out of everything! You are fucking rodents to me!"

The Indestructible Book Jesus moseyed along with his worthless books toward BookSmart.

"Hey, Saami, did you see that?" asked Chitchee. "When I blew my acorn, Undone Buttons got five bucks from The Indestructible Book Jesus. Did I do that too?"

Saami hoisted one eyebrow suspiciously at Chitchee. He handed him a poorly-rolled, thin-as-a-toothpick, pin joint. They passed it back and forth twice before Chitchee choked on the rice paper spitballed around the grain of marijuana.

"Good thoughts, good words, good deeds," said The Indestructible Book Jesus over his ragged shoulder to his even more ragged brother.

"Lewis & Clark," sounded aloud Chitchee. "This will be fun, Saami. Think of it as a Lewis & Clark expedition for food stamps."

(Chitchee had read DeVoto's *Across the Wide Missouri*—Clark's memorable entry, "killed a mountain lion for breakfast."). A hawk trolled overhead crucified against a grey cloud. Chitchee and Saami watched the diesel-sputtering #6 bus a block away, approaching them like a chicken ridding itself of parasites in a dust bath, kicking up clouds of exhaust.

"We have to get you food stamps," Chitchee consoled Saami, "or you won't be able to afford drinking yourself to death at the book store anymore."

Blocking the bus stop, a white Dodge van had partially parked on the curb.

A gray pall cast over the scarps of the alpine city buildings and the gray nothingness permeated Minneapolis with the gray goo of AI disaster stories. The railroad tracks, the railroad ties, and the worn-out windows seemed to feel it. Although high, Chitchee caved into feelings of sludge. The bus itself looked like someone's last roach.

#6 busdriver, Lily Holmgren in a gray uniform cardigan steered the wheel: the front door folded and opened. Shouting from her perch, Big Mac-faced Lily leaned on her #6 horn, honking it like a thousand Canadian geese with kazoos in their beaks.

"Oh, I'll go tell them to move it," said Chitchee, suddenly feeling a lot better and skipping over to the van. "Window down, window down, hello?"

Chitchee knocked on Spartak Bok's window to no avail. He blew his acorn.

"Yes, sir?" asked Spartak Bok, rolling down the window, not recognizing Chitchee because he didn't look up.

"Could you move your van, please?" asked Chitchee, looking homely and plain. "Me and my bus here are going to get Saami food stamps so he can drink more freely."

"Yes, sir," said Spartak.

U-turning in front of the bus and then parking behind the bus, Spartak fiddled with his seat belt and boxes of ammunition.

UPTOWN EXPLODES

Saami high-fived Carlos and Cesar Leon in the front seats. Katreena sat by her sons. She saw Torg across the street and thought of waving, Torg sitting cutely in his own way, covered in urine. Undone Buttons waved his petition for spare change in the air and cursed the birth of the universe. Linda Rolvaag, in her flowered hat and floral dress and boxy purse of white leather at her side, sat in a front seat. Linda beamed at Saami, who jumped and landed next to her.

Behind Saami, with exact change Chitchee boarded the #6 bus triumphantly.

"There you go, Lily! Exact change, for your beatific smile!" said Chitchee at the top of the stairlet. "Is there a tip jar? Lily! You should stop by the book store sometime. Aloysius is always talking about you. He says that your big round face reminds him of a sweet potato pie. Wait up though, here comes Randy Quaalude and Susquehanna Stanton."

Chitchee pinched and tore the transfer between his thumb and index and turned around to look for Saami. Smackdab, Chitchee stepped into a quarrel, and such carryings on as who shot John!

Courtney Kirkwood, over her art stroller, confronted Katreena Polk, who wore tight sparkling jeans and a sequinized pink top that read "Pink On Top." Here are some excerpts:

"Faggot!" "Fuck yo' ass bitch!" "You know what I'm sa'in'? I'm sayin' fuck U!"

Melusina and Kriemhilde were scared stiffs, filled with liquid fear in their front seats.

Randy yelled for the bus, stopped, lighted a cigarette butt, and burned the tip of his nose. Every miserable farce behind every depressed face contained a novel, a story, or a poem of tragic beauty. One saw profound acts of Christian kindness on the #6 some days, on others manslaughter. Chitchee could not remember what street the "Welfare" Building was on. It wasn't even called that anymore, was it? He rubbed his forehead with two fingers until his floaters floated off. Food stamps had once been issued from the Ramar Building on Franklin Avenue; now it was Century Plaza. Someday *that* would sound old, he figured, and it would be called the more eschatological Millennium Plaza. It wouldn't be the Twin Cities, it would be the Triple Cities, having grown a new branch from a budding suburb. Chitchee remembered: Health and Human Services. But what street? Chitchee gazed out the bus window like a Labrador. His own "Our Town" did not look familiar. A defamiliarized, Shklovskian Minneapolis. Who was this Slavsky guy anyway? And what about Bakhtin, Lukacs, and Roman Jakobsen? Well, they can get their own food stamps.

Nowhere to sit, looking down the aisle from the front to the back, straphangers with hands in their nooses, Chitchee glimpsed the kaleidoscopic ark of humanity. He read the thoughts of each passenger, which was tedious, trivial, or a shattering waterfall of tears. Ruminating loops of fear passed behind the eyes of: teenage outpatients on their last trip to the cancer ward, metro-proles going to work for the best years of their lives, and confidential informants looking for scraps of information for scraps of food. Chitchee noticed that Kennedy in the back seat chortled at the previous altercation. Five seats in front of Kennedy on the other side sat Lake Street Rodney, absorbed in an old Gygax role-playing game in which Rodney played twenty different characters all at once, all interactive as a crowded bus.

"Wait, busdriver! Randy is coming! He went into McDonald's!" yelled Susquehanna from her wheelchair, a prototype from before WW I.

"Sorry!" said Lily. "The bus's platform is broken! I can't lower it. Something to do with the hydraulics. I think they all evaporated."

Randy untangled himself from McDonald's, unaccompanied by his gnarled, warty blackthorn shillelagh. A cigarette always hovered over him somewhere like a dragonfly. He had probably, *probably*, been selling prescription drugs, the wrong ones, from his fanny pack. In his off hours, Randy acted as a sidewalk superintendent for the Uptown neighborhood, roamed like a rabid and incessant weasel, swacked litter bugs over the head, and jabbed them with the sharpened copper tip of his walking stick poisoned with "curare," which turned out to be an off-brand peanut butter. When this 90-pound tunnel rat of skin, ballistic stitches, bones, and a few teeth caught people littering, he came down on them like Moses on the Israelites—bolts of anger rained down, green tracers burst from his eyes, and whispering tigers ran from his wrath.

Chitchee looked out the bus windows. Randy couldn't lift Susquehanna's wheelchair. Chitchee stepped off the bus to offer a hand. Lily shook her head angrily.

"That's what falling in love is like, Lily," said Chitchee, stretching and scratching his yawning arms, "building a bridge that meets in the middle."

"So Chitchee, how were those Klonopins?" asked Randy, his skeletal frame close to an X-ray of himself when he grabbed the wheelchair's handles and lifted it again.

"What Klonopins? I bought Ativans," claimed Chitchee, lifting Susquehanna's wheelchair from the bottom toward the bus.

Randy had recently invited Chitchee over to his apartment to buy Percocets. Curious, Chitchee crawled through the flotsam/jetsam layers of Randy's veteran cavern. Randy wanted to show Chitchee something extraordinary. The "extraordinary" turned out to be an old Acorn Archimedes, which came with *Space Invaders* on it.

When Randy powered on the Acorn, the Windows '95 logo parted through the clouds and whooshed like a synthetic pipe organ.

"Did you see that?" asked Randy and bounced from his bed of trash. "Holy fuck, did you see what happened, Chitchee? Fuckin' wild shit! Fuckin' A bomb! You see that wickedness?"

"Yeah," said Chitchee, "you started your computer. Holy wickedness."

That alone caused Randy such heartfelt joy, such heartfelt joy as Chitchee had never seen (nor would he ever see) over a *computer*.

"Randy," said Chitchee, "you know what? You're an angel!"

A few tears flowed from Chitchee at this poignant moment over the irony of Randy's sublimity in a trash hoard. And for an encore Randy clicked on an icon. The icon contained a file for *Dark Side of the Moon*, which his grimy hand clicked on with a grimy mouse-hand.

"Hear that! Listen to that!" said Randy, his eyes big as glass paperweights—his mouth all ovals and saucers.

To Randy, his Acorn Archimedes contained and dispensed miracles; to Chitchee, his friend Randy contained and dispensed miracles. Chitchee bought a couple perfunctory Ativans for the inevitable rainy day of pain and isolation.

"I didn't sell you Ativans, did I?" asked Randy. "Wait, how did they make you feel?"

"I don't know yet," said Chitchee. "I took one half an hour ago, so I'd be okay with going downtown for the welfare interview. If they weren't Klonopins and they weren't Ativans, what did I swallow? Randy!"

"Did I sell you the green pills or the orange pills?" asked Randy. "What did they look like? Tablets or capsules? Were they those see-through jobbies?"

"It's a miracle we're alive," said Chitchee, foreseeing an imminent death for Randy and his sloppy drug deals. "I didn't *think* those were Ativans. WHY DIDN'T I CALL POISON CONTROL HOTLINE? 1-800-222-1222. Randy, what did I take?"

"I don't know, let me think," said Randy, reaching for his stub. "Yes, let me think . . . what is E exactly? Were they the Blue Dolphins going around?"

"What is E! You're kidding!" said Chitchee with a swimmer's face surfaced from an Olympic dive, opening his eyes. "E is Ecstasy! You mean I just took 3,4-Methylenedioxymethamphetamine?"

"Uh," said Randy, "are you feeling ecstatic?"

"No," said Chitchee. "Ecstasy doesn't make you *ecstatic*, it makes you *empathic*; but if they called it Empathy, it wouldn't sell."

"True, then, no worries!" said Randy brusquely. "You got a good deal. What's the beef? Another great deal brought to you by Randy Johnson from Wisconsin."

Chitchee, with his hand on top of his black wool cap, moved it around, sliding concepts around in his brain.

"What about that weed I gave you?" asked Randy.

"I know the weed was for free," coughed Chitchee, "but it was so bad, I was going to ask you to take it back. Was it weed or *was it Memorex?*"

Randy charged himself with taking care of Susquehanna (and lately Chitchee had seen Randy in the neighborhood pushing Susquehanna to Hum's Liquor). Her backpack, strapped to her backrest, contained a ring binder of her 84 allergies, which at last count was 85. Most of the time, Randy and Susquehanna bussed to Liquor Lyle's and drowned in the local suds with the local sots, feasting on pickled herring until pickled like herring with sundry homeless locals no longer with us, the tide washing them out at their last closing time.

"Busdriver, do you go to the McDrunkard's in Dinkytown?" asked Randy. "Or the McDoper's downtown?"

"I sure do," said Lily. "I can take you all the way to Leech Lake if you can pay me in walleyes. Uff da on you. Get in!"

Susquehanna, in her wheelchair, grabbed the antique rims of her dilapidated wheelchair. The wheelchair collapsed. The wheels had no more structural support than a plastic trellis for mignonettes. One old rubber wheel bent inward, pigeon-toed like a bad grocery cart with uneven wheels at Rainbow Foods. Randy grabbed her shoulders.

"Randy!" cried Susquehanna. "Don't!"

Chitchee lifted her by the ankles. Terror framed Susquehanna's face when her proprioceptors told her her torso was in mid-air.

"I got her!" said Randy to Chitchee. "Set her the fuck down! You goddamned fuck!"

"Stop helping!" cried Susquehanna. "You're not helping!"

"Don't worry, I got you babe," said Randy defensively, drunkenly fumbling the cigarette stub he had stuck in his mouth before it popped out again.

Randy looked for the cigarette stub while holding the collapsed wheelchair. Chitchee snatched the smoldering cigarette off the sidewalk and handed it back to Randy.

Lily watched. She had been ahead of schedule but the clock ticked. Several passengers suggested they go now. Like right now. Susquehanna's legs withered in Randy's hands and her blouse snagged in the wheelchair, which Chitchee carried onboard, not seeing the shredding of Susquehanna's blouse in the broken wheel, which fell off.

"I got the wheel!" said Chitchee. "We're good to go, Lily!"

"Busdriver," said Katreena Polk, watching over Carlos and Cesar Leon. "I got serious business to tend *to*."

"Randy! Where are we going?" said Susquehanna. "I'm sorry, driver, if he used the 'n' word he didn't mean it. He's a white man!"

"I didn't hear anything," said Lily. "Come on, come on."

Lily always had a handgun under her seat, but was afraid of its repercussions. It was easier to disarm the passengers with her double-barreled, hearty hamburger helper "hello."

Carbureted carbon fumes coughed out of the metro-auto pipes. The #6 hulked north on Hennepin. When Chitchee looked down the center aisle, he telescoped another dimension, unfolding before him like an infinite bus.

An unholy host of crows, robins, chickadees, finches, and sparrows surged into the sky at the same time Chitchee jumped, concussing his head into the ceiling and knocking his beanie off. An ear-shattering explosion ripped the sky's giant sheet of foolscap. Someone screamed like a sacrificial pig. Then Chitchee saw everybody else jump. After him, a second later. He pictured himself: he had lurched. The aisle had lurched.

The bus woggled like a puddle duck with a wounded foot.

A car bomb had exploded within a block, the blast radius spreading out in ripples from Uptown. The passengers jumbled out of their seats into the aisle, fell, and tumbled like molecules in a giant beaker that an enzyme had speeded up.

Debris, chrome, cement, glass, aluminum, and human flesh roiled above the Uptown McDonald's. Caved storefront windows and capsized parked cars lined the east side of the block. The blast tossed the bus shelter like a bird cage, the birds flattened against the DeZign windows, whose showroom splintered into smithereens.

A parked #6 bus, ahead of schedule, in front of BookSmart, shielded the book store's windows from the blast. Aloysius looked like a child with a pirate's treasure map, prowling around the basement unable to find *The Waste Land*, which someone had ordered off Amazon—unable to find the Poetry section because Saami moved it around to discourage Yardley.

Nothing remained of Croffut Gleet but a cleated racing shoe at the door stoop of the MAC store half a block away across the street. The hairy partial foot in the racing shoe beat like a human heart. Spartak Bok had been incinerated, but for his hands, feet, and body parts festooning Aveda's windows at Lake & Hennepin.

Corky Skogentaub threw open his office window in the Yggdrasil building.

The Uptown Theater's doors had blown inward, bending like palm trees but not breaking.

And the #6 pulled over and quaked. Suspended in an eclipse, the passengers felt numb as cotton. Everybody looked around, wondering whether the bus had been run over by a bus. But the bus, sticking to its schedule, under Lily's firm grip, plowed ahead like a cut earthworm.

In plain view of Hawk Eye (panhandling outside Club Miami), Croffut had crawled under the white Dodge van parked in front of DeZign, the furniture showroom for the stars. Croffut's remote control had given him tendonitis earlier. He had pulled a hamstring getting his racing socks in his cleated shoes, which affected his concentration when he affixed the homemade bomb under the van and attached a pressure-sensitive fuse. The tube was hard to handle because of the cramped quarters. Sweat and oil combined to drip over Croffut's face, and glass rocks needled his back through his racing shirt. He couldn't remember how the circuit attached to the bomb itself. His twiggy little fingers trembled. He tried again to connect the wires. He wired the firing system to the fuse, which depended on the roll of a little blob of mercury in between the little switch.

Spartak had returned to Club Miami to pick up a payment from Viktor, who deemed the payment of any debt extortion. Upon realizing that Viktor wasn't there, Spartak launched a barrage of profanity at Nestor, already in a continual plague of jealous rage against LaDonna. Nestor took a step backward from the bar, fearing contagious brain damage from Spartak's frontal lobes.

"My father stepped out to run an errand to US Bank," said Nestor, texting Croffut Gleet: *the coast is clear*. "Spartak? Viktor just texted. He said to wait up. The drinks are on the house."

Nestor looked across the street and washed his hands with Purell hand gel and hot water.

Wearing a satin bowling jacket, cleated shoes, Dickies work pants, and little leather gloves, Croffut locked his racing bike to a street sign with two locks. U and chain.

"I'll wait here. Oh, give me a Courvoisier. The most expensive one. And leave the bottle," said Spartak, sitting on the swivel stool.

He snorted cocaine powder with a tubularized hundred dollar bill and coughed a fit all over the Club Miami counter. He waved off Nestor, who wasn't going to help *Spartak*. Nestor merely wanted to run a soapy, terry cloth rag over the area.

"The air quality is bad today," said Spartak, fisting his chest twice.

"Actually, carbon dioxide is essential for the environment. . . ." said Nestor, slowly pouring a dram of the V. S. O. P. into a cognac glass for Spartak. "I don't know what all the fuss is about. Do you? The AAAS has been bribed by the solar and wind power sharks. So of course they want to drive the coal and oil industries out of business. This isn't Maxwell's equations. It doesn't take a rocket scientist to corroborate the fact that excess carbon dioxide is devoured by oysters. They love the stuff. Plankton need it to survive. But the scientific establishment doesn't want you to know that excess carbon dioxide is drained off by calcium carbonate. It feeds vegetation and lowers the temperature—although it only accounts for .04% of the earth's atmosphere, because without it every man, plant, and animal would die of thirst. How do you like that cognac?"

"It's not doing anything," grumbled Spartak.

"Wait," smiled Nestor, "the greenhouse gas corporate models are all based on Venus. Anyone with a telescope can see that Venus is a false model for Earth. Venus has a weak electric-magnetic field, and the Sun's solar field destroys it easily, because Venus is so slow. It's all a scam. But you have to be super intelligent to understand all this."

"No," said Spartak Bok, lifting his head up from the counter and finishing another line of cocaine. "You would have to be a fucking idiot to understand all this."

When Spartak, bottle of Courvoisier in hand, stormed back to the white Dodge van, he slammed the door (Croffut heard the car door slam), thrust the key in the ignition, and turned the tumbler to the right.

The last thing Spartak saw before transmogrifying into McNuggets was the McDonald's golden arches—below him.

Smartphones frantically searched for answers like barnyard fowl for seeds.

"Does anybody know where the Welfare Office is?" asked Chitchee with an asking face toward the entire bus, which was blank. He smiled wanly.

Everyone looked up and stared past him, through him, and around him. He drew out his acorn cap and blew his high E. A flock of hands went up like ducks and geese and pointed in the same migratory direction.

"Okay, thanks, everybody," said Chitchee.

The explosion had after-effects of worry, concern, and anxiety—only increasing in intensity by everyone talking at cross purposes with excited tongues imagining all the theories about the explosion. "I gotta get my stick!" said Randy. "God damn, it's in McDonald's! Driver! We need to turn around."

"I don't gotta *do* anything!" declared Lily. "Nobody's turning around."

A round of appreciative applause surfaced faintly, broke up, and faded fast.

"Gotta?" asked a clapping, matronly patron Melusina to a patronly matron Kriemhilde.

"That's not good English!" said Kriemhilde. "Where did he graduate? Gasoline Alley?"

"Hah, hah," said Linda, "I guess he wasn't brought up right like he ought! Say, do you gals know my husband, Saami? I'm so proud of him. Did you know he is the first one in his family to ever get a job?"

"Oh shucks, you're the best, 'da," replied Saami. "Do you need a dollar for the Dollar Store, 'da?"

"No," said Linda, cuddling her man. "I went early this morning while you were chonking in the bathroom. Oh wait, I want to get off here! Spaghetti for dinner?"

"Sure," said Saami, slumping. "Why not? Why not celebrate Christmas early and get it out of the way?"

Libor Biskop, sweating profusely in his winter parka and wool cap, holding giant baggies of air he had gathered from the frozen foods coolers at Lunds, jumped on the bus, looked around afraid, and shouted:

"I think I have it! A quantum mechanical solution to the squaring of the circle problem of the ancients, using group theory and ordinary differential equations—building upon Ramanujan! Can I borrow a dollar from somebody?"

Libor jumped out the back door and perspired and almost expired on the sidewalk. He inhaled from one of his plastic bags of cold air, walked back to the front of the bus, and pounded on its door.

"Hey Libor, pay as you get on, no fare beats on my Viking cruise line!" said Lily. "You know what to do."

"But I don't have the correct change, driver! I only have a five," Libor said squarely from the sidewalk. "Can you wait while I go get change?"

A roaring belly laugh answered for Lily. The bus unmoored and pulled away.

"I could have paid for him!" said Chitchee, raising his hand.

Libor Biskop ran after the bus, pounding on its side.

"That will only enable him!" said Lily. "By means of co-delinquency."

Chitchee opened his window and thrust his arm for Libor Biskop to grapple.

"Come on, Libor, come on!" goaded Chitchee. "Run, buddy, run!"

Lily did not go off schedule for anyone. She would drive over the Grand Coulee Dam to make her stops on time. Her pay review was coming up, and she needed the money for Beda's gene therapy to cure Beda of the white racism she claimed she had inherited like Dioxin from her mother.

Libor refused the human contact of Chitchee's warm-blooded hand. Lily broke out in hives when she saw Chitchee leaning out her window. She scolded and threatened Chitchee, who gave up, pouted, sulked under the reprimand of Lily, and sat down.

Chitchee jumped up and faced the pilgrims.

"Listen up, everybody," said Chitchee. "Do you all want to hear a joke? I got this from Soren Kierkegaard. A woman came to the door of a baker to beg for bread and the baker said to the begging woman, 'No, mother, I cannot give you anything. There was another mother here recently who I had to send away without giving anything too: we cannot give to everybody.'"

Blank silent stares straight forward without a nod.

"Woo-wee," said Chitchee. "What's everybody been listening to? 'Gone with the Wind?'"

"I got the joke," said Cesar Leon. "I think Bertrand Russell is funnier though."

Confusion and panic (sirens chimed in a chorus of harpies) dominated the traffic while Lily drove on the MTC timetable.

"Sounds like a gas main exploded in front of McDonald's," said Lily, having talked to headquarters. "You're lucky I picked you all up on time. I probably saved all your lives."

"Let's hear it for Lily," said Chitchee, "for saving our lives!"

Blank silent stares straight forward without a nod.

"Yay, Lily!" said Chitchee, clapping to encourage the others.

Echoes of silence.

Every pasty face was pasted to a cell phone or pasted to its own thoughts. Chitchee stared along a longitudinal line out the front window and watched traffic slug ahead at a caterpillar's pace.

"Hey, Saami, we're really on a roll now," said Chitchee over his shoulder. "I wonder what that exploding gas main was about?"

"What. Eh," mumbled Saami, his eyes skyward, "Verrrr."

"Life in the big city, don't cha know?" laughed Lily like a Wife of Bath.

"Look at Lily!" laughed Chitchee. "She's like: *sew 'em up and throw 'em back!*"

The sound of sangfroid humans chattering and trilling pleased Chitchee's ear.

Kennedy's scratchy laughter reached the front seats; Rodney ogled Gygax; Katreena brooded over her two kids; Courtney lost herself in thoughts of revenge; Melusina, Kriemhilde, and Linda contemplated the cheapness of the clothing draped on the raggedy riders; Randy and Susquehanna catnapped; a student stepped off the bus at the wrong stop for Metropolitan Community and Technical College; Chitchee gazed at the world of Dagny's "Corporate Asshole Penis Tarts." Was she thinking of him?

Downtown Minneapolis worked with its ears budding, mouths eating, eyes tiring, and bodies displaying brands like Boss, Emporio, Zegna, and Lauren. To Chitchee the men looked like giant *boys*—starched, gorbellied, and corpulent in their Hilfiger shirts with cuffs. He zoomed in and out with his eyes measuring their straight-edged skyline haircuts embedded like fractals in the skylines of skyscrapers.

"Is that how lawyers look nowadays?" asked Chitchee. "Miserable?"

Offices with faceless names like 225 South Sixth Street, 717 Mall, 90 Seventh Street, and One Point Two Two Financial Plaza also looked miserable.

Larry Sangster and Corky Skogentaub looked about as conscious as softballs pitched toward the Hennepin County Government Center, briefcases full of class-action lawsuits and multi-million dollar settlements. They rehearsed their fake lines like bad actors for the Hennepin County Attorney.

"Hey, Larry, don't look so glum!" Chitchee yelled out the window.

Chitchee cupped his hands and formed a heart.

Larry Sangster heard construction. Larry looked up and saw: hard hats with power tools, loud radios that glowered in silent white majority music, and pissed-off eyes like roadblocks. Drills filled a thickening tarry wind, manned by raspberry-shaped faces under lemon-peel helmets.

"Oh well," thought Chitchee. "You had to love humanity, especially when you didn't have a single thought in your head."

#6 bus driver Lily tried to lower the platform again, but the #6 bus sighed, sank, and expired. A thick gray hydraulic lake pooled underneath the tires of the #6. The front end knelt forward, the right side of the bumper touched earth.

"All right," said Lily, setting down her radio-phone. "Everybody out! We have no brakes."

"What kind of a bus has no brakes?" asked Toby Pfeiffer, rolling forward to catch the bus. "Where did you last see them?"

"There will be another #17 in six minutes," said Lily. "You can catch a 12 or a 4 one block over in 7 minutes. Those of you who need a 7 or a 5, check your local listings. Everybody OUT!"

Melusina and Kriemhilde stretched their arms and legs and strolled arm in arm to the IDS Center for monthly bus passes. Lynx-eyed Katreena admonished Carlos and Cesar Leon to stay close. Courtney was coming down with pellagra and would eat chalk soon. Kennedy matriculated out the back quickly. Rodney bumped into Libor. Bedraggling himself to the bus, adding only more entropy to the universe, and reaching out for the stop, Libor threw a desperate, horseshoe-look at the #6.

"Out of service, Libor," said Lily, unstrapping Susquehanna.

Susquehanna stood up, grabbed her wheelchair, and walked off the bus.

"Thanks, busdriver," she said, "you know we're not spring-loaded chickens anymore."

Susquehanna, helped by Randy, reseated herself and Randy shoved her chair forward by her handles, stub in his Popeye mouth. They walked to Nicollet Avenue. Next to the Neiman Marcus storefront, they entered a Celtic-stenciled, plate-glassed pub with an Irishish name like O'Donnegans, or O'Doonagahoolies, or O'Hoolihannigandoonigan's.

Libor scratched his head with a slide rule. Lily scratched her head.

The rear end bumper of the #6 dripped like a gutter, eavesdropping green dropped blood drops. The green pool of blood transmogrified into the squealing wings of flaming, wart hog-headed bats and flew off.

HEALTH AND HUMAN SERVICES, CENTURY PLAZA

Saami and Chitchee examined the bumper's grille, looked at each other, and walked.

"Ya, Saami," asked Chitchee, "if BookSmart is going out of business, why do you still work there?"

He swigged a Phillips half pint, dropped it in an ashcan, and held his nose: "Where else can I drink myself to death on the job?"

"Are you suicidal?" asked Chitchee.

"Not at all," said Saami. "I can't afford to lose my apartment."

"Fair enough. That's pragmatic, if not heroic. What's the inside skinny on BookSmart? Will the store make it to Christmas?" asked Chitchee. "Because if it's a lack of innovation, there are TED talks for that. In fact, there are TED talks on how to give TED talks for that."

"All I know is that there is something awful fishy going on in our basement at night," said Saami. "I'm guessing the landlord is filming underage snuff movies for the Fraternal Order of the Police or the Illuminated Members of the Third Eye or high-ranking S & M dungeon thumpers with vampires in their blood. But the lighting is terrible down there for making movies. Have you noticed the equipment that keeps showing up at night? They painted the room red, then it was black. Aloysius won't talk about it. When Club Miami first opened next door to us, Aloysius went over to meet the new neighbors. He came back with a dislocated wrist, a black eye, and an amputated toe."

"You mean he got that drunk?" asked Chitchee.

"No, but one night I was up late watching porn on the computer, and I heard something going on in our basement. There were thumpers down there and they had some gal gagged—might have been Native American. I could hear . . . I heard them . . . I got the fuck out of there."

"Are you sure?" asked Chitchee. "I didn't hear Diana Pierce or Paul Magers mention anything about that on KARE 11."

"Then, one night, as I was watching porn . . . and I'm only going to tell you this once . . ."

Chitchee took off his black woolen beanie, scratched his chest through his red plaid flannel, and hooked his index on his lower lip. He turned around. He had to admit that his daily routes—averaged over the year and put down on paper in a connect-the-dots fashion—resembled the neural networks of a nematode.

The Minneapolitan gray skyscrapers and brown brick apartments played goblins and gremlins with his cortical cortices.

"Viktor's thumpers brought in a prostitute one night, and I think they raped her there. I swear. Where she ended up, I have no idea . . . and that's how they got the knife inside Aloysius."

"What knife?" asked Chitchee. "There's a knife inside Aloysius?"

"Oh Lord!" said Saami. "What is wrong with you? I'm not going to repeat myself!"

"Saami? Are we friends?" cried Chitchee. "You have no moral backbone. You didn't call the thumpers? But I guess you rationalize everything and blame the world for your suicidal drinking."

"What's wrong with that? Got any better ideas?" asked Saami. "Linda wanted me to pick up some popcorn."

At the word "popcorn" Chitchee laughed his insides out over nothing. He corn-popped back to the night he bought a two-pound bag of Jolly Time Popcorn at the SuperAmerica gas station on Lyndale Avenue South from Phyllis, and he wept when he heard Whitney Houston sing. He knew who Whitney Houston was, "The Voice," but he had never "followed the Voice." He didn't know the name of the song, but it reminded him of the movie, *The Way We Were*, which he had never seen. It sounded too sad to watch and Chitchee was an easy crier, although as grown as he would ever groan. Chitchee's emotional structure collapsed. He fell to the floor when he speculated: what if Whitney Houston *starred* in *The Way We Were*? Later, just the *name* "Whitney Houston" could cause him to well up like an onionhead!

A veteran-looking, surplus U. S. Army-jacketed man in jeans, and capped by a trounced Minnesota Twins baseball cap, asked Chitchee if he was okay and offered to get him some toilet paper from the bathroom as soon as the key was available, *as soon as the prostitute gets out of there*, and Chitchee gets off the fluorescent-tiled floor with its corpse-like glow. Chitchee choked and thanked the stranger. Yet another act of kindness witnessed in a SuperAmerica gas station. How did he get there? Prostitute, U. S. Army, Whitney Houston, Jolly Time Popcorn, prostitute . . .

Was the Good Samaritan with the Twins cap *Hawk Eye?*

The landmarks downtown had moved, stranding Chitchee with no more foresight than that of a Malagasy jumping rat, which is about a yard.

A middle-aged white man with gray, soft cactus needles for hair, his hair parted down the middle, his gray ponytail straight down his back, and his mouth a double-bladed mustache, screeched out of a liquor store off Nicollet Avenue. He wheelchaired straight for Chitchee and Saami. He wore a black Paul Revere, tricorn hat, and loose camouflage pants, which had split at the seams because of a plaster cast on his right ankle. Two slack, unenthusiastic American flags poked out of his handlebar grips.

"Got five bucks, assholes?" asked Paul Revere.

"Why?" asked Saami, with the indifferent eyes of a hog butcher punching the clock.

"I can't work because I got injured at work," said Revere. "And uh four black teenagers stole my backpack, and I have a broken leg from when I lost control of my pickup driving home from deer hunting in Champlin, and I got caught in a flash flood in the Minnesota River Valley, and the truck crushed my leg."

"Jack?" asked Chitchee.

"Don't talk to Mad Jack Apple Jack! Fuck no!" screamed Saami, smacking his head in a rush of palm-slaps—Chitchee couldn't walk one block without bumping into somebody he knew or meeting someone he wanted to know and then inviting himself over for the next religious holiday and backyard barbecue.

"Chitch, let's go," said Saami. "I'm getting the shakes! Oh Lord, I'm not going to make it. My goose is cooked. Look at me, a cooked goose with the shakes!"

"Jack Mattson? The bully?" pursued Chitchee. "From Minnetonka High School?"

"That's the name, don't wear it out!" said Jack. "Got ten bucks? I have to get to the airport. I have to get to Chicago's O'Hare for a video conference on Dzus fasteners."

"Remember me? Chitchee Chichester!" said Chitchee, eagerly wanting to be loved and to love everyone.

Thirty years.

"Oh y-e-eah . . ." said Mad Jack Apple Jack in a dream.

Jack Mattson's glory days flew past on the robin wings of youth. He used to strut down the high school corridors like a giant robin red breast looking for bookworms. He shoved Chitchee into a locker again and again. He lighted and tossed a Black Cat firecracker at Chitchee's throat. Every day he called him "femmo," "la Queer," and "mo-ey lass," and Chitchee woke up every morning in cold sweats afraid to go to the school bus stop. He feigned colds, flus, and pneumonias. He couldn't tell his mother about it without looking like a mouse.

Jack stroked his inchoate goatee and scratched his pumice sideburns as a high school actor would to signify a rumination. Chitchee reached back for his wallet with the idea of handing his old high school chum a bygones-be-bygones five-dollar bill. Jack asked Chitchee what he did for a living, hoping it was "pushing a broom," which was Jack's profession in fact. When Chitchee said he wanted to open a used book store, Jack said:

"So you never gotten anywhere in life either! Good!"

"Also, I'm working on a novel about the future," said Chitchee, "but that's going nowhere."

"Why?" asked Jack. "Nobody's going to read it."

Chitchee froze. He closed his cowboy wallet.

"*What* did you say?" asked Chitchee.

"I said no one is going to read your faggoty-ass, pussy-faced, cum-swallowing book!"

"Yeah?" said Chitchee. "Then you're not getting my five bucks, you're only getting three of the five of my bucks, bucky!"

"Yeah, then I guess you're a Jew too!" said Jack, getting up from the wheelchair.

Chitchee thrust Mad Jack back into the wheelchair. By lifting the front wheels and dumping the chair like a little red wheelbarrow, Chitchee tumbled Jack ass-over-tea-kettles onto a church's front lawn.

Mad Jack, with his oversized torso, stood up despite his cast, like a gored ox. He charged Chitchee headlong into the rose bushes that bordered the green grounds of the church.

"Hey! Mad Jack Apple Jack! Get back here, you forgot your backpack in the aisle!" said Einar Steinkampf, the liquor store owner, holding an old lime green backpack at arm's length, which was unzipped. "Hey, what's in here? It sounds like—hey you stole this Phillips from me!"

"The fuck! You calling me a thief, Stinky!" said Mad Jack, limping towards Einar. "I'm not no thief."

"You stole this vodka from me!" said Einar. "And left it behind!"

Dougal, Mjollnir, and Nicky Fingers slow-marched towards Chitchee like a toy snake made of wooden cubes.

"Is this the pheromone trail for handouts?" asked Chitchee when he crawled out of the bushes, exhilarated by the smell of roses, laughing instead of crying for emotional relief.

The Three Grasshoppers bent their knees, hopping from the vector of Health and Human Services. Mjollnir had a PhD in Loafing Engineering circa 1968, Dougal never worked a stroke in his life, and Nicky Fingers was actually a conservative and hated the very idea of welfare—he preferred outright burglary.

"Hold him down!" said Einar, who kicked the legs out from under Mad Jack.

Mad Jack lost his balance. He fell with his mouth and eyes open and helpless as a baby backwards snapped the back of his head, jerked on the clean sidewalk.

"Hey you guys, can you give me a hand?" yelled Einar.

Mjollnir and Nicky Fingers hurried while Dougal moseyed, his Red Wing boots clumsily large because they were too tight in the first place.

"Open his mouth! Chug this, Mad Jack!" said Einar, who had the well-anchored arms of a wrestling coach—the kind of wrestling coach who fought in the Korean War hand to hand with charging Chinese Communists out of ammunition.

"Don't hurt him, sir!" said Chitchee. "He has a human soul!"

Mjollnir, Dougal, and Nicky Fingers (stealing Jack's wallet) held Jack down on the sidewalk. Einar angrily inserted the open bottle of Phillips vodka into Jack's throat and force-fed him the vodka. Mad Jack gurgled and fought back with fists flying, but the heavy cast weighed him down. Einar's well-anchored arms pinned Mad Jack like a butterfly. Saami lay prostrate on the lawn and thrust his fists into the grass, bored by all the commotion; he produced a Sudoku booklet from his pocket, set it aside, ripped out chunks of soddy grass, and threw sod at the church's steps.

And the squad car arrived with Officers Weatherwax and Weatherwax, sirens flashing, fresh tires screaming up the curb. The thumpers piled out smirking because they knew all parties involved and Einar was all for pressing charges.

The hand-locked, head-locked, and full-nelsoned Mad Jack kicked, spit, and writhed.

"Hey, you asshole thumpers, if I resist arrest, can you hit me up with some of that there ketamine again?"

Choked, trapped, and thrown in the back of the squad car, Mad Jack squirmed, his curses attenuated into a helpless, vengeful silent glare at Chitchee from the back seat window.

"Hey, Chichester! I would have broken your face, but I didn't want to break my parole. Write that down. Am I in your book? You should write a book about me!" said Mad Jack as the thumpers drove off, leaving his mad smile up in the air like Silly String from an aerosol can that could talk: "Hey Chichester? I'm sorry!!"

"All right, Jack," giggled Chitchee. "Apology accepted!"

"How do you know Mad Jack?" asked Saami.

Saami and Chitchee circled around the Health and Human Services building one way, then another, then changed their minds again, then regretted changing their minds again, and then Chitchee said:

"Mad Jack? But there are at least three Mad Jacks in Uptown. Mad Jack Apple Jack Mattson from Excelsior, Mad Jack Barley Cake from Mound, who wears the Viagra baseball cap, and Mad Jack Harry Snatch, who moved here from Cedar Rapids, who wears the T-shirt that says 'Anti-Science Guy.' How the hell do you get into this building? It's too modern. It's so modern it's pointless."

He blew his acorn whistle and there appeared Hassan Abdi, an elderly bald man with an orange beard and a benevolent wave of his right hand.

"You're from BookSmart!" said Hassan.

"Yes," said Chitchee. "Your name is Hassan, right? Do you know if this building has a door? Or do you have to climb an oak tree to get into it? Is there a door?"

Hassan pointed the way and that way Lewis and Clark went looking for food.

Chitchee and Saami operated the lift. A security door buzzed, clicked, buzzed and then clicked. Hungry, hungrier, and ego-depleted, Chitchee and Saami stumbled into a waiting room that looked like an airport check-in area. They walked up to the "ticket counter."

"Is this where we check in our baggage?" Chitchee asked the security guard, Bobblehead, who said nothing, not even "cookie, cocoa, bus."

"Typical security guard! Just stick a badge on him, point him in the general direction, and he's done," continued Chitchee—hurt that not even Bobblehead acknowledged his existence. "Saami, I'll wait over here while you get your number."

A general-issue television hung in the corner on chains, showing the repeating Cable News Network broadcasts with the breaking news repeats. The crawler scrolled left to right with Standard & Poors rated stock prices beaming at the slumped guys in foamy shoes rearranging their nuts in their drawstring, gray Walgreens sweatpants.

"Spaghetti and meatballs," said Saami to an employee.

BREAKING NEWS: *Explosion in Downtown Minneapolis . . . Police have not ruled out Terrorist attack . . . two dead, four injured . . . one in critical condition . . .*

"I'm not your case worker, but what is going on in Uptown?" a polite young man asked, his eyelashes wet and stuck together like little isosceles triangles.

"Spaghetti and meatballs," said Saami. "Got any?"

Voices in the lobby entered the office waiting room in the form of shouts. More excerpts:

"Faggot!" "Fuck yo ass!" "You ever read a book bitch?" "I never seen you in the book store!" "THE FUCK OUTTA HERE!"

Elbows flailing and asses bouncing, Katreena Polk and Courtney Kirkwood flew at each other's throats. Bobblehead discreetly shuffled to the vending machines.

"Hey, is that any way to treat a fellow human being, Katreena?" intervened Chitchee. "You should act in such a way as you would want all people to act. Each of us is endowed with reason and from reason springs our own moral law from within. Or so Kant says."

"Chitchee, shut up, you'll get us both kilt, capital T," said Saami, closing his eyes then falling asleep with his tongue out.

"You know what I think of that?" said Katreena, hustling Carlos and Cesar Leon to her side. "I think you're right and I'm gonna set my ass down and let this shit blow over. Now what the fuck is going on with the TV and Uptown?"

Courtney grumbled, angrily grabbed her number, sat down, and looked up spellbound at the TV.

BREAKING NEWS: *Authorities have recovered video footage of a suspect wanted for questioning about a car bombing that occurred about an hour ago in the Uptown area of Minneapolis . . .*

The film clip shows a white Dodge van illegally parked on the curb. A #6 bus, a big dull red vehicle, waddles into view: the front door folds and opens. Flannel-shirted Chitchee walks into the frame and is seen talking to the bus driver. Chitchee is seen walking over to the white Dodge van. Chitchee is seen knocking on Spartak's window to no avail. It looks like an obvious drug deal. Chitchee shifts his weight from foot to foot, looks up at the sky, and rolls his eyes. When Chitchee looks up toward the perched camera, the footage stops.

. . . Police are looking for this man . . .

Chitchee's face is zoomed on like a pizza from Pizza Lucé with mozzarella cheese, green peppers, black olives, red onions, Genoese salami, Italian sausage, and Neapolitan pepperoni.

. . . The Minneapolis Police Department is asking for your help in finding this man connected with a double homicide at Lake and Hennepin that took place this morning at 11:20 p.m. The MPD said they are looking for help identifying this man. Police are speculating that he might be a radicalized Palestinian. Terrorism has not been ruled out . . .

A man, moving like a funky, walking bass line—strutted into the waiting room, looked at the TV, looked at Chitchee, and then looked at Bobblehead, who had taken up his guard's position under the suspended TV.

On TV: Chitchee is leaning into the van's front side window. He is seen reaching into his pocket, he is seen placing something near his mouth. He is seen walking out of the frame. The white Dodge van is seen leaving the frame and is seen driving back into the frame.

Chitchee's captured face is zoomed on again again, enlarged to fill the screen with eyes, nose, and mouth. Chitchee saw blackheads on his nose he never knew he had.

Chitchee sank, glanced over his shoulder, and pulled his black wool beanie down over his eyes.

Anyone with information about this man or the possible bombing should call the MPD Homicide Office at 612.751.2889. He should be considered fully armed and extremely dangerous.

Bingo! Saami's number, a horse jockey's bold number, rang a bell.

"Second thought," said Chitchee, his cap over his eyebrows. "I'm sick of TV. Too many repeats. Piggyback?"

They hurried through a security area, through a buzzed door, past Bobblehead.

"My family originated in Hibbing. Have you heard of Hibbing?" asked Saami in a confrontational way. "I dare you to have heard of Hibbing!"

"Yes, but I don't need to know about Hibbing," said Astrid Eskola, her name on her engraved desk-plate.

"Hibbing," said Saami, "is beyond the seventh gate in Hell. H. P. Lovecraft imagined it. It's real name is the corpse-city of R'lyeh . . . nothing to do in Hibbing . . . is all I'm saying."

"Hibbing," said Chitchee, over-excitedly, streaming with sweat, looking around for cameras, "your parents must have liked hibbing, because they had you."

Astrid constructed a mechanical smile with no teeth in it and sipped her coffee.

"Astrid?" interjected Chitchee. "Do you know Dagny?"

That was a coffee spitter.

"Why?" asked Astrid, super slowing it down , and setting her coffee cup down quickly.

"She's great, Dagny Knutsen, isn't she?" asked Chitchee. "She mentioned your name! I'm meeting her for coffee at The Sick Joke Cafe as soon as Saami gets a bag of food! Coincidentally, this is synchronicity. Dagny and I get along great! When we slow-danced, she reminded me of an armadillo. In a beautiful way! I think I love Dagny! And *you* must be the one who likes to smoke!"

When Saami finally finished his forms, Astrid quickly issued him bus tokens and a provisional version of an EBT card.

"Saami," said Chitchee, grabbing Saami's elbow outside, "I have to leave the country. Where is the airport? I was on TV! I'm wanted for terrorism again!"

"Oh, Lord!" said Saami, throwing his hands up as if he kicked a kick ball. "You're not important enough to be followed! Ask this guy!"

Fishing hat, fishing pole, faded, shapeless Oshkosh overalls, checker-boardish, buffalo plaid flannel shirt—top button buttoned, Sausage Man had turned the corner and waved hello with a nod.

"Sausage Man! Am I important enough to be followed?" asked Chitchee with the heebie jeebies, pulling his black wool cap down around his face. "There are cameras everywhere!"

"I don't follow you," said Sausage Man with a halo of naivete.

"Now *you're* being followed, Sausage Man. I'm following you! The eyes have us. We're being read like a book in broad daylight. Why do I feel so weird?" asked Chitchee. "Everything is floating in the floating world. But I feel better now."

"*Man ain't nothing but a lying porpoise, hee haw,*" said Sausage Man. "EE-AW! Gabble rabble doo dah, a rabbababba."

"You see," said Saami, "you've got nothing to worry about! Nobody wants you."

Overheard voices puffed above a Peavey Plaza bench.

". . . and so then he gets pulled over in a cab . . ."

". . . how do you get pulled over in a cab for being drunk?"

". . . yeah! how do you?"

Mjollnir and Nicky Fingers discussed how stupid Dougal was, Dougal agreeing with a slap happy face at his stupid fame.

"How drunk is that? Pulled over for being drunk in a cab!" said Dougal. "Sometimes I even surprise myself!"

"Dougal," said Nicky Fingers. "We were talking about Mad Jack, not you!"

"Oh," said Dougal, "well, it's still funny as hell! I don't have to be Mad Jack to laugh at myself, do I?"

"You're imagining," said Sausage Man to Chitchee in a brotherly way, sober and understanding as Mencius to his disciples. "When I was in the Army, first reports were always thrown out."

"But the FBI is looking for me," protested Chitchee. "I'm on a terrorist watchlist!"

"Because they like you!" said Sausage Man. "And they want you to have a happy life!"

"You know," said Chitchee, "you might have something there! Maybe *you're* the FBI! And I *don't* have anything to fear! Nobody wants *me*. I feel great all of a sudden!"

The wind's face frowned because it had a chill, and the wind was tired from running in every direction, and Chitchee felt sorry for the wind. Spots appeared to him on the sidewalk that weren't there. Sprinkles frizzled the air. Stratus clouds scraped bottom overhead.

Saami looked up at the raindrops and picked up his pace. Chitchee heard crunches in some leaf litter. Sausage Man tagged along.

"Hey, you guys, look at all the acorns," said Chitchee, astounded at the windfall under his feet.

He picked up an acorn and removed its cap. He rubbed the acorn on his flannel shirt tail.

"Make a wish!" said Sausage Man.

"I wish I had no criminal record," said Chitchee.

"Done," said Sausage Man, waving his fishing pole at the sky like a hillbilly wizard.

"Sausage Man," said Chitchee, tugging at Sausage Man's arm, "what if the oak tree that hatched this very acorn encoded a book in this nut? What if the encoded book was the translated, pre-written story of the growth of a nut? Maybe to the oak trees, we writers are the oaks producing the books, the books we store up for the winter."

"To feed the unborn unicorns," added Saami, sharing a joint with Chitchee, who shared it with Sausage Man, who passed on it.

Sausage Man removed his fishing hat, removed Chitchee's black wool cap, plumped the fishing hat on Chitchee's shaggy head, and handed his fishing pole to Chitchee with a fresh Vienna sausage at the end of its hook.

"Now, *you* are Sausage Man," said Sausage Man, bare-headed, who handed Chitchee back his beanie, flaunting a live bus transfer from his upper overalls's pocket. He hopped a bus going north.

Saami said he was walking to the Lunds grocery store on West Lake Street to splurge with his provisional EBT allowance on a huge spaghetti and a huge meatball shindig with Linda in celebration of his food stamp Eat Better Tonight windfall. In passing, he noted that Chitchee had some real losers for friends. Saami also planned to generously patronize Henn-Lake Liquor, mistakenly thinking they accepted EBT. He selected lush red wines that only a lush would go for until he was red in the face. Lushfully considering how he could blow half of his handout on lush Italian wine and half on "sketti and some hangerger" at Lunds—even if he threw it all up later—Saami shook his head at Chitchee's loser friends. They were a "bunch of drunks who drank like a bunch of drunks." Saami hinted they might all be friends if they were all equally drunk at the same time, drinking the same wine as equals with the same buzz on, feeling the same blood alcohol-content, and playing the same video games without much luck.

Chitchee, wearing a fishing hat and carrying a fishing pole, and Saami entered Loring Park.

"Why are we going *this* way?" asked Saami.

Chitchee didn't hear him. Chitchee felt his consciousness drifting when he shared another joint with Saami. A street light, illuminated by the traces of eternity, revealed the infinity of another lost time. The mirror of what we think is the Real, he reflected, looking at the liminal pond in Loring Park fringed with reeds, rushes, watergrasses, and marsh lilies.

"Where did you get that weed?"

He was a momentous abyss between a moment and a mountain.

"Saami, I'm weirded out," said Chitchee, looking over his shoulder; the moisture in the air curled his hair, and on the sides it looked like hickory bark. "There is a white squirrel over there, that's weird. Okay. Oh, God! And an all black squirrel. What if they were fake? Fake squirrels with cameras inside. There are only gray squirrels in Minnesota. Eastern gray squirrels. That's what I am, and I'm being persecuted for it! Ha, ha, ha. I feel better for laughing. Oh, I forgot I took that Ecstasy! Randy! No wonder people treat happiness as a mental illness! It really marginalizes you!"

"Oh, Jesus," laughed Saami with a deep growl at the bottom, "you really *are* nuts!"

"What do you mean?" asked Chitchee. "You make it sound as if everybody calls me nuts behind my back. My friends all think I'm nuts? I better go to the 5th Precinct and get my name cleared by those pistachio-eating thumpers before they lock me up in a looney bin for being too nuts out there."

"Yeah," said Saami, "you're on your own if you wanna go to the 5th Precinct. I got beat up by those thumpers for biking on the sidewalk without a rear reflector."

"I'm sorry," said Chitchee and gave Saami a parting, overly heart-felt hug.

"So long," said Chitchee. "Nice working with you, if I never see you again."

Saami shook his grinning head at Chitchee, which looked like a human skull mug filled with frothy beer for a "Skol!"

THE SICK JOKE CAFE

Chitchee age-progressed everyone he knew into their deaths, coffins, and graves. Each consciousness was a book of success, failure, love, and hate. How did each character develop? And succumb to a death-bedded body, surrounded by a hundred thousand people or nobody? He imagined Dagny dead. If only he knew judo.

Chitchee shuffled along Lyndale Avenue South, followed by squirrels working for the NSA, to meet Dagny at The Sick Joke Cafe. He turned around and blew his magical acorn cap. Nothing happened. No one looked up. What if the magic only worked when he was in a state of good thoughts, good words, and good deeds? That must maybe be it.

He knew he was in love at first sight with Dagny. The auger boring into his heart was like an Archimedes screw. Once she got to know him better, she would certainly swoon. Women lived for love and men who knew judo. Financial security, pension plans, savings accounts, credit cards, cars, new clothes, and vacations never entered into it. It was *the individuality of the individual* that mattered the most. He would tell her, he would insist on it, and drill it into her. Her opinion of him wouldn't count, because he carried the truth in his heart.

Everyone in The Sick Joke Cafe had groomed themselves into an unconscious flock during a called-off mating season. All the males wore the same clothes as Chitchee: black or blue jeans, black sneakers, flannel shirttails out, black T shirts, beards, and boxy glasses.

"Look at all those hipsters in black caps, black jeans, flannels . . . geez," Chitchee said aloud to himself. "It's like listening to a guy talk to himself. At least I'm unique, wearing my fishing hat."

"Hello," said Alex, "I'll be your server for the first half of your dining experience. Here's your folding chair and you can sit anywhere."

"Do I need to check in my fishing pole?"

"No, you can keep that," said Alex in *his* black knit cap, slunk back on his head like a snood (bringing to mind a giant black slug eating his skull), black jeans, black high tops, fluorescent shoelaces, and a black T-shirt with a white orc from Warcraft (for accent).

"Hey, Alex," asked Chitchee, "have you heard anything about an explosion near McDonald's Uptown? Like a gas main exploded? Or a suicide bomber wanting to end all possible happy meals blew himself up? Or anything about the explosion in Uptown?"

Maybe the whole wanted-for-murder thing would blow over. He could hide in The Sick Joke Cafe safely. No TV either.

"No," said Alex casually, "but I always figured no one would bomb that McDonald's because the whole neighborhood hangs out there."

"Yeah, that would be like bombing People's Park," said Chitchee. "Oh, thank you God, I feel better already! I can hide in here."

"'s up?" asked Alex, bringing in a more professional tone.

"Okay, I'm expecting," said Chitchee.

"Oh, that is so cool!" said Alex. "Do you know when you are due?"

"Soon!" said Chitchee. "She'll probably have an iPod, and she'll be listening to jazz and possibly be-bop, Bird . . ."

Alex's smile fell like an oak leaf, absorbed by its own shadow.

" . . . tattoo on her sleeve of a carp, tattoo on her chest of something red like blood or roses or bloody roses. I don't know if she might have piercings, she wears high tops and crazy sneakers. Eye color? I don't think I've even looked in her eyes as yet. I'm a shoe gazer, but I was looking at *her* shoes, not mine. Not that—" said Chitchee, gazing at his own worn-out Reeboks. "To tell you the truth, I don't know what she looks like."

"That's okay," said Alex. "I'll keep an eye out for her anyway."

"Wait . . ." said Alex, ". . . is her hair lopsided? Or high and tight? Dreads? Do you think she tints her hair mauve, teal, or chartreuse?"

Chitchee googled the room. He gave Dagny a "reminder call." She picked up. Chitchee heard a whistling sound when she inhaled smoke like a faulty intake valve.

The young women—incredibly varied in dress, creatively dazzling in bohemian combinations—blinded Chitchee by their palette of chromes and accented accessories; but the men, the men were almost all bell-curved at no more than about thirty years old and sported beards (thick, scraggly, knee-length, floor length). Some sported waxed-tip mustaches that ended in shiny, lead pencil points. Some antediluvian fossils had braided soup strainers tied to their goatees. Some teens had whispers of a few teensy-weensy chin hairs. And each guy sat transfixed in front of a sleek chrome MacBook and made Kombucha-inspired beats. A similar expression grew on all the guys' lumber-jacked, fixed-gear faces, faces expressing tinctures of dejection. They had discovered the carrots in their salad hadn't been sliced with the right brand of mandoline. Maybe they were unable to name a feature film nobody had heard of. Maybe being a Gourmand Gandhi (dressing poor, eating rich) wasn't all that it was cracked up to be?

"Is there a dress code for men?" asked Chitchee, covering up his clean-shaven chin with his elbow.

"Not officially," said Alex, with consolation, while rooting in the lost and found box, "but usually we prefer the men to have facial hair . . . and we do have some fake beards."

"Can I get one?" inquired Chitchee, looking into the box. "Preferably a strap-on beard along the lines of a Biblical dwarf (were there any?). Ginger, if you have it."

When Chitchee affixed a long red beard to the lower half of his face, Dagny entered The Sick Joke.

Chitchee inhaled rose petals or shampoo that had been scented for gardenias, or bergamot, or angelica, or some other scent he had no idea about.

"What smells so good?" asked Chitchee. "I hear a 'choir of carousels.' Is that Herbal Essences? That's a Proctor & Gamble product and they funded the Institute for Advanced Study at Princeton."

Chitchee pecked her on the cheek (must be musk on that mask), but she parried with her forearm and a disgruntled half-smile fell from her. Her good spirit flew off like a startled heron.

"Let's sit down and order," she said, adjusting to the half-flap, "and eat food. And then I have some reading to do. How embarrassing. You show up stoned for a first date? What are you on?"

"Wait up," said Chitchee, carrying his folding chair and fishing pole behind Dagny and her folding chair, while Dagny looked for an open table.

"I really blew that marriage of mine," said Chitchee to Dagny's back and neck. "I ended up preferring me and my friends to my wife and her friends, especially after she blew up at me for double-bagging the groceries. She found it sooooo difficult to separate the two bags later, she said—*that* drove her crazy. That bad Seinfeld episode was a poison thorn between us for years. It seems funny now though."

"That's nice."

"I double bag everything. And a bag without handles is not even a true bag. Are you a double bagger? Dagny? Hello? There's an open table over where that crew of musical lumberjacks is plagiarizing by themselves."

Dagny and Chitchee plonked down at a picnic table—another awkwardly-bored, married couple whose marriage had been drawn from ice to isolation.

Chitchee kick-started their meet up with cold-pressed waters in recycled spaghetti sauce jars—Prego jar for Chitchee, Ragu jar for Dagny.

"So, what do *you* believe in?" asked Chitchee. "You go first."

A silence sprouted like unwanted hair.

"What?" asked Dagny, looking around. "What do you mean? Believe in?"

"God?" asked Chitchee, looking at the menu. "What if suddenly all the books in the world were blank? Have you ever wondered whether the universe was somehow secretly connected, Bell's theorem and all, wired in a way we can't comprehend with our limited five senses, our limited four dimensions, our Wasabi To Die For. That sounds heroic. The Quinoa Reeves, The Nothing To Kefir But Kefir Itself—it all sounds DELISH!"

"The Nothing To Kefir But Kefir Itself is the bomb," said Alex, drily distant, sensing Chitchee and Dagny were not breeding.

"What's the narrative on the bacon?" asked Chitchee with an academic air, adjusting his eyeglasses under his fishing hat.

"The bacon is thick slab, and it is awesome AF!" said Alex alertly. "I've heard some alternate discourses that it's wack, but generally the customers say it's a-m-*A-A-A*-zing!"

"What comes in your steamed buns?" murmured Dagny.

The room fell silent. Somebody snorted. Cell phones flew out of backpacks.

"What? Did I say something funny?" asked Dagny, looking around hurriedly over each shoulder.

"N-n-n-nnn-o!" said Alex and Chitchee overlapping.

Dagny threw her cardboard and magic-marker menu down.

"You have borscht?" said Dagny.

"The borscht is hip, if only because it is made of beets," said Alex.

"How's the basmati?" asked Dagny and sneezed.

"I bet it's Sikh!" laughed Chitchee. "Is the eggplant legit?"

"It's dope," laughed Alex. "I've got a GIF of it on my phone. I'll run back to the kitchen—"

"—that's okay! Is the cactus salad lazy or tasty? I don't mean to needle!"

Dagny laid down her menu, with a look of folding in a card game.

"Punning seems to be the meme here!" said Chitchee.

"What *is* a meme?" said Dagny.

The room froze and fell silent as snow. Cell phones perched like texting blackbirds. Already Dagny's remark was on someone's Facebook update, ending with "Can you believe it?" And ten Likes.

"What isn't a meme?" asked Chitchee, standing up and addressing the subdued communal room.

The Sick Jokesters and other *habitués* thought for a second, gave Chitchee the proper hipster Bad Housekeeping Seal of Approval, and returned to walking their beats on their MacBooks.

Dagny produced her Carousel cigarettes whose box version she placed on the picnic table as a reminder to herself to have a smoke as soon as possible.

"Carousels, those are good, aren't they?" asked Chitchee.

"I don't know," said Dagny.

"Come on, man," said Chitchee. "You must know! You smoke so much that I can hear your smoking on the phone even when you're not smoking."

"You cannot," said Dagny and sneezed.

"Cold pressed water in a recycled Ragu spaghetti sauce jar for you and cold pressed water in a Prego spaghetti sauce jar for you, and here are your eggplants."

"Oh, you changed!" said Chitchee.

"Yes, I prefer to be called 'Alice' until closing time," said Alice, setting down a plastic basket of bread. "And here are your non-gender rolls."

"Which do you prefer," asked Chitchee, "he, she, they, or y'all?"

"He is fine!" said Alice. "I don't want to be difficult."

Do you prefer 'guy' or 'gal?'"

"I'll go with 'guy,'" said Alice.

"Sounds good!" said Chitchee, making notes in a notepad. "And along with that, do you want to have a sex change, no change, or continue to cross dress with a name change or without a name change?"

"Hmmm . . ." said Alice. "I think I want the *no sex change* but *with* the name change—and a glass of water! All this chatting!"

"Here," said Chitchee. "Have mine! So Alice, tell me, what have you done with your life up to this point?"

"Well, I drank a glass of water," said Alice. "I'll process that and get back to you dude."

Alice wore a rayon, red-on-black blouse, buttoned down the middle by bakelite buttons, the blouse fitting nicely over a tartan kilty dress. He had black and pink hair, wore pink lip gloss, and eyelined his eyes like an Egyptian temple cat. Chitchee looked surprised (pleasantly), and he complimented Alice on his gold earrings—tiny gold wind chimes, which re-tinkled tintinnabulations from an Arvo Part piece for porcelain tea cups.

"This place is so cool," said Dagny.

"Yeah," said Chitchee, "nice place to go to get away from *The Great Womble Hunt*."

Dagny didn't so much *smile* at Alice as she "quoted" a smile for Alice; her smile was a "quotation" of a smile for a smile.

"You two have been so ni-i-i-ce . . ." said Alice, "you should come see my band Pepsi Beaucoup. Well, it's not my band. It's really Mono's band. Do you know Mono Boondalicks? Rock aesthetician for *The Daily Beehive*? He's a local influencer. He's in the band but doesn't sing, play an instrument, or write lyrics. He doesn't contribute anything. Except lectures. And we have a lot of ex-members from Krab Z n T, Lil DJ T-Bop, and Crapping Kangaroo coming and going."

"What kind of music?" asked Dagny. "I need some new music. I'm sick of jazz. It doesn't grab me anymore. I need a human voice to touch my soul. Like Billie or Nina."

"Mono describes Pepsi Beaucoup as 'immanent rock.' Trance, post retro, proto dubstep, symbolist, skeletal metal, genre neutral," said Alice. "Sort of like Stickleback Cupcake or Fanzy Thangs Lost in a Hurry—if you're familiar with their work?"

"It sounds as if Pepsi Beaucoup," said Chitchee, "is a combination of Cocteau Twins, Fugazi, Liz Phair, Dead Can Dance, Talk Talk, and St. Vincent."

"What are you talking about, Chitchee?" asked Dagny from a register lower down in her throat, about ready to choke on phlegm. "You don't know what you are talking about! You're pulling band names out of your ass to pose as a hipster."

"I'm trying to be helpful!" said Chitchee, a confused look on his face like a skunk quietly shitting carpet tacks.

"Anyway," said Dagny. "I know Crumb from Stickleback Cupcake. And Ice Z Fl*y Spec from Fanzy Thangs. Where are you playing?" asked Dagny.

Chitchee pouted a pale pink rainbow.

"Club Miami," said Alice. "You two should go! Both of you should go!"

"We just got here!" said Chitchee.

Dagny growled. Her face registered a suppressed hostility.

"Ugh, I can't!" said Dagny.

"Yes!" said Chitchee.

"I quit there," continued Dagny over Chitchee. "I used to work there. Make sure you get paid in real money, not swag, up front!"

"You don't get paid?" asked Alice.

"He pays by percentage of the door, so he will give you the knob and keep the door. Viktor is a Nazi rat," said Dagny, half-twisting the words, shamed by their mere enunciation. "The life of that greaseball is the life of a fascist rat in the Year of the Greaseball Fascist Rat. He owes me two weeks pay. He asked me to meet him at Ruby Tuesday's parking lot in Southdale, and he would pay me in gold coins. Pieces of eight he called them. And then he promised me a notarized map of the buried pieces-of-eight on Boom Island."

"Here are two free comps for Pepsi Beaucoup. If you guys can't make it, I can go get you my complimentary CD," said Alice, stroking his long hair with a claw-hammered hand and combing fingers. "It's called: *Can't Wait To Drop You Like An Atom Bomb*. I know that sounds negativelandish, but actually it sounds more like early Sonic Youth or late Love Monkeys or even posthumous Love Monkeys I guess you could say. You know? The band that committed suicide together by jumping out a window in London and at the same time? Oh, and we'll press vinyl soon and 100 wax cylinder copies. Then South by Southwest in Austin next summer."

"That sounds great," said Dagny, who seemed farther away as Alice walked farther away. "I used to go out with his son, Nestor."

Dagny wound a strand of her luxurious hair around her little finger, tapped the ends of the strands, thrust her hair back to forget about it, and sealed that hair with a birch bark barrette (chopstick through it), which put her hair up.

"What?" said Chitchee, leaning forward. "Nestor's seeing my ex."

"Nestor? Shut up!" she almost laughed but censored herself. She sneezed. "The manager at Club Miami? Nestor got so mad at me because I couldn't hit the bull's eye at Bill's Gun Range. He's into his music. His music bores me. It's like sterile metal. Besides, he's distantly related."

Dagny's cell phone mumbled. Dagny scooped up her Carousels and walked outside to smoke on the phone. Sadly she walked back, sat down, sneezed, and said that Club Miami called. Her last back pay from Club Miami had been located and was ready for pick up.

"You keep sneezing, do you have allergies?" asked Chitchee. "Are you okay?"

"I have one allergy," said Dagny. "Acorns. Yeah, it's kind of weird."

"Acorns? You're allergic to acorns?" asked Chitchee. "Are you serious? You're seriously kidding! You mean I'm never going to have another relationship? Is that what you are saying? That's it? My elevator speeches keep going to the 13th floor. I can't give up acorns. Can you wear an inhaler? All the time for the rest of your life? We don't got this, girl! Just when the Ecstasy was kicking in? I don't want to be alone for the rest of my life, do you? Or you? Or you? Or you?"

Chitchee stood up and addressed the rooms:

"Raise your hand if you prefer to neither love nor be loved unconditionally," cried Chitchee. "You see? For the sake of Allah, don't jilt me Dagny!"

"Is there a bathroom?" asked Dagny and excused herself—if she had to smell her way there. "I have to blow my nose on some Kleenex—and then throw up."

"Okay," said Chitchee, "I'll stay here and guard the food."

When Dagny returned, she had set her mind on leaving, packing up, and paying quickly. Chitchee grabbed the fishing pole, held on to his fishing hat, ran out the door, and yelled:

"Hey! Who do you think you're *not* talking to?"

"Well, that was nice," said Dagny, fast walking so that her elbows were in his face. "It's nice to be able to talk to someone who has some individuality."

"You noticed!" said Chitchee.

"Of course," said Dagny, smoking, clearing her throat from smoke, and clinging to her cigarette like it was a dying raft, "not many people have the courage to cross dress like Alex."

Viktor had asked to meet Dagny at Southdale Mall in his white Dodge van in the parking lot designated "PIGEON." He promised to take her to his ATM and withdraw her cash from the ATM at the Mall. Would Dagny be interested in Prince's first Casio? Which Prince gave Viktor on his birthday—not Viktor's birthday, but *Prince's* birthday! Did Dagny know that Viktor went to high school with Prince's mother and dated her before she met Prince's father John? Viktor used to take John for spins around Lake Minnetonka and talk to him about making a movie about John's son who would make bank. According to Viktor, Viktor was famous in *Crawdaddy* for convincing Prince to drop basketball and pursue music instead. It was quite the hard sell. And yet Dagny expected to be bludgeoned to death by Viktor not only in the Southdale Mall parking lot, but also in the Ridgedale Mall parking lot for good measure. To feel safer, she asked Chitchee to escort her to Club Miami, to walk her Uptown, and to help her collect her back pay in the form of something called money from Viktor at Club Miami.

"What makes you think Viktor will kill you?" following Dagny, Chitchee yelped.

"What makes you think he won't?" asked Dagny, elbow in Chitchee's face.

Now that Chitchee was in love with Dagny, what did he care about anything, much less an Uptown tangled, torn, and smoking from smithereens of shattered glass, contorted aluminum, chrome, iron, smashed engine block, and spare parts hanging from the clouds. DeZign, the epicenter, was a tabula rasa—struck by a meteor, looking like Vonnegut's Dresden. A St. Bernard had been seen flying backwards. On Lagoon Avenue, they saw fire hoses worm down the block. Traffic lights blinked and/or blanked. Utility poles leaned dangerously, stretched to their limits, and a transformer broke off, crashed, and sparked hysterically. Chunks of vomited pavement forked out of the intersection. The bus shelter that barreled into DeZign had flattened the customers exiting onto stretchers. McDonald's fallen arches lay flat in the intersection. Dale the Raging Librarian stood in front of Walker Public Library, disappointed because he had expected *more* damage, given the enormity of the explosion, and concluded he was looking at a mere scratch, compared with jungles he had fought in.

". . . Skip Skipperton here . . . an explosion in Uptown Minneapolis occurred just hours ago . . . perpetrators of this horrible act of mayhem . . . we don't . . . it's kind of chaotic . . . all we have are first reports . . . police had been saying they were looking for a male suspect in a red flannel shirt and black wool beanie but now they are saying he is no longer a suspect and that a woman in a hijab seen near the scene was acting suspiciously and is wanted for questioning. They will release a video of her soon."

Rival news teams from WCCO, KSTP, KMSP, and KARE collided, setting up heavy equipment. Reporters descended on Lake & Hennepin, where eighteen squad cars barricaded the area, blocked off detours, and directed traffic manually. A Department of Public Safety helicopter and an unmarked helicopter floated like soap bubbles over the floating world in which Sausage Man appeared from around the corner.

"Sausage Man," said Chitchee. "What do you make of this?"

"It's all a hoax," said Sausage Man, transfused with certainty, taking back the fishing pole and hat like shaking hands. "It's what they want you to believe."

Although the 5th Precinct thumpers had cordoned off Carousel Square on Hennepin Avenue, Dagny and Chitchee entered Club Miami from the alley next to Kinko's parking lot. Structurally, Club Miami suffered not even a splinter. No one on the harried Club Miami staff knew anything about Dagny's call, nor did they care to talk to the press—all eyes had scurried across the street. Neither Viktor, nor Nestor, nor any manager was in the main office.

A new server, Clara, told Dagny to go into the main office and look around "because everything is in shambles right now." TVs at the bar, tuned to The Local Crime Channel, asserted: "so far no group like ISIS or al-Qaeda has claimed responsibility for this heinous and despicable act of cowardice."

In the main office, a rack of keys dangled on a pegboard. Enumerated and labeled white solar disks on the key chains identified which magic key led to which magic room in the pyramid.

Chitchee read "Basement" inked on a key's white solar disk and he slipped the basement key into his pocket, looking away from Dagny. She rooted around but recoiled with surprise and disgust.

"What are you doing here?" asked Nestor.

"Looking for my backpay," said Dagny. "What is it supposed to look like?"

"Who said you could be back here? Clara? She's about to get fired," said Nestor. "I'll look for it. Come back tomorrow! Are you hanging out with this Mongoloid now?"

"Yeah, why?" said Dagny, her dromedary eyelids lowered in case Nestor threw sand in her eyes. "He's not Mon-go-loid. What are you talking about? You're the Mongol."

"He works in the failing book store next door," said Nestor. "How smart can he be?"

"You know, Nestor, I've known you so long," said Chitchee slowly and continued quickly: "Sometimes I find your brutal truisms propaedeutic toward further instruction in respiritualizing my morale by an enantiodromiatic reversal of opposites . . ."

"All right, we'll go," said Dagny, her eyes undergoing space dilation. "I'll come back tomorrow."

Chitchee asked Dagny to wait outside Fratelloni's Ace Hardware while he shopped for Tomcat mouse traps for his apartment, because Dan the Maintenance demanded proof of the presence of a mouse, which cleverly absolved Dan of fixing the resident infestation of mice.

Once inside Fratelloni's Ace Hardware, Chitchee had a copy of the Club Miami basement key re-shaped on their lathe; in the confusion the key copier didn't notice DO NOT DUPLICATE.

"Oh, Dagny, I walked off with this office key by mistake," said Chitchee in an innocently sweet light when she was smoking outside. "Could you bring it back tomorrow so no one notices?"

"I guess so," she rolled her eye-whites to the sky like water-boiling eggs. "Not that I ever want to go there."

Chitchee and Dagny walked down residential lanes to avoid the terroristic threat of Lake Street. And the neighborhood continuously updated the hue and cry on neighborhood crime watches, blaming the most visible "Mom Pants" liberals they could think of.

"McDonald's has been obliterated!" said one. "Everyone is dead. Everyone except that thyroid-eyed goofball who walks around analyzing The Hobbit for the meaning of life. He walked out of there like Buster Keaton without a scratch. He didn't notice a thing!"

"Carousel Square is on fire," said another on his front lawn. "The looting is spreading downtown. The local crime watch is reporting rioters being flown in from Mogadishu. And guess what? Obama doesn't care! He just doesn't care! I guess he hasn't evolved enough yet. He's too busy trying to start a race war!"

Minneapolis was a tinderbox, with its wood-framed duplexes doubled down every alphabetical avenue—packed together so tightly, you could reach out and shake your neighbor's hand, if your hand wasn't on fire.

"This morning I saw a suspected terrorist bike down our alley," said yet another, "and he looked like he was looking for somewhere to stick a bomb."

"Say?" asked another neighbor on her lawn. "They're saying there's a link to a Mad Bomber sighting at The Tin Fish on Lake Calhoun, which was connected to a drug deal, which was connected to a Vice Lords' gangster initiation involving a doxxed false

911 and a dyslexic, ex-Hell's Outcast confidential informant's wrong address that led to the police's taking the lives of a family of four, their dog, and a newlywed couple next door, who died of smoke inhalation in another one of those drug busts gone wrong. Although police claim they found a knife buried in the sandbox of the newlywed couple's backyard."

Chitchee stopped to talk to whoever stopped him, but Dagny in her cardinal P. F. Flyers kept flying ahead of him like he's her paparazzi.

NEW WORLD SUNRISE MASSAGE AND SPA
Licensed Masseuses, Shiatsu, Foot Rub, Appt. Only, Walk-Ins Welcome

"I'd love a good back rub," said Dagny.

"We should go up there," said Chitchee. "I've heard of this place, but I never knew where it was, because I never cared! Snorri's girlfriend works there as a receptionist, Madison. I knew there was a New World Sunrise Beauty Salon, but I didn't know there was an upstairs where they give massages! Let's see how much they are!"

"Nah! Too much money for something you can do yourself," she said.

"You mean you are ready to engage in ribaldry?"

"No," she said. "We'll have to have the talk."

Chitchee grabbed her hand. She pulled it back. He punched the buzzer.

"Hello?" asked the speaker.

"Madison?" asked Chitchee, looking up at the camera like a child who is spinning around to get dizzy from spinning. "What's going on up there? Is there a prostitution ring up there? Can I join?"

"Fuck off, Chitchee!" said Madison. "What do you want?"

"I wanted to let you know, Uptown McDonald's is no longer pimping," said Chitchee sadly. "They broke the mold when they made that McDonald's."

"Got it, thank you!" said Madison.

New World Sunrise Massage And Spa did their business in a run-down walk up, above the New World Sunrise Beauty Salon, flourishing with manicures, pedicures, and hairstylings under death clouds of toxic, chemical-smelling, automotive repair fumes in a cubist room of chrome and mirrors.

Upstairs from the beauty salon, vaguely Asiatic airport decor dotted the massage rooms with decadent, Orientalistical velvet Elvis Buddhas, potted bamboo plants, and the Chinese characters for good luck, prosperity, and filthy lucre in large gold slashes on red-walled scrolls. Paj guided the new girl Reina through the rooms (Rosamie and Luv had the dayshift off) but the problem was language. Reina had no English (she spoke Tagalog) and Daisy Vang hammered out a high-strung, nervous Hmong—about something that had happened and might happen again.

Reina was pleased to smile along with Daisy as long as Daisy was pleased.

"Snorri has been talking about suicide!" said Madison, checking her maquillage for miscues. "He's worried to death about losing his job."

"That awful," said Daisy Vang. "You poor thing, yeah, I know how you feel. I hate when men make threats of suicide like that. It can really bum a girl out. Dump him. You don't need a boyfriend like that! He must be a bummer."

Daisy stroked Madison's platinum hair.

"But I love him," said Madison. "He thinks too much, that's all. And he's cute as the devil with a big dick."

Snorri confronted Chitchee and Dagny leaving the New World Sunrise Massage And Spa foyer. Snorri shifted his weight from foot to foot and blocked their possible departure.

"Aloysius closed the store early," said Snorri. "He's afraid of the thumpers arresting him after curfew, as soon as there is a curfew."

"The thumpers?" asked Dagny, chewing on a licorice-twisted strand of hair.

"Martial law," said Snorri, brushing Dagny aside with his eyes. He took a deep breath. "It's on the way. Rumor has it that a Saudi national hijacked a helicopter from Flying Cloud Airport and flew it straight into Victoria's Secret. No one knows for sure what the hell is going on."

Snorri anxiously wiped the sweat off his palms on his jeans and threw back his dreadlocks and their extensions.

"The right wing channels," he continued, "are *predicting* more Saudi terrorists flying head over heels into giant brassieres. Sexually-repressed Wasabis no doubt. Pissed at the world and the world's underwear. And who benefits? Dick Cheney and the Texas War Machine. And who benefits the terrorists? Dick Cheney and the Texas War Machine."

"Yeah, I think I heard about those giant brassieres getting busted. What next," said Chitchee. "But the version I got was that a Tamil Tiger drove a Galactic Pizza electric car into the Lake Harriet Bandshell when he fell asleep at the wheel during a *Prairie Home Companion* rebroadcast from 1997."

"Okay, fine," said Snorri. "Do you take anything seriously? This is deadly serious. The U. S. is under attack by terrorists, but the terrorists are *US*."

"Snorri, brother, I'm telling you," said Chitchee, "us is all we have."

"Didn't you hear Solomon? Civilization has collapsed," nodded Snorri, "and you seem to think it's just another P. G. Wodehouse and all you can talk about is Bertie Wooster and Gussie Fink-Nottle and Aunt Agatha—well, Jeeves of course. There is the whole *Psmith* series. Have you read those? No? Mr. Blandings—I have to admit for Gestapo, Woadhouse was pretty funny."

"Snorri," said Chitchee, "for a guy so obsessed with security, why are you so insecure? You are security. Whatever happened to you in the past is dust in the bin. But you have to get over this obsession with getting fired. We all get fired someday. We all love you, you know that. You can work in my book store. You'll never suffer for lack of work. I have greater aspirations than appears here."

Snorri was touched in the heart and felt he should hug Chitchee, but he was forestalled by Chitchee, who had thrown himself at Snorri and clasped him.

"Even Aloysius loves you," continued Chitchee, overflowing with love for his fellow man—the mammal whose candle-eyes are fired by their own mortality.

"Come on, man—that's enough love for now," said Snorri grimly moved. "Blech!"

He pressed the buzzer on the intercom. "Madison?"

Snorri vibrated and swam away up the stairs in his blue jean cut-offs.

Dagny sneezed. And sneezed again.

"Bless you," said Chitchee, "unless you are coming down with something—you don't need positive reinforcement for catching colds. "

He touched Dagny's hand to hold, which she swatted away like a cloud of nits as they walked back to her place. They strolled far apart through an empty parking lot, where the wind was sweeping aside the litter.

"Oh, Dagny," said Chitchee, "those fallen oak leaves, like young children chasing each other, oh the delight of being a child again. I have to chase those oak leaves!"

They necked on Dagny's couch, but their lovemaking broke off.

"Don't go there," she said when she felt his hands.

"*Come here, woman!*" said Chitchee. "*I'll catch you by your heaven-sent ass! You're in my hypnotic power!*"

She pushed him away.

"I'm not particularly attracted to you."

"To tell you the truth, I'm not particularly attracted to me either."

"What?" asked Dagny.

"I won't do you no harm, easy sweets," said Chitchee. "But I want *to kiss you all over you, inside and out, everything and anywhere.*"

"Huh? Wait a minute."

"We can make pancakes instead," said Chitchee, wiping a tear from his lower lid caught in his wetted eyelashes. "Baby, I can wait—you're so beautiful. Do you know anything about bonobos? Geese, swans, eagles, geese, and beaver mate for life. I *think* beaver. Did I say something? Baboons, bats, and kings have exclusive harems. Bonobos don't give a fuck—they give a lot of fucks—five times a day—all-over-the-map giving fucks."

Chitchee opened Dagny's refrigerator door.

"Do you have any blueberries? I love those little things with passionate abandon."

Then the cupboards, one after the other.

"Where is the maple syrup around this joint?" he asked.

With a great deal of gnashing and exertion, Chitchee opened a fresh bag of Old Dutch tortilla chips. He spread peanut butter on a home slice, layered Old Dutch tortilla chips over the peanut butter, and clamped home slice #2 over the embedded Old Dutch tortilla chips. When he chewed, the Dutch chips flew from his mouth to the floor.

"Then there are the hygiene issues," added Dagny.

"I've balled a lot of chicks," said Chitchee, "but I don't got the drip or the herp. I guess *lovers have to be con artists . . . to convince each other . . . love can exist.*"

"Where are you getting this dialogue?" asked Dagny. "What are you up to? You're weirding me out."

"I ain't up to nothing, darling," said Chitchee. "But you make me holler, wow whee! *Darling, I'm so tired of this stupid, faithless existence. Tell me the truth, tell me why you're here, tell me everything you are.*"

"What are you on?" asked Dagny.

"I thought we were going to have 'the talk' about sex," said Chitchee. "The libido is so strong, they could have made it a little weaker, for our sake!"

When Madison watched on closed circuit TV her Snorri bulldozing up the steps, she felt conscious of her piercings: tongue, lips, earlobes, eyebrows, and nose.

"Oh, here he is now! Shhh . . ." said Madison to Daisy.

When Madison buzzed in Snorri, Sausage Man, fishing hatted and poled, stepped out of a heavily-scented back room and into the lobby where he coughed up patchouli particles as thick as dust in a flour mill.

"Thank you, have the nicest day!" said Daisy.

"Ja ja ja, hee haw, oink oink oink!" said Sausage Man choking, passing a face-stiffened Snorri struggling on the stairs. "Hee haw! I'm going to have the *daisiest* day, Madame!"

"That was weird," said Pakpao, walking out of the back rooms. "That man asked me a lot of personal questions, but didn't want to be touched."

"Some men are like that . . . soft and lonely," said Daisy. "Next time he show up in French maid's outfit. You see."

Reina formed a heart out of tea leaves by the tea machine and smiled happily.

Snorri grunted disgruntledly and worked his way up the stairway to Madison. He walked into the parlor's parlor and looked like a caribou stag whose thick neck upheld a glass-eyed, mounted-on-paneling stare at Madison.

"I didn't interrupt anything, did I?" asked Snorri. "You didn't *do* Sausage Man, did you?"

"*THAT* guy that just left?" said Madison. "Why would you even think that?"

"I'm a jealous guy is why. Who's the new girl? Anyhoo, I better start looking for a job. BookSmart is belly up," said Snorri with a feverish, fitful paranoia so that when he heard the buzzer, he shook. He looked around again.

"Aloysius is completely *non compost mentis,*" continued Snorri. "He wants to sell lemonade at the front counter. He can't function anymore! It's depressing and I can't sleep anymore under these conditions . . . I feel like death on four wheels . . ."

"Oh," said Daisy. "I'm sorry for your boss."

"He has to step down from his command, Daisy," said Snorri, "and let Noel run the show. I'm telling you right now, BookSmart—it's like "The Charge of the Light Brigade"—if you know your history of the Crimean Peninsular Campaigns."

"And we don't," snapped Madison.

"Can I fill out an application?" asked Snorri, anxiety oozing out of the pores of the Norseman's athletic body at the thought of fishing around for a new job.

Shocked, the whole room adjusted in silence to the purport of this statement.

"I didn't want to say it aloud, but cripes," continued Snorri, ignoring his own previous remark, "I'll tell you what it's really like. Thermopylae. Spartans sitting there brushing their hair—Xerxes's army like thunder over yonder and—"

Closed circuit cameras revealed a small head, a big nose attached to it, and the legs of a fly. Daisy and Pakpao looked over Madison's shoulder.

"Can I help you?" said Madison over the intercom.

"Cocoa, cookie, bus," said the tiny figure.

"Figures," said Snorri. "Bobblehead."

"Free smells?" squeaked Bobblehead.

In the fish-eye lens, a wall-eyed Bobblehead's nose bloomed from the fusiform face area.

"What-t-t-t-? I think you want Jimmy Johns!" said Madison. "If you like patriarchal, union-busting, scab-covered, fascist sandwiches."

"Cocoa, cookie, bus," repeated Bobblehead, rubbing his nose with the palm of his hand.

"Bobblehead?" added Madison. "Katreena doesn't work here anymore. She went back to school to finish her degree in Economics. We have Reina for massages now."

Viktor Martensen picked up Bobblehead and chucked him into a parking meter cop writing out a ticket, who, stunned at the audacity—connived to keep his job by looking for a candy bar.

Viktor laughed, eyes spasms of delight beaming at his business associate Izzet "Izzy" Mutulugulu.

Izzy, as wing man, was a Turkish Hulk underneath his black leather Burberry while standing in pointed Oxford Fluevogs and sporting a black LaCoste golf shirt. Izzy's once gaunt face had bloviated into a peach-tinted dirigible: for the eyes, two dashes and for the mouth a long double dash. His body weight itself expressed a protest against confinement of any kind—never mind all the skulls, bones, grim reapers, coffins, bleeding arrows, and stabbed hearts like warning labels on rat poison, which decorated his flesh with endless death trips.

His immanence rippled out in waves from a body gone to suet.

"It's goddamn me," said Viktor. "Viktor, and I think you know what I'm here for. Open up this damn door! I paid for this door! This is my door! Goddamn bitches! Buzz me in or I'm going to bust down this door!"

Snorri crouched behind an aquarium; so his severed head, like a Chinese inkstone, became part of the fish tank. Looking around the waiting room of tranquilized fish in fish tanks that glowed green with algae, his saccading eye movements behind the toy fish (*Crossocheilus oblongus*) did not blend in well. But Viktor and Izzy walked past Snorri, who looked like a submerged *fu* dog with his bronze jaw in a grimacing smile open.

"If anybody asks you, Daisy," said Viktor, looking shaken and walking toward the back rooms with Izzy. "I've been here all day."

Snorri tippy-toed out the door and down the steps discreetly.

"Except I went out to a verifiable food shelf," continued Viktor, "when I heard the news that McDonald's had been looted by fucking Somalians—Nigerians—Mexicans—all of them combined—what's the difference? I raced back here to protect my business interests. Where is Katreena? I've got a score to settle with her."

"She quit," said Daisy. "Remember? She went back to school to study Economics."

"Oh," said Viktor, licking his glistening lips, "so now you are going to roll out the big fat three syllable words on me! She's uneducable, uneducatable, uneducationable—she's black! Blacks don't study Economics!"

"And she wants *me* to get my credits together and go back to MCTC," said Madison, "or enroll at the Aveda Institute to better my mind. Maybe even Environmental Science."

"That is one ugly fucking aquarium, I noticed it on the way in," said Viktor. "What mind? Never mind!"

Viktor reached inside his coat, withdrew a compact, snub-nosed Glock, fired at the aquarium, which inundated the lobby with gallons of water and goldfish.

"Then I guess it's Katreena's lucky day!" giggled Viktor. "Tell her I'm looking for her!"

Aloysius drove home early in his Trailblazer, his car payments tending to drive him off the road with distraction.

Feeling smaller than a skinned flea and wondering why his daughter Aubrey never called him back about Viktor's book, *Quantum Biscuits*, Aloysius snapped open a cold Grain Belt Premium beer, placed it back in the fridge, and couldn't find it later. Aubrey was probably with a boyfriend, about time, of course. Aloysius's eyes lowered to half-mast, eyelids fluttering. He drifted: she probably found a nice enough guy—great, if he likes the Allman Brothers; okay, if he doesn't. Vietnam was one really bad version of Woodstock. And you would have thought Gregg Allman shot himself in the foot when he shot himself in the foot, but he didn't. Another two drum solos. Aloysius was exhausted forever.

Aloysius jerked awake, skydogging at the wheel of his Trailblazer, dreaming his drum solo. He reached for the Grain Belt Premium. Fully awake he stumbled into his grimly, unclean fridge, extracted a cold Hamm's beer, returned, flipped the can open, flopped down, and dozed off again to the soft strains of breaking news—a car bomb detonated in Beirut. He woke up again sprawled, watching Season 14, Episode 11 of PBS's *This Old Body* and then woke up in the middle of Episode 14 of Ken Burns's 24-hour documentary *Mom's Apple Pie, The Lattice Pie Crust*.

"Listen up, you hippie faggot, where is my book? *Quantum Vision*? I need you to borrow me your car, and I want Aubrey's number so I can give her something," Aloysius heard in his dreams. "I'll be moving some more things into your basement, and if anybody touches anything, they motherfuckin' die. I'll torch them like when we lit cats on fire when we was kids playing with gasoline on the driveway."

"How do I pay my employees?" Aloysius remembered saying, "even minimum wage, which is what?"

"Which is too high and socialist. Pay them in cockroaches, I could care less. I hear Minneapolis has a lot of cockroaches, but they were here before I got here! Here's the thing: Forget the back rent. I'm giving you free rent. And I'm paying your rent. I'm putting Aubrey through four years at St. Awful college! I'd like to meet her. And you protect the basement with your life. Make sure nobody goes down there. Nobody but me, the cops, and the Club Miami workers. Got that, mallard head?"

"St. Olaf's," mumbled Aloysius. "The tuition and fees are way overdue now. I'm two months behind on my townhouse and car payments and my credit cards are maxed."

"Whaaaaa-a-a-a-t?" asked Viktor. "I'll pay you, don't worry. *You* and all your long-haired butt buddies at the book store. Look, all I have to do is write the check. Don't worry, Aubrey won't be kicked out of the sorority house. Is she good looking? I might be able to hook her up at Sunrise. She could be sitting on a gold mine."

Sitting bolt upright, Aloysius looked shocked, bitten by a baby moray eel (gulp). Aloysius didn't recall closing his eyes. But when he did nod off, a spider happened to catch the opportunity to weave a winter-wide web from the wall to the side of Aloysius's left cheek. The Doors, they weren't a band, they were a band's banned band hallucinating being a band. And then another web appeared over the cave of his mouth to catch the tiny white moths falling in. Aloysius walked to the bathroom and splashed cold water on his face, thinking he was now awake enough to go to bed. Lily Holmgren's phone number fell out of his shirt pocket onto the floor, and he kicked it under the bed; he floundered in bed, position after position like a plastic, sliding 15-number slide puzzle for children. He marched back to the living room couch, sipped a warm Hamm's, and watched a ham-faced Tony Robbins infomercial crawl by at worm speed on TV. Aloysius was dreaming of an old-fashioned, tin ice-cube tray with a definite clamp. Aloysius pulled up on the clamp, and all the teeth fell out of Tony Robbins mouth, and those sparkling teeth, as he interpreted it, were inspired by the cold water Aloysius had splashed on his dry face.

"Three things will get you killed: sleeping with my wife, stealing one of my Porsches, and anything else that happens to cross my mind, slave!"

Aloysius recalled thrashing in the middle of the night. Maybe he dreamed it. What has Viktor said that he hasn't said before?

Aloysius thought: did I hear him right? There was a murder in Uptown, right outside BookSmart? No way. Are we out of bookmarks? No way, because that way is way in the way of the way, wa-a-a-ay!

ASSOCIATED CLINIC OF PSYCHIATRY

In the waiting room of the Associated Clinic of Psychiatry, Noel Schoolcraft read an old, aging, wrinkled *People* magazine about the Hollywood starlet, the Minnesota-born Samantha Airedale, who had opened up about her suicidal depression, drug addiction, and locked-in-the-bathroom syndrome in her best-selling memoir, *I'm Never Growing Up*, soon to be a major motion picture with a budget of $12 million produced by Lionsgate Films, but Noel could not connect to her variety of depression, her heartbreaking addiction to codeine, and her locked-in-the-bathroom syndrome, which tragically curtailed a good many possible relationships, especially with some well-known stars in the industry. But when her co-star and ex-boyfriend, Dustin Duesenberg, of *Why Grow Up?*, stole her gerbil and when ransomware appeared on her MacBook Pro demanding $372,000 for the gerbil . . . it was a big deal in Hollywood circles.

Depression for Noel, he traced to: BookSmart's failure to thrive, the dumbing down of NetFlix, social media narcissism, the death of the Gracchi, the rise of Caesaropapism, and Dick Cheney and his War Machine. *Failure* when Noel was a teenager—*that* was inconceivable. He thought depression was a nebulous, self-indulgent act used by goldbrickers to get out of *real* work. There was something dishonest about depression and he treated it suspiciously as a new ailment—especially if Samantha Airedale was making money off it, although Noel himself was a big fan of hers and had seen all her pictures.

Why wasn't the Enlightenment at work? The Enlightenment was down. Noel looked at the Enlightenment next to him—coughing, broken-hearted, unalive—faces like boiled red potatoes, emotions swallowed by whales of despair, and children blubbering or about to blub in a few seconds. Kleenex boxes waited at strategic spots. Noel felt like society's fat, chewed up, spit out, and politely evacuated to the paper plate's scalloped edge. On every table of the waiting room, was a *Mpls. St. Paul*, a monthly magazine devoted to reminding miserable, unenlightened wretches in waiting rooms how much the wealthy in their "home town" enjoyed galas, operas, and dress balls without them—the good life, the great life—*la dolce vita*. He filled out his PHQ9 strategizing possible consequences for wrong answers and dashed through it to show off to the other patients he wasn't the crazy one.

"How was *that* for a little bit of alacrity? Eh?" asked Noel rhetorically, handing in the form to the blue-toothed receptionist.

Noel sank in his chair sinking into depression. He perused an article about Spofford Larsen Dumbarton, whose *nom de plume* was Mono Boondalicks, a successful painter, art critic, and recently rock critic, who also had attended St. Louis Park High School. Mono flaunted his personal success in his Liberace vest, tuxedo, black and pink bow tie, and green tennis shoes while holding a laboratory-sized snifter in his *Architectural Digest* living room, an *Artforum* on a DeZign coffee table. Photographs of Mono's modest home on Lake Minnetonka, where the paintings of boats on his living room walls and the actual boats tied up to docks beyond his French windows matched the Dufys on his walls. Mono was also going out with Samantha Airedale. Noel sniffed and turned the page.

Looking closer at the Who's Who, Noel recognized Viktor Martensen, Lawrence Sangster, and Corcoran Skogentaub, arm in arm with various Weegee-looking socialites in the intense lighting that transformed their faces into putty. Mayor R. T. Rybak, Carl Pohlad, Yanni, some Daytons, some Cargills, and a sprinkling of Pillsburys.

Noel imagined Samantha Airedale naked, posing with a gerbil, and then he positioned her in the tittiest position possible. Her boobs were probably small, but might surprise him with their improbable hugeness, but then her long legs—when he heard:

"Noel?" asked Dr. Box toward the waiting room. "Come on in."

"The book store is dead," said Noel efficiently, "and there is nothing I can do about it. Just when something possibly good happened. Well, you probably don't want to hear about that."

"No, go right ahead, we have nineteen minutes," said Dr. Box. "If I seem uncomfortable, it's my sciatica acting up."

"I'm worried that I met a woman I like," said Noel, "but I don't think I'm financially secure enough to ask her out."

"Ask her out?" asked Dr. Box.

"Well, ask her out to a, *vis a vis,* marriage ceremony," said Noel. "Or at least a step by step non *ad hoc* process by which to attain marriage. I was thinking that a flow chart would help. You know, like, third date: go to first kiss. Third kiss, go to . . . slick, huh?"

Dr. Box stared straight ahead, forcing a smile out of a frown when he looked up from his old-fashioned clipboard.

"It's a bit of a culture clash with Ye Young. She's Korean. But I'm going to get her to watch a lot of quality American cinema, like Criterion, to acculturate her to my tastes, starting with all the Alfred Hitchcock movies, especially *The Birds* because of the obvious Minnesota connection, which we can watch together, after reading *Hitchcock / Truffaut* together, and discuss over trail mix. Who doesn't like trail mix? I hope she likes trail mix with her *kim chi*!"

"How did the Lexapro go?" asked Dr. Box, a kindly but frankly harried psychiatrist, who always was relieved to see Noel because Noel never seemed suicidal, although his scorecard on Noel of tried antidepressants displayed insignificant figures: Celexa 20 mg., Paxil 20 mg., and Zoloft 100 mg.

Noel had been ashamed to tell anyone he had been seeing a psychiatrist. He would take his meds, feel better, quit his meds, feel worse, take new meds, feel better, quit his meds, feel worse and worse, then after a month of Lexapro, which he hadn't liked, he flushed all his antidepressants down the toilet, wondering whether the residue would leach into Lake Calhoun and lift all the boats.

"Yeah, it went pretty good," thought Noel to himself in a flat monotone head voice.

Pretty good *if* you threw out the Lexapro, the long walks in Lakewood Cemetery, the drawing up of several invalid wills, the walking on the hand rail across the Washington Avenue bridge, and the male fantasy that Ye Young could save his life. If she spurned him, he imagined his emergency call to the automated suicide prevention hotline:

"*Welcome to One Two-Don't Do it! All our current representatives are currently busy. To expedite the waiting process please use the following options: If you are feeling suicidal press One. If you plan to use a gun press Two. If you plan to use a knife press Three. If you plan to jump off the Washington Avenue bridge press Four. If you plan to use all the options at the same time press Five. If you are still alive press Six. To get back to the main menu press Star.*"

"It didn't go. I quit a month into it," said Noel, "because I had some bad side effects. My uh uh uh what do you call it, libido, weak to begin with, simply evaporated! Not my libido, but all the aggregate libido in the world evaporated. Everybody had no libido. Nobody had libido. I was a cardboard widget—I quit taking the Lexapro, and then I felt really bad, really bad. I had no energy. I sat there watching *The Birds*. It didn't seem real—it was like a message from the future. I couldn't concentrate. I kept thinking: then what were the crows? The crows of allegory? The crows of Van Gogh's madness in Dr. Who's TARDIS? My mind flew with the crows. They seemed to be laughing at me: Hah! Hah! Hah! Never mind. I think I might have added ADHD to my list of woes."

Noel bungled his Lexapro withdrawal, sitting in an empty space with death rays beaming into and out of his eyes. Streams of panic over mere existence swept him up, tore him from his orbit, and flushed him into the center of our galaxy. He would have done any drug to escape that horrible morbidity. Any insane act would relieve his limitless pain—if only he could have slit his own throat with a complete set of Ginsu steak knives. He didn't want to tell his psychiatrist, because he didn't want to upset him.

"Maybe we should try Adderall," said Dr. Box, distracted by an escalator of pain going up and down his legs and back.

Sure, thought Noel, whatever Adderall *is*. Let's try them all! Out of twenty, one antidepressant should work in the next hundred years.

"Adderall? It sounds like a laundry detergent," said Noel from a vacant hollow in his heart.

Noel wanted to witness the phase trials of Big Pharma when they tested these *soi-disant* "antidepressants," so he could tell the guy in the white coat with the active ingredient not to skimp on that part of the drug. Double that, asshat, don't be a skinflint, that is the drug. What's it to you? The rest is filler. Adderall? That has 'water pill' written all over it. Another revolutionary placebo from the people who brought you Corn Chex. And then wait a month for the effects? Noel could get high with the entire BookSmart staff in a matter of minutes on marijuana. Marijuana made him paranoid though. He couldn't smoke it without seeing Dick Cheney leading a Metro Gang Strike Force and St. Paul's Sheriff Bob Robinson battering down Noel's apartment door—no warrant, no due process—smashing everything to bits that couldn't be auctioned off later and breaking Noel's ankle in a cruel twist of sadistic power, ultimately meant to prevent Noel's having children. Noel feared his hauling off to a privately-owned Panopticon Prison Compound. Sheriff Bob Robinsons guarding every cell in St. Paul . . . guarding the political prisoners and black anarchists . . . Sheriff Bob Robinsons all along the watchtowers . . . Sheriff Bob Robinson, principal shareholder in Prisons, Inc., using Noel as a Persian footstool.

"Do you have trouble concentrating?" asked Dr. Box.

Noel loved Dr. Box for the sanity of his dealing with mental illness. Dr. Box's very reasonableness was a relief. His emotional neutrality was an oasis that held fresh air and spring water for Noel, who worked with a bunch of loonies and sold books to a bunch of even bigger loonies, who was reciprocated for his good will with nothing but quarrels, arguments, and ultimatums, asking Chitchee over and over, because Noel had forgotten, why Chitchee had never seen *Groundhog Day*.

"No, yes, no, I mean I can sit in a corner and read for four or five, well, four hours anyway," said Noel, sounding like two people interrupting each other.

"Adderall is for ADHD," said Dr. Box, adjusting his spine, but not complaining about his sciatica. "But we can try it. If the SSRIs aren't working."

"But, after five hours, my concentration is pretty much shot, Dr. Box. The book store is shot. I don't know how it survives. The owner keeps it all inside. It's like he has some deep dark secret hidden way down inside. I don't know where the economy is going. My car keeps breaking down, and I have to keep borrowing my dad's Ford Focus to get to work. I can't seem to finish Caro's biography of Lyndon Johnson, *Master of the Senate*, if Caro could ever finish it. Because I'm always thinking about Ye Young. And then I sleep, but can't sleep."

"What is it you want to do?" asked Dr. Box, shifting around to appease the inflamed lumbar region in his back.

"I want to write like Steinbeck," said Noel.

"What have you written?"

"Checks."

"What about computer programming?" asked Dr. Box with his eyebrows arching.

"Computer programming? Of course, there is always computer programming. Join Pharaoh's army if you fail. There's a suggestion. That hadn't occurred to me. I'll look into it."

Noel's eyes fell out like orange pips to the floor from an orange when he realized Dr. Box did not really know him personally—to suggest that—offering the bromide of going back to school to learn computer programming. The Internet had *murdered* the book. It was the new idiot box and Noel was dead set on thinking outside it. The Internet was an insane asylum you couldn't get out of.

"I want you to start using social media, get on Facebook, Instagram, and Twitter—and make friends, because I don't think you have any. Before you go, name one friend you love."

"Chitchee Chichester."

Dr. Box laughed, "The name itself—sounds like everybody's friend."

"He'll do," said Noel, getting up slowly, "*in a pinch*!"

Noel gripped and read the new scrip, congratulating himself for his witticism, which was payback for cold Dr. Box's invalidating his soul. Why didn't the guy respond to his jokes?

"Samantha?" asked Dr. Box toward the waiting room.

Noel's eyes popped when Samantha Airedale brushed by him. Noel's heartbeat beat offbeat as he drove off in his Ford Focus to the Walgreens next to Kowalski's on Hennepin. He picked up his prescription, hopped in the car, and switched on the radio:

"Traffic is backed up from 1-94 back to the 10th Street exit, so there is decongestion all through Minneapolis."

"I could be dating Samantha Airedale," he said aloud in a hurry.

After popping two 10 milligram orange tablets, he parallel parked on the Mall, backing over the curb into a tight spot—to the applause of a ragabond vagabond mad camp of dropped jacks.

"Hey, Harry Potter!" said Mad Jack Apple Jack. "Drive much?"

Noel took the jeers in stride. It was understandable *qua* legitimate criticism. Noel was in the encampment's windshield's range of vision and one of nature's legitimate objects of thought. The area was cordoned off, he didn't know why. Actually what was Dr. Box thinking? Noel had plenty of friends from high school, although he couldn't name them aloud when put on the spot like that—that wasn't fair or equitable. Wasn't that a taunt of Socrates? You know how many cows you have, but not how many of your friends are cows? Noel hated the very idea of Facebook. Facebook was a Chitchee thing. Noel's style had to be ramped up. His research on the Internet suggested he find his own scent, buy a pint of Calvin Klein eau de parfum, use coconut hand lotions for ash, perfume his armpits with oregano body washes, line his sandals with charcoal pads, place a spring meadow sachet in his underwear, stuff eucalyptus leaves up his butt, and have Snorri apply a Roman strigil to scrape off Noel's excessive sebum or so-called body cheese.

Noel had tried to give Facebook a "Like." He added every possible Facebook friend going through kindergarten back to the womb. He surfed mindlessly on Facebook until he reached the ultimate dead end, which was always a selfie of a grown man in diapers who looked like Har Mar Superstar. Then Noel received a notice from Facebook to identify his own friends in their photos, and it was multiple choice: he had to score four out of five or his account would be suspended. Every family in Minnesota looked the same. They all had picnics. All the men at the picnics had arboreal beards. Even the picnic tables had been bought at the same Wal-Mart. Noel felt nervous, then euphoric, then antsy, then galled, then touchy, and finally shaky. He knew he had taken too much Adderall.

Was he supposed to take one twice a day or two once a day? Thrown off key, he didn't feel like radio. He forgot to KBEM all the way to work, guided by the MnDOT traffic reports, whose helicopters provided a useful and democratic public service. But nearing Uptown he sensed something wrong.

Why was the back door locked? Noel wondered. Aloysius slept his head off and overslept the whole day? Noel entered cautiously, turned off the alarm, turned on the lights, brought the till up from the basement, turned on the computer, and opened the front door hoping to take advantage of all the foot traffic. There must have been a terrible accident. It had happened before when Blue-And-White taxi cab driver in a rush killed a suburbanite in the crosswalk on her way to Club Miami.

Noel noticed the contour of a TV-dinner tray by BookSmart's front door. Hubel and Wiesel popped into his head, because Hubel and Wiesel always popped into his head whenever he noticed he had noticed something coming toward his head like a frisbee made of razors.

On the TV-dinner tray sat a red plastic frisbee with lemon sugar cookies arranged in a scalloped circle. A bent-in-half, prismatic index card read in bold black Sharpie: "SMOKING HOT LEMON SUGAR COOKIES" under which Noel saw $2.00 crossed out and $1.00 scrawled in graphite below that.

Noel toyed with writing a novel that combined all the popular themes he could think of: the Titanic, Custer's Last Stand, Jack the Ripper, baseball, and murder. Could you have a novel where the passenger list on the Titanic—through a mix up in alternate historical time travel— included George Custer, Napoleon, Jack the Ripper, Babe Ruth, the Ku Klux Klan, Salvador Allende, Rasputin, Caligula, Castaneda, *and* Washoe? Then work in the Mexican Revolution, the Bermuda Triangle, the I Ching, Cinderella, and Robert Caro? Contemplating a novel such as this, he wondered whether this plot had already been done. So many novels had already been done, in fact all of them. He went online to research (on EBSCO? JSTOR?) what's been done and undone.

"Aloysius? It's Noel at the store," said Noel into the store phone's mouthpiece rimmed with crust from someone's dried Nescafe saliva as he carried the tray of lemon sugar cookies toward the utility closet, the receiver on his shoulder like a violin.

"How are the lemon sugar cookies selling?" asked Aloysius. "Are you writing all the sales down? Oh God, I overslept. No, I didn't. I took a nap. Oh yeah, Noel. There was an explosion across the street today. I forgot to tell you I closed the store early. Take the night off! Have a good one!"

"What happened?" asked Noel, looked out the window, turned on WCCO radio, streamed CNN on the Dell, and contemplated a smartphone purchase from Target.

Noel, careful to not let Aloysius hear the locking lock sound of the closet, locked the lemon sugar cookies in the utility closet. He itched all over with an aggrieved impatience—the world spun too slowly and needed a swift kick so all the dictators would fly off. Waiting for Aloysius to call back with an answer, Noel disinfected the keyboard with the last of the Lysol, downloaded the inventory (lately alphabetized according to first names by Aloysius which Noel corrected dutifully), clipped his fingernails to the nubs, broke a sandal strap, and speed-read the day's sales.

"There was an explosion," said Aloysius, falling back to sleep.

Aloysius's dry lips licked themselves dry. He had dreamed of a Thanksgiving turkey and deserved a traditional and patriotic nap in front of a Vikings-Lions game. Wild turkeys covered the gridiron. The punter Snorri missed the punt completely. Ariel picked up the live ball and ran for an open-field touchdown, called back for holding. Wayne Fontes, the head coach, received the kick-off, ate the flubber-filled football and floated over the goal line.

"It wasn't pretty," said Verne Lindquist. "But that will put the wind back in Detroit's win column."

"Where is your section for World Literature?" asked Mono Boondalicks, startling Noel so that his glasses almost took wing on the wings of a midnight owl.

"World Explosion? What?" said Noel, adopting his professorial tone, agitated and pumping his nervous knee up and down and then the other knee.

"Hello? World Literature? Heard of it?" asked Mono. "Over here!"

"Aloysius, I have to get off the phone," said Noel, miffed and clicked off. "Do you mean *world* opposed to *regional*? It would make more sense to segregate *regional,* not *world* authors. You seem to be implying, basing your view on a kind of American exceptionalism, that *our* privileged position determines what *world* literature is."

"You're challenging me? Oh, really!" said Mono, who glowed with sunburned-looking cheeks and windswept gazes.

Mono's face, always a little mask-like, was hung with an aesthetically-chiseled expression of passionate romanticism. He wore a Byronic dress shirt with two buttons open at the top. He swiveled around in tight-as-tight, butt-tight, hip huggers to swerve with his verve. A sexually evocative soul patch throbbed under his lip. The buttonless collar of the shirt was from a different collar era, seemingly pretentious, but ironically pretentious, making meta-comments on the self-reflectivity of making pretentious comments in a decade of decline as seen in shirt collars. Mono had the perfected profile of the young Antonin Artaud and his handsome Gallic-Gallimard pose lacked only the hand-under-chin photograph of a first-time author—*auteur moi. Genial.* Mono was the song of the nightingale to many women; he was everything Noel wasn't to Samantha Airedale, and they had gone to the same high school in which they were still competing.

"Do you speak French?" asked Noel, feeling his heart pound, his face flush, and his mind race.

"No, I'm from St. Louis Park," said Mono. "What do you think?"

"Oh! Spofford Dumbarton!" said Noel. "You're in this month's *Mpls. St. Paul!*"

Mono shrugged himself above it.

Noel sniffed for Mono's intellectual weak spots.

"And the name Mono? It's——?"

"DID YOU READ THE ARTICLE?" asked Mono. "Mono refers to monophonic, which is how rock sounded in its golden age. Stereophonic is pure bullshit. That's all over-produced George Martin bullshit. That's all multi-track Beatles studio bullshit. That's not rock. Rock is raw. Raw, raw, raw. It's like football."

Mono's two-button openness distracted Noel. But Mono's non-button down, largely ironic shirt collar drove Noel to the point of crowing madness. The button-fly, hip-huggers were also complete bullshit. Mono's nightingale eyes (Noel wanted to gouge those out with a Sharpie) were that of a neo-liberal, repressively-tolerant clown. Noel labeled Mono's poetic air as that of aesthetic dung, which had dropped, hook, line, and sinker from Mono's ass, the ass of a pundit who supported the Propaganda Model of mass media.

And now he's got Samantha Airedale! Where was she? MAC? Minneapolis was a big deal if Samantha Airedale was in Minneapolis visiting Minneapolis because she was from Minneapolis!

"So what do you do nowadays besides—besides carry the right books (deBord, Lyotard, Baudrillard) around to impress the opposite sex in bars where you shout all night in a dark corner until you realize no one is there, and it's closing time? *What pretentiously illiterate band are you in now?*"

"Did you read the article? I thought you said you read the article all about me. Why are you asking me these questions? I'm in Pepsi Beaucoup, why?" asked Mono, his coals stirred to anger, a spark in his eyes conflagrating like old *StarTrib*s inside Noel.

Dragon's blood red blood cells of anger burst within Noel.

"Pepsi Beaucoup? Pepsi Beaucoup? Heard of us?"

"What I thought! Aha!" said Noel triumphantly. "Never heard of it! Thank God!"

Mushrooms of sweat mushroomed on Noel's entire racing body, a slightly hostile twitch on his right upper lip. Noel's milli-sneer was absorbed by Mono's consciousness.

"Did I detect a milli-sneer," asked Mono, "on my sneer-o-meter?"

"No," said Noel, "but check your snob-o-meter!"

Noel looked at Mono with an unformed question. His schoolboy round eyes evinced no emotion. Adderall rushed through Noel's sympathetic nervous system, epinephrine pinballs volleying up and down his spine in ricochets.

"Do you have a degree?" asked Mono.

"Of course," said Noel, trembling in his hands and voice. "I have 98.6 degrees in political science. I am a *bona fide* anarcho-syndicalist. Top that, bitch!"

Beda Holmgren carried in a paper bag of books to sell.

She dumped them on the counter without saying a word. She was trading cowries and seashells as a sales rep for the Sea People.

"Are you sure you are wearing clean underwear in case you get into an accident?" asked Mono, eye to eye, with Noel. "I'll ask you again. Try to concentrate. Where is your World Literature section?"

"Yes!" said Beda. "I stand fully 100% behind that question. I know you don't have a World Literature section. I know this store like my own backhand. And I will not argue this point. I choose not to. I stand in solidarity with this nice guy."

"WHAT THE FUCK DUMB QUESTION IS THAT? WHERE IN THE WORLD IS THERE A LITTLE SHELF LABELED 'WORLD LITERATURE' in any world book store?" yelled Noel.

Chitchee blew a high-pitched whistle from his acorn cap like a Mississippi steamboat.

Noel grabbed Chitchee's wrist and twisted it. When the acorn cap fell, Noel squashed it flat and said:

"Knock it off! That is so fucking irritating!" said Noel. "What? Are you a fucking squirrel? When are you going to grow up and quit pretending you're the honorable schoolboy?"

"But," said a hurt Chitchee, gathering up the pieces of the acorn cap, "one of the definitions of *life* is causing 'irritability.'"

"Well," said Noel, "I guess that means *you're* alive."

"Every book store I've ever been in," continued Mono, stroking his thick hair back with his palm, looking shocked, indignant, and outraged, "has a fucking section for World Literature! I was just in Elliot Bay, and they had one! Then I went to Powell's and they had two! There are book stores in the world you have never even dreamed of, sitting in your little rat-hole selling rat-holed books. I always go to the Strand, meet up with friends I know who know Phillip Roth or his work or those who know of his work and appreciate its art and we always discuss World Literature late into the night in the East Village with people like Blondie."

"How about if I took a weed whacker and mowed your head flat like an abandoned baseball field?" asked Noel.

"Why would you say that?" asked Mono. "Why would you say that? My hair is . . . my hair is my Primo Levi! *That's* who I wanted! *The Periodic Table*!"

Chitchee lurched for the trade paperback under the counter, but Noel book-blocked him.

"We don't have what you want, but you know what? I'm going to build a shelf for World Literature anyway, just for you, Mono! Even though you are the kind of neo-liberal, repressively tolerant clown who turned a blind eye to the massacres our administration condoned in our client states of El Salvador and Guatemala!"

"Maybe!" said Mono. "What the hell is a Neo-liberal, repressively-tolerant clown? Somebody in this 'book store' please tell me!"

Beda Holmgren stood patiently examining the same five paperbacks from which she had removed the bookplates with her fingernails. Grisham, Grisham, Clancy, Clancy, and one James Patterson. Minerva walked in hurriedly like a hail-storm she needed shelter from. She held her two fists up to her face, smiling and shivering, uninterested in the pontificating Chautauquas one tripped over at BookSmart when Noel worked.

"And I bet *you*, Mono, are the type who *would* be guilty of war crimes! The type of hypocrite who would be brought before a War Crimes Tribunal and hanged for hypocrisy!" said Noel.

Mono himself hail-stormed out the front door, leaving his glare behind, its after image a discarded hula hoop on a blacktopped playground.

"Why did you treat that nice gentleman like an asshole, you asshole?" asked Beda Holmgren.

"Yeah, Noel, why *are* you so fucking rude?" said Minerva. "You iced that perfectly nice, well-dressed guy. He dresses really well, you know! Does he need a seamstress?"

Noel reached for an empty plastic bottle of lanolin Snorri used for leather bindings, squeezed it out like a fart, set it down, grabbed Aloysius's Lubriderm, and moisturized his hands out of nervousness.

"Do you have an Empathy section yet?" asked Minerva. "And why not?"

Noel tucked in his tuckered-out shirt tighter.

"Don't tell me," said Minerva, "you *had* an Empathy section, but everybody ripped on it, so you had to tear it down—I've heard that one seven ways to Sunday!"

Noel offered 2 bucks for four of the paperbacks, but not the James Patterson, to Beda.

"Why didn't you want *this* James Peterson?" said Beda, sensing Noel's state of mindful concentration shattered. She might squeeze an extra quarter or two out of him because of that. "What's the difference between this James Patterson and all the other James Pattersons? Aren't they the same? Besides, I think I bought one of them here!"

"Well then, I guess you made a big mistake!" said Noel.

Beda's cheeks bloomed. She pitched the priceless, worthless Patterson at Noel's head and ran. Minerva darted after her. Beda cried outside.

Noel grabbed *Trance Formation in America*, walked outside, and showed Beda.

"Well, at least it isn't a completely worthless book store," said Beda, with a philosophical tone softening her tone. "Can you put it on hold for me?"

Gollum walked past Noel and into the book store. Gollum was a short bald man with white side tufts, blue eyes as big as snowballs, a baggy and striped shirt, baggy brown trousers, mud-puppy brown loafers, and ears sticking out like Phil Spector's.

"Do you have any more books on Stoors?" asked Gollum.

When Noel returned he saw unveiling teeth like protruding bone spurs, sharpened by diamond-studded rasps.

"Where?" asked Noel, his voice fluttering with emotion, after he had placed *Trance Formation in America* on hold for Beda.

"I've read all *The Lord of the Rings* trilogy," said Gollum, "and I want to read more about that Gollum guy. Isn't he really the hero of the sacred opus? A tragic hero! Hamlet, Oedipus, Arthur, Gollum!"

"That would be downstairs in genres," said Noel, getting on the computer.

"Where? Could you be more specific?" asked Gollum.

"Downstairs is downstairs," yelled Noel. "I'll get you directions."

Noel Google-mapped the downstairs and printed off the directions:

1) Head north through world history toward literary criticism go ten feet 2) take the first right past European history go twelve feet total twenty two feet 3) continue toward Churchill pile about five seconds 4) turn left at military history three seconds 5) continue three feet past science fiction about a second 6) now call for help because by now I'm sure you're totally lost and pissing in your pants 0 feet 7) turn around in circles finger up ass ten seconds 8) Middle-earth will be on either your right or your left total time spent thirty minutes total distance .012 mile.

"There you go," said Noel, blushing for the first time ever. "Have at it."

"Thank you, my pretty," said Gollum, snatching it greedily—and disappearing.

"You see," said Noel to himself, "pop culture is totally taking over. And it is no substitute for World Literature."

Noel had let himself down; he had lost his self-control, his prime virtue. And there was no way he could continue with Adderall. He was ashamed of himself. His rational enlightened model of himself crashed.

After work, Noel walked to his car, the Ford Focus—and was deep in thought.

Monstrous giant brown bats on the green knoll watched Noel's approach. He blinked. The hoodied bats squeaked at him and drank Blech's with long red tongues and their eyes glittered from evil eyelids.

"Hey, everybody!" said Mad Jack Barley Cake, waving his Viagra feed cap. "Harry Potter is back!"

"Where's what's-her-face?" clacked Mad Jack Apple Jack. "Did she stand you up?"

Ignoring the drunken *claque*, Noel for a second wondered why the corbeled trees had looked like gargoyles. The grass smelled like burnt hair and the sepia of stable dung.

He felt like crying a lake of waves, which was a drowned Ye Young's weeping.

"Oh I bet she '*stood*' him up!" said Mad Jack Harry Snatch, elbowing the air and hooting. "Whoever she is!"

Mad Jack Harry Snatch tore off his shirt and threw it into the bushes.

"She left him with a peckerwood," guffawed Mad Jack Barley Cake, "peck a wood, peck of Peter's wood, if Peter pecked a Potter up his ASSHOLE! You never read Harry Potter, you dumb fuck?"

Mad Jack Barley Cake tore off his Viagra feed cap and crammed it on Mad Jack Harry Snatch's head. They rolled around, revealing the round torsos of ostrich eggs, and their whiter guts with the whiter sheen of an eggshell's insides.

"No," said Mad Jack Harry Snatch, "but I got as far as Hogwarts you motherfuckin' asshole, then someone at the safe bay stole it from my locker."

Eager to avoid all confrontation, Noel jumped in the Ford Focus, assured the windows were rolled up and the doors locked.

"Hey asshole," said Mad Jack Barley, "got five bucks?"

In the rear view mirror of the wine-dark night, Noel saw the outlines of crows on power lines. He blinked.

The crows wanted money, and they were coming after him.

Noel spent a sleepless night.

Noel had offered his Adderall to Aloysius.

"Sure, Noel, I'll give it a try, it can't do much harm, can it?" asked Aloysius. "Helps you concentrate, eh? I guess we could all use a little more focus around here."

"Everybody is different," said Noel. "But can you tell me one thing?"

"Sure, buddy," said Aloysius.

"Why does the store continue to fail although the numbers are up? I do the books you know! And everyone in Minneapolis loves our book store and—I don't understand—"

"I can't say why, but from now on, you're not doing the books," said Aloysius, grim, glum, and seriously morose. "There are no more books. The book store will continue off the books. Until further notice. And tell the guys the landlord will be storing some stuff in our basement, which we are not supposed to touch or we die. That's an order! Don't question it! Less talk, more elbow geese."

"More elbow geese?" ventured Noel—timidly to be clear.

"You know what I fucking meant!" yelled Aloysius.

LAKEWOOD CEMETERY

Autumn had brushed hazel and gold over Minnesota's lakes and icy shores with its foxtails, rushes, and cattails when the Canadian geese began honking their horns, slow as pot-bellied saurians, wedges in the sky, squadrons migrating at night. Leaving behind the herringboned needles of serried evergreen, the frosted leaves had fallen, blushed, and died on the sidewalks. Auroras and trepidations of solar winds had swirled by. The nightjar's *awk awk* had echoed over the plaintive parking lots.

The air's chill presaged the pain of a deep, dead freeze.

Chitchee gazed blindly out the BookSmart window at a white Dodge van and wondered whether the game of life was a prisoner's dilemma, which said that by cooperating, both sides came out on top—unless both sides were in prison, and then they would come out on the bottom.

Chitchee closed *Theory of Games and Economic Behavior* and lifted it with two hands into the air above.

"It's over my head!" he cried. "Look, everybody! Game theory over for Messieurs Von Neumann and Morgenstern."

Chitchee danced from an overflow of pent-up energy.

Chitchee leafed through the other book he had been reading and narrating to himself: "I was at work. I looked out the window. I was reading Yukio Mishima's *Confessions of a Mask*, which is about a Japanese boy/homosexual/sadist/suicide who grows up with a taste for European religious painting in WWII Tokyo."

Wrote Mishima: "It was all the same to me whether the war was won or lost."

Mishima was working in Tokyo during Hiroshima when he wrote of the citizens on the streets of Tokyo:

". . . going about their business with cheerful faces."

Later, Mishima is *jealous* of a girl *who has fallen in love with Mishima* . . .

Chitchee danced saying, "Do you think Mishima could dance? I wish I had a block-lettered narcissism like Mishima! What nuts for a nut! I would have let Mishima fuck me up the ass even if he was a fascist prick! And then would I flip him over like a pancake and return the favor—and then we would dance in the moonlight and then—."

"You're closing early tonight, so I stopped by five minutes before the early closing!" said Raven, his face an ironic filter. "I didn't hear that! Anyway, why were the fuzz here last night?"

"Aren't the thumpers here every night? I don't know, I didn't work last night," said Chitchee. "Maybe it has something to do with that last terrorist attack on Uptown. They still don't know who killed Spartak Bok."

"Oh, the thumpers know—they don't care," said Raven triumphantly because his antennae were infallible feelers of information. "It was Croffut Gleet obviously. The guy whose own mother threw him off the Hennepin Avenue Bridge when he was two. Croffut Gleet, that ass wipe. Who set him up though? It's a cover up by the 5th Precinct of that ass wipe with the cops' asswipe, for sure, because it was the thumpers themselves who wiped the pavement with Spartak Bok's ass like ass wipe. But why? They try to make it sound like it was al-Shabaab's ass wipe. But I'm sure that Spartak Bok wasn't paying out the local thumpers enough ass wipe to wipe their asses with. So they wiped the ass wipe's ass. They splatted Croffut Gleet like rabbit roadkill. The thumpers tricked him into dying. Life in the fast lane caught up to Croffut Gleet, that ass wipe, and it ran him off the road—like ass wipe."

"Maybe I should get my own car," said Chitchee. "Or a good book on cars."

"How about *On The Road?*" asked Raven.

"Nah, that's okay," said Chitchee. "I read Mad Jack Kerouac when I was ten. Since then, I haven't really done anything, except waste time, not knowing enough about cars either. I'm possibly too timid for cars. Possibly. I've been a coward all my cowering life. But if I had some venture capital, an angel investor . . . I don't even know how to *ask* for 30,000 dollars. How do people get away with things like that? And where do you get a rabbit's foot these days? Is there a Magical Thinking store in Carousel Square?"

"No, but I can get you a real rabbit's foot," said Raven, "and if you visualize it with your third eye and you really want one . . . a Magical Thinking store will appear!"

"Figuratively, yes, but I really want a figurative rabbit's foot," said Chitchee, "or maybe a four-leaf clover would do."

"Four-leaf clover?" admonished Raven. "What! Sure, and a box of Lucky Charms! That's ridick, but a rabbit's right foot . . . and it has to be the right kind of right rabbit's foot, right?"

"Yes, a leftist rabbit's foot won't do, it would be un-American," continued Chitchee, setting aside Mishima and the rabbit's foot idea. "Anyway, the 'fuzz' are here every night."

"You mean Officers Weatherwax and Lowry? Those dips!" said Raven. "Those are the guys who had all the complaints. Weatherwax stuffed a Lakota Oglala in a trunk and went to McDonald's inside and ordered cheeseburgers. Weatherwax Tasered that African American kid who was twirling yarn on a knitting needle outside the YMCA and killed him. Then he went to the I-HOP for blueberry pancakes. I guess torture whets their appetites! Insurance covered the Godzillian-dollar civil suits as usual. The city is almost bankrupt from settling out of court. Police have taken all the money. And Weatherwax got another trophy larger than Tiger Woods."

"Whoa," said Felix, walking into the store.

"Are they the guys," asked Chitchee, reconstituting a powder-dry memory by stirring in water for milk, "that shot the Somali girl outside Hard Times and then went inside and ordered farmer's omelettes with extra hash browns?"

"Whoa," said Felix once inside the store.

He dropped his wire cutter from the inner pocket of his black leather duster onto the redolent, white pine wood flooring.

"Whoa," said Felix once on the floor.

On his days off, Felix gothed himself, eyelining his eyes' lash lines with tiny strokes of his tiny black Revlon brush and applied faint eyeshadow to his round eyelids like snails' shells when closed and when open like mourning doves. And for that he loved Revlon.

"No, those were some other thumpers in a different precinct, nothing to do with it, totally different, you're not listening to me," said Raven. "Okay, *dude*, here's the thing: aliens landed in Lakewood Cemetery last night. Didn't you hear the sirens last night? One of the ETs ODed and went ASAP to the ER at HCMC. But keep it under your HAT!"

"The aliens were looking to score heroin?" asked Felix, standing up and placing the wire cutter back in his inner pocket with other items from a burglar's tool kit.

"It really *is* an opioid epidemic!" said Chitchee, looking at Felix. "Who knew?"

"They don't want you to know," said Raven, looking at Felix with incredulity. "So don't tell anyone!"

"Why are you looking at me?" asked Felix, looking at Chitchee and Raven.

"Aliens landed in Lakewood Cemetery? Sure you weren't on mushrooms—?" asked Chitchee, turning to Raven.

"I'm always on mushrooms," said Raven, reading Chitchee's aura and looking directly through Chitchee.

"So it wasn't the mushrooms," said Chitchee.

Raven said nothing, because whenever he had to read an aura, he went into a preoccupied trance like a tourist checking into a hotel.

"So Raven," said Felix, "don't you think you might be getting too old for . . . well . . . you know . . . things like mushrooms?"

"I just started doing them fifty years ago!" said Raven, uncrossing his eyes. "So I figure I can keep doing them for another good two or three hundred years . . ."

"But what if you get addicted?" asked Felix.

"Oh," said Raven, "I've got the cure for that."

"What?" asked Chitchee.

"More mushrooms," said Raven.

Raven thumbed his thumbs under his arms. He chewed confidently on a stalk of grass.

Felix, capping his water bottle, looked at Chitchee. The cap to his water bottle flew off when he threaded it the wrong way. The cap bounced off Chitchee's nose onto the floor. Chitchee looked at the floor from over the counter.

"Come on, you guys!" said Raven. "Get your Wheaties!"

"Hey, you guys," said Felix to the floor. "Was Terence McKenna ever on the cover of a box of Wheaties?"

"Whoa," continued Felix, standing up with the cap, "that cap was a long way down!"

"So, what were the aliens *doing* in Lakewood Cemetery?" Chitchee asked, puzzled.

"Oh, come on, you guys," said Raven, shaking his head, the corner of his mouth worming around in a little smirk. "What else would aliens be doing in the middle of the night in Lakewood Cemetery? They do what they always do. Collect DNA samples from bone marrow, clone false identities for fake life insurance scams, and then register their dead souls to vote for their own candidates in local elections to defeat the zombie candidates, who are always against the vampires of course. You didn't know that? Christ, you work in a book store, Chitchee!"

"Wait," asked Chitchee, "can we unpack this? Is there a zombie running for Mayor of Minneapolis, or is it a vampire running *from* a zombie who is running *from* the Mayor of Minneapolis?"

"A zombie *is* the Mayor of Minneapolis, but he will be running *against* a vampire! I told you," said Raven, his exasperation at its asymptote. "The *zombie* knows that all he needs to get re-elected is register the false votes of the *undead*, and then shoot a silver bullet through the heart of the vampire that lives in Lakewood Cemetery. How many times do we have to go over the existential threat of aliens, vampires, and zombies?"

"It's McC . . . sl . . . osh," said Saami, stewed as prunes in a prune stew, slugging up the stairs.

He stopped and looked around, having heard footsteps, which disappeared into apparitions, then reappeared when he continued climbing the stairs.

"I heard McCosh following me," said Saami. "Ghosss-hhh. McGhost is down there. The book store is defff-initely haunted by a gho-hoo-ost."

"Saami," said Raven, "ghosts? Really? Ghosts? Let's be rational! Come off it, man!"

Raven browbeat Saami with a painfully sweet and sour mixture of concern as the older and wiser brother.

"I heard . . . him . . ." stumbled Saami. "He must like whips and chains like the ghost of Christmiss pissed."

"They say McCosh never lost a book except one, Saami," said Chitchee, trying to look facetious for Saami. "For which he wanders the earth eternally trying to remember where he put that book. Maybe he *was* down there looking for that book."

"Poor man!" said Saami. "God, life, she is tough, a tough nut on crack for everyone. Welcome to the bungle, mister."

Saami looked lost. He had gotten off on the wrong bardo and the elevator doors had closed behind him.

"Don't we all wander the earth eternally until we die?" said Chitchee. "That's why we are all ghosts before we are born. Then we are born as baby entelechies. I never thought I could use 'entelechy' in a sentence! Another milestone for me!"

"Saami, you're hearing the Club Miami people in their basement, bleeding through the wall," said Felix. "It's music bleeding through the walls. That's another local band bleeding through the walls."

"No," said Saami. "It's McCosh. I heard him in our Middle-earth section rooting around. I know he's down there middling about."

"Saami, you have to quit drinking," said Raven. "You're seeing doubles now. Everyone is concerned about your drinking. What can we do? You have to quit. We're waiting for you to hit rock bottom."

"I *am* Rock Bottom," said Saami, flexing a flabby bicep. "There's nothing to hit. It's rock bottoms all the way down through all the other rock bottoms and even then there will be another rock bottom brewery selling rabbit piss at the bar! So what's your fucking point?"

"Quit drinking, Saami," scolded Raven. "I know your drill: last hurrah, lost weekend, rock bottom, repeat."

"Let's activate! Show us this McCosh, Saami!" said Chitchee.

After Chitchee performed the ritual of transcribing the daily totals and other closing procedures, he, Felix, and Raven followed Saami, who shushed, and led them, walking on a staircase of water. They were careful not to step on the earth and scare off all its ghosts.

"See?" said Raven. "Nothing! Another wild ghost chase!"

"Keep going, McCosh is down here somewhere," insisted Saami, "looking for his roots. I have a funny feeling this is his root cellar."

"Seriously? Maybe we should try the tunnel system going toward Lakewood Cemetery this time?" asked Felix.

"That's it!" said Chitchee. "McCosh is probably coming *from* Lakewood Cemetery! If we find his grave there, then we will know for sure that McCosh doesn't like our store, and that's why BookSmart is always failing *under his curse*. He's the Fisher King from *The Waste Land*."

Saami embraced Chitchee.

"Smart," said Saami, smiling as widely as his muscles allowed themselves to be stretched. "I'm so glad you like Stephen King."

The four of them confronted a small vestibule three-quarters dark. Food-stained, chessboard-trousered restaurant workers in heat waves of thermonuclear radiation scrambled in foot races. Some in hats of expanding paper soufflés barked orders at dishwashers in showers of grease. Chefs boiled in fits of anger blamed dishwashers over scalded frying pans with scalded faces themselves.

Chitchee pointed to a corridor that led to a storage room.

When the squawking Club Miami employees no longer hurried back and forth into and out of the walk-in coolers, the four explorers scooted past.

"No sign of McCosh as yet," said Raven.

"Well, keep going, he couldn't have gotten very far," muttered Saami.

"Maybe he is a slow ghost, putting on weight now," said Raven sarcastically.

"You're so cynical," said Saami, "and you will just never change. Never."

Felix dropped his water bottle. When he bent down to retrieve it four black flashlights tumbled out of his inner pocket.

"Whoa, the flashlights!" said Felix. "Okay, everybody grab a flashlight!"

Flashing their flashlights, they illuminated the door to the storm sewer system, which Felix popped with the bolt cutter as Raven clawed his thick red beard with a backstroke, and with some satisfaction that he had done his Royal Canadian Air Force exercises that morning. He helped Felix wrench open the KEEP OUT-signed south submarine door. With a little bit of elbow grease, they pulled it open.

The four dogged down on their hands and knees.

"I know McCosh is down here," said Saami with wounded pride. "I smell his book droppings. They're like yeast infections. Hey, who turned my flashlight off? That's weird. Flashlights don't turn themselves off!"

"Unless they just died!" said Felix. "Whoa, this is getting creepier by the minute."

"Ghosts don't have ghost droppings, Saami, come on," said Raven.

"Yes they do," said Saami. "I've seen them. You're one!"

Raven and Saami heard Felix push the manhole cover to the side on the pavement.

"We're in Asimov's 'Nightfall,'" said Chitchee.

Northern lights roared above their upside-down heads. The local stars in the night sky yawned over the dead cemetery as if the stars were sleeping in a bed of dreaming.

They crawled onto the white asphalt pavement of outer space, one by one, into the moonlight, their flesh white as sprouting seedlings. They heard a girl sobbing, dopplered away in echoes. Jeers dangled from the bone-white, winding branches of the birch trees, looking like skeletons of hanged wind. The wind blew (there was no girl, the wind was the girl) through the tops of the spruces' whorls, and the breeze below covered a battlefield of stone men, frozen because of a magic spell like the betrayed and massacred men in *One Thousand Nights and a Night*. Obelisks, like soldiers in an army of urns, approached the visitors. Grave markers, under the command of a mausoleum, stood behind them. Against the full round moonlight, the x-rayed silhouettes of the maples and oaks looked like giant hairy flies. The moonlight bounced off the giant flies' legs covered with sticky stars.

"Why is my flashlight off again?" said Saami. "Heck, I didn't do that. McCosh did that. He's here. I just have a funny feeling. Seriously—a funny, funny feeling. THE WORLD WAS CREATED BY DEMONS!"

"Ariel is playing with you, Bottom, " said Chitchee.

"What does that mean?" asked Saami. "Nobody ever fucked with my bottom. Listen, Chitchee, stick to what you're good at! Stick to your Shakespeare and all that rot!"

The clear moon was a watery womb while rabbits and hares galloped and galumphed, crashing blindly behind the lunette markers—up green hills, through silver woods, and down black slopes. The tombstones were shaped like the fingernails of buried-alive giants. In his mind's eye, Chitchee witnessed the resurrection of sleeping grave-bones, heard their hushed lullabies with his invisible body, and sensed with his own living feelers the static of a far away faerie land where Oberon controlled the waves by whispering.

(Is that the Hagia Sophia over there? whispered Chitchee.)

"Yeah," smirked Raven, "we crawled on all fours to Istanbul! Hey, there's McCosh over there, nyuck, nyuck, nyuck!"

"Did you hear that?" said Chitchee. "You guys, this graveyard is crawling with living people. What kind of graveyard is this?"

Melchizedek, his feet tied by rope, hung upside-down from the beam of an oak tree's branches. He smoked a hand-rolled cigarette unconcernedly as a goat, surrounded by devil-worshipping children, witches, warlocks, wizards, and clowns. His wrinkles dried up the deltas across his cheekbones, his neck running red with a rash he had rubbed raw as a rock. Melchizedek gazed strangely and fixedly at Chitchee. The white-satin sheen of an arachnoid star vanished into the hub of a black hole's web and then a supernatural tingle crawled up Chitchee's spidery, web-like spine.

"She died young, unloved, and off her medication," recited Minerva, reading aloud from her manuscript, "martyred by her own broken heart, which she nursed like a stillborn baby in a world of white demon men, always stalking her for her beauty, the same not nice men who buried her alive in Lakewood Cemetery on the night of the day of the end of her life. Damn! Well, the end—of the dead, that is. The day of the night of the end of the dead, I meant to write. Sorry it took so long to get to the ending, sorry everybody! Sorry if I ruined everyone's evening with my chicken tracks! It wasn't my best outing. It's only a first draft. Forgive me!"

"Don't put yourself down so much! That was *so* awesome," said Beda to the audience. "Oooooh! Awwww! Give it up for Minerva Singleton! Now all you have to do is—get it out there, Minnie! Walker Library will definitely want it, right Dale? Dale? And BookSmart will sell it on consignment like all the other book stores in town always do for their favorite authors."

"Chitchee!" yelled Felix. "Where are you?"

The circles of carousal, out of square, drifted.

Felix, Raven, and Saami strayed down the flickering lanes, the moon a sputtering, tungsten, low-watt bulb filled with the white shadows of the past.

Chitchee felt a presence, a being watching him. McCosh was high up in the night sky in a Goodyear blimp, looking down at him with eagle-sized binoculars.

Chitchee scratched his armpits, palping for buboes and pustules. He walked, encountering sudden cold spots. A carriage door slammed. Spanish black lace. Operatic masks on chopsticks. Venetian masqueraders from the set-piece ballroom of a Russian novel where the leads meet, court, spark, and later die in pools of blood after a silly duel of some kind.

Chitchee felt himself to be vanishing and reappearing, a ghostly electron-clot of blood condemned to impermanence. Music transfused the grass-sweetened air. A gibbering goblin played a scordatura violin with the disdain of a Scheherazade dancing a scherzo. Her see-through muslin dress of printed belladonnas, white thorn apples, and the purple-spurred, shooting-starred petals of nightshades, revealed that it was Beda. And her friends with ratted-up hair, swirling skull and crossbone tattoos, chains, and covenous grimoires danced in a circle to a mixtape on Dale's boombox of old Dr. Demento radio shows while the others turned green drinking, their happiness growing green with *La Fee Parisienne* absinthe.

Upside down, hair like the gnostic feathers of a fallen devil, skin white as a Dresden figurine, Melchizedek lectured (or thought he lectured) a cohort of ghouls in blue jean shorts, rose-cheeked gremlins in leggings, and moon-fleshed gnomes with shaved heads, hunkered next to Davanni's pizza boxes and weak beer cans.

"Chitchee!" yelled Felix, Raven, and Saami, alternating in overlapping rounds.

The palaver of revelry under barren trees branched outward in ciliary arteries, distracting Chitchee, who saw a book on the ground: *Tales of Hindu Devilry.*

"Hey, Melchizedek, what the Haystacks Calhoun is going on here?" asked Chitchee.

"Oh," said Melchizedek, flicking his cigarette butt and talking upside down in smoke rings, "it's our Walker Public Library Book Club Meeting."

"What is the book club book for this month?" asked Chitchee. "*Vikram and the Vampire?*"

"What?" asked Melchizedek. "How did you know that? HOW DID YOU KNOW THAT? There is no way you could have known that!"

"I was listening to the Ukashic record the other night," said Chitchee, grabbing Melchizedek by the hips. "Dr. Demento played the whole thing."

Chitchee spun him like an upside-down quark.

"Help!" moaned Melchizedek. "Dale! The Raging Librarian!"

"What is it now?" asked Dale, emerging from the shadows. "Can't I even piss in peace and pass out somewhere in quiet, ever? What am I, fucking Mr. Wizard?"

Dale the Raging Librarian wore a flowing black lace dress with a Spanish mantilla. Saami, having bummed a beer, stumbled around the clearing, calling for McCosh.

"Hey, Melfloozedek, seen any *ghosts* by the name of Oshkosh McCosh tonight?" asked Saami.

"BookSmart is here!" said Melchizedek. "And it's Sam Boney, the little elfgrin! I seen *aliens*, Little Elfgrin, but I ain't seen a goddamn ghost since *Topper* went off the air!"

The distant cenotaphs ejected a burqa and a black hijab.

"Got the T-bone," asked Chitchee, "but ain't got no mashed po-ta-to?"

A cloak whisked through the graveyard like a guilty spirit, a spirit of sable and dark forces exhaled from a fissure in the underworld.

"Any new books by any aliens *of note* come in lately?" asked Melchizedek. "Notice I say *of note*!"

"Only the usual unusuals," said Chitchee. "Forteana from over a hundred billion galaxies. Usually in poor condition though, I must admit! These advanced civilizations don't know how to pack books in a box."

"Beware the white noble flower in your future!" said Melchizedek, white hair flowing like snow over the heads of the grass blades until his angular momentum approached zero, although his head remained less than a meter above his x-axis. "In the blooming fields of winter!"

"Okay," said Chitchee. "But why is Dale the Raging Librarian here?"

Dale crossed his arms.

"*# ?F^# /*] *U!=K @!," said Dale, chugging another beer and tossing the Blech's beer can on the pile. "Fucking chaperone duty for the Walker Public Library horrible book club. It's fucking bullshit is what it is! Like I have to prevent these guys from calling forth demons? Don't tell anyone you saw me here! I am officially ghosted tonight!"

Felix's mouth resembled a day-old bagel. He felt a "whoa" encrust his mouth when he tripped over Dale's empty Blech's beer cans. He fumbled to the cold earth.

"There goes your McCosh in a burqa and hijab," scoffed Raven, who pulled out a pair of cheap 10 x 42 binoculars, swiped the horizon with them, and scooped Felix off the ground.

Felix's eyes followed Raven's eyes pivoting toward their object.

"She's running around the cemetery like a giant black bat in a hijab!" laughed Felix, elliptically ellipsing himself into semi-hysteria.

"And she's carrying something like a shoebox, like in *Nosferatu*," said Chitchee. "Is she stuffing the shoebox in her backpack?"

"Do you mean the *Nosferatu* of Dreyer or Herzog?" asked Felix, abruptly sober and embarrassed. "I actually met Werner Herzog at a Walgreen's, the one on—"

"Why would McCosh wear a burqa and a hijab and skulk around Lakewood Cemetery like Jason without a goalie's mask?" asked Saami. "None of this makes sense. And why are the Avengers here? And Ninjas? And Wolverines?"

"McCosh moonlights as a vampire," speculated Chitchee. "With an army-surplus entrenching tool."

"And Pennywise?" popped up Pennywise with a clownish flourish, mugging it up in the background of a selfie and falling backwards over Dale's beer cans.

"Watch where you're walking!" said Dale. "You fucking fuckstick! Cosplay bullshit! Have any of you reached puberty yet? Hard to tell!"

"Melchizedek, when are the aliens coming?" implored Beda.

"I'm guessing they're going to cancel," said Melchizedek. "Dale, can you get me down from here?"

"Cancel?" asked half The Sick Joke Cafe's clientele, worming from the woods, their dark eyes like iced oysters in propped-open shells, dressed like the very gremlins Chitchee had seen these gremlins sketching at their tables at The Sick Joke.

Dale chewed on a nail. He climbed the oak tree, pulled out a machete, and sliced the rope in one blow, sending Melchizedek to the ground.

"*Those aliens were a kind of solution*," said Chitchee.

"Grandpa?" asked Felix.

"Felix?" said Melchizedek, the sound of a hoary, croaking gate in the distance slammed.

"Did you escape from the nursing home again?" asked Felix.

"Listen up everybody," bellowed Raven. "If the aliens do come to pick up their shit tonight, *do not look directly into their headlights*! That's what Syd Barrett did, and that's when he stepped through The Door . . . forever . . . and that's—"

"Here comes a car! Security!" said Melchizedek to his followers, who scattered to hideaways well rehearsed.

"Grandpa! Wait up!" said Felix. "I've got to get you back to the home! It's past your bedtime I'm sure."

"Bedtime?" said Melchizedek like a spark. "I'm just getting up to make the toast now!"

Behind the driven wheels of the Lakewood Cemetery security vehicle sat Heinie Heinemann merrily whistling "She'll Be Coming Around The Mountain" and tooling down the dark lanes. He plunged through the enormous complex of monuments, mausoleums, small parthenons that looked like poultry houses (angels abounding in repose on top of them with wreaths), and evergreen trees touching the thistledown stars. Heinie mulled over *Crash*, whose aesthetic totality Toby had atom-smashed with his caterwauling cavils. Heinie day-for-night dreamed: how the house lights went up, how Emily the manager escorted Toby the Intruder, who cried out all the way to the sidewalk, protesting his innocence like the daughters of Sejanus led to the gallows.

"And we didn't even get comps! Criminee!" Heinie exclaimed aloud and immediately thought: "If only I had married homely Leggy Peggy Magnusson with the bluebottle-blue eyes and the ability to drink like a beluga—four oceans of Schlitz Malt hidden in her thin, sleepy hollow legs stretched out on the beach, next to her mom, who was from Florida, an artificial blonde with an artificial tan at an artificial beach from an artificial state. Oh yeah, her mom. Delores Something Something."

Heinie kicked the brake and stopped to catch his breath. With switched-out cheater glasses, he spied a burqa silhouette (with a North Face backpack) boosting up the Lakewood Cemetery wrought-iron fence, a six-foot tall palisade of spear-points. She perched and shimmied down onto the 36th Street sidewalk, which stunt she executed in a particularly athletic and skillful manner.

Chitchee sniffed around the cemetery for McCosh's grave, reckoning that it should be near the manhole. He stepped on a dead brown bat. Rabbits multiplied like people. What if McCosh showed up in a kerfuffle?

Chitchee wrestled McCosh to the ground like Jacob's angel:

"What does it take to run a successful book store?" asked McCosh.

"30,000 dollars and a rabbit's foot?" asked Chitchee. "I don't know. I don't know anything."

Chitchee's eyes shaped teardrops from the teardrop shape of his eyes, and the midnight breeze played a piano sonata by Shostakovich on the tear-shaped tombstones .

"Give me the title of a book," said McCosh, with his crazy red hair flowing, "and if I can't find the book before the first of the new year, I will grant you a book store."

"*Perri the Squirrel*," said Chitchee.

"How about *Vikram and the Vampire*?" asked McCosh. "I know where that one is."

"I have that one myself," said Chitchee, watching a brown bat flap its wings over the grave markers, the holes dug in the ground, and the black hills. "The version in Somadeva's *Ocean of Streams of Story*."

The smell of fresh dirt from the freshly dug earth smoldered in Chitchee's nostrils with the damp, wooly warmth of woody mushrooms. Heinie thought to double back and around for a little look-see in case the shadowy spirit of *Iblis* from the fires of *Jahannam* nipped back to Earth, because Iblis could level Minneapolis with one black, fell sulphuric breath. The Lakewood Cemetery security vehicle wheeled back around and silhouettes darted and dodged behind gravestones.

A rabbit, unaware of death only minutes away, waited for her chance to emerge, browse, and graze.

"Okay," said Saami, "Raven, you can take your hand off my shoulder. Security's gone."

"My hand isn't on your shoulder," said Raven.

"Oh, are you fucking with me? Shut up!" said Saami.

Melchizedek's disciples sounded like a sheep-shearing contest in a megachurch, copping hiding places Heinie never knew existed. He might work on the incident report later when he needed something to do in between portable electronic chess moves, whose pieces lay on the car floorboard like flood victims. And there was no use chasing Melchizedek. Old Melchizedek needed to get out once in a while, once in a blueing moon, poor old committed wanker. And Minerva, Beda, and The Sick Joke Crowd. Let the children have their say!

Saami turned (a big brown bat?) and looked (meow?) at his shoulder. A bat gripped Saami's shoulder. Its black leather wings were tucked in. Saami saw a tiny black canvas chair, folded up with the chair legs sticking out, and a bat sitting in that chair. Its oily ears were pointed; its teeth bared like upper and lower scythes; and its throat was like the underground tunnel system they had crawled out of. When the brown bat's mouth dropped, Saami croaked like a giant frog with a little man stuck in his craw.

Saami took off running—he didn't gauge the speed of the Lakewood Cemetery security vehicle curving round the bend. Heinie's slammed brakes squealed, squishing a rabbit that changed directions ten times, right before the car launched Saami on the curve of all summed-over paths with enough spacetime to fly over the hood in a single bounce and then fly up toward the full moon in a full embrace. Saami was like a child grasping its mother only to fly back down and *land wrong*. Off center, thunk, crack, on the lane's asphalt, grunting, ba-bam. He lay moaning on the grass, clutching his shoulder.

The Great Bear had swiped Saami down to the ground with its giant Bear's Paw.

A clown's mask of pain revealed Saami's true face like a new mask with gaunt, grimacing circus cheeks.

Chitchee screamed like an apparition screaming at an apparition.

"AGGHHH!" screamed Chitchee, tears masking his face. "Somebody! Call Security! I'll start compressions!"

"No," pleaded Saami, a tear droplet in the eye suspended. "No, PLEASE NO! I don't need compressions. Don't touch me, don't move me! I'm paralyzed!"

Heinie unfolded his cramped, wizened body from the company car ("Any books by Emanuel Lasker come into BookSmart lately, Chitchee?" first thing out of Heinie's mouth).

Raven sauntered over and examined the dead rabbit like a rabbit doctor. Felix bolted after his grandfather. Felix tackled Melchizedek ("No! Don't take me back!") when his grandfather tripped over the silhouette of a rabbit, which was Dale's beer cans of Blech's, which sliced Melchizedek's already grass-stained, baggy blue dungarees at the kneecaps, leaving behind red scrapes and raspberry bumps of blood.

"You see, Saami," said Raven over the dead, run-over rabbit. "My magic spell worked! It always does . . . eventually! You guys never listen to me."

"Because we're tired of your saying we never listen to you," said Chitchee. "Come on, call 911! Somebody help! Paramedics! Somebody with a car?"

"I have a car," offered Heinie, leaning on the car and cleaning his eyeglasses with an orange, serrated chamois cloth. "Is Saami badly hurt? I tried to get out of his way but he ran into me like a goddamned rabbit."

"Oh, he'll be fine," said Raven, pulling his one-hitter out. "It's only a separated shoulder. I've had lots of those before. Bah!"

"The pain, pain, pain, the hate, hate, hate," cried Saami. "I can't afford an ambulance. GOD! Oh, fucking god, no, oh. AHHH!"

"Raven," said Chitchee, "can we snap the shoulder bone back into the socket like it's a piece of LEGO?"

"If you hold him still," said Raven, picking up Saami by the scruff of the neck like a naughty kitten, "I can pound the bone back. Hey Beda, a little help?"

"What's going on, Raven?" asked Beda. "By the great god Pan, did someone get hurt? I heard human cries—what can I do to help—oh! Oh. It's Saami. Hey, everybody let's go, it's only another very average white male. Saami the rude dude who works at the book store dude: fuck him!"

"Beda," said Minerva, feeling slighted, "I thought we were going to burn copies of *Lolita* tonight and burn NAY-bo-kov in effigy! And I thought Pepsi Beaucoup was coming for the reading too."

"I guess not, babe," said Beda, "thanks to Saami."

Raven pounded Saami's back. Chitchee braced Saami. Raven was perplexed about his best friend's screaming. Where were the thank yous? You help a friend out by pounding on his dislocated shoulder and all you get is a bunch of screaming monkeys, and they didn't want to feel better, because if they did, they would thank Raven, the reincarnated sorcerer from Lappland, who has droves of magical reindeer at his command. But to the world at large, Raven was only a little tin-can gardener with a little tin can. Feeling sorry for himself, Raven worked in a garden where the flowers didn't want water.

"Grandpa Weatherwax!" yelled Felix.

Melchizedek hurdled over a defunct garden fence of croquettish, wickety half-moon hoops.

"What about curfew?" asked Felix. "You're running out of time!"

"Not just time, but space too!" said Melchizedek over his shoulder.

"I have to," continued Raven, unfolding from a snap-buttoned sheath a small silver crescent, "cut off the right foot—or is it the left—under the full moon with this Buck knife."

"Stop, Raven!" yelled Chitchee. "Don't mutilate the rabbit! It will bring us bad luck! That rabbit will have a limp in its rabbit afterlife and curse my book store like a pissed off Noel!"

"Not if you use an elk-antlered Buck knife soaked in a tincture of sage blossom and then dried next to a coyote tail in a reindeer-antlered ashtray," said Raven. "Get out of the way! Stand back! You said you needed a rabbit's foot! You've always said you wanted to open your own book store, Chitchee! This is your big chance! I'm telling you! It's now or never! Take it from me, the game is afoot!"

Holding the grisly stump, blood drops a-drip and a-drop, "I'll take this home and treat it with my Hasbro taxonomy kit and preservatives. And the next thing you know you'll find thirty thousand dollars. You don't believe me? You're just like Dougal! Every winter he gets frostbite on his toes and I keep telling him to wear sphagnum moss socks. And he refuses to take my advice to wear sphagnum moss socks!"

"We have to dump off Saami at HCMC . . ." said Heinie, motorizing the engine and rescuing the 1970s chess pieces, which he packed into the portable chessboard. "I'll have to call it a draw. We can go now folks."

Heinie postponed his chess game in imitation of Paul Morphy and stroked his chin like a budding but sensitive potato.

"I'm going to stay here for the after-party," said Felix. "Pepsi Beaucoup is coming to play 'Monster Mash,' and Mono Boondalicks is supposed to explicate it, or provide another abstract exegesis of it, or whatever it he does so reconditely as to litter us with lit-crit and his romantic lack of humor. If, if that's okay, I mean I don't want to be disrespectful toward rabbits. Or any fellow mammals, really. I dreamt I had sex with a rabbit once. Weird, isn't it? I have an affinity to (for?) furry warm-bloods. That's okay, isn't it? That's not weird, is it? Where is my water bottle? I dropped it. Whoa! Way over there by that red fox!"

"Fee-Lix!" said Emily, surprising her own tones hidden in those two syllables. "Is this your water bottle? Are you on your water break? The midnight movie is getting out soon!"

"Whoa!" said Felix. "The red fox is white Emily! Another animal altogether!"

Emily's aborted hug caused Felix's eyeglasses to eject, drop, and lose an arm on landing. Felix crunched the arm when he tried to hug Emily in return, but she found the tiny, silver screw for Felix's glasses in the moon's albedo.

"Hey! Emily!" yelled Heinie. "I wanna rain check on *Crash*! *Crash* the *movie* crashed!"

Saami tried to smack his forehead with the palm of his good hand. He couldn't move. So they tossed him in the back.

"Hey fellas, I hate driving at night. I can't see a thing," said Heinie. "I'm sorry if I hit anything."

"That's okay, Heinie," said Chitchee. "Do what you can in the dark during an emergency."

"Take the back roads," said Raven. "I know them all. We can veer around Nokomis and drive up Minnehaha and approach HCMC from the back."

"What?" asked Heinie, crowding his shoulders over the wheel. "I can't see!"

"It's a knight's move around Nokomis," said Chitchee, "a bishop's move up Minnehaha, and then castle to HCMC!"

"Heinie," said Raven, "don't listen to him! Take a right, right here, uh, wait, you missed it. Turn around, make a U-ey!"

"We're on our way to Iowa!" said Chitchee.

"Iowa! No!" Saami groaned and died. "I can't take Iowa! Let me die in Hibbing, oh God, please! Don't stick me in Iowa!"

The ghost Saami gave up, chilled, and flew back inside him.

"Can we stop off somewhere and break into a liquor store?" asked Saami, smacking his forehead.

Past the massive, brutal pillars of the hospital at the registration desk, the inpatient nurse, in a shrinking violet-purple uniform, looked blithe, cheerful, and upbeat. And familiar.

"I guess you'd have to be really happy to work in a depressing place like this," said Chitchee to the nurse.

She smiled with pretty little teeth. Chitchee greeted all the nurses to see if they all had pretty little teeth.

Saami couldn't fill out the necessary forms properly, so Chitchee and Raven helped Saami with recalling who he was, where he lived, and where he had hidden all his action figures. Saami would not cooperate. He claimed it was only a scratch—pointless to stay overnight, which would cost thousands if not tens of thousands of dollars, which would force him to sell his action figures. Besides, Saami had to work the next day and swing by Henn-Lake Liquor on the way to work.

When Chitchee offered to work Saami's shift, Saami went into: "I can't ask you to work for me, unless you want me to ask you. Then I could."

Saami looked at Raven, who shrugged.

"Here's some Ambien to help you get some sleep," continued Chitchee. "I've always wanted to practice radical hospitality. So here you go, Saami, free dope!"

He kissed Saami on the forehead. Saami smacked his forehead then smacked Chitchee's forehead.

On the way out Chitchee pointed politely at the recognized nurse:

"Shuwen Qu! I remember you," said Chitchee. "*Shui Hu Zhuan*! Ha, ha, ha!"

Shuwen Qu smiled with a schoolgirl wave as if a tree sparrow in her hand flapped frantically to get free.

Saami looked like a cartoon of himself: the boy frowning with the thermometer in his mouth, the boy who had to stay home from school with an ice pack on his head. He smiled an arc of 180-degrees like a Katzenjammer Kid. Ensconced in his hospital bed sheets like an eel in a bed of eels, wriggling around the Sargasso Sea, he reeled out of bed. He looked wistfully out the misty window.

"It looks like a frame out of a Steve Ditko," said Saami. "It has a Dr. Octopus vibe."

Saami swallowed the thin white pellet of Ambien and awaited the bus of sleep that never came.

Saami strolled down Hennepin Avenue. And his shoulder was not broken. Was not. It was scratched. He had been winged. Over him the Minneapolis skyline towered, the excited windows glowing with warmth. Springy rainbows, packed in neon boxes. Against the sky salient Mondrian edges and razor-sharp Cartesian coordinates outlined the girders of downtown finance.

Saami crept along a dark, residential street, black as a coal scuttle.

A bruising white and livid light smashed his cerebellum from behind. Rassled, rolled, and batted down, Saami sprawled forward onto someone's lawn, his mousey ears bleeding. Some night revellers near the CC Club heard gunfire and encountered a bedraggled Hawk Eye, who demanded the soused and soaked sprouts call 911, 411, 311, and 111. Someone had been mugged, lying on the ground, over there, bleeding. "The guy who works at BookSmart, I've seen him there anyway," said the guy who called 911 as if Dispatch would respond with, "Oh, you mean Saami? Everybody loves Saami!"

Saami lay dead by some blister-barked, bistre-colored crabapple trees, next to a bare-bulbed tulip patch of wounded hearts, buried red and white.

The baby's skull propping open Saami's mouth spoke:

"Wherever you go, Saami, you will be a Minneapolis."

2825 FREMONT TERRACE APARTMENTS

The silvery peals of leaves in the autumn trees faded and the crystal prisms of spectral snow above the wet sidewalks waltzed and dissolved. Tubular grain elevators reflected the golden tubes of the sun. Office towers and commercial sugar castles (with big Sullivan windows) awoke to a November frosting. Over night, each blade of autumnal grass, each unfallen and fallen leaf, and each evergreen needle had been rimed and rimmed with whiskers of ice.

Also whiskered Aloysius paced outside BookSmart, chilled, puffed a gasper like a dove-tailed joint, and again called Chitchee, who woke up slowly, if at all, when he heard an electronic chirp.

"Chitchee, I'm locked out," Aloysius unpleasantly swallowed the loud flow of traffic. "You don't have my keys, do you? Saami must have the keys."

"Who is this?" asked Chitchee. "What the hell! Were you just expelled from an uncreated Paradise, and you are calling me from an area code east of Eden? Just kidding!"

"What? Chitchee, I can see someone in there," muttered Aloysius, seeing from behind his own breath his own cold smoke. He paused away from the phone, his attention diverted, and returned: "Hey, maybe the burglar will let me in."

"See if it's McCosh!" said Chitchee, checking the mousetrap he had set in the kitchenette on the top shelf of his bare, contact-papered cupboards, the top shelf bare but for the peanut butter and unused paper plates—saved for a special occasion, and the uncanopenable canned goods Kennedy favored him with.

Chitchee had placed the mousetrap out of reach so that he would not hear the coiled bar snap the mouse's spine—all too much of a reminder of the Reign of Terror, Committee for Public Safety, Robespierre, and the Year One. Poor Antoine Lavoisier, remembered in America only as a mouthwash nobody remembers. Nevertheless, twisting and turning through his usual sleeplessness on the floor, Chitchee felt a mouse scamper up the length of his body towards his nose, forcing him to sleep sitting up with the lights on. He didn't want a two-mouse night.

He called Dan the Maintenance Man, who called right back, waiting to be pissed off. Dan said that a lot of MPG apartments had mice. That it probably didn't happen anyway, that it was probably a dream, because a lot of apartments had had the same dream! Besides, without mouse tracks and paw prints it would be hard to prove the presence of mice, unless they installed "mouse cams" in every MPG apartment. Chitchee should be thankful he didn't have rats in his underwear.

When Dan mentioned "rats," Chitchee felt boneless rats' claws scurry up and down his axons like ratlines on a mental ship. The gnawing, the chewing, the cannibalistic butchery. Chitchee stood over the toilet in case he was sick, which he wasn't, so he lay down on the floor, eye level with a copy of *1984*.

"Still there? Saami called in sick," said Aloysius. "He thinks he was mugged last night around 3:30 by three Somali girls. Or something. With pumpkins. On roller skates. I forget the minor details."

"Mugged? On his way home from work? By three Somali girls? Pumpkins on roller skates? But—" said Chitchee, seeing a tiny gray mouse zigzag into the studio.

With the phone caked to his ear, Chitchee reached for his acorn cap and puckered his lips.

"Yeah, he's in pretty rough shape," Aloysius on speakerphone said with some discomfort, smoking a smoke that curled upward out of Chitchee's earpiece, Chitchee whiffing tobacco and coughing out curly shreds.

"Hold on, boss man," said Chitchee.

When Chitcheee blew the acorn cap like the winding horn at Roncevaux, blowing pitches beyond 20,000 hertz into painful shrieks in any mouse's ears, Aloysius's neck hair stood on end, each hair shrieking like the mouse that zagzigged under Chitchee's front door and ran down the Fremont Terrace apartment hall, paws over its bleeding eardrums.

"Aaaaawwwwwww (cough) gggggghhhhhh . . . owwwwww, so I don't have keys to get in and Saami was supposed to open! I'm—"

"I'm taking you off speaker phone now," said Chitchee, accidentally turning on the flashlight instead, snapping a selfie, ordering an Uber, and joining Instagram. "Wait, what's going on with my phone?"

"—locked out, buddy. Wait a second. Here comes the burglar. Maybe I can get the burglar to let me in."

"Hello?" asked Chitchee.

Chitchee scowled at his phone. The line croaked. He banged the cell phone on the kitchen counter and the mousetrap's guillotine fell. He scanned the steel-cut Quaker Oats, Riceland rice, Goya beans, pinto beans, Nescafe, granulated sugar, noodles, flour, salts—iodized, non-iodized, semi-iodized, and sea—and not a speck of pepper. Famished and exhausted, Chitchee fought back the yawns but dropped back to the floor "to close his eyes for a second" with the phone to his ear like an umbilical cord. He would have loved to fall into the introverted orbit of a book, but milliseconds and a few brain waves later . . . later . . .

"Aloysius, can I use your potty?" said Hawk Eye, looking up from his squat outside Club Miami.

"Sorry, Night Sea Journey," said Aloysius. "I'm locked out."

"Night Sea Journey! That's not my name," said Hawk Eye, plucking for his discharge paper. "Is it? I better check."

Again Hawk Eye showed Aloysius the same dogeared, hard-bitten official form with the official number on it that Hawk Eye validated his existence with before an imaginary jury of twelve.

"It's Owen Rasmussen, but everyone calls me Hawk Eye."

Hawk Eye was resentful and invisible as a veteran of the Vietnam War coming home—except when he hooked up with Randy Quaalude. They hauled off like snake-bitten mongooses and got good and fucked up, visibly blissed invisible, and then Hawk Eye reached out to people who didn't like him and avoided him like Dr. Octopus.

"Here," said Hawk Eye, "this is to prove to me I served again. Three tours. DD214."

"Oh, he served," said Officer Weatherwax, who strolled up Hennepin Avenue and snatched the DD214. "What are you up to, Hawk Eye?"

"Oh, just resting, Officer Weatherwax," said Hawk Eye. "I was out for my daily constitution. Which has kinda been helled with lately."

"You know," said Officer Weatherwax, double-taking with a rebound look and a look of moving on, "you can't panhandle around Uptown anymore."

Officer Weatherwax handed back the DD214, rested his claw back on his utility belt, and his black serge pants sagged a bit further.

"Uptown Trade Council complained," said Officer Lowry. "You're bad for their business. You're scaring away the rich folks with all your crazy signs and languages."

"Brother, it burns," said Hawk Eye with an abdominal pain that had no immediate cause.

Hawk Eye chewed the black hepatic sore warted on his lip.

"I want to talk to Aloysius standing here though," said Officer Weatherwax. "We had—are you okay, Aloysius? Aloysius, you seem—we had a—have you ever taken LSD? Aloysius?"

Aloysius gulped his Adam's apple with an ascorbic little sob.

"Why? Are you selling? Actually, eons ago . . . ago . . . ago I did . . ." said Aloysius, uptight around thumpers no matter how well he knew them as acquaintances.

"And the store is—" said Officer Lowry.

"*Everything's* fine," said Aloysius, holding his elbows together as he blew up his fists with his warm breath. "I was out late last night, looking for the all-night Halloween parties I wasn't invited to! Then I went home, teepeed my own house so no one else could, and hit the hay late around ten. I'm waiting for someone to let me into my own store."

"Aloysius," said Officer Lowry, adopting a tone of conciliation, "we had a report from Dale of some stolen books from the Walker Public Library. Now you wouldn't be buying books stolen from the little library down the street, would you? You guys? From a deaf mute guy known as Undone Buttons?"

"Nope, never heard of the guy."

"Never?"

Aloysius shrugged. He made the face of one who had very thoughtfully considered smelling a volcano but ran instead. The shape of his dried-out lips expressed concern and they promised, as he pursed them tighter and tighter, that he neither knew anyone of that ilk, anyone of that appellation, or anyone in the unbuttoned world of anything.

"Because if you *are*," said Officer Weatherwax, leaning with his chest out, his chest newly-invested in bulletproof Gore-Tex. "I'm going to bust you down to your nuts, Assguard!"

"His name isn't Assgaard, Officer," said Hawk Eye. "It's Night Sea Journey. How do you like them apples?"

"Christ!" said Aloysius. "Well, butter me up and call me a biscuit because—I—am—!"

Torg pushed open the crash-barred door to BookSmart from inside.

"What are you doing out there in the cold, Aloysius?" asked Torg. "I need you in here to man the register."

"What the heck—I thought I was locked," said Aloysius, "out?"

"The door was open when I got here," said Torg. "And it was busy, and that deaf-mute guy Undone Buttons—whew! funkier than grandpa's underwear—with those really thick, shiny Marvel comic books he always swipes from Walker Library? He was here waiting impatiently, pestering customers to buy stolen Barnes & Noble gift cards and cursing a lightning blue streak because no one would."

Aloysius looked at the thumpers and the thumpers looked at him.

"Come on Hawk Eye, let's go, we'll give you a pony ride up to the corner on Lyndale & Lake by the Falafel King," said Officer Lowry.

"Oh, okay, thanks much," sighed Aloysius, crunching the sand pebbles from his eyes.

Officer Weatherwax dogged Aloysius into BookSmart.

"Who, Torg?" asked Aloysius. "I don't know any deaf-mute guys."

"Okay," said Officer Weatherwax. "Where did the deaf-mute guy go?"

"I guess," said Aloysius, "he heard you coming."

"Whoever he was," said Torg.

"Officers, I don't buy stolen books!" said Aloysius. "I don't have a big bank roll like James Laurie on Nicollet—"

"—that asshole—" quipped Torg.

"—or Tom from Midway Books—"

"—another asshole—" cut Torg.

"Torg!" said Aloysius. "Officer, I'm not that desperate. All I do is open the doors in the morning, let the sunshine in, and the wheels roll off by themselves!"

"We like you, Aloysius," said Officer Weatherwax, leaving. "Just keep it clean!"

"There were already people in the store when I got here," continued Torg. "Your mother Ariel wants you to call her, and you're supposed to call Lily Holmgren, who is wondering why you never call her back, but she said she still loves you. And that clown who looks like a clown was here and he wanted to know if you are officially or unofficially open or closed. Are you?"

"Was it that Ronalds McDonald's type guy?" asked Aloysius, pinching his face like clay back into the shape of his usually worn face. "Oh! Saami forgot to lock the door! That's what happened! I feel much better. For a second, I thought we couldn't open the store! Say, Torg, would you mind standing here while I boogie to McDonald's? Want anything?"

That the night before Saami floated his teeth (on the clock), Chitchee had squelched out of loyalty. Nor any mention of rabies. No aliens to speak of in Lakewood Cemetery. No ghosts, no tunnels, no Somalis in burqas digging up baby graves for cash on the Silk Road. Mummies is the word. *Ta Sin*.

"What's that smell?" asked Chitchee, his mouth squared into a trash receptacle.

Chitchee sniffed the way into his bathroom. His bathtub of dirty water had backed up with floating broccoli, carrots, onions, cauliflower, and stewed kale in the black slurry of a garbage disposal's undigested sludge—of someone else's Drano and dreck. The old pipes were always rotting, rotting all the way back to the Roman Empire, Dan the Maintenance Man had once hypothesized to Dan the Caretaker, who seemed to be impressed by this classical allusion to a movie. All the pipes in Minneapolis disintegrate every year anyway. Growing back, rotting, growing back like an evolving fungus. It was ol' Mother Nature destroying everything within reach like a baby.

Chitchee killed a centipede with the rolled-up, blank pages of what had been his future, his novel *The Hell Hound Chip*. The fossilized centipede attached to his manuscript looked edible—a source of quick energy and fun he thought—microwaving it and eating it absently. He would throw out the dead mouse after it had dried.

Saami had popped Ambien, two ten-milligram tablets, not one, dressed, wobbled home for a shot (that turned into a firing squad) of vodka, blacked out, and merrily headed out for last call at the Uptown Bar, although it had closed at one o'clock, although he remembered standing outside the CC Club to take a leak.

"How come Saami didn't open?" asked Torg.

"Saami? He was mugged last night by a 30-something Somali big mother," said Aloysius, looking to see if his *kantele* was still in his hold pile. "With pumpkins!"

"I've been mugged fifteen times by dozens of thugs, and I never missed a day of work at the Department of Public Safety," said Torg, brandishing an unlit cigar he bought at Carousel Tobacco in Carousel Square. "And one time I was left for dead, screaming on the sidewalk in a pool of blood at the bus stop. A big galoot punched my left eye out through my glasses, but the worst pain was when I saw the bill from Hennepin County Med. 4,000 dollars. Don't ever take an ambulance! 10,000 dollars for the first mile! You are better off flying to Luxor and shitting all over the Valley of the Kings."

"Okay, Torg, thanks buddy," said Aloysius, easing slowly into something scalding like a hot bath, "for the heads up, and thanks for opening the store and answering the phone and taking down the messages. So go ahead and pick out a book for yourself under 4.99."

"Books on tape on vinyl in here?" asked Torg, who had never ventured beyond the shallow end of the front counter.

"Here," said Aloysius, grimacing at his wallet. "Take five ones."

Torg waved him off. "Anything for an old friend, Aloysius."

"You're right," said Aloysius. "So who is this old friend?"

"You are!"

Torg waved him off angrily on the second wave, completely astounded at the man's incredible depth of oblivion—*they were complete and absolute strangers.* And Torg had waived the five bucks!

(Torg had called the FBI from the community phone at Lunds Grocery Store on Lake Street to report on Zalar Gossick, who had indeed blinded Torg in one eye one night at a #6 bus stop. Zalar robbed him of a stack of Braille Big Band albums checked out from the downtown library, his wallet, his ATM debit card, and Minnesota ID. The sight and sound of Zalar in BookSmart triggered in Torg a paralyzing fear for his life and a trickle of urine on his BVDs, which he adjudicated over and decided wasn't so bad; but he would have to change his BVDs on the morrow.)

"Yeah? FBI guy? T. O. undercover here. I wanted to inform you that Zamart, the rat-faced weasel, seems to have lost an important Family Photo Album," paused Torg, standing on a chair and facing the Lunds checkout lanes and aisles, "and from what I gather—from an inside source who leaked this . . . Yes, I'm almost done with the phone! The weasel-faced rat's name is Zamar or Zamart Ghostwick or Gooseneck! Or something Greek to me. Is this line secure? Maybe we should meet by Lake Calhoun inside a tree. I will corroborate the name and get back. Over. I am now maintaining radio silence . . . and out . . . 10-4."

"Yeah, go ahead," said FBI Agent Hillswick to himself, eyes somersaulting in backward flips, listening to his messages, and swatting an unknown insect crawling across his desk.

Hillswick sat stone-faced before yet another scrambled signal from yet another scrambled egg-mouth "busting" suspicious-looking individuals who looked homeless, acted out of line, lay down on a park bench, carried a package with an unusual number of vertices down Lake Street, or smirked on the bus like a cow.

A THIRTY-SOMETHING SOMALI BIG MOTHER

Aloysius was dead by now, dead with his mouth open too, so shocked by life as to be done with it—burgled of everything . . . Chitchee scrambled for his black beanie acorn cap and the acorn caps he had painted black as his jeans, which he front-pocketed in his jeans . . . he thrust a *Qu'ran* in his back pocket . . . what if the burglar figured out there was no money . . . faced with only that last bit of blue cheese in the fridge, if it hadn't evaporated into the ultra violet already . . . there was no telling what retaliative, retail destruction a band of junkies could do . . . with a rented U-Haul full of used books no one wanted except Half Price books which didn't want them either . . . Chitchee's apartment shivered . . . the world was getting colder . . . he was used to feeling cold in tiny studio spaces but not really . . . he froze like a cherry in a stone . . . sleeping in sleeping bags for body heat under a soak of vodka . . . with his socks on . . . the big house he had shared with LaDonna was drafty but warm as the touch of her flesh . . . now the registers around his studio baseboards felt dead cold to the touch . . . maybe the scroogilistical landlord didn't turn on the heat for November? Who was the landlord, he didn't even look! Turn on the oven . . . the heat will pour out . . . small enough space . . . Chitchee hoped the stove could serve as a space heater . . . space heaters blew up electricity bills and fuses . . . yeah she is a space-heater, uh oh here she comes . . . waiting for warmth. Jog in place? The heat died two feet out. No, the oven didn't work. Boil water until blood coagulates. Sex with Dagny: how he had crushed on her and why? His coldness destroyed his poise with her. All because he had a new white pimple of desire on his nose, and the self-consciousness from that gummed up his spontaneity with Dagny. Haircut, car, retirement plan. That morning argued for sunny metaphysical statements of nonsense, meaningless rhymes, and bowls of clichés. He loved clichés because he liked to mend them. Worn out for a good reason they were once new. "The ship plowed the sea" at first was fireworks. "Where did you get that? What else do you have up your tunic? You're blowing my mind with these radical comparisons. Ships and plows? I have to sit down. Amazing!"

The image of Aloysius lying lost in his own Norwegian blood hampered Chitchee's concentration. Prowler at large in BookSmart. Like Moosbrugger in *A Man Without Qualities*. Old *OMNI*, new *Wired*. Can't define anything without making a mess of things. Words under the sheets and between the covers. Too cold to get up and book. I am the gray goo I read about in *OMNI*, the end of the world . . . self-replicating nanobots and Von Neumann machines and not even a decently-heated apartment . . . so we eat all the greens of the word salad those fascist capitalists implanted in us with their hell hound chips . . .

Chitchee pieced his thoughts together in this way, not so much a stream of consciousness but a discontinuity of quantum biscuits.

Garden apartment windows, clouds budding in gray, leafy curves, the sky drizzling hexagons from the low black nimbostratus, a few cold snow drops here and there melting on the sidewalk. Sunshine another brand of soda crackers. Freezing. Frozen. Silverfish on wall. Frozen Silverfish Sticks. Preheat the oven to 475 degrees. Stuff backpack with Snickers bars, spiral notebooks, a thermos of last night's coffee, moribund apple, dead Cavendish banana, and a chunky hunk of day-old French bread someone gave him.

"Do you want a relationship?" Dagny had asked Chitchee's acorn-shaped face. "How many relationships have you had? Do you know what your sperm count is?"

"I want to love someone who loves me and vice versa. Isn't that what you are supposed to say? What should I have said?" Chitchee asked himself. "What should I have—"

His neighbors' blasting monotonous stereos at four in the morning and picking fights in the hall came back to him to explain his lack of sleep.

"Gloria, you remind me of Empress Lu, the wife of Liu Pang! So why can't the frat rats next door to me in #110 have their arms and legs chopped off and their bodies thrown into an outhouse sewer? And their golf clubs thrown down after them?"

Later he returned Gloria's threatening messages about his threatening messages with another threatening message. No reply. Chitchee replied to her non-reply with a non-reply, gauging his silence to fit her silence.

He called his Congressional Representative Keith Ellison who, Chitchee claimed to Gloria, bought a book at BookSmart, unlike Gloria who seemed to "gloria in her illiteracia" and was "caught up in a spinster wheel running after the gravy." He regretted leaving that insult on her message system. He would visit her office and beg forgiveness. Kiss her thorny ankles. He couldn't *expect* her to read Sima Qian! Hadn't she planned to buy a planner, when the whole plan blew up on her?

The feeling of anxious, impending doom dimmed his mind when he decided to withhold the rent he didn't have in order to smash this broken, capitalist, trickle-up racket. And then wait for his mom to send some money. Paisley maintained a post office box in Wayzata for him, but why pay for his own boxed-in box surrounded by fraternity puke, spermed Trojans, beer cans, pizza boxes, daisied underwear, and broken windows? The boxed-in occupants had no respect for neighbors, quite the opposite: they were in their boxes, pressing the levers for their pleasure centers to light up in order to start their hooting like drunken owls.

"Dan, #110!" said Chitchee. "They punched out all their windows, broke all the hall lamps, and tipped over the coke machine in the lobby."

"Gloria said that was okay because they are white."

He had complained to Dan the Caretaker in the middle of the night. Dan the Caretaker said anyway Gloria quit or was fired. After Chitchee had complained about #110 he turned his attention toward #106, a small outpost of 20 guys, whose car speakers made the building shake and burst sewer pipes underground. Both brotherhoods retaliated by taunting Gloria in the hall and blew belches of beer and smoke in her face. On one side Chitchee had crack jocks and on the other jockstraps. Now the referee was forced out of the ball game and ejected. Now MPG would never respond. Dan the Caretaker skirted the issue and was afraid and shaky. The dealers next door were as massive as the Oakland Raiders' offensive line, and they tried Chitchee's doorknob every night to intimidate him from making another noise complaint.

Chitchee wasn't intimidated one bit, but to be on the safe side, he unscrewed all his light bulbs. If the guys in #106 broke into #108, they would be in the dark where Chitchee could Cretan axe them with a baseball bat, one by one, like hitting fungos . . . same went for the crackers in #110 next time they pounded on Chitchee's door with golf clubs and hooted like drunken owls for a fist fight.

Chitchee in his personal library sat like a live football on the 50-yard line of a Packer-Raider Super Bowl rematch.

Chitchee threw on his black leather jacket, grabbed his gloves, and ran out the front door.

Watching his breath condense into silver powder, he thought of Mr. Popper's penguins waddling along. Penguins like ornithological bonobos. A shivering feeling of having forgotten something. Oven off. Easy off. He had forgotten to take out the stinking garbage and had to run back quick. He grabbed the garbage and walked toward the dumpster. He waved hello and yelled "Dan!" After no response, Chitchee looked closer: it was Dan the Caretaker, not Dan the Maintenance Man. Dan the Caretaker almost scuttered off, looking like Peter Rabbit. He wanted to avoid Chitchee's chewing off his ear and gnashing it like bloody gum, but he was aware that Chitchee's bathtub was clogged. Dan stood frozen, conflicted. For that matter, Dan the Maintenance Man had been rather aloof since Chitchee mentioned that he had voted for Obama. They had been rather chummy, but suddenly Dan the Maintenance Man's distance was pure Ice Nine. Their relationship had been poisoned. It had been light over easy, now it was as muddled as dumb mud. Chitchee fretted over possible causes. Was Dan the Maintenance Man so opposed to the opposition as to have lost his plumber's mind? Dan the Caretaker also avoided Chitchee, he noticed. Maybe he feared Chitchee's talking about Diderot, D'Alembert, or even Ben Franklin; so Dan the Caretaker was no philosopher either. Lately, when Dan the Caretaker happened to bump into Chitchee, they stopped, quarreled silently, and moved on. Dan the Caretaker squished in his ear buds, pretending to be listening to a TED talk on Innovation. Chitchee shunned Innovation at that moment. He had been waiting for Dan the Maintenance Man to fix the bathtub drain and the kitchen sink until he was sick in the face. What if Dan died? He looked for dead Dans in the *StarTrib* online obituaries.

"Dan, have you seen Dan?" asked Chitchee.

"I don't know anything right now," flinched Dan. "I'm listening to a TED talk. Innovation."

Dan pointed to his podded ears.

"How many TED talks on Innovation can there be?" asked Chitchee. "Can't they think of something else to TED talk about? Innovate a new TED talk on innovation and then TED talk that TED talk to death and then keep innovating new innovating TED talks . . . Is that the deal? What a goddamn rat race!"

Dan the Caretaker did not want to address Chitchee at all; he shook his smiling (obligatory) head, slowly removing the black earbuds from his ears (as if they had gotten tangled), which they hadn't. He fidgeted them nervously like a rosary. Dan the Caretaker might never get the wires disentangled. He might have to take the earbuds into the earbud store. Could he build a better earbud? *Innovation*, Dan! Start with a new name!

"But Dan the Maintenance Man can fix just about anything," said Dan the Caretaker.

"I agree, he just about fixed my bathtub drain and he just about fixed my kitchen sink," said Chitchee.

"Well, I don't know about that, you'll have to complain to the landlord. And he lives on a three-story yacht off the coast of the Antilles Islands and never responds to his registered mail."

"He doesn't work?"

"He works. He works on his tan."

"Okay, well if you see Dan, Dan, can you send Dan?"

Dan wasn't going to tell Dan. Dan did not like to deign to Dan; it caused resentment and emotional chaos in Dan, who, as Maintenance Man, ranked higher than a talentless layabout caretaker. Dan was a Dan's Dan, so Dan and Dan never hit it off in the scramble to amass prestige, status, and honors at Fremont Terrace apartments. The "first Dan" haled from Osakis, the "second Dan" from Mahtomedi; geography alone pitted Dan against Dan. Social relationships were of a finer silken thread than Charlotte's web and tempers flared when a filament threatened to break and need repairs.

This Armageddon with the Dans exhausted Chitchee to the point of nervous collapse. He slumped back to his cold studio, Danned to death. He broke out a small, thin wall mirror. Chitchee had squirreled away the precious Peruvian for a snowy day, squirreled away Kennedy's cocaine find. One line down. Two lines down. His head felt like a lighted sparkler. Paranoid, he feared Gloria storming in with the Fire Marshall Bill saying that all the books on the floor are a fire hazard. And then they would all spontaneously combust. No, Gloria was gone, remember? Well good riddance he said to himself. I feel good. I can do another line. No Glorias to hold me back now! Upsy daisy, sssssswwwwttt!

Chitchee heard a knock on the door. He recognized the knuckles of Dan the Maintenance Man. Besides, no one ever knocked. They usually just broke in.

"Dan, you are alive! *Marhaba*!"

Chitchee's nose bled a bulb-shaped line of blood. He thrust his head back, toilet paper in his nostrils sponging up blood; while opening the door to #108, he eyed Dan the Maintenance Man like a sideways, government mule. Chitchee pointed at the stove without looking at it or Dan.

"The pilot light always goes out," said Chitchee.

"Well, it's on now," said Dan defensively. "Problem with the bathroom sink?"

Dan walked into the bathroom and turned on the faucet.

"Nothing wrong with it!" continued Dan. "The bathroom sink always does that. It's an old building from the '70s."

"Try the kitchen sink!" said Chitchee.

"Nothing wrong with that either, it's just a little slow—in the winter."

"And the heat register?"

"Nothing wrong with that!"

"It doesn't work."

"Nothing wrong with that! Landlord hasn't turned it on yet."

"Why?"

"Because he never turns it on."

"How about my nose? Nothing wrong with that?"

"Actually," said Dan, examining with the refined eye of the plumber, "that *is* leaking blood, you should get your nose fixed."

"Okay, thanks Dan," said Chitchee. "Who fixed your nose? It looks a little better now. You know, I was thinking we used to click. But now, there is estrangement between us. Was it something I said? Was it because I said something against Hobbes?"

"Uhhhh," said Dan, looking askance, "I'll get around to fixing the bathtub later—try not taking a bath for a few days. That shouldn't be too hard."

Chitchee allowed Dan a head start, scurried out the door, and flew under one long cloud that tickled all the way down his phlegmy sore throat like ugly snot going backwards.

Cowboy-hatted Mad Jack Apple Jack's wino-red eyes ran together like flies going at it. He slumped on Fremont Avenue against a factory wall whose ventilator shaft spewed hot, sheet-metal gray air, his blue jean jacket ripped by wolves. Chitchee kicked his boots and asked if he was okay. Mad Jack fluttered with an apology, drowned out by an intake-fan. Chitchee gifted his black fur-lined gloves to Mad Jack's exposed solar plexus. Then he ran off to rescue Aloysius. What if Aloysius had been recruited by al-Shabaab? No, Aloysius would never have the energy to blow himself up!

Spindling down the avenue, thrusting his dentures in his threadbare pocket, and picking at the nits in his scalp, Undone Buttons, in his buttonless, shredded gray overcoat, threatened traffic. Claiming he was deaf and dumb, he sold the free bibles he stole from Treasures Await to flashy folks in Maseratis. He handed out hand-written business cards. If the commuter drove on, Undone Buttons spit and swore a dragon flame. The thumpers were so sick of the angry bird they left him to his own snares.

Undone Buttons, thought Chitchee, I wonder what he reads? Spinoza's *Ethics*? A guy like that? "Neither can the body determine the mind to think nor the mind determine the body to motion." For that matter, Undone Buttons probably never bothered to read the directions to Act II Microwave popcorn or even bothered to cook it.

Undone Buttons accosted Chitchee with a note requesting funds past due, with a late fee added on. What was causing Undone Buttons's frenzied aura, reincarnated from a water-skimming insect that looked down for the first time and drowned?

"Normally," said Chitchee, smiling typically, "I don't like to loan out money, dear Buttons. Nor do I lend my books. Samuel Johnson said: nobody reads the book you lend them. Here's a couple bucks. No need to pay me back."

"Pay you back? You look like a fuckin' faggot rodent!" said Undone Buttons. "I'm not going to pay you back! Fuck you and your fuckin' rodent bullshit."

"Comrade, you are caught in the orbit of *samsara*!" said Chitchee. "Everyone has the right to a beautiful life. Give me a hug. I am a hugging machine like Temple Grandin constructed—"

Undone Buttons spit a green wad in Chitchee's face.

"K," said Chitchee. "I didn't see that coming!"

The wet spray hardly phased Chitchee, saliva so light he barely knew it was there when he wiped it off with a leather jacket sleeve and coughed into his leather elbow. Undone Buttons fumed at the Uptown world of store-shoppers to and fro with bags: bulging grocery bags, double-bagged double-handled branded bags, bags plain and plastic fancy, and sparkling paper bags with glittering fancy clothes tissued inside them and receipts ensconced in Hapsburg rococo curls. The bags and the baggers bagged their consumer goodies (a century of bags) oblivious to the world's slaughterfest of poverty, war, and famine. They were passersby to Undone Buttons's life wreck. Looks as blank as garage door windows Undone Buttons took as "fighting words." The blank looks of the middle class white as the Oil of Ofay were jabs, jibes, taunts, and attempted stabbings while he walked on hot coals in Death Valley. The idle suburban shopper struck Undone Buttons as a slow looter, because the slow looter bought luxury items manufactured in a cobra pit in Calcutta where the children and old widows worked and died like rats in sweatshop factory fires, while Ganesha from the banks of the Jumna elephant-walked down the boulevard of suffering, jingling his gold coins in his jangling jute bag, and the Monsanto-monopolized cotton fields forced the farmers to guzzle their own Roundup to escape debt with excruciation, death, and the poor family left behind screaming.

Snapped out of this hybrid of daydreaming and sleepwalking, Chitchee's thoughts, curled up in their curled-up dimensions, reset to normal. He quick-stepped into a froward-frowning Hawk Eye, freewheeling ambly-shambly back from The Falafel King in order to panhandle outside BookSmart to catch the crowd, de-brunching from Club Miami.

Aloysius looked okay, but he tuned his *kantele* not okay, and set it on a shelf.

Chitchee heard Noel's worried voice:

"Saami, can you possibly come in later?"

Noel gripped the store phone like a military commander in a war room, anxiously at the same time using hand signals to communicate around him.

"Are you up to it? If you're not able to walk, I can pull a double, okay, take care," said Noel, sentimentally welling up for a moment.

When Chitchee approached, Noel's tears dried like a gully in a hot Grand Canyon swale.

"What? Ok, ok, ok. That's what I said," said Noel. "Weren't you listening and taking notes? I have to go."

Noel hung up on Saami like he was a wrong number for the second time.

"Chitchee, that was Saami. He just got out of HCMC. I guess he was mugged, beaten, and hospitalized by the CC Club—"

"The entire CC Club beat up Saami?" asked Chitchee in wonder. "What could he have said to the waitress this time?"

"Don't be absurd!" said Noel. "This is serious! He woke up in the hospital and can't remember what happened. He said he remembered leaving his hospital bed—walking—he saw a big white flash—and then he was in a hospital bed. He's going to be a little late."

"A mugger got him?" asked Chitchee.

"He told Aloysius he thinks a group of some about thirty-something Somali grandmothers on Rollerblades jumped him from behind and smashed him over the head with Halloween pumpkins, left him for dead and propped a baby's skull in his mouth," said Noel, spinning his eyes toward Chitchee, "if you can believe that."

"Maybe it's a message from the future," said Chitchee. "But thirty pumpkins? That's the part I don't get. From where? A Somali gang of thirty-something grandmothers on Rollerblades out jacking pipsqueaks on Halloween . . . unemployment is that high, alas. *Did you say a baby's skull?*"

Melusina and Kriemhilde poked their heads out of the Cooking and Crafts aisle.

"How many times do I have to say it?" asked Noel. "I already said what I had to say. And I said it. I said it once, so I said it twice! The point is, Chitchee, not to go around repeating yourself. Just don't repeat yourself. Repeating yourself degrades the level of discourse in the Age of the Internet when no one even says hi anymore because of all the texting, Facebooking, and YouTubing."

"What?" asked Chitchee, confused. "I text, Facebook, and YouTube every night at work, and I say hi. Baby skull? Was I a-hearin' you right? Did you hear that ladies? Mel, Hildy! A BABY SKULL! Sick, sick, sick."

Noel looked at his fingernails.

Then Chitchee looked at Noel's fingernails. The silent as nails treatment.

"Noel, friend, listen to me," said Chitchee. "If your signal to me was degraded, you might actually *want* redundancy in the system. As you well know, in information theory there is the Shannon formula for that."

The entire store heard a "NOT gate" SWITCH in Noel's brain.

Noel blocked Chitchee's speech-act as unworthy of response. Noel couldn't have a decent conversation with a Millennial— so it was not worth talking to anyone. The day a Millennial is worth saying hi to—*that* would be the Millennium. The voice of reason has been drowned by the Internet surface chatter of Millennials who could not say hi *even once*, forcing Noel to repeat his forced greetings over and over. He gave up communicating with Millennials, who never noticed his silences anyway—they were so busy blowing him off with the silent treatment whenever he even looked at them.

"Earth has been destroyed, not by capitalist monopolies, but by *StarCraft*," said Noel.

Noel's mouth and lips whisked to one side of his face as if kissing the Pope's cheek.

CHITCHEE LOVES TO
STRAIGHTEN BOOKSHELVES

Saami was laid up for weeks. Chitchee rolled up his red/black flannel shirt sleeves and commenced to do what he loved most—alphabetize the bookshelves. Chitchee removed dust jackets of hardcover collectibles and wrapped the dust jackets with mylar transparent covers. Helping out Snorri, he repaired bindings with wood glue. The recently arrived books, Chitchee Goo Goned. He scraped off (with his thumbnails) the previous price stickers, and scrubbed off the stickumish and residual glue, carefully using economical sections of Bounty paper towel and making sure Aloysius saw that he was being frugal with the "good stuff." A little more elbow grease and he was ready to apply his protestant work ethic to work, the same work ethic that caused Max Weber to have a nervous breakdown and contemplate suicide.

Downstairs he straightened the shelves and brought the AWOL books back to attention. He carried Bobblehead's massage book back to where the guy could sniff and find it. He returned Jason Unterguggenberger's fave *And I Don't Want To Live This Life* to the unsettled groups of musical bios. So, one by one, Chitchee inspected every spine, checked condition, and mowed down the rows, row after row. He had to know where every book in the store stood. The *arete* of a simple book clerk he strode for. He had to master every aspect of the book business before opening the covers of his own book store, Ulysses & Sons.

He smiled to himself: yes I love this book store too. *Dhikr*. He dusted off History (Ambroses, Tuchmans, Braudels), which covered the north wall; and Military History (with plenty of *Jane's*), which stood in the northeast corner for the (usually not-so-buff) military buff. Chitchee checked up on the Family and Medicine and tussled with the Psychology section, thinking to divide it into: historical, psychoanalytical, cognitive, and "happy" books by: Maslow, Csikszentmihalyi, Goleman, Gardner, Levitin, Gladwell, for examples. He refreshed Sociology, which was in the northwest corner with *Nickel and Dimed*, *Pedagogy of the Oppressed*, *The Power Elite*, DuBois, Fanon, Marx, Said, Kozol, and Coles. He tidied up the mass mess spread across the south wall: True Crime, Unbelievable Crime, Mysteries, Science Fiction, Fantasy, and Horror, with proper kudos to Edgar Allen Poe (who had single-handedly invented half the basement's genres). Chitchee feather-dusted, swept the cobwebs, vacuumed carpets and runners, replaced light bulbs, chased the ghosts away, burned sage to aerate the metaphysical plane, and sat down on a lumpy, bloated, garagey chair that passed gas when he sat on it. He stood up and pulled off the seat cushion and discovered a chemical-smelling periodical, *Giant Tits for Gentle Yanks*. Are you kidding? Did Bobblehead stash that?

Chitchee expected to meet interesting writers at BookSmart. He stuck his head in the bathroom and cleaned the toilet with Lysol and Scotch-Brites. Who knew who might be pissing and shitting here someday? And Minneapolis had a cohort: Tim O'Brien, Louise Erdrich, Heid E. Erdrich, Roberto Bly, Jim Klobuchar, Sigrid Underdaswetter. Robert Pirsig had lived nearby briefly. John Berryman suicided off the Washington Avenue bridge. Chitchee always walked on the north side of the bridge out of respect for contagious vertigo, recalling James Wright's: "But he was not buried in Minneapolis/At least./And no more may I be/Please God."

"In blaming Minneapolis, Wright was Wrong," Chitchee yelled. He thought there were other great writers associated with Minnesota (more than you could shake a spear at) who did not suicide off the Washington Avenue bridge onto the icy ground: Gordon Dickson, Bujold, Simak; then Neil Gaiman on Team Dream Haven; then Steinbeck who drove through Golden Valley with Charley; Sinclair Lewis running down Main Street chased out of town; and there were a lot of successful mystery writers too, John Sandford, Vince Flynn, Steve Thayer, and included in this group was Garrison Keillor, admiring whom was certainly a mystery. Wanda Gág, Kate DiCamillo, Brenda Ueland, Sigurd Olson all had the itch to write in the snow.

Chitchee anticipated meeting professors, scholars, academics, editors, publishers, poets, intellectuals, and artists of bohemian genius. To no avail. But someday, Solomon Deressa would come back, because so far, Chitchee had met only one published writer, the already forgotten Amharic poet, the only man of letters to fit the bill of the endangered "man of letters," the Oromo exile of Powderhorn Park. But Chitchee hadn't seen him in a worrisome while—not even over at the Rainbow grocery store's produce, where he used to be found, a Walt Whitman in the beets and yams. Where was Quetzalcoatl? Chitchee asked around but no one knew where he lived. What about a number? The sacred ibis of Thoth was not a number.

Chitchee straightened the last leaning book and made haste for the bathroom. He loved the bottom of the ladder where he could just about lick the bottom rung when he stood up straight. Feeling good, Chitchee might restart *The Hell Hound Chip*, although he never tired of never starting it, and he never tired of talking to captive strangers at bus stops about never starting it. It was too good to start. He also erased LaDonna's angry reaction when she suspected that he erased the whole book while editing. He lied his way out of that by copying passages from *A Song of Ice and Fire: A Game of Thrones* and leaving the pages around to look like a revised version of *The Hell Hound Chip*. She picked up a page and said of it:

"A lot of first drafts are as bad as this! Don't feel bad about changing professions! Being a writer is complicated. It's not for the old and faint of heart. Are you *sure* you still want to write? Plenty of writers say they write, but write nothing at all. Have you ever thought about that? Was it Laura Ingalls Wilder who wasn't discovered until the day she was deader than a a doornail on a plank bed—or was that Darger?"

Chitchee's mind carouseled forward (as he flushed the cleaned toilet) in squares. As soon as he caught up on his bills (he might have to sell some books), he would take Dagny somewhere fancy like Mickey's Diner. Even if it cost him a whole Blue and White.

Dagny had already exported Chitchee from the "attracted to him" file to the folder labeled: "males." That included: "not cute, not my type, nothing behind the eyes guys, hope he's not a creep, he's a creep, hope he's not a stalker, stalker, hope he's not a serial killer, serial killer, restraining order information, more forms, last will & testament, list of witnesses and notaries, tentative obituary, and DNA samples of all ex-boyfriends."

Chitchee knew he was in perfect equilibrium with Dagny. His love for her was immense and words for it were only measuring the sky with fittable spoons. What a great team they would make—*once he established eye contact with her*. Chitchee, walking toward the utility closet, thought he was hand in hand with Dagny. He gave the neighborhood bathroom a once-over for stashes of acetone-smelling periodicals, spent cartridges, drugs, and guns. Chitchee, scrub-brush and Soft Scrub at hand, reckoned cleaning toilets was as respectable as any other job in the bathrooms of the galaxy. He Comet-cleaned the porcelain sink and toilet, and Pine Soled the mirror with a streaky rag. A Vietnamese busdriver once claimed Ho Chi Minh cleaned bathrooms on steamers for seven years and washed dishes in Marseilles for another seven, but that sounded too Biblical to be true.

Finishing up in the bathroom, Chitchee visualized his sampo cloth karmically wiping clean everything karmic from his karma. He felt inspired enough to go up to the front register and write something. Torg had encouraged his writing too, after a fashion. Torg had listened to the audiobook of *50 Shades of Grey* (suggested to Torg by Dale the Raging Librarian to get rid of him), and Torg confronted Chitchee point blank:

"Why don't you write any old trash like *50 Shades of Grey*? And throw the trash out there?"

"Throw the trash out where? Sort of like space junk? Launch it into orbit? Okay Torg, you're On!"

So Chitchee opened a new Word Document (Aloysius was at McDonald's dodging Lake Street Rodney or Kennedy), typed, printed, and read aloud:

"*After our passionate lovemaking on the beach, I realize there are people all around. Christian, fluent in ten languages, apologizes to the entire Riviera. Then he rubs sunscreen over my exposed breast while kissing my lower lip. His strong and supple fingers work the sunscreen into my tanning breasts, and then he takes a dab and proceeds to coat my nipples with sunscreen. My eyes roll back in my eyelids with their ridiculously expensive eyelashes, and the aroma is awesome and tangy as the waves splash. I say I love the smell of the sunscreen. Christian leans over my mouth and whispers, 'That's not sunscreen, that's my sperm.'*"

"Do you mean trash like that, Holmes?" asked Chitchee.

"Not bad for trash," said Torg, sucking on the rhyming calabash, which he lifted in his hand like an after-dinner toast. "But it's going to need some sex to spice it up."

"Yes, old kidney bean, the world would be perfect, if it weren't for sex," added Chitchee, "but if it weren't for sex, the world wouldn't *be*."

"It's dead anyway," Torg shrugged.

Aloysius arrived from McDonald's and saw Snorri reading the obituaries.

"Snorri?" chirped Chitchee. "What's in the news? Any fresh murders out there? You know, jealous ex-boyfriend purees ex-girlfriend in a Waring blender, waits for the next light rail, places head on tracks, body found in woods, next town over."

Bubbling with an effervescence after this remark, Chitchee for no reason felt transported and translated into the 108 languages of paradise, which then, all at once, became one language, and eventually one word: mother.

"Robo-break," he announced and danced, singing "Next Town Over," featuring a lot of echolalia and pregnant silences . . .

Left, right, open left palm, open right palm. Doing the ol' Capek robot. Stopping, starting, stooping, standing. Chopping vegetables for stir fry. Head ratcheting, invisible gears. Then flat 2-D. He contorted in a Mobius striptease. He stopped. Conscious of the store's eyes on him (tears brimmed to his waterlines), with his hands, Chitchee formed a Theravadan bowl into which he thrust his face.

"You guys I can't do this anymore," cried Chitchee. "I lied, I'm not really a writer! I can't keep lying like this. My whole life is a lie. And I am so sorry I lied to the entire store, and will probably continue to lie, lie like a poor, poor politician, a pitiful, pitiful politician, talk talk talk balk balk balk bo-bo-bo-brok cluckle cack—"

"Lakewood Cemetery," said Snorri, looking askance at Chitchee, "is being burglarized by a very, very disturbed Somali woman. Just sick, just ughaggh! She must have lost her mind because she couldn't find a job. I don't blame her. The job market is *that tight*. Did you hear about this, Aloysius, about the job-tight Somali woman who went insane because there were no jobs out there for the unemployed to work? Poverty destroys minds and torches civilizations—"

"—what?" asked Aloysius. "Do the Vikings play the Bears next weekend? Do you know, Snorri?"

Snorri shook his head and donned his heavily corduroyed, cookie-buttoned coat. Extra large and stiff cookie buttons stuck out stiffly until he buttoned all the cookies in their cookie-cutter holes. And thus he achieved a smart look for the long depressing bus ride home.

THANKSGIVING SALE
AT BOOKSMART

But do you know what Noel did? Noel offered Snorri a ride home! And it was in Noel's father's brand new Lexus, because Noel's Ford Focus was in the shop with a cracked engine block. Noel's father Roger, who always supported his son with love, had found a good deal on a Honda Accord from Cars With Heart and intended that for his son's Christmas present. In the meantime they could share the Lexus, which they enjoyed for its excellent acoustics.

"Thanks, Noel," said Snorri, "I really appreciate it. Nice car too. Smooth ride. You can't even hear the outside with the windows rolled up!"

Noel smiled proudly, conscientiously monitoring the traffic attacking him personally. Once in a while, Snorri slammed his foot to brake. And Noel reassured Snorri that he was a Class-A driver and never had an accident or ticket.

"No problem! And listen to the stereo on this puppy! *Dance, McCobb*! Saint Song. Ye Young turned me on to this piece of classical for Halloween. It's kind of morbid, but I found a disco version that was more upbeat. I have to crank it. Stand back."

Disco Danse Macabre unwound like a loud black thread off a giant Singer sewing machine winding its multiways in all possible degrees of freedom through the interior of the Lexus.

"I know you don't want to talk shop talk," yelled Snorri, "but can you appreciate how hard it is for me as an empath to work at BookSmart?"

"You're an empath?" yelled Noel. "What *is* an empath? Is that like an indigo baby unicorn?"

"You didn't know that about me?" asked Snorri with a minted taste of condescension in his all-knowing look. "That's why all the customers give me such a royal pain in the ass. Oh, I thought you knew that. Oh. Go figure."

"So then," said Noel slowly, "is that why whenever Chitchee sets up an Empathy section, you tear it down?"

"Oh, come on!" said Snorri. "You don't know? Well, if you don't know, I'm not going to tell you . . ."

They drove on in silence with a loud stereo. Snorri directed Noel to take a left. Noel faced a back alley of dumpsters, dented ashcans, garbage for free, garages filled with antique computers, big box television sets, bicycle thief leftovers, and bushes reduced to thorns.

Aloysius worked at the computer screen, busy-looking, (he had his Ben Franklin glasses on), busy looking up *kantele* tablature for the Kinks. Or any song in D major. Chitchee sang "Lola," without the words, *a capella,* and after a few choruses Aloysius inexplicably felt ill, down-cycling into oblivion. He drove his white Chevrolet Trailblazer home to have a beer and a fresh Carousel cigarette, leaving Chitchee to hum in the store by himself. Chitchee called Saami, but Saami's phone was not in service (according to the authority of a depersonalized poindexter at the end of the line). He had learned a lot from Saami, he thought, while absent-mindedly missing the cradle of the telephone receiver so it was soon not in service.

Chitchee walked off, picturing Saami in Saami's perfect *Saam City*.

Saam City is a Turko-Romish Jerusalemy Tokyo of video game parlors, anime theaters, and manga stores. The thumpers are caped super villains. Life-size Japanese action figures swerve through space on beer and pot and Radiohead. Window-shopping shops are designed by H. R. Giger. Street-corners blare Ozzy on the Ozzo speakers and ozzybody on the street is on beer or pot and queued to multiplexes for royal audiences with the next movie from the eternal King Stephen. But oh no, superhero fans! Here comes an impossibly-scaled, rock 'em, sock 'em Meiji nationalistic Godzilla, stomping on the urban-ugly, Joe Coleman-drawn streets of a William Gibsonian red light district/jack hacker shack. Godzilla is going to disrupt the Tokyo premiere! He hates foreigners and especially Stephen King. But oh yes! A giant, fishnetted, cantilevered Betty Page appears over the skyline (Yukio Mishima and his army of patriots attack Betty Page's stiletto heels with their ancient and perfect steel swords). Betty Page grabs Godzilla from behind, strangles "they" (it's a gender unspecified non binary Godzilla), plants her heels, and then tosses Godzilla into the sequel.

Around eight o'clock, Spiderman appeared in a webbed red torso, a red mask with eye slits, and blue leggings. He had a black spider on his chest. Mouth masked, eyes lensed with goggles, spider gloves, and red rubber boots: all there. Spiderman matter-of-factly walked around the maroon counter into the EMPLOYEES ONLY area as naturally as if he worked in a book store for spiders and sold spider books.

Hawk Eye had drifted in behind Spiderman.

"Halloween must be late this year," said Kennedy, looking up from *The Memory Book.* "Nobody told you all the machinations were over?"

Kennedy curled up into a ball with his asthmatic laughter, which sounded like Chitchee's kitchen faucet choking on the first rushes of water in the morning.

"What's up with the cosplay, Saami?" said Chitchee. "Aren't you a little old for that?"

"You're never too old for getting murdered," said Saami, pulling off his mask to look at Chitchee.

Chitchee screamed.

"E-gadzooks!" said Chitchee. "What happened to your knobby little face?"

"Yeah, I know," Saami added with an expression of guilt, which revealed contusions, bruises, purple eyelids, and a missing tooth.

Saami and Chitchee shared a fatty of "Raven weed" in the back alley. They used the "method of relay," taking turns to watch the register, back and forth, and no that wasn't obvious to the customers, but the real problem with Chitchee's getting high at work was his losing empathy.

"Some forty-year old Somali mothers did that to you," said Chitchee, "with their pumpkins?"

"I better put this mask back on," said Saami.

"Grow a beard," said Chitchee. "And then you will be as handsome as ever."

Customer: "Do you have *The Tao of Leadership* by John Heider?"

Stoned bookseller Chitchee: "If you have to ask for *The Tao of Leadership* you'll never attain the Tao of Leadership. The Tao doesn't lead, manage, or compete with Toyota. Nor does it wind up unread in the Self-Help section. But if you like *The Tao of Leadership*, you'll love *Quantum Biscuits!* Which isn't out yet, but we do have *The Tao of Pooh*. We *always* have *The Tao of Pooh*. And the sequel *The Poo of Pooh*."

Customer: "Oh, I don't want *The Poo of Pooh*."

"Oh, so you're going to pooh pooh poor Pooh?" asked Chitchee. "Poo on you!"

Salah Mohammad and Hassan Abdi, regulars, walked into the store arguing Somali politics, and their love for their favorite subject always tore them apart.

Hassan was bald as a fireplug with a henna beard and talked loudly and worked as a translator. Salah was a thin and quizzical (with the posture of a question mark), well-dressed, stylishly quiet man with a shy look behind his polite glasses (he was always cleaning the lenses), and he worked at Hennepin County Medical Center as a nurse.

"*Nabod*," said Hawk Eye, turning around. "*As salaam alaykum*."

Hassan and Salah froze. "*Alaykum as salaam*," Hawk Eye mumbled.

"You speak Somali?" said Hassan with a sort of challenge.

Hawk Eye begged off, claiming his linguistic abilities were limited to confrontational "hellos" in twenty languages. Chitchee suggested he incorporate the "hellos" into a polylingual cardboard sign for "spare change," which they could find on the Internet, but Hawk Eye demurred.

Arguing Somali politics, Hassan vociferated and Salah disagreed; both walked up and down the stoic aisles until they realized that the more heated their politics, the less they knew what they were talking about; and then they kept going at it. Hassan's mood burst like a fish out of water at the beach in Mogadishu, where in fact he had been mistakenly shot by a teenager—shot in the arm so that he had to drive one-armed to capture the kid, drive him to his parents (whom Hassan was related to), and demand shillings.

"Chitchee," said Hassan. "You Americans can speak only one language, why is that?"

"Because bwain damage boss," mouthed Chitchee, stone-grinning and giggling like a tickled Poppin Fresh Doughboy.

Cameron McCocky strolled up to the counter and smiled half-ironically.

"Can I help you?" Chitchee addressed him, laughing at him.

"Do you have *Scan Her Darkly* Philip K. Dick because I'm on a phillip kick day, dick, I'm philliping for a fickle k. dick, I'm looking for *The Scanner Book*, man," said Cameron, fingering his mouth like clay to work the smirk off his face. "By Phillip Kaydick."

"That's perfectly understababandible," said Chitchee, "for a horselover of fatness!"

"No, I'm not sayin', I never said," said Cameron with a sharp fork in his throat. "You Dickle Day Fuckin Dickfuck! I'm a Kickle Dickle Fay Fuckstick on a fuckin kick for a Lickle Spittle Dickle Stiltskin—what are you looking—did you know—I love to read, it's a perfect way to kill time. Isn't it? Okay, I'm a little drunk. When some motherfucker steals your bitch, bitch. Where is that other guy?"

Hassan looked on with detached horror. Chitchee knew Hassan lodged yet another example of Western decadence in his indignant memory. F-bombs in his Muslim ears sounded like explosive booby traps.

"Yep, brain damage, Hassan," said Chitchee, his half-shut eyes incarnadine incarnate. "Most Americans are too old to learn a second language or master a first."

Everybody had a good laugh, even though no one thought it funny, but it was weird enough to qualify for funny in a weird way.

Cameron snaked around for Ye Young or Noel.

"Where is that mousey, geeky, pencil-necked, cucking . . . but first another drink at Club Miami to drink it over with."

Whore, bitch, cunt—only three words left in Cameron's drunken, slurring Logos.

"I'll tell Ye Young you stopped by! Thanks for stopping," said Chitchee, "your bullshit!"

Chitchee played Copland's *Our Town* and felt the inner warmth of *tapas* and—oh how much he loved his friends and co-workers at the end of the night when it was always impossible to express this feeling—then he Saami-smacked his forehead.

"Why did I say that? I should have suggested a book. Patanjali's *Yoga Sutras*!" said Chitchee aloud like a scold. "I can't help anything I do or say. Maybe I should go over and buy him a hot cocoa. Maybe I can go even cheaper and console him with lemon sugar cookies. There might be some broken ones. And I'll leave Aloysius a note with an offer to buy them, hoping he will write off that debt as a business expense, getting me off duty free."

Suddenly the store was empty, empty as the Milky Way spinning around in dark matter carousels and the sleepers were dreaming and the pony planets were dreaming up and down the universe too.

"Here we are," said Noel, pulling up to Snorri's house in the back alley. "Happy Thanksgiving, Snorri! It's not easy for me either, Snorri. Aloysius is selling Thanksgiving Day lemon sugar cookies he bought at Lunds—selling them at a dollar apiece! It's so embarrassing for a professional book store like BookSmart—"

"A world renowned book store like BookSmart," added Snorri.

"As soon as he leaves for home," said Noel, "I immediately put the lemon sugar cookies in the utility closet and then put them back before I lock up—it will look like I left them out by mistake. How's that? Eh? Brilliant?"

Snorri, with the door open, half-getting out, caused the cold air to whirl and snow to dissolve on the cushions inside.

"Noel," said Snorri, "we have to navigate this 'perfect storm' together if Aloysius's idea of diversifying our portfolio is selling lemon sugar cookies! If the City Health Inspector finds out, we're all going to be out on the tiles before Christmas."

"And who keeps bringing in all those books on empathy?" asked Noel.

"Chitchee does," said Snorri. "He feels sorry for them."

"No one's going to buy them," said Noel. "They're going to end up in the dumpster."

"Where do you think he finds them?" replied Snorri.

"Well, now what do we do with them?" asked Noel. "Could we put them on a cart and set them out on the sidewalk for free?"

"Are you kidding?" said Snorri. "Seriously? Do you know what kind of flies that books on empathy attract? I should know, I'm an empath!"

"So," said Noel, hoping to avoid a long goodbye. "I don't know where the store is going frankly. I better get going though. It's cold outside, aren't you cold?"

"I was thinking," said Snorri, keeping the door open and half getting back in.

Noel turned the car off.

"Let's you and I buy out Aloysius! Then hire Aloysius back as our Saami, after we fire Saami," said Snorri excitedly, having given the matter much thought. "We have to let Chitchee go. I love the guy to death, but he might even be *bad* for business to be honest, he hasn't learned a damn thing; moreover, he hasn't been of any use to anybody beyond the 'mind droppings' of comic relief like a class clown on a small town merry-go-round, do you know what I am saying? I know I recommended him—but the other day he and Saami reeked like a peculiar hybrid of blue diesel, purple kush, and orange cream indica. I know that because only a professional nose like mine could detect that—besides I bought a nugget of it the other day. It should still be in my pocket. Yeah, there it is."

"Snorri, it's cold," said Noel. "My dad expects his Lexus back soon."

"Oh, yep, I understand," said Snorri. "I'm going! Goodnight, take care, night, thanks, take care, bye-bye, talk to you later, yep, bye now."

Noel heard the door shut.

He turned up the gain on YeYoung's *Disco Danse Macabre* and tooled down the alley of yet another memory lane, past the peaceful houses and movie-glowing apartments like electric candles with electric moths warming up to the screens. He reflected on the foggy, misted-over windshield. With this almost Tolstoyan good deed of self-sacrifice in the can, Noel felt good about himself, Snorri, BookSmart, Thanksgiving, life, and YeYoung. Noel detected tiny knocks. The knocks grew louder and closer. Noel wondered whether he had topped off his father's gas tank with the wrong grade gasoline. Maybe he was running over potholes. Maybe danged rabbits had wrapped themselves around his wheels. Sometimes abandoned kittens hid in engine blocks. Maybe he was banging garbage cans. The drum machine, isn't it? He turned the music off—and he heard the xylophone's bones rattling. When Noel slowed to make his turn onto the main street, he noticed a piece of corduroy in the passenger side door.

Snorri stood outside, pounding on the passenger side window.

"What are you doing out there?" asked Noel, reaching over to open the door and releasing Snorri's corduroy jacket lapel, caught in the Lexus car door.

"My God!" bellowed Snorri. "Didn't you hear me? My jacket was caught in the car door! I've been screaming for hours, what seemed like an hour, for someone to call 911! Did you do that on purpose? You almost killed me!"

"I'll give you a ride b-b-b-backwards, if that h-h-h-hhelps," said Noel, overcome with emotion.

"No, you better get the hell out of Dodge," said Snorri, mopping his head sweat off with his ripped corduroy sleeve and seeing blood stains on his jacket, which meant paying for dry cleaning too. "Actually I called 911, and I gave the thumpers a description of your car! Are those the sirens now? You better get going. I can crawl home. I'm not getting in that Lexus death trap. Happy Thanksgiving."

"Happy Thanksgiving," said Noel.

"Oh," said Snorri, re-opening the door, "and thanks for the ride."

"Sure," said Noel.

Noel drove slowly down every side street he could find . . . parking, waiting, starting up again, then creeping home exhausted. Oh the Thanksgiving Day lemon sugar cookies—they're in the utility closet! I forgot to put them out for the morning! Aloysius is going to find them in the utility closet, unmoved from the day before. Oh, happy holidays!

MURDER ON THE BOOKSMART EXPRESS

Chitchee looked out the apartment window, waiting for the MJB coffee to drip from the coffeemaker he forgot to plug in. Chitchee heard a rustling of paper. Immediately he knew: another rent increase! He knew that sound! When Chitchee threw open the apartment door, he saw Dan the Caretaker's guilty shoes like scared rabbits running up the stairs to get away.

"Dan!" said Chitchee. "Caretaker Dan! Dan, I love you! Come back!"

A door slammed.

Dan's footsteps dripped in echoes down the anonymous halls of doors, carpets, shoes, other Dans, and other Dans' shoes.

"Another late fee for a non-emergency maintenance request?" Chitchee read the letter Dan had slipped under his door. "And a late fee for the late fee? What the fuck is this? ComCast?"

MPG's itemized charges for non-emergency repairs included all the unperformed but requested repairs, which required processing fees for HQ in the Yggdrasil building, because every mouse-sighting, maintenance request, and complaint had to be logged into the computer and deleted the next day.

"Oh, my Jesus!" said Chitchee, clutching at his crotch to stop from urinating while he danced around. "The rent just went up $450 from $650 to $1100, plus retro billing and then henceforth for water/sewer/snow shoveling fees, if I 'so choose' to stay while MPG 'refurbishes' my studio with a bar and wine rack—oh, perfect—I'm gonna wanna get bombed after throwing all my money on a wine rack."

MPG gave Chitchee ten days to decide, giving him notice to give notice to their notice of giving notice, which he had never noticed before. He pissed into the toilet bowl, but felt more exhausted than relieved afterward. Having to vacate the premises, he groaned and groaned and groaned laboriously and wept.

I have to throw some of my books into the dumpster, but it's always like suddenly I'm playing God with books: this book isn't so bad, I'll keep that one, this book I know someone wants (even though they don't, I'll force it in their hands and bug them to read it) oh, and I have two of this one, well, I bought it twice, and this book? IS amazing, I didn't know I had it, that one is pretty interesting, and this book in this box is a great good bad book and this is getting me nowhere, and oh no there's more over here and the kitchen cupboards cram-jammed, and the linen closet overflowing with classics of world literature, text books, and science projects.

Starting over, I have to toss out the Encyclopedia Britannica but there's a book-length article on languages I want, and fifteen years of Scientific Americans—two hours have gone by and I'm reading flat on my back paralyzed, reading a book on how to move your books, and it's pretty good TOO. I could save myself some trips if I placed my unwanted books in boxes by the dumpster, because inevitably The Indestructible Book Jesus will come along and bring them to BookSmart. Then he will haul all my books to ME. Then I buy them, pay out The Indestructible Book Jesus, and BookSmart has increased its inventory, and we're back in the black!

No, Chitchee sat down on the floor and cried, but the well was empty, and the ducts were dry. As if snow fell from his eyes. He had to move out. How? Who if he cried out would help him move his shit? He sobbed, and he stifled the next sob. He splashed his face with cold water to wash off the despair. His washed-out face hung on his skull like a hat on a rack. Night had fallen, although it was afternoon. Winter days in Minnesota split into thirds: afternight, twilight, and night. He clawed through some more boxes for a while, but stopped and stared at a box, because he saw that it was a black hole. He placed all the books back in their boxes. Then he lay down and stared at the ceiling, motionless as a fallen, beaten dog.

Snow flurries dusted down—frost on the window panes, hoarfrost on the utility poles—and rime rimming the Viking fork-beards, trimmed and untrimmed. Cirrostratus sheets of ice had left a pall of gloom in the open casket air of Minneapolis, the overcast citizens with no more expression to them than pincushions without pins. Shoulders down, Chitchee skulked by the purported human beings, dwarves, and trolls gray as chain-link fences. Each face had two minus signs for eyes and one minus sign for the mouth. Winter dogged on. Chitchee's Reeboks barely noticed the snow crystals floating like lotuses because he himself dissolved in lotus puddles. The frosted eyebrows of the Minneapolitans looked shocked by another early winter, a winter re-

realizing they had aged so quickly they would only grow older, frostier, colder, deader—and be forgotten snowfalls.

Skeins of ice, thin as sheets of graphite, stretched and yawned over the potholes, and the windshield wipers wiped the drizzling snowflakes with repeating, crickety stridulations. Every early-onset winter brought Chitchee half-frozen tears of rain, because the prospect of freezing to death for the next six months re-brutalized his body memory. The gray sidewalks carried the gray and graying pedestrians on Hennepin Avenue in gray overcoats like giant juncos. Some of the younger juncos wore junk coats with a flatness of face that suggested a dead, abandoned ant farm. Clutching collars, long gray beards appeared to head south. The Vikings with their long gray beards sensed the change in pressure, feeling it with their fingers in their sensitive, porcupine beards.

A north wind picked up and blew the McDonald's wrappers like xanthinic and carotened maple leaves down Hennepin Avenue into the margins of the gutters. Chitchee loved to watch the wind vomit trash. He laughed at all the garbage flying around like the Valkyries to Valhalla—and the garbage was laughing along with him. A kind of black day of death had threatened to burn Chitchee to cold, wet ashes inside, but his natural good spirits buoyed him at the thought of no thought. Look at that fire hydrant! It had a certain thusness. A sort of fellow feeling. Back to the fire hydrants themselves. Wasn't it one of love's blessings to be gifted with life on Earth? Absolutely Axiomatic!

There was Snorri in the distance, and how happy and wonderful Chitchee felt at the sight of an old friend. It was an event worthy of a Chinese poem written by a moonlit exile.

Snorri's black beard was black rust in the shape of a lobster pot.

He had set up two heavy stanchions, which cordoned off the sidewalk pedestrian traffic and detoured that population into BookSmart.

"Chitchee," said Snorri, outside BookSmart with his official, guarded face. "We have to get more people in the store. Before I die!"

"Before you die?" asked Chitchee. "No!"

Band-Aids swatched Snorri's fjordic face.

"Sir-ma'ams, the sidewalk is temporarily closed until further notice," said Snorri to the barbarous herd.

He scratched scratches on his thorny, horny-knuckled hands. A couple dreadlocks were missing.

"Oh, don't die on me, Snorri!" said Chitchee. "I'm eternally grateful that you recommended me for the job here."

Snorri pushed back on Chitchee's approaching hug.

"Chitchee, please. We're professionals! Can you keep a secret? Well, Noel is out to murder me," said Snorri, holding out his bloody jacketed arm. "See that? And look at my face. It looks like I tangled with a cougar."

"Oh," said Chitchee, "it looks a lot worse than that! It looks like you tangled with two cougars."

"See that?" said Snorri, ripping a Band-Aid off his face, pulling his face off his face.

Snorri's jaw, replete with teeth, had a gash that blossomed like an orchid tickled by a bee.

"Can I touch the wound?" said Chitchee. "I'm an empath. But you knew that."

"Who says you're an empath?" asked Snorri. "There can't be that many empaths. Who isn't an empath? I'm an empath, but who cares? Chitchee, *Noel is trying to kill me*, don't you get it?"

"No," pouted Chitchee, rubbing his black wool cap around on his head; he pushed his glasses back at rest on the bridge of his sniffling nose. "I don't believe you."

Snorri stood speechless, profused sweat, and wore his ripped corduroy jacket like a bloody toga. He champed on the crowd with his fork-lifting jaw. There was a black polar bear with extensions on its hind legs guarding BookSmart. Snorri brandished a left-behind umbrella, which he intended as a cattle prod.

"When jobs are on the line," said Snorri, "the butterfly switch-blades come out. Simple scarcity. Smith, Ricardo, Marx. I thought you knew that. What was your degree in? French? Come over here, between you and me: *Noel tried to assassinate me last night*! I suspect he's plotting a book store coup or an Unholy Alliance with Saami. Which side are you on?"

"I'm on the side of history," said Chitchee.

"I knew I could count on you," said Snorri. "Thanks, man."

"Now reverse that!" said Chitchee.

"What?" asked Snorri. "Excuse me, I see potential customers!"

Marten Martensen, thin-skinned as an onion, wore his black, box beard and flowing white moustache with a shrewd pride.

His mandatory frown mandated a lipless straightedge and then it took dramatic downturns at both vertices. His rectangular beard defended some hidden goal, and he watched, with thinning corneas, you closely for telltale sudden moves, moves toward your blocking his hidden goal.

"Sir, the intersection is closed," said Snorri. "You'll have to go this way, through BookSmart, and out the back door of BookSmart."

"I'm not walking through BookSmart! I'm 82 years old and—" said Marten, whose neck crooked forth like a Canadian goose attacking a rival Canadian goose.

Marten's chin pushed his lower lip and jaw forward.

"Give it a rest," said Snorri. "And get in there and check out our books! It's Thanksgiving time. Please. Let's give thanks for all the books we have—and shut up!"

"Why don't you shut up your shut up?" asked Marten. "Goddamn son of a bitch!"

"There is a line to get into Club Miami?" asked Edelweiss, out of countenance.

Edelweiss Hillswick hurried up to her brother, Marten, buttoned her winter overcoat, grabbed his arm, and buttoned his winter overcoat. She held his gloved, leather hand. Bundled up in velvet black flock and a matching black toque, she was the mirror of everybody's old country grandmother in Minnesota—pleasantly plump, white raisin face, oven-dried lips, black glasses, white curly hair, fleshy nose, fleshless gums that curbed her smile, and black square shoes like cinder blocks.

"I don't know what to do anymore, Marten," she continued. "Viktor is out of control—he won't listen to me. And he's so rude to me. The lies! Gosh!"

"Is this the Canadian goose's *mate*?" thought Snorri. "Are they a shoplifting *team*?"

Snorri extracted from his torn corduroy jacket the body cam his father Hjalmar bought him at Snorri's insistence to provide extra security for BookSmart. He clipped the little black box to his bloody, corduroy lapel. Powered on, the body cam recorded the 82-year old Marten's pinched face (if it went to court).

"Young man, who do you think—" said Edelweiss. "You can't film strangers. Are you the police?"

"Everybody," continued Snorri, "into BookSmart. BookSmart is a book store! Heard of it? You saw the movie, now look for the book, let's go! *Schnell*! You asked if I was police, Madam? Well, I *was* a security guard at the Target in Edina, Sons of Norway, and the Swedish Museum. Also Lake Harriet Elementary for one day. To be brutally honest, I didn't like the hours. The hours seemed really long! I've never been big on *long hours*. Long hours . . . from what I've gleaned from military history—well, don't get me startled! Started!"

"Startled on what?" quipped Marten. "Sanity?"

"We're not here for your kerfuffles, young man," said Edelweiss. "We are going to lunch with my nephew, Viktor Martensen."

"Come off it," said Marten. "You must have heard of him. He owns all the buildings on this entire block. That's all. He's on the cover of all the local magazines. That's all. He's only writing his autobiography. Heard of it? Or maybe you don't read much!"

"Sir, that is not the way to address an educated member of the lower-middle, sinking working class. I am only trying to educate Grandma Grannies like you or yours and bring you up to snuff," said Snorri, picking his ears with a BIC pen cap and scraping out excess wax.

"Oh, so we're not civilized?" asked Marten, the Canadian goose, spitting out feathers of air, arching his neck, and looking for other Canadian geese.

Snorri examined the black BIC cap with the earwax scraping lodged in the black BIC cap's groove.

"Have *you* read one book in the last year?" asked Snorri, adjusting his extensions with a flick and a toss back.

"That's none of your beeswax!" said Marten, recorded on the body cam.

Snorri played it back over and over, admired it, and showed it to Marten and Edelweiss.

"That's none of your beeswax!" said Marten on Snorri's body camera. "That's none of your beeswax! That's none of your beeswax! That is none of your, none of your, bees . . . waxwaxwax . . . beesbeesbees . . . beesbeesbees . . ."

"My brother has an internal bowel condition," said Edelweiss, watching Snorri's playback of Marten's irritated head bobbing, "wax bees, wax bees, wax bees."

"I read books, okay, get it?" erupted Marten Martensen. "If you must know, *Lone Survivor*!"

"There must be a million potboilers like that downstairs somewhere," said Snorri with a casual air. "Frankly, at your age I wouldn't get started on something you'll never finish. We do have a copy of *Life After Life* lying around here somewhere."

"What!" shouted Marten.

"You don't have to get moody, sir," said Snorri. "You could get Kubler-Ross instead!"

"But we are famished," said Edelweiss with an open, pleading mouthful of air.

When Snorri flicked his BIC, the earwax ball flew into her mouth and gullet, and she choked. She spit and spit and spit, head down, waving her arms for the passing moviegoers to back off. Snorri didn't see exactly what happened.

"You mean the Uptown Theater ran out of food?" asked Snorri. "I find that hard to swallow."

"We didn't want to go in there because of all the smoke pouring out," said Edelweiss.

"Yeah," said Marten, "the bonehead who works behind the counter there burnt the popcorn. He forgot to put in the oil. We told his supervisor, Emily. He's fired."

"I see," said Snorri, feigning to ponder this. "Actually, we are selling Thanksgiving Day old lemon sugar cookies, dollar apiece. Smokin' hot! You can't get any cheaper than that. Well, except at Byerly's. Go figure. We have plenty of cookbooks too with pictures of food in them."

"Why would we want pictures of food?" asked Edelweiss.

"There's this little thing called Facebook, heard of it?" asked Snorri. "Chitchee? Could you show this illiterate couple around the store? They probably haven't been in a book store since the invasion of Normandy. I mean the one by William the Conqueror."

"We need to use your bathroom!" said Marten.

"And Chitchee? Remember," continued Snorri, shoving the octogenarians into BookSmart, "always take the customer to the bathroom."

"You mean shelves?" asked Chitchee.

"I mean shelves!" said Snorri, slapping his hands together and re-posting himself. "That's why we need uniforms!"

"To pin your Star Trek badges on?" asked Marten.

Chitchee led the cold couple into BookSmart.

"I'm so sorry, you guys. He's a little stressed," said Chitchee, herding the couple toward the bathroom, "because someone wants to murder him."

"Who? *Who* wants to murder him?" asked the two octogenarians together with a shared, irascible unbelief.

"Can you keep a secret?" whispered Chitchee with a serious face and serious look over his shoulder.

Chitchee wriggled an eyebrow at the brother and at the sister, then the other eyebrow at the sister and then that eyebrow at the brother.

"The murderer is BookSmart's manager, Noel Schoolcraft," said Chitchee with a curious, scurrilous stare. "Snorri thinks Noel has been *radicalized*."

"Awkkk!" spit out the gooseneck. "OH! Of all the—let ME kill the guy myself! Let me at the son of a son of a bitch! I'll strangle him with my colostomy bag and hang him from the Foshay Tower!"

"Sir, no!" pleaded Chitchee. "We can't have the book store floor covered with blood and shit and littered with dead bodies like *Titus Androgynous*. Go out the back exit by the bathroom! When you're done farting around in there with fecal matter, you can get to Club Miami out through the BookSmart back door and then take an immediate left."

Courtney clanked off the #6 bus with a backward holler at the bus-driver, not seeing that Lily Holmgren had aimed an imaginary trigger finger at Courtney's bitchy back.

The line outside Club Miami dog-legged around the corner beyond MAC down Lake Street.

"What is this, Studio 54? Snorri?" called out Courtney. "Is Cher here?"

Courtney, pushing a wheelchair filled with a stainless steel sink filled with scrap metal, wheeled toward Snorri.

"Hello, handsome!" said Courtney to Snorri. "What's a girl gotta do to get some attention around here?"

"Buy a book," said Snorri.

Her crush (it slapped her face again that morning and it had gone on for years) on *Snorri* woke her up again. And for *Snorri*, she had donned her lucky wedding/funeral/cocktail tea length gown of tourmaline-purple silk, embroidered with white reindeers. She wore red rubber boots to go with her glazed purple-as-purple-rain lipstick. Snorri, Snorri, Snorri, every second, third, and first thought . . . oh Snorri, last time ever I saw your square face, oh that was a heatwave burning inside my core!

"Why don't you shove *me* into the book store, handsome?" begged Courtney, bringing together her strapless, bare shoulders and sort of bringing her knees together as if she were the bride stripped bare, shy and standing before her wedding featherbed made of cuddly down.

"Not you, Courtney!" said Snorri, prodding the outflow of elderly drones from the Uptown Theater. "Didn't we trespass you from the store?"

"Not that I recall . . ." said Courtney. "Trespass? Maybe somebody who looks like me. Look, here, Snorri. I made a bust of Aloysius for Thanksgiving—for his being such an all-round good guy to the neighborhood. Yes, we've had our moments, but I never took his threats that seriously! It's a bust, you see. And um I was wondering if I could do *your* bust, Snorri? I'm pretty sure I could take your measurements if I could wrap my arms around your broad chest and shoulders to get an idea of your bust size."

"Sir," said Snorri, looking over Courtney's bare shoulders. "BookSmart is officially open for today's sale! Happy Pre- and Belated Thanksgiving Day Weekend! Books! Books for Thanksgiving! Courtney, could you move over a bit, you're always in the way of customers. Half off double the price of two books! Thanksgiving Day sale!"

"Why should I be trespassed?" objected Courtney, sounding sadly hurt. "That's funny. I haven't been trespassed in a while. Hmmm?"

"Well, no offense," said Snorri, "but maybe you've run out of stores on this block to be trespassed from! I mean after all. There's a smaller pool of trespassable stores to draw from, statistically, for you. You're running out of stores to be trespassed from, that's all, you understand. Is that what *Black Swan* is about? Statistics and ballerinas? Wait   complaining about ascorbic prices, wasn't *that* you? Throwing a *Junie B. Jones Coloring Book* at the owner's head, calling him a fascist, a sadist, the second coming of Manson, and a cheap, stale, gigantic lemon sugar cookie, wasn't *that* you? *Not* checking in your old art school crap in the allotted three minutes, wasn't *that* you?"

"Hmmm," said Courtney. "Me? Some other Courtney prolly!"

"Yes, you!" admonished Snorri. "Come on, don't let the cold in!"

"What are you talking about, handsome? I always check in my old art school crap in the allotted time," said Courtney.

"Oh, hi Courtney!" said Chitchee.

"Don't I, cutie?" she continued with Chitchee, facing him.

Snorri slammed the door behind her shut.

"Sometimes the allotted time," continued Courtney, "takes a little longer, for a regular Minnesota gal, who loves someone with her aching heart."

"How was your Thanksgiving, Courtney?" asked Chitchee. "I set aside a 243-piece RoseArt sidewalk chalk set for you. It has glitter too! It's a suitcase full of chalk!"

She thought for a second. "Chitchee, thanks for at least thinking of me!"

"You are welcome!" chirped Chitchee.

"I guess it doesn't matter," said Courtney.

"Thanksgiving?" asked Chitchee.

"IT WAS FUCKING—" squealed Courtney through her poorly-insured, sour teeth, "—TERRIBLE!"

"Wh-h-h-hy?" asked Chitchee, inflating the long vowel.

"Ummm . . ." said Courtney, "because I was on the bus sitting in the front and looking out the window at Lakewood Cemetery, when the lady acrost from me says 'What are YOU looking at?' I says 'not YER ugly face!' all Hell breaks looSe! The fucking #6 driver-BitCH pulls over. It took forEVER to get here! What can you DO? It's a crazy world. Yeah, bunch of FUCKING LOONIES OUT THERE!"

Aloysius accepted Courtney's "Homage to Ignatius [sic]" with a grateful look of ginned-up gratitude. The sculpture *Ignatius* was a mumble-jumble of iron blades from an old push mower and razor-sharp scraps of sheet metal from a ninth-grade shop project turned in late.

"Thank you so much, Courtney. It's very nice," said Aloysius. "Did you have a nice Thanksgiving? It sounds like you did! I'm placing this piece of work in the utility closet for now for safekeeping—where we put works of art like this piece. But it really belongs in the Minneapolis Institute of Art next to Jade Mountain (if it hasn't eroded). Or in the Otis elevator [preferably going down, he thought]. Or maybe out in their Ro-tundra! Help yourself to a Thanksgiving lemon sugar cookie, Courtney. There should be some sugar cookies left over from last night on the TV dinner tray by the door. Dollar apiece, but for you—half off! You're never going to get a deal like that again!"

"Minneapolis has an Institution for Art, in Minneapolis?" asked Courtney, who feigned appreciation for the appreciation— and the pause acted as a refreshed ticket to see more of Snorri, oh Snorri.

Aloysius recognized his head from among the blades and held the bust at arm's length, careful not to cut himself on his own head. He blew out a big sigh as if blowing out birthday candles, and he walked toward the utility closet carefully.

"*I* don't see any fucking cookies," said Courtney. "Snorri?"

"The cookies should be out there!" said Aloysius over his shoulder. "Chitchee! Ask Snorri where the lemon sugar cookies are! We probably sold out last night."

"Snorri!" said Chitchee to Snorri on the street. "Do you know where the Thanksgiving Day old lemon sugar cookies walked off to?"

Aloysius unlocked the utility closet, threw open the door, and saw the untouched lemon sugar cookies on the TV dinner tray. What did it mean? Aloysius ate one. What did that mean? This wasn't high school algebra. Noel was supposed to put the unsold cookies back in their packages with the receipts. *They weren't that stale.* That kind of cookie always tastes a little stale anyway. That means: NOEL KEEPS THE LEMON SUGAR COOKIES IN THE UTILITY CLOSET. Why? What did *that* mean?

After carrying back the lemon sugar cookies on the TV dinner tray to the front of the store, Aloysius panicked at the contours of Larry Sangster and Fjard Gardet together crossing Hennepin Avenue. Aloysius clunked down the tray by the front door. He ducked under the front counter, but bumped his forehead and grew a goose egg.

Courtney picked up a lemon sugar cookie, thought of Snorri, and munched it without thinking of paying; with her tourmaline sleeve she tore the crumbs off her purple-as-purple-rain lipstick.

Snorri pushed Chitchee back into the store, following him inside.

"Chitchee, what are you thinking? They're right here by the door, are you blind?" asked Snorri quickly under his breath. "Are you crazy? You're worried about lemon sugar cookies? Listen to me: Noel wants to kill me. NOEL WANTS ME DEAD!"

"Well," said Chitchee, "he thinks you're an idiot, but he doesn't want you dead. But don't tell Noel I said that he said you're an idiot!"

Snorri continued looking over his shoulder.

"Don't you know what that means, Chitchee? You work in a book store! He wants to eliminate us all and keep the store for himself! What was that knocking? Watch your back, trust no one. Not even Aloysius! I love the guy to death, but it's like *I, Claudius* around here. I ate one lemon sugar cookie last night, but Noel refused to put them out . . . why? Ask yourself that! You don't have to be Agatha Christie to paint in the numbers. He took chemistry in high school, so he can find his way around a chemistry lab with a Bunsen burner. He is good with numbers. I'll give him credit for that."

"Is Aloysius here today?" asked Larry Sangster, helping himself to a lemon sugar cookie, looking at his iPhone, determined not to make waves or allow the waves to drag him down by the ankles. Larry put away his phone, looked at his phone, and put away his phone.

Larry in a black Eddie Bauer parka over a navy blue suit and blue tie approached Chitchee, who stood behind the maroon counter thumbing through books.

"Hey, I ate one," said Snorri, his whole brain looping and counter looping with alarms and air raid warnings. "Wait. What did I just do? Oh, my aching God!"

"What's wrong, Sugaree?" asked Courtney, munching her lemon sugar cookie and admiring Snorri, who had propped himself on the counter.

Larry looked at Courtney.

"Me? Nothing," said Larry, his lemon sugar cookie digesting. "Why?"

"I wasn't talking to your mug, smug as a bug in a dirty rug," said Courtney.

Chitchee saw Larry's blue suit twitch—Larry's cell phone was on "Vibrate" over his heart. Viktor's call vibrated in Larry's parka pocket.

"Start compressions!" yelled Chitchee. "Larry's having a heart attack!"

Chitchee ran around the counter and grabbed Larry from behind and threw him to the floor, cookie in hand.

"I'm fine. Everything's fine," said Larry as he hit the runner. "It's not a heart attack!"

"Thank God!" said Chitchee, with a helping hand. "Has anyone ever told you, your blue eyes are the blue of the *Alcoholics Anonymous Big Book*? Maybe it's a sign from the future!"

Stay calm, Larry told himself. Maintain cold air of priestly piety. Finish complimentary lemon sugar cookie as a "goodwill" token cookie like a business card. Eat stale cookie. Eat stale business card. Don't move. Make sure no bones are sticking out.

"Ah!" said Snorri, seeing an oncoming tsunami. "I have realized everything! Noel POISONED the sugar cookies last night! NOEL LACED THE LEMON SUGAR COOKIES WITH ARSENIC LAST NIGHT! HE WANTS US ALL DEAD SO HE CAN TAKE OVER BOOKSMART! I wonder if he has been reading Agatha Christie lately? Do you think?"

Snorri parted the shower curtains of sweat from his eyes.

"Sir," said Snorri to Larry. "I would caution you to not . . . don't eat any more lemon sugar cookies. They've all been poisoned. One probably won't kill you per se. But *caveat emptor*."

"Larry," said Fjard, edging away and pointing, "I'll be downstairs with the spider webs looking for Griffin's web. Get the reference? Larry? Get the joke?"

A large furrow creased Larry's forehead. The ceiling was very far away. Furthermore, when he swallowed his chin chinlessly, his thin upper lip revealed teeny front teeth. His round, almost spherical cheeks flashed white, blushed pink, and paled white. When he thought about it, he felt faint. He thought to pass out, so Larry clung to Torg's back at the counter, and Torg pushed him away.

"Don't breathe on me," said Torg. "I don't want what you got!"

"Larry!" said Chitchee, running from around the counter. "You're having a heart attack for real this time! Let me pound on your chest!"

"WE'RE ALL GOING TO DIE!" cried Courtney. "OH NO! HOLD ME, SNORRI!"

Larry struggled like a Prometheus to be released from Chitchee's clasp.

When Courtney saw Chitchee grab Larry, she grabbed Snorri from the back, caressing him for comfort and warmth.

"Are you having a heart attack too, handsome?" asked Courtney.

"Can I help you find something, Courtney?" said Snorri, feeling Courtney's hands like giggling kittens stamping on the softness of his chest.

Snorri tore Courtney's little mitts like giant Band-Aids off his chest.

When Larry declared himself okay again, Chitchee threw him to the floor.

"Good to hear," said Chitchee.

"You know what?" said Snorri. "*Noel probably planted that car bomb too!* Funny how the police have no suspects, isn't it? *Qui bonobo?* That was simply a diversion. That was only a sideshow to start a witch hunt for a fishing expedition to cover up a coup chasing its own tail. Bastard! Noel! That Bastard of the Universe! The double-crosser wants to cut us all out of the picture, take over the store, and declare himself the once and future McCosh, as it were. Mercenary Caesar bleeding heart-fucker! It's always those real quiet guys. Like Cassavetes. Okay, then I'm Brutus! I'm Brutus. And I will save the book store, democracy, and the rule of law—if I have to fall on my sword and call 911. Such is my oath. Bound by mine honor. My honor is my bond, my James Bond—"

"Your phone . . ." said Larry, getting up from all fours on the floor. "Snorri, where's Aloysius? His phone has been . . . poisoned all morning! I mean busy. I can't ever get through to you guys! I mean. Poisoned? What's going on here? Really? Whew. I feel so . . . faint. Probably, I'm okay. It's just some organic chicken soup I ate. Okay, I'm okay. Go away Chitchee! You BookSmart Mongoloid! Don't touch my suit! Get away from my suit."

Fjard Gardet, in his plump, cranberry North Face down jacket over his suit, minus the suit jacket, looked at his iPhone (a gift from Viktor), entered the upstairs, and carried a Tom Clancy tomette while looking like Tom Clancy.

"So," said Chitchee, "what have you got there, *The Hunt for Red Vagina*?"

Fjard frowned in a dash.

Behind that dash, Fjard's thoughts careened wildly until . . . *that guy*? Is that the guy who was at all those Hennepin County Library book sales? I remember we were at Southdale Public Library and he reached around me, and it was really crowded, people pushing and shoving me, and he sticks his goofy smile in my face like a horse snaffled by a bit with its tongue out. Then he said looking at my pricing scanner:

"Don't you know a MIT University Press book when you see one, Scanner Man? Oh Scanner Man and the Scanner Clan! Hey, all you legitimate book dealers! Scanner Man is here! This is the end of the used book trade! And he doesn't know 'M,' 'I,' 'T' from 'S,' 'H,' 'I,' 'T!'"

Behind Chitchee's smile, Chitchee clicked on "Fjard Gardet" and "Scanner Man" . . . and thought . . . *same guy*! I was so nice to that guy even though he reached under my arm with his pricing scanner in hand, his arm poking out, and I looked like an octopus while he grabbed the donated trade paperbacks. Scanner Junior untied my two shoelaces, and Scanner Miss tied them together.

Even then he scowled in my face like a vituperative viper and I let him bite me!

Scanner Man was not the type of Scanner Man who would back down from being called Scanner Man even if he was Scanner Man. The grudge had not healed—it never would. The general public has no idea about used books, where they are used, how they are used, and who uses them for what nefarious purposes, and who will stop at nothing for a vintage Pocket Book from the 50s in a collectible baggie.

"Did you talk to Aloysius, Larry?" asked Fjard.

"Aloysius was pimpin' here a minute ago," answered Chitchee. "But he must have jet. Plus the phone is always off the hook. And they keep charging us! Can I help you, Larry, find a book while you wait? We need to unload: *Tuesdays With Morrie*, *The Seven Habits of Highly Effective People*, *The Road Less Traveled*, and *The Power of Now*. Not now? Not into power now? How about: *Who Moved My Cheese*? We've got a million of those! It was *really* popular."

"No thanks. Can you put this one on hold for me?" asked Fjard.

"Seriously?" asked Chitchee.

Snorri walked behind the counter and kicked Chitchee's leg. Chitchee grabbed his shin.

"Hey," said Chitchee, scribbling on a yellow post-it, "did you ever learn how to work that Scanner, Scanner Man?"

"Oh, that's it!" screamed Fjard. "THIS PLACE IS GOING *DOWN*! THIS PLACE DOESN'T KNOW ITS PLACE ANYMORE!"

The phone rang. Aloysius's hand reached out to hang it up.

"Where is he?" asked Larry. "Is he here or not?"

"I mean he might have gone home to his abode of bliss to reread that rare Ahearne book on collecting rare books, what do you mean?" asked Chitchee. "I mean where is he supposed to be? Sitting here waiting for the next colostomy bag to walk through the door?"

"I mean I thought I heard the phone ring!" said Larry.

"Well," said Chitchee. "It's recharging."

Aloysius coughed.

"What was that?" said Fjard.

"That was the message machine coughing," said Chitchee. "When you hit this button, you hear Aloysius cough. Noel was going to turn it into an app. Like this!"

Chitchee kicked Aloysius and Aloysius coughed, crouched under the counter.

"Yes, like this!" said Chitchee, kicking Aloysius.

Aloysius coughed again.

The phone rang. Aloysius's hand reached up to hang up on it.

Chitchee pie-eyed a white tarantula hand walking around the counter and slapped it so hard that it fell off the counter.

"Spiders are getting out of hand these days!"

Larry faced the front door.

"Sirs, gentlemen, please," said Torg, "could you please not block my blocking the door? That's my job. I'm the greeter. That's why they call me THE FACILITATOR."

"Fjard Gardet from the bank just," said Larry to Snorri and Chitchee, "*just* called your number a minute ago and your store phone *did* ring! Damn it! It wasn't off the hook! Tell Aloysius to call Viktor when he decides to quit hiding!"

Smartphones thrust into inner Eddie Bauer pockets, Larry and Fjard exited to the sidewalk, where Larry's smart-phone dogged him with ring-tones again and again.

"Hello, Viktor? Yes. I'm here!" said Larry, looking at Fjard. "No, he went home! What am I supposed to do, kill him with his own poisoned lemon sugar cookies? Jesus Henry Christ, Viktor, it's Thanksgiving. Oh, okay, I'm whining. Yeah, you're right. Sorry. Talk to you later."

"He's gone now, Aloysius," said Chitchee, looking out the window. "You can come up for air."

Aloysius sprinted toward the bathroom to induce vomiting the arsenic-laced lemon sugar cookies. Noel had gone bonkers-berserko. Aloysius grabbed the locked bathroom door, shook the brass knob and, with the other hand, frantically rapped his knuckles white, asking:

"Is somebody in there?"

"Yes," said Edelweiss, standing outside. "He'll be done in a few minutes."

"Wait your goddamned turn!" said Marten from the bathroom. "Don't give me your Minnesota nice bullshit! You're going to rush a nice old man with your nice bullshit!"

"Open the darned door!" said Aloysius. "I'm dying! I've been poisoned!"

"By who?" asked Marten. "The manager, Noel Schoolcraft?"

"How did you know?" asked Aloysius, a sense of eerie bewilderment stealing over him as if there were crazy bats flying behind his eyes. "How did you know THAT? What is going on?"

Aloysius felt faint and he held on to the Poetry Section.

"Aloysius!" said Edelweiss. "You've aged! How are you?"

"This isn't happening," said Aloysius. "But the wall is the wall. The floor is the floor, attached to the wall, right?"

Larry and Fjard had sneaked around the block to re-enter BookSmart from the back door by the time Aloysius crash-barred, dry heaving, through the back exit to throw up in the alley by the dumpsters.

Aloysius had his finger down his throat, seeing Larry and Fjard.

Marten fixed his colostomy bag, opened the bathroom door, and strolled outside with Edelweiss.

"Auntie Edelweiss! Thanks for stopping," said Aloysius. "Have a good one!"

"More fake Minnesota Nice? From our own estranged nephew no less," asked Marten. "We proved that wrong again, didn't we Edelweiss? Hah, hah!"

"Ja, we did at that! Yes, we did!" laughed Edelweiss, hooking her arm around her brother's arm as they entered Club Miami's back door.

"They really need to beef up their security with guards to protect the customers from their employees, " said Edelweiss. "Horst should work here."

"I *had* the rent, fellas," said Aloysius, sleeving some upchuck off the corner of his mouth. "But I misplaced it, you guys, what can I say?"

"Again?" asked Larry. "Another 6,000 dollars *lost*?"

"It's in a book somewhere," said Aloysius. "I've always had a bad memory going back to I don't know when."

"Aloysius," said Fjard, "nobody wants to see you circle the drain like a hairball, but why didn't you follow the general 25% rule that everybody else obeys? Never go above 25% of your gross monthly income for rent."

"For that to happen," said Aloysius, "we would all have to be coke dealers."

Larry and Fjard traded long looks of disgust mixed with disbelief.

"Aloysius," said Larry. "Plenty of coke dealers could never pay their rents."

They muttered away muttering, Fjard to his Hummer; and Larry to his vintage AMC Gremlin, its hood, a shield dented by a Red Cross knight with a cardioid fist, both cars presented from Viktor in lieu of what he owed them. Aloysius darted back inside, intending to cash out the till and run across the street. He paused to avoid Lake Street Rodney making paces toward Walker Public Library to research Celtic torques, Ogham tree alphabets, Scythian motifs in the folk art of Brittany, Incan *quipus*, and the seashell languages of Mali. Aloysius ran out the front door to McDonald's to get something solid in his stomach to "even everything out." When Kennedy saw Aloysius ordering at the McDonald's counter from Kaylee, Kennedy gathered up his gym bag of deals (deals old, deals new, deals borrowed, deals blue), gleaned from his circumlocutions after lengthy machinations of matriculating to his favorite conjunctions, scuttled across Hennepin, and rolled into BookSmart, in search of the "soft target," Chitchee.

The pushover shelved the sticker-priced, used books stored under the maroon counter.

"What was all that ruckus about, Snorri?" asked Chitchee, an armload of books pressed in a stack against his anxious, asthmatic, and ailing lungs.

Back and forth, Chitchee dumped the books expertly in rows on top of day tables and immediately customers browsed the titles, looked at the book spines, and flocked together like sheep to graze.

"You mean you don't know?" said Snorri. "You didn't know that that's our landlord, Larry Sangster, from the MPG HQ! And Ford Guardette, our personal loan officer from US Bank? We're going to lose the book store! That's what that means."

"Snorri," said Noel, "that's not true."

"It's NO-EL!" said Courtney, emerging from Children's Books. "He's by the collectibles now! RUN FOR YOUR LIVES! He's got a car bomb strapped to his back! THE MANAGER HAS BEEN RADICALIZED!"

Noel sat on the bar stool behind the counter of collectibles, measured the angles of earshot he needed to estimate the customer base, counted out twenty or so customers, opened the Accounts notebook, and aligned himself like a ledger to study the ledger.

"My word," said Kriemhilde, approaching the maroon counter, to Noel. "Did someone say there is a suicide bomber in the store? My goodness, that's not good! Did you see a suicide bomber walk into the store?"

"Someone said he was by the collectibles!" said Melusina, emerging from Cookbooks.

"I didn't see anybody," said Noel, looking around his area for a dropped pencil.

"I think it's the radicalized manager," said Kriemhilde. "He wants to blow up the store and himself, so he can take over."

"Could you go ask the manager if he has seen the suicide bomber for us?" asked Melusina.

"I am the manager," said Noel.

All the customers sprinted for the front and back door exits.

Chitchee blew his acorn cap. The sound Chitchee kissy-whistled stopped everyone in their track shoes, sneakers, heels, flats, and boots.

"There is absolutely no truth in any of that," said Noel.

"Why not play it safe . . ." said Kriemhilde.

". . . and believe a lie!" said Melusina.

All the customers trickled back with gum stuck to their guilty soles.

"Look, Snorri," said Noel, "we're not going out of business. We're all caught up on our bills. Business is picking up for the holidays! Everything is paid for—except the rent, which Aloysius promised was being taken care of so . . . if he can remember what he did with it . . ."

"Wait a second," said Snorri, "while I turn my body-cam back on. So, testing, testing, you, *Noel that is,* are saying that BookSmart is actually worth a lot? Worth it enough, that you, Noel, would *die* for it? Okay, stand back a little, so I can get you in the picture, Noel. Are you listening to me? Back up some more. Move the stool back. More."

"Why?" asked Noel.

"So I don't CHOP YOUR HEAD OFF!" intoned Snorri. "THAT'S WHY!"

All the customers sprinted for the exits, dropping all the books in their hands to the redolent, white pine wood flooring.

"Snorri," said Noel, "we're not losing the store!"

"BookSmart declared bankruptcy?" asked Kennedy. "No! Did I overhear what I think I appreciated? Then can I actually hold my hold pile? Isn't that why it's called a hold pile? Can I hold my hold pile *one last time*? I'd like to say a valediction to it. When is the sale? And all the books in hold piles, and will they also be discounted *at the sale rate* on the last day? COULD I PUT THE ENTIRE BOOK STORE ON HOLD AND BUY IT FOR NOTHING ON THE LAST DAY?"

"I heard Aloysius is losing the store!" exclaimed Lake Street Rodney when he charged into the book store. "That's the rumor going around Walker Public Library anyway! Where's my hold pile?"

"Lose the store?" echoed Noel. "We're not losing the store!"

"Easy for you to say," said Courtney, "WITH A BOMB STRAPPED TO YOUR BACK!"

"So you *don't* lose a book store when you *don't* pay a book store's rent?" asked Snorri, woodenly, a wooden sailor on the wooden deck of a wooden ship in a glass bottle.

"That's how slumlords get the money to build more slums," continued Snorri. "Otherwise, it would be more profitable to burn down BookSmart for the insurance money."

"Ever heard of *Greek lightning?*" interjected Torg. "It wasn't invented by the Turks for nothing! The owner is probably planning to throw a bomb through the front window any day now."

"He doesn't have to," said Courtney. "The manager will bomb the store for him."

"And save the owner a bomb," said Snorri. "Go figure!"

"How do you know that, Snorri?" asked Noel, slamming the pencil from behind his ear on the maroon counter and breaking the pencil in half. "You don't know any of that! Kennedy? Could you come over here for a second please? Kennedy, *don't* repeat what you just heard. And don't say anything to Aloysius about it!"

"Of course, but update my hold pile for now," said Kennedy, leaving the store. "I won't repeat what I just heard . . . *not exactly anyway, not word for word, anyway, not ad verboten.* Oh, and, just to be perspicuous, do you have the *actual* date set for the *official* going out of business sale? And how will the sale be proliferated in advertisements?"

Torg cramped up. Wincing in pain, he clung to the maroon counter. Neck muscles stiff from his trying not to look noticeable. The idea of losing BookSmart triggered Torg's colitis. Or there *was* arsenic in the lemon sugar cookies and Noel played dumb, because Noel was smart enough to be dumb. Sneaky, that one.

"You okay?" Torg heard as someone coughed behind him.

"Not really," said Torg, gripping his gut and smiling in pain. "I heard BookSmart was going out of business. Nobody is supposed to know. But don't say anything to that IDIOT Aloysius about it! He's not supposed to know!"

"Aaaawwwwgggghhhh."

"Oh," said Torg, turning around, "uh, you ARE Aloysius!"

Aloysius glanced a pan-flat glance at Torg. He walked back to his desk, feeling like the Farmer with the Dell. He ate to re-normalize his stomach's biosphere with French fries and a Jumbo Coke.

"Say, Noel," said Aloysius, treading softly past Noel's workstation and going outside for a smoke. "You didn't happen to somehow lace those lemon sugar cookies with arsenic last night, did you?"

"Aloysius!" said Noel. "Of course not! You don't believe me?"

"Not really!" exclaimed Aloysius. "Hey, where is my wallet?"

"You left it at McDonald's probably."

"Yeah," said Aloysius. "You're probably right. I'll be right back."

"Hey," said Snorri, who watched Aloysius depart and re-read *The Uptown Messenger.* "What's this about Saami? He made the news!"

"Minneapolis resident, Zalar Gossick, . . ." read aloud Chitchee, looking over Snorri's shoulder. Chitchee snatched *The Uptown Messenger* out of Snorri's hands, ". . . was charged with robbery and assault in an attack on a 39-year-old man, Benjamin 'Saami' Rolvaag, who was attacked at approximately 2 a.m. near Pleasant Avenue and 24th Street, one of a series of assaults on pedestrians in the Uptown neighborhood that have left several with concussions. The attacker in each case left behind in the victim's mouth a baby's skull. Charges say the attacker punched Benjamin Rolvaag in the head repeatedly and then took his wallet, which was empty. He said nothing before the attack, blindsiding Benjamin Rolvaag with three or four rapid punches, police said, with a blunt instrument. The blows broke Rolvaag's nose and several facial bones, according to the complaint. Police believe the attacker is linked to the recent spate of Lakewood Cemetery burglaries. Owen 'Hawk Eye' Rasmussen drew a pistol and fired three times at the robber, who ran to a nearby car. Witnesses saw the car drive off and were able to tell police four of the six characters on its license plate. Investigators who were already looking into other Uptown assaults showed Rasmussen photographs of the suspect, and he identified him as the attacker, according to the complaint. Zalar Gossick was charged with first degree aggravated robbery and third degree assault. Under questioning after his arrest Thursday, he denied that he was responsible for a previous graveyard robbery, but added, 'I got shot at the other night by an old-ass white dude and got a hole in my Slave Raider T-shirt,' according to the complaint.

Zalar Gossick was also picked out of a photo lineup by the victim of an October 9 robbery, according to the complaint. A vehicle registered to Gossick's roommate, Alma Weatherwax, with whom Zalar sometimes lives in the 3700 block of Stevens Avenue S., matched the description given by the witness after the attack on Benjamin Rolvaag.

A search of the vehicle turned up books on Charles Manson's Family, a .40 caliber Smith & Wesson, the remains of children's skeletons, some as young as two, stolen from the crypts of Lakewood Cemetery, the complaint said. A Minneapolis police spokesman said Zalar Gossick could face more charges from other Uptown assaults and burglaries, including Lakewood Cemetery. Zalar Gossick is on parole for a 2008 Hennepin County robbery and a Redwood County home invasion. It's still not entirely clear how police were led to the suspect, but two 5th Precinct patrol officers found information helpful to the case, said 5th Precinct Inspector Jonathan Weatherwax. 5th Precinct won a department award in 2008 for crime reduction and this year again leads the city in crime reduction."

"Do you have a magic marker I could use?" asked Hawk Eye, wafting into the store—uncombed, unkempt as an unmade bed, and his herky-jerky body a bent, untwined coat hanger. "I heard the store is closing and Aloysius has to declare Chapter 11 or he will be swimming with the loan sharks."

"Hawk Eye, you're one of my many, many heroes! You saved Saami's life!" said Chitchee, hugging Hawk Eye's chest and pinning him right and left as if the thumps were medals. "It's all in *The Uptown Messenger*."

"Not really," shucked Hawk Eye. "I was wandering around and saw the whole thing go down. That's all. It's not like I'm going down in the Anals of History. Mind if I use your potty?"

"Go ahead," said Chitchee. "You deserve it!"

Chitchee had called LaDonna repeatedly, because rumors about her disappearance and abduction scared him. Chitchee checked his messages.

"Chitchee? Calling you back," said LaDonna, her voice disembodied on Chitchee's voicemail. "It's LaDonna. I'm in an elevator. I'm okay. I lost a few days. I was talking to Madison at Club Miami. The next thing I knew I was staggering around Famous Dave's. And Carousel Square security called the cops, who took me home. I'm with Madison now. Everything's okay. So you can leave me alone now."

Chitchee dialed LaDonna's number and heard her groggy, muggle-headed voice, "Go ahead leave a message—if you have to." Chitchee hung up puzzled and asked Snorri about it.

"What? She can't be with Madison," said Snorri. "I just saw Madison at Bryant Lake Bowl. And she didn't mention anything about LaDonna."

"LaDonna," said Chitchee, leaving a message. "I talked to Snorri, who was just with Madison. Here's Snorri!"

"LaDonna? I know Madison went to her mother's house for Thanksgiving in Gooseberry Falls and then to her weirdo dad's in Waseca. So I know you can't be you! I think you dialed the wrong number!"

Snorri hung up and handed Chitchee the phone back, and it rang:

"Quit calling me!" yelled LaDonna. "You're creeping me out, you asshole. Leave me alone. Don't *ever* call me! I don't want anything to do with you! Get out of my life!"

Chitchee jumped backward as if a piece of industrial equipment had short-circuited, completing the circuit by hurling him into a wall of books. He conked his cerebellum, saw stars, and sat on the motionless swivel chair waiting for Aloysius, wallet in hand, to return.

"I am talking to Madison, Chitchee," said Snorri, looking over his shoulder toward the bathroom. "Careful with those books, sir! She doesn't remember being at Club Miami with LaDonna. Go figure eight that out! She said it sounded like something Reina once said. Reina remembered once getting into a white van outside Club Miami with a thumper who was going to give her a ride home. It was Reina or Paj, Madison wasn't sure. But the girl woke up in an abandoned basement with gallon jugs of water and boxes of books all over, but she couldn't remember anything. She doesn't speak English too well. Someone gave her a ride home. That's all she remembers. She remembers seeing gallon jugs in the back of a van."

"What?" asked Chitchee. "Am I dreaming?"

"Look, Chitchee," said Hawk Eye, passing Snorri on his way back from the bathroom and mumbling through his dry, cracked lips: "If you ever need a .38 Special, I'm keeping a Derringer in your bathroom. It's above the toilet. In the acoustic tiles."

"It is an honor," said Chitchee, kowtowing, "from a scholar and a sharpshooter."

Chitchee was thrilled to be awarded such a prize, but he heard fear neurons firing volleys. What if the .38 Derringer accidentally discharged a round? A mouse could trigger it. Active mouse shooter in Poetry. Then what? Dead bookworms all over the store.

Saami walked up the stairs and dropped his jaw. Chitchee looked to see why. Zalar walked past BookSmart's front window. Zalar turned to his right and unfolded his middle finger. The signet ring was engraved with baby skulls. Torg's wiggling ears pinned themselves back, sensing a walking ambush. Chitchee ran for the Derringer in the acoustic tiles, but Snorri had occupied the bathroom with an upset stomach and kidney stones. Chitchee hopped outside with Torg. They watched Zalar lumber into Club Miami.

Aloysius careered out of McDonald's, holding his Jumbo Coke refill, having recovered his wallet from Kaylee, the counter girl, who didn't rip off "Mr. Have a Good One." The bifold of the billfold's coin case, cardholder, and ID window were all sufficiently empty of cash.

Aloysius galloped back to BookSmart so quickly he appeared to passersby to be a thief.

"Why was that guy giving the store the finger?" asked Aloysius, panting.

"We didn't have *Man's Search for Meaning*," said Chitchee. "Was that you making that whistling sound trying to breathe?"

Aloysius swallowed this, Adam's Apple elevating up and down,

"Wait, I know we have a *Man's Search for Meaning* around," said Aloysius. "I'll go run it out to him and see if he is still interested."

Aloysius found a used copy of *Man's Search for Meaning* under the maroon counter, placed it on the maroon counter, hurdled over the maroon counter, ran down to the intersection of Lake & Hennepin, and looked around like Fran Tarkenton (whose offensive line had collapsed) for Gene Washington running downfield.

Hours passed and no Aloysius.

The phone rang and Chitchee picked up the receiver:

"BookSmart!" greeted Chitchee. "Feed the need to read! Buy a book, we need money!"

"If I can't have her," said the veiled voice, "you can't either."

"O. J?" asked Chitchee.

"You know who it is," said the caller. "And I'd hate to mess up that beautiful face of yours."

"Hey, Snorri! Telephone!" said Chitchee. "It's for you, beautiful."

"I'll be right there!" said Snorri. "What's Aloysius *doing* out there?"

Aloysius ran in front of cars and streamed through traffic.

"Look at him," said Chitchee, "He's early LA Jim Morrison on Orange Sunshine."

"Whose dick did you suck to get that job?" heard Snorri, blinking as soon as he sat down.

"Saami! It's for you!" said Snorri. "And it's not Linda!"

"Who would be calling me? I must have won a contest! Which one? Hello, Halifax? Canadian Cruise Lines?" asked Saami excitedly. "I'm packing my toothbrush for Nova Scotia right now!"

"You are one dead fucking cunt," said the voice.

"You must want Noel," said Saami. "Hang on!"

"Hello? Ye Young? Hello? Ye Young?" asked Noel, pushing the accounts notebook away. "It's Noel."

"Fucking pro-fucking-gressive, fuck you. . ." said the voice. "Femnist ass-licker!"

"Whoever you are," said Noel, "if you have a problem with Simone de Beauvoir or Susan Brownmiller or our Feminism section, you could at least have the gonads to meet me in the Lunds parking lot for a debate!"

Noel hung up. Then he picked up and added:

"Instead of this sucker-punching, 4chan backwoods bullshit!"

He slammed the phone on the counter.

"Hey, you sissy Chichester, *now* am I in your book?" laughed Mad Jack Apple Jack to himself, sitting at the Club Miami bar and flashing his loose gray smile and bleeding gums. He handed back the flip phone to Nestor. "The pussies next door bought it! Book-reading cry babies! Yeah, now they will all need *sensitivity training*. Oooooh, we're so smart, we read boooooooks! We're Puro-Eons!"

Mad Jack Apple Jack placed his hands, which were square as matchbooks, over the bar and played a dainty piano piece with his pinkies crooked in the air. He choked on his own isolating, mad-capped laughter.

"Your hands are shaking," said Nestor, drinking pulpy orange juice. "What's with all the locals with their tremors and their shuffling gaits as if they were machine learning how to walk? It's because their substantia nigras have collapsed after heavy, daily boozing. I'm a bartender, but I don't mind weeding out the weak in the survival of species! Bottoms up, Mad Jack!"

Nestor slid Mad Jack his drink. Mad Jack sobered up a second to catch the tumbler sliding toward him and when he held the drink before his eyes, he lighted up like a plastic Christmas candle from Walgreens and smiled broadly like a toothless moonbeam.

Aloysius bounced into the book store like a live, glowing tennis ball:

"Wow! I took one of Noel's energy pills! Wow! I feel as fit as a top hat! Wow! I ran down to Lake Calhoun, but I couldn't find the guy! Wow! He must have rented the last kayak!"

Aloysius cranked out twenty ankle-snapping, crackly push-ups, endured ten tired jumping jacks, groaned through half a sit-up, and was down for good with a downwardly collapsing dog. He stood up woozily and threw *Man's Search for Meaning* onto a new arrivals table, the pages fluttering like doves ascending the sky.

"All right you guys, huddle up," said Aloysius, catching his breath, wheezing like a death rattle, and barely audibilizing.

Chitchee blew his acorn cap, blew the socks off everybody, and caused customers to plug their ears with cupped hands.

"Are we still in a hostage situation ummm still?" coughed Ivan Von Volkov, emerging from a corner in Fiction, coughing like a backing-up bathtub, and regurgitating sludge. "Is the suicide bomber still in collectibles? That was the last I heard."

"Attention! All staff! Mandatory staff meeting!" yelled Chitchee, quite pleased with his acorn technique.

"I'm s-s-sorry," said Aloysius, staring holes in space at the redolent, white pine wood flooring, "but I'm going to have to let everybody go. I can't . . . p-p-p-pay . . . you any more."

Chitchee raised his arm to ward off a blow. Snorri scratched his ear with a BIC pen. Saami closed his eyes and clenched his fists. Noel looked away.

"I'll work all the shifts myself from now on," said Aloysius, thrusting out his chest. "I can do it all. I don't know what it is, but I have tons of energy. I feel like a brand new man, like Jack LaLanne! Okay? Everybody? We'll get there! Good job!"

Aloysius coughed and almost sat down on his readers. He reached for the old McDonald's Jumbo Coke. He swigged it. Some of it bubbled out his nose. Coughing, he looked lost.

"Are you sure?" asked Chitchee. "Ten in the morning until midnight every day?"

"Aloysius! Really?" asked Saami sadly. "Eight days a week?"

"I knew this was coming," said Snorri, shaking his head. "I guess we will all have to become sharecroppers."

"What about if we all worked for free?" asked Chitchee.

Noel arched a look at Chitchee (who arched back). Noel was silent, nauseous, burpy, and stunned. At the same time he plotted, planned his plan Bs, foresaw obstacles, and overcame the obstacles.

"What was all that whistling about? Was that a siren?" shouted Ivan from the Poetry section between Byron and Cavafy, shelving books himself.

Ivan's red Sorel hiking boots' boot laces were all over the floor like a spilled can of worms. His blond beard, blond hair, and blond eyebrows portrayed a shabby, flaccid Volga boatman waking up in Lenin's tomb after a bender in Kiev.

"I thought *they* were coming for me with hammer and thongs," said Ivan.

"Why would *they* be coming for *you*?" asked Chitchee, attentively listening.

"Mayakovsky, that's why!" his voice was so clogged with mucus that Chitchee went to get a plumber's snake to clear it out. "According to my mother, we're related, not by blood, but by neighborhood."

Aloysius stared at Ivan for his undermining intrusion.

Not too long ago, Chitchee had gone to Ivan's apartment on Bryant Avenue and 32nd Street. Ivan had arranged all his books by the year *precisely* in the chronological order he read them day by day: Baudelaire, Marx, Balzac, Malraux, Zola, Comte, Engels, Proudhon, Mill, Goldman, Morris, Hugo, Gorky, Wilde, Zamyatin, and a row each for Lenin, Trotsky, Stalin, and Nikita Krushchev. He had written meticulous notes on index cards filed in Hush Puppy shoe boxes whose Basset Hound logo he resembled. He had post-it notes under each author with miniscule footnotes to himself and the start and end dates for each book read.

"Heavens to Murgatroyd!" exclaimed Chitchee. "One look at your bookshelves and I can tell you are autistic, schizophrenic, and Aspergergic—in equal thirds. I just love it!"

"Yes," said Ivan. "They diagnosed me a year ago."

"You mean you have been misdiagnosed all your life?"

Ivan stroked his blond goatee with the back of his hairy forefinger.

"No one ever came over here and looked at my bookshelves," said Ivan, "except you."

"Excuse me, sir," said Aloysius. "We are having a company meeting."

"Well, I'm a communist, so can I join in the discussion, comrade?" said Ivan, loudly scraping crud from his throat.

"Not right now," said Aloysius. "Okay, where was I? I want to thank you guys for all the years—"

"Well, I published another book of poetry," said Ivan. "I'll put this one in your poetry section. I noticed the other ones are gone."

"Excuse me," said Aloysius. "I'm really sorry, I want to apologize—"

"I don't know about *apologizing* for your poetry section, it's pretty good," said Ivan. "But I do know I can work here. Could I fill out another application?"

"You already filled out *all* our applications," said Saami. "We don't have any more."

"We're not hiring," said Aloysius.

"Really?" said Ivan, pondering. "Look at all the books coming in. There is no reason *not* to hire. Can I get an application anyway? I can work here because I can read here and bring in lots, lots of business."

"What if," temporized Chitchee, "I fetch your *last* application from last week. And you can run to Kinko's, make ten copies, and apply ten more times?"

"Well, I *am* writing a book on Khrushchev's early career as a cow herd, which served him well later when he was put out to pasture."

"We're not hiring," said Aloysius, frustrated.

"That doesn't matter. You see, I like it here. And I can work in a book store," said Ivan. "I always wanted to work in a book store and write poems. You don't seem to understand me."

"We're not hiring," said Snorri, crossing his arms.

"Oh, I don't care about that so much," said Ivan. "As long as I can work here."

"We're not hiring," piped up Saami, "because—because—you see—we're not hiring just *anybody* who wants to work here. If you *want* to work here, that's an immediate red flag."

"You mean I'm hired?" asked Ivan.

"And there is a hiring freeze in observance of National Hiring Freeze Day," added Saami.

"But I'm a famous poet!" said Ivan.

"How so?" asked Aloysius with his stuffing knocked out.

"Well, wherever I go I hear people reciting my poems by heart," said Ivan. "And my book of poems, *What the Wasp Said to the Tobacco Mosaic Virus Before The Battle of the Somme* went on Amazon yesterday."

"Ooh la la," said Chitchee. "How can you be famous overnight if you only published the night before? And everybody on the streets is quoting your poems?"

"Frankly I was a little surprised, myself," said Ivan. "But there are many things, Mercutio, that heaven and earth will never know anything about. As Shakespeare is quoted as saying."

Snorri snorted like Ferdinand the Bull at heaven's gate impatiently: "Can we get on with this?"

"Oh ok, I don't want to interrupt anything," said Ivan, farting loudly so that his loose pants seemed to flutter with a broken, brown wind. "But do you have Kropotkin?"

Stares.

Farts.

Kropotkins.

"I've never heard of National Freezing Day," continued Ivan on a melancholy cloud of disappointment. "Freezing Your Ass Off Day, now *that* I've heard of."

Ivan and Chitchee shook hands again and again and parted . . . then several more taffy-stretching goodbye goodbyyyyyye goodbyes elongating arms between them, the farewell taffy stretching . . . goodbye, catch . . . and release! Ivan stopped, turned, thought of a poem, walked out the door, walked back in the door, and said "goodbye."

"Aloysius," said Chitchee.

"Yes?" said Aloysius.

"Is it because of the lemon sugar cookies?" asked Chitchee. "The city health inspector found out, didn't he? I bet you 'Ol'

Colostomy Bag' complained! Damn it! We should have poisoned him!"

"Let's drop the subject, Chitchee," said Noel.

"Yeah, you're right," said Chitchee. "It's too explosive. Those lemon sugar cookies were certainly the bomb though. Is that what broke the camel's back? We didn't diversify our portfolio fast enough—and now we have to pay with our jobs!"

Chitchee cried like a rowboat swamping in waves of emotion and then hugged Snorri.

"And possibly our lives," said Snorri.

Snorri's eyes like two oxen unyoked at the sight of Chitchee's overwhelming emotional state.

"True," said Chitchee, heaving a heavier sigh. "At least when you are poor, you know who your friends are."

"Yeah," said Snorri, "because you don't have any."

Chitchee dried his tears on Snorri's extensions.

Aloysius unscrolled his plan, which resembled a Song Dynasty painting for its use of empty space. Staff (excluding Chitchee) could work for the rest of the paid work-week schedule; after that Aloysius would take over BookSmart as a one-man book store and work a 108-hour work week, covering all positions and shifts. And he would finish off all the shifts for that night and close early, because he needed to get some shut-eye before working 14 hours tomorrow.

Chitchee's book face smarted. The staff pinched their coats and jackets from off their hooks. Dispersed on the sidewalk, the staff took a tennis court oath to keep an eye on Aloysius. Stoic Aloysius never shared out his emotions. Nor did they. What was really going on inside him? What was going on inside all of them? Sturdy Minnesotan stock never appeared weak, indecisive, or soft, and that went for the men too.

Head down, ears pierced with cold, and looking like an overgrown black-capped chickadee, Chitchee stamped his Reeboks on Hennepin Avenue and warmed his toes.

"I'll miss you guys," said Chitchee, sniffling and about to have a seizure.

"Even though we paid you in books?" asked Noel.

"Even though we used you as bait?" asked Saami.

"And then conspired to get rid of you?" asked Snorri.

"Why kick a dead horse?" asked Chitchee.

They froze saying frozen goodbyes for another hour or so and split with splitting headaches.

Aloysius grasped for the shaking apricot bottle of Adderalls, strung up the CLOSED sign, locked the crash door with the Allen wrench, sat in his swivel chair, popped another 20 mg., rolled up his sleeves, and priced out books. The old college gridiron visualized itself before his tired, old eyes: hut, hut, hut, running down the stairs, packaging books, running up the stairs, answering the phone, making the play calls, buying books, pricing books, (and what if The Indestructible Book Jesus pulled up?), helping customers, taking customers to the empty shelves, and selling customers the empty shelves.

Frets tabbed his forehead when Aloysius thought of Aubrey's unpaid-for college education. That was the most important thing. Wherever he looked, there she was, beautiful again. Aloysius so wanted his daughter to have a better life than he had and at this rate, it would be too easy. With his face in his hands, Aloysius caved in; he wept uncontrollably, but he caught himself, cried, and stopped crying.

UPTOWN THEATER

Migrained for days, Chitchee never walked outside, except to Rainbow Grocery store twice. When the temperature dropped, he refused to get up. Facing a forcible removal, he couldn't move; he considered starving himself to death like Gogol. But first he would talk to somebody, preferably somebody he knew better than Gogol.

He remembered Felix. He loved Felix.

Walking forward into the teeming nightfall, Chitchee looked apprehensively at the cold streets everywhere. His mind was nothing but the sounds of creaking floorboards. The distressed branches of oaks croaked in the lowering wind. Brick corridors of slowly moving, funereal traffic reflected Chitchee's mood. The leafless, bare boughs predicated the harsh winter they pointed toward. Shut-ins whose windows framed obituary photographs glanced down at Chitchee. The hangdog buildings, always for lease, with drooping eyes, stared with dejection at the boulevard. Elegiac trees prayed to an exhausted sky. Chitchee marched forward through the snow slogging down on his shoulders.

Felix worked that night.

Felix looked to have shrunk since his house on Pillsbury Avenue had burned down. Smoke inhalation permanently damaged his roommate Lyle's brain, caused by his own forgotten cigarette. Not soon after that another friend "from the punk days," who had Alice in Wonderland syndrome, jumped off a balcony in the IDS center onto a Crystal Court table and died with a broken neck. Then his friend Rachel, who worked at Ragnarok's, died of opioid poisoning at her sister's wedding reception. Although Rachel had a prescription for Xanax, she wasn't known to have been on opiates. Felix himself had been in and out of the ER or Urgent Care twice in the last month.

Chitchee walked into the Uptown Theater lobby, doffed his wool black cap, and slung it on the concessions counter. The combers of his uncombed hair rolled forth in breakers. The beanie fell to the floor with a flop. Chitchee planked his hair back down and preened with grooming swipes.

"I had a breakthrough using squircles!" said Libor Biskop.

Libor emerged from the darkness of the inner theater, smothered inside his giant, white L. L. Bean down parka, under which he wore khaki shorts, knee-high navy blue socks, and oxblood Oxfords, his eyes growing as big as his glasses.

"Squirrely squircles!" cheeched Chitchee. "How did you do it?"

"Hobbes was murdered for his solution," said Libor. "Why should I tell you? You'll go there!"

Libor zipped up his zipper to the last tooth on his L. L. Bean down parka, creating the expression of a hanged man.

"All I want from your book store is a copy of the Rhind papyrus," said Libor.

"Libor!" said Chitchee, brightening up. "I don't work at the book store. I got laid off! You know, I always admired you for walking up to the Wells Fargo teller, demanding all the money in the till, and then asking to open a savings account—while you waited for the #6."

"Don't confuse me," said Libor. "There is a link between set theory and string theory. And I'm not in the habit of discussing my work with laymen. All right I'll tell you: you add extra dimensions to the rounded squares of implicit, entangled structure— and you get *quantum biscuits*!"

"Oh no," said Chitchee, his eyes as large as family popcorn bowls.

Libor looked for the next bus to chase. Chitchee knew Libor liked to give the bus a head start, betting that the bus driver would let him on for free—out of a possible respect for the horsepower per yard per man-hour Libor invested in chasing buses.

Felix commiserated with Chitchee by the crawl of one eyebrow.

"Oh, I'm really sorry, Chitchee," said Felix, dropping the popcorn shovel full of orange popcorn, which emptied onto the floor.

Felix searched for the misplaced corn broom.

"They don't hire anyone over 50 anymore," frowned Chitchee. "They don't want anyone with wrinkles, stretch marks, or broken bones. Everybody wants someone younger to exploit longer. 50 has flies. Faces after they undergo spontaneous symmetry breaking are no longer tigers in the night. I could say that, but I won't."

"It's human ineffability," said Felix. "What about becoming a goose herd? And you would have your nights off to write."

"Yeah, I *goose* so. I could do that," said Chitchee, slowly lifting the smile to his mouth, "but I'd rather open a book store on the Moon and take my chances there! But whatever God brings me I will accept with a loving heart."

"Odd duck! I ordered a bucket of popcorn eonsssss ago," said a customer, rumpled, red bow-tied, and red suspendered under his blue suit jacket.

His voice had the comatose quality of a sleepwalker asking for directions at a crowded intersection like Lake & Hennepin. Shaggy eyebrows, spiky eyebrows—he was *all* eyebrows in fact.

"Felix, I'm not even a writer," cried Chitchee, "I made that up so that people would like me. You can't be a writer if you can't lift a pencil. Who was I kidding? A real writer is successful like Robert Bly. Even a mediocrity like Garrison Keillor is something."

The customer's eyebrows resembled Karelian birch trees and curled like bark at this comment.

"People *like* you *do* like you! Not like me, because people like me—*don't* like me . . ." said Felix, turning and holding a Jumbo Coca-Cola overflowing cup. "What the whoa, that was woefully fucked up!"

"Hello? I ordered popcorn," said the splenetic eyebrows, cutting swathes of space away left and right. "Is the popcorn ready, YET?"

"I'm *getting* the popcorn," fumbled Felix. "I can't find the corn broom to sweep it up with. Here's a free Coke I wrecked. Do you want it? For free. On top of the house. Emily said we could do that. And by the time you finish that, a new batch of popcorn will have arisen."

Felix bobbled the Jumbo Coca Cola and the river delta of a strong brown sugar god with ice cubes flowed across the concession stand's counter.

"Stop!—whoa—oughtta be ready soon, sir," said Felix, mopping the counter with movie flyers.

"When LaDonna," continued Chitchee, mopping the counter with movie flyers, "discovered I was only submitting blank pages to publishers—she felt betrayed, rightly so—but I had nothing to say! What is there to *write* that hasn't already been retailed into tripe? What is there to *be* that hasn't been retailed into servitude? Art for art is as impossible for me as it is so easy for Minnesota legends like Garrison Keillor. So I'm an artist, by not being an artist? Is that Dada?"

"I don't know," said Felix, ringing up the charge on the cash register, which did not respond. When he shook the till, the till shot out on the floor. "It's hard to control Dada."

"EXCUSE ME, POPCORN?" said the customer, frequency modulating. "HELLO? I'M MISsSsING MY MOOO-VIE."

"Why not buy the book, based on the movie, if the movie doesn't even compare with popcorn? Or buy the book the movie is based on, if the movie is good and skip the popcorn?" said Chitchee as an aside. "What *is* the movie? *Hannah Montana Likes Her Popcorn Buttered?*"

"I'm sorry, sir, will you settle for a free hot dog?" asked Felix, kicking a broken hot dog under the cupboards.

"Do you guys know anything about customer service? You don't know who I am, do you? Radio Hall of Fame? I have a *Peabody*."

"Oh," said Felix like an actor acting out a laugh, "is that to go with your Pea*brain*? Ka-BOOM! I couldn't resist. You were a sitting duck, sir. Sorry about that, Guy. Um . . . okay maybe not kaboom, but Ellllll Ka-*bong*!"

The customer glanced at the ceiling. He pressed his lips tightly together in anguished restraint. If he were any hungrier, his teeth would fly out of his mouth with infected claws and shred the face of Felix: ribbons of blood, Potemkin sliced beef, and vultures on the red carpet would result.

"Anyway," said Chitchee, boxed in by the Sno-Caps, Whoppers, and Milk Duds in the vitrine display case. "Anyway."

"Popcorn?" Felix scooped popcorn with a shovel and filled a paper boat and handed it to Chitchee.

"*Danke schön*, so for now . . . can I work here?" said Chitchee, munching a single popped corn and savoring its delicious, puffy flavor. He smacked his lips. He looked for old maids that had half-popped and molarized flat the crunchy kernels like steak-meat.

"I'm really good at customer service," continued Chitchee. "Watch!"

He offered to share with the customer half a popcorn boat:

"Popcorn? I never got anywhere in this life, how about you, sir?" Chitchee asked the customer. "Do you think it's because I have these epicanthic folds? That's the end product of an accident on Chromosome 7, and that's because of a deletion of twenty genes. Fate prefigured my fate pre-written on a heavenly scroll signed by the moving hand of Al-*lah*."

The customer, a mouth of growls, blew breath upward as from an exasperated, squeezed Aeolian windbag, and shook his eyebrows, like docked Viking-prowed long boats over-washed to the gunwales.

"Or is it the calloused hand of custom," asked Chitchee, "that makes us weep?"

He poured the popcorn boat of popcorn down his throat.

"Excuse me," said the customer in the bedside voice of a chaplain's last rites. "Can I get a candy bar insssstead of the popcorn? Do you know who I am, look, do you need another clue? Doesn't lutefissssk ring a bell, doncha know, hello, lefse, Lutherans, Sven, Ole, hello?"

"Popcorn's almost ready," chirped Felix. "I'll bring it out to you when it's ready, piping hot! Piping, smoking hot popcorn! Pipe-smoking hot popcorn, popcorn, we're all born for popcorn! Wait! Sir!"

"Where's the manager's offisssse around here?" asked the customer.

The customer roved to the entrance door, spied on the movie, and marched back to the concession stand.

"Upstairs! Wait! I could give you the kernels, sir," said Felix. "You could pop the kernels at home and then send us a check, would that do? I'll throw in some weird orange, Nepalese un-iodized, saltless salt. I'll get your address in a second, if you could wait another second. And after that, a second second second. Wait! We can't let you go away starving to death from the concession stand."

As Felix rounded the corner, running from behind the counter and running in slow motion like an instant replay, replayed slower each time, he tripped ("Whoa!") on Chitchee's black woolen beanie's dehydrated bat shape and flew to the floor, the yellow-orange, tear-dropped kernels spraying like corn stones in a corn storm over the red carpet.

"I concede my concession," said the customer who walked hurriedly, glancing at his watch and striding up the sweeping staircase to the manager's office, where Emily sat drawing sketches of gremlins, the same gremlin over and over she always drew lately. When she looked up, the same gremlin stood before her, and she pushed backward in her manager's chair, startled.

"Why are you sitting there drawing bats?" asked the customer.

"Whoa," said Emily, "they're gremlins, not bats! And somebody has to draw them!"

"I want to talk to your supervisor," said the customer.

Up rose the occasion, and up rose Emily.

"Go ahead," she lied, not even looking up, concentrating on her art. "He's downstairs making popcorn."

"What was that guy's problem?" asked Felix. "It's only popcorn!"

"Popcorn, popcorn, popcorn, but he likes it," sang Chitchee, and he danced spasmodically like a go go dancer choreographing popping popcorn. Chitchee's spine straightened. Then his eyes bolted upright.

"Uh-oh, Felix?" asked Chitchee in the peak aha moment before plateauing. "You know who that was? THAT WAS GARRISON KEILLOR! I grew up with *The Prairie Home Companion*. I forgot how I loved that show—"

"—at a safe distance I hope—" interjected Felix. "I kinda loved how I forgot that show!"

"Oh no, I insulted Garrison Keillor! He *is* the State of Minnesota! I didn't recognize him. He looked a hundred years older than his high school graduation picture. What else can go wrong? He's going to hate me! He's never going to book me on his show. I could have been reading empty pages on *Prairie Home Companion*; that audience will laugh at anything."

"What do you think he does all day?" asked Felix, peering up the stairs for the customer's whereabouts.

"He owns a book store on Selby," said Chitchee, sleeving off the sweat perspiring from dancing.

"Wherever that is," said Felix.

"If it's not in Minneapolis it must be in St. Paul. What's it called? Uncommon Grounds? Common Roots? The Root Cellar? The Sixth Chamber? The Fifth Element? I forgot! Anyway, he's got plenty of dough to lutefisk with all day long. He's not starving to death. What is lutefisk anyway? Does it have something to do with the Aquatennial?"

Chitchee watched the hull of his own small, unmoored bookshop Ulysses & Sons drift out in a Viking sea burial on Arctic Sea currents eventually ramming into Greenland, litorally.

"Chitchee," said Felix. "Uh ho, here comes Emily. Somebody's done for."

"Felix!" said Emily in her full-blown goth gear, dark blue eyelids, creosote black everything but for the barn owl-white face. "Can I talk to you for a second?"

On Chitchee's interior movie screen, he panhandled next to Hawk Eye outside Club Miami. Chitchee held a cardboard sign squiggled with dried-out Sharpie:

LOOKING FOR INVESTORS IN BOOK STORE
NEED $30,000$ DOLLARS WILL PAY IN BOOKS
AND NEED 'SOMEONE' TO SHOW *ME*
POWER POINT, ADOBE HUT ILLUSTRATOR, XCEL, AND
KOOKLA KHAN'S ACADEMIE DOMIE THING

"Um," said Emily, "a patron has complained to me. I gave him rain checks, but he intends to complain to the District Manager. Don't worry, the District Manager has a crush on me."

"Well, who doesn't, Emily? Anyway, it was all my fault," Chitchee cried. "I distracted Felix from his job description. I'm sorry Emily but I lost my job—the only job I ever loved. What's left for me? Can I work here?"

"Okay, you are nuts, I can see that!" declared Emily. "I wanted to thank you, Felix! That was Keillor again. I wanted to say: Good job, you two! But really Chitchee, you're distracting Felix from his next dropped object."

"Oh, ok," said Chitchee, examining his hands. "I'm not cut out for plumber, carpenter, mason, lathe operator, hand model, trapeze artist, escalator captain, elephant hypnotist, dog park lifeguard, laugh track technician, asteroid realtor, wah wah wallah, or anything, but I can sell candy to big babies!"

The moviegoers bundled up and exited the Uptown Theater into the early nightfall behind Garrison Keillor who might be going home to "book-block" Chitchee for the missed box of popcorn. What if "Guy Noir" had masonic friends on the police force? Or the Fusion Center? The Illuminati? Or the Members of the Third Eye? What if Keillor was "connected?" Chitchee thought . . . looking at his hand's veins, wrinkles, freckles . . . I'll be thrown off the Hennepin Avenue Bridge!

"Okay, Felix, I have to go," said Chitchee, slipped outside, brushed the snow off, and said, "Hey Felix, it's snowing."

"Corn," mused Felix to himself, vacuuming the carpeted lobby floor, not hearing anything, staring at the red carpet and noticing every bruised patch and every spilled seed-kernel of corn glowing radioactively. The Dyson had unplugged itself from the wall socket, but Felix thought the Dyson broke and he took it apart. Emily plugged it back in, and Felix jumped in a shower of sparks, his eyes flashing with sparks. He tripped backward on the black woolen beanie again.

"Whose is this?" Felix asked Emily. "Oh! It's Libor's. I better get this to him so he doesn't catch pneumonia."

2001 HENNEPIN AVENUE SOUTH

Chitchee needed a mentor. He looked to Solomon for guidance. Or Ivan Von Volkov as Krishna's reincarnation. Where were these lovers reciting Ivan's love poems while they hung upside-down off their balconies like vampires squeaking odes to snowflakes. Where? Chitchee saw only the colorless snow that washed clean all the stars from the night sky and the skyline's skyscrapers that hung off the gutters like dirty icicles glowing in the night.

Another eternal winter in Minneapolis: her avenues rutted with puddles, potholes, and muddy snowbanks; her snot-green ridges of ice on the roads; her darkness around the dawning street suns; and Chitchee before the image of an old lover, when who should Chitchee see but his old and dearest lover, LaDonna DeLaVelle D'Galactica!

She fast-walked and ran as if chased by a snow plow down Hennepin Avenue. She stuffed two white terrycloth towels into a square garbage receptacle. She snow-plowed smackdab into Chitchee.

"CHITCHEE!" exclaimed LaDonna. "I made that call because Nestor forced me. He had a gun to my head. Nestor made me say that crap."

"What's up?" asked Chitchee, padding down his pockets. "Hey, I forgot my acorn cap at the Uptown Theater. My favorite black beanie."

"Nestor locked me in the basement, nailed the door shut, and wouldn't let me out until I said *I love you Nestor* to him through the door ten times. He's insanely jealous of you!"

"That makes sense," said Chitchee. "But Nestor keeps getting smarter and smarter than me until it's like I'm walking on the giant web of a schizoid spider when I talk to him. Can't he *learn* to control his insane male sexual jealousy like all the other insane men who can't?"

"There she is!" yelled an older man to a younger man bubbling up from a parking lot.

The New World Sunrise Massage And Spa owner Daisy Vang, with Reina, Paj, and Bobblehead (far behind) had rounded the Aveda Store on Lake Street.

"Crazy lady stole!" shouted Daisy Vang in a red silk robe undulating with mountainous dragons over long underwear.

"Do you want these 'love' stickers I stole?" asked LaDonna over her shoulder as Chitchee jogged with her. "You can have them!"

He read one: "Your heart knows the way."

Chitchee peeled one off and stuck it on his forehead.

"Yah harse nose the hay! Where did you get those?" asked Chitchee, running to catch up.

"I got into a little spat at New World Sunrise Beauty salon," said LaDonna, "because the Empress Dragon Beautician bitch burned the fuck out of me on a tanning bed and revoked my five-session package, no refund! Then she said she is selling the tanning beds in two days anyway. Lie! And *that* after roasting me like a pig on a spit! So I cased the tanning bed room, and grabbed the goggles, towels, and this roll of 'love' stickers. Quick, run across the street, catch the #6 before it takes off!"

Once on the bus, LaDonna casually tossed off:

"When I made for the door, her bodyguard ran out of the office after me, 'Stop, police, she's got a love roll!' Her son is blocking the door. I squirt him with a spritzer and go 'you can suck on this, slicky boy, and you can keep sucking on it until it comes out your asshole!' Her bodyguard pinned my arms back, but I somehow hair-sprayed him into a tanning bed, but the Dragon Lady was already waiting for the thumpers to arrest me. I ran right past her like she was standing in butter."

"They jumped on the bus behind us!" said Chitchee.

"I have squared the circle!" heard Chitchee. "With other dimensions."

Libor Biskop ran after the #6 bus.

"Implicit structure!" said Libor from his big white parka like a moon-fed moth. "I squared the circle with the equation of the universe, using the fine structure constant, Newton's G, the Planck constant, e, i, ?, and the Biskop constant. Glashow was wrong, Witten was right," he panted, "I have it," he wheezed, "the universe in one," he coughed, "algorithm. By squaring a quantum circle.

Call Steve Weinberg with the good news, again."

Chitchee snapped the bell-cord to stop the bus for Libor. LaDonna pulled it twice, negated the first pull, and said, "Wrong stop, driver!"

Chitchee pulled the cord again:

"Stop! A Nobel Prize is getting on the bus!"

"Don't let any Nobel Prizes on the bus!" said Mad Jack Apple Jack from the back where he sauced with Mad Jack Barley and Mad Jack Harry Snatch, who stood up, took off his winter coat, and showed off his olive, arm-pitted T-shirt, which read Anti-Science Guy.

The three saucy, taunting grimalkin leer-kats ground everybody's nerves into gunpowder.

"Hey, Chitchee! Don't pull the cord for anyone but yourself, or I will have to kick you off the bus!" said Lily. "I mean it! And you in the back, SHADDAP! You're distracting me and I'm running behind the weather."

"The fields of force," said Libor, talking to himself while he ran, "plus structure to equal the raw twistor manifolds that emerge from the implicate properties of quantum gravity and entanglement . . . what else could it be? David Bohm wasn't mad, everybody else was!"

"You're the boss!" said Chitchee, giving the bell-cord two tugs to signal agreement and the bell-cord broke. And the bus stopped.

"I have it," said Libor Biskop calmly. "But I have to write it down before I forget to call Andrew Wiles or any Russian like him."

Felix pulled out his Stingray bike with its sparkling ribbons around the banana bars. The pedal on the right had lost its grip and fell off. Felix bought ten Percodans which turned out to be Xanax from Randy, but Felix ate them anyway and with a face shiny as a tumbling gemstone he sped off on his Stingray the wrong way, then turned around. Felix forgot he had no brake pads on his brakes. He braked with his shoddy sneakers on the tentative ice sheets. The loose handlebars slid forward and the front tire slammed into Libor's jumpy lunge toward the door of the #6 bus when it stopped.

"You forgot your hat, Libor!" said Felix.

The Stingray fell on top of both of them.

"I'm wearing my hat," said Libor, feeling to see if it perched there. "No, it's right here in my pocket."

"Maybe that's someone else's hat," said Felix. "And this one is yours."

"No—they would have to be entangled for that," said Libor, crawling backward in terror from Felix. "I have to get to Kolthoff Hall at the U. to verify my calculations experimentally with someone doing their homework there."

"My bad," said Felix.

When Felix pedaled back to work the chain came off, the other eroded pedal broke in half, and upon arrival the kickstand flew off when he kicked it.

"We will call that your break, Felix," said Emily, who was vacuuming the red carpet with the reconstituted Dyson.

When Lily looked up at the interior rearview mirror she saw Chitchee and LaDonna stand up, while Libor climbed onto the bus's front bike rack without Lily's noticing. He never had bus fare; he was "allergic to it" was always his last ditch excuse. And when the New World Sunrise employees boarded, LaDonna shoved Chitchee backward and out they stepped from the back exit, facing the bus's opposite direction. The bus drove on through the punctual night of falling snow, the bus's front bike rack clasping Libor to its bosom.

"Let's go to my place!" said LaDonna.

They jet across Hennepin Avenue to a bus shelter, sat for a while, recrossed Hennepin Avenue for the next bus, and sat in the front seats with their good transfers.

Dagny Knutsen in a back seat read *Beneath The Underdog*, looked up, and met the gaze of a man who slurred down next to her:

"What are you reading there? Something I should know about it? Something about me? Look me up in the back. They call me Mad Jack the Fourth for some mad reason."

Dagny examined the face of a man who had spent his entire life at a permanent peep show and only crawled out of the Faust Theater when it was forced to shut down.

Dagny continued to read: "*Maybe lovers have to be con artists on this poor earth . . .*"

"ASSHOLE!" shouted Dagny, changing seats and seeing Chitchee and LaDonna through a keyhole. Steam arose inside her thrifted winter coat.

"You stole that from Mingus!" yelled Dagny.

Wool-capped heads swiveled in gyres.

"Who stole from Mingus? Mad Jack the Fourth? Dude, you gots to go, FUCK OUTTA HERE! Get the fuck off the bus!" said a collective gang of four.

Lily let it go. She was late. Mad Jack the Fourth was bombed. And Dagny did not notice Mad Jack the Fourth getting tossed off the #6 bus, because her heart was white hot. Red hot. White when looking out the window, red when she saw Chitchee and LaDonna get off the bus together. Holding gloved hands like laughing school children on a swing set! Celebrating? What about me? Chitchee broke the clasp of their hands by searching all his pockets. LaDonna watched Chitchee poke in all his and her pockets. LaDonna took her hat and pulled it over Chitchee's ears. And then he kissed her on the lips, which caused Dagny's sidelong glance to return to the page although the page was vague with a mist. Dagny squeezed her eyes together until the upwelling blush faded; she sensed clearly that love crept back into her heart. LaDonna's smile alluded slyly to something going on between those two exes. So what, Dagny didn't care. Then she cared. Hate, love, hate, love, madness, barking . . . it was like trying to get through *Nightwood*.

She considered the oyster: He was: poor, unclean, unreliable, sentimental, clumsy, narcissistic, mean, sarcastic, lazy, and even his intelligence seemed to hurt more than help. On the other hand he could be frugal, tidy, loyal, practical, deft, altruistic, kind, and as openly loving as any artist devoted to talking about his art as she had ever met. She had rejected many clumsy advances. Why were they rhyming now? Her mind kept turning with a carousel of images of Chitchee, and she felt sick from the delirium of the fixation. She had no chance of intimacy with Chitchee. But what the fried chicken fandango was going on with her? She was coming down with something she hadn't had in a while. A sort of love plague, a viral aphrodisiac, a deadly crush. A crushed rib-cage over an absurdly, wronged beloved. Her mind was a fracas. A crush was the end of a love relationship, not the beginning, because ever after the crush was a devilish corpse that intervened and forced her to say all the wrong things, act in all the wrong ways, and suicide bomb all her plans for sexual and creative harmony. She couldn't get Chitchee out of her head. Looping, looping, looping. Like a circle in a square, like a heartbeat laid bare. Far from being the ultimate loser, he was unique, fascinating, and very creative. She groaned aloud at what could have been the biggest mistake of her life.

"OH GOD!"

"Whacha readin, pretty woman? G-r-r-r . . ."

"Excuse me, I'm getting off here," said Dagny. "I'll try not to step on your deflatable ego, you old bugger."

She got off the bus, revering Chitchee, but obviously he was back with his ex, the pretentious LaDonna. Well, they matched like a comfortable old pair of galoshes. Dagny could not compete with a Metropolitan Opera house diva. Dagny imagined she needed a new overcoat to do that, even if LaDonna was a born cheater. Dagny's fit of jealousy carried her as far as the wet, soft snow that was plastered on the facade of LaDonna's brick apartment building. Fleece upon fleece of a whiteness enveloped the two-storied, gabled, wooden-framed houses with snow; and the four-storied brick flats down Hennepin Avenue described two unbroken, white lines converging at a theoretical single ice crystal in all directions. Cracks in the brick facade resembled inflamed, heroin-collapsed, in-between-the-toe veins. Chitchee didn't see the poverty. He was an idiot, and she was an idiot for not realizing he was an idiot when he talked about opening a book store. He couldn't even open a bag of Old Dutch tortilla chips. She was over him. It passed. Mark it: read.

In the first snowfalls every year, Chitchee saw only the snowy curves of snow drifts, sculptured Henry Moore's reclining nudes, odalisques of ice, and beds of erotic snow. He loved winter and the first heavy snowfalls. Winter was merely Spring upside down. The snow blossomed and grew flowers of ice in your front yard. By the frozen lakes, surrounded by balsam fir, green spruce, and white pines on the horizon, the bony broadleaves seemed a mirage of summer. Looking up, Chitchee hunted with Orion the white tigers created from snow-packed moguls whose roars were the wind blowing them all away. Then the cold air was so clean and pure he heard the clink of glass bottles a block away—someone threw out a bag of bottled empties and the dumpster shut.

LaDonna grew up in a Lake of the Isles chateau. Her wealthy, adoptive parents bought multiple houses like house progressions: ordinal home, second house, cabin on the lake, and summer house . . . and then LaDonna's and Chitchee's house in Northeast, LaDonna's house by Powderhorn Park, and finally her Uptown studio in a rickety-staircase apartment building whose fire escapes looked more dangerous than the fire and where the neighbors and small town tenants appeared tight-lipped, suspicious, burly, snow shovel-bearded, hipsterish, hairy as rams, bristling with opinions as with stray cilia, and possessed with an exclusive puritanism that constrained their pleasures to a trickle from a needle or a glow from a screen. Where did they all go, those party monsters from the 1970s, when the "recreational" drugs were marijuana and LSD? Did they graduate to cocaine and heroin, or other "occupational" drugs? And their children become the skinny meth heads who would grow old and play bingo for crystal in New Hopeless and Racoon Rapids? Chitchee examined the building's dilapidated midden piles of gigantic, squirrel caca bricks, the yard dotted with dead trees hung with ghostly plastic bags, and the cornucopias of overturned trash cans by the curb.

"This is an MPG building," said Chitchee.

"How did you know?" asked LaDonna.

"I see all the signs," said Chitchee.

They entered the musty halls and the carpeted hallways with their dogeared, worn-out, third world Mr. Bojangles's shoes on welcome mats, which had worn out their welcomes and said nothing.

LaDonna's studio lay cluttered with clothes on every stick of furniture, having emptied out her closets, which were nothing but hangers, each a different type. The vinyl broken couch, covered with her purchases from Saint Sabrina's over the years, nursed her cat, Marvin, cuddled up like a ball of black and white yarn in a cushion's indentation, which it had scratched to death.

"Let's take mushrooms and celebrate the arrival of winter," said Chitchee. "Like the way we were."

Her reddish-black corrugated curls of hair spilled down her chest when she tossed off her winter coat and cap and unraveled her ten-mile long colorful scarf of a burning rainbow, irised with purple skies and gold epaulettes.

"No," she said, slowly adjusting her jewelry's delicate metrics in a floor-length mirror, "pfff! How about Phillips vodka?"

"Sure, why not?" said Chitchee. "Do you have any pickled herring to go with it and shrimp cocktail sauce to go with that?"

Her fortune teller's rings adjusted, she shook her head.

"No, all I have is some Ecstasy that my friend Frenchy gave me," she said, securing her earrings' large fiestaware crescents. "We might as well do *them*, because I'm going into treatment tomorrow—and besides you know how I hate anything to do with reality! I can't live like this anymore. I'm getting old. See these labio-nasal wrinkles?"

"No, you look great, you look 45," said Chitchee. "You could probably get away with 43 or 42. Real men don't care about looks much. Just so long as you bear a cousin's resemblance to your mother."

"Who is my mother?" cried LaDonna. "That's just it!"

The colored light from a colored glass lamp played on her lower lip, then two dots of star-white light appeared in her pupils.

"Who is everybody's mother?"

Come to think of it, Chitchee thought while watching LaDonna pour Phillips vodka, they didn't have anything in common.

LaDonna hated seasons, trees, cows, flowers, succulents, grass, anything to do with nature poetry or landscape painting—it was all bunk. Artificiality above all, she loved leopard skin capri pants, turquoise stilettos, pointy sunglasses with rhinestone studded arms, bakelite square rings. Strange taste was her only taste. Everything green that grows? It grew out of its own grossness.

LaDonna never enjoyed Chitchee's mystical bent. He used to pray to God to hate him and to strike him down with hideous skin diseases to "strengthen his inner I" against the world. Drinking only bottled zumzum water, fasting, trancing, sleep depping to the music that drove her crazy, and reading books by Ibn Tufayl, Mulla Sudra, and Suhrawardi—all of it was unpronounceably alien to her. On the coffee table, the Yes! Catalog, the one with the Persian miniature of Haroun al-Raschid, especially moved her to vomit anger.

"What are you doing?"

"Dissolving my ego."

"Well, do it in the other room."

"Okey dokey."

"It's not as if you had an ego!" she called out.

"You don't understand. The thing is: *man must be made perfect* . . . according to ibn Arabi . . ."

"Sounds like a perfect waste of time to m-e-*e-e*!"

Whenever LaDonna had to decide between two courses of action, she turned her lips like a cross-bill's beak, placed her hands on her hip bones, and looked at the floor.

"I'm going to work on the car," she uncrossed her lips and yelled into the bedroom, "because the electronic fuse system turns the headlights on at night."

"Maybe it's an enlightened Volkswagen," he had said.

They swallowed their capsules of Ecstasy. They opened two bottles of Blech's beer—the Phillips vodka stood drained. Chitchee suggested a toast to LaDonna's going into treatment.

"Do you even know me?" said LaDonna.

Silence.

"Like I know my own hand," said Chitchee.

Silence.

"How do you know your own hand?"

"What does that mean?"

"What does what mean?"

"What you just said."

Silence.

"No."

At first, the flesh of her face with its makeup looked like wet clay or a shield.

"Excuse me for interrupting," he said.

"Interrupting what?"

"What you just said," said LaDonna.

"What did I just say?"

"I don't know because you interrupted me."

Silence.

"I love you," said Chitchee, bursting with tears from every pore. "I'm so lonely and burnt out and old. And you're so beautiful and miserable too! I need someone to hold my hand."

He hugged her like a little boy hugging his mother, and his body softened like a stream carefully carrying lily pads.

"I think I'm starting to feel something," said Chitchee. "Like I'm going to sleep! I'm so tired, I don't think you bought Ecstasy. This feels like At . . . i . . . van . . ."

LaDonna was a phantasmagoric Scheherazade as Chitchee's perceptions shifted and slid back and forth—in and out of dreams.

"You were saying," said LaDonna, yawning and falling asleep.

LaDonna awoke to Chitchee's hand-written poem on the Whirlpool refrigerator:

While the blueness descends from the stone cold clouds and the embrace of a guitar germinates gently in the stinko paleozoid gingkos I am waiting for the bus with my transfer my life in between two stops, two full stops, sentenced completely to the beautiful sun like a billboard that reminds you of your being reborn as a praying mantis with its head cut off an insect suicide so invisible am I to the strangers providing my optics an alien from inner space I get on the bus and talk to my neighbors with love for you LaDonna

LaDonna tiptoed from the shower as Chitchee was leaving, holding the doorknob. Apartment hunt/job search day had dawned on him: he didn't know *how* to look for an apartment or a job anymore. It was as all over his head as the sun, and moon, and stars.

"One question," he said quickly, feeling a trickle of perspiration run down his arm and drip off his fingertips like raindrops down a bus's window pane, "did we actually fall asleep around 9:00 last night? I have a vague recollection of feeling opiated, but I fell asleep. Your 'Frenchy' is fucked up. What's that knocking sound? Is someone here?"

"Don't you remember talking about my parents?" she asked, turning around to confront Chitchee.

"Your latest obsession, locating and meeting your biological parents . . . why?" he asked, looking up at the ceiling. "I loved your adoptive parents. They were fine people and supported us, even though we were fuck-ups and losers."

LaDonna had a vague idea that her mother once had an incarcerated husband—a Vietnam War veteran. And from another relationship, Jen had twins. That was with her high school sweetheart, who one day disappeared with the twins.

One night one twin walked into his sleeping father's single parent bedroom, placed a brown paper bag over his own head, and hanged himself from the light fixture for his father to see upon waking up. The other brother graduated from drugs to petty crime to real crime until he had a bed reserved for him at the local reformatory. He ran away and never came back. His father never cared for him—no more than a rock. The father left Texas for Florida to join a church. After Jen divorced him, she never talked to nor saw him again. Eventually the father of her twins eluded all capture by becoming a minister. Jen herself became devoutly Christian, actively involved herself in Wayzata Community Church activities, and there she met Wirt, whom she passionately loved and wanted to have a child with, but he couldn't, which is when they called Lutheran Social Services and discovered Donna, who had been confiscated for child endangerment and lived in an institutionalized home, which no matter how she distorted it, was an orphanage for orphans, ages 5-18, each cut from the world and alone as barnacles on a wooden pier.

"Did you roll your eyes at me?" said LaDonna.

"No! I wasn't rolling my eyes at you, I was rolling my eyes at the ceiling."

"I hear something too," said LaDonna, looking over her shoulder out the window of snow-gowned oak branches. "What is that knocking sound?"

"Why do you even want to find your real parents? Who cares about *real* parents? Your parents are everyone twenty years older than you. Your Mother is Mother Earth, your Father is Mr. Pie-in-the-Sky. Everyone is either One or Zero. One is alive, zero is dead. All women are sisters. All men are pigs or dogs. So everyone is your mother or father or daughter or son or labradoodle or pig-dog!"

"That's such a cliché! You don't understand! And it's not my *latest obsession*," she said, the last two words flaring up with a change of heart, "*Charles.*"

She used his real name to taunt him from the open wound at the bottom of her heart, which was draining her own essence down a rathole. The miscarriage. It was always the miscarriage, leaving them two halves of a broken heart.

A snowball climbed up to her window and fell back.

LaDonna looked out the sash window, saw Nestor standing in the snow, and threw open her window.

"Throw me the key," said Nestor, cupping his hands in an upside-down heart.

LaDonna formed a T with her hands.

She searched yesterday's jeans draped over an armrest, both pockets, and then jumped into the same jeans, zipped up, brushed her hair, and looked in the mirror. Chitchee looked for a moment at LaDonna, whose anguished forehead wrinkled like tally marks—a diagonal slashed through them right to left.

"Chitchee," said LaDonna, "you never really understood this pain blocked inside me, ever since the separation. All the pain of separation from my real parents. It's like being separated from Allah for a Muslim."

"Al-*lah*? Oh, that separation," said Chitchee, removing his hand from the door knob. "Maybe your real mother doesn't want to be joined. Maybe you'll find her, and she's homeless in a trailer park, or making a porn film in a Miami motel room with a swinging dick named Brad from Ypsilanti, smoking phencyclidine on Schilling's parsley flakes—but why you should have ever hooked up with the most arrogant man on Earth—"

"Get out! Jerk! *Ifrit!*" she said, slamming the door behind him. "Don't ever come back!"

"Huh?" said Chitchee through the slammed door. "I was talking about me!"

He peeped through her peephole, placing his heart sticker on the heart-shaped brass knocker.

LaDonna rushed to the open window, but Nestor was only secondhand prints in the snow. LaDonna ran back to her front door.

"Chitchee, come back!" said LaDonna, quietly but loudly. "You'll have to never come back through my kitchen window. And I forgot the stairs are broken! Like you said: the MPG landlord is a giant cockroach and never fixes anything! I wouldn't want you to get hurt! Try the fire escape."

"Now can I roll my eyes?" said Chitchee.

Looking down at the tracks of snow where Nestor had stood, Chitchee crawled out onto the MPG fire escape, slipped on the icy slats, and felt the scaffolding move. The zigzagging, cast-iron fire escape, which had been eroding from the brick walls for irreparably lost years, inched out cockroach-like from its mooring. It was definitely an MPG building, one of Viktor's finest creations in the great chain of being.

While Jason Unterguggenberger walked huddled down Hennepin Avenue, the snow fell like soft tennis balls defying gravity. Pine, spruce, and fir trees accumulated the wet snow on their branches, haloed in blue, purple, and gold. He waved once disconsolately at Chitchee with a hand like a dead snowflake. He had a black eye.

Slats broke, popped out, and flew to the ground, falling at Jason's sneakers.

The entire fire escape came loose. Chitchee looked over his shoulder, hanging on by white knuckles without gloves to the cold, iron railing, and he prepared to fall and die.

"Chitchee!" shouted Jason. "Why are you hanging from a fire escape? Aren't you cold?"

"Jason! Where did you get the shiner?" asked Chitchee, his legs barely able to tap-dance on the railing of the fire escape on the second floor. "You're not suicidal, are you?"

"MPG fired me," said Jason.

"Out of a cannon?" asked Chitchee, losing his handles.

"Sucks," said Jason.

"Real shit bro," said Chitchee. "Can you catch me if I jump? I don't think the fire escape can hold my weight . . . much . . . longer . . ."

"Has Grant Hart been in?" asked Jason, taking off his headphones.

"I don't know, I don't work at BookSmart anymore," said Chitchee, his Reebok toes unable to support his dangling hulk.

Chitchee pounded his gloved fist on the brick wall and yelled.

"HELP!"

A window opened. A goth girl held a candle in a sconce out the window and whispered:

"Dude, you're ruining my vibe."

And the window closed.

"Sorry!" said Chitchee, tapping lightly on the window and talking to a black cat.

Melchizedek's Ensorian face floated over the cat's shoulder.

Chitchee let go of the fire escape.

Nestor opened LaDonna's window and deduced the entire event. He had seen it all from the beginning of time. She had lied again! The snow was like hot ashes, but the cold air froze Nestor's black locks like spiderwebs.

"What was that idiot doing here?" said Nestor. "You slept with your ex? Why would you do that? I'm not good enough? Who else are you sleeping with? I'm telling everyone on Facebook what a whore you are!"

"That should drive the men away!"

The glow in LaDonna's cheeks faded like the smell of roses.

A window slammed shut behind which shouts were heard.

"Let's walk to Walker," said Chitchee, feeling his body for broken ribs, "before we get much older and need walkers for Walker. Old age wasteland! They're all shirt-waisted! Jase? I feel so sorry for your job loss! Where are you going to run to, Johnny Too Bad?"

"Back to the storage locker, where else?" said Jason, drawing in his mouth and biting the lower, already bitten-through, dried-out lip tissue.

"Now, *I* need a storage locker," said Chitchee as they talked and walked together into the antechamber of Walker Public Library. "I'm getting evicted and I just got let go from BookSmart. How does one obtain a storage locker? Hey, Jason, do you need a roommate? Split the utilities, if there are any!"

WALKER PUBLIC LIBRARY

After the Walker Public Library won an award for The Ugliest Library in the United States, the Walker librarians dutifully installed a display case to commemorate this honor with various photographs of the building, the poured concrete slabs, the library windows looking up to the street level like an insectarium, and the overall architecture from a micro-brutalist Le Corbusier who had squeezed it out his backside. On the longest day of summer, no sunshine entered the building. In the carrels were a lot of homeless men reading Rowling randomly. The transient souls positioned their chairs for their posed moments, knowing they could get away with pretending to read even while snoring. Head jerk, look around, go back to the cave of sleep, hibernate in the smoke of winter dreams, and hide with the descending sun.

Chitchee melted like a candle in the Walker Library lobby. He looked over the photographs of the country's ugliest library— its gray, cinder-block box, as an aesthetic form was like biting into a chocolate and finding the creamy center to be a liquid paste of concrete, sand, and road salt. And yet it was a home and a nest, because he escaped his neighbors' threats at the Fremont Terrace Apartments. Walker Public Library was Chitchee's research center, his Institute for Advanced Study, National Archives, and arXiv.org. He knew all the librarians: Maryanne, Tom, Stock Market Dennis, but mostly he interacted with Dale the Raging Librarian, who had a long black and gray ponytail and a ferocious moustache shaped like a wharf. He wore a flannel shirt, a black T-shirt, and faded Levis uniformly every shift. On the job he moved about like a pair of angry scissors. By the end of the night he was a hatchet with blue eyes. He had worked at the Minneapolis Central Library when pneumatic tubes filled with call slips (with the patron's requested call number on them) flew down a chute to one of six workstations for six pages, one of which was the bombarded Dale. Overworked, pissed, and super subordinate to every clown in town, he pulled out the call slips, crumpled them into balls, and chucked them in the corner: "I left the sweatshops behind me in Asia, fuck this!" instead of placing the call slip in the book he had fetched and sending the book back up the dumbwaiter. The call slips accumulated in a mound politely referred to as "Dale's Downtown popcorn." His supervisor, fed up with the surplus of popcorn, re-upped him, and shipped his angry butt to Uptown, Walker Library branch.

Jason quickened to the Express Internet computer station and he stood in line in puddles that had waxed large from the snow dragged in on snow-covered footwear and damp, frieze overcoats.

Chitchee helloed Dale and tiptoed past a round table where Coca Cola Man, a homeless, deaf, diabetic man with combed-over hair, thicker than Plantation Blackstrap Molasses with streaks of white sugar in it, sat face-planted. Arms forward over the library table with plastic tanks of Coca Cola everywhere, his giant mop of hair absorbing the library table's puddle of spilled Coca Cola, Chitchee slipped two dollar bills under his hand. For all anybody cared Coca Cola Man was dead. Coca Cola Man had been re-charting Minneapolis weather tables from the last hundred years for what seemed a hundred years and it had aged him a hundred years. He spoke to no one ever but sometimes nodded at a mute woman with Moebius syndrome and a backpack, who did nothing but walk all day everywhere in silence year round.

"Congratulations, Dale!" said Chitchee, shaking Dale's hand. "You work in the world's ugliest library! I want to check *The Guinness Book of Records* to see if you're in there!"

"Not the world's ugliest library, only the *United States's* ugliest library," said Dale, scraping books off the floor.

"You're so modest! I love that about you!" said Chitchee. "Are you hiring? I lost my job."

"You don't want to work here," said Dale, stroking his soup strainer and stubbly chin. "The ceiling leaks, and the roof is caving in—below the parking lot, above the middle study area over there by Coca Cola Man."

"Oh, really?" asked Chitchee.

Chitchee secured that particular table under the structurally weak, rotting chunks of concrete ceiling immediately, figuring if the roof fell on top of him, he'd have a lawsuit that would pay for Ulysses & Sons, if not his wake.

Chitchee walked into the neighborhood bathroom, where the urinal overflowed with fecal liquid, stools, and turdy balls. The shoes of another homeless man scruffled, stalled in the stall, his pants around his ankles—seemingly waiting to come out. Over the sink Undone Buttons looked in the mirror, his pants thrown in the corner, a brown streak burbling down his bare leg. Through the looking glass, he saw Chitchee. Chitchee saw Undone Buttons in the mirror, who looked surprised that anyone should intrude upon his private ablutions.

"Undone Buttons," said Chitchee, with a smidgen of soft butter in his doting tone, "what's up with the green apple splatters?"

"Fuckin' library faggot!" said Undone Buttons. "Get the fuck out of here, rat-fuck-face!"

"You are hardly in a position right now to espouse your homophobia," quipped Chitchee. "What do you think this is, Buttons, the downtown Central Library? Love ya, man, but get your shit together! Have you ever read *The Great Gatsby*? All we can do is swim upstream, with water up our noses, and I forget the rest. I suggest you join a book club. Walker has one. I'll go sign you up!"

Chitchee turned around and walked off to notify the security guard Bobblehead, who was playing with an eyeless teddy bear in the children's corner. He gurgled to the eyeless teddy bear like a broken toilet.

"Cocoa, cookie, bus," said Bobblehead when he saw Chitchee approach.

Bobblehead, chief head of library security and crowd control, tucked in his shirttail and said that Chitchee should defer 'book club' questions to Dale the Raging Librarian, who was listening to a crook-necked Linda Rolvaag complain about the voice in her head, emitted from WCCO's talk-show host Ruth Koszlak. There was an aerial hidden in a shotspotter and there was a receiver in Linda's molar. The frequency was tuned directly to her "life signature." At times, Barbara Carlson on her cell phone cut into the conversation with her urgent babble, driving Linda to drink herself into the gutter.

"Like a party line," Linda complained to Dale's steel-jacketed eyes, "when there used to be operators . . . and people!"

"Linda," said Dale, feigning concern over the burgeoning fracas at the Express Internet computer workstation where Jason stood in line with headphones blaring *Candy Apple Gray*, "what you just said is just a chocolate chip on the entire pile of shit we got going on here."

Minerva and Beda on the one Express Internet Walker Public Library claimed twenty minutes as a couple although they always bogarted the terminal past the single person, ten-minute time limit anyway. Their argument with another couple standing behind Jason carried them outside to the sinking parking lot and snow banks. Chitchee followed them upstairs and outside. Beda twisted the girl into a headlock and bloodied her nose while her boyfriend watched, and Minerva vowed to never, never go out into the world again—unless the Uptown Theater premiered a new Jane Austen movie as pretty and time-consuming as the last outing.

"Go, Beda!" she cheered unconvincingly.

Chitchee ran downstairs to the dim lobby after seeing he could do nothing, but there were already two more people on the Express Internet and three more people waiting impatiently in chairs pissed, their boots splashing in puddles around their boots. Jason had disappeared.

Chitchee informed Dale of these events, but Dale said sorry he had eaten too many of Frito-Lays's Fritos to get up and do anything productive about production quotas except brush deep-fried, cornmeal crumbs from his Nietzschean 'stache. He ended with:

"And since I found a burnt black Frito in the bag, I consider it my lucky day!"

Chitchee wanted to read La Bruyère and wait for the roof to collapse. He had meant to read La Bruyère, Lichtenberg, Gracián, La Rochefoucauld, and Cioran—all in a row as moralists and apothegm jewelers. Head jerked, Chitchee heard a laugh track. Mad Jack Apple Jack with a mini-TV was watching *Family Ties*. And Mad Jack Apple Jack sat next to Ivan Von Volkov, shoes off, snoring with his open mouth swallowing the fly specks that fell from the ceiling. Next to Ivan's black-socked feet, tall stacks of books on the Soviet Union piled up in a mess for Dale to clean up.

Bobblehead, cradling his favorite eyeless teddy bear, walked up from the children's corner and asked Mad Jack Apple Jack: "What's on?"

"You're standing in my light!" said Mad Jack Apple Jack.

"Who cares?" asked Dale.

Dale grabbed the teddy bear from the security guard and hurled it back to the children's corner.

"Turn that shit off, this is a library," said Dale, snapping off *Family Ties*. "Fucking garbage!"

"Hey, whaddya doin' man?" asked Mad Jack Barley. "It's a free country!"

"What is going on?" asked Mad Jack Harry Snatch. "That's his personal liberty! That's in the Constitution where it says 'I can watch whatever I want.'"

Chitchee jumped for the available Express Internet computer terminal, curious to see if there were rooms for rent in the Uptown neighborhood.

The security alert system activated when Undone Buttons, now wearing a Boston Celtics green cap, carried in plain sight a *Webster's Third International* through the RFID security gate. And Bobblehead had waved him through.

"It always does that when it detects something!" said Bobblehead.

Dale's neck hairs bristled and stood up. He stroked his mustaches; he goosed his neck like a mongoose. He flew after Undone Buttons.

"That's not for checking out, asshole," said Dale, prying it out of Undone Buttons's hands.

"Fuck you, you motherfucking mongoose—"

Dale grabbed Undone Buttons right hand and bent its thumb backward until Undone Buttons yowled, falling backwards to his knees until his thumb broke. Undone Buttons screamed death threats and Dale pretended to call 911 while eating Fritos.

Chitchee was on Craigslist eagerly looking for a cheap, but beautiful apartment. He imagined such castles as never filled the air. There was one prospect on Lyndale Avenue South:

"There is a motherfuckingshitton of storage space in here. I'm talking motherfucking hidden cabinets to narnia and a storage space like the wonder years in the basement. Speaking of the basement, management has been talking about levelling up the laundry sitchuation. They probably mean new/more machines. (Currently, laundry is $1 per machine). Oh—they're gonna be putting some motherfucking bike racks down there, too. There is no off-street parking for resident—but don't let that deter you from this fine-ass abode. I've never had an issue parking within half a block away but I can't tell you how many fools pussied out of this place because of the parking sitch. I mean, come on. It's *eat street*. No one can find parking on Nicollet during the *day*. Idiots. This apartment has been pretty cool in the summer, even without any AC—except during that gross bullshit heat wave. August. Ugh. In the winter, it's super warm and cozy. Hot-ass Bitches love being super warm and cozy. Bitches also love kitties. And the cartridge shells on carpet all gone swept under the bridge."

A deaf mute man resembling a starving, hollow-eyed El Greco walked behind Chitchee, stood in the corner, sucked his thumb, and then screamed as if a super hot peanut butter sandwich had stuck to the top of his mouth.

"'en minu'e! 'ime!"

An old bald Teutonic hobo, with a creaky dolly of his worldly goods, meditated in the magazine corner and sucked on a Slo-Poke, his bags of groceries from the food shelf spread all over the flood-stained carpet like a basement picnic. And for no reason he barked like a dog.

"Oh, it's good to be back in my library," said Chitchee, serenely gazing at his surroundings, "where I can think!"

Chitchee picked up an *Uptown Messenger* and a *Daily Beehive*, walked back merrily to his ceiling-doomed table, and buried himself in the local want ads.

The Three Grasshoppers walked into the library lobby. Stumbling around, Dougal, Mjollnir, and Nicky Fingers grinned foolishly. Chitchee waved them over, having not seen them since Bobby & Steve's truck towed them in Skooge's '65 Chevy Bel Air station wagon to the impound lot.

"Chitchee, what are you doing, man?" asked Dougal, his hair and beard purple.

"I'm waiting for the roof to cave in," said Chitchee. "I heard the building is structurally deficient and could cave in at any moment. So when it does I'll be buried alive, but I'll be rolling in four-leaf clover all the way to the river bank with the moolah-lah-lah!"

"Really? Mind if we join you, Chitchee?" asked Nicky.

"Have a seat," said Chitchee.

"Did you hear what happened to Dougal, Chitchee?" asked Nicky.

"What happened to Dougal?" asked Chitchee, pushing away his *Uptown Messenger*.

"They amputated his toes," said Nicky. "Show him your toes, Dougal."

"Are they purple too?" asked Chitchee.

"Hah!" shouted Mjollnir.

Mjollnir's short, sharp laugh was the crack of a whip, surprising everyone around with its violence, and just as surprisingly, Mjollnir, blanketed by his long white winter beard, fell asleep in his plastic, egg-cupped chair.

Dougal revealed a sealed jar of human toes floating in formaldehyde. Dougal had been passing out drunk by Lake of the Isles overnights for years—even through the winters. The moisture in his boots had turned to ice one night when the temperature plummeted below zero. Dougal hadn't taken a shower for so long, he hadn't noticed that his feet had turned black from frostbite. HCMC shook their heads but prevented the gangrene when they examined his stupidity. Allowed to keep his own toes as a gentle reminder to cut back a little on his tippling tendencies, Dougal showed them off as toe trophies.

"Are you guys hungry?" joked Dougal. "Mjollnir, wake up, it's feeding time at the Minnesota Zoo."

Mjollnir opened one giant whale's eye.

"What did you do that for? I was dreaming I was at the State Fair selling weed to "BB" Robbins—the thumper at the RNC who fractured my jaw and gave me a concussion when he kneeled on my back with a chokehold and another MPD thumper kicked my head in," said Mjollnir going back to sleep, his head about to fall off his shoulders.

"So?" grinned Dougal.

"And then me and you were in Florida picking oranges with Tiger Woods."

"So?" grinned Dougal.

"Then we were all at Burning Man. There were topless girls dancing . . . but I had forgotten my bifocals under the orange trees in Florida. I was on the grass looking for them, when Elton John stepped on my hand and said, 'Those are mine.'"

"What are you guys doing?" asked Jason.

"We're waiting for the roof to cave in, so we can afford to go to the next Burning Man," said Chitchee. "With our bifocals."

"Do you want to go check out my storage locker now, Chitchee?" asked Jason.

"Oh, yeah," said Chitchee, who heard snoring.

When Dale the Raging Librarian popped and cracked his knuckles next to Ivan's railroad track ears, Ivan aptly snored awake. Ivan looked around the library at the lounge chairs shaped like abridged chesterfields. Each departmental chair was held by yet another homeless version of Ivan, whom Ivan either knew, knew of, or had collaborated with.

"I guess that's enough research on Lubyanka Prison for one night," said Ivan.

Ivan zipped up his parka and dragged his heavy boots like bulging suitcases toward the exit until Isaac Deutscher's *Stalin* beaned him in the back of the head, cocking its spine when it kerthunked. Ivan turned around and fuming Dale launched Katyushas from his deeply-bunkered eye sockets at Ivan, both guys' eyes bristling wide open. Ivan licked his nicotine yellow teeth, pondered the wounded *Stalin* on the floor, and soothed his scraggly-fraggly Van Dyke with petting strokes.

"Oh that was you, Dale," said Ivan. "I wanted to ask you, where is your Gus Hall section?"

"Put your books back where you found them, you pencil-necked twatwaffle!" said Dale, kicking over the entire stack of unshelved books.

"It's not like I work here," said Ivan.

"What do you think this is, Ivan?" asked Dale. "The Library of Congress? As if *Congress* ever read a fucking book in their crock-of-shit fucking lives of lying shit!"

"Now, Dale," said Linda Rolvaag. "Calm down, you know for the love of country, you know our political leaders sacrifice their families and family life when they are getting it on in Washington."

Dale half-winced on his left side toward Linda in acknowledgement of his accepting her message, but ultimately discarding it like a call slip from a pneumatic tube. He upped stakes and stalked into the men's bathroom. He shook up Walker Public Library when he shouted through the roof, the ceiling cracking like the walls of Jericho.

"I'M NOT CLEANING UP THIS FUCKING SHIT!"

SEWARD NEIGHBORHOOD

Chitchee and Jason-under-headphones bussed past basins of bars and uplifted ranges of churches and back down to bars again until off Central Avenue, they de-bussed outside a Latvian-owned, stand-alone hardware store. It stood like a frozen streetcar in a row of cocktail lounges. They stood in a frosted time-frame from Svensk. A thorough bass of bars and saloons beat a foursquare march through the snow of Northeast Minneapolis. Scarlet cardinals and powder-blue jays dotted the plowed parking lots of white and black cars. Beer bars with their pitchers and glasses of Grain Belt, rimmed and brimmed with hoppy froth, quenched the potatoey guys in gray parkas, alpines, pork-pie hats, and black overcoats. You could pretty much hear them salting their stale but edible jokes from winters past. Faces bleared and bleated with warm glows that ended in kisses for their cozy, Winona Ryder-looking girlfriends (because Winona Ryder had something to do with Minnesota?) with upturned noses, eyelashes for eyes, and sugar beets for cheeks. Chitchee bought Jason a Blech's beer in one of these bars. Chitchee ordered a Blech's for himself as an afterthought. It tasted sour and gave him a floaty headache. He envied the carefree couples and wished he were one. Unjustly marginalized for his disability, he sketched the outline of a murder mystery on a napkin: love at first sight, murder at first crack, kisses, bullets, kisses, set ups, double crosses, kisses like bullets, kiss this, bang! Title: *Murder for Love.* Jason asked if that meant it was "non-fiction." And off to Jason's lived-in storage locker they traipsed and tripped along in the snow—to one of a raft of storage compounds, composed of strip malls of stuffed garages, packed to the rafters with infinite stuff. The complex of lockers blended with the woods, the wild turkeys, and the nearby condominiums in 1970s Revival of Revival style. They jostled an enormous Vizio Quantum 65-inch flat screen to make room for two bodies on top of the random lot of boxes thrown pell-mell.

"I thought you were living with your girlfriend," said Chitchee.

"Baby kicked me out when I couldn't pay my half of the rent, because fucking Sangster fired me," said Jason. "I was doing my job and I found a dumpster filled with these boxes that were like chemistry sets. And they were all filled with microscope slides, little eye-droppers, plastic baggies like for collecting insects, and stacks of unfilled forms to fill out. There must have been hundreds of them. I brought the kits home and put them on Facebook to sell for extra cash. Then at six o' clock in the morning, we woke up to pounding on our front door. The door shattered into splinters before we could answer. Thumpers poured in and arrested me for drug dealing. For evidence they removed all the Facebook chemistry sets, our large screen television, my mother's jewelry, and my baseball cards. When I got out of jail, fucking Sangster told me I had been fired for job abandonment. MPG couldn't cover my last pay period with cash, but would pay me off with a large wide screen television instead, which I had to pick up at Club Miami or settle for nothing. And when I got to Club Miami, I saw a 65-inch Vizio Quantum! So I guess it all worked out in the end. Such as it is."

"Talk about a deal," said Chitchee. "No warrant? What were they looking for?"

"I think they were looking for the right address, which was supposed to be for Vice Lords, but the CI must have been blind because the Vice Lords lived down the street. They even had Vice Lords on their mailbox. Obviously not me. How goddamn stupid can thumpers be? Then they asked me how I got my hands on all the rape test kits from 4th Precinct."

"So the thumpers throw out the rape cases before they go to trial?" asked Chitchee.

"How should I know? I got off easy! A friend of mine lost his parents to thumpers due to the smoke inhalation from their 'task force gang' flash bangers. They murdered the old couple over forty pounds of marijuana, and his parents were in their 80s, and never smoked anything. Except grenades."

Having spent one trial night in his clothes, next to Jason's sweaty socks, jugs of urine, and doggie bags for his excrement, which stank like a sewer of roadkill excreted from the ass of the selfsame roadkill, Chitchee rolled out from under the flat screen HDTV.

He sneaked from the storage compound into the morning's freezing fog.

Chitchee, wearing his fleece-lined, red Buffalo plaid shirt, his worn black motorcycle jacket, a blanket-sized, knitted scarf, black bean-colored beanie, and ugly orange nankeen mittens, canvassed Seward neighborhood in South Minneapolis for a room to rent, a place to shelter for the endlessly winding winter ahead. But nobody walked around looking for anything *like* FOR RENT signs anymore. Search engines, websites, and emails had eliminated the need for eyeballs, hands, and faces, so his prowling around the Seward neighborhood looked suspiciously like prowling around the Seward neighborhood. And yet, he wanted to move to an edgier neighborhood, because Uptown had lost its edge when McDonald's eliminated their patio.

Now Chitchee could add dollars and cents, but he could not budget household finances. Funnel clouds whirled those dollar signs and decimals away like melting hailstones in the rain. Chitchee understood the history of the 13.7 billion year-old universe; he had tracked the KOBE, the Wilkinson Anisotropy Probe, and the Hubble Telescope, but without Paisley's covert remittances he'd be floating down the Mississippi River with the final eviction notice in his orange mitten.

Echoes of footsteps appeared in ellipses of time as he walked down long residential lanes, dominoes of low bungalows alike as the bird-feeders. Some houses were dolled up with elaborate aprons of gardens, some with William Morris-style, stained-glass tree hangings. Most had front yards of bare-branched birdless trees with hanging wind chimes. Under the usual overcast, iron-gray, lowering stratus quo sky of Monotonopolis, Chitchee found himself lost. Feeling fairly freakishly warm (temperature in the upper 20s) that day, Chitchee watched the wind mosey past him at a negligible five miles an hour.

Therefore, he could at least knock on a few doors to see if they had spare rooms. He said he was quiet and would eat in his room. The neighborhood clicked on Next Door's website, twcrime.com, and Citizen.com, scanned scanner groups, checked their bolted locks, and informed 3rd Precinct of his presence while Facebooking and tweeting at the same time. Chitchee toured the houses besieged by years of countless winter snowstorms, shovelfuls of snowy sidewalks, and elaborately snowed-over gardens manned by trolls and flamingoes. The flamingo beards refracted light through their icicles, the radiation of flat screen 65-inch Vizio Quantums transmitting rainbows from dark dens.

"Good job!" yelled Chitchee, echoes slapping back at him.

He needed a plan. Option 1: get on a Greyhound bus to New York City and see what happens. Option 2: marry some old bat and hope she likes silly, seedy homeless guys. Option 3: there was no Option 3. It was either: Option 1 or Option 2 and neither of those was an option.

Mini-lighthouses with flat screen 65-inch Vizio Quantums transmitting rainbows from dark dens fanned across the snowy quietism, the sidewalks deserted, and the streets empty as thought. And look where the past had gotten him! His damn past followed him everywhere. What if BookSmart were replaced by StreetSmart—what would a store called StreetSmart sell? Nunchucks. Brass nukes. You'll never go broke selling guns in America. In fact, why don't we sell off the public libraries for public gun shops? That would subsidize growth in firearms manufacturing and create gobs of jobs in the security sector—prison construction, undertaker software development, surveillance analysis, and elementary school pathology.

After getting nowhere, Chitchee sat in a snowbank, cried, and wept. Confused, he didn't know how to find an apartment—it was like trying to find love. If he went home, the neighbors wouldn't let him sleep; if he complained about the noise, the bully decibels redoubled.

Street lights glowed glowworms of glowing blue.

MPD thumpers from the 3rd Precinct slowed down and looked at Chitchee slowly, then sped up when he looked at them like a white ghost from the snow. The whole neighborhood looked blacked-out. Everybody had driven home in rush hour to sit on the couch and watch someone get fired on *The Apprentice*.

By walking alone, Chitchee stood out like a house fly in clam chowder. Followed by the 3rd Precinct, he ditched into an alley behind some stodgy, stucco frame homes with white-trimmed windows, dark interiors, and odd V-shaped antennas on the snowy roofs. It started snowing again as the air grew warmer, which fattened the snowflakes. He darted into a dark alley of ashcans, dumpsters, and asthmatic trash, trapped in scrawny cranberry bushes. The headlights of two men getting out of a Toyota Camry attracted him. They opened their trunk. They lifted an awkward Hefty bag and lugged it into the cranberry bushes by a row of old ash cans next to a beer can-stuffed, rusty dumpster. When the Camry motored out of the alley, Chitchee edged closer to—not a *polyurethane* bag—but a *vinyl* bag with a zipper. An outline of a human body in a fetal position formed. Never one to be put off by digging through other people's garbage, Chitchee plucked off his orange mittens. He yanked on the zipper. The zipper balked at the dried brown residue, forcing Chitchee to pinch and yank with greater force on the zipper.

"One, two, three," he yelled, "infinity!"

The slider came off in his hand. The zipper broke.

Blood spurted across Chitchee's face in sticky globules. A man's arm fell out like a flank of beef. Chitchee reeled back from a bruised, skunk-eyed head. Under the black jilbaab, the man's flesh had twisted into the cotton cloth. Wounds like giant clams surfaced. The corpse had spit out its teeth, if it hadn't swallowed them. Gasping, sweating, and looking around for neighbors, Chitchee reached for his cell phone. Which wasn't there. Pocket after pocket he checked. Not having his Android on him he was less than human. He couldn't move—no Android—he had no legs, only forelimbs like an octopus. He was Cthulhu. He felt dead and couldn't breathe. His eyes were white, all white, and froze open.

"BookSmart!" said Zalar from inside a resinous, fossilized amber.

Zalar, returning to consciousness, wiped from his eyes a wax paper film and stirred his broken limbs to get up. Looking up, Zalar contemplated the world and sky in different directions. Zalar looked straight at a comatose Chitchee.

"Not you again!" said Zalar. "Any more Manson books come in?"

Zalar's loose, waggling teeth filled his bloody mouth, which emitted a single, bloodily-rooted tooth that bounced red into the snow. Chitchee picked it up and handed it to Zalar.

"Here, you dropped this," said Chitchee.

Chitchee fled on fleet heels toward the street, his heart racing ahead of him. Mimosas of blood flecked his face. The Toyota Camry had boomeranged his way, barreling toward him down the alley and knocking ash cans over. Police sirens oscillated in his curling eardrums. Chitchee gamboled through a no man's land: between two dark, one-story, no-one's-home-looking cottages. Tripped on a child's sled, he heard a volley of large bird dogs alarm their owners. Then the entire neighborhood of watch dogs barked: the website watch dogs, that is: CitizensFirst.com, LocalCrime.com, OutsideYourKitchenWindow.com, ScaredOfEverything.com. Chitchee leapt into a broken, stand lamp, straightened up the lamp, and ran for hell, always only two steps away from homemade and homebrewed Stasi. Responding with alacritude, 3rd Precinct squad cars zoomed past the alley. Judging by the whooping sirens, Chitchee pictured thumpers turning around and driving down the alley of snow-banked garbage cans and dumpsters, looking for him. He turned around and face-to-faced with the Toyota Camry. Izzy Mutulugulu was at the wheel and Viktor Martensen in the passenger seat. Izzy leaned into the car horn.

"GET OUT OF THE WAY ASSHOLE!" yelled Izzy, a blood clot taking shape to strangle him.

Chitchee collected himself two blocks over. As he re-traced the last memory of his cell-phone memories, his memory clicked! He had left the Android in Jason's storage locker. A bakery advertised itself with the incense of bread, along with the chalked specials of bread in cents. Chitchee poked his black wool beanie into a Ukrainian cafe with red-and-white plaid checkerboard tables, hunched over by plaid, checker-shirted working class, unfriendly faces forgettable and all alike as rolled oats. Oh perfect anonymity! Ah! He drank in the beautiful tunes of fresh butter on toast, marmalade jam, sweetly frying bacon, grape jelly, blueberry pancakes, and mushroom and garlic omelettes. Before he ordered his coffee and old-fashioned donut, his server stared with horror at the dried blood on his face.

"Are you bleeding?" asked the server.

"No, why?" replied Chitchee quickly. "Am I covered in blood or something?"

Chitchee dreamed out the window and saw his reflection (freckled with blood) and beyond his reflection he saw a Finnish appliance store of light fixtures, which was incubating under lights and light bulbs. Next to that, his sensorium registered a dilapidated wallflower of a beauty salon next to a Polish barbershop of nearly-blind old barbers, charging next to nothing for a trim and a shave.

"I just got out of that barbershop over there across the street," said Chitchee. "Poor old Pawel's hands were a little shaky. A couple razor cuts. It's nothing really. It's just ol' Pawelsy."

"That old barbershop has been closed for years," said the young server with a voice as old as she could muster.

"You mean I paid that guy ten bucks to stab my cheeks for nothing?" joked Chitchee, his eyebrows lifted like a crow's wings. "I'll have a black coffee and an old-fashioned donut 'well done' and more napkins to wipe any evidence off my face!"

The server told the manager, who told the owner, who called the thumpers.

Chitchee lipped his torrid coffee. He stood up and admired the wall of photographs, which re-animated the old days of Minneapolis's pool halls, the popcorn-and-peanut basement bars, and the women and men in fedoras, toques, overcoats, and neck-tied flannel shirts. Across the street Viktor Martensen and Izzy Mutulugulu walked toward the corner, laughed about something painful, and nodded toward the Ukrainian cafe Chitchee sat boxed in like a squirrel.

MEMORY LANES

Chitchee plonked down five bucks and sallied next door to Cyryllo's Roller Rink with Coca Cola machines of green-bottled, pony cokes. He bought a Coke, tried to look normal, and calmed down by placing a BIC pen in his mouth, which forced a smile and a memory of LaDonna. Coca Cola Man was face planted on a table surrounded by two-and-a-half dozen pony cokes, his hands outstretched and shaking, his mop of hair coke-soaked. Chitchee gazed under the bangled disco lights, spiraling sequins, and raindrop rainbows that played over the holy roller rinkers. A pair of thumpers walked in, looked around suspiciously, picked up Coca Cola Man's head off the table, and let it drop with a bang and a snort. Chitchee ran onto the skating floor, broke up a couple holding hands, and the trio traversed in circles to a wheezy Hammond B-3 organ playing "Love Hangover." He sidled out the door and burrowed into the nearby Memory Lanes bowling alley. The customers tippled Old Milwaukees in wiener-red booths shaped like train compartments on a Pullman. Girls wore black leather, string-tied vests, gaping-hole fishnet stockings, and hair of colored yarn; guys wore significantly death-black T-shirts, flannels, floppy wool hats, tattoos, and short black trousers that reached mid-calf, exposing endless tattoos. Either birth-sex might be shave-headed or hipster-haired and bearded, tabled with half-eaten onion rings. Pints of brown ale and red plastic hamburger baskets with big green dill pickles floated by a hungry Chitchee. He heard his stomach meow.

"What are you doing here?" asked LaDonna alone in a red booth.

Her glass frames flashed her ivory cat's eyes while she nursed a Campari.

"I was out for a haircut," said Chitchee. "Do I have blood all over my face? I thought you were going into treatment. Nestor gave you a ride to Hazelton?"

"No, wait, turn toward the front door," said LaDonna. "Well, good, you can hear Nestor's band. He's playing a tribute to Buck Owens, Henry Mancini, and John Wayne. He plays every instrument in his band. One at a time. Brilliant!"

"A series of virtuoso solos?" asked Chitchee, his lips tented up at the corners. "Brilliant! I have to hear this!"

"You were right about those pills too!" said LaDonna. "Those *were* benzos! Sometimes you really *are* as smart as some say!"

"You found the E and took it with Nestor," said Chitchee, sitting down in the booth across from LaDonna, "so that you might feel empathy and try a little tenderness for him?"

"How did you know *that*?"

"I can see through your eyes," said Chitchee, "to your other Self."

"Well, you're wrong," she said. "He wouldn't take it with me. He had something else in mind. Fame. He's a monkey for recognition. Although he said he wanted to take a drug called *fame* if only all the carping clods in Minneosta would just wake up. I think I want to study Arabic again and go back to school. And read *Conference of the Birds*. Don't tell Nestor, he hates Arabs."

"*Conference of the Birds* is in Persian, remember? The U. doesn't teach Persian anymore. Persian bit the budget dust when the Board of Regents pole-axed the humanities and the General College program to pay for restructuring their secret research into God knows what."

"I'll teach myself Persian and then I'll teach it to you and the world! Don't tell Nestor, he hates Persians too," said LaDonna.

"That's okay," said Chitchee. "Arabs hate Persians, Persians Arabs. Hatfields hate Persians. Arabs hate McCoys. And so on and scoobie doobie doobie. An hour ago I witnessed an attempted murder."

"Well, look who's here, who'sis fuckin' hoosier?" asked Viktor, lazily pointing his thumb at Chitchee, unworthy of the effort of extending a thumb for a bum.

Viktor and Izzy broadened like Broadway stars into the bowling alley in their black leather, full-length, Italian great coats, and loose belts like razor strops trailing down.

"Chitchee," said Chitchee, offering his hand to shake, but when Viktor looked at Chitchee's hand—he saw the carrion leg of a hyena covered with flies and maggots.

"You look familiar!" continued Chitchee, with a withdrawn hand. "Were you ever in a fucking Scorcese movie? Hey, didn't I just see you two fucking guys careening down a fucking back alley in a fucking Toyota Camry fucking? Fuck! Care to join us? Hey now, hey now, we're in a Tarantino fucking flick! Like *Reservoir Dogs* except Madonna is right fucking here."

"Do you think Sean Penn gave her good head?" asked LaDonna.

"Move in, *Chee Chee*," said Viktor with a hornswoggling snort and a high-pitched titter.

Izzy's face was slack buttocks. His thin upper lip flatlined. From his tattooed neck upward it looked as if Izzy were wearing a spittoon inside his head.

"As far as you know, *Snitch-chee*," continued Viktor, the corners of his mouth pinned back to reveal tiny gold mines, "we've been sitting at this table for hours. *Hours*. Got it? *Hours*."

"Got it, this table is *ours*."

Izzy sprang forward, but Viktor pushed him back.

"But why?" asked Chitchee. "Is it for another alibi?"

Viktor blinked askew.

Izzy felt the gnat hairs tingle on the back of his neck. He itched his back, because his shingles blistered sight unseen.

"Nobody insults my family, Izzy, not like that," said Viktor. "Can you believe Zalar told Nestor he was tone DEEF and shit? Izzy, only I can do that! Because Nestor's my shit. Even if he whines all the time—he's my shit!"

"Tone deaf, someone said Nestor was tone deaf?" butt in Chitchee. "I know Nestor. He's not tone deaf, he's people deaf."

"Nestor is genius," said LaDonna to Viktor. "Manic bipolar, he's disorder. Like Van Gogh or Brian Jones, he was born with a musical paintbrush in his mouth. You know what I mean. His IQ is higher than the best musicians in the Twin Cities. Higher than a kite! Nestor plays twenty instruments. He writes symphonies on the toilet. If only he could find a decent producer."

"Zalar insulted Nestor?" asked Izzy. "How?"

"Right to my son's fucking face," said Viktor. "Zalar, the big mouth, telling everyone in Club Miami all Nestor's songs sounded like 'Jukebox Hero.'"

"Zalar knew too much," said Izzy.

"He spewed too much," said Viktor, feeling a little jolly giggle rise in his gorge, which triggered a snorting fit. He cleared a nostril into a napkin, crunched the napkin, and dropped it under the table. "The dildo breath was nuts, wearing a HIGH-jab and Somalian women's clothing—like a Transylvanian whaddayacallit!"

"Are you guys talking about Zalar *Gossick*?" asked Chitchee. "That poor lummox must hate himself for being so hateful. Did you guys ever notice he has no theory of mind? Especially after you bludgeoned him to death with a tire iron. Maybe people with no compassion should be executed right off the bat."

Viktor looked overlong at Chitchee's face for sparks of irony.

"Everyone always said Zalar had an abusive father," said Chitchee, leaning forward to whisper into Viktor's ear. "Zalar's father . . . used to hang sausages off a fishing pole like Sausage Man and have his son bob for sausages at mealtimes to make him tougher."

"Not true," said Viktor, scowling. "That was *me* with my son Nestor. How did you know that?"

"Because I can't see through your eyes to your other Self. You don't have one!"

Chitchee shrugged like a mummy.

"But did you have to put Milk Bones in his Flintstones lunch box?" asked Chitchee. "We never heard the end of that one. Did you have to torture your own son upon a wheel that would never end in anything but more torture? For you, for him, for everyone around?"

"So what about the sausages anyway?" asked Viktor. "It worked, didn't it? It made him tougher for when the kids at school called him a pussy and beat him to a pussy pulp! I was in law school and we didn't have money for food. Now look at him! He's playing in a fancy bowling alley."

The stage was set for Nestor's one man band. He smiled like a mother sow over her farrow equipment: pedals, levels, mikes, amps, pre-amps, and speaker stacks. Sound check. Feedback. Cables crossed.

"He can play twenty instruments faster than Prince," said LaDonna. "And he's getting his own Vevo."

"Right, LaDonna? LaDonna, you look all relaxed," continued Viktor, looking at LaDonna. "You look like you need a back rub. Wanna go for a back rub?"

Viktor paused to pinch the black cankerous sores on his rosey, vulcanized rubber lips.

"Then *what* did *Zalar's* abusive dad do?" asked Chitchee bemusedly. "Oh yeah! That's right! Zalar's dad was so abusive, his twin brother hanged himself from the light fixture over his dad's bed for his dad to see when his dad woke up. Funny how memory plays tricks with your abusive dads! I'm sorry, Vik! How am I supposed to keep straight everyone's sordid Family Photo Albums? It seems like everyone-I-know's dad was a racist, sexist, homophobic, sociopathic drunkard . . ."

Everyone heard 18th-century crystal chandeliers land on the bowling alley lanes then realized they had heard thunderous strikes from hooking bowling balls.

"I can't hear myself," said Nestor to the microphone, staring at the monitors in disbelief. "Hello, testing one plus one equals two . . . hello? Can you hear me? Minnesota morons . . ."

Mono Boondalicks from *The Daily Beehive* had walked into Memory Lanes unannounced (or so he felt). Nestor squinted when he saw Mono. Their rivalry was political, intense, and irrationally sexual—because the two local musicians had often crossed paths and fought for the affections of a mutual love interest. Since they both looked alike, they usually styled their hair differently. Mono's hair was lush, better groomed, and styled, whereas Nestor's was more of an overgrown shaggy garden. Mono had a naturally athletic physique; whereas Nestor tended toward scrawniness, beefed up with precise supplements, lifted weights under precise regimens, and repeated work-outs in front of the mirror with a notebook of his progress.

Nestor was nervous unlike his usual overconfident smartest-man-in-the-room self, and a snow-cold sweat crowned his forehead. Tentavitis infused his jerky confusion. His posture was choppy, and when the bowling alleys with their pear-shaped pins exploded like rock quarries—he flinched. He kept muttering and muttering, talking to nobody in particular. His random audience stood back and gave him their politely lifted eyebrows.

"Sound check!" continued Nestor, lecturing the bowling alley. "Hey, fool! You see? Minneapolis isn't worthy of any genius at all. Not enough sleep. Ecstasy does nothing for me. I'm permanently dopamine-deprived from playing before too many fools. That means I need to inhibit my norepinephrine levels because of fucking Minneapolis! I need to be numb to play. How am I supposed to release melatonin from my pineal gland after I've been fucked by Minneapolis? This wouldn't happen in Chicago."

Nestor's smile dripped off his face and onto the stage and formed a puddle under the microphone stand. Nestor stared at the puddle—his eyes spiral staircases leading upward and downward. He shook his right hand to rid himself of a cramp that wasn't there. His legs looked stiff as crutches, and he marched like a parade soldier to take a few steps.

"Can I borrow your phone to call work, LaDonna?" asked Chitchee. "I left my Android in a storage locker."

The microphone clicked on and Nestor's voice transformed its amplitude into a scream of righteous indignation:

"Fucking sound check guy! YOU MORON, DON'T YOU KNOW WHO I AM PRETENDING TO BE? HEARD OF BUCK OWEN?"

Everybody looked over their shoulders at the strung-out "Buck Owen" from elbow-crowded tables and bowling lanes.

"Hey, Nestor!" said Chitchee on his way out the door. "Can you play 'Jukebox Hero?'"

On the snowy sidewalk, Chitchee called 911 from LaDonna's cellphone and reported an attempted murder, a Toyota Camry in an alley two blocks over from Memory Lanes, the license plate number, and the two walruses getting out of the car, one of whom was Viktor Martensen, the famous local mogul. The other man Chitchee described as having skin like unleavened, tattooed dough. Or if you prefer, his skin resembled the back of an Ace playing card with water damage. And that man was "probably the corporate raider Carl Icahn, but fatter." As a matter of fat, the corporate raider was fatter than a "pierogi stuffed with sauerkraut, onions, and mashed potato, stuffed inside another pierogi." Two executives threw the bag of body parts into a dumpster. Typical hedge fund shit. But there was a man with a soul inside the body bag. Zalar Gossick. He was wearing a hijab. He needed immediate medical attention. He looked like a Damascene political prisoner who took a blood bath under the interminable Assad gulags.

"And guess what? The two murderers like *In Cold Blood* are sitting in my booth at Memory Lanes right now," said Chitchee. "Hurry. I'm going back in there to stall them in their stall."

Chitchee demanded he remain anonymous because his father, Finkle Chichester of Deephaven, Vine Hill Road, had always yelled at him to never, never volunteer information to the government, because "those are enemies of the people, who pretend to be our elected officials, but only exist to steal our guns and our right to bear arms against them."

"Thank you, 911," wound up Chitchee. "Will it be long? I have some errands to run after the stake out."

He powered off LaDonna's cell phone.

"Stake out, sir?" asked 911 to a dial tone. "Hello?"

"*Jukebox Hero*," sang Chitchee in a Funky Chicken past the stage where numerous sound system difficulties persisted for

Nestor, perplexed at being so high off the ground.

Chitchee returned to the table where drinks had arrived. Viktor was stuck to his cell phone.

Two thumpers from the 3rd Precinct, Officers Boosalis and Weatherwax, thumbs in belts like Hollywood cowboys, walked into Memory Lanes.

"Should we order something, Izzy?" asked Viktor. "I'm starving to death. Like one of them Ethiopians you used to see in syndicated commercials."

"I don't want anything," said Chitchee. "Can I peck over your leftovers?"

"Another Campari for me," said LaDonna. "I'm not hungry. I'm on a diet. Of Campari. I actually feel really good right now. Why doesn't Nestor?"

"His Ecstasy rejected him," said Chitchee. "Besides, he's obviously got 'crack lip.'"

Finally, there would be justice, thought Chitchee. He sighed a breath of fresh air like freshly baked and buttered bread. The two thumpers veered toward Chitchee's booth, but their duty belts weighed heavily on their hips, causing them to look more like Western gunslingers.

"You thumpers are fat, *fast*, that is. That fat moved fast to get here that fast," said Chitchee. "Here are your guys! Take them away!"

"What guys?" asked Officer Boosalis.

"The guys I made the 911 call for," said Chitchee.

"We didn't get a 911," said Officer Weatherwax. "Do you have an ID on you? We would like to talk to you."

"Who?" asked LaDonna.

"You!" said Officer Weatherwax. "Who do you think I'm talking to, Donald Duck?"

The thumpers, with stomachs rolling over their waists like watermelons, escorted a docile LaDonna out to a squad car, smoothed her into the back seat, and Officer Boosalis looked at her criminal record from her ID.

"That's her, the Daisy Vang robber."

LaDonna felt a knocking sound echoing through her spine.

"What is that knocking sound?" she asked, looking out the back window.

"Is there someone in the trunk?" she asked.

The two thumpers looked at each other and drove off with LaDonna.

When Chitchee excused himself for the bathroom, Viktor plucked LaDonna's cell phone off the table. And Chitchee sneaked out the door while Nestor played "Jukebox Hero."

"He called 911 on the bitch's phone," said Viktor to Izzy. "When the retard comes back, let's show him St. Anthony Falls."

Chitchee walked a long way back cold to Jason's cold storage locker, recovered his cold phone, and read the text cold from LaDonna's cell:

where did you go come back we go picnic st antony falls

Come back LOL haha is this jukebox hero :(

SOUTHDALE LIBRARY BOOK SALE

The United States Marshals Service had declared Chitchee a fugitive and tied a yellow ribbon across his front door. Over the "Obama remark" alone, Dan the Maintenance Man could have changed the lock on him, but maybe Dan hadn't gotten around to fixing anything.

After breaking into his apartment, he inventoried: bread, rice, peanut butter, milk, coffee, popcorn, a pot, a frying pan, a fork, a wooden bowl, a microwave, two plastic glasses, and two coffee cups. He boxed books. He picked out *Berlin, Alexanderplatz*, found the quietest corner in his bathroom next to the still-clogged bathtub, and plunged his 36 decibel-rated earplugs like oakum into both ear canals.

"I'm going to be another Franz Biberkopf, if I don't start buying and selling books again," thought Chitchee, "and make some fresh bread."

Chitchee used to forage for books up and down Minneapolis and turn them around on Amazon. LaDonna hated his collectible clutter. She secretly sold his books, which caused a certain distancing when Chitchee found out his complete *One Thousand Nights and a Night* had been sold for dope and hepatitis C.

Books were awash in Minneapolis as agates on the North Shore. Chitchee scoured garages, back alleys, dumpsters, and piles of garbage for the Logos. Chitchee used to rifle Goodwills, ransack Salvation Armys, pillage St. Vincent's, and raid Treasures Await. He went at Arc's Value Village and Savers like a hungry, Malcolm Lowry-pariah dog for marrow bones.

Chitchee's face was a familiar face among the familiar faces at every church rummage sale from Hopkins to Columbia Heights. At dawn, he used to line up at estate sales (usually greeted by a nearly dead couple with a nearly dead smile) and crept around the dead china, crystal, antiques, and jewelry boxes like a deadpan vulture at a sky burial. He biked to every library book sale in the Hennepin County system. He became acquainted with other book buyers and heard stories about the other book dealers and what they collected.

When Sheldon Clark the occult book dealer from St. Louis Park died, his mother advertised the sale of her son's occult books. Cars parked outside her house a day before the sale. The Magus book store scout with black fingernails drank absinthe the night before the sale with his green contact lenses in. He banged on the bereaved mother's front door for a preview, barged in to use a bathroom, then bought everything but the crumbs on the kitchen table. The "green-eyed scout" died later under mysterious circumstances . . . crushed to death by his own electric garage door . . . and the entire occult library went missing, only to turn up in Figueres, Spain in the basement of the Dali Theater and Museum years later, and no one could explain why.

One day, when Chitchee was waiting in line at the Southdale Public Library sale, a tall middle-aged man with slicked down black hair, moustache, and mirror shades—sort of like you would see on an Army Man doll—showed up with a new device. It was a Hewlett-Packard handheld scanner. Although the scanner could "read" barcodes only from 1972 onward, it automatically plugged the digits into the Amazon marketplace search bar and showed you all the listings. Was it a penny book or a real find? Soon, this "Scanner Man" showed up everywhere in the used book trade. He scanned every book at every sale and looked up every barcode. At first no one paid him any mind, because no real book buyer slicked down his hair, dyed his moustache, or froze you in his mirror shades. Most book buyers had been book people: they had unkempt, mad hair, gray cowboy pony tails, shaved monkish heads, or asymmetrical balding patterns; as for the women, they were all book potatoes, au gratin, hashed brown, or Crinkle Cut—and they were polite as potatoes.

Then the past masters started talking about Scanner Man and his Scanner Clan as "cheaters," "imposters," and "b-holes."

"Who is Kate Di-Ca-milo? Is she good? Dad?"

[Raspberries and sniffs from the old book dealers]

"I want this one: *The Tale of Desperado, Desperado*, er . . . can I have it? D-a-a-a-a-d!"

"No!" said Scanner Man. "Look for W. E. B. Griffin! And don't give me any lip!"

One morning Scanner Man rafted the entire Scanner Family Robinson into the mobbed Edina Public Library sale, little scanners everywhere, each epsilon held Suzuki-style scanners in their little hands. The old book hands were slow and too polite to respond at first.

Chitchee glimpsed a handful of Stanislaw Lems with the distinct, ivory HBJ covers and he reached around Scanner Man (evidently green as gooseberries). Chitchee uprooted all the Lems (always a good idea) like a clump of bunch grass. Then he latched onto three Milan Kunderas with one hand and two Orhan Pamuks with the other hand from the other side, bagged them in his Lunds grocery bag, turned up a row of Mermaid drama books (including Lope de Vega and Calderon), and cleaned up with ten Classics of Western Spirituality (including Meister Eckart, Saint Hildegaard, and Saint Theresa of Avila (love!)). He frosted the cake when he swept twenty red and green Loebs (including Pliny's *Natural History*) into another Lunds grocery bag he had snapped open quickly. Scanner Man looked at Chitchee:

"Did you steal a *Moosewood Cookbook* out of my Lunds bag?"

"No! Why would I? I'm shopping for good reads, like you, Scanner Man," said Chitchee in a pantomime of hurry. "Besides I already grabbed a *Moosewood Cookbook*, a *Joy of Cooking*, a Harold McGee *On Food and Cooking*, and three inscribed, hardcover *Kitchen Confidential*s by Anthony Bourdain! I don't need another *Moosewood*, Scanner Man."

"What's wrong with using a scanner? I'm putting my kids through St. Olaf's with this," said Scanner Man, looking into his Lunds bag of books. "My *Moosewood*! My *Moosewood*! Someone took my *Moosewood*!"

"Dad, my scanner isn't working," said Scanner Junior. "Can I go outside and wait by the car?"

"We charge extra for scanners," said Melusina, the librarian, who with her sister Kriemhilde, always volunteered to run the book sales at Southdale Public library. "I've got a bad feeling about this guy. I don't even think he's from Iowa. He looks like a game changer and I don't like the cut of his jib."

"He's the new wave," nodded Kriemhilde. "And it stinks like the new greed. Ummm-m!"

Melusina and Kriemhilde pretended that library book sales were for the very senior citizens whose delights in life were browsing for cook books like slow bottom feeders, pleasure-reading craft books, cat-napping with tea-cozy mystery-thrillers, tripping to Mitford, and attacking the ambitious epics of James Michener.

"Oh dear, oh dear, is it safe to go anywhere anymore in Minneapolis?" asked Kriemhilde, setting out books from boxes under tables on tables. "He looks like Dirty Harry with those sunglasses!"

Melusina tracked sales with a No. 2 pencil on a lemon-lime legal pad and sensed the negatively-charged atmosphere building up Van de Graaff charge.

"That will be one hundred dollars even!" said Melusina.

"That's outrageous! You raised the prices on me when you saw me coming!" said Scanner Man. "It doesn't say anything here about *no scanners*. Show me where in the Minneapolis City charter it says anything about *no scanners*! That's discrimination when you say *no scanners*!"

"Do you know what I have to say to that?" asked Melusina.

"What?" said Scanner Man.

"*Tough titty!*" said Melusina.

Kriemhilde held an imaginary shovel, loaded her imaginary shovel, and threw the load over her shoulder.

All the Ahearne-class book collectors split their sides laughing. A few of the older women roared with laughter and others tittered like skipping stones on a mill pond.

The two sisters retailed this episode and passed it down to their grandchildren as a Christmas chestnut. It grew into a chestnut tree. Every Christmas Eve or so at Granny Mel's behest all the grandchildren gathered around the fireplace of sweetly-burning birch, candy-cane red stockings, and mantelpiece of mistletoe to hear the traditional retooling of the family legend.

"So your Grandma Mel, that's me kiddos, who used to be a librarian at Southdale, was selling books that Southdale Library didn't want for various reasons. Some were too old, some were too common, and some had nowhere else to go. So your grandmothers, Hildy and *I*, not me, but *I*, or *we*, but not *us*, wanted to find a special home for every book without a home, because a book without a home is a very sad thing, isn't it? Yes, it is. How would you feel if you didn't have a home? A home where your parents loved you very much? You'd be like kittens left in a box in the middle of the highway. I mean to the *side* of the highway. That would be *not nice*. Not good. Yes, that would be sad.

So there I was, we were, Grandma Hildy and I, in a ballroom that seemed as big as a palace, and the men and the women were dancing at all the books on sale. Like a Russian wedding. And we all know weddings are good, don't we? Arm in arm 'clogging' broke out, not kitchen clogging, that's a different clogging, no all the bathtubs in the village were successfully draining. Clogging is dancing with funny shoes. No, the funny shoes aren't telling jokes. And there was plenty of eggnog with nutmeg, or eggmeg with nutnog, if you prefer. So EVERYONE was happy. Every villager could have plenty of books and literacy would not die out because of the Internet. It was like a village fair! And the girls wore dirndls, pelisses, and colored sashes and all the lads wore nankeen trousers, clean white shirts, and ice cream cone hats with real ice cream.

Out of a dark cloud descended a man on a galloping bolt of lightning, and he had a magical weapon he called 'Skannrot' or 'Skonner' that darted out tiny, thin but coherent beams that melted whole winters and made them whole summers.

There I was face to face with Scanner Man, whose magical device read the label on every book in the library or the world for that matter. Skannrot whispered to him how much money he could sell a book for. Anywhere in the world! Even up the branches of the Amazon where the Big Bezos lurked behind the evil Gates of the castle walls of TimCooktu, where the iron cauldron boils over with the boiling children who will be eaten, once turned into an AmAppMicroGoo pie.

And I told that cheap-ass, I mean Skonner the Mon, the sorcerer, he had to pay a little extra for using a modern scanner, because it wasn't fair for a village fair, you see—no one had ever relied on magic to judge a book by its cover. In those days, because everyone read books, not particularly good ones maybe, especially as the eyes grew dimmer, the ears larger, the teeth tinier, the noses droopier, and the car keys lostier, we didn't accept so readily the social construction of reality as a result of capitalist commodification. Whatever.

'Pay a little extra?' bellowed Scanner Man in anger. 'You mean like a tax that only *I* pay? For what? To support the lazy rounders in the village who won't work if they don't have to?'

Scanner Man, with his muscular broad forearm and whip hand, swept all the books and the cash box off the card table. He swore, that's right he *swore* out loud bad words. In a library!

'The prices are too high here, you witches,' continued Scanner Man. 'I'll have to sell my daughters to US Bank and my sons will have to pull bank jobs to rob them back just to buy a single *Moosewood Cookbook*!'

Then Scanner Man picks up his books and drops them right on top of Grandma Kriemhilde, Hildy that is, the one who makes the cinnamon sugar sticks for the root beers remember and . . . ummm . . . don't they always smell goo-o-o-od? Yes? Of course, yes! Oh my goodness! Scanner Man drops over Hildy's head Sandburg's *Lincoln*. Do you believe it? With *Lincoln*? No, he didn't pick up Mr. Lincoln and swat your mother over the head with President Lincoln himself. It was a book *about* Lincoln, a whole bunch of books *about* Lincoln. Books that preserve his memory. No, not like his brain is preserved in the book itself like a box you open up and there is Lincoln's *brain*! No! Don't think like that! That would be eeeeuuuwwwyy!

So your grandma Melusina leapt up and kicked Scanner Man in the throat and your Grandma Hildy hurled him into a wall of books where that guy from Midway Books was hogging everything as usual with his wife. Scanner Man cried that he needed to make enough money on the Internet to pay off the dragon that was keeping his kids from going to college. Then yours truly, Grandma Melusina, said to Scanner Man, 'Tough Tetons, Scanner Man!' And I squeezed his throat even tighter than before, and then I kicked him in his middle like a nutcracker. Mmmm-hm! The security guard, your uncle Horst, tossed him out, but your grandmas Melusina and Kriemhilde spent a week in the Plymouth workhouse for assault and battery. Just like Thelma and Louise. Which is a story for another story."

In reality, Chitchee brooded: winter was never far off, spring was always far away, and summer ended with the State Fair. He didn't wait for the court date or the hands-on eviction itself. He could throw everything himself in the snowbank—household goods in boxes and notebooks in bags. Immediately after he had applied for unemployment, he received an official notice from the State of Minnesota to report to a mandatory job placement meeting. The State of Minnesota had the perfect dream job waiting for him at Lake & Chicago. He foresaw a menu of book store jobs to select from. They might send him to the work site directly from the Workforce Center. He would spruce up with a non-gray scarf and make sure his long underwear didn't show. He needed his résumé printed off.

When Chitchee looked at the MSN Minnesota weather forecast for the week, his PC clone's Window screen froze and turned blue.

Then his back-up desktop tower died with an early version of his résumé on it. Luckily, he had saved his résumé to floppy. He found the floppy and downloaded it to an old Samsung laptop once connected to dial up, copied it, and emailed it to himself. That attachment he downloaded and copied, but Microsoft Word posed a password problem. He remembered he had used someone else's Microsoft Word's registration number, but who, when? Microsoft Word prevented him from reading his Microsoft Word. His scattershot password guesses locked him out of the entire job market in three tries.

Claiming computer fatigue and a bad cold, he called in sick to the Workforce Center, choking on the Workforce Center message machine. Would they get his message? He had wrestled an alligator twice his body mass to print his résumé! Another Microsoft Word was $200, but how else could he write a résumé? Meanwhile his phone died. The old Samsung laptop wasn't charging because the power cord was broken, or the adapter, or the power strip, or the wall socket, or Xcel Energy had frozen solid into a block of ice. Without electricity, how would he know whether a ferocious blizzard had shredded the power grid or buried the local utility poles up to their transformers? Unless he owned a transistor radio with fresh batteries (double-checked) and a flashlight with fresh batteries (also double-checked) on hand to hear the snowstorm warnings, he wouldn't know the weather! At last resort, he looked outside.

Afraid he had mortally offended The Workforce Center's Control Central, his conscience attacked him with ill-tempered knives, scattering his wits like feathers. Chitchee! Remember to buy a Motorola transistor radio and triple A batteries—Energizers or Duracells. Locate Radio Shack on MapQuest. Locate MapQuest. Locate dead résumé on dead computer. Or die. Behind on his rent, fees, and surcharges, he resolved not to pay any of it. He tried to imagine Dostoyevsky on Blogger or Nietzsche on Yahoo Geocities.

He ran out the door into the freezing cold. He knew the MPG lawyers had his nuts in their briefcase folders if he showed up at the HC Government Center courtroom; for that matter they had BookSmart's nuts in their briefcases too. The Opus Group had easily annexed Dinkytown without a fight, because the land grabbers hired the money grabbers to kick The Book House to the curb to 1316 4th Street. And in full view of the ghost of Melvin McCosh, who had no power against developers.

Looking out the #21 MTC bus window, Chitchee escrowed $50 for each Mad Jack to move his books, with Aloysius's permission, into the BookSmart basement. The rooms, studios, and fine-ass abodes on Craigslist he had looked at could not accommodate his library of 3,000 books. The BookSmart basement seemed boundless and infinite as the ground of Being itself. Kennedy said his house had a room for rent—somewhere in Northeast Minneapolis, and Kennedy wasn't on a lease that he was aware of.

WORKFORCE CENTER, 777 EAST LAKE

Chitchee found himself running down Lake Street to the unemployment office on Lake & Chicago. The steamy meeting room jostled and fumed with recently laid-off IT departments from Wells Fargo, US Bank, and Twin Cities Federal, thrown there because of the subprime mortgage crisis.

Fjard Gardet, his mirror shades on, sat in the front row, turned to Astrid Eskola, and asked her:

"W. E. B. Griffin?"

"No, thank you," said Astrid Eskola, kissing the air to one side in a gesture of thought, doubt, and avoidance. "I'm vegan. And I'll never eat an Egg McMuffin."

"How about Clancy?"

"Not into serial killers, thank you," said Astrid.

Astrid swished her pursed lips away from him, looked over her shoulder for another chair, and re-seated herself when Gloria Skogentaub marched into the room.

"Sorry, I'm late," said Chitchee. "Gloria! It's so good to see you alive! I heard you were fired! Hugs?"

"Have a seat, Mr. Chichester," said Gloria.

"Chichester looks like the kind of pickled jerk," whispered Fjard to Astrid, "that likes to ask questions at the end."

"Look at all the people who lost their jobs!" said Chitchee. "Is this the end of the American Empire and the beginning of the Second Weimar Republic?"

"No!" said Fjard. "It's the natural boom and bust cycle. It all trickles down in the end. I'm not worried. I think I have a job with MPG! I shouldn't even be here!"

Gloria bored everyone's pants and pants suits off with her pep talk. Every man and woman stood naked before their own sinful, terminal boredom. How to find employment, search job boards, and appreciate the importance of networking, networking, networking could not have meant less.

The cauliflower-headed, fat, and little IT businessmen who sat in the back row to plug into the outlets looked like white-collar galley slaves with laptops of spaghetti code. The Information Technologists typed Word pages of useless notes for Gloria while looking at Facebook for job leads, which ended with another fat guy in diapers looking like Har Mar Superstar. Everyone hoped to get out early, which was only possible if Chitchee didn't ask idiotic questions at the end. Gloria handed out a sheaf of handouts to be passed around the meeting room, which dead-ended on Chitchee's desk. He passed the stack to his neighbor. Gloria handed out a second, third, and fourth handout that went over the shoulder of Fjard, because Astrid paid him no mind—he punished her by absolutely ignoring her presence and depriving her of the handout on financial depression, suicide prevention, and bankruptcy.

"Has everyone gotten a handout?" asked Gloria. "There are more handouts to pass around before we continue."

"You're handing out handouts?" asked Chitchee. "I never got a handout!"

Gloria presented another sheaf of handouts and handed off the handouts to be handed off and everybody took one and handed off to the others, the others. An IT cauliflower head in the back brought the stack up to the front and started the whole process over. More and more handouts were handed out—no one read the titles. No one thought to stop passing the handouts around for fear of not being a team player. Gloria walked to and fro from the room to copy more copies for more handouts and came back with more handouts, this time starting from the other side of the room. Sheet after sheet, desk after desk—pigeons of paper fluttered about and flew around the room. Airdropped leaflets in Gloria's war zone rained down like propaganda from World War II's Operation Cornflakes.

Chitchee raised his hand.

"Yes?"

"I haven't gotten a handout yet."

"Yes you have!" said Gloria. "I see the handout on networking right in front of you!"

"Oh, that kind of handout!" said Chitchee. "I thought you meant free money! Okay, then what exactly do you mean by 'networking?'"

The question exasperated Gloria.

"Can somebody else answer this?"

Gloria stopped like a roadrunner in front of Fjard's desk.

"It means ask around," said Fjard Gardet.

"Ask around who?" asked Chitchee. "Hey, you cauliflower-headed IT businessmen in the back! Know of any book store jobs? On the bus routes? If the bus routes still exist!"

Gloria's frown lines deepened at her nasal bridge, with two incisions at each corner of the hypotenuse of her mouth, and they continued straight down to her jaw and neck, making her jaw look detachable like that of a ventriloquist dummy.

"Are you good with a coffee scoop, Mr. Chichester? Can you pour coffee into different size cups? No?"

"Why is your makeup so bright?" asked Chitchee. "Did Thomas Kincaid come out with his own line of *giclée* cosmetics?"

"Mr. Chichester, I need six references from you on this form," she demanded of Chitchee.

Gloria stood over Chitchee to make sure he didn't hand around all the handouts again.

The others filled out their forms. They handed them up to the front row safely.

"Six whole references?" cried Chitchee, pleading eyes wide open as a lambkin.

"For you, Mr Chichester, first names are good enough! You know, Peter, Paul, Mary, Puff, the Magic, and the Dragon, there! That's six, now give me that form!"

"Ok, Glore, you're the pit boss," said Chitchee. "What about emergency contact numbers? What happens if I'm at work and I get shot by violent sectarians?"

"Then you fill out the forms for getting shot at work by violent sectarians!" said Fjard Gardet. "Don't be an asshole, Chichester!"

"Gloria, don't listen to Scanner Man," said Chitchee, ignoring Fjard with a parting wink, "I heard in Greece they had a law on the books until 1995 that if you were hired before 1995 you didn't have to learn to use a computer. Side by side the computer-trained, information technologist worked on the computer and the senior employee sorted through stacks of paper until the stacks of paper disappeared, leaving the senior sitting there, with a job, with a desk, and next to the information technologist with the computer skills. Side by side. Are there any jobs like that? Just sitting there? Could *this* be a job if I sat here all day? I *mean* what do you actually *do* all day?"

"No," said Gloria. "Are there any other questions? Somebody else raise their hand!"

"Gloria! Question! In death penalty states," continued Chitchee, "does the public executioner ever call in sick? Like: 'Spock? This is Kirk. I can't make it in today. I got that stomach flu.' 'WHAT? You're supposed to kill that guy at midnight!' 'Can't I use a sick day? Tell him I'll do it tomorrow! Like he's going to be pissed? Can't you get someone else from a temp agency?' 'NO! Bones is in Cancun! Scotty is on sabbatical.' 'Scotty is Jewish?' 'Kirk, get your ass in here!' 'Can't the prisoner do it? Can't he do something constructive for once in his life?'"

"What are you even talking about?" said Gloria. "Do you need to see a doctor? Was your mother experimented on with LSD?"

"Let's assume she was," said Chitchee, leaning back in a relaxed position, "then what color would my parachute be?"

"You wouldn't have one," said Gloria.

A thousand wrinkles ensued.

"Chichester here is a classic 1960s casualty, classic," snorted Fjard. "I know. I was there. The runaways to San Francisco for 'free money' and 'free love'? They all came back with needles in their arms and syringes in their wombs. I saw a docu-drama on NetFlix."

Chitchee didn't qualify for unemployment. He needed a permanent address to get the job for the permanent address. He stayed after class and gathered up the handouts, which were all over the floor, stepped on, and wet, but usable on the backsides.

"What a score!" he told Gloria, who gave the scrap paper to him. "Don't worry, I'll find work. I'm opening my own book store someday. Ulysses & Sons will wipe out illiteracy, yours included, Gloria, *inshallah!*"

THE HOUSE OF EDELWEISS

Once Chitchee had matriculated to the nearest Arby's in Northeast Minneapolis, he was supposed to call Kennedy. Renting a room in a boarding house was an adventure for Chitchee. He cherished the winter's city streets, which were intimate with all his thoughts, feelings, and passions. Even though the weather seemed a simulacrum from between the third and fourth ice age, Chitchee laughed through the snow toward downtown Minneapolis (when the bus didn't show up). Especially in winter, long walks enthralled him for he seemed on a mountain top in the Himalayas looking down at a model of reality. The model was snow-covered and included city offices, old dance halls, half-star hotels, abandoned tramp camps, alleys webbed with crystalline lace, Edwardian glazed bijoux, marquees overhanging placarded, icicled acts, cast-iron theater crowds in black frocks and furs, bar-hopping marshmallow parkas in and out of skyways, steamy beehive dives, apartments with dingy television consoles tuned to the Weather Channel's stationary radar, and the viewers' faces like spellbound test patterns. Chitchee rappelled and clawed his way past ice-lined crevasses in the glacial cliffs of rat trap-shaped windows. Warming up in a groggy ramp lined with Sports Utility Vehicles, F-Series trucks, Accords, Corollas, and Civics, Chitchee pictured the emigration of the original Peat Bog People trekking west looking like missionaries from a religion of alcoholism. The descendants of the Peat Boggers heard sermons in wet houses for the hopeless-beyond-hope stumblebums, pass-out artists, and vodka-bottled blue babies. And that was good too. The Peat Boggers stayed indoors all winter long and drank themselves to death in bed with the Weather Channel transfixedly on. That was normal, given the weather! The wet houses saved on gas money for the thumpers too. Blech's brew cans everywhere, ice-bearded dead bushes, and tossed-up brown bags in the bare-crowned trees. A hundred years ago Chitchee too would have been living under a Hudson Bay blanket in a plaster-walled, chicken-wired rooming house or a balloon-framed prairie house, never far from calling hogs, steering cattle, and bleeding chickens. And the drifting soil of limestone and granite to remember him would be swept away.

Kennedy had said (Chitchee thought) that the boarding house was near an Arby's. And next door to a "Sugar Cookie Castle." Chitchee walked in a circle that brought him back to Kramarczuk's Sausage Company.

"Sausage Man! I know you!" said Chitchee, overjoyed to see his familiar sausage face stacked on top of other remembered sausage faces like a totem pole. "Is there an Arby's near here?"

"Use' to be a Burger King near——," said Sausage Man. "Are you German? Because we were German. No, now, you're thinking of the Taco Bell that was a Taco John's next to the Taco King John's. That became a Taco Burger Tower, but they're all condos now with nice names like the Taco Burger Towers."

"Okay, thanks anyway," said Chitchee, looking at the street corner of masonry flecked like kielbasa with coriander seeds in the brick.

Chitchee warmed up his icy red fingers inside Kramarczuk's (his favorite restaurant besides McDonald's) and entered Kennedy's number.

When Chitchee heard an old woman's voice—that of Mrs. Edelweiss Hillswick, he realized he was on a landline with the State of Minnesota. After twenty minutes, Kennedy picked up the phone and told Chitchee the street address, but Kennedy was going to REI for "snowmobile sartorials, goggles, and other excessories."

"You're in, my friend! Prevaricate on over and Edsel Wise can give you a screening preliminary for the first round perfunctory."

Chitchee pictured the typical nice and sweet old landlady, Mrs. Edsel Wise. He packed a grin as square as an icebox for her. He would regale her with his charming wit and bangles of panache, but he lost his sense of direction when he met up with an eerie snow drift in a bizarre ice formation. LaDonna always berated him for never knowing where the sun was in the Milky Way. He walked the Soo Line and Great Northern railroad tracks, railroad ties meeting at vanishing points like witches' hats. Chitchee jogged in place to create warmth. When the cold wind blew, stainless steel razor blades shred him like a giant soft Muenster cheese. Nevertheless, he thanked God figuratively for the awakening frost. Winter's joy lifted up his heart like a ski jump at moments like this. Also, living in Northeast Minneapolis would be great, especially when Spring tilted into view and the ice went out.

Chitchee identified the Sugar Cookie Castle! Its porch was fronted with a sad harridan dressed up like a red cabbage and her sister a bigger red cabbage, who was really her husband in overalls, not her real sister, because her real sister then stepped out to see the commotion, and she was a tower of silage, and she wore a fedora hat that made the house smaller.

"Trying to get somewhere?" said the husband. "Show me your face!"

Spruce and pine trees showered snow down Chitchee's nettled neck when he cut through the front yard of the Sugar Cookie Castle, tramping like a snowshoe hare.

"Who are you, the Demjanjuks? I'm looking for the House of Edelweiss. Heard of it?"

"Over there! We couldn't tell if you were black!" said the first red cabbage. "Sorry! We got the PulsePoint alert app. So we thought there was a black man in the alley. But Edelweiss gots one next door anyway! And he's a real black!"

"A real black! Thanks!" said Chitchee. "You're a lifesaver . . . after all!"

Chitchee knocked on the front door where Kennedy lived. Whitish snow webs trimmed the domino-shaped window panes. Picketed with a fence of cavalry-pointed stakes, the half-timbered Gothic-Tudor house had pheasant feather-colored chimneys, pillared uprights with little roofs, balconies, nooks, and dormers. Or it was a Queen Anne with a bust corset. Or it was a Victorian mansion with elliptically-finned gables, glassed-in porches, and crow's nest windows—the whole house was as crazy as a church organ on stilts.

He knocked on the knocker until it was a joke. As he was about to leave, an image developed—formed from a page out of *Scary Stories to Tell in the Dark*. A mannish woman with a blue and silver complexion behind the black walnut door stared through Chitchee with a frosty glare, her misbegotten face above the knitted pink shawl. She waved her pale hand like a willow wand.

"Are you a ghost?" asked Chitchee.

"What do you want?" she asked. "Are you Russian?"

"Do you have a room for rent?" asked Chitchee, blowing warm air into his fists.

"Are you the guy coming over?"

"I think so," said Chitchee. "I usually am."

"Did you read an advertisement?"

"No! I called earlier. *Kennedy* told me about it."

"The black?"

"Yes, he's from Kenya."

"No matter what people think of his skin color, he pays his rent on time."

"That's good to know!"

"But I only have room for one snowmobile in my garage."

"Kennedy has a *snowmobile?*"

"Are you sure you are a friend of Kennedy? You look more like a friend of Zalar. Zalar was the good-looking local boy with the good manners. His father and brother came by and got his things. So polite. He moved to Uptown to be closer to work. You're *not* a friend of Zalar?"

"No—I want to rent his room, I think."

"Sorry. I can't help you, child. It's already rented."

"Mama! To who?"

"To Earl. A Christian from Bozeman. He's a sausage company canvasser for Kramarczuk's. He just moved into that room. I have another room though. Earl's old room."

"Can I look at that?"

"I guess so," she said, opening the door. "Take off your shoes and socks! Gudrun shampooed the living room carpet. Smell it! It's fresh. It's still so damp, so I'm asking you to take off your socks so you don't soak your socks in soap."

Chitchee hopped into the three-story frame house, which overflowed with the smells of boiling potatoes, pork knuckles, red cabbages, and burnt white toast. Serpentine antiques and stuffed furniture spilled into side rooms for lack of space, because the living room (trellises of camphor wood and teak tables aside) had bottled the chintzy days of spiritualism in a set piece, period room. Looking like Eusapia Palladino herself, Edelweiss plumped down in her upholstered Sunday chair, and Chitchee sneezed a Wurlitzer of children's songs repeatedly from the cat dander that danced up a storm when Edelweiss spun down.

"Inhaler?" said Edelweiss, returning from a drawer filled with inhalers. "Asthma runs up and down the family tree."

Edelweiss Hillswick wore a dress shaped like a root beer barrel and coughed into her armpit. The doors were for dwarves, the steps for elves. Every room seemed to be in a curled-up dimension, the roomers inside playing cat's cradles at the Planck length.

In a pastel, floral, house-aproned shirtwaist, rocking on a Windsor rocking chair which rested on the freshly-shampooed, braided throw rug, Gudrun Knutsen silently crocheted. She rocked in front of the nearly turned-off television tuned to 1959. Muenster cheese and Saltine crackers on a panhandled Bavarian bread board, Edelweiss presented to Chitchee.

Edelweiss drew back as an afterthought:

"You're working, *sicherlich*?" said Edelweiss sternly and drew back with callous aforethought. "You don't sweat, you don't eat."

"I sweat! I'm working in Carousel Square," he lied. "At the chocolate shop. Ragnarok's Choklit Stoppe. Have you heard of it?"

"I've heard of Carousel Square," said Edelweiss. "That's an old movie."

"Carousel Square," said Gudrun, her spine shivering. "It sounds so exotic! Is that by Treasures Await?"

Muenster cheese and Saltine crackers on the panhandled Bavarian bread board feasted a hungry Chitchee, tucking in a nugatory dinner.

"And," began Chitchee with an air of distinction and conclusion. "And I plan to go to MCTC in the fall and double major in something. I can get a job as a translator at HCMC, which I can get to on the MTC. MTC to MCTC and then MTC from MCTC to HCMC."

"I see," said Edelweiss bitterly and hobbled off in cement shoes.

After Edelweiss returned with a bulging Family Photo Album, she dropped it on Chitchee's surprised lap.

"Let me show you some pictures of my family," she said.

Chitchee waded through more and more photographs. Page after page of the three-story history of a house several paint jobs ago. Hillswicks, Martensens, Knutsens, and Weatherwaxes. And there was her brother-in-law, Michael, whom she had had to place in a nursing home in St. Louis Park, where he scarcely recognized her anymore. Maybe he didn't want to, said Chitchee.

"Does your brother-in-law sometimes wander off and wait for aliens by the delusional grave of his confabulated brother, the book dealer Melvin McCosh, because Melvin will take him back to his home planet of Melchizedek, which is where Michael was given his new name? I wonder if it's the same Melchizedek that I know?"

"Poor man!" said Edelweiss, trembling, and here she paused, because a couple more evocative words would make her cry.

"You gaslighted him, didn't you?" asked Chitchee. "It would have been easy to poison him slowly with the old arsenic wallpaper trick to inherit this old three-story house. You don't have to answer if you're guilty."

Chitchee looked closer at the photographs mounted in pasted black corners, and he noticed that Edelweiss either had had twins or had been adept at trick photography.

"Twins, huh?" asked Chitchee. "Well, wait sort of. It looks like someone has an inky thumb. Some of the faces are black-faced out."

Chitchee picked up the entire Muenster cheese and with his two large buck teeth he gnawed it like a rodent; and then he shred all the Saltine crackers, crumbs cascading onto the family heirlooms and snowing all over his red staid plaid check flannel.

"Arthur and Henry," said Edelweiss, looking over Chitchee's shoulder. "Both of them had no offspring. And then Waldtraut, Kriemhilde, Melusina, Norberta, Ilgenfritzi, Thrania, Klausina, Retz, Wee Willi Peter, and . . . who am I leaving out? Oh, Wheezer! Wheezer died in his crib because the genes were getting thinner at that point I do believe. Kriemhilde and Melusina turned out to be librarians and didn't go into law enforcement, the family tradition. So sad. We have such a tradition of law enforcement going back . . . to the beginnings of law itself in the forests of Germany probably!"

Chitchee looked at his watch. He was going to have to get high soon.

With another Family Photo Album on his lap, Chitchee tried to identify Arthur, Henry, Waldtraut, Kriemhilde, Melusina, etc. But he could not distinguish any of them from the other blocked-in, Kodak kids on the black-and-white, Hoover era-looking block. All the children had been lined up to sit like canned goods on a shelf in an old general store, all about as sunny as Boy Scouts trapped in an Appalachian coal mine. Store after store fronted the block of two-story brick buildings. The lower layer was family-run shops and the upper layer their living quarters.

"Henry and Arthur. For twins," she sighed, "they never got along like twins are supposed to! They always had to compete like those Jews. God bless their souls."

"What's this certificate?" said Chitchee, picking up a cursively-elaborated, calligraphically-scripted diploma off the carpet.

"Oh, that must be Henry's. His pilot's diploma. He used to fly until he broke his thumb at Flying Cloud trying to land one of those little planes when the wheels got stuck. One of those dingy little planes you used to see on Sherm Boen's *Aviation Today*. That was our favorite show right after church. Here in this house. On that TV. Oh my, that must be fifty years ago. I miss those days so much . . . Kitsch-key, do you know what it's like to be a woman who's lost her husband and best friend, and nary a day goes by without thinking of him, without seeing him in his favorite rocking chair, where Gudrun is sitting on top of him right now!"

Gudrun smiled cutely. A little guilty shrug punctuated her expression.

"Don't cry, Edelweiss," said Chitchee. "You're going to make me cry. And do you know what it feels like to have your own father disown you because he labeled you a Mongoloid idiot?"

"Only from what you just told me," said Edelweiss, opening a drawer beneath the drawer of inhalers, a drawer of generic cheaters. "Inhaler?"

"I'm good," said Chitchee.

Chitchee went into a song and dance about previous employment: he had helped harvest corn up in the Red River Valley, mined for iron on the Mesabi, and loggered up in the Porcupine Mountains selling horseradish donuts. Chitchee squirmed as he lied, dividing himself in half, because he felt his heart was on both sleeves at all times, and the lying faces he made in reaction to every objection Edelweiss made were beyond his volition to keep in poker-faced cement.

"Change jobs a lot?" said Edelweiss, adjusting a new pair of square glasses that at least weren't broken.

"I want to immortalize my friends in a Family Photo Album like pressed autumn leaves too," said Chitchee, trying to sound profound. There is always something profound in having nothing profound to say. "What did you ask? Change jobs? Yes and . . . no. Because . . . *maybe there are no steady jobs to be had in today's economy because of leftist, radical bankers in New York City*."

"Good answer!" said Edelweiss.

Gudrun applauded.

"Edelweiss," said Chitchee, feeling his confidence dilate outward toward all beings, "the powers that be are army ants marching in droves and we are the tropical rain forests being eaten alive."

Gudrun licked her lips and winked at Chitchee. Edelweiss puzzled a look.

"I'll take you up on that inhaler now," said Chitchee coughing. "Edelweiss."

She didn't hear him. Chitchee pretended not to have said anything. Silence.

"Silence too is language."

Silence.

"Hmmm . . . It's undecipherable! Where were we? Mankato, awwwwwwggkkkkhh," continued Chitchee. "Yeppers. Sioux Falls, Fargo, Aberdeen—I've cased them all for jobs. I'm a bit of a rover. But I've never been to Idaho."

"You say you are a rover? You must have lots of get up and go to go out into the world and say 'Welcome to my world, I am a rover!'" laughed Edelweiss.

Edelweiss turned to Gudrun who smiled back, echoing the word "rover."

"And gung ho, especially to go to Idaho!" continued Edelweiss. "Where there is nothing!"

"I-da-hoe!" laughed Gudrun, stamping her feet from her Windsor rocking chair, "and there is nothing there. Exactly!"

Chitchee leaped to the balls of his feet. Over-joyfully! He slipped into a cap-and-bells, court jester performance. Again he was the natural born fool. He grabbed Gudrun and they foxtrotted. Age had not curved Gudrun's spine yet, nor did Chitchee mind or notice the calcium deposits on her yellow fingernails. Then they sat back down.

"Oh, that was healthy," said Chitchee. "The old Idaho foxtrot! And here my old man wrote me off as The Mongol From Mars!"

"More idiocy he!" said Gudrun.

Sitting on his shawled chair (all the furniture wore shawls he noticed), Chitchee heard the front door slam. The cold wind's carriage wheeled into the living room like a Faberge droshky.

"What's all this about Idaho?" asked Bobblehead, shaking off the snow from outside. "Did something happen in Idaho today?"

"Chitchee, this is my nephew Horst," said Edelweiss. "Horst works security. He has degrees of expertise in security and espionage. He went to Northwestern Bible College for Archeology. He reads books and especially magazines all the time. Did you remember to pick up the Nestle's Quik? Take off your socks, we shampooed the rug."

"Bobblehead?" asked Chitchee. "Here I thought he was the poster child for the Shinders porno section."

Bobblehead wore himself out taking off his boots and sat down on a shawled, overstuffed chair, his arms on both armrests. He removed an inhaler from an inner parka pocket and inhaled.

"Cocoa, cookie, bus," he said. "But I'm going right back out! Besides, I'm too tired to take off both socks."

Fanning himself for sitting down too fast, Horst inhaled from his inhaler.

"Horst this is the new lodger," said Edelweiss, "and this is Horst. Horst's baby pictures are not in these particular albums. Horst is in the Knutsen boxes. The Family Photo Album is something our family has always cherished like the old family recipes for sausages. Horst used to live as a caregiver with my brother-in-law Michael. His branch of the family leans more to the Weatherwax side, which my daughter, Waldtraut, married into after Waldtraut's first husband, Angus Knutsen (he owned I, Spaetzle in Circle Pines) died horribly when he fell asleep on a chair lift at Lutsen . . . he never woke up . . . mein Gott . . ."

She coughed for a moment of silence, her hand over a queasy stomach. She made the sign of the cross, knelt, and prayed.

"He froze to death?" asked Chitchee while she was praying. "Nobody noticed? Is he still *on* the chair lift? Angus is a skeleton going around and around in circles with a lift ticket clipped to his rib cage?"

Horst scrunched his face to not cry.

"I don't want to talk about it, Kitsch-kee," she inhaled, crossed herself, and stood frozen. "Angus and Waldtraut had only one offspring, Horst, the world security expert, who got into Brown, but since transportation was an issue getting to Mendota Heights, he withdrew in the first week. Waldtraut's son, Arminius "Mutz" Weatherwax, whose aunt-in-law was *me* who married his grandmother, I mean his grandfather! I mean! The point is . . . about the monster, Arminius, Arminius "Mutz," the less said . . . *schweinhund* . . . and then Rhonda Rasmussen. No fear of the Devil in Rhonda! She's in a better place."

"Hell is better than this place!" said Gudrun.

"Hell is a better place than this place?" whispered Chitchee. "Holy cow, you two don't get out much! Where's the nearest skating rink?"

"Mutz the Schweinhund," said Edelweiss, "married Pembina Brisbee, who went to prison for what she did to Arminius. We called him 'Mutz,' we should have called him 'Putz,' he was a weird child, born with antlers . . . and he lived in Sleepy Eye and worked at a Hirshfield's or a Kresge's, or one of those Mel's Fleecey Flarmy things. They had a kid. That was the kid whose father's revolver blew up in his hands. Not the kid who was dropped like a crumb into the Mississippi."

Gudrun screamed:

"I jabbed myself!"

"What crumb?" asked Chitchee, turning the leaves two at a time of the tenth Family Photo Album on his lap.

"I don't want to talk about it!" said Edelweiss with a Beethovenian finality of tone. "Gudrun! Can you bring out the other boxes of Family Photo Albums? I don't see any Knutsens or Martensens or Weatherwaxes in here! Where . . . are all . . . the trips . . . to Heidelberg?"

Gudrun, who had been crying, stood up, saluted Edelweiss, and sat back down.

"Oh, I'll get them, soon as I catch my breath," said Edelweiss. "My husband Heinrich was from New Ulm and after he was decorated for serving his country with full military honors, he worked for the Bureau of Criminal Apprehension in St. Paul, which is where we met. Oh, I miss him so much every day! Oh, the honeymoon in Pfennigstadt . . . excuse me . . . now he's buried in Lakewood Cemetery . . . while I go to the powder room."

A hearing aid dropped like a crabapple from Edelweiss's ear. When Chitchee went to pick it up, he stepped on it and crushed it. But it still worked and Edelweiss hobbled off with her damaged hearing aid in her hand.

"Cocoa, cookie, bus," said Bobblehead to himself, with the smile of someone whose real smile wore off waiting too long for a snapshot and with a hint of doubt about the photographer's competence. "*Tantchen Edelweiss* will be back soon. She always comes back. She has to. This is her nest. This is where we eat her toast."

Bobblehead grinned with nothing to do, quite content with nothing to do like a child playing with his fingers; Gudrun rocked in her Windsor rocking chair. The crochet needles in her hands looked like extra-long witchy fingers.

"Are there any more crackers here besides myself?" asked Chitchee.

Croffut Gleet's car bomb went off in Chitchee's head when Edelweiss returned and dropped the next cardboard box.

"I heard that! You're a sketch, Kitsch-kee!" laughed Edelweiss, slapping her root beer barrel-dressed thigh, howling out a Saltine Cracker crumb with Krakatoan laughter: "Heavens! Horst, help yourself to cheese and crackers and join us!"

"Oh, I would *Tantchen*, but I have to go back out," said Bobblehead. "I forgot to pick up the Nestle's Quik at Lunds and then I thought to swing by Shinders for anything new by way of reading matter."

"Like Horst's father before him, Angus—"

"The one on the chair lift who—"

"—had to go on life support. But without a living will. Then in the hospital he caught an infection that ate his skin. The whole organ of skin collapsed and ate itself."

"What a terrible way to die! It must have been like burning at the stake, like a witch, to death," said Chitchee, his face and mouth churning. "Just the thought of it! I'm choking! Help! Inhaler!"

"He's not dead," said Edelweiss. "He's been on life support for years like that. They stood Angus on his feet in a giant pickle jar, where he floats around, locked up inside himself, unable to blink or eat anything but krill."

"Angus is going around and around that chair lift at Lutsen in his mind forever? Like a scene from Euripides?" asked Chitchee agape. "I forget which one. He could be Pentheus in a modern stage production of *The Bacchae*!"

"I don't want to talk about Angus anymore. Maybe later," said Edelweiss, crying into her armpit.

She added a sniffle to her sniff.

"Hugs!" said Chitchee, standing up with arms outstretched, accidentally kicking a brindle cat he didn't know was there—to he didn't know where. "Sending love!"

"Eow," said Edelweiss, feeling a hug from Chitchee.

Bobblehead stood at attention and Chitchee hugged Bobblehead, who was shivering with tears.

"No, I'll be all right," Edelweiss inhaled. "Careful, the cats are coming out. Horst likes to go to rare book stores and look for rare books, which for some reason he rarely finds. Sit down, Horst, you're stirring up the cat dander and confusing the cats."

"Yes, *mutti*," said Bobblehead, stifling a last sob.

An Angora jumped on Bobblehead's lap.

"It's a rare book store, I have to say," said Chitchee, "with so many rare books in it that you can rarely find the rare book you are raring for!"

"Horst," said Edelweiss, "saw Uncle Michael in a book store called HalfSmart Books near the Junior League building, if that's still there."

"Michael? Michael *Weatherwax*?" asked Chitchee.

"Yes, but he goes by the name of Melchizedek as you know."

"Melchizedek?" asked Chitchee, drawing down his eyebrows. "Yeah, he's around. He hangs out in Lakewood Cemetery, if that is still there, waiting for the aliens, *if they are still out there*. Edelweiss, your brother-in-law started a new religion in the old folks home, and now he has a cult following that would follow him to the moon. He has become a sort of God."

"Heavens to Betsy Ford, no!" Edelweiss blushed, then coughed into her hand. "How's your inhaler doing, Horst? I have more spacers. Is everybody good? More Saltines? Get 'em while they're hot!"

Chitchee coughed into his cold hand and waved off and waved off again the unfinished crackers in shards on the Bavarian breadboard, then he changed his mind:

"Okay!" chirped Chitchee. "I am ready for seconds. Are those inhalers still going around?"

"Gudrun," said Edelweiss, "see if we have any more of that white Muenster cheese in the fridge, would you be a dear?"

"It's purple now," said Gudrun, returning with the Bavarian panhandled breadboard, Saltine crackers, and purple cheese on it.

Chitchee stood a Saltine cracker on its lower vertex, then flicked it with his middle finger so that it would spin like Katarina Witt. Instead it took off like a missed field goal.

"Shank you very much," he said, embarrassed when he stood up to recover the pooched cracker.

"On the Himmelreich side," continued Edelweiss, "the Hillswick side, that is, because the name was changed at Ellis Island. They might as well have changed all our names to 'Ellis Ellison from the Islands.' Those were American traitors, changing people's names like dirty underwear. Anyway . . . my daughter Hildy had seven with her husband Andersen Anderssohn. Seven. One after the other like a machine gun. Knut, Anders, Demetrius, Graziela, Zosia, Tag, and Eisen. Bang, bang, bang."

Edelweiss fished up another Family Photo Album from the box she had dropped with a big bang in the living room on the freshly-shampooed, braided throw rug by Chitchee's bare feet.

"*Einen Augenblick*, let's see," muttered Edelweiss.

She stood lost looking as if over bins of old monstrous potatoes with sprouting Argus eyes.

"Ilgenfritzi married the *Norski* Roald Rasmussen. Klausina married the *Hungarian Polack* named Biskop. Retz married the burly red *Russkie* named Volkov . . . that makes for . . . the branch that lives in Isanti and Detroit Lakes. Norberta married an Asian doctor from Eveleth, Li Ang Wangah, he tok like this hello how aw you, a doctah. She never calls. Thrania married two times, first to that awful Varoom Supermanian and then another darky from India. And then Little Willie Peter, who never married after a botched, penile-enlargement surgery left him sterile. Wait, I forgot one. Thrania always had a thing for Hindus and married another awful Hindu dark-skinned fellow, Vinnie, Vinay, Vinay—"

"*Veni, vidi, vici?*" offered Chitchee.

"Heavens no, he's not a wop!" she laughed as if a clown had tumbled into the room. "At least he wasn't one of those pizza slicers from Little Caesars or wherever. This guy's name was Deep. *Deeply* atheist. Being a Hin-Doo for Christ's sake!"

She made the sign of the cross.

"Was it *Fairview* that botched it for Little Willie Peter?" asked Chitchee, noticing that most of the Gothic-bound tomes on Edelweiss's shelves had to do with bugs or tanks.

"No, it was Wee Willie Peter himself with a mail-order forceps from Ronco operating on Wee Willie Peter's . . . [dead air]. I don't like talking about the botched vasectomy, period. I don't want to talk about it," said Edelweiss, clutching the pectoral staves of her dress near her coronary artery. "Melusina had her eight buns in the oven. Chippo, Pancake, August Frederick, Lazar, Sackgasse, Birchard, Oola, and Dammit. Dammit was born in the family three-legged, eagle-clawed, enameled bathtub because Melusina couldn't get a ride to St. Mary's Hospital in the blizzard of some damn year or other . . . Gudrun? Fetch me the other boxes of the Himmelreichs and Hillswicks Family Photo Albums! There might be eight or ten still in the attic unless Earl moved them!"

Gudrun nodded, disappeared, and returned, lugging sloppy, broken cardboard box after sloppy, broken cardboard box into the time-capsuled living room, which had turned its face to the wall and croaked. Gudrun dropped a heavy box. On all fours she pushed it forward with her head and arms toward Edelweiss's black, block-shaped shoes. More and more boxes were on the way. Gudrun dropped another box and fell on top of it with an outstretched hug. Edelweiss harrumphed with a slightly triumphant smile.

"Gudrun!" said Chitchee. "Let me help you with that! How many more boxes are there? Oh my God, we need a dolly. Gudrun, you will break your back!"

"Can you at least massage my shoulders? That's what my nephew Horst usually tries to do," said Gudrun. "He's got the hands of an Indy race car driver."

Horst blushed rouge and stood up so fast he coughed his inhaler across the living room floor, bouncing to rest under a shawled love-seat, awakening two sleeping cats there who ran off on hotfooted tiptoes looking up as if the ceiling might cave in.

"Which brings me back to those cousins in Wisconsin," continued Edelweiss, unfolding a street map of Milwaukee from the 19th century.

She gripped a dull red plastic flashlight (her cataracts were getting bad) in one hand, whose thumb triggered the switch back and forth, and she held an inhaler in the other.

"Those Zorro-Austrians," she inhaled and continued. "They sounded and looked like creatures from a black Martian lagoon. The Ardeisheers. The Artie Shaws? They are the lost tribe of this family. One of them said they were actually *Aryan*. They are no . . . any Aryans . . . in Eye-ran anymore than there are Jews in *Ireland*! The Ardeisheers were Orientals. You could tell by the way they had that Mongoloid look. Oh I am so sorry Kitsch-kee. I didn't mean to cast slurs on your birth defect. It's okay to look a little retarded nowadays, because there's no such thing as euthanasia anymore. They have surgery for that, I betcha, at the Mayo. You poor thing. Can you see okay? I'll put you in my prayers."

On Edelweiss's orders, Gudrun fetched more Lunds bags of loose papers, birth certificates, death certificates, medical examinations, and church records—enough documentation to wallpaper the house a dozen times over. Gudrun admired the handsome new lodger with the charismatic disability, maybe *because* of the disability. The outsider she always liked; and she let it be known that her eyes had tears of sympathy for him, eyes awakened. She collapsed over the next box without a sound. Another cat ran off startled, its padded, trochaic forefeet flying.

"That's okay, Edelweiss!" said Chitchee. "Epicanthic folds never bothered me like they bothered people like you. In any case my body was built to last a lifetime. Oh no, Gudrun's down! GUDRUN! Quick, Horst, bring me some *sal volatile*, if you have any."

"She'll be okay. She's a one-horse dynamo!" laughed Edelweiss, holding her ribs back from falling out. "What a stitch she is! Oh, she puts me in stitches!"

Chitchee picked up Gudrun by the waist and carried her to her Windsor rocking chair, from which a tabby leapt like a flame with extended claws downward onto the living room rug.

"It's nothing," said Gudrun. "I forgot to exhale."

Gudrun picked up *The Horizon Book of Needlepoint* and contemplated the next stitch; she examined her pattern; she looked and scrutinized the pattern until she was in it.

"Look! It's a Carousel Square pattern! Oh, goody gum drops! Allow me to work my old-time magic!" continued Gudrun. "Ariel wants this by Christmas for my nephew, who has scholarosis from reading oceanography books under poor lighting in his store. His back is so bad from eye strain that when he sits down his disks slip out of his spine—left and right like flying saucers from his Lombardy region. Poor man, he could have been a great Jacques Cousteau."

"Heidelberg! Here they are!" said Edelweiss. "Heinrich's grandparents! *Der Alte*! Look! Here's the house Herman built. He was a master woodworker, joiner, and master mustard plasterer. He lived in the cellar of that house for the rest of his life. Only coming up for air at family funerals. I don't know how he ever met his wife Emma Wald, except she was the neighbor girl, half his age, but she was a very mature fourteen and a half for fourteen. In those days there was no age for age anyway."

"How does one become a . . . plastered . . . mustard . . . masterer?" asked Chitchee. "Where were we? Danzig? Do you have any depictions of the dying Germanicus? By the way, this cheese board has met its Waterloo."

Chitchee picked up the panhandled Bavarian bread board and hand-swept all the crumbs of Muenster cheese and Saltine crackers into his mouth and all over his flannel front; and then he stood up, brushed off the crumbs, and handed the licked bread board to Edelweiss, who set it down on the braided throw rug next to Gudrun.

"Melusina had eight pups minus two that died in the helicopter crash. Her second husband, Orthwein Weatherwax, who is a shirttail relation through my brother's wife's side of the Weatherwaxes, through my sister-in-law's uncle. Wait, is that right? I can't remember who my relatives are anymore! This is hideous, hideous!"

"Imagine you're a Zen master with no thoughts Edelweiss! What's the difference?"

"Aging is the damned difference!" said Edelweiss, recovering. "Waldtraut who died of—"

"Non-Hodgkin's lymphoma," said Bobblehead, mechanically absent, "pancreatic cancer. I think the chemotherapy and radiation killed her though. Excuse me, I have to go lay down. I'll run out later for cocoa powder. When the wind dies down."

"But her sisters are alive, last I heard," said Edelweiss cheerfully. "So Ilgenfritzi and Rolaid are retired and live in Robbinsdale in that bunker complex underground with their five gallon buckets of pinto beans, separated egg whites, and fortified potatoes, living like naked mole rats for the Rupture . . . anyway I don't talk to Norberta, the slut. I'm not really sure where she lives. Aging ages you, not to worry! I hear about Norberta through my daughter-in-law every other Christmas. I think she is a librarian or a libertarian. Or is she a croupier at Treasure Island? I can't keep up with all the newfanglements under Obama. Not one of us, you know? Or did I already say that?"

"Who is a slut?" asked Chitchee. "Could we explore that line of inquiry?"

"So I have six grandchildren through Mel, after August Frederick and Sackgasse died under a helicopter crash on Gull Lake when the rotors caught a great horned owl, and then the tail rotor fishtailed down and the helicopter crashed on top of them while they were fishing for sturgeon with live leeches peacefully before they were obliterated. The pilot lived, lived in Stillwater that is. Then we get to the eighty-four great- and grand-children, counting nieces and nephews, and I'm proud to say that forty-two of them are cops."

"You have 42 great- and grand-children on the police force?" asked Chitchee.

"They *are* the police force," said Gudrun with a grim grin.

"Ja, ja, ja," said Edelweiss, handing Chitchee a Lunds bag of charts and graphs. "And all dar-r-r-rn good cops! The kind you'd want your daughters to marry over and over!"

"Have you read a lot of Claude Lévi-Strauss? His *Structural Anthropology*?" asked Chitchee, kinship charts held up to the low-wattage light bulb he had difficulty reading under. "Does this line here indicate intermarriage between cousins? Where is the key . . . to this madness? So the green line represents exogamous, first cousins, wait, I'm missing a kinship chart. Are we almost done? My own family tree is boring enough. Wait a second, it looks like we are related."

Chitchee allowed his arms to fall at his side and he stuck out his flat tongue to represent exhaustion.

"Oh, we can pick this up later," said Edelweiss, disappointed and insulted. "Gudrun, can you bring the rest of the Family Photo Albums by this gentleman's room later? I think you will fit in nicely here. It's one big happy Family Photo Album here as you can see."

"No," said Gudrun. "We don't have a dolly. The *Wart Hog* borrowed the dolly and never brought it back. And he stoled Kennedy's gas can from the garage."

"I'm sorry," said Edelweiss, getting up slowly and sciatically, brushing off the crumbs that came from Chitchee, "you wanted to see the room! Let me show you your room! I got carried away. Anyways, you can see how the Himmelreichs have proliferated, how they have paid back their country with hard-working, patriot-loving patriots' blood, sweat, tears, toil, and other stuff. They would never betray their country for a dime! By marrying outside your bloodline, it gets weaker that is—"

"Racism," interjected Chitchee, "did you know, was institutionalized with the rise of the Nation State for imperialist plans of conquest, because you can't do someone wrong unless you think he is inferior, before or after the wrong."

"What is a Nation State?" said Edelweiss, her skeleton hand on the railing, paused. "Is that like a . . . Napoleon thing?"

"I think it's what we used to call a country," said Chitchee, standing barefoot at the bottom of the stairs. "But if you call a country a Nation State it suddenly has a really big army. All I know is that I'm always careful to display my love for my own country, once in a while. I wasn't cloned yesterday. Patriots are not patriots after they get shot by the patriots who shoot them."

"It's important that the human race be as smart and strong as possible, don't you think so? Horst and I were talking this morning about the importance of equal but separate races. Is that someone knocking outside?" said Edelweiss, looking heavily brow-ridged, although her white eyebrows had already fallen to the floor and been sucked up into the Hoover vacuum cleaner under the Clinton Administration.

Libor Biskop, with a winter coat, black wool cap, and his gloved hands holding a corn broom, ran up the stairs. Libor stopped, turned back, and holding the corn broom, ran back to his room.

"What's all that knocking noise?" asked Libor, standing in the door of his room. "I can't think! Is a wildcat moving into the room above me with a teletype, Edelweiss?"

"No," said Edelweiss. "There shouldn't be a teletype. Zalar moved out."

"It won't stop!" said Libor, standing in the middle of his room, followed by Edelweiss and Chitchee. "I had a breakthrough in loop quantum field theory but I didn't write down the equations! They got knocked out of my head by that banging! Do you hear that?"

Libor drove his corn broom handle into the ceiling.

"I can't think down here!"

Plaster showered down. The corn broom handle had drilled clean through the low stucco ceiling. The lath and plaster crumbled like a dried-out wedding cake.

Edelweiss and Chitchee climbed the stairs and opened the door into the small room, from which the noise had emanated. The window was open (Chitchee smelled cocoa butter, pineapples, Hawaiian beaches). Bobblehead was naked next to a pink, boxy Victoria's Secret bag. He was sitting in front of a vintage National Geographic article on Sudan. He was looking at a bare-breasted village woman who had copper bracelets around her neck like a Tesla coil and a giga-electron volt smile of salt-white perfect dentition.

"Horst!" said Edelweiss. "This is a no smoking room! You'll burn the whole house down one of these days!"

With his legs splayed beneath him like a tree frog, a jar of baby Vaseline on a Vaseline-saturated bath towel next to him, and Libor's corn broom handle from the room below entered into Bobblehead's Vaselined rectum, Bobblehead sat, cock in hand. He let fall his lighted cigarette onto the flammable oil slick of a towel. Pools of flame leapt up and danced in fantastic shapes on Bobblehead's face when he saw more pools of flame. Bobblehead jumped up, wiped his hands on the flaming towel, and shook the fire out of the towel, rapidly increasing its chaotic motion with his shaking it. He wrapped the burnt towel around his waist. The broom handle wormed back into the floor like an unscrewing screw. There was a quarter-shaped hole next to the bare-breasted village woman who had copper bracelets around her neck like a Tesla coil and a giga-electron volt smile of salt-white perfect dentition.

"Horst! This isn't your room! I thought you were going out for Nestle's Quik! Shoo!"

Horst ran out of the bedroom, down the stairs, and secreted himself under the kitchen sink with the boxes of Spic and Span, burnt towel around his waist, and buried himself behind boxes of Fels Naptha.

"Gudrun!" shouted Edelweiss down the stairs. "I need you to clean out Earl's old room and closet! Horst has had another *accident*."

"Anyway," continued Edelweiss. "This is the room for rent."

"I'll take it," said Chitchee.

"Don't you want to look at the closet?"

"Does it go to a magical land?" asked Chitchee.

Chitchee saw the clothes of the Old White-Haired Man in a Teener's Costumes bag in the closeted closet when Edelweiss threw open the closet door.

The closet contained: spats on the floor, a homburg on the top shelf, a long black overcoat on a scarecrow hanger, National Geographics piled in the corner, and fishing poles.

"What's all the smoke?" asked the tenants as if Lakewood Cemetery had emptied out for a zombie movie in Loring Park. "Is there a toaster on fire? What the day heck is it? Don't we supposed to have to fire extinguishers in every room?"

Gagged with dying, hacking snores and deathly, throaty coughs, coughed their lungs up and out, gasping like heavy smokers, their ancient TV sets set on sports they knew nothing about, or their radio tuners glued to 8:30 WCCO for the next tornado touching down in Sherburne County.

Out of the basement, Edelweiss's lodgers streamed out.

"Form a bucket brigade everybody," said a lodger no one had ever seen before until they recognized the raspberry bumps on his nose.

"Gudrun's burning toast!" said Edelweiss. "Everybody go back to your rooms! *Wie immer*! We were only toasting, everybody!"

"Toasting everybody," the lodgers muttered. "Okay, it was toast." "We're toast." "Don't fear the toaster . . ."

"I apologize for Libor," said Edelweiss, adjusting her old Mother Hubbard gray bun. "But he was a boy genius. Half-Hungarian to the bone and marrow. Of Mag-weird stock. Madmen or geniuses. They all play tennis like lunatics. And they multiply like golf balls on a driving range. He hasn't been the same since he opened up that twelve-year old can of paint when he was working his way through the Physics Department at the big University. The paint in the can was twelve years old. When he breathed in the paint fumes with his asthma, his left side froze. When he reached for his slide rule, the right side froze. He went into a coma for a year, clutching the slide rule in his frozen right hand. He had to drop out of the University. He couldn't do any more physics problems than he could write his name in alphabet soup. Wait, this *isn't* Zalar's old room. *Your* room is on the third floor, the next floor. Sometimes I totally forget where I am! Aging. This is Zalar's and Earl's old room. But Earl moved into the attic to be closer to God. I must be losing my mind! Your room is on the third floor."

"I think you must be losing my mind too," said Chitchee, with difficulty breathing and a rib cage-shaking smoke fit.

"Your mind too?" said Edelweiss, catching her breath and ascending Machu Picchu on all fours. "Wait, slow down. I haven't been up there in years. Is it still there?"

"When did you last see it?"

Chitchee walked up to the third floor to view his room.

"Yep!" he called down. "Still there!"

"Are you in the program?" said Libor Biskop, having emerged from the third floor bathroom, turning the corner in a winter coat and black winter cap.

When Chitchee peaked into his new "can," he saw that Edelweiss's idea of good taste was a carpeted bathroom with tank and seat covers, an ashtray on the tank, an ashtray with strike-on-the-box Diamond matches.

Edelweiss coughed abruptly.

"What program?" said Chitchee, walking back down toward Edelweiss.

"Deep State Witness Protection!" said Libor with a tremulous voice and pale as a new shoot. "That's how they got Zalar!"

"Libor! Don't listen to him, Chitchee. He sometimes thinks he's Rudolph the Red-Nosed Reindeer on *The Burl Ives Christmas Special*," said Edelweiss, sitting down on the stairs, her knees wide apart.

"BROUGHT TO YOU BY NORELCO!" said Libor with a smile so big it haunted Chitchee to the grave.

Chitchee wondered about bedbugs. He grafted the smile of Libor onto the face of a giant bedbug.

Gudrun crept up the stairs, carrying a duster, a bucket of Lysol, saddle soap, a bristle brush, Glade, and Air-Wick.

"No rest for the wicked," said Edelweiss.

"But you're sitting!" said Gudrun, trudging upward.

Chitchee intuited something unreal or uncanny about this house: the house was "staged," the people were actors, and the actors were characters one might find in an otiose romance novel at Treasures Await. Cold sweat fed Chitchee's anxiety, which palpitated his heart and erased his lungs so that the walls were breathing for him. He sensed the boundaries of his sense of self erode when he opened the unlocked, unlockable door to his prospective room and saw Sausage Man.

"Say! I think there is a squirrel in the house! Don't you know man ain't nothing but a lyin' purpose?"

Sausage Man white-knuckled the room's walls like they were doors.

"I heard acorns running up the walls," he said and walked out.

Chitchee glanced around the empty room for a second look. What choice did he have? What was there to look at? He would take this room, because he was all roomed out from looking at rooms.

While at the top of the third floor landing, Chitchee heard Sausage Man:

"Where's all the stuff I left in the closet?"

"I don't know," said Edelweiss. "Why?"

"60,000 dollars of why," he said.

Chitchee stepped backward into his room, knuckled the walls a couple times, crept back to the top of the landing, and heard:

"Viktor threatened to beat Brady to death with a tire iron because he tattooed him with a Jerry Lewis tattoo instead of a Marilyn Monroe tattoo too," said Edelweiss, sounding tired and bored as Saltine crumbs. "He threatens lots of guys with tire irons these days. It's true, he's getting worse. He listens to no one. He's beyond my control. And beyond Marten's control. He's jazzed up again on that cocaine stuff. He said to Marten he suspects *you* of *turning* Zalar. None of this family . . . sits well with me."

Chitchee cleared his throat to announce his having eavesdropped.

Chitchee had been duped by Sausage Man, Edelweiss, and Kennedy into believing and living in a House of Lies. And here he was lying to a family of liars. Everyone he knew had been simulated there to lie especially for him to lie to. A free-floating anxiety made up his mind to get hammered on Blech's to reduce his cortisol and adrenaline levels and consider looking for a wet house instead of a dry one. That was his own *maya* he decided and dismissed it with a laugh.

So he paid Edelweiss in cash for the first week, and after he doled out 50 bucks each to the 4 Mad Jacks to move his books and condiments into the BookSmart basement, he wanted to rest in his new room. Stretching out on the creaky bed, hands behind his head, he dreamed ahead and anticipated living at this Planck length.

Sometimes he heard sniffing under his door—usually before the ten o'clock news when Edelweiss watched her favorite newsman, the crushed-on Don Shelby, who she mistakenly called "Dave Moore" because she hadn't noticed that Dave Moore had died and that Don Shelby had taken over the anchor position on *WCCO 4 News at Ten*.

And this is how we spend our short time on Earth, pretending that we don't have a short time on Earth? Chitchee started drinking screwdrivers of Phillips vodka and Tropicana orange juice even to *want* to be inside Edelweiss's depressing sober house and untangle his hair from another family tree.

He drank secretly with Kennedy—with or without "Dave Moore" and his thirteen cultic house cats with heads like gigantic garlics—Dave Moore's face on them furry as flies.

One night, feeling drunk, lonely, and suicidally vacuous he sought the human contact of Edelweiss, Gudrun, and "Dave Moore," and walked downstairs to catch the news, cats raking their backs up against Chitchee's shins, leaving behind scurf, sneezes, songs, and bugs.

"And finally," said *WCCO 4 News at Ten*, "we'll leave you with this!"

A fishtailing, snowbirded '65 Chevy Bel Air station wagon was pushed out of a moonlight-colored snowbank by Mjollnir, Dougal, and Nicky Fingers. Skooge spun his wheels. Dougal grabbed his back in agony and stepped on a red-faced shovel, whose handle whacked him in the face. And everyone laughed, *jada jada jada*, "that's Minnesota!" and Gudrun echoed, "that's Minne-so-what-da!"

Later, Gudrun scratched (not knocked) on his room door and insisted she deliver three, freshly-found Family Photo Albums filled with Weatherwaxes. She returned to the chintz-wallpapered closet Edelweiss provided her with, along with a chenille bedspread. The next day: Gudrun, scratch, scratch, scratch. She insisted on cleaning his room. Chitchee wiped his eyes and opened his bedroom door to the smell of the downstairs kitchen radiating particles of burnt toast, melting dairy butter, and burning Jimmy Dean's frozen pork sausage breakfast patties made from real sausage.

Gudrun surprised Chitchee one morning in her skimpy nightie with a plate of marzipan-and-caramel danishes, snowed-over by sugar frosting, brown sugar, and cinnamon. They each picked off the frosting and ate that first. Then Gudrun pulled Chitchee down onto his sleeping bag spread on the floor. Without even thinking Chitchee made love to Gudrun. Her cherry face glowed with the freshness of Spring. Her body he held dear like the air of Spring after winter's vast devastations. Her open-mouthed kisses were like the minnows you used for bait.

Which brought to his mind the mystery girl from next door who kissed him when he was five. Had it been Gudrun? There never would be an answer.

Instead when he connected soul to soul with Gudrun like two facing, mating squirrels, he read some enormous pain in her past, a spiritual wound with a history going back to childhood.

"I was framed for that murder," said Gudrun. "If you heard about that already."

"No," said Chitchee, his arm around her bare shoulder. "No one told me you were a murderer."

"My husband beat me, that's why I'm like this," said Gudrun. "Three concussions and a permanent traumatic brain injury."

She told Chitchee she was framed for the murder of her son. The police didn't believe she had been raped. Her husband Henry didn't believe her either and he threw her down the very same stairs in The House of Edelweiss. Gudrun was sent to St. Peter's and wound up at the Shakopee Correctional Facility.

Chitchee told Gudrun that his wife LaDonna miscarried four months into pregnancy while taking a bath and found the two fetuses in the bloody water because they were plugging the drain. And that was followed by a DUH, community service, schizophrenia diagnoses, methadone, buprenorphine, and divorce.

"LaDonna always said," said Chitchee, "the purpose of life is living for the purpose of others whose purpose in life is living for you."

"A wise woman, that LaDonna," said Gudrun. "Where is she now?"

"Treatment."

"The treatment center in New Brighton? Maybe she'll give us a free tour of the plant."

Holding hands under the sheets, ashtray over the sheets, having opened the window only as wide as a white tan line on a woman's bare shoulder for fresh air, they smoked Carousel squares and blew alternate smoke rings through each other's smoke rings from their Carousel squares.

Gudrun had been raped with carrots in a snow fort she had been lured into by a next door neighbor who promised her a root beer. The memory of that humiliation continued all through junior high and then one of her relatives raped her at a family reunion in Minnehaha Park, a knife to her throat if she talked—by Minnehaha Falls.

"I had the child out of wedlock. I presented the baby to the father and while we were walking together, he threw the baby off the Hennepin Avenue Bridge before I could stop him. He told the police I did it. That I was insane. The judge believed his story and they sent me away for twelve years."

"WHAT? REALLY?" Chitchee jumped. "The judge believed *him?*"

"Yes!" said Gudrun. "Every woman I've ever known has been abused and then accused of lying about the abuse."

Gudrun left Chitchee's room crying, leaving a crying Chitchee behind her.

Chitchee lay in bed thinking. If Earth were weighed down with all the suffering it bears, it would disappear. He pondered his relationship with Gudrun. A white-throated sparrow and a Canada yellow warbler met on a hundred-branched, hundred-year old oak tree, and had to part ways at the sight of Edelweiss stomping through the woods, her breath hot with the grease of

Jimmy Dean's pork sausage breakfast patties and a BB gun in her arm to shoot at birds for nickel-and-dime target practice. Since Gudrun was twenty years older, Chitchee feared being labeled a dirty young man, a grave robber, and a necrophiliac—Hester Prynne with a "N."

"No-o-o-o-o!" he banged awake like a door.

Startled, he heard the door's: Scratch, scratch, scratch.

"I want you to have this pillow," said Gudrun, wearing go-go boots to keep her feet warm and a skimpy teddy, bare. She let go a laugh, her words dancing out of her mouth: "I made this one for you!"

It was a picture-perfect pillow of Carousel Square itself, knitted, crocheted, and embroidered in red, green, and white, although the resolution resembled something from the early days of video games with chunk by chunk pixels—but it contained *baraka* or *baraka* flowed through it.

"Carousel Square!" said Chitchee, his heart buoyed up with this gift. "I love it! It flows! Good job! I'm touched to the heart by your work of art. But this belongs in the rotunda of the National Archives or the Museum of Questionable Medical Devices, the Bakken, or somewhere over the rainbow!"

"No," said Gudrun. "It's so you!"

Chitchee, moon-faced, eyeballed the pattern of the Carousel Square pillow, seeing himself within the reality of its representative cubic building, nested within a larger sphere, nested within a larger cube, nesting a white-throated sparrow and a Canada yellow warbler, flying off when they heard a crash squarely in their round faces.

"What was that?" asked Chitchee. "It sounded like a dumpster lid in a prison yard."

Gudrun peeped out Chitchee's window.

"He's back!" said Gudrun. "The Wart Hog!"

A white 2009 Porsche 911 Carrera had rolled into the driveway.

When Viktor climbed out, Gudrun dropped to the floor in a dead faint. Chitchee splashed warm Tropicana orange juice on her face and she revived.

"Am I in Miami?" asked Gudrun.

She bounded to the window, constantly bobbing in and out of the frame.

"Chitchee, what's he doing in the garage? Is he siphoning gas?"

"Hey, I bet this would look good in BookSmart's front window," said Chitchee. "Gudrun? What do you think? Gudrun? What the Heckle and Jeckle? Gudrun! Are you okay? What are you looking at?"

"I need a glass of Ocean Spray Cran Apple," said Gudrun, slamming the door on her way out. "You don't love me. I can tell."

Chitchee stumbled into the dim hallway after her. Sausage Man—wearing a lampshade, which he had somehow modified into a Hunnish *pickelhaube*—crashed into Chitchee.

"Gossick?" asked Sausage Man.

"Chichester," asserted Chitchee. "Remember? Gossick moved out and some Earl from Christendom took over his room. How long have you lived in this house, Sausage Man?"

"Yes. *I'm* Earl. Earl from Bozeman, Christendom. Oh. Oh! Say? Have you met any nice German girls in the neighborhood yet?"

"No," said Chitchee. "You'll have to take me around and introduce me. And I guess Spring is going to be late too because 'the wooly bear caterpillars were pretty crunchy this year.'"

"Say?" perked up Sausage Man. "The price of German potato salad has gone down at Frisch's. It used to be 99 cents a 14-ounce can, but if you buy two say, you can get them for 79 cents a can. Say? I just remembered now a sausage I ate in Canada twenty-seven years ago with a German girl on the Yukon River. My father ate a lot of sausages. I think he passed down the sausage genes."

"I see," said Chitchee, abstractedly looking off, "and then your epigenetic markers for sausage consumption caused you to eat so many sausages that *you became your own sausage*."

"And," said Sausage Man, his expression that of a man stirring a barrel of mustard with a harpoon, "those sausages, like Vienna schnitzels and Sauerbraten and Braunschweigers—they cause you to remember things, you know, like German girls! Say? Pretty soon the moss will be blooming. And then that bee will be back."

"Did you say a *bee*?" asked Chitchee.

Bobblehead, terry cloth towel over his bathrobed arm like a wine steward, had a chin already lathered with shaving cream (his can of shaving cream had been stolen when he forgot it there) and he was walking into the third floor bathroom for the second time in his life, trembling like a bee himself creeping before a virgin source of nectar.

"I didn't see a bee, I tell you!" said Sausage Man. "I was watching an epic. Epic on the ice of the Ant-ar-tict! Fell asleep. Woke up! Bee on my nose! Stings the very tip of it—urt-hurt—hurt—oh. That's why I'm wearing this hat. To keep the bees off my nose for when they get here! Say? Do you know any German girls who like sausages? You haven't seen my fishing poles have you, neighbor? They were in my old room. Next to some old clothes in a church bag."

"No," lied Chitchee, scratching his chin. "Excuse me, something is burning."

Chitchee, smelling the burnt cinnamon raisin toast from the kitchen, descended the musty, carpeted staircase, stair steps fraught with now over fourteen balding, mangy cats that cuddled up to his shins and clawed his jeans.

Instead of screaming or sneezing, Chitchee stood over the kitchen sink and poured a glass of Ocean Spray Cran Apple for Gudrun.

"Is that you Earl?" hollered Edelweiss. "Oh, it's you, Churchy Churchill, never mind!"

"I'm getting a glass of Ocean Spray Cran Apple juice for Gudrun," said Chitchee. "Want any cranny, granny?"

"Well, no," said Edelweiss, "should I? Are you my sister's keeper now?"

"Well, yes," said Chitchee. "Shouldn't I be?"

Chitchee rubbed his eyes with both forearms like a cat sleeping in a bright bedroom, stretched his arms and legs, yawned, and unfolded in a star-shaped pattern.

"Okay, Mrs. Hillswick," said Chitchee. "IF that is your real name, IF this is your real house, and IF this is really Minneapolis and not some strange, alternative universe like St. Paul—point blank, blammedy blam—WHO is the Wart Hog? I do believe he owns Club Miami and Carousel Square and he plans to run BookSmart into the ground and reopen it as a cathouse for cops."

Twenty cats scattered into every available cranny, crouched, and curled up like balls of yarn.

"Have I shown you Heinrich's medals? Have a seat—if you're not too busy chasing warthogs through the snow."

Rocking in Gudrun's Windsor rocking chair and drinking Gudrun's glass of Ocean Spray Cran Apple juice, Chitchee witnessed Edelweiss launch an air attack on Hitler. He had "no real military training in strategy like the Great Frederick or Charles the Something of Sweden," or so her "dear Heinrich always said." Where were the danged medals? She told Chitchee he could affordably buy anything Adolf Hitler ever owned just around the corner in Fridley. There were swap meets where Edelweiss had bought Hitler's: Schnapps glasses, Meissen sugar bowls, Chantilly lace doilies, zircon nose hair clippers, and spent cartridges found in THE bunker, with the rest of his bunk. Evidently, Edelweiss's cats understood more about military strategy than Hitler *and* Kaiser Wilhelm II combined.

"You know what they said about the Kaiser after he put the poison gas industry on a wartime footing?" asked Chitchee. "The Kaiser was on a roll."

"I don't get it," said Edelweiss.

"Neither did Justis Liebig, poor dumb Hun. The fertilizer guy? Have you read *Silent Spring* by Rachel Carson?"

"I don't read books by Heebs," said Edelweiss.

"Edelweiss!" said Chitchee. "I just had a vision of you young and yodeling, clad in lederhosen, eating Muenster cheese and Saltine crackers, halfway up the Matterhorn, in your tungsten-colored, flying sidecar, filled with house cats, spraying deadly pesticides every which way, with swastikas falling from the sky directly into your open mouth as you lose control and lunge off the road into the valley below. You aren't wanted by Interpol or Simon Wiesenthal, are you? Your husband Heimlich was in the War? I take it he died in action on the right side? Prince Valiantly?"

"S-h-h-h-h . . ." said Edelweiss.

Kennedy stomped into the foyer and shook off the snow from outside.

"B-r-r-r-r . . ." announced Kennedy as a formality.

Edelweiss planked her finger on her lips and whispered:

"There is only ever one War. The rest are all skirmishes in the War for Global Dominoes."

"Hey, where did Gudrun go?" asked Chitchee, leaping almost up, but falling back down.

When Edelweiss removed her finger from her lips, Chitchee saw Gudrun's lips, Dagny's lips, and LaDonna's lips. He tallied every calibration on the upper lip and lower lip of Edelweiss. Chitchee imagined the tongue in her mouth and then the mouth, which swallowed him whole as he free fell, head over heels in zero gravity, down a deepening tunnel. He zoomed out from the other side of the tunnel up Gudrun's vagina.

"LOOK!" air-horned Kennedy, "at the Cheerio faces we have in our *hacienda*! HOLA!"

Kennedy tapped the snow off his new Klim snowmobile boots from Dick's Sporting Goods. Obviously tipsy when he was drunk, everything he said sounded like a huge surprise over a loudspeaker.

"This is an extraordinary encounter, doubtless I am assured! It smells indubitably like Welsh Rabbit in here! It's a Welsh Rabbit gathering, I GATHER! "

"Oh, isn't Kennedy a riot," laughed Edelweiss in a forced way, looking over at Chitchee in his Windsor rocking chair, expressionless, and depressed with rings of anguish around his eyeballs.

Chitchee gripped the empty glass of cran apple juice for Gudrun, feeling like imprisoned splendor.

"Named after the most overrated President after Roosevelt, but *our* Kennedy speaks English, doesn't he? At least not like the real hydra-headed Kennedy clan: hellaw frawm hawvawd yawd maw fawthaw is a mackeral snawwwper!"

Gudrun bounced into the room like a ping pong ball—spry as a spring day, all sunshiney April, tulips, peonies, and buzzing insects.

"Gudrun! Are you okay?" said Chitchee, getting up. "I was going to bring you a glass of Ocean Spray Cran Apple juice but Edelweiss pigeon-holed me with a bunch of her racist shit, and I had to drink it!"

"Excuses, excuses!" said Gudrun, rocking in her rocking chair.

While Kennedy negotiated with Edelweiss about his late snowmobile fees, Chitchee pulled Gudrun aside.

"I'm sorry, Gudrun, I've been thinking about us. I have to cut it short."

"Oh no!" implored Gudrun, pleading, clinging to Chitchee, and afraid to let go for the abyss below. "YOU'RE GOING TO CUT OFF YOUR PENIS?"

"Gudrun!" said Edelweiss. "Let's talk in the kitchen! Excuse us!"

Chitchee and Kennedy climbed the stairs and entered Kennedy's hole in the wall.

"Kennedy!" said Chitchee, fitting himself into the DIY pawn shop that was Kennedy's rat-packed garret. "Did you know Sausage Man lives here?"

"In the affirmative!" guffawed Kennedy, coughing heartily. "Dumb old white crazy codger? He turned the attic into his own dormitorial. He goes around here with a lampshade on his head and a sausage sticking out of a duck-hunting hat to keep the bees away! Isn't that the guy who goes matriculating around town and tells everybody he's Robert Bly? He fooled me like a deer in the headlights! He's probably eaten too many sausages, too many sausages, kckckckck! Only in Minnesota. Eh? Maybe he's Canadian. He's definitely from the Outer Limits. He gave me a finder's fee of two hundred dollars for recommending you. Was that you? No! It was Zalar. Another tall weird white guy. What is it with you tall weird white guys?"

Chitchee looked at the two tin cans of unlabeled food not even generic enough to say FOOD on them.

"And since when could you afford to buy a snowmobile?" asked Chitchee, moving aside mounds and mountains of self-help books (from A to Z).

Chitchee inspected other tin cans for their health benefits—so many were dented and punched in their stomachs. He appraised a white bag of white corn chips labeled STALE CHIPS. He reviewed and set aside a pint crate of whiskered blueberries covered in spidery webs of mildew. He made no offer on the half loaf of Wonderbread (the other half he had rolled into balls of dough but had not eaten so they sat in a row on a shelf). He sifted through a myriad of shiny, serrated packets of mayonnaise, ketchup, and mustard from Wendy's, Arby's, and McDonald's respectively.

"I came into a forebearance," said Kennedy, who smiled with a wheezy, guilty laugh over this forged friendship, which also produced saliva bursters at the corners of his smile.

"What? Who? Finder's fee? What are we talking about?" asked Chitchee.

Chitchee opened the bag labeled STALE CHIPS, his hand perched to dive in with his long white fingers to snatch from the white bag of white corn chips a white corn chip. He held the chip to the light to admire the water of its diamond. He kissed it and asked:

"What? Sausage Man? He paid you for what?"

"For a finder's fee!" shouted Kennedy. "Are you taking notes? That is nothing compared to the six thousand dollars I found in *The Memory Book* by Jerry Lewis and Tommy Lee Bradshaw."

"You mean—OWWW!" yelled Chitchee, grabbing his jaw and crying baby tears. "I broke a tooth. I broke a tooth. And I don't have a lot of teeth to spare! Do you have Ibuprofen?"

"Yes, yes, yes," said Kennedy. "How many do you want?"

"All of them," said Chitchee.

"Exactly," said Kennedy, feeling his own eternally sore, inflamed, flaming, and tooth-aching molar, "but you do understand you were in dentures to me for that much already? The bag of pharmaceutical I found stuffed in the futon outside by the dumpster? I inherited that property, all but in deed and kind. So now, at this temporality, we are finally on the same equilibrium of a playing pitch, *per se*. Anyway, it's all been *expenditured* and *investitured* into a sleek, mo-to vee-hicular Arctic Cat. And it runs on answered prayers."

"Then let's give the Cat a test run to a Blockbuster and pick up some French DVDs," said Chitchee, looking wistfully at the gray clove chipped off an old tooth. "So I can start learning French and go to Paris and speak English."

"How about a watch?" asked Kennedy, handing Chitchee a little white box.

"Wait a second," said Chitchee, massaging his jaw.

Then Chitchee opened the white box, looked at the watch, and pulled out the instructions typed in font 2: "Made in China . . . 3. Do not wear it in puissant electric field. 4. The watch can bear normal shake but not hard shock . . . 8. The watchband is made from resin, so If you find white powder on the watchband, wipe them off with cloth, the powder would not cause any hurt to your skin and clothes. 9. The resin-made watchband may aging, crack or break when bear sweat or damp . . . 12. The watch is made of precision part, don't open the cover by yourself. If there is water smoke or drips inside the watchcase, ask approved specialist to disassembly and repair. 13. Keep well the operation instruction."

"I'm thinking about going back to school, starting over at a community college like MCTC," said Chitchee, placing the watch in the white box and into Kennedy's hand. "I'm sure all the old clocks are still working there. So I won't have to keep well the operation instruction. I can't even afford to keep time now."

"Well," said a rebuffed Kennedy, taking back the re-valorized *Chinese* timepiece, "do you mean to take real classes in broad daylight or night classes playing gin rummy with a bunch of old Geronimos . . . without any teeth at all or maybe one . . . smoking rum-flavored cigars . . . in their diapers like the guy who always shows up on Facebook with no friends and looks like Har Mar Superstar?"

Kennedy's ridiculous grin was for piling up pillows in a corner onto which he would throw himself like a kid.

"It depends," reflected Chitchee. "If I'm not too old to get financial aid. Languages, Kennedy. The future is in communications. Maybe I can handle French. Then open up a French book store inside the New French Cafe in the Warehouse District by the Monte Carlo or at Snelling & Stinson on Central, because there probably aren't a lot of French book stores there. Who was Snelling? What kind of name is that?"

"Sounds like some guy left out of a Charlie Brown Christmas," said Kennedy.

"You know what, Kennedy?" said Chitchee in a dream. "I bet I could take business classes somewhere and learn how to run a book store into the ground myself. Everybody has to do something spectacular, don't they? The other day I looked at the self-actualizing, Maslovian pyramid, and I thought: hey, I haven't satisfied even one stage on the pyramid. I wake up crying a lot lately—not that the Maslow's Pyramid of Needs is worth killing myself over! And then I'm so nervous about paying for my future, I can't think from A to B anymore. I need real skills—like in data entry levels if those jobs are still out there!"

"I can procure language films," offered Kennedy, feeling and looking expansive. "Linguistic marvellations. Especially French. Frenchez-vous Anglais, Monseignor? *You take the French* and I'll ascertain you the cinema. Hot DVDs by the buttload. Two bucks. My friend sells them, but I can get you a discount. My buddy, my man, I can't remember his name. French something. French. Frenchy."

"Frenchy?" asked Chitchee.

"Yes! But . . . how did you *know* that?" said Kennedy, making a casual gesture for the Phillips vodka in its brown bag.

Chitchee absorbed himself in watching Kennedy's hands lose all control in screwing off the bottle cap, so that the bottle of Phillips vodka had delirium tremens too.

"Do you think he has *Amelie*?" asked Chitchee, biting the spandrel between thumb and forefinger. "Where can I meet this Frenchy?"

"You really *do* belong in more academious settings! Or graduating at Harvard with an honor roll. You are *extremely* well-acquainted with the sphere of computer books and knowledge of all the areas of precision learning . . . why aren't you a great thinker?"

"I wanted to be a great thinker, but I never got my big break."

"Here's to Phillips vodka! Old Edsel will never know. I used to be soberific, but living in Minnesota is hardcore. I never made friends in this harsh climate."

"Kennedy, I'll be your friend!"

"Oh," said Kennedy, surprised. "No thanks."

"Why *is* this vodka so cheap?" asked Chitchee.

Chitchee wet his whistle, took a pull, swigged, and elbowed himself up for a full-snort until Kennedy reclaimed the bottle.

"You don't have overhead on the cork for one," said Kennedy, handing Chitchee the Phillips vodka twist-off cap instead. Kennedy got drunk on a dime. The drunker he drank the more dramatic his cantankeritis grew. He spoke louder and louder. The whole neighborhood heard him talk. His voice rose like plumes curling up from Mount Kilimanjaro. "That's what I love about this country. Everybody is constantly inventing new machinations and MAKING MILLIONS OFF THEIR WORTHLESS LITTLE WIDGETS!"

"Kennedy, chill . . ." said Chitchee, calmly placing his hand on Kennedy's shoulder.

"Between the two of us, we ought to come up with a widget is all I'm exclaiming, and Old Frenchy . . ." paused Kennedy, taking another pull straight from the bottle and mopping the sweat from his forehead with an old sock. "Ol' Frenchy sets up shop at the Wendy's across from the Popeye's Louisiana Kitchen on Lake Street near the Uptown Pawn shop that the Hispanics levitated with the equity from their Taco Rocket business. Anyway, Frenchy is there at night holding court with his pomp and circumlocutions of destitution amid packets of Hellman's mayonnaise . . . packets of Hellman's mayonnaise . . . and this is called A LIFE?"

Kennedy looked at Chitchee who was laughing a long time. Was he waiting for the tell of an echo of recognition from Chitchee that packets of Hellman's mayonnaise were somehow funny-in-themselves or A LIFE was so unbearably painful it was unspeakable?

A bad conscience cudgeled Kennedy around the shoulders and he asked:

"What's your name again?"

"KENNEDY!" yelled Chitchee.

"That name belongs to me," said Kennedy, pulling away and looking tricked. "I think you got distracted."

"Chitchee! You don't even know my name!"

"What's in a name?" said Kennedy. "Unless it's a *brand* name!"

"Maybe if we all had brand names, we'd fare better! Hey, I know! Let's take out your Arctic Cat!" said Chitchee excitedly. "And go *cherchez le Fr-r-r-enchy*! We can go on a bipolar expedition!"

"Were you ever married?" asked Kennedy.

"Yes," said Chitchee, "but I think I might be done with all relationships. Now I just want to watch my grandchildren never grow up."

"So you are not gay?" asked Kennedy. "And you don't have any children anywhere?"

"I don't have children. LaDonna miscarried twins. That ended me. God has cosmically censored me twice. I'm not really a completed human being. So what?"

"We can't all have children," said Kennedy, saddling his eyes that reflected a botched love affair somewhere along the line. "God made it that so. Or there would be too many. Children, children, children fighting for survival. Anarchy, street-fighting children throwing bombs, blowing up toy stores, children, children, children amok and running havoc."

"Let's get out of here, I've got cabin fever," said Chitchee. "Let's go ice-fishing! I saw a bunch of fishing poles in the closet downstairs."

"I saw those too," said Kennedy. "But I already pawned them!"

"Let's take your Arctic Cat out for a spin!" said Chitchee. "Let's go on an endless roller coaster ride of joy! Let's go outside and embrace the universe with all the love left in our old hearts."

"We cannot perform that maneuver as yet, ahem," said Kennedy, sucking slowly on an unsavory and salty white corn chip. "I don't have gas money. I need a gas can! Someone stole my gas can from the garage. Gudrun said it was the *Wart Hog*. Besides, you can't just matriculate anywhere. It has to be ten feet away from the street's avenue of discourse. And I need a driver's fee license title, certification of some particular kind, and four valedictions of my current address."

The lower eyelid twitching, Kennedy eye-measured the active volume of vodka remaining in the bottle and tilted it for another view. His hand trembled. He guzzled the last swig-a-swig, drippety drop, took the cap back, and carefully licked its liquid grooves.

A bright hope of inspiration ignited the fire in Kennedy's eyes:

"*Annihilation* is *creation*. At the end of all the revolutions *God* will become *Earth*. And *humankind* will cry out in *rebellion* that God enslaved men to make them tools of his amusement so men will retaliate by making God the SLAVE to their *technology and ideology*. Look it up on your Wacko-pedia."

"I believe you, man," said Chitchee. "But what brought that on? *You* should have been an orator at Harvard Divinity School, Kennedy, yourself. You could have been a saint! A very loud saint. Probably turn the hair of the church choir gray. But you have the articulation for the matriculation, my friend!"

"What are we doing here? Living in Min-nee-a-Police," said Kennedy, smoothing out the corrugations in his forehead and looking at the floor.

Ashamed but not ashamed of bloodshot eye contact.

"Where should we be?" asked Chitchee. "Doesn't every seat in the universe have exactly the same view? It's like the play is consciousness, but we always forget that we are watching it. Reminds me of *dhikr*. Real existence is allegorical, layered with meanings and meanings beyond meanings. 'Good are all the religions/Better is the Knowledge/That best of course/Is one Emptiness.'"

"Oh, it's not about that! I took the finder's fee and I put money above friendship to you," said Kennedy. "I needed it for rent!"

"Kennedy, are you crying?" asked Chitchee, giving him a brief gentle hug like a parent carefully inquiring into the child's pain. "Where is the pain? All right, let's go peddle that stolen iPhone of yours for gas money."

The two grown men wiped their tears away. They tiptoed down the stairs past the "old bat" with her batty tea cups on her teak side-table and the rest of the batty tea room from a time when our great grandmothers wore millinery and lily-white hats like sailboats. Ghosts from Edelweiss's era lived in her mind—she peered through nostalgic tears at the aproned waitresses who marched around stately restaurants like Army nurses carrying tea cups.

Edelweiss stood forward from her rocking chair with her back curved in the shape of the rocking chair, not of a Bell curve but more of a Pareto distribution, the area under the curve bunched at the shoulders, with a long tail going down her spine. She poked her mother-of-pearl inlaid, rosewood cane at the RCA television console in a duel.

"These newfangled cockamie contraptions," said Edelweiss, exhaustedly sitting back down, "don't sit well with me for one Iona. Ow! Gudrun, when are you ever going to finish making me that pillow for—excuse my French—my dare-ee-airrre? The Andrews Sisters are going to be on . . . some day!"

Chitchee and Kennedy slipped and stumbled, shodding their sneakers heaped by the black walnut front door in the dark.

"Gudrun, can you hold the antennae and stand by the television set like a Christmas tree until the Andrews Sisters come on? And then stay there for an hour?" asked Edelweiss in her painful Windsor rocking chair, enviously looking over at Gudrun rocking in her Windsor rocking chair. "And while we are waiting we can listen to Mitzi Gaynor's *Christmas Album* on the Magnavox."

"But the Andrews Sisters are dead," said Gudrun. "The Mitzi Gaynor is cracked, Edelweiss. It is cracked. Remember when the *Wart Hog* refused to play Bridge with us last Christmas and then sat on the stereo record album with his big fat crack?"

"Who has a big fat crack? Who, me?" joked Chitchee with a thickly maple syrup grin. "Goodnight ladies, we're off to see the Blizzard!"

Chitchee was closing the smoked-glass, black walnut front door when Gudrun caught hold of Chitchee, layered in his winter coat and three flannel shirts like a multilayered candy bar.

"Just between us," whispered Gudrun, "you're being followed."

"By who?" said Chitchee.

"The Earl of Bozeman. He's not in the picture."

Gudrun twitched a tiny muscle under her eye.

"Sausage Man," whispered Gudrun, "is Edelweiss's son. He's paid to live here and follow you."

"Why?" asked Kennedy.

"You are," said Gudrun, pointing her finger from her eye to Chitchee, pointing back at her eye, and creating an Aleph out of three fingers, "plotting to overthrow the United States government, aren't you? Because if you are, you're my hero!"

"What?" said Chitchee, bending down to kiss Gudrun on the lips. "Isn't everybody plotting to overthrow the United States government? Especially Congress?"

"Do you have to go out in the freezing cold?" whispered Gudrun, dreaming in his eyes. "Please help me. I'm in danger for my life here."

"Yes, but this is important, Gudrun," said Chitchee. "Kennedy and I are going to meet a Frenchman about my learning French. I'll be back soon with a DVD we can both watch on a DVD player. Scratch me up later. You'll love it. It's about a French girl who speaks French in order to meet a cute French guy. And a lot of cute French stuff happens, in French, but since she knows French, and she is really astronomically cute, she isn't too worried about anything when the movie ends. Oh, I forgot my Carousel Square! I wanted to show it off to friends. It's the only Christmas gift I'll get this year!"

"It's for your book store," said Gudrun with a tiny wink of scrutiny.

Chitchee ran up the staircases, two at a time, bounding with his feet turned into claws. A house of mice flew through the air and cats continued snoozing in the corners. Sliding back down the banisters into the living room, Chitchee carried the partridge feather-stuffed pillow, encased in the colors of a blazing chariot wheel's rainbow fires.

Chitchee awkwardly crammed the Carousel Square, brick-shaped pillow into his Jansport backpack.

"If you don't miss me now," cried Gudrun, "I don't see how you'll miss me when I'm gone!"

Edelweiss and Sausage Man looked at each other as if at the reading of a family will and then discovered they had been cut out of it. They held cinnamon-raisin, buttered toast, frozen stiffly when Gudrun turned around and screamed after the front door slammed:

"No! I didn't do anything! WHY ARE YOU PUNISHING ME?"

The smoked-glass, black walnut front door shut behind Chitchee and Kennedy and they cut like diagonal slashes of infinities through the ice-faced sheets of layered gusts, knocking them back in waves into a weightless sea of snow, Kennedy's scarf flying off his neck and wrapping itself around Chitchee's head.

The distantly approaching #10 bus arose like steam off Lake Superior. Then disappeared.

"*Hear my bus a-comin'*!" repeated Chitchee over and over. "Said: *I don't hear my bus a-comin'*!"

"We missed it!" said Kennedy, replacing the scarf around his neck.

"Check the schedule," said Chitchee, his hands like ice-balls in frozen mittens, "if that is still there."

"Central Avenue," said Kennedy. "#10. Is it six o' clock yet? Riverside to Cedar? No. We want Nicollet. Let's walk."

When they walked a half-block, the #10 bus sped by them. They ran crazily to the next bus stop, fortunately filled with frozen stiffs, giving Chitchee and Kennedy enough time to catch up and get on. But when they stepped off the #10, the wind picked up more gusto. No matter which way they turned the wind slapped their open cheeks. Propelling forward in the dark down Marquette Avenue, they downturned offers for discounted transfers. Waiting silently, they stood like shivering, giant commas at the bus stop for a #5. In frozen silence, they exhaled crystal streams of cold air, forming warm, popcorn-shaped puffs. Once on the sparsely-passengered #5 bus, they had their transfers punched.

"Yeah, Kennedy," said Chitchee, looking out the ovoid window, "how do I know this Frenchy connection isn't wearing a wire? I should have grabbed Hawk Eye's Derringer! This is already too much film noir!"

"I never thought I'd see the day I'd look at money and say 'Wow, money!'" said Kennedy, smiling wistfully as if to pick his teeth but couldn't afford a toothpick.

Kennedy shrugged, smiled, looked out his window through his own reflection, and felt the pain attenuate slowly so he could breathe normally.

"Or the day," added Rashid, having overheard from the back and moved up, "I'd be arrested for biking without a rear reflector! It went to a jury trial and I lost because the thumpers lied through their perfect teeth. Then I lost my job and then I was evicted. The landlord forced his way into my apartment to shut off the circuit breakers, claiming he was preventing anarchists like me from taking over the building. These Minneapolis landlords don't need knives, they have lawyers."

"Yeah, it's not Lake Woebegone," said Chitchee.

"Garrison Keillor," said Rashid, "I bumped into him outside the Uptown Theater. When I said hi, he stared at me like I was a type of Hawaiian sea snail."

"So?" asked Chitchee.

"So I said to him," said Rashid, "if you can't say hi, go back to your fucking Lake Woebegone, asshole! Learn to tell a fucking joke that's funny! Any blacks in Woebegone? No? 'Coz they all took one look at all the motherfucking confederate flags around your frozen Lake Woebegone in hell, and went: *We-be-gone*, motherfucker!"

"I'll run inside Wendy's," said Kennedy. "You stay outside until I give you the signal."

The bus crunched on the crunched snow, stopping on a crunch. The frozen wind rushed up the corrugated steps of the bus to warm itself.

"All this for fucking *Amelie*?" asked Chitchee, looking at icicles hanging outside Wendy's.

A frost obscured the roast-beefed indoors, the frost climbing the plate-glass in hills and bounds. When Chitchee breathed out, he created more misty hills and misty bounds.

Snow cleaned the air, and the cleaned air tasted clear, bright, and sharp on Chitchee's tongue. He blew hot breath into his lightly-clenched, curled red fingers carefully taken out of his orange mittens, and it hurt to get the feeling back in his hands.

"Frenchy isn't home," said Kennedy huddled outside, plastic spoons, napkins, and Hellman's mayonnaise packets stuffed into his pockets. "I inquired of the manager, Craig. Craig said Frenchy moved back to the McDonald's by Hiawatha. Not only is that a false narrative but it's not true at all. Because I KNOW Frenchy utilizes *that* McDonald's for his summer residency in the 3rd Precinct. In that way, the 5th Precinct will forget his identity."

"No! No Frenchy?" said Chitchee. "There goes the *Academie Francaise*!"

"Maybe college programming for computers at MCTC *is* the right thing for you now," conjectured Kennedy. "It's not like you're going to swarm the barricades and breach Harvard any time soon."

"I should take another gap year off," said Chitchee, so cold he almost screamed. "Here comes a bus, I think. Is that a snow plow? It's a snow plow! I AM FREEZING! Hurry up yo' ass, bus! Don't make me put my foot up yo' ass, bus! Kennedy, I'm hungry, aren't you?"

"Don't worry," said Kennedy. "I have an 'in' through a back door at a food shelf in West St. Paul."

"Kennedy," said Chitchee. "I can't see digging tunnels underground to rip off a food shelf in West St. Paul, wherever West in St. Paul is."

"We don't have the tools," said Kennedy. "We'll have to dig around for those. Damn! So can you get me the substance? You know! The stuff. The green matter. The green magistrate. I can't keep riffing for it with all this riffle raffle. Undone Buttons, Motherfuckin Green Eyes, Mad Jack Appleflap, Mad Jack the Barley Toad, Mad Jack This, Mad Jack That . . . everyone we know is mad! They are all lost souls, like us! Why is that?"

Chitchee could get weed from Raven, but Chitchee would have to leave a nuanced, purple-coded message on Raven's message machine, whose cassette ribbon had worn itself out into transparency and static; then they would have to wait two astrological signs minus a house of Venus and a retrograde Capricorn divided by two Gemini for the actual drop off time. The drop off had always been in BookSmart's bathroom ceiling. By standing on the toilet and pushing up on one square of the acoustic tiles you could stash stuff in the ceiling.

"Riff raff, like us?" Chitchee asked Chitchee, because Kennedy was lost in thought.

"Do you think we will all be snatched off the street someday and placed in mental wards?" asked Kennedy.

"Given enough madmen," said Chitchee, seeing their bus.

Kennedy stepped aboard the #23, and there sat Lake Street Rodney, Undone Buttons, Motherfuckin Green Eyes, and Mad Jack Apple Jack huddled together in the back seats reserved with a sign that read LOST SOULS MEET UP.

"Look! Who needs mental wards when we have public transportation? More riffle raffle like us!" exclaimed Chitchee, following closely behind Kennedy, finding a clean seat, sitting behind Kennedy, and leaning forward to hear Kennedy.

Kennedy stretched his legs out across the seat, boots in the aisle dropping snowmelt, and he intoned excitedly:

"Here's the deal: I asked Frenchy to sell my own Vicodin prescription, which I appraised at an estimated value of $120. He said sure, here's a hot iPhone for collateral, replacing the previous hot iPhone 3 he pawned on me. Which I never got activated. But Frenchy absconded on the megabus to Milwaukee, and didn't come back for a couple weeks. And when he did come back he professed he only got $65 for the Vicodin. So he starts postulating, 'Can I have the iPhone back? It's worth way more than I thought! It's worth $165!' So I lied. I told Frenchy that I already sold it coincidentally for $65 bucks. Frenchy conjoindered: we will call it even, if you get me a book from your book store on how to pick up women and you buy another iPhone from me at $50 (the only thing wrong with it is the screen is cracked). But I'm absconding again on the megabus to Madison, Wisconsin in two days."

"So, you're thinking that Frenchy already moved the *Amelie* DVD?" asked Chitchee, looking at the frosted window, tracing shapes he had seen from Lascaux, and seeing the shaman with the reindeer head-dress, hand-print, and thumb-print.

"It could have been snapped up like the wind," said Kennedy. "Frenchy is a five-star maestro salesman. He could sell the Brooklyn Bridge to the Brooks Brothers and win it back off them in a poker game. That's the kind of advanced skill set we are talking about here. He's gifted with that peculiar kind of magic-selling snake oil. He lies even when his lips aren't moving. A lot of his sebaceous smoothness and chiconnery, he prevaricated from a bunch of books on dealing he fished out of the BookSmart dumpster."

A frozen Hawk Eye gimped onto the bus like a gate-legged table.

Hawk Eye had the bad habit of guessing the ethnic background of everyone he met and impressing them with a few words he picked up in his capacity as a Navy Seal behind all our enemy lines on secret missions, shouting decoy hellos.

"Are you Japanese? *Kon'nichiwa?*" Hawk Eye immediately asked the bus driver. "Are you Korean? *Annyeong? Annyeonghaseyo?* You're Chinese? What the hell are you?"

"Vietnamese."

"Oh," Hawk Eye paused dejectedly. "They only taught us how to curse in Vietnamese."

"You betcha," said the Vietnamese bus driver.

"Do you know what I heard about *that* guy?" nudged Kennedy, looking straight at Hawk Eye and forcing Chitchee to look straight at Hawk Eye in synchrony. "A Vietnam vet who works at the Veterans Administration told me that guy used to cut a little hole in his stomach and funnel it full with gunpowder to stay awake on monthly patrols with no sleep, but now he cuts open his stomach and fills it with gunpowder so as not to fall asleep because of the horrendous flashbacks."

"Hey, Hawk Eye," yelled Chitchee. "Hawk Eye, do you cut yourself and pour gunpowder in your wounds?"

"Bullshit! Where did you hear that?" asked Hawk Eye, working his jaw back and forth and touching the black sore on his frozen lower lip.

"Kennedy here," said Chitchee.

"I sleep like a god-damned, shit-assed baby," said Hawk Eye, sitting down in front of them, looking over his shoulder, and whispering, "did you get my you-know-what . . . the . . . hand . . . gun . . . the Derringer."

"I never got it," said Chitchee.

"You didn't see anyone leave BookSmart with a loaded Derringer did you? I left the Derringer there for you."

"No," said Chitchee, "but I'm going over there to give Aloysius a pillow for Christmas. I'll ask him if he's seen any Derringers go out."

"I suggest," said Kennedy, looking over his shoulder, "we pick up some Kemps ice cream at Rainbow Grocery and we advert the subject of firearms for another menu . . . um they say we scuttle a language every fortnight, so if you temporize too long, French won't even exist!"

As Hawk Eye slowly thawed, he pondered this truth statement with a seriously industrious face like a platypus working hard at whatever it is platypuses do.

"*Mon Dieu*," thought aloud Chitchee, and he felt himself getting a little louder the more he melted and the more the lakeshore of his memory unfroze itself.

Chitchee stood up in the aisle and announced:

"Hey everybody, in a hundred years, we will lose 5,500 languages . . . leaving behind about five hundred languages . . . and that should dwindle by the year 2200 to about twenty or so languages, and then one big language by 2300 . . . and that mono-language will get simplified to a pidgin in another hundred years . . . and then it will become a super-complicated programmed artificial code for language bots, and human beings will be clinging to Facebook with their last two hundred words like: "block," "troll," "clickbait," "set to private," "deactivate," and "delete account." And then all the lights will go out, and the computers will take over in a cyber coup, thinking that we're bugs or tanks . . . and kill us through the nano-particles in our thumbprints. And here we are, Rainbow Foods, it's our stop!"

The sparsely-seated bus with Undone Buttons, Motherfuckin Green Eyes, and Mad Jack Apple Jack broke up to get off.

"Stay warm!" the Vietnamese bus driver laughed.

"We must love one another or die," replied Chitchee with LBJ's Texas Twang.

As the bus took off, Chitchee had second thoughts, staring ahead of himself at the snowed-over, icy sidewalk.

RAINBOW FOODS GROCERY STORE

Chitchee and Kennedy, not warm enough yet and covered with snow, traipsed into the Rainbow Foods grocery store like Rosencranz and Guildenstern onto a stage-lighted *Fiddler on the Roof* already in progress. Immediately, Chitchee saw that his Fremont Terrace next door neighbor, Washington Spelz (so his mailbox had read) from #106, was in the bakery section. Chitchee dashed off for the meat section, bypassing produce and cutting a dash up the aisle of brown rice and beans labeled "International." Chitchee crossed his fingers mentally. With any luck, the meat counter, a brightly-lighted slope of steaks, pork chops, and chicken breasts, might have discounted chubs of tube hamburger with advanced expiration dates—marked down three dollars. Chitchee knew that the night manager, Cave Man, sensed him, and imagined him through the two-way mirror to which Chitchee waved hello.

"I know you're in there somewhere, Cave Man!"

"Hi Chitchee," said the mirror backwards. "What's new?"

Chitchee looked up, startled that the two-way mirror had talked back. He continued to eye the ribeyes, admiring the portions and proportions of healthy and unhealthy beef when Nicky Fingers T-boned him in the T-bones. As usual Nicky despaired for dough and a friend. He said he was fresh out of the Plymouth workhouse where he checked out five books a week from the county library system, but gangbangers yelled shit all the time, so he had to read at night, yelling shut the fuck up every time he turned a page in the book *The Birth of the Prison* by Foucault.

"So what were they shouting?" asked Chitchee, curious.

"More Triple Crown! Fuck, if I know! Those gangers!"

"Those T-bones look good, don't they?" asked Chitchee, no longer curious.

"Chitchee, did you hear what happened to Dougal? The gangrene spread, Chitchee."

"Yeah, you told me."

"They had to chop his toes off. Power-sawing right through the bone. He got to keep his toes in a giant Kimchi jar of formaldehyde, Chitchee."

"Yeah, I know, Nicky, remember he showed me his toes in the library?"

"Hack-sawed his toes off, I think it was a hacksaw—"

"Hack-sawed his . . .," said Chitchee. "You mean they don't have power tools at HCMC by now?"

"Have you seen Dougal lately?" asked Nicky. "He's really losing his memory. And Mjollnir, he's a hippie from the last Ice Age. He didn't have any memory to lose. You know Nestor, right? Seen him lately? Noel hates me, but Aloysius thinks I'm great! He lets me watch the store when he needs to go out and get a burger or something. Whatever happened to Jeff? Did he die? Or did he move in with the Chameleon Slut Monster? Did you ever know that one guy, Matt, seen him? Did he die? Have you seen Mike? Or Brad? Mike the Bouncer at Augie's. Do you know any living Dans? Seen any of them lately?"

"Settle down," said Chitchee. "Nobody ever dies around here."

"Chitchee, Dougal showed me his feet—where the gangene is spreading—like raw tube hamburger, three dollars off, with foot fungus. Yechh! He's a goner, Chitchee."

"Well, I guess," said Chitchee, "but no one ever accused Dougal of trying to walk the straight and narrow."

"That was cold, Chitchee," said Nicky. "Chitchee, for you. Cold. I always thought you were too nice. Anyway, they don't fool around, those doctors at MCTC. Gangrene spreads like fireballs. Your flesh burns up, turns to black pus and mush, and it's all swishing around inside your body like maggots. Can you imagine maggots chomping on your wiener, like, and your wiener falls off, like, and before the maggots can get at it, a brown recluse fucking nails it? That's what it's like. But you're right, who cares? Are you interested in some SD cards for cheap, Chitchee? How about a candy bar, buy that, Chitchee?"

"Not right now, maybe when I get my tax returns back from 2005," said Chitchee. "I'm sorry, Nicky, that life dealt you a worthless hand. And you're reduced to stealing cheap junk from gas stations like a magpie."

"Geez, Chitch, I wasn't asking for your pity!" said Nicky. "I wasn't asking for any pity from the bourgeoisie."

"Sorry," said Chitchee.

"Where are you going? I thought you wanted to buy these brand new SD cards, Chitchee!"

Chitchee plowed down the aisles boustrophedon-style.

"Kennedy!" hollered Chitchee. "Where are you? How are we going to buy ice cream if we don't sell your hot iPhone somewhere?"

Kennedy, gripping the bucket of Kemps ice cream, stood stiff as a heron in line at checkout lane 2 looking embarrassed. The whole store's eyes had him under a microscope. He crouched behind an artfully-colored, cute bag of awfully-flavored potato chips.

Standing up straight like a human periscope, Nicky looked around for Cave Man, who, by evidence of his absence, was still red-in-the-face from protecting the meat in the meat section behind the meat mirror because he knew the meathead Nicky Fingers had only been using the meathead Chitchee as a screen for casing the meat case. Nicky had been trespassed from Rainbow already for running out the door with a rotisserie chicken in a white bag and two onions only to be tackled cleanly by the manager Michelle in the parking lot, where he claimed the chicken was already dead so he didn't think they wanted it.

Courtney Kirkwood was a new cashier, wearing curlers in her hair. Chitchee walked around the check-out counter and sneaked up behind her.

He hugged Courtney a huggy-bear hug—lifting Courtney off and on the floor up and down.

"Snorri?" asked Courtney, rebalancing into her aerial ballerina slip-ons unsuccessfully. "Oh! Chitchee! It's you! Put me down! I thought you were Snorri!"

"Hi Courtney, I didn't know you worked here!" said Chitchee.

"You'll make me lose my curlers! I *have* to work here after Governor Pawlenty slashed my food stamps and my medical. Now he wants my rent credit too. The legislature cut the bus routes so I can't get anywhere. And now I have to pay for the Twins baseball park, but our city-wide referendum rejected it, which Pawlenty vetoed soze he could stuff his buttered face with more lobsters and look down his buttered chin at us from his VIP Lounge with his triumphant crooks. He might as well go around all the Section 8 apartments and take a box-cutter and slash the wrists of us fixed-income folks. Why do all the politicians in Minnesota hate us? What did we ever do to them? Did we interfere with their Winnebagos? Like it's *Death Race 2000* out there with their Winnebagos! And all the loony politicians are running us over on purpose!"

"What else can a politician do with his life?" asked Chitchee. "What if everyone had to run for their lives all the time?"

At the front of Courtney's #2 check-out line holding two off-brand colas bigger than scuba tanks was Chitchee's other Fremont Terrace neighbor Towey Levins, the Green Bay Packer fan turned University of Minnesota Golden Gopher fan, dressed as Goldy the Golden Gopher. Towey Levins had a full shopping cart of ten thick-crust, boxed Green Mill pizzas. He looked ensconced in University of Minnesota Golden Gopher regalia—maroon and gold sweatpants and a Goldy the Golden Gopher maroon knit cap with a golden pom pom.

"I guess you like Morehead State," said Courtney.

"You mean the University of Minnesota," said Towey Levins.

"Minnesota State, Meathead State, I get 'em all mixed up!"

"Looks like you get a lot of things mixed up," smirked Towey Levins.

Courtney made a meowling growl. Kennedy smiled.

"That's some dope shit," said Washington Spelz, the crack-dealing neighbor in #106 with his red-rimmed pomegranate rinds for peepers gazing at the scuba tanks of generic cola.

"It'ssshh not a dumb sss—shirt," said Towey Levins.

"I didn't say it was a dope shirt, you dumbfuck!" said Washington Spelz.

"Fuck you, asshole, you said dumb not dope!" replied Towey Levins. "Dumbfuck!"

"You dope-shirted douchebag," said Washington Spelz. "I never called you no dumbfuck, you fuckin' dumb-assed douche bro."

Towey Levins was walkinginging away mutteringinging about goinginging to "get that fucker in the lot."

"Hey, Charlie Brown!" said Courtney.

Towey Levins froze.

"Hey," said Courtney, walking after him, "you—"

Towey Levins, his back turned toward the opening glass door, dropped the Green Mill pizza boxes, swung around, and sucker-punched Courtney and the blue curlers out of Courtney's hair.

"Boom!" said Towey Levins with his punch

"—forgot your soda—" said Courtney on the floor's rubber mat by the automatic doors.

"Don't call it soda!" said Towey Levins. "It's called 'pop' in Minne-sooota!"

"Security to Register 2!" said the crawled-back Courtney into the microphone and out the speakers. "May Day! May Day! Register 2!"

Chitchee collected Courtney's blue curlers off the floor while Courtney casually turned to Kanishka Amma and his extended family, who were placing their groceries on the conveyor belt and watching their smashing loaves of bread get more smashed.

"I love India, and I have no control over that," said Courtney, frowning at the backed-up, exotic vegetables cascading over the counter to the floor, the sight of which helped her regain her composure until the unrequited Cave Man walked by frowning judgmentally at his lost love again. She couldn't get fired for smashing groceries—even if Cave Man sometimes hated Courtney for rejecting his advances in the meat department.

"I always watch India," said Courtney. "Jadpoor. My favorite show. Does your father know English, your brother? I don't want to say anything stupid!"

"This is my mother, she is a retired Professor Emeritus of Anthropology from the University of Heidelberg," said Kanishka, placing his reading book on the check stand while producing his credit card. "She studied Comparative Religions under Mircea Elieade at the University of Chicago; she has a Ph D. from Harvard in Archeology; and she was a lecturer at UCLA with Marija Gombutas. My distinguished mother is visiting from New Mexico where she was recently invited by Murray Gell-Mann to the Sante Fe Institute after she received her MacArthur Fellowship."

"How do!" said Courtney. "Are these Brussel sprouts? Look at all this vegetarian fruit! I know you people worship elephants, but you have lions there in India, don't you there? A lady scientist is protecting them. I'd love to go there and be a lady scientist protecting lions. Even if I have to pray at shrines to gold mice! No worries, I have to pray at shrines to the gold mice *here*! Or they will evict me and cut off my medical assistance."

The entire over-extended Amma family scrambled to open paper and plastic bags to catch a marching army of plums, oranges, bananas, jackfruit like giant goiters, smashed blueberries, kiwis, guavas, mangoes, and a rearguard of pomegranates wheeling in.

"Do you have a Rewards Card?" asked Courtney, glancing at the floor of plums, oranges, bananas, jackfruit like giant goiters, smashed blueberries, kiwis, guavas, and the rearguard of marching mangoes and pomegranates falling and dying on top of the wounded. "It always does that when I'm here!"

Courtney scratched a nail on an emery board and used a fingernail clipper to clip off the one chipped, broken Revloned nail.

"Hey! Kanishka! Jim Corbett!" said Chitchee. "*The Man-Eaters of Kumaon*! Read that one?"

"Are you calling them all cannibals?" asked Courtney. "That's prejudiced, Chitchee. Better be careful with politically correct cannibals hunting us down. Do they look carnivorous? See for yourself. All they eat is smashed fruit. And Jim Corbett there ain't no nickel and dime bumshow. His mom is a retired Embolitis of Anthropology at the mercy of the University of Archeology in Chicago and went to LA with Mary Bea Arthur from Harvard. And she knows Bill Murray from an institution in Sante Fe."

"Have you read *Vikram* yet?" asked Chitchee. "See? I never forget a book with a face!"

"Ha, ha, yes," said Kanishka. "You remember me *and* the book! But do you remember the riddle?"

"Not really," said Chitchee.

"Who doesn't like a good riddle?" asked Kanishka.

"Me," said Chitchee.

"A daughter's grandmother," said Kanishka, "is married to the son of the daughter's grandfather. How?"

"Now I'm going to have that *ouroboros* in my brain all night!" said Chitchee, who saw Larry on an iPhone business call. "Hey, Larry!"

Kanishka's family made for the exit with a full shopping cart.

"Cheating on your wife again, Larry?" yelled Chitchee. "Wait, Kanishka! What about a Diwali Thanksgiving next Thanksgiving?

Make a mental note of that."

"Okay," said Kanishka over his shoulder. "I'll see you around!"

Chitchee hopped on the moving conveyor belt for a free ride, which halted. He hopped off. He broke it.

"I got it to stop!" said Chitchee.

Larry was mentally disheveled, his pink Arrow shirttail was out. At his side, Reina from New World Sunrise Massage And Spa, looked like a little girl who got lost in her mother's walk-in closet, while trying on her wardrobe, mirror-wise, for fun. Larry threw jelly beans in a plastic bag, flipped his arm around Reina, and warned her not to listen to "el local loco loser," who had the "wrong Larry." Larry bundled her off, Reina looking scared of the cold parking lot.

Kennedy suggested going to Carousel Square after they dropped off the Carousel Square pillow at BookSmart for Aloysius, because Chitchee didn't need a pillow—besides it was hard as brick, and it would look great in the BookSmart window. They could share the Kemps ice cream at the marble-topped tables outside Ragnarok's Choklit Stoppe in the Carousel Square atrium, which was open all night.

"Sorry about the wait," said Courtney, "everybody."

Then she grabbed the microphone.

"Everybody! Quit getting in my line!" continued Courtney. "This isn't a fucking popularity contest—just because I'm young and beautiful."

"Is Carousel Square still *there?*" Chitchee asked Kennedy. "A whole *week* has passed since I passed by Carousel Square. Maybe it declared bankruptcy. By now Martensen could have boarded it up, sold it to who knows who, who replaced it with an identical Carousel Square, doubled the rent, gutted it, then boarded it up to be sold to the next sucker born that minute as an Uptown bargain. Or maybe it flew back to the Pleiades with Captain Melchizedek at the controls."

"And ran out of zero fusion rocket fuel," added Kennedy, "and crash landed in Lakewood Cemetery."

"A-ha, Al-*lah!*" said Chitchee. "Y-a-a-a-ssss!"

They could stay warm outside Ragnarok's Choklit Stoppe, because Ragnarok's Choklit Stoppe's chained and locked, marble-topped tables were left out at night after closing, making Ragnarok's a good place to "matriculate various business machinations in the prospects of financing the gas lackage situation, which was needed to get the Arctic Cat road soluble."

"Didn't ol' lady Edelweiss have gas cans in the garage?" asked Chitchee. "I thought I saw some."

"She did," said Kennedy, "but someone stole them like that Mickey Fingers friend of yours I saw by the steaks, who I don't want to know either. Don't introduce me to your friends, or I'll be dodge-balling them all day long everywhere I go! We'll have to buy gas cans with the proceeds from the iPhone sale parsleyed ahead into further . . . deals . . . it would be nice to pick up, you know, the thing, the merchandise, the rope, the alfalfa, the communion boat, the green uhuru, the gathered magic, you know, the Xbox360."

"Raven might walk by with a little something . . ." said Chitchee.

"A little something? Jesus! Shhh . . ." Kennedy flinched, looked around the Rainbow Grocery store at all the checked-out people, ducked below the check-out counter, and then strained his neck for hidden cameras. "Don't say 'a little something' in Rainbow! They have secret tape recorders wired all over the place, waiting to be ACTIVATED by 'A LITTLE SOMETHING!'"

"If Carousel Square," said Chitchee, feeling pinched and reprimanded, "*does* go out of business again, only to be replaced by a Target on the ground floor, and a condo up to the clouds, who would notice?"

"Only the termites," said Courtney. "Just the 5 gallons of ice cream for you then? Perfect for a nice cold winter's night. Carousel Square is gone now, didja say? Oh, perfect. So much for the assholes at L. A. Hole Fitness. It's just Kemps ice cream for you big suspenders then? Okay?"

Larry Sangster galloped into the Rainbow Grocery store; he looked mugged by his own ghost.

"Did I leave my phone here?" asked Larry, the sweat drooling down his forehead like Christmas candle wax.

Outside a pissing contest had transpired between Chitchee's two neighbors from the Fremont Terrace Apartments.

"Did someone call for security?" asked Bobblehead. "Present."

Bobblehead wore the gray, synthetic weave of a uniform drowning him, shirt bunched up, belt sliding off his hips, large eyeglasses that gave you the impression of a house-fly version of Yves Saint Laurent, and heavy-handed shoes that clanked like dreadnoughts.

"Someone stole my iPhone!" said Larry Sangster, his terra firma dissolving into a brown slush beneath his Kenneth Cole lace-ups. "I set it down on the counter. I just had it. I just saw it right here! It's an iPhone! For God sakes! An iPhone! Someone call the FBI!"

A patrol car ramped up the curb. It emitted Officers Weatherwax and Weatherwax.

The altercation intensified to the point that #110 Towey Levins in his Goldy the Golden Gopher suit had his ID on him but #106 Washington Spelz didn't. #106 thought he had his wallet on him, but when his slow arm was busy reaching for his wallet—kaboomadee bam!

"Excited delirium!" said Officer Weatherwax.

Washington Spelz was spread-eagled on the hood of the squad car, his jaw grimacing, chin digging into the hood.

"Get him, he's a bad apple," grinned Towey Levins.

Free to go, Goldy the Golden Gopher invisibled himself, returned to the fraternity party at Fremont Terrace, drank himself toward intoxicated death, grabbed all the girls' private parts, ate a whole Green Mill pizza in one sitting, fell down some stairs, passed out, and threw up like a fire hose on someone's couch.

Lights and noise from the thumper's patrol car inside Rainbow Grocery scattered little children with their little fingers in their little ears. Some cried, some were scolded for crying. Bobblehead couldn't wait for it to end, because he was crying too.

"Somebody call for more cops!" said Larry, unable to believe that the squad car was more interested in Washington Spelz and drove off.

Kennedy double-wrapped the Kemps ice cream in two plastic polyethylene bags and dropped it into two Rainbow Foods paper bags with handles. They walked past Washington Spelz staring straight forward in the back of the squad car.

THE iPHONE INFINITY

Shuffling onto the tricky, black-iced sidewalk's iced-over Lethe, the two picked their way across a snow-banked Hennepin Avenue, under shining street lamps that stood entwined with Christmas wreaths of evergreen. The pine tree's branches were covered with illuminated white caterpillars. Globe bulbs in glass-enclosed, Victorian lanterns allowed one to see that BookSmart had an OPEN sign on the door, but it was covered with snow that sometimes calved off in clumps.

Aloysius slept exhausted in his office chair, bedtime getting earlier and earlier in the descending darkness of winter nights.

"Chitchee? Kennedy?" asked Aloysius, dumping his Walgreen cheaters on his nose and re-setting the open book of Robert Frost on his lap. "What are you doing out there in the freezing cold? It is *Ice Station Zebra* out there!"

"Merry Christmas, Aloysius!" said Chitchee, taking the Carousel Square pillow out of his backpack.

"A pillow?" said Aloysius, scratching his head with admiration. "Thanks much! I'll put it in the front window where everyone on Hennepin can enjoy it!"

"I thought you'd love it!" said Chitchee, hugging Aloysius, who dropped the pillow like a slippery, scaly, vicious arctic salmon.

"Look how cool it is, it's a crocheted tesseract," continued Chitchee, picking up the pillow. "It's a square, but it's a cube. It's a cube, but it's a cube within a cube. So it represents the n-dimensional space we are in!"

"Ok," said Aloysius. "Thanks much! Like I said, I'll put it in the window. Have a good one, guys!"

"And," continued Chitchee, picking up the pillow and unable to bend it, "if you bend the pillow you can mimic non-Euclidean, Gaussian geometry and get relativistic effects!"

"I could give it to Viktor the landlord as a Christmas peace offering," said Aloysius, "come to think of it."

"Keep on truckling!" commented Chitchee. "You are the man!"

Chitchee and Kennedy walked into a headwind from all four directions. Whichever way they turned—the icy wind flensed their exposed skin. Their scarves over their palimpsest mouths reproduced their mouths in mouth-prints of ice whenever one of them yelled something like a hunting call through their scarves. They slodged into the whale-mouthed entrance of Lake & Hennepin's Carousel Square.

"Do you think he liked the pillow?" asked Chitchee. "I have a soft spot in my heart for that pillow. And for Aloysius for that matter. He's done all he can to keep Minneapolis a thriving, intellectual Mecca and . . . yeah, I have funny feelings about that pillow."

"Gudrun," said Kennedy, "wanted you to appreciate it. You hurt her feelings. I am almost positive she wanted your self-approbation. Why didn't you see that?"

Chitchee was terror struck at Kennedy's correct assessment. Chitchee couldn't believe that he hadn't appreciated Gudrun's pillow enough. Stunned at his own lack of empathy, he bit his hand and shouted to the deserted mall:

"Hang me!"

"Sorry, Kennedy," continued Chitchee. "Life is so *brief*, it's barely worth mentioning; at the same time, life is so *endless* you never want to stop talking about it."

Then Chitchee and Kennedy stamped their frozen toes and feet to shake off the snow. A frosty, shivering brick mall, itself a brick in the vast landscape of brick malls, shivering in a brick-malled country, greeted them and their condensed breaths. Chitchee puffed into his artificially arthritic fists, red and pink as frozen tulips. He worked the red blood cells back into his arteries. Two jumping jacks and a push up did nothing. Chitchee walked in circles, shivering in a delayed reaction, while Kennedy walked counter-clockwise circles, both staring at the mezzo-tinted tiling pattern of the faux floor, the verdigris dead fountains with spinach in them, and the bright chandeliers without lights. Everybody knew that Carousel Square always bucked its small business owners off its merry-go-round of chained-together chain stores, while it somehow remained "vibrant," "revitalizing," and "gentrific."

Chitchee and Kennedy sat down at a wrought-iron, marble-topped, out-of-kilter coffee table (paper wadding under one fleur-de-lis table leg), its three chairs facing the atrium. They witnessed their breaths because a trapped automatic door at the entrance pushed frozen air inside.

"Chitchee!" heard Chitchee.

"Raven, you're up early!" said Chitchee, smiling a tired smile. "It's not even midnight yet. Do you know Kennedy? Have you guys met?"

"Kennedy?" asked Raven, shaking the red icicles off his red beard, his blotched red cheekbones under his woolen, flap-eared hat lined with caribou belly fur.

The long red icicles dangled over his heavy woolen overcoat when he unbuttoned and asked Kennedy:

"You knew Kennedy *wasn't* assassinated by Oswald, didn't you?"

"President Kennedy?" asked Kennedy. "How *did* he die?"

"He committed suicide, where were you?" asked Raven, sitting down with authority on a wrought-iron cafe chair.

"In Kenya," replied Kennedy, "waiting for the Queen to matriculate her ass on out of there."

"Look at the Magruder film, it's obvious. Come on, Chitchee, you work in a book store! Tell him!"

"But *how?*" asked Chitchee with a wrinkled nose that expected to sneeze.

"With mirrors," continued Raven. "All that can be done with mirrors. You work in a—"

"Raven," interrupted Chitchee. "I don't work in a book store. No one works in a book store anymore—except Aloysius who doesn't work in a book store either. Aloysius couldn't pay us anymore. I know the whole neighborhood loved BookSmart, but we couldn't pay the rent for some unknown reason I know all about, which I'd rather not discuss—because it could get me killed. The Fraternal Order of Police could snatch me off the sidewalk and throw me off the Hennepin Avenue Bridge!"

"Oh, brother!" said Raven. "You sure come up with some real doozies!"

"And *I'm* a musician too!" said Chitchee.

"That's not good enough to be thrown off a bridge," declared Raven. "You have to be in the musician's union to be thrown off the bridge by the policeman's union."

"I'm sticking with selling books," said Chitchee, urged to bite his hand and scream out of uncertainty. "Books are what I know for sure."

"Chitchee, I *told* you," said Raven. "Americans don't read books—Americans read *palms*. Americans don't read anything! They read Tarot Cards and tea leaves. That's why BookSmart should be a Tarot Card reading room that sells metaphysical tea-bags and spiritualized minerals—like that famous shamanic healer Torsten Tripspittle, and he's not even Native American! He lives in a mansion on Lake Minnetonka and sells quack remedies to the rich bitches in Wayzata. He might as well be printing off his own money! And I *told* Aloysius to branch out into wellness woo woo, palm readings, and healing talismans, but he wouldn't listen to me!"

"Was he asleep?" asked Chitchee. "Was he lying there like a goldfish at the bottom of a goldfish tank? Sometimes you have to hold him down and force his eyes open to make eye contact with him."

"I don't think he fell asleep," said Raven, "until I started telling him about Moldavite's protective powers!"

"He's a little off his game after all the daily extortions, blackmail, and death threats," said Chitchee. "He owes so much back rent that the landlord is holding him hostage, so that BookSmart can be a front for Viktor Martensen's global, burgeoning criminal empire."

"I knew that," said Raven. "But none of that would have happened if he had placed the *Moldavite* I gave him under his pillow!"

"Weird! I just gave him a *pillow* to put on top of the Moldavite!" said Chitchee. "Isn't that weird, Kennedy? Weird! That was either synchronicity or a message from the future about synchronicity . . . Anyway, my wingman and I wondered whether you could front us some *purple nuggets of amethyst from the capital of Kashmir.*"

"*Weird!* And I was just going to stash a nugget for you in the BookSmart bathroom above the toilet in the acoustic tiles in case you asked me that," said Raven. "So weird!"

"Really?" asked Chitchee and Kennedy both getting up to go to BookSmart's bathroom.

"But I went to Cheapo instead," said Raven. "And I met this super cool cat at Cheapo who knows you. We were both going for the used Coltrane CDs in jazz. We both wanted *Live at the Village Vanguard*. They only had one copy and he said I could buy it, because he was actually in the audience! He saw Coltrane play in person in Greenwich Village. So I thanked him and gave him that rabbit's foot you didn't want for a good luck charm. At first he refused."

"He refused a rabbit's foot?" asked Chitchee.

"Can you believe it?" asked Raven.

"Anybody want to buy an iPhone?" asked Nicky Fingers abruptly as if barking loudly outside a circus tent and tied by a rope to a stake.

Nicky's face was a composite of every Minneapolitan, thirty-something musician—every averaged-out, MOR, white-banded, blue-eyed guitarist who has ever been caught off-guard in a black-out, while his f-hole guitar was being stolen from the back of his band's bland van by some guy who looked exactly like him.

"Chitchee," said Nicky with his overly-familiar friendliness, "check out this iPhone I have for sale! And who is this? I don't believe I have had the honor of an introduction yet, Chitchee? Chitchee? Do the honors?"

"Oh, Nicky," said Chitchee. "This is Kennedy, who doesn't want to know you, and this is Raven, who is better off not knowing you."

"An honor and a privilege, my good sirs. Kennedy and . . . sorry I didn't catch your name, was it 'Radon?' Chitchee, check it out. I have to take a mad whizz you guys. I'll be right back. Here are some really dope SD cards I figured you all could use, for sale! I bought too many by mistake! Make me an offer, Chitchee! Those are some top-of-the-shelf SD cards."

Chitchee looked at Kennedy. Nicky trailed up the escalator followed by five security guards from Carousel Square in their bright, white, cotton, and buttoned shirts with Eagle Scout-looking badges on their biceps.

"Nicky stole Larry Sangster's iPhone," said Chitchee. "Larry is BookSmart's landlord! Let's see what's in the blackmailer's email!"

"Better yet, download it onto one of those SDs," said Raven. "Quick, before that Mickey Snickers comes back. Ha, ha *diabolically clever.*"

"Where does the SD card go on an Apple?" asked Chitchee. "iDunno. Here's the thing: just give him yours, Kennedy. And we can keep Larry's."

"He'll know how to differentiate them," scoffed Kennedy.

"Kennedy, can I see the iPhone you got from Frenchy?"

Kennedy pulled it out and threw it down.

"Do *you* want to buy an iPhone, Raven?" asked Chitchee.

"Not until I sell this baby first," said Raven, looking around.

"Oh no!" said Kennedy. "I want no part of this! I did not hear that!"

Raven threw a silver .38 Derringer on the marble-topped table.

"What are you talking about?" asked Raven. "*That's* my baby! Not a real baby!"

Chitchee and Kennedy returned from reeling back in their chairs.

"Where did you get *that*?" asked Chitchee. "The bathroom at BookSmart?"

"How did you know that?" asked Raven, shocked.

"Above the toilet in the acoustic tiles where I hide my . . ." said Raven, his gloved hand screening his lips from the satellite cameras orbiting Carousel Square geo-synchronously.

"That's Hawk Eye's," said Chitchee.

"Okay, you take it," said Raven, giving the Derringer to Chitchee under the coffee table. "I don't want it anyway!"

Chitchee stuffed the .38 Derringer in the inner left pocket of his thick black overcoat, which had replaced his black leather jacket for the sake of its "layerability."

The three of them hunched together over Larry Sangster's iPhone, reading his open email accounts, exporting them, sharing them on the Internet, and converting them to PDFs when the front doors of Carousel Square blew open. The wind shoveled snow into the lobby, a swirl of ice around the shovelful of Randy Quaalude, his icy walking stick, and his beat parka.

"Frenchy!" said Kennedy.

"Randy!" said Chitchee.

"Milo!" said Raven.

"Guys!" said Randy.

"*Randy?*" asked Chitchee. "*Randy* is the World's Greatest Salesman?"

Randy was "Frenchy" at Wendy's, but he was known as "Milo" at Arby's and "Randy" at McDonald's Uptown. Evidently he hadn't gone to Madison or Milwaukee on a megabus or a pogo stick or on the piggy back of a giant piggy bank.

"Kennedy, do you have my iPhone?" asked Randy. "I can't afford the megabus until I sell that."

"But where's my 120 dollars?" asked Kennedy with an indignant look. "For the Vicodin? I'd rather have *that* than the iPhone 3 you gave me for collateral. You owe me $55."

"How do you figure?" asked Randy, hunching forward with his arms out, surprised.

When Kennedy pointed to Larry Sangster's iPhone, he took a deep breath for a possible peroration, but a frazzled Larry himself bumbled through the front doors with the new Filipina girl from New World Sunrise Massage And Spa—Reina. Larry looked like a lab rat that, immediately after the removal of its hippocampus and place cells, had been placed back in a water maze.

"Chitchee," said Larry, "can I borrow your phone? It's an emergency. Someone stole my phone."

"Sure, Larry," said Chitchee. "At least you remembered my name, that was nice of you!"

Larry quickly dialed *#06#. Viktor would chop his hands off if he found out what was going on. Larry had to act quickly—though too befuddled after Shiek's, Rick's, and DreamGirls (and the other ones) to think. Reina's only language was Tagalog, which was of no use. Larry scribbled in ink his IMEI on Reina's neck. Then he typed in his iCloud and password bank password and deleted his porn, passwords, emails, and identities.

"I have to do a Find My iPhone first, don't I?" Larry wondered aloud. "I have to call IT Corky before I change MPG passwords. Hold on, Reina. Oh, you don't know what I am saying. I don't know what I am saying. What more could I have done to ruin my life than what just happened to me? My entire life is entangled with that iPhone. I just lost my life. This is attempted murder! My God, my phone. That phone just stole my soul!"

"Hugs?" asked Chitchee. "Maybe you shouldn't have invested in the iPhone Infinity, or whatever it's called. Maybe it's a message from the future."

Larry loosened his tie, poked at his own phone, and then set the phone on the marble-topped, out-of-kilter table in order to search his wallet for his plastic money.

"Anyone for ice cream? We have here our own Holidazzler in the offing," said Kennedy, who handed out plastic spoons (Kennedy set down his iPhone on Larry's table next to Larry's iPhone) and place-set napkins on the table for the luscious dessert Kennedy served.

"Ice cream castles and carnivals of winter delights," said Kennedy, wishing he had sprinkles for the highly-anticipated scoops. "Who wants a scoop? Put out your hand for a scoop."

"Go away," said Larry, looking for something in his wallet, to Kennedy. "And she doesn't want anything from you either."

"Hey, who's the hot chick?" asked the returned Nicky, pointing with his stolen, pronged, ski-hatted head toward Larry's "chick."

"Come on, let's go, Nicky Fingery," said one of the five Carousel Square security guards, two of the closing ranks behind Nicky for a show of force.

"Oh, c'mon man, you guys know *me*. I wasn't doing anything but window shopping," said Nicky, the All-American boy in the back alley shooting for marbles, "and trying to get out of the raging cold out there guys . . . come on . . . I'll freeze to death . . . have a heart! I'm Minnesota nice!"

"Nicky Fingers? Out the front door! You were trespassed a week ago!" said the security guard with the two more guards escalated closer behind Nicky in the show of force.

Nicky stood alone outside. Chitchee ran and handed Nicky the iPhone Randy gave Kennedy as collateral.

"You forgot your phone, St. Nicholas," said Chitchee. "To help you out, I'll give you five for the SD—and I want some candy bars, because the SD card is obviously ripped off from Target, Walgreens, or CVS, along with the candy bars you always swipe from the Holiday gas station across from Jefferson Elementary or the SuperAmerica on Lyndale. The card depreciated because the previous owner paid nothing for it, and Apple doesn't take SD cards."

"You need a micro SD card and micro SD adapter with an iExpander," said Nicky. "That's all! I can go get you one. And then all you have to do is download the app from the Apple store. And for your Wi-Fi use AirStash. Hey, this isn't my phone," said Nicky, turning it over. "Are you pulling a fast one on me, Chitchee, that's not like you! You've always been nice to me!"

"It was an iPhone 1, 2, 3, Infinity, wasn't it?" asked Chitchee.

Squad cars kettled Carousel Square. They parked like magnets on a white board, every which way. MPD thumpers jumped out, entered Carousel Square's front doors, and talked to the Carousel Square security guards.

"Well, whose phone is it?" asked Chitchee impatiently because cold air had seeped into his overcoat like a waterfall of ice down his chest.

His eyes teared up automatically with rivers of salty, prickly icicles. His fingers felt pinched already. Soon his toes and fingers would fuse. Chitchee and Nicky stamped their feet and blew cumulus clouds at the icy sidewalk, their conversation freeze-framed. The icy breeze snipped and cut all lines of communication, negotiation, and reconciliation, so Chitchee and Nicky both knew to cheese-pare their sentences down to one word utterances or use sign language.

"I want my phone back." "It is back." "Where?" "There." "You stole." "No, that was you stole." "Not so, Chhhhhh-iiiiiiii-tttttttcccchhhhhh-eeeeeeee." "Yes, Na-na-na-nn-nnnnnicky!"

Thumpers escorted Larry to one squad car and the Filipina girl, Reina, who cried tears that froze solid as opals on the way— to a separate squad car.

"That cake-eater was arrested for stealing his own phone," mocked Nicky before tramping off in the snow and bitter cold. "I hope the thumpers torture him like they tortured me. They ruined my life, so let the thumpers ruin his privileged life. Bourgeois bougie bullshit artist!"

The "bullshit artist" vomited into the backseat of the squad car and retched so violently he induced the weak-stomached Chitchee to chyme in with Larry's Lobster Bisque and stomach of pink rainbows. Chitchee heaved his heavenly ice cream and Holidazzling treat into a snowbank and he bit his mitten. Kennedy made a disgusted face with onionized eyes. Raven donned a told-you-so look on his face. Randy whacked the snow-banks with his walking stick all the way home, smoking another Carousel to get there.

THE ANGRY BAGEL EMPORIUM

"Good morning Minnesota! It is minus 7 degrees, and with the wind chill factored in, it's a *balmy* negative 18," said the crackling, sarcastic boom box, shuddering in Chitchee's cold room on the third floor of the House of Edelweiss. But this was the red-letter day he had been waiting for. His passion for Dagny had carried him to the brink of stupidity. He had to declare his undying love for Dagny and offer his hand in marriage. He would have to end his relationship with Gudrun, painful as that might be. He should take Gudrun to The Sick Joke Cafe and with the utmost aplomb calmly tell her: "Gudrun, it is over. Someone else had already captured my heart before I met you. And my heart always tells me to follow my heart." And then he could introduce Gudrun to Dagny so they could all be friends.

The FBI had raided MPG headquarters by now, he figured. How much more evidence could he give them? Did he have to breastfeed the FBI? Maybe they were a little slow on the uptake or it was Christmas.

Chitchee pulled his black wool nightcap down to his ear lobes. He fell back to sleep under his sleeping bag on the bed. He smiled, thinking of Larry's iPhone as hard evidence in his backpack, which warmed up his hopes in the cold bedroom of his flesh and thoughts. Chitchee looked outside his window and clapped his hands for joy at the gorgeous, young snow reclining on bare branches. The forestry reminded him of both Samuel Taylor Coleridge's winter poems and *The Fractal Geometry of Nature* by Benoit Mandelbrot. When the snow flocked the evergreens white it also clumped on the power lines in little stupas. Whited algorithms of blazing snow branched in the snowy distance while the branching of the snowflakes in the air reiterated the branching of the evergreen's branching boughs, limbs, and needles. He inhaled the winter scent of mint from the air outside his window, on which the panes had hoar-frosted with icy ramifications, beyond which silver-filigree ganglions and branches stretched into other silver-filigree ganglions and branches and knotted themselves together like newly-wedded dendrites.

Fascinated by these patterns, he rooted around in Benoit Mandelbrot's book. Having entered *The Fractal Geometry of Nature*, he lay back on the lumpy, doughish bed and devoured the book like homemade brown bread and butter. His almond eyes lighted up and danced enchanted.

After eating an Old Dutch tortilla chip (chipped in the shape of a coastline made of corn) he had picked up off the floor, he prepared physically and mentally like Parzifal for Minnesota, with his newly-purified soul in his winter armor: thermals, top and bottom, tight T-shirt over his butterfat gut, long-sleeved cotton shirt, loose T-shirt #2 over that, a plaid flannel shirt, 501 jeans, Target sweat socks (which didn't wick well), previously salt-lined Reeboks, three thin sweaters, a long black baggy wool overcoat, thick leather gloves lined with orange wool gloves, ear band, black wool beanie, small gray scarf, and then a knitted plaid scarf as large as a windsock to cover the space between his chest and his eyes. His mobility approximated the absolute immobility of absolute zero. But Chitchee was, hands down, the luckiest and happiest man alive.

"*I'm getting married in the morning,*" he sang and then sneezed.

Who has never seen snow, nor felt the embrace of the blue arctic wind, and felt warmed by the golden rays of the sun? Chitchee looked at his black Reeboks. The salt lines on them looked like the coasts of Norway—white chaotic salty teeth, cutting tiny fjords into his imitation leather dress/work/play shoes. He scraped off the salt lines, erasing the Mandelbrot sets. *Zähle die Mandeln.* Chitchee threw open the black walnut front door, greeted winter in all its glory, and stood amazed as he was by *Infinite Jest*, bemazed marvelously. Great art: it stops you in your tracks. Then he walked through the untracked snow: the snow fluffed on his shoulders like eiderdown pillow feathers. And in his ideation he continued through the marmoreal monuments of rolling hills and furrowed avenues, giving Minneapolis, with its rime-covered maple trees, maple tree branches, and maple tree twigs, the look of a Mandelbrot set itself. How like snow angels the children made snow angels in the snow. And while the same snow squeaked into the dried fractal cracks in his salty soles, he walked in Laetoli-like boot prints on sidewalks unshoveled.

Chitchee drew in his arms, preserving angular momentum "like a figure skater pulling in her arms," but sensed his fingers had frozen; so he balled up his pinched fingers into fists inside his orange wool gloves. Chitchee bussed to Lyndale and Franklin and hoofed it to The Sick Joke Cafe.

The drying air had stopped manufacturing snow, but the icy glassy slippery sidewalks made him slip when he walked too fast unfastidiously. He looked down and inspected the booted snow prints like arrows of time that had stepped before him. The House of Edelweiss had been a great call. He thought if he could split the rent with Dagny, she could learn to love and marry him, and they would have money to spare at the end of the month for SD cards and various vitamin delivery systems known as food.

"Dagny," he called out when he turned up West 22nd Street.

Dagny smoked her self-rolled cigarette, and then she punished the stub harshly with a summary execution. She saw him and walked inside. She had smoked with an abruptness that implied to Chitchee her anticipation of the arrival of her Parzifal and his heroic deeds, because life was beautifully pre-arranged so as to maximize the greatest good for the happiest people. Probably according to somebody.

The Sick Joke Cafe had changed ownership, names, and goals. It was the Angry Bagel Emporium, and the new owner, Viktor Martensen, CEO of MPG, wanted to replace it with a jet ski shop ASAP.

The brick building of the Angry Bagel Emporium looked the same: it contained the same broken curtain rods, drapes at half mast, and the air conditioner about to fall to its death. Snow covered the trim and gables and the black urethane, which covered the same windows, flapped so loosely that the wind could pirate the black sheets any moment. Poorly-clad teenagers in ripped jeans and crummy jackets shared pouch tobacco and cigarette stubs, milling and mulling about on the sidewalk. They poked around for their cached stubs in the snow bank.

Chitchee was in love—a wounded, festering spurned love with medieval fevers, night sweats, and the dreams of epic, stick-figure heroes. He sleeved the snot off his face, upturning his nose with the back of his wrist, and then he, his heart fit to burst, jaunted inside The Angry Bagel Emporium: same old flannel, plaid shirts, dark wool caps, MacBooks, MacBook Pros, and steamy haze sneaking in the door in search of Dagny herself. Chitchee looked around and saw Dagny (sitting in the middle of a Smith Brothers convention) clearing off her crumb-covered table, which was covered like all the tables with butcher's paper and crayons instead of tablecloths.

She too had fallen in love, finally accepting him for himself.

What would she want from him besides his love and his half of the rent?

Table after table of sauerkraut *kinder* sat cozily in the frozen-in-the-frost-bitten silence. Students plunged in threnodies over social media firestorms. And the foggy sighs frosted the storefront window. Russian dolls wobbled around Chitchee and threaded by him angrily. Body heat stoked the hot-house, cubed rooms. So hot, so hot, some had stripped down to their long black underwear to cool off. Steam and fog arose from the floorboards as if The Cure were on stage. It was the same fetid, footed air of the Lake of the Isles's warming house next to the skating rink. At every table, every budded artist drew the same angry gremlin over and over in a frenzy of frustration, never getting it right, leading to a collective resentment at being left out of a gallery and left behind at The Angry Bagel Emporium off Lyndale Avenue South in Minneapolis's 5th Precinct. Every MCAD classmate the envious artist knew was already in Rome, Paris, London, New York, San Francisco, or Chicago. But Minneapolis? The gremlins at every table grew more realistic, more flibbertigibbety, and darker than nightshade in a dead heart.

"What the fuck do you want?" asked Rashid, finger-tipping his beard's stunted sunspots that refused to grow out.

"A rabbit's foot," said Chitchee.

"You came to the wrong place for a rabbit's foot," said Rashid over the chip in his shoulder, manning the espresso machine of a WW I submarine. "It's hell in a very small space right now. And the whole world is fucked!"

"That's all right," said Chitchee. "I wasn't expecting much of a heaven in a very *big* place. But could I please have an End-of-the-World pot of symbiotic, probiotic green tea with chaga, cordyceps, and lion's mane?"

"No, you can't! Here's a coffee. Two fifty. Now get out of here. New owner has a 'no chat' rule now. Dagny's in there," added Rashid, which was a friendly slip on his part, because interacting with customers was verboten.

The new owner flatlined such extra favors for customers, and he especially didn't want friends, neighbors, and gargoylish gremlins hanging out in his cafe doodling unconscious monsters with hideous, heinous, hairy faces.

"It's bad enough, being reported by every given neighborhood smear artist on NextDoor, UptownScareWatch, TrueCrimeWedgeNeighborhoodInformersBoard, and the 28thAndAldrichOutreachPanphobicSnitchGroup, but Viktor Martensen, the new owner, is out buying pepper spray for the off-duty five ohs he's going to hire for all the police reports he expects from them."

Dagny fidgeted, uncomfortably bedeviled by a pebble at the bottom of her thermal socks. Chitchee sat down and fidgeted in a mirror of silence, sensing the pebble at the bottom of her thermal socks. Of course, she was nervous about his presenting her a too-expensive engagement ring.

Alex showed up with an ashtray-gray face. He wore castanet earrings that were castanets, insectoid sunglasses, and scrubs. His hair was so haphazard he looked lost, because the new broom had swept so clean it destroyed the entire ecosystem that had gone into the new broom that had swept so clean. A girl with tie-dyed hair and dressed like a maypole cried into her cell phone; texting with her dynamite thumbs so quickly, she blew up the receiver's cell to hell and sat pigeon-holed in a pigeon hell.

By the frosted front windows, two MacBooked MCAD students argued over a common electrical outlet. The argument and the socket flared up in sparks. A light bulb exploded when Ivan Von Volkov, moving a leaning floor lamp, tripped on an adapter and power cord. He tore the three-prong from the socket. The wall-plate dangled by a single screw, revealing the bare plug like a white hog's nose.

"Do you care if there is MSG in everything?" asked Alex.

"Does it matter if I do?" asked Chitchee.

"Frankly, no."

"That's okay, Alex," said Chitchee. "Monosodium glutamate addiction? Have you heard that Hazelden has two new wings for that? One for ruffled and one for plain."

"Hey, you guys," said Ivan. "I'm gay!"

"So?" said Chitchee. "Let us know when you have a sex change!"

"I'm sorry, Chitchee," said Alex, "but if the owner catches us laughing, we'll get fired. We can't even cross-dress anymore . . . we're getting *uniforms* tomorrow. And they're *so* ugly, so brown and ugly . . ." Alex was breaking up . . . "Brown? Are you kidding me? Blech! The new owner was in Georgia and bought an allotment of old Confederate Army uniforms from a grand nephew of Robert E. Lee's."

"Confederate uniforms, here, why?" asked Chitchee. "Are they trying to put this place out of business?"

Chitchee's eyes teared up after he saw Alex almost crying when Alex walked away with Chitchee's order for a slice of pumpernickel bread.

"Who's the new owner?" Chitchee asked Alex, upon his bringing the bread.

"Viktor Martensen is his name," said Alex.

That was it! Viktor Martensen had a master plan: he planned to own Minneapolis and no one could stop him.

"Why were you so rude to that guy?" asked Dagny, not moving a muscle but still growling. "It was like you were angry at him for coming out of the closet!"

Chitchee looked up and frowned, "Ivan? I think he can take a few razor cuts, Dagny. I'm his friend. Ask his mother Vera how I helped him open a savings account, because he didn't understand what a debit card was. At first, he thought that ATMs gave out free money."

"Well, I don't believe that either," said Dagny. "You obviously hurt his feelings."

"Dagny, two bebop musicians are standing on a street corner," said Chitchee, "passing a joint when a fire engine races past and the one turns to the other and says 'God, I'd thought they'd never leave.'"

"That's not funny," said Dagny, her mouth shut straight-edged as a block of wind-packed snow in an igloo. "You hit my un-funny bone with that one. I'm in a relationship now with someone who actually loves me for who I am."

Ivan in the other room read aloud his love poems, his harsh voice travelling everywhere as from a mouth and tongue coated with gelatin and cornbread.

And he gagged on every tobacco-greased rhyme that his larynx ejected.

"What?" asked Chitchee.

Dagny slowly scraped her rolling eyeballs off the ceiling with a putty remover.

"Chitchee, do you know what love is?" she asked.

"*Bit O, Bit O Honey*," sang Chitchee.

"Are you listening to me?" asked Dagny when her eyes changed from half masts to black sails with pirate flags.

"Of course, I know what love is," said Chitchee with a sinking feeling. "It reminds me of the story of Li Fan, the Chinese knight and troubadour of the Sung dynasty, who had become 'caught between divided loyalties' in an affair of the heart. Unable to stand it any longer, he literally ripped his heart out. Once in the marketplace, he approached a woman, who was selling only heartless vegetables, and he asked her if a man could live without his heart. She said no. And the Chinese knight and troubadour of the Sung Dynasty Li Fan dropped dead."

Dagny fingered a bit of dead, dried-out lip. She spit politely a squiggle of tobacco shred from a previous smoke.

"Right there on the spot . . . the knight of love keeled over dead as a crooked nail," said Chitchee. "Crushed like a stink bug, having ripped out his heart."

"Have you ever known true intimacy with a woman who loves you?" asked Dagny.

Dagny's narrowing eyes contrasted with her nose. Her silence took the shine off her lip gloss, if she ever wore lip gloss. A sudden desire possessed her now. To hurt the innocent.

"You have to ask? Why are you twisting your napkin into double helixes?" asked Chitchee. "And then Li Fan's lady love from Hangzhou died when her servants lost their footing on a steep path in a mountain pass and sent her palanquin packing into a ravine, ass over tea-kettles."

"Everything reminds you of something you read," said Dagny. "That gets old even if you don't."

"Everything exists to appear from a children's book, doesn't it?" asked Chitchee. "Or so I once heard."

"I saw you with LaDonna the other day getting off the bus," said Dagny.

"I'm sorry, Dagny," said Chitchee. "It was a chance encounter at a bus stop. We didn't have sex. But neither one of us remembers that. We accidentally took Ativans instead of Ecstasy because poor Randy can't think worth a rattle anymore. I think he's traumatized from when his entire platoon was mowed down in Dak To or some hole we never should have poked our nose in. Or something he never talks about. So you see nothing sloppy or sweaty happened. So if you will marry me, we can pick out a wedding dress and order the cup cakes tomorrow."

"Are you all ready to order," said a new server, "or are you still arguing?"

"We're still arguing, thanks," said Chitchee. "I can't seem to read people. What language are they written in? Does anybody here know?"

Chitchee watched himself like a hawk over a cornfield. The gremlin inside him made him say the most devilish things, even though he knew they were wrong. The confidence drained from his face and catastrophe loomed ominously on the horizon of his eyebrows.

"She kicked me out of her apartment," continued Chitchee. "She hates my ever-lovin' guts! She never wants to see me again. Remember, we tried to have children and failed? She has to hate me or she would love me. Are you jealous?"

Dagny clenched her jaw, ground her molars, pulled her hair out of her eyes, and spindled a strand on her finger as from a spinning wheel of multi-colored yarn.

"Nobody 'accidentally' takes Ativan instead of Ecstasy," said Dagny with the skepticism of a great horned owl when she looked at Chitchee. "If I read that in a book, I'd say 'bullshit.' Hey, speaking of bullshit from a book, why did you steal lines from *Beneath the Underdog*, my favorite book? Did you think I wouldn't notice his pick-up lines? How could you think I'd be bowled over by an old white guy masquerading as Charles Mingus? Do you secretly crave rejection to justify my rejection of your rejection of my justification of your rejection to redeem your ego?"

"Okay, we're *not* getting married! See if I care! Skip the courtship, the gifts, and the relationship. Why bother? We're squirrels running through trees. One squirrel is as good as another! I'm out of here!"

"The simple fact is," said Dagny, "you don't have medical or retirement or a pension plan or an address and I'm sick of being broke! I can't support my own mother!"

"Neither can I!" said Chitchee.

"My mother has to live with her brother's mother-in-law," said Dagny, "because she had a closet to stick my mother in like an old corn broom."

"Well, as for me, I've been busy with putting the finishing touches on finishing *Quantum Biscuits*," continued Chitchee, "for BookSmart's landlord, if he is still there. When *Quantum Biscuits* makes the New York Times bestseller list—I can save BookSmart! Don't you understand? *Quantum Biscuits* could be my big break, not Robert Bly or Garrison Keillor. You're not listening. Viktor Martensen's blue wall is crumbling! Okay, where did you meet your someone special? *The Match Game*, *OK Computer*, *Tinder Vittles*, or *Bumblebee Tuna*? You have the look most men adore, so I'm sure you didn't have to search too far afield for a boyfriend. Is he a rock star?"

Dagny gripped her fork to stick into Chitchee's tiny heart like a meaty marshmallow and roast it over an open campfire's flame.

"How far can a painted turtle travel on a winter's night?" asked Chitchee.

A long silence took root between them. They searched for pleasant or hurtful things to say, unable to make up their minds between the two . . . whether to escalate toward revenge or downward toward forgiveness.

"Where did you meet this . . . 'somebody' to love?'" asked Chitchee after the long silence.

And 'somebody' had a negative spin to it when Dagny absorbed it.

"Here," said Dagny firmly. "Alex. And Astrid Eskola. It's a three-way open relationship."

"Oh, I see," said Chitchee. "Like Beauvoir, Sartre, and Brigitte Bardot."

"You never took me out, you never bought me a gift. A woman wants to be loved. A woman wants to be eaten. *And you can't love,* Chitchee. There is something wrong with you, Chitchee Chichester. You're like all men with their starving dog stories."

"Did you mean *shaggy* dog stories?" asked Chitchee. "What's a *starving* dog story? I think you meant to say *shaggy.* Let me explain the derivation."

"How are you two doing?" asked another new server (since the last had been fired), Aubrey Aalgaard. "Are you still arguing?"

"Yes, thank you," said Chitchee. "Aubrey! You're working here? But where is Alex or the other server I pissed off?"

"They recused themself, full disclosure, it was a conflict of interest issue they said, and I guess they wanted to avoid any possible binary, you all know?" smiled Aubrey with sincere apprehension.

"I thought you were at St. Olaf's studying the bio-history of pollen," said Chitchee, pushing away his water, pulling it back, and taking hummingbird sips.

"I dropped out to work here," said Aubrey. "That's why I didn't have time for *Quantum Visions.*"

"*Quantum Visions*? I thought it was supposed to be called *Quantum Biscuits*? Uh-oh. It's too late," said Chitchee, throwing down his black wool cap on the table, his hair like inky waves of wheat. "I sent the publisher the corrected galleys already. Now I'm waiting for Sheryl Z. Goombah at AuthorHouse to send me the free copies she sold me—and my chance for a spot on Car Talk to be announced."

"How have you been, Dagny?" asked Aubrey, throwing open her arms for a hug.

"Oh, all right, I guess," said Dagny, shrugging through the hugging.

"You two know each other?" asked Chitchee, his head jerking back so that his black wool cap slid.

Chitchee slid it around on his head again, pulled it down over his eyes, and took it off.

"Cousins," said Dagny solemnly.

"My grandmother Ariel's sister," said Aubrey cheerfully, "is Dagny's mother, whose brother Angus was married to Waldtraut, whose mother's brother's son, Viktor, is how we're related through marriage to Viktor Martensen, who . . ."

"Through Uncle Angus who died," said Dagny, bored to death.

"He's not dead, remember?" asked Aubrey hopefully. "He might recover consciousness."

"He'll be dead—even if he regains consciousness," insisted Dagny.

Aubrey's face waffled between mournful reconciliation and electric shock.

"Then Auntie Waldtraut remarried," continued Aubrey, smiling bravely. "And *Waldtraut* married Uncle Michael Weatherwax. One of the Weatherwax sides of the family. Poor Waldtraut, I feel so sorry for her, she should have never married, because she had to deal with Arminius."

"Arminius," said Chitchee. "Michael? Melchizedek?"

"No," said Aubrey. "Arminius *Paul* Weatherwax."

"Paul?" asked Chitchee. "*Paul*? Paul from the House of Harkonnen? Where does it end? On the planet Dune? For that matter, where does *Dune* end? If it's still there!"

"Excuse me? You're talking about our *family*," said Dagny. "Hello? Look, I told you I was related to Aloysius. He's my cousin. You weren't listening. I'll write it down for you."

Dagny picked up a nearby purple crayon and drew on the butcher's paper a purple cloudberry bush. She filled some of the leaves with names and arrows. She crossed out several names and wrote other names on top of those. Branches grew into other cloudberry bushes with names on their leaves and with green arrows shooting in all directions. She picked up a nearby amber crayon and listed names and surrounded them with leaves, which attracted more arrows from cloudberry bushes of crossed-out names and crossed-out bushes with married, deceased, and uncertain status annotations in brackets.

Two cloudberry bushes formed eyes and another bush formed a mouth and the assemblage was another angry gremlin. The brackets appeared to be wings of a newly-fledged gremlin, and a little brown bat flew off the page when Chitchee looked at it.

MCAD students cheered when they saw Dagny's sketch, because each student knew in her heart of hearts she could do better and each was duly inspired for ten more minutes of inspired gremlins, looking so real they breathed.

"Okay Chitchee? Are you listening? My real father Knutsen died of leukemia when I was five," said Dagny as she continued filling in the features of a bat without recognizing the bat. "His first and last names were Knutsen. My mother worked as a housemaid at a house in Northeast to support us. Pretty soon her employer forced himself on her, but his wife caught him and brained him with a old toaster. She ended up marrying his son, another asshole. That's the family history, asshole after asshole, back to the first asshole in the garden of Eden."

"I see," said Chitchee, "so your family tree was cut up for cord wood a long time ago?"

"Then Henry married your mother to protect her?" asked Aubrey.

"Protect her from what?" asked Dagny.

"From Henry's father Heinrich?" asked Chitchee.

"Not exactly," said Dagny. "Henry beat her like a cave man. He accused her of sleeping with his cousin, when in fact his cousin raped her. She got second-degree murder, but I know she didn't do it. They took the kid away. For 'cheating,' her husband threw her down a flight of stairs. Broke her jaw and two ribs. Ever since she got out of Shakopee, she hasn't been able to take care of herself. Her landlady Edelweiss takes care of her. Her short term is gone. She's in her second childhood, acts all dotty, turns into a floozy, and evil men take advantage of her."

"Didn't she call the thumpers on the cousin?" asked Chitchee.

"You don't understand," said Dagny, with her cheeks sucked in as if smoking. "All the thumpers *emerged* from between the legs of Edelweiss, more or less. And all the Hillswicks."

"And the Weatherwaxes," said Aubrey, paling with shame and blushing at the thought of her shameful guilt made public by the blush no one noticed for her having almost left out the Weatherwax branch of the family from the Family Photo Album.

"So," said Chitchee, "all the thumpers in Minneapolis and St. Paul, all the bobbies, all the Sheriff Bob Robinsons of St. Paul, and all the Robert 'BB' Robbins of Minneapolis were hatched from the eggs of Edelweiss?"

Dagny drew noodles on the fetched scratch paper. Aubrey filled in blank areas, using the rainbow-colored pencils taken out of the community chest of art supplies. Aubrey wrote with stylized hearts that said: "Love" and "Gratitude" while Dagny wrote in block capitals: "Evil cannot be redeemed."

The girl with tie-dyed hair and dressed like a maypole, wobbling by, looked on with interest and commented on Aubrey's talent: "Dope."

"That *does* look interesting," said Ivan, holding his cupped hand out without the coffee cup in it. "Am *I* in there?"

"If you stand there long enough," said Rashid, leaning over the counter, "you will be."

Everyone previously dodging Ivan in one room returned to the other room. They worked on their angry gremlins, which progressively turned into labyrinths, snakes, squirrels, and bats.

"Heyggghh," said Ivan, coughing up mucal sludge, tasting it loudly for all to enjoy—its fascinating consistency gulped down. "If you find *my* Uncle Pavel, who was born sometime in the October Revolution, I think *I* can link you to the House of Harkonnen."

"I think I'm ready to order," said Chitchee. "Do you still have water?"

"The pipes aren't frozen," said Aubrey, "as far as I know."

"So for me, the water always comes first," said Chitchee, "and three avocados."

"I'm sorry," said Aubrey, "the boss doesn't believe in avocados."

Chitchee lifted his arms to the elbows in dramatic despair.

Dagny's shy gaze caught Chitchee's shy gaze.

He had lost Dagny.

"We weren't even going out together," said Dagny. "Why are you so sad?"

"We weren't?" asked Chitchee, his voice cracked like a window hit by a brick. "But I love you, Dagny!"

"Oh," she smiled for once, "you do not!"

Chitchee's broken heart was crushed.

"But you should come to Alex's show," said Dagny, picking up confidence.

"I never cared for you anyway," he said to himself.

That was obvious as the red heel in the hole of his white sock.

"Pepsi Beaucoup is playing for a book signing at Club Miami," continued Dagny, a note of optimism in her tenor.

"It must be for the *Quantum Biscuits: Six or Seven Keys to Success* book signing," said Chitchee.

Aubrey had been kicked out of her dorm. Aloysius had been promised Aubrey's college education by Viktor, not a Lincoln penny of which Aloysius had seen. Nevertheless Viktor, in lieu of payment, offered Aloysius substitutes: Greg LeMond's racing bicycle, a herd of alpacas from the Andes, wall paintings from Herculaneum, Fra Angelicos from Brazil, espresso machines from the Crusades, a crystal skull that once belonged to Charlemagne later determined to have been a paperweight of Nero the Roman Emperor, a Cheryl Tiegs poster (signed), a Crackerjack box of moon rocks, and the world's smallest hand-held neutrino detector, which Viktor stole from CERN when nobody was around.

To make ends meet, Aubrey served at The Angry Bagel Emporium *and* Club Miami. *When* she would get her undergraduate degree was up in the air, up in the stratosphere, and on the way to the hundred moons of Jupiter.

"So there is no money in the entire family," asked Chitchee, "for Aubrey's college education?"

"There's only Gudrun on my side of the family," said Dagny, "and she never gets paid except in kittens."

"Gudrun?" gulped Chitchee, sliding back in his chair. "Is Gudrun kind of a manic pixie of an uncertain age?"

"*Do you know my mother?*" asked Dagny.

"Well," said Chitchee, pulling his black wool cap down over his face.

"Well," said Dagny. "She's kind of cute for an old lady. And she's a mom's mom."

"Well," said Chitchee, pulling his black wool cap up over his face. "Oh well."

"But," said Dagny, leaning forward, "she is extremely vulnerable. And men sense that and take advantage of her. So help me God, the next Wart Hog that tries to seduce my mother, I will hunt him down, strangle him in his sleep and—"

She picked up the table knife. She thrust it into the wooden table and the blade broke.

"—I'LL CUT OFF HIS NUTS AND THROW THEM IN THE FUCKING GARBAGE DISPOSAL!"

She smiled at Chitchee, who was rubbing his greasy hair, looking around for the menu, which he picked up.

"Dagny, you heard Auntie Gudrun's not doing too well?" asked Aubrey, pulling a Christmas card from her back pocket that had stuck to her cellphone. "She sent me this Christmas card, 'Dear Outside My Walls: 2009 has been another worst year of my life: hearing voices, night terrors, night sweats, locked-in syndrome, incubi, succubi, fuccubi, you name it—life is a prison where you are all the guards, all the locks, all the keys. The inmates murder, rape, terrorize, and assault one another because there is no tomorrow. Existence is merely the existence of the passage of time, and the passage of time is the passage of the waste of existence. The passage of waste is indeed the meaning of existence. And the waiting for death is excruciating around Christmas time. Have a Very Isolated Christmas Like Me, Gudrun Knutsen.'"

"Last year," said Dagny, smiling a bit. "Mom sent out all these statistics from the World Health Organization on undernourishment and starvation, ending with 'You won't *go* to hell for eating their Christmas because you are already *in* hell for eating their Christmas. Oh, yes. I know some things. Like a hundred million things.'"

"Was that last year's Christmas card or the year before?" asked Aubrey, looking to check her email on her smartphone because she thought that staff had already received their Confederate Army butternut-dyed uniforms. "Gudrun's Christmas cards are some of the bleakest commentaries on humanity ever penned."

"Aubrey, you're fired!" said Viktor Martensen in his silver-and-black chinchilla coat, standing next to their table. "Sitting down on the job when there are customers waiting to order from the brand new menu? And you're on your phone like a typical millennial? And it's too bad. You're kind of cute. You know I was only trying to help your father pay off his debts! Is this the loser from Book Smart again? Is this your newest loser boyfriend, Dagny? Don't look so sad, Aubrey. Think of it this way: you'll have that much more time for *Quantum Visions*! I'll pay you back for that, once things settle down here. I'll have plenty of liquid. Maybe we can meet for coffee."

Aubrey ran to hide her face behind the three-story, pineapple cream cheese/coconut shred/cinnamon carrot cake in the once sparkling display case whose fuse had blown.

"Dagny, talk to your mother lately?" asked Viktor, plumping down next to Chitchee.

Beside a tan torso, cheek-by-jowly chops, cold-sored lips, icy teeth, neotenous baby eyes, hair smelling of the successive coats of Grecian Formula that had varnished the curly furrows of his shingling, Viktor had developed a thick, ochre crust to his peeling potato skin.

"She doesn't have to answer that, Big Man," said Chitchee. "Big Man, are you listening?"

"Why are you everywhere I fucking go, Richard Speck?" asked Viktor, reaching for something inside the front pocket of his chinchilla.

"Maybe because I'm your biographer?" asked Chitchee. "*Viktor Martensen: Quantum Fascist or Psychopathic Weasel?*"

Chitchee jumped. A pit viper with red-hot teeth had bitten him. When he withdrew his hand from his flannel shirt, he witnessed his own bloody fingers.

"You stabbed me?" cried Chitchee.

"I owe you one, Dagny, for quitting on me! I don't like quitters," said Viktor, snorting his nostrils clear and standing up to go. "Tell your mother to watch her back. She's a thief."

"Fuck you," said Dagny. "Your days are numbered too."

"Why did you stab me?" asked Chitchee. "THE OWNER STABBED ME! I'm bleeding!"

Chitchee stood up, lost consciousness, and saw the Holy Spirit. He instinctively reached for his cell phone to take a selfie.

"We'll see whose days are numbered," said Viktor. "Now get out of my jet ski shop! Get up! You disrespected me!"

"Should I call an ambulance?" asked Aubrey, crying from behind the counter.

"Ambulance?" asked Chitchee, regaining consciousness and instinctively reaching for his wallet. "Is that covered by MN Sure, Minnesota Care, Medical Assistance, Hennepin County, Health Partners, Allina, Medica, or not? Do I have time to call my provider? What is a provider? Whatever happened to doctors?"

"I accidentally poked you with a razor blade, that's all, you pussy!" said Viktor, grabbing Chitchee by his belt and flannel shirt collar—in order to fling him outside.

"You deserve *respect*?" asked Dagny standing up. "Fuck you, CUNT! Ass-licking bitch! You and your MPG crooks with their college degrees can go to hell!"

"I'm going to kill you," said Viktor to Chitchee, Viktor's boxer's hands lifting Chitchee to his feet, "if you don't leave now."

"Fuck you," continued Dagny, "and your sports cars, celebrity pals, and your moneyed mansions, and fuck your private jets! They are all lies! Your promises are lies, your existence is solid waste from a shit-for-brains sewer! Nothing but lies are shit out of your mouth, open sewer! Rapist!"

"GET OUT!" said Viktor, angrily hurling Chitchee at the door, every word of Dagny's incorporated into harming Chitchee, as if Viktor thought them the same person.

Aubrey minced into the room radiating chirpy thoughts and said:

"Oh look, I found some avocados after all, y'all!"

Dagny plucked up a carefully sliced-in-half, sea-salted avocado off Aubrey's tray, clasped it softly, then smashed it into Viktor's eyeballs.

When Dagny tore at Viktor's eyeballs and gouged away, Chitchee grabbed her by the waist and tossed her into the table they had given up.

"Stop, Dagny," said Chitchee. "You'll kill him! Let due process take its course, we can settle all this peacefully in a court of law. I told the FBI all about him. We have to trust the American criminal justice system—whatever that is. I didn't want to have to tell you, but I think there will be reward money for my turning in this crook. That then would have been the dowry."

"Have a very isolating Christmas" said Dagny, a smugly satisfied grin superimposed on her smile—alternating with it a current of smile/grin, grin/smile, smile/grin . . .

Viktor wiped the green gunk like insect guts from his face, stomped downstairs to the utility closet, ran back upstairs with a twelve-gauge shotgun. Thunderheads boiling behind his mountainous, brow-ridged eyebrows, he bawled:

"I'll get you back for that, you dead cunts!"

On second thought, unable to breathe, Viktor walked wheezing back downstairs, hid the shotgun, and had to use his inhaler.

Chitchee felt inspired to kiss Dagny, Aubrey, Alex (who decided to walk out), and Ivan (who froze and pondered asking Chitchee for a book store job) while an apathetic customer watched from the check-out counter and waited for Chitchee to quit hugging customers and leave the table free. The apathetic customer hugged Chitchee, grabbed Chitchee's table, sat down, and drew in a frenzy on a fresh piece of butcher's paper, the contoured, finely cross-hatched face of Viktor in the manner of a melancholy woodcut.

A crumpled napkin winged past Chitchee's tearful face.

"Sorry, I don't have any more hugs to give, Rashid," said Chitchee.

"Don't forget to tip double the usual," said Rashid, "because the white racist owner takes half the tip jar for his white racist nose candy."

"I heard *that*, *Richard*," said Viktor, grabbing a Reddi-Wip can from the industrial refrigerator and slamming the door so hard a wire rack inside collapsed. "You're fired too. All of you get out of here! The cops are on their way!"

Out on the sidewalk's tiles of ice, Chitchee, Dagny, Rashid, Aubrey, and Alex re-grouped in their own carousel square, producing mammatus clouds above them when they coldly spoke.

"I'm sorry for acting so crazy everybody," cried Dagny, her face in her gloves. "I'm overwrought."

"That crazy was sane!" said Chitchee.

"Babe, you were magnificent," said Alex.

Dagny seemed to be moving back and forth between little snowshoe-shaped tears and dry ice.

"Do you need a hug Dagny? Here," said Alex.

Dagny had swerved from Chitchee to Alex.

Aubrey cheerfully deflected the whole situation, hoping against hope Viktor didn't see her steal the remaining two avocados in lieu of payment for the Spring semester. She had never stolen anything in her life. She would never steal the crumbs off her own cookie! But she already thought of returning the two avocados tomorrow or at least leaving them at the front door with a sorry note. She smiled out of habit and forgot and forgave the past as always.

Aubrey was aware that her father wasn't washing his blue jean wardrobe anymore. Dinner was peanut butter and jelly sandwiches on Wonder Bread, economy-sized boxes of Old Dutch potato chips, and six-packs of Blech's Light. He didn't look at his *kantele* anymore. His Beatles CDs sat unspun. His town house crawled with spiderwebs. Mousing around (with arthritic knees lacking all synovial fluid) BookSmart, he was keeping the doors looking open, but he was also being attacked by a lower lumbago, no pillows helped, and he went home early every night. He didn't qualify for any medical coverage or he couldn't figure it out. She needed more time to restore the tabs on Aloysius. She intuited her father's cortisol levels, fearing he had lost BookSmart and everybody in it so she could study pollen grains. And the guilt was killing her.

"Yeah, good job, Dagny," said a jovial Chitchee. "Always take the customer to the shelf and smash an avocado into his face."

"That pig head with the pin brain?" asked Dagny, walking in the other direction with Alex and Rashid. "You don't know the *half* of his perverted acts."

"Oh," said Chitchee to their vanishing grins, "don't be too sure, because I was going to say something clever, but I lost it. I don't really feel like looking for a job now."

Then Chitchee slipped on the icy pavement. Looking up at the sky and Aubrey's nursey face when she pulled him up, he thought not of the fable of the frog boiling slowly to death in water, but of the frog slowly freezing to death in the water crystallizing to ice in his veins and brains.

"Is that why Edelweiss black-faced her husband's head out of all the family photos?" Chitchee asked Aubrey.

Aubrey smiled and said she didn't know, happy that she didn't know, happy if she did know, happily.

CAROUSEL SQUARE

Chitchee woke up like a giant cairn heaped up high for the blackbirds to rest their feet on. The wind outside his third-story window bleated. He woke up as a blue whale and couldn't roll out of bed. When he heard thickets of clustering blackbirds outside his window, he remembered he needed a job soon. The snow's diaspora from the North overnight had made shapes that shifted the earth into albino crows, rabbits, squirrels, mice, and bats, all white as the bare-naked birch trees and pine woods that housed them.

All his clothes were in his laundry pile. He was so tired and weak he skipped wearing his underwear and slipped on his 501 black jeans. He moved slowly like a dream, unable to convince himself his life was worth chasing after. Everything carouseled around him in meaningless square circles. Chitchee couldn't live in Edelweiss's boarding house without drinking himself into Korsakoff's syndrome, cirrhosis of the liver, and a face like Moussorgsky's. He had a taste for Bombay gin after reading about the gin craze in 18th century London, but he could only afford Phillips vodka, chipping in.

He could move downtown!

When he got off the #6 bus Uptown he froze and the air sucked the lungs out of his body.

He looked at the Laurel Avenue Apartments off Hennepin, by MCTC, but large centipedes like drunkard's stitches crawled out of the bathtub's drain. The neighbors in these fleabags and flophouses had oval and zitted faces like deviled eggs; and they rolled over on their bed-cots, snored from their broken bugles, and struggled against freezing by frequenting the local saloons with other small beer loons, chatting with bullheaded barkeepers, avoiding fights with Yakky, and hoping for a soft and sudden death after a long, friendless, and pointlessly hard life.

Chitchee cried at the absurdity of his passivity before all the passive suffering he saw. Dagny had inflamed Chitchee's depression. Nothing lifted his spirits from the tabled flatness of a cockroach's back he discovered in the bathroom of the Drake Hotel when he looked at a room there.

At the intersection of Lake & Hennepin, the WALK sign took so long a herd of reindeer could have crossed the street. With frosted eyebrows and rimed eyelashes, he stole into Carousel Square—every little baby hair on his face frozen white. Into the Figlio's Italo-Americano restaurant bathroom, he sprinted for a bursting, emergency pit stop. When he unzipped—he screamed. Figlio's host jumped backward and broke a wine rack. A drop of urine had frozen Chitchee's penis to the zipper on his 501s and his zipper had train-crashed into his circumcised penis.

Coincidentally, when the overloaded wine rack of wine bottles smashed on the floor and a deserted Carousel Square heard the smashing wine bottles that Chitchee thought his frozen penis had unleashed, Chitchee relaxed, felt much better, and waited for his penis to thaw until he realized the sounds and smells from the occupied stall emanated from Undone Buttons. So Chitchee booked with renewed purpose and job-hunted the mostly empty big box and small box stores to see if *anyone* was hiring.

After making the rounds, Chitchee saw everything in a new-as-blue light.

For one thing, *Snorri* worked at White Sox 'n' Sandals. He wore white socks, sandals, blue jean shorts, long underwear over his black hairy legs, black braided extensions down his back, and Fellini sunglasses.

The store had been empty all day long.

"I had to do it," said Snorri, wiping dark chocolate off his fingers with his tongue. "Go figure. Saami is over at The Rabbit Fern Store. Drunk as usual. Go figure."

"I'm tired," said Saami at The Rabbit Fern Store, crunching the stem of his already eaten chocolate-covered strawberry. "I got a free chocolate-covered strawberry at Ragnarok's because I know the manager, Astrid. I trade rabbit ferns with her for Americanos and I'm about due for a refill. Do you think she would like this giant jade plant from Madagascar?"

The Rabbit Fern Store—Saami smiling like Captain Morgan on the Spice Rum bottle while watering the rabbit ferns with a diligent spray bottle although the bottle had been empty all day long—was empty too.

"Why not? I'll bring it over there, I know Astrid," said Chitchee. "I have to work on my applications. I'll give it to her and bring you back your refill!"

There was an always-failing specialty store across from Figlio's Italo-Americano restaurant and Ragnarok's Choklit Stoppe was the current victim of the Carousel Square rack rent. Chitchee hunkered down at a drafty, wrought-iron, wobbly table outside Ragnarok's Choklit Stoppe and filled out applications with various colored pens and pencils for: the Wrangler Roast 'n' Boast, the Big Earth, the Admiral Sushi, Pavloni's Italian Grinders, SUP the What'sa Cooking Place, the Potholder PitStop, the Belt Buckler, the Cuff Link Kiosk, the B Fruity Juiceria, Gummo's Cummerbunds, Bill's Improbable Beef, Little Tweezer's Eyebrow Clinic, the Malibu Tanning Sensation, Carousel Tobacco (Torg was there maybe if you could see him in the smoke), Pizza-n-Kwiet, and Daisy Vang's New Age Cuticles of Cutiest Cuteness.

"Are you writing a book in the middle of Winter? What's it about? Summer?" asked Randy Quaalude, invading Chitchee's marble-topped table and knocking it with his shillelagh so that it wobbled three times.

"No, Randy," said Chitchee. "I'm looking for a job. I'm back to Carousel Square one."

"Looking for Oxy?" asked Randy. "Benzos? Xanax? What about videos?"

"Not now, Randy," grunted Chitchee. "Besides, the *Amelie* video I bought from you wasn't *Amelie* at all. It was porn, and it wasn't even French porn. It was one of those dumb bunny Playboy soft focus, swirling negligee, montage jobs. I watched it at Walker Library, but when a crowd formed behind me, Dale kicked everybody out and kept the video."

"He kicked my ass out of Walker three times. Didn't Kennedy tell you?" asked Randy, pulling out his dentures for a quick look-see. "I only sell *porn* videos."

"Oh," said Chitchee. "Good job, Kennedy! No, he forgot to mention."

"Hey Chitchee, you want a job?" asked Susquehanna, zooming and zeroing in on Chitchee's table.

In her new, motorized wheelchair, instead of the old manual kind, Susquehanna sat up straight and alert.

"Mirabal needs a bird sitter," said Susquehanna.

The buskers Kaspar, Howlin' Andy, and their friends also roosted at Ragnarok's Choklit Stoppe by Chitchee's table. Howling Andy played Bert Jansch's "Angi" on a beat-up guitar. Kaspar, whose passing resemblance to Prince often caused a double take, distributed 4-track cassette versions of his original songs with hand-printed lyrics in each personalized baggie.

Minerva sailed into Carousel Square—a happy grand birdmother! One of her parakeets had hatched an egg! Her birds glided around her apartment at night while she smoked weed nervously in her bathtub and blew the smoke down the bathtub drain to play it safe. The mere mention of Raven who sold marijuana by the eighths, sub eighths, nuggets, sub nuggets, and molecules would cause the DEA to scoop her up like Kemp's ice cream.

She feared FISA camps where they would detain and remove her ovaries, replace them with nano bots, and coat her with a permanent bio-film. Minerva passed a note to Chitchee: "Where is R?" She sniffed around for cameras hidden in the plethora of rabbit ferns and jade plants in plastic brown pots. She saw the white shirts of the night security cruise by the staircase to the second level. She withdrew the note and chewed it and ate it.

"I don't know, Minerva, but I saw him a couple days ago," said Chitchee, looking over his applications. "He's usually up all night astral-traveling on business. Raven must have a pretty low opinion of humanity, because he believes humans can't get to the moon, but tiny lizards can easily hurl through wormholes to get to Earth."

"Shhh . . . he might hear that while he is dreaming himself into a murder of crows. You know . . . the vibrations of it . . . he's psychically attuned to thought-prints of bloodshed. Sometimes when you see the crows completely envelope a bare elm or a telephone pole—that's him!"

"What? Are you kidding?"

Susquehanna charged inside Ragnarok's Choklit Stoppe for an outlet when the kitchen-aproned manager, Astrid Eskola, walked out looking to chat.

"You're open?" laughingly asked Chitchee.

"We're open!" said Astrid, looking over the sea of friends not ordering anything, but occupying marble-topped tables. "We're just not getting any business."

Astrid asked Chitchee whether BookSmart was going out of business too like all the small businesses in Carousel Square and while conversing, she sanitized marble-topped tables and cleared dishes.

"The official version is: we're still open, but we're cutting back on store hours to protest Daylight Savings Time," said Chitchee. "Don't tell everybody, but the actual book store was kaputt before I was even hired! It will have to be one of Andersen's

Imagined Communities from now on."

"Do you mean," asked Susquehanna, drowsily merging toward Chitchee's marble-topped table, "the affordable housing by Lyle's Polonaise Room? Are they hiring? I wouldn't mind a job of the imagination. We ain't no spring chickens anymore—"

A dossier of allergies in a ring binder for a pillow, her medications causing her to fall asleep without warning, she fell asleep in mid-sentence at Chitchee's table, head down.

Susquehanna awoke startled with stage fright when Astrid shook her shoulder.

Susquehanna passed around photos from her recent colonoscopy. Astrid, who looked down at them, arms akimbo, twisted her mouth like a sideways kiss, too sideways to be a genuine kiss.

"Are you okay, Susquehanna?" asked Astrid. "Let me get you a chocolate turtle."

Astrid fetched a tray of chocolate turtles that Libor Biskop had measured for rads and then had run from glowing with excitement.

Astrid sampled out a dish of chocolate turtles. She walked table to table offering the samples. She sat down next to Chitchee, because, she said, he was the kind of guy you had known all your life after meeting a week ago. Seeing that Chitchee had a lot of friends, Astrid figured Chitchee might draw in a lot of much-needed business, because Carousel Square was going under again.

"Why don't you work here?" asked Astrid.

"Really?" asked Chitchee with ingratiating, grateful, self-serving, and cringeworthy thanksgiving. "Hugs?"

"Well, no," said Astrid, twisting her mouth like a sideways kiss, too sideways to be a genuine kiss again.

But Astrid did hire Chitchee on the spot. Starting him the next day, she would inform Vinay Deep, the owner, of the new hire. They desperately needed to cover the hours Carousel Square demanded on the lease too. The previous chocolatier, Rachel, had died at her sister's wedding reception. She had mixed OxyContin, Xanax, and alcohol before passing out next to her passed-out married sister on the hotel room bed. Her sister woke up but Rachel did not—she had foamed at the mouth. After Rachel's funeral, an incessant gloom cast its clouds of contagion over the little chocolate shop. When Chitchee mentioned Rachel's death to Randy, he froze and Chitchee never saw him again. Susquehanna eventually moved into assisted living in Linden Hills. He conjectured, from talking to the apartment manager who had thrown Randy's home computer in the dumpster, that the news of Rachel's accidental overdose triggered Randy's accidental overdose or it could have been coincidence. Eventually Ragnarok's Choklit Stoppe failed, only to support another failure, Maud Borup, Inc another chocolate shop "with attitude" and even less of a reason for its useless existence in Carousel Square.

Chitchee was duly excited and fully ionized for his new job. He planned to read everything extant about chocolate—the Aztec codices, the *Popul Vuh*, Joanne Harris's *Chocolat,* and he vowed to make Roald Dahl's *Charlie and the Chocolate Factory* his vademecum. If he lived like a leaf-cutter ant and ate only chocolate turtles, he could open Ulysses & Sons in five years, courtesy of *Theobroma cacao.*

But his co-worker, Beda Holmgren, cultivated her own body odor as Earth's natural perfume, her Eau de Mace. She was training Chitchee the next day when Vinay scooted into Ragnarok's Choklit Stoppe, can of Reddi-Wip whipped cream in his hand. Vinay drew from the till and drove home in his Trailblazer to Roseville dissatisfied at his lowly position on the ladder of success— and already thinking the new hire was not pretty, looked stupid, and stank like green onions.

Vinay Deep was an impeccably tidy man with dark, massive, undecimated hair. He wore shield-shaped, wire-rimmed glasses—and his eyes were blank as milk. His wife, Thrania, managed Ragnarok's and Ragnarok's sister store, Viking Sweets on Grand Avenue in St. Paul off Rice Square. Viking Sweets also served hot chocolate, sold fudge, and peddled gee-gaw, gift-store gifts for out-of-state relatives whose idea of Minnesota was an endlessly snowy expanse, forming a whiteout that caused green-eyed sled dogs to disappear into their own traces.

Vinay cared little for his own chocolates. But his eyes re-animated like eels in a kiddie pool whenever talking about local sports (and he could go all the way back to Alan Page and on and on). He fretted about the X report every hour like Droopy Drawers, and indeed the drawer was drooping. But Vinay perked up at any mention of the Minnesota Vikings, giving him another chance to say that Randy Moss had dated his daughter; not only that, his daughter had done Bobby McFerrin's hair. Or his daughter had gotten into Randy Moss's hair or Bobby McFerrin's hair or his daughter had gotten into bed with both men at the same time while they did it in her hair. And it was not so much *names* he dropped as names he *dangled.*

Celebrity was more Lakshmi than Lakshmi, a better form of wealth, to Vinay. He collected mental autographs and cherished any random encounter with the famous, first or second hand. For instance, in California at a party held in Sly Stone's mansion for which Sly pulled a no show at his own house, because he didn't own it, Vinay had been on the same front lawn as Patti LaBelle. Vinay once asked Curtis Mayfield for a cigarette. Vinay had been at the same airport as Les McCann, standing in the line one over from Vinay. Vinay had been in a Mill Valley record shop when a member of the original Santana band purchased an album by Miles Davis. Then Vinay bought the same album by Miles Davis and loved it so he could retell the story. Vinay's favorite customer was Jerome, who worked at Rainbow Laundry on Hennepin, who had gotten the order to wash Beyonce's clothes, because she was on tour. Vinay then had the honor of knowing Jerome, who had fondled Beyonce's underwear.

The very same Jerome had seen Prince at New Power Generation.

"I met Prince at a party," said Chitchee.

"No, you didn't," said Vinay. "I kind of doubt Prince is floating around without bodyguards at the parties you go to. You probably met someone else!"

Chitchee agreed to this possibility. He enjoyed learning from Vinay (a celebrity vane in an April snow storm): how to make lattes, cappuccinos, and espresso drinks. How to serve slices of cake and sandwiches. How to tare weigh the chocolate pecans and almond clusters. How to clean the espresso machine with Puro. And, above all, what to do if Prince shows up.

Vinay demanded that his employees bubble, sparkle, and burst with joy. Vinay prided himself on his education—as people do who aren't sure if they have a real one, because he went to the U. He learned there how to tare-weigh people for importance by their connections; and those without wallets were simply not true sports fans in the All-American sense of meaning Business.

"I don't think the Vikings need a new *stadium*," said Chitchee, making a Sicilian mocha for himself. "I think they need a *Taj Mahal*, where they can rest up and have village girls exercise for them, while the Vikes drink mead from onyx-studded, gold goblets. Unveiling virgin courtesans fan cooling zephyrs across their banquets of roast venison, lamb, and goose. And then maybe they could win a Monday Night Football game. Sorry Vinay, but though the Vikes put on a strong first quarter, they get smeared in the second, and then come out at halftime determined to not get hurt. They sustain massive injuries, not from playing, but from seeing who can get in the door at the nearest strip club first."

Vinay never forgave Chitchee for this offensive foul, this offsides, this five yards backward, and another five yards for the outrageously racist and sexist remarks. Vinay had no connection with a "Taj Mahal" or "virgin courtesans." That was racism and sexism, pure and simple as the hate crime that would soon follow. Chitchee had been so blatantly rampant and egregious at the outset that Vinay planned Chitchee's quick undoing. Vinay immediately connived with Thrania over the phone to plot the redneck's downfall from grace—how to get rid of the new hire quickly and politically, for he "lacked all initiative, had no sense of urgency, smelled like a rat's armpit, lied to him about Prince, and exhibited the kind of everyday racism you find in all Americans, not to mention Thrania's own grandmother, the old white boot." The Deeps planned to secret-shop Chitchee on a shift he shared with Beda, then fire him "at will" for body odor, because that was known as "cause." Vinay feared to fire Beda (he feared her outright) for her body odor, foreseeing a discrimination lawsuit like Brown vs. Board, because Beda would shout "Fire" in the Supreme Court Building if she had to, which might tarnish Vinay's reputation as a successful entrepreneur. People were saying Vinay Deep could be the next Viktor Martensen, whom he was related to by similar Prince stories.

But, if such bad publicity came around to bite Vinay's ass . . .

Vinay was watching Chitchee count the sugar packets, the cups, and the cellophane packets when a customer approached Chitchee.

"'ey man, do you have potato chips?"

The customer was a meticulously-laced dandy with blue sunglasses, looking out over his paisley caftan.

Vinay saw Prince and secreted himself, hiding behind the pillar and unable to think how to approach "his Majesty."

"No, but if we did they would be delicious," Vinay whispered, sweat filming his forehead with an anxiety that made Chitchee nervous for him.

"No, but if we did they would be delicious," repeated Chitchee, confidently nodding with a plastic smile of approval.

Vinay gave Chitchee the OK sign, but his okay was a slug nickel in a nickel slot. Vinay seemed to be rehearsing what he should say, his hand outstretched to shake Prince's hand, but his hand was shaking, trembling; he caught his hand with his other hand to make it stop shaking and bit his hand.

"Can't eat just one!" cracked Chitchee with a wry, dried-out smile.

"Especially, if you don't have any," said Kaspar (who was a night busker), knuckling the marble-topped counter with two short raps. "Later, bro'."

Kaspar smiled, backpedaled, and walked out with a carefree saunter.

Vinay groaned and fell to his knees in paroxysms of agony.

"Why did you say 'Can't eat just one?' WHY DID YOU SAY THAT? He's not coming back! Prince is never coming back! Oh my God, do you even *know* who was just here?"

"Why wouldn't he come back? He's here every night," said Chitchee. "He plays outside Carousel Square."

"Where did he go?" asked Vinay, taking off his glasses and cleaning them with a shirt tail and looking for a cleaning fluid of any kind. "He plays outside? Have you lost your mind? You basically kicked Prince out of my store! My store! Is that him? What was he wearing? I didn't get a good look, I thought, my vision is so bad, damn . . . you should have given him the espresso machine for free! You could have at least introduced me! He seems to have liked you! Why would he come back to this chocolate hole-in-the-wall if he knows we don't have potato chips? You should have told him we're out of potato chips but there's a shipment of potato chips coming in from Puerto Rico within the hour! You idiot!"

A woman entered the store.

"Can I help you?" asked Chitchee. "We are out of potato chips. But we are getting in a shipment of potato chips from Puerto Rico within the hour."

"But we don't carry potato chips," said the customer. "Look, here's what I want!"

The customer read off an index card: "Give me a latte with a pump of grapefruit juice for the bitter-sensitive taste buds at the rear of my tongue. For the sour and salt-sensitive receptor sites of my tongue's filiform and circumvallate papillae, I'd like 1/4 pump cookie dough. For the sweet responsive buds at the tip of my tongue's circumvallate papillae, I'd like 1/2 pump Kahlua, 1/2 pump vanilla, and to eat—a toffee square cut into thirds. It's for my husband."

"Yes, ma'am!" said Chitchee, hurriedly set in motion like the espresso machine of the espresso machine.

She glared when Chitchee said "ma'am," but she appeared thankful as she was receiving the cup and saucer offered to her as a latte, minus all the pumps and toffee square cut into thirds.

Vinay burst out of the back storage area of supplies, threw his apron to the floor, and jostled the woman jiggling the steaming hot latte, frothy with a heart design Chitchee had created out of steamy milk foam especially for her delectation.

"Please move!" said Vinay. "Please get out of my life, woman!"

She emitted a piercing, high-pitched cry.

"Why were you standing there, Thrania?" said Vinay. "Was that on purpose? To block my getting to meet Prince? God, if we had a daughter I'd offer her hand in marriage to Prince! What am I saying? Why be stingy? I'd just give him my daughter! Why haven't you given me a daughter to give to Prince yet? I'm sure he'll be back! If we're lucky, we could have a daughter by then! We better get to work!"

Vinay stood outside the gated, grated wrought-iron doors. He looked as if someone had stolen the tip jar. He greeted Astrid who walked past him, stopped, and looked down at the floor.

"Why is there coffee all over the floor, Thrania?" asked Astrid. "Chitchee, can you get that mopped up?"

"Yes, ma'am!" said cheerful Chitchee.

After Chitchee mopped the floor, he cut the toffee square in thirds, careful not to rip his see-through plastic gloves. Order after order, Chitchee ran around in circles to impress Vinay, which had become impossible. Vinay and Thrania had a silent dinner at Ruby Tuesday's, and then he and his wife drove home to Roseville, where Vinay and Thrania watched vintage episodes of The George Michael Sports Machine. Vinay couldn't follow the bouncing balls because every time someone fumbled, Vinay fumbled. Vinay fumbled in front of the head coach Prince. Vinay blamed Chitchee for the missing of his missing blocks.

Shankara's *Crest Jewel of Discrimination* and *The Life of Ramakrishna*—that's what I should be reading Chitchee thought.

"Hey, Astrid," said Chitchee, "Vinay is batty. Vinay thought he saw Prince here!"

"Again?" asked Astrid, wryly twisting her lips, her eyes darting into corners for dirt to sweep. "Here's the thing, Chitchee: all the minimum wage earners in Carousel Square barter with the goods in their store to supplement their low pay. Only Kitchen Window makes a profit and can pay the rent, so the new owner's plan is to make Carousel Square a giant Kitchen Window and then we would have a corner in Kitchen Window as a subsidiary."

"Our lives are in the hands of anonymous investment groups?" asked Chitchee.

Astrid looked at the rings on her fingers. Chitchee looked at the rings on both her hands.

"That's a lot of spouses you have on your hands. Are those all wedding rings? Where did you get that one?" asked Chitchee. "Is your name Draupadi? Or do you mean J. Hudson's Jewelers is trading diamond rings for chocolate-covered pretzels?"

"No, Sassy gave it to me, you don't know Sassy? I'm surprised you don't know Sassy. You know everybody, and you don't know Sassy?" asked Astrid.

"Who?"

"The creepy guy who wears a hijab," continued Astrid as she swept the corners of the shop with her corn broom. "He dresses like a Somali woman sometimes. He hangs out in the mall and gives all the girls jewelry. He kisses their hands, asks for hugs—he was always hitting on the girls at Heartbreaker."

"What does he do for a living?" asked Chitchee.

"He's a teacher," said Astrid.

"Does he have really hairy armpits?" asked Chitchee.

"He gave me this ring," said Astrid. "Actually, I'm going to J. Hudson's to see if Sassy *really* bought this. And then I'm going home. You'll be okay—it looks like all your friends are here."

Libor Biskop spread out his correspondence course over two marble-topped tables, notebooks disproving the General Theory of Relativity and approving the General Theory of Squaring the Circle with Perpetual Quantum Tunneling. Linda Rolvaag walked into Ragnarok's for another sample coffee of the day (from Tegulcipa) and poured the sugar of the day into it from the sugar canister of the day, whose lid she had removed for the day. She sobbed because Libor had picked on her and "he wasn't supposed to do that." The Three Grasshoppers had heard that Chitchee worked at Ragnarok's so they dropped by for free samples with Dougal's formaldehyde toes in a kimchi jar—because the library was closed (rolling papers quickly fell on the floor by their feet or parts of their feet). Saami greeted Linda after Saami had smuggled into Ragnarok's a 6-feet tall horsetail fern and traded it for lemon squares and almond bark. Snorri in his black cut-offs, Birkenstocks, and long underwear, walked in the door, bearing a pair of damaged, striped black socks that had silhouetted profiles of the Carpenters, for trade, in the hopes of scoring a hot, peppery chocolate made with real bar chocolate. Libor ran inside Ragnarok's and begged permission to hand-dowse the bags of chocolate-covered potato chips for their radioactivity (and then he would decide how much he didn't want any).

Walks in Aubrey Aalgaard, concerned but not upset, but not really *too* concerned about her work record and never depressed as ever, though a little concerned about the fact that The Angry Bagel Emporium had fired her for sitting down on the job, cell phone use, and insubordination to her superior. Nevertheless, she shone like a sunny Samoyed in a four-winds hat, looking like a knock-kneed yearling: her sandy hair was gold-braided and twisted in withy plaits over a bright blue scarf that matched her irises' sky blues. She handed Chitchee the Ragnarok coffee cup, saw it wasn't completely clean, stopped, asked for a napkin, wiped the traces of former Aloysius sips from the world, requested a replacement lid, clasped it, and handed the recycled cup respectfully to Chitchee.

"Another depth charge, please," said Aubrey, apprehensively satisfied. "And you don't have to give me a deal. I want to pay the full amount. I have nothing to barter."

She busied herself by sorting out all her spilled-out, spare change (which she usually saved for panhandlers) on the marble-topped counter.

Chitchee, by looking out Ragnarok's window facing Hennepin, saw Aloysius outside BookSmart, pacing outside and wearing only a jean jacket. Aloysius hotboxed a whole Carousel cigarette without thinking. Aloysius walked back inside BookSmart without realizing it.

"Aubrey, thanks for paying for the publishing of the first hundred copies of *Quantum Biscuits*," said Chitchee. "Do you think Viktor will still pay us back?"

"I don't know, I'm so worried about my dad," said Aubrey, "he's trying to do everything at once with a million arms."

"We are *all* worried about your dad," said Chitchee. "Your dad has been Lord Shiva to Hennepin Avenue for ages. Better yet, he's the Avalokitesvara of Hennepin and Lake and the Kuan Yin of Lake and Hennepin. And it seems he's dying every day, but he always bounces back! He has grits and okra too! He can do it all."

A phone rang with the ringtone of alarm bells. Everyone turned around, jerked convulsively for their own phones, jumped into their backpacks, looked for Carousel Square Security smoke detectors, or they pretended they didn't hear anything.

"Hi Dad! What? Call 911! Listen to me! It's not ten thousand dollars! No ambulance ride cost ten thousand dollars! What do you mean you're okay now? Oh my God, Chitchee, that was my Dad. He thinks his heart is racing."

Chitchee skipped closing procedures for the store and, without cleaning the espresso machine, kicked everyone out by quickly dimming the dimming switch. He locked in whoever wouldn't leave.

Aubrey and Chitchee ran diagonally and parallel through the intersection.

Aloysius breathed. He lay on the floor, stood up, and walked—but only bent over like a fishing rod that's hooked a fish. He had aged thirty years in one stroke. His face had been drawn and quartered. Since he absolutely refused an ambulance, Aubrey fetched her car. They sped to Hennepin County Medical Center's ER, where Noel, chewing and biting on his lower lip, met them at the entrance of HCMC. Noel held gloved hands with Ye Young, who chewed and bit her lower lip. Noel, Ye Young, Chitchee, and Aubrey helped Aloysius walk into the warm air of the building

The curtained hospital room opened out onto a hall where the nurses and doctors visited room to room: tableaus of grief in one room, joys of recovery in another.

Dr. Li Fan stepped into Aloysius's bedroom. The ring on his finger revealed his recent marriage to the nurse, Shuwen, who gave a slight bow of recognition to Chitchee, following Li Fan to the bedside of Aloysius. Saami and Snorri, having properly closed their deserted stores, taxied to HCMC to attend Aloysius's bedside, if he was still there.

"Have you been experiencing a lot of stress lately?" asked Dr. Li Fan, calibrating Aloysius's vital numbers and heart signs.

"No," said Aloysius. "Why? Do I look a little worried? You don't have a Coke machine, do ya, Doc?"

"Yes, he has, Dr. Li," said Aubrey, various "s's" creasing her forehead, drawing together her blonde eyebrows like worrying purse-strings. "He's running a giant book store by himself."

"Well, okay," conceded Aloysius. "I didn't want to tell you guys, but I guess the owner Viktor doesn't get along with his son Nestor and—"

"The prick who thinks he's a genius?" interjected Saami, rolling his eyes.

"Which prick who thinks he's a genius?" asked Chitchee. "There's the prick who thinks being a prick is being a genius, that's Nestor Martensen, and there's the prick who thinks being a genius is being a prick, that's Mono Boondalicks. There's Libor Biskop who is a prick because he lost his genius when he smelled a can of twelve-year old paint, and there's—"

"Okay, okay, Chitchee, hold off on the roll call of genius," said Aloysius. "Really the only genius in the room is—"

Everybody leaned forward, thinking their name would ring out in the heavens and shake the stars with fame, renown, and recognition.

"Aubrey!"

A slight decrease in air pressure was registered when everyone looked at Aubrey, who blushed when everybody stared at her incredulously.

"I should have told you before," continued Aloysius, "that Viktor called me today. He plans to make BookSmart a bar and give it to his son Nestor, the Club Miami manager. I will be Nestor's bar-back—at minimum wage and we will split the tip jar. It will be called BarSmart. Viktor said to hell with Minnesota. It's all cornfields. He hates Minnesota. I guess because there are too many laws, and the taxes are over his head like a field of corn. So, he says!"

"What!" yelled softly Aubrey, looking around so as not to disturb. "BarSmart? That's awful!"

"That's Saint Awful!" said Chitchee, his hands of prayer over his face except for the eyes, which popped at the same time he convulsed.

Hollow groans emerged from Chitchee's stomach. He bit his hand. He ran out in the hospital hall and vomited when Jason Unterguggenberger, his flesh tone a colorless wisteria, headphones on, was walking down the hall by Aloysius's room.

"Hey, you guys, I just saw an alien!" said Jason, clasping his green robe in the back with one hand while stepping around Chitchee, who then went to apologize to the janitor.

"The alien is on the fourth floor!" said Jason. "He OD'ed!"

"We're closed, Jason!" said Snorri.

Jason smiled, reading Snorri's lips, and walked away, rocking.

"No one," said Aloysius, his arms resting on the bed sheet wrapped over him neatly, "hates Nestor more than his own father

Viktor. I guess it shouldn't surprise us that Viktor calls him a POS! What a piece of work Viktor is! I don't even know the guy and he's telling me his own son is a talentless fuck, a completely tin-eared, heavy-metal doodlebug. I don't know Nestor, he's probably a really nice guy—if the biggest bastard in the world is your father, and he disowns you out of some strange envy, and then announces that he's not playing favorites because he cut everybody out of his will!"

"Doesn't Nestor have a thing for your ex, Chitchee?" asked Snorri solemnly when Chitchee, swishing water down, walked back in the room. "Pardon me for prying of course, but Madison told me they are codependent enablers of the worst kind . . . on the rocks all the time . . . or some such deal?"

"*Who* rocks?" asked Ye Young.

"Not us," said Aloysius, feebly, making a feeble joke that garnered an enormous response, levitating the hospital room's mood with inflated hilarity.

"If Viktor turns BookSmart into BarSmart—Aloysius," said Chitchee, "maybe you could get us all jobs as bar-back *assistants*?"

The general consensus of the white-coated doctors, stepping out of the way of the janitor attacking their shoes with his mop, was delivered by Dr. Li:

"Aloysius, you had a panic attack. You'll have to stay overnight, so we can give stress test in the morning."

"Hey, Doc!" said Aloysius to Dr. Li Fan, leaving with the RN Shuwen.

"Yes?"

"Good job, thanks man," said Aloysius, both thumbs up, recovering his old smile—the old smile he pulled from the old valise of smiles he had in his mental closet from long ago.

Aloysius told Chitchee if it came to eviction or homelessness, Chitchee could sleep in BookSmart's basement at night if Chitchee agreed to leave in the morning or work for free when Aloysius arrived to open the store around ten. Aloysius would keep the keys and let Chitchee in and out for walks like a dog.

"Oh, thank you!" said Chitchee.

He hugged Aloysius as everything on the hospital bed flew off it.

The shared green curtain between the two beds coughed, extending outward.

"Hey, there is someone behind this curtain!" said Chitchee, yanking the curtain back.

"Nestor!" said Chitchee. "Behind curtain number two! What are you doing here?"

"What does it look like? Practicing pentatonic and Mixolydian scales?" asked Nestor, quietly running his fingers over his knee; and the tilt backward to his head suggested he had been cheated out of his inheritance, out of spite.

Everyone who had gathered around Aloysius's bed tacitly replayed their conversations about super-sensitive, super-intelligent Nestor on their mental recording devices to check who said what offensive remark.

"I was stabbed," said Nestor. "It was a steak knife."

"So was I! Your dad hates you like he hates me?" asked Chitchee. "Is Viktor your real dad? How do you know you're not an accident?"

Nestor lay recovering from what Chitchee blurted. Nestor's eyes were blue and black. His lips were purple. He looked mauled.

"Could you be more specific?" asked Chitchee. "What kind of steak knife? A filet mignon steak knife? That would be like a butter knife. Were you at Murray's?"

"Somebody dosed our drinks at Club Miami," said Nestor apathetic as a coal biscuit.

"Sure it wasn't you?" asked Chitchee.

Emotions to leave stirred quietly across the field of vibrations.

"I'm afraid I'm not following you," said Snorri. "Who are you, or should I say whom, are you referring to with the word 'our' or 'us?'"

Nestor's lips twisted like long red jalapenos, and he looked up at Chitchee with pity.

"Are you going to be okay, buddy?" asked Aloysius to Nestor.

"Oh, as soon I get over being a talentless fuck," said Nestor, looking out the hospital window at the Minneapolis skyline.

The snow fed the Mississippi River and roofed the slate and shingled houses with ice.

"Looks like a house is burning out there!" said Nestor with a wry satisfaction. "Morons all—out there! Mostly liberal snowflakes, of course. You can tell by the way they have all been brainwashed. Everyone in this hell hole of a town can go to some other hell hole of a town for all I care. Hah! The king is dead, long live the king. What does that mean anyway? What's that from, an Elvis song? Chitchee? You're good at the useless facts of bunk history."

"It refers to *The Golden Bough*," said Chitchee, "or its thesis. Or *The White Goddess*, but there the woman castrates the old king with a sickle and beheads him with a scythe. You should ask Marija Gombutas. She shops at Rainbow I hear."

"You're not talentless," said LaDonna, who stood up and yawned. "Oh! All your fans are here!"

She held Nestor's hand and stroked his little fingers.

"You know I wouldn't have stabbed you unless I was messed up on GHB, don't you?" continued LaDonna.

Everyone quaked a little in his or her own way, glaciating out the door, and for Chitchee it was a good time to leave awkwardly too.

"GHB," said Nestor. "I'm probably dehydrated from that in my drink and my sleep cycle being off from too late a cup of coffee, giving me that twinge in my gall bladder this morning I told you about before breakfast when I drank that bit of bad water. And then it was Walgreen's orange juice from a frozen concentrate made in China! Why did I poison myself with Chinese orange juice? Baby, can you call the nurse? I want her to check my levels for dopamine, serotonin, and the electric potential at the synapses in my fingertips. To see if I can still play keyboards better than Prince."

"You look so sad!" mirrored LaDonna.

"The thought of letting someone like a doctor tell me what to do about my health! I must be getting old," said Nestor, shaking his hair forward and looking cross-eyed forward for gray hair. "That's like a weatherman telling me about climate change. What's the world coming to?"

Everyone but Aubrey left Aloysius's bedside, and she drew the green curtain to rebuild the partition; Aubrey fell asleep as soon as she sat down on the chair, which the nurse Shuwen had provided.

"I wasn't flirting with Yakky at DreamGirls, baby, last summer! Is that even possible?" asked LaDonna.

She leaned over Nestor and kissed his smooth forehead, smoothing it gratuitously with her scarred, needle-pointed hands.

Nestor had sustained a broken arm on the sidewalk outside DreamGirls on Hennepin Avenue in the erotic heat of the neon night last summer when Nestor had words with a guy on a Harley, and then another guy on a Harley, and then another guy on a Harley, who had picked up LaDonna off the ground by her waist and claimed her as his squeeze.

Chitchee bundled into his coat, bundled into a frozen bus, in which everyone was bundled, and the bus bundled off into a winter thunderstorm.

Chitchee stepped off the exhausting bus, the empty bus, exhausted. He ambled like a dead man into the nose-piercing cold, the ice-pricking needles of ice injecting him with electric shivers. Running for shelter from the cold, he made ready to scream through two scarves wet with perspiring curses. But the unstarred sky floated like a large ash-black snowflake, sooty-fresh supplements leafing down like fragments of a larger, unwritten confession.

"Oh, my God," said Edelweiss in her stout housecoat, ear muffs, and steel-toed marching shoes. "My house is burning down!"

Chitchee hustled in a huddle to the House of Edelweiss, hurrying at a pace that would have ended in a frozen gallop—but for the blaze of sirens blasting the air.

Fire hoses aimed thin quicksilver arcs into the bedrooms. Windows poured flames upward from the attic like hell hounds barking on fire. On the roof, black cumulus smoke. Fire trucks, whose ladders leaned on a window next to twenty-foot flames, dwarfed the dwarf-like fire crews in yellow and tarpaulin-black, the yellow of yellow-jackets. Ambulances shrieked and fire rigs flickered in the splinters of the white, orange, and yellow flames.

Bobblehead slipped on the roof in Gudrun's nightie, falling in a barrel roll onto a snow bank. Libor, sheathed in his fur-trimmed parka, though pant-less, sobbed so hard he hyperventilated and the wind was knocked out of him as if with a baseball bat. The ghostly inhabitants of a cave with Sausage Man leading them out coughed into the crowd where paramedics triaged them in well-trained units.

Gudrun's shade was in the draped window of Chitchee's bedroom.

"Gudrun! Get out!" Chitchee shouted.

But I'm naked, she seemed to be saying, *I can't go out*. The house's blaze released a fire storm. And the ash bounced down like the feathers of a gigantic, fairy-taled, black swan onto the white snow. Drapes surrounded Gudrun with ghostly hands. And she vanished, flying toward heaven, passed out from the loathsome fumes of smoke the house exhaled.

A mad squirrel ran screaming into the House of Edelweiss.

Something like a two-by-four upended Chitchee at the black walnut front door and smacked him down cold with an echoing skull. Kennedy had draped Gudrun around his mastiff shoulders like a terry-cloth towel. He had blindly head-butted Chitchee, who woke up on a stretcher seeing one side of the House of Edelweiss reveal the ribs of the burning, balloon-framed house. The house collapsed into itself like a giant brown bat drawing in its wings and exhaling smoke. One neighbor said he saw lightning strike Edelweiss's roof. Another neighbor reported seeing suspicious-looking taggers run to a waiting '62 Corvair. *Good Morning, Minnesota* reported that the fire was under investigation, but that was the last anyone heard about it. In the end, the lodgers pointed their fingers at Bobblehead for smoking in bed, but Kennedy swore he smelled gasoline.

THE RESURRECTION OF THE INDESTRUCTIBLE BOOK JESUS

Everyone escaped safely with minor injuries and henceforth Chitchee slept in the BookSmart basement. He lost everything he owned in the fire except the books he had already deposited in the BookSmart basement, after his virtual eviction from Fremont Terrace Apartments.

He woke up in BookSmart's overstock and storage area, walked over to Carousel Square, received his firing with aplomb, and walked back to BookSmart. Exhilarated, his life was so simple that all he had to do was roll off a couch and climb upstairs; he prayed to Jesus that the money to open Ulysses & Sons would snow down from Heaven soon.

"Register is broken," said Saami to Chitchee. "We will be closing early. Calculator broke too."

Saami wore a money-changer belt that a hot dog vendor at the Old Met Stadium might have worn, the vendor selling deliciously bland hot dogs from his steaming hot cooler, the grimy, Kelly green apron underneath.

"Books, hee-yuh! Git yer smokin' hot books, hee-yuh!" said Saami.

"What happened to the register?" asked Chitchee, astonished.

Chitchee's round white face was blank as a plate on a plated plate shelf.

"It snapped," said Saami, digging a thumbnail into his soul patch. "I ran a Z report instead of an X report or an X report instead of a Z report. It's all alphabet city to me! One of them is for the morning and the other is for a solar eclipse, or something? The head cheese can fix it when he gets back to normal. I've already hit every button twice. It doesn't matter anyway, because there are no sales yet. And if there were sales they would come out as imaginary numbers for the imaginary book store where I imagine I'm working in my imagination with you. When I was growing up I always imagined myself working in a book store, but then I thought later I must have imagined it."

"Get a grip on yourself, dreamer!" said Chitchee. "We have to keep BookSmart open for Aloysius. We'll get by without a cash register. The first step toward hope is always absolute hopelessness. We have an abacus in base 2 in the basement too. I'll go get it. It's never over."

"So you looked at my books, boss? Maybe I came in too early for payouts?" heard Chitchee and froze in his sneaker steps.

"Okay," said Saami to The Indestructible Book Jesus. "I looked at your books. Here's ten bucks to take them back."

"Wait, Saami, let me look at his books!" said Chitchee.

Torg blew in through the front door as if goosed by the winter wind. He pivoted and swiveled, riled at the ill treatment of his vulnerable blind body by something as cruel as cold chance. Torg's savant-like sensitivity to odors detected seven molecules of paint on a house painter. The fumes decked him. He smelled acrylic mixed with the sour smell of an eggshell finish. The smell tanged against his nostrils' walls and inflated his face like a clammy gherkin soaking in pickle brine and vinegar. He sneezed as if by a remote control.

"Isatvastra?" exclaimed Torg. "Is that really you?"

"Torg?" asked The Indestructible Book Jesus, diligently unpacking boxes of books for his probable pack of cigarettes. "I thought you died and went to seventh heaven."

"I did, but it was just more rip-offs up there," said Torg, smiling harshly, which was a tell that his life was fucked. "So I came back because I got a better price for aluminum cans here."

"Holy Indestructible Book Jesus!" interrupted Chitchee, looking through the boxes eagerly. "Look at all these trashy bodice rippers! We have to have these, Saami! Women love these!"

"Not Beda! She probably hates them passionately and wants to rip the covers off them," said Saami, watching Chitchee paw excitedly through the boxes Saami had skimmed and dismissed.

"Very funny," said Chitchee. "She's the one who always asks for them."

Torg looked around the store. Where was she? His she. Her he. What was her name? Caressa? Carissa? Carrie Ann?

"Have you ever been in love, Indestructible Book Jesus?" asked Chitchee.

"Hey boss, you sure ask some good ones," said The Indestructible Book Jesus too busy to look up from his strict regimen of dragging in the boxes of unwanted books and dragging out the boxes of unwanted books while Skooge circled the block for hours in the '65 Chevy station wagon, looking for parking in the snow banks and losing his tracks in time.

"I grew up on a farm," continued The Indestructible Book Jesus, standing on his shovel for a rest. "But for a while my pops ran a combo gas station/Zoroastrian fire temple in Wisconsin, where I was a gas station attendant. You never forget your first one. Or any of them really, boss. How can you ever forget a woman?"

He sighed, thought for a moment, and returned to his boxes, looking like a calf-roper at a hobo rodeo.

"Care to spill your guts in a book store?" asked Chitchee, unloading more pulp from the pulpy boxes.

The Indestructible Book Jesus turned misty-eyed, wistful, and soft focus:

"It was an ice cream thing at the Interfaith Church of Unitarian Ice Cream—I forget what they called the damney thing. Peg was visiting relatives who ran Sweetser Oakes Dairy, and we got to hankering one night on Lake Orange. And then another twenty nights. But damn if she wasn't already hitched. She left for Minnesota. I heard she later married an astronaut related to Walt Disney. Her family so liked me that they hired me on, washing milk bottles for 65 cents an hour. Then I was in charge of ice cream production, earning the position of Ice Cream Plant Manager of the Month in 1965. I worked for Sweetser Oakes Food Company for more than 40 years. I designed new plants for Sweetser Oakes. And then Windows 95 came into the office. It was like when a bobcat encounters a bear. And we tangled. So when I had a stroke in front of my computer in 1997, I retired. I couldn't sit around though, Torg. I got antsy to work good thoughts, good words, and good deeds. Social! That's what they call it. An ice cream social. And the name of the church had something to do with infinity."

Chitchee's face was a book. The creases and the bumps on his forehead were the water damage on the book's dust jacket. He watched The Indestructible Book Jesus upload Skooge's '65 station wagon. It fishtailed into the intersection.

"Every book is a seal looking for an air-hole in the ice to breathe through," blurted Chitchee aloud, bit his hand, and sneezed, which triggered "The Ants Go Marching." Chitchee diligently priced and shelved books as usual. "*The little one stops to suck his thumb . . .*"

Night had appeared magically like a trick.

"Good job, everybody," said Aloysius, sadly adverbing farewell from his saddle-bagged eyes. "I'm going home for a smoke, Southern Comfort, and some Allman Brothers."

"Oh wait," Aloysius continued, watching TV. "I already *am* home!"

The Aalgaard TV was always ON even when it was OFF. Aloysius liked to fall asleep in front of the TV. He tuned to the Big Bang on a dead channel, basked in the white noise of the black body background radiation, and dreamed of a different universe, where the evil that men do was not done.

"I'll be back to work tomorrow, right buddy?" said Aloysius to the refrigerator. "After all, Noel was right. I *am* a significant member of the community. And as Snorri said, a book store is like a famous educator like . . . like . . . are there any famous educators besides Dr. Seuss? And as Saami said . . . what did he say? He must have said something. We used to talk a lot over the years! I have to admit, he's been as loyal as an egg. Anyway, Minneapolis sure does love her book stores. I'll go with that for now."

"Hello? Are your closed minds still open?" asked Grover Gossick, his face pinched red by his numbing scramble from a Blue and White Taxi. "The knowledgeable conservative is back to tell the progressive agents of the Red Terror, I'm back! You know, like Arnold? You gotta love Arnold! I said you gotta love Arnold! The Governor of California!"

A pin dropped. Big Bang!

It was Big Bangs all the way down.

Grover wheeled in his relic Keeler Polygraph, the same one he bought at a garage sale in Prospect Park for five skins from Arthur Hillswick of Hillswick Investigations, LLC detective agency, licensed, and bonded. Arthur Hillswick sold it to Grover and threw in a striped box of striped, bendable straws. Wheeling the Keeler Polygraph on the red runner in front of the maroon counter, Grover had vindication on the tips of his lips, tasted revenge, and stared with a hollow, icy grin at Chitchee.

"I told y'all I was coming back with the Truth," said Grover, "and I kept my promise as a man of his word, y'all!"

"Has anyone ever won an argument with you?" asked Chitchee. "Or cared?"

"Finally," said Grover, "I'm going to prove to Minneapolis and *y'all* that this communist book store is owned and operated by the Communist Party. All book stores are. And so are you, Powderhorn Park poofdahs! Why is it they love me at Battlefield Books on Highway 7, but when I come here y'all call me a liar? Answer me that, Manager Mao!"

"Face it, Grover," said Chitchee, plugging in the Keeler Polygraph into the wooly, mammoth-haired power strip, "Stalin killed Communism. You're chasing your own rainbow."

Noel volunteered uncomfortably to prove he was not a member of the Communist Party. Grover wired Noel with electrodes. Ye Young held Noel's hand, and she expected electrification any moment. She looked closer at Grover's hair, black and white and phony. His mustacheless beard jutted out like a shiv sharp enough to kill a prison bull.

"It looks bogus," said Ye Young. "It doesn't look scientific. Is this a creative science project?"

"This is America," said Grover, who smiled like an adder with two heads and no tail.

Grover stared at Ye Young, and Ye Young stared unmoving and intently at the unmoving needle on the polygraph.

"As if a woman would know anything about science," muttered Grover.

Noel's eyebrows leapt up with Grover's assertion.

"But I'll admit—something is wrong with the calc-, calistrations—it might have gotten bumped on the way in. The needle isn't moving. Hmmm. Of course, you don't believe in dinosaurs do you? That old hoax? I suppose you grew up in China believing in evolution. The Miller-Urey experiment was proven to have been faked. I myself am the proof of that. The Milgram experiment solidly proved that not only are most human beings weaklings at administering pain, but that the strong will be ostracized for their strength. She has magnets on her!"

"I don't know where this is going," said Noel.

"The lives of strong babies are so sacred that if you disagree with one like me your seed must be made void," said Grover, "that's where this is going."

Grover itched his beard, a white stripe from ear to ear like a footballer's chin-strap, clean shaven below the nose to above the jawline. He scratched his neck's beard with the backs of his fingernails and waited for the needle to budge. He flicked it with his finger. A drop of sniffled snot landed on the device's ohmmeter.

"With you," said Noel, "the only thing that matters is that all the so-called *weak* babies be exposed to the criminal justice system, which provides the jobs that keep the prison systems going—just so long as the jobs are profitable enough to melt the polar ice caps—creating other jobs—more and more jobs out to infinity—finally putting the angels to work—"

"Nash equilibrium?" asked Ye Young. "Is this—?"

"Chitchee," said Torg dreamily, "have you seen that one woman who was here? You know her, with that hauntingly silky voice. You know, the satin doll with the great . . . chest?"

"Exactly!" said Grover, looking at Torg. "Yes, in a certain sense, as long as the polar ice caps keep melting, everything will be okay. Because there ain't no such thing as no O-Zone or free lunch! Unless you are sitting around an O-Zone hole waiting for a welfare check! I am sorry for your loss of sight. I actually have the cure for that."

"Your mind has been intentionally left blank," said Torg, jerked from a pleasant, nice and slow dream, slow dream-dancing to the music of Ella Fitzgerald and Joe Pass.

"I have the remedy for your blindness," said Grover to Torg. "Prayer to Jesus! Black mold did that to you. Black mold, which is spread by Communists. Black mold sandwiches eating us and our sacred nation every day with extra mustard. Black mustard. I pray to the Stars and Stripes. God hears my prayers. I made a deal with Him."

"What? Through the ozone hole?" said Torg. "*You* can take an American flagpole up your arse hole!"

"You're talking to a Navy Seal, half pint!" said Grover. "I served with Jesse Ventura! Thank me for my service!"

Beda and Minerva (a head taller behind her) climbed the stairs from the basement, Minerva looking unable to resist Beda's emotional pull on her rounded shoulders like a tide.

"Where *is* your subaltern studies section, Noel?" asked Beda. "Or is that too far left to ask a neo-liberal? I don't see *any* new metanarratives in your store. Or meta discourses of the meta binaries on women as imagined geographies. Why? I think it's because you and your right-wing book store patronize the subaltern class. At the same time you are guilty of the "O" word. This book store is superstitious, quaint, outmoded, irrational, submissive, let me finish—and I don't need any of your right-wing, mansplaining manterruptions!"

"Why do *y'all* dress funny?" asked Grover, eyeballing Beda's fresh labrets. "You know? You people with your pants down around your bee-hinds!"

Beda looked at Noel, Grover, Chitchee, YeYoung, and Saami, who was bravely and carefully organizing the books Beda brought for Saami to form into REJECT piles.

"Nope, can't use these Beda!" said Saami. "We don't need any more *Kite Runners*."

"Saami! You took everybody else's *Kite Runners*! Why not mine?" asked Beda.

Beda looked betrayed, bewildered, and bumped.

"You, sir, asked me why I wear what I wear? Because throughout the whole of human history," continued Beda, "men have determined my clothes. And if you can't dress like Catherine Deneuve the French snobs spit you out like chew! Then they chew you out like spit! And you know why I eat the things I eat? Because throughout the whole of man's history, men ordered the canon of cooking. Haute cuisine? Male. Peanut butter and jelly sandwiches. Female. All the French cooking schools? Men posing as women for the highest pay grades! That's why I only use Julia Child's recipes, because she didn't whore herself out on street corners to the five-star pimps in the world's best Michelin brothels, force-feeding dead white male meat down our mouths—every time Minerva and I go out for a bite!"

The front door banged and shook.

Yardley Singleton trudged into BookSmart under a cloud of dark steam and snowflakes. He wore an impossibly-orange snowmobile suit, which looked like a prison jumpsuit, standing in oversized, lock-stitched, sealskin mukluks. He had the face of a teddy bear on a hunger strike.

"So why should *I*," continued Beda, pivoting back to Minerva, "feel *ashamed* if I don't like dead white food shoved up my ass! And then be made to wear the shirt off a dead white man's back?"

Hurt, stepped on, and shoulders stooped, Yardley Singleton walked straight into Minerva and hugged her.

"Dad! What happened?" asked Minerva.

"All I have left, Minerva," said Yardley, stepping back and hugging Beda, cheek to cheek. "I had to move into the Drake Hotel where there are so many cockroaches in the bathroom, you can't even open the door! I was evicted by MPG for "cause." Too many books. Fire hazard they said. And then they said all the graffiti in Minneapolis was done by me."

"Why didn't you call me?" asked Minerva.

"Go on," said Beda, with her eyebrows up and surprised, dimpling her forehead with concern.

Yardley continued: the Vietnamese caretaker came by one day for an inspection of all the MPG apartments, starting with Yardley's at 7:00 a. m. She asked him where his TV was. There were too many books in the apartment. Yardley got pissed, she got pissed, fire marshal came over, more pissed, Yardley called a pissed-off lawyer who advised him to take it to court and piss on it. Yardley took the whole pissing match to court, Yardley said his books were service animals, he lost, the judge pissed on him, then pissed on his books, then Yardley got so pissed, he pissed off the court fees, slapped all his tweedy-twilley, Cambridge suits from Bloomsbury into a pissed-off storage locker, and he split the pissing fees with some pissed-off ol' pisser named Jason the Pissed Off Argonaut, whose execrable taste in music was out-rivaled by his execrable taste in everything else.

Then Yardley booked a room at the Drake Hotel downtown.

"Excuse me," said Grover to Yardley, "for talking while you are swearing. We can proceed now, Noel. The needle is now moving, and it says all the liberals in this room who voted for Obama are all liars. Well, I guess the experiment is over. And again I was perfectly correct! I deserve credit at least for showing *y'all* y'all brainwashed."

"Thank you for your service," said Chitchee.

"You're seven miles behind me, son," said Grover. "I've answered more questions in my lifetime than you *dreamed* had answers."

"We done here?" asked YeYoung.

"Yes, y'all, the Keeler is a little buggy," said Grover, "but I bet Dan the Maintenance Man in my building would take a look. They say he can just about fix anything."

Recently recovered from a fractured vertebrae, a bruised kidney, and two cracked ribs, Zalar looked racoon-eyed. Zalar secreted himself into BookSmart. His skin was a white film of alcoholic sweat. And his too-small parka grew his hands out, because he was wearing the wrong parka. He had abrasions on his nose and forehead.

"*Marhaba*," said Chitchee, "Farag, Fargo, Farrago the Pure One, or whatever your enigmatic name is today."

"You fucker," said Zalar, looking around BookSmart, making minotaurian, miniaturized faces. "I heard the Family Photo

Album showed up here!"

"It showed up," joked Chitchee, "but we sold it to an undercover FBI agent. This guy here!"

Chitchee flipped his thumb toward Grover.

Grover's eyes recoiled and rocketed from their sockets.

Grover's flesh melted from his bones and formed a puddle of glue.

Zalar "v"ed his first two fingers, gestured to poke out his own eyes, turned his hand, and stabbed his two fingers at his father's eyes.

"What are *you* looking at?" asked Zalar. "Hey, you look familiar. Waaa-i-i-t."

"Zalar!" barked the purple Irish wolfhound outside with the mulberry beard and mutton chops. "Where'd ya go, buddy?"

Dougal, a purple hairball, lost his duck-egg wire rims minus one lens, upchucked over Hennepin Avenue, and hunched-over coughing up purple hairballs. He barked up the evergreen-wreathed lamp post outside Club Miami. Baggy-parkaed and baggy-jeaned in his loose-laced Red Wing boots, Dougal bolted himself to a NO PARKING sign—where he stood, floating up to his purple eyeballs. He felt the looney sign embrace him warmly. When he kissed its cold iron ironically, his lips froze to the metal. He had to leave his lips on the NO PARKING sign when he pried his lips away.

"Zalar?" asked Grover. "Son? Wait!"

Zalar stumbled out the BookSmart front door, fumbled past Dougal, and tread scurvily back into Club Miami's dark, loud foyer and portiered vestibule. The bouncer stood up from his stool.

Viktor had hired his friends from the Minneapolis Police Department for a hundred dollars an hour to work as Club Miami bouncers, and his best friend Sergeant Bob "BB" Robbins had been best man at his wedding for which Viktor reciprocated when BB married Daisy Vang.

Sergeant Bob Robbins, nicknamed Big Bob, or "BB," had averaged 17 complaints a year filed against him over twenty years for excessive force, excessive force, and excessive force and each time he was exonerated, exonerated, and exonerated—maintaining his perfect record, review after review after review. To Viktor, BB never whined—BB was real Minnesota gopher gold, and for BB, bouncing a mixed-race bar like Club Miami was yet another opportunity to try out a new pepper spray on some whining moron.

"Hey, loser," said BB, busting out of a black, bat-faced Club Miami-logoed T-shirt from Club Miami. "I trespassed you!"

Zalar reached into his armpit and sprayed armpit sweat into BB's face.

Zalar dropped to his knees, not knowing what hit him.

BB escorted Zalar to the gutter and dropped him there.

"Chill, man," smiled Dougal. "Peace out, man."

When Dougal placed a brotherly hand on BB's shoulder, BB tripped Dougal and kicked Dougal in the head and Dougal screamed. When Chitchee heard this, he adjusted his black knit wool cap and ran outside in his flannel. BB kicked Dougal's head for kicks in the head again.

"You're going to kick a man with no feet when he's down?" asked Chitchee. "You're hurting the guy! You're the bum's bum. Stop!"

"Gotta a problem with that, white boy?" taunted the thumper. "True dat, huh?"

"I didn't do anything!" said Zalar, writhing on the ice. "Fuck you, pig!"

BB lifted a stun gun like a metallic crab's claw from his belt and zapped Zalar on the neck by the jugular. With his heavy, weight-lifting, wrestler's hands BB twisted Zalar like a bendable straw man, who, already on a slippery patch of ice, backwards flew—on the back of snow-banked Dougal. At least, Zalar's fall was broken by landing crosswise on Dougal, who softened Zalar's fall like snow.

Beda rushed BB with her pepper spray. BB punched her in the nose and face.

"Have your lawyer call my lawyer!" smiled BB, revealing his gap-toothed front teeth from which he squirt spit on Beda. "Problem is: my lawyer is the Hennepin County Attorney!"

"Hey, you okay, Zalar?" asked Dougal, with bleeding lips. "Let's get you inside Club Miami for last call!"

BB flattened all his responses as if a dumb rock fell on his head.

"No fuckin' way," said BB, "you're getting in Club Miami."

His neck was stiff and belonged to a giraffe.

"What the hell is going on out here?" asked Viktor. "The customers are complaining! Oh, I get it. It's Zalar. Hey Izzy, give me a hand with this piece of shit! Let's take him down to the basement."

Beda's aerosol froze upon release into a galaxy of golden flakes, which glittered in so many manifold ways it blew back into BookSmart. Minerva ran outside without her coat on—wearing only a blue pleated skirt and a bare shouldered middy blouse she had sewn that morning. Minerva unfastened Beda's Taser from her Sam Browne belt.

BB planted his feet like roots shooting out rhizomes beneath the permafrost.

"Who's this skinny . . . MINNIE?" asked BB.

The Taser's electrodes fastened on BB's bat-faced, Club Miami T-shirted heart.

BB groaned and spiralled in a whirlpooling, swirling curl to the ground.

Chitchee dragged Dougal by his Red Winged boots and Minerva dragged Beda by her wrists into BookSmart.

"Dougal! I heard you got the ol' gangrene!" continued Chitchee. "And they amputated your feet. You can't have mine—if that's what you're thinking!"

"Saami!" said Minerva. "Throw me the Allen wrench so I can lock the cash bars! Hide me! I'm scared!"

"QUICK, Saami, THE CLUB MIAMI BOUNCER IS COMING!" said Chitchee. "Minerva saved our lives!"

"Huh? Oh, all right!" said Saami, mad at all the work he had now that Chitchee ordered him around too. "I guess so. Lord, so much drama in a little book store. Love them or hate them, you have to deal with them."

Chitchee reversed the OPEN sign to say CLOSED.

BB lifted himself off the icy sidewalk, shook off the stars, worked the shock out of his muscle tissue, and walked into Club Miami, revenge firing his blood.

"Chitchee, man," drooled Dougal from his bushwhacked purple boosh and booshy beard—smiling like a five-year old splashing in a marble basin of holy water. "I'm okay, I have my hands. I'm smashed. I got into the Hallmark School of Mortuary Science Photography in Boston. I'll show you the ladder of acceptance."

So much purple hair surrounded his face, his head was like a white-eyed Susan with purple petals radiating outward. Dougal produced the folded letter of acceptance from his back pocket.

"Hey Dougal, Congratulations!" said Chitchee. "I'm always happy for a friend who can turn his life around. And around. And around. And."

"Thanks, man! Here's my financial aid letter of acceptance," said Dougal.

WANTED BY FBI: CHITCHEE CHICHESTER
For Violation of Anti-Riot Laws, Conspiracy, Intent to Distribute
Un-American Literature.
Chitchee Chichester should be considered dangerous because of known propensity to incite
violence, class conflict, and mayhem. Capable of explosives. Last seen wearing a hijab.

Then in purple, clumsy, broadening felt strokes: **&10,000 dolars rewar money** was written on the back side of another copy of Chitchee's unwanted poster.

"You're the man!" said Dougal. "You're my tuition and fees. Don't worry I'll split it with you. This is dope. So how do we collect? That's what I was coming over to ask."

Dougal gave Chitchee the knucks and Chitchee gave Dougal the fist and then Dougal gave Chitchee the bumps and then a secret handshake like the children's game "First Comes Love," and then a Roman handshake, another slap, then a Masonic grip, then inter-linked pinkies.

The handshakes exhausted Dougal and he collapsed.

Grover helped Dougal arise sympathetically and spun him toward BookSmart's front door.

"There you go," said Grover.

"There I'll go! I'll go out the back door," said Dougal. "Who won the game? What time is it?"

"Dougal! Do you need a place to stay?" asked Chitchee, pulling Dougal out of a snow bank next to the BookSmart dumpster in the alley.

"No, I have my Palace by the Lakes," said Dougal, buttoning up his overcoat, the buttons out of sequence—he had to start over with the button count. He couldn't out-figure the clever buttons. No gloves. Lost them. "Where do you think I put those financial aid posters? Is this my coat? It's called a willow tree. Hey, anyone seen my feet? Hey, Chitchee, maybe you should go to Boston and be the photo-graver instead of me!"

Dougal stumbled out the back door and dodged back into Club Miami, where Nestor, who was the last person to ever see him, served him.

"Hi Shitchee!" said daisy-eyed Linda, kicking snow up the snow-banking alley from the back entrance. "Go-go-go inshide! Is Saami on break yet? I brought him his favorite jug. What are you doing freezhing out here?"

"I'm looking for Dougal," said Chitchee as if he wanted Dougal's autograph in the alley. "Do you know Dougal? Which way did he go?"

"What he doesssh he look like?" asked Linda. "How would I know him?"

"Purple hair, purple beard, purple teeth, no feet, can't walk straight, can't see straight, kind of looks like a big dumb friendly stoned puddle duck and keeps falling over every five feet because he lacks two."

"Could you be more shpeshific?" asked Linda, slipping on the ice.

Linda's black wool beret fell off, revealing hair blonde-white as whipped cream, the soft flesh of a larva, cheeks pink as poached eggs, and teeth like 5,000 year-old megaliths.

"He soundsh like a nishe guy!"

Linda hadn't worked since September. She had been running the Lady Slippers Gang out of Brainerd—plucking lady's slippers from Minnesota state parks, wearing pink shag and sherpa slippers, a pink Pink Floyd top, and cut-offs, while tooling around in her Fleetside pickup truck. Confronted by the Ginseng Gang, who had an inside fence working for Pandolfo's Arts and Crafts Store at Bryant and Lake, she also received an anonymous death threat on a business card attached to lilies in cypress wreaths delivered by Bachman's florists, who were in on it.

Chitchee helped Linda out of the snowbank. Linda had sprained her wrist, trying to break her nasty fall. Chitchee carried her inside in his arms to the black leather couch, next to Madison, who had shown up to sit around and read a book on a winter's night in a quaint and cozy little Parnassus without wheels.

"Saami!" yelled Chitchee. "Your super gorgeous wife is here!"

"Oh, honey," said Saami, hugging his wife like a honey child. "Now there's two of us!"

Hawk Eye knocked on the locked front door of BookSmart until he, in his Twins cap and Army jacket, shivered in the door, shivering inside, and passed an old man whose head was down on the maroon counter. Hawk Eye tripped on the extension cord to the Keeler Polygraph, yanking it out of the now gray-haired power strip that Saami had threaded under the counter.

The old man looked up, alarmed.

Hawk Eye asked the over-exasperated Noel, Ye Young sitting next to Noel behind the counter, for use of the potty again. Sitting on the potty, Hawk Eye realized he had walked by his mortal enemy, nemesis, and anti-self.

Hawk Eye flushed the toilet and exited BookSmart's back door and walked around the block to let a cooler head prevail. Then he crouched outside Club Miami for spare change.

"You again?" asked Viktor, Sherman cigarette between his sore-capped lips. "God damn it! You are scaring off customers, you fucking scarecrow. I don't believe you are a vet anyway, because even if you were, you lost the war for us. What was the matter? You didn't know how to fire a rifle? Too chicken to pull the trigger? Cluck, cluck, CLUCK!"

Viktor finished his Sherman, bulleted two shots of snot into Hawk Eye's face, flicked randomly the half-smoked Sherman at Hawk Eye, and quipped over his shoulder at Hawk Eye:

"I'm going to get rid of you once and for all, if it's the last thing I do!"

Grover, packing up his Keeler Polygraph, had the same realization as Hawk Eye at the same moment almost as if they were the same man: Grover hadn't seen Owen Rasmussen since Grover walked back, forty years ago, from the Municipal Liquor Store in Excelsior at the corner of Water & Lake with a bottle of Southern Comfort for Jen and Thunderbird for himself—not to mention the four-fingered Colombian ounce, two lumpy dovetailed joints, and loose Zig Zags inside the grass baggie.

Married and the father of two boys, proud Grover strolled to the Budweiser kegger on the Excelsior commons like the

Wyandotte rooster clucking, "*The gin is mighty fine but them biscuits are a little too thin.*" Grover revved like a Dodge Charger that had taken a Charles Atlas course.

Grover watched Jen Gossick screwing Navy Seal Owen Rasmussen on the beach facing Lake Minnetonka toward Big Island.

Grover dropped the bottled bag. And he never looked back, if you omit the countless times he did. As if to be in love one time was to have a fluttering third rib forever. With face dropped, he walked home, sat on his porch, and pointed a .22-caliber rifle at his head. He asked God for a reason to live. Waiting for the answer, he walked back inside to the kitchen and absorbed himself in Thunderbird. I know what to do: I'll kill them!

He ran down to the Excelsior commons with his .22. The beach was empty but for gulls with their cuck-cuck-cuck. He changed his mind. Grover promised God again he would turn his life around, so Grover packed his suitcases, grabbed the twins, his .22, and his 12-gauge; and he drove down to Texas to stay with his older brother, Clyde, a Texas Ranger, until he figured out what to do with his new haunted life. He tormented his conscience for not killing Jen and Owen like termites in the act of coupling—what a great legend that would have made! He reasoned any Minnesotan jury would acquit him for his poor soul. After being deported for his unauthorized missionary work in China, Grover returned to Minnesota. He wanted to hunt down Hawk Eye although Grover had forgiven Hawk Eye in his heart of hearts once or twice. He smiled a broad and hollow watermelon grin when he heard that Hawk Eye had finagled a helicopter at the Minneapolis airport but crashed it into a lake, killing two fishermen fishing for sturgeon.

And there was the man himself, lighting a conflagratory, inflammable, burning inferno of a cigarette. Hawk Eye had seen the same inferno in Grover's cold stare.

BookSmart's back door banged.

"Where is fucking Zalar?" asked Viktor in his D Con-blue bosom of badges, blouse of tin stars, and impersonating uniform. "He's over here. I know he is."

"I think he went downstairs for more Manson books," said Chitchee. "Since when did you become a thumper?"

Viktor's smile was that of a carpenter who keeps his nails in his mouth, while he hammers the lid of the coffin shut.

"If I told you that," Viktor chortled, blowing his nostrils out to each side, "I'd have to beat you with a tire iron."

"Spare change?" asked Hawk Eye, squatting in the dark outside Club Miami. "For a veteran?"

"I know a veteran when I see one," said Grover, waiting for a Blue and White. "And you're no veteran! I should know. I was a Navy Seal and I had the honor of serving with Governor Jesse Ventura."

"Is your name Grover?"

"What if it is?" said Grover. "I *work* for a living! And I don't take handouts!"

"Oh," said Hawk Eye, trying to stand up, but failing. "What do you *do* for a living?"

"I play the banjo at the Shakey's Pizza Parlor in Minnetonka," said Grover. "And it ain't easy for an old sinner like me."

Grover sealed in his emotions, his heartbreak unspoken. He didn't know himself anymore, because he was going to the real Hell for the pain he caused everyone he had ever known.

"You cheated me in that snowmobile race down Water Street, Governor!" said Hawk Eye, trying to stand up again to stay warm. "You cheated me out of Jennifer. You stole my girl when I was a young man. Now I'm a basket case. I'm panhandling in the snow for goddamned powdered potatoes!"

Hawk Eye remembered seeing Jennifer Van Roo in the middle of the night, waking up on a three-month patrol again near the DMZ and the western border in the cordilleras. Where his entire platoon was ambushed and wiped out. The nurses were all angels. And they reminded him of Jennifer. The thought of Jennifer had nursed him back to the World. For his action the Navy awarded him with all the medals he had recently sold for crack.

"Who threw that snowball that made me lose the race?" asked Hawk Eye. "One of your friends, that's who! Who threw that snowball? Whoever it was, I have cursed his very soul from the beginning of time."

"Jennifer must have thrown it," said Grover. "I don't know of any snowball anyway. Besides, that was so long ago. I barely remember that snowmobile race. That was the '60s. Do your own thing. Rising crime. Breakdown of the family. New York Times sabotaging the War. Walter Cronkite waving the white flag on national TV. Jane Fonda in bed with Moscow. Church attendance down. Those were different times. All standards flew up the chimney. So I don't remember you. Pretend we never met. Jennifer is long dead, but she has a daughter who doesn't look like her. Here's my Blue & White cab."

"Hey pal," said Hawk Eye, "don't walk on the black ice!"

Grover turned his back and, walking away, looked over his shoulder.

An ice ball hit Grover square in the face.

Grover slipped on the super slippery patch. The Keeler Polygraph fell and Grover nailed the back of his head to the sidewalk. Grover heard his cerebellum crack and he lay paralyzed.

Zalar looked around, noticed he didn't have a coat on, and walked back inside.

"Leave me alone," said Grover. "I don't need a doctor! It's not progress to live beyond one's allotted life span. Only a progressive would think that. You've got to die from something."

Hawk Eye hurried into BookSmart and called 911. Chitchee craned his neck to see out the front window. When he heard an ambulance pull up, he heard his ringtone.

Hawk Eye walked outside and told the paramedics that Grover slipped on the "glaring ice."

"I have to answer this, you guys," said Chitchee to Noel and Saami. "I think it's my mom checking up on me. You know how moms are! They're ten feet tall and bulletproof! That's why they always live forever! Is everything okay, mom?"

PAISLEY

"Chitchee, this is Finkle Chichester. Your mother is dying, she asked me to call you," said Finkle. "The doctors say she hasn't long to live. Maybe only a couple days. She's at Methodist Hospital in room 323. She asked me to call you."

"Where is my mother?" Chitchee asked Finkle after signing in with security, when he found the room, still stunned that his own father had called him.

"She's in there, Charles," said Finkle and exited the room.

Finkle looked drained. His hair appeared as a mere afterthought, and his once florid, ruddy glow had been smoked and ashed. Unshaven, he wore the ashen gray of charcoaled lumps of coal on his chin in patchy necessity. Finkle Chichester: aged and shrank like a poked spider. His skin loosened and drooped off his scarified cheekbones. The Finkle face looked like an old, rat-eared Bible; and the tooling was the wrinkles, the gathers, and the foxed cheeks. Finkle did not look hostile. Righteous indignation must have arisen in him against his own anger.

Paisley Pug lay twisted up in the sheets and the catheter. Her eyes had glossed over with a clear gel that formed second eyelids.

Paisley's nurse-in-charge Inna informed Chitchee that Paisley had a rare form of meningitis, which had entered her system via a mosquito bite. The virus had vectored from inside the guts of the bug that bit her. Then she had a stroke.

"A bug bite? When? Where? A stroke? How?" cried Chitchee, falling on the shoulders of Inna. "Human life is more fragile than a clot of blood? This is unbelievable!"

Chitchee roared like a lion shot through the heart, his tears the blood of his heart.

In the awkward embrace of thanking the RN for her care, Chitchee knocked his chin on a wood board that fell on the floor. He bumped his nose on the back of her head when she picked up the dropped board, reminding Chitchee of Spartak Bok and Viktor Martensen. Clenched-fist punches.

Chitchee pulled up a chair and sat by Paisley's IV-supplied bedside. He wasn't sure if she could hear him. She blinked when she rolled her head his way, her eyes rolling in and out of sleep or death.

"I LOVE YOU, MOTHER!" shouted Chitchee, looking into her eyes and holding her cold hand. "Forgive me, I wasn't the best of sons for you and dad. Thank you for secretly supporting me all these years, so I could keep writing empty pages for nobody. You can't die!"

"Not your da'," said Paisley, slurring as the words drooled out.

"What?" asked Chitchee, his ear up to Paisley's last breaths.

"Your real fath' . . . named Isa Bahram Jem. Met at social bonfire one night Lake Superior. I was a Tam O' Shaoyanter. His family was Zoroastrian. We did it. I was young once. It was good," she said and fell back to sleep. "Twenty times over."

Chitchee kissed her forehead.

"I heard all that!" said Finkle, in the middle of telling the Russian nurse Inna in the hall that if worse came to worse they should call Washburn-McReavy.

Father Finkle was sterile, which he could never admit *or possibly even know*. Chitchee guessed that his mother conceived with another man to protect the pride of Finkle.

"Chitchee," said Paisley, lucid for the last time, "my only regret is that we never opened your little book store Ulysses & Sons. Don't cry. No one on Earth wants you more to live than those passed above it, where I'll be soon. Don't mourn me for your own sake, because that's all you would be doing. Somehow the dead live more than the living, while the living only invent new ways to die. I know you don't believe in God, but God does. And as he has looked over me, he will look over you when my is over pilgrimage. You made me laugh, when others made me cry; you gave me love, when others gave me hate; you comforted my soul. When Finkle found me out, I needed the comfort of a mother by her son. That comfort kept my candle burning in my darkest hours. You were that light. I always knew you would be an ambassador of that light."

Paisley looked to the wall to see the green numbers on the Welsh Allen machine, while Chitchee kept reassuring his mother that she would beat this thing called death.

Nurse Inna re-entered the unit, leaving Finkle in the hall, asking a housekeeper in green scrubs where the bathroom was.

"I feel so guilty," said Chitchee, "that I didn't reach out enough to say that I loved you mother. You gave me the gift of give and take. I learned from you the love of—mother? Mother? MOTHER!"

Nurse Inna placed two fingers on Paisley's radial artery. Paisley's face was aquamarine. As soon as Inna pressed the call light, "CODE BLUE!" filled all the intercoms.

"CODE BLUE!" said the mechanical voice as flat as a square sphere.

While Inna deftly applied the tubing of the ambu bag, Chitchee's fluey nose ran like a broken spigot and blood flowed down his chest. Inna slipped the wood board under the mattress for the Lucas machine. The resuscitation team ran in the room with their crash cart, like a big red Craftsman tool chest, squealing, with assistant nurses and the hospital recorder curving in behind the nurses.

Weeping with a hollow wail, Chitchee slunk to the floor.

"Vere is all this bluud coming vrom?" asked Inna.

"Is she delirious again?" asked Finkle.

"CODE BLUE!"

"Is she getting enough oxygen?"

"Nee-yo," said Nurse Inna, breathing a deep current of breath, her brown eyebrows consternated into triangles. "She's dead."

"She coded," you could hear from the hall.

When Nurse Inna called for a wheelchair, Chitchee stood up, threw her aside, and threw himself across the corpse, blood from his nose on the floor. He wept in dry heaves and sobbed uncontrollably.

Chitchee hugged the bluing corpse, her sheets splattered with Chitchee's nose blood. Blood stuck to the sheets, pooled over the bed, and dripped to the floor from the soaked sheets. He had no idea how he had given himself a bloody nose.

Having gotten turned around, Finkle indecisively looked around at the nurse's assistant and ran into the hall where the nurses' stations provided little pancreas-shaped pools of light on the gray tile. Light stretched out like a red ribbon splitting the lime-green curtains and lobbies where anxious families sat on sterile furniture.

Chitchee's arms opened to embrace his father.

"I love you Dad, no matter what," said Chitchee. "Because you're my real father."

He hugged for the last time (he somehow felt it) the soon to disappear Finkle, soon to be a tear, a whisper, a flicker, an echo.

"I have to confess, Chitch," said Finkle as he released himself from the hug he had embraced Chitchee with. "I got a call from an old friend one day. Grover Gossick. He alerted me to your radicalizing activity at the Shakey's Pizza Parlor on Highway 7. I called the FBI. I told them you had been radicalized. You might be making explosives and wearing a radical hijab. Grover told me you lived in Neo-Communist Party Uptown, where the anarchists and big government liberals live. The FBI never returned my calls. I got angry. I plastered posters of you all over the neighborhood. I had to do my civic duty, you understand? Because I loved you, son!"

"I forgive you . . ." said Chitchee.

"I wanted to hire a private investigator to follow you too," said Finkle, "take pictures, gather information on your political activity . . . but, watching you, just now—you truly loved your mother . . . your mother . . . everyone loved Paisley."

Chitchee threw himself across his mother's body and wept and sobbed uncontrollably. The nurses pried Chitchee off his mother.

Finkle crossed himself, saying: "Mother? Mother? Mother? MOTHER? Mother."

Chitchee ran a dirty washrag under hot, soapy water; with the clean rag he cleaned and then kissed her cold feet.

FBI: BROOKLYN CENTER

Ordered to appear at the Hennepin County Government Center where the plaintiff Corky Skogentaub planned to hang Chitchee in front of the hanging judge in small claims, Chitchee felt extremely cozened and contorted by MPG's unreasonable rent hikes, fees, lack of repairs, lack of heat, lack of plumbing, and lack of sleep due to incessant noise.

Chitchee re-read the forwarded letter and let it fall to the floor of the bus. With all the official debris, threatening letters, past due bills, and other testy numbers that determine a life, he persisted against a universal backdrop of meaningless spacetime. Life was a glimpse of paradise between a rising sun and a setting sun—and finally Chitchee accepted his mother's death as a natural ending to nurture. Therefore she would live through him, grow through him, and come to fruition through him.

But he located his old copy of *Final Exit,* thrust a Hefty bag over his head, and when he couldn't breathe he ripped the bag off his head, and lay there shaking, trembling, and sweating. He couldn't kill himself, because he still had his mother to think of.

Ulysses & Sons needed an angel investor, a business plan, a CEO, a decent vending machine, a large dumpster, and a US Bank willing to ignore the fact that Chitchee had no credit. He didn't understand that you paid interest on your credit card to get more credit cards to pay interest on. It was a wonder he knew how to advise Ivan Von Volkov so much about something Chitchee knew nothing about.

Viktor Martensen had no problem taking out a Wells Fargo loan to install fish tanks where women servers swam in string bikinis and go-go flippers. Viktor borrowed the idea from the Persian Palms bar that Corky Skogentaub recalled from Slow Siggy's stories of the good ol' shoot 'em up days of gangland Minneapolis. "In those days, we had real gangs," said Slow Siggy, "because they were Yids and Micks and wore ties." Shortly after generously accepting the loan, Viktor failed to file a required financial report to Wells Fargo, which had loaned him the $500,000 to keep Club Miami's fish tanks afloat.

Wells Fargo sent out the newly-hired auditor, Fjard Gardet, to survey Club Miami's inventory, which had served as the loan's collateral. When Fjard Gardet walked into Club Miami, BB threw him out and barred the door. BB was "under orders" by Mr. Martensen to not let anyone from Wells Fargo inside. Outside, Izzy and Yakky threw a blanket over the Wells Fargo auditor. They tossed him into the company's white Dodge van, threatened him at gunpoint, drove him to the Hennepin Avenue Bridge, and suspended him by the cuff links over the Mississippi River. Fjard agreed to retire from Wells Fargo and move to Idaho.

Wells Fargo turned to the courts, which designated a "receiver," Turn It Around Twin Cities Management Group, to pony up the money to repay the bank. Larry claimed that mice ate half the relevant documents and then pissed on the other half. Some of the uneaten records showed Club Miami had lost $663,957 in the first eight months of 2009.

Chitchee's iPhone dump of Larry's email had alerted the local FBI's computer experts in darknet and cryptocurrency. FBI Agent Henry Hillswick looked at the files of Larry Sangster's iPhone and laptop with little interest at first; however, after a Behavioral Analysis Department review, Henry finally realized how many millions of dollars were sloshing around the Martensen People's Group, which he had been tracking and stalking for over a year.

A flood of indignation, bordering on revulsion, swept across Henry's brain, backwashing. He scrutinized Viktor's brazen criminality. Henry justified swiping Viktor's fortune because Henry felt morally justified in swiping Viktor's fortune. Henry could buy a 6-passenger Lear jet and fly away to Bozeman for that matter. Henry looked at his extended family with a hyperbolic frown, drawn down at the endpoints under the negative curve's focus. And Edelweiss? His platysmic muscle played quivers across his neck. He contemplated a cyber heist. He would quash records and squelch traces. He thought: where is my computer? It's been stolen!

Halfway out of his chair, his eyes like Hollywood posters, Henry realized the computer was right in front of him. He emitted a humph. So absorbed had Henry been in his contemplative computer, he had believed he existed in his computer without his computer.

Viktor's name popped up earlier in connection with a credit card scam. Someone at MPJ or MPG had helped Spartak Bok mastermind a credit card scam, which had already netted $832,000 in bitcoin. Henry computed on paper his computer forensics specialist salary, expenses, mortgage, two cars, and Bozeman. The records of payments from Corky Skogentaub bitcoin account to pay for the murder of Spartak Bok were enough evidence for FBI Special Agent Henry Hillswick to feel tempted.

When a VPN server in Singapore thrashed Corky with emailed death threats, Corky's buttocks pooled together. His sweaty MPG office chair made suction sounds whenever he opened his Microsoft hotmail messages. Then the ransomer blackmailed Corky into handing over passwords, pin numbers, aliases, and email accounts. Corky balked. He faced a slow death by a variety of torture devices favored by the Spanish Inquisition and officially endorsed by North Korea.

The hacker posted Corky's address, pictures of Corky's kids, his wife, his bank account numbers, his social, his first grade classroom picture at Moose Lake Elementary, three love letters from Courtney Kirkwood, and a file of every porn site he ever clicked on. Corky chewed the micro-thin flaps of flesh off his lips and chewed them over and over, unable to finish his warmed-over, re-heated, flaccid, chilling, and ransom-ward Triple Mac.

Cold Chitchee convulsed off the bus right outside the egg-carton windows of the bomb-proof FBI branch building in Brooklyn Center. He adjusted the bright red vinyl winter jacket he bought at Treasures Await for such an occasion: Chitchee's own clothes struck him as fairly crisp, clever, and comfortable. He wore a checked flannel, shirt tails out, and black Levi jeans and the bright red vinyl winter jacket from Treasures Await. And then he saw someone else walking by on the sidewalk, wearing the same flannel shirt, black Levi jeans, and a bright red vinyl winter jacket from Treasures Await.

"Oh my God! I look like crap!" Chitchee yelled at the stranger, who thought he was mad at him.

Once inside the bright interior, Chitchee approached the stodgy receptionist:

"I look like a storm drain, don't I?" asked Chitchee. "I would have been better off if I had worn a clown suit and neck-tie and skipped the clown suit!"

"I don't see color," said the desk information agent.

"You see in black and white, in grayscale," said Chitchee. "Smart! To tell you the plain black-and-white, I won't want color after I throw out this second hand, sore thumb of a bloody jacket. I'm going back to basic black."

The FBI receptionist ushered Chitchee eventually to an FBI interview room. Chitchee sat before Henry Hillswick. Table and chairs were so minimally functional as to have been sketched onto a storyboard with a few slashes of an artist's pen.

There Chitchee sat, drawn with a few slashes, on a sort of frigid deck chair that bounced when you leaned into it—then bounced you back forward as if you were eager to spill the beans across the iron-gray, iron, and wide table.

A clove of garlic over his eye? Chitchee thought. He placed Henry Hillswick in his mind's eye. Did the second Henry match the first Henry? Chitchee replayed images of the unfriendly man whom he had encountered on his first day at BookSmart, whom he mistook for Sausage Man. Didn't Sausage Man take his picture?

"Is this your office?" asked Chitchee. "I thought you would have more degrees on your wall than a small-town barber. Did you go to school? It doesn't matter! I came to ask you for a loan!"

True, Henry had a Bachelor's Degree from Princeton in Political Science and a Master's Degree from Columbia in Geology.

"This is a meeting room," said Henry, flipping through a folder that had cellophane tabs about every five pages, while everything about Henry emitted to Chitchee the word "fundamental" as in "fundamental decency" and "fundamental honesty" and "fundamentally good cop."

The photograph on Edelweiss's mantelpiece was ancient, but Chitchee remembered the face of Arthur, the twin, he thought. Had Chitchee confabulated this FBI Agent with his twin brother, who was Sausage Man? The locals, often of the stock of Stockholm, especially the older men, looked the same as twins anyway. Age eroded their features into kinship. They walked and talked as alike as the rubbed-off pips on a die. Who could tell them all apart? It would be like being introduced to a herd of reindeer. Were they all that different? Evolution expressed the branches of a single organism underneath it all.

"We can discuss the loan part later, I'm guessing," said Chitchee. "How did you break your thumb? Don't tell me! I bet it was in a plane crash at Flying Cloud Airport when the wheels got stuck!"

"How did you know that?" asked Henry with a disinterred, disintegrating grin.

"A little drone told me," joked Chitchee.

"Do you think this is an episode from *Law and Order?*"

"Without the commercials," said Chitchee. "Where are the vending machines? I bet you guys got some good ones."

"Are you willing to be a confidential informant?" asked Henry. "Would you consent to wearing a wire?"

Chitchee pulled out a baggie of Cheez-its, munched a munch of munchies, and, when he saw the cheddar orange crumbs on the table, swept the crumbs back in the baggie.

"Do you mean like in *Law and Order?*" asked Chitchee.

Henry showed Chitchee how the defunct Nagra worked (an old one he had in his bottom drawer), how the tape thread, how the buttons worked, and how to tape the tape recorder to his chest. (The idiot was buying it.) And his parting instructions to Chitchee were:

"Remember, Deputy Agent Chichester, you only have an hour to record, so don't waste precious magnetic tape."

Henry looked and sounded bored. His face looked sealed with boredom at birth. Henry henceforth had carried that boredom stamped on his face like a purple birthmark for the rest of his unrewarding, unrewarded life.

With Viktor behind bars, Henry could safely disappear and spend the rest of his days playing checkers in Bozeman with his mother Edelweiss, who had played her own cards perfectly to entrap Zalar, Kennedy, Chitchee, and hence Viktor, the main quarry, who Henry had yet to connect to the murder of Spartak Bok. The whack was obvious to Henry as it was unsolvable and case-closed to the corrupt thumpers at 5th Precinct.

"Oh, and Chichester, you come back with the bacon, and I'll come through with the corn."

"Oh, now we do sound like we're on *Law and Order*," said Chitchee. "With your experience in law enforcement, I bet you could write extremely realistic, first-hand scripts for them."

"I tried," said Henry. "It turned out that's not what they were looking for."

THE CROWS

Sequestered in BookSmart's basement, Chitchee lay on the cold couch. He wore the tiny antiquated tape recorder taped to his back, because it tore too many hairs out of his chest to keep it taped frontally. He couldn't waste expensive FBI magnetic tape. The Feds account for every stitch of every inch. He practiced turning the Nagra on and off; he pretended to scratch his back; he play-pressed the playback on his back with a play-scratch.

Chitchee picked up at random an Oxford University Press book: *The Cinema of Loneliness*. The dust jacket was a down and out, dorsal-crested *Taxi Driver* shot of Robert De Niro in a concrete district of alienated anxiety subtitled: *A Study of the Cinema of Penn, Kubrick, Coppola, Scorsese, and Altman*. Inside the book he found a bookmark, which was a coupon for the Hooters in Burnsville: Shrimp . . . Clams . . . OYSTERS . . . (Cleavage & Clam chowder off 35W). He picked up Donald Barthelme's *60 Stories*. At random he read: "Some fathers, if you ask them the time of day, spit silver dollars."

"Let me point out that what an artist does is fail." He set it aside for later. He grabbed R. Buckminster Fuller's *Critical Path*, which had a chronology of scientific milestones in the back, but page 352, listing Leonardo da Vinci's Formidable Inventions, ended with the "perfect whorehouse."

Leonardo da Vinci designed the perfect whorehouse? What was a perfect whorehouse?

Through the vaulted underground door, Club Miami trafficked people between the two establishments. One business was thriving, the other business dying. A parasite had attached to all the books in BookSmart, draining them of their life and blood; it pumped fresh, oxygenated energy into Club Miami. Club Miami exploded every night with new clientele. It raced in popularity by leaps and bounds past the Nankin, Brit's, the Local, and the Town Talk Diner. Another First Avenue. *City Pages* voted Club Miami best new restaurant, best new night club, best new place to meet new people, tallest bar, most interesting bathrooms, best of all possible worlds, and best bar after The Rainbow Bar to replace The Rainbow Bar. Nestor had been booking more, not necessarily better, musical acts, and he culled them from the bands he hated most, bands which had played at First Avenue, the Turf Club, the Viking, the Fine Line, and Palmer's. The more the back-room lap dancers danced and the more the crazy chefs drank, the more positively-charged reviews multiplied and phosphoresced as beacons to the Minneapolis club moths.

A clattering in the walls made Chitchee fast-twitch. He heard a nest of senior mice discussing plans in Spanish.

Chitchee's skin beat rapidly like his whole heart. Hidey-holed behind the dank couch, he crouched like Jacob in Rebekah's womb. Voices trailed off into the ceiling. A door slammed, leading down flights of daedalian stairs into secret passageways. He crawled out of hiding and cast around for something better to hide behind: Mommsen's *History of Rome* was solid. Prescott's *Histories* was a good brick. And Runciman. Three volumes. Folio Box Set *The History of the Crusades*. Needham's *Science and Civilization in China* (although six volumes long, it really picks up in volume 4, part 3, *Civil Engineering and Nautics*). He immured himself behind these word castles and added a last minute Plutarch's *Lives* as the drawbridge.

"I don't want *that* in *my* club," Chitchee heard Viktor say. "Hey, you stupid spics be careful with that! *Ha-blah Julio Inglesias?*"

Chitchee clutched his Spanish dictionary of slang like a clawed nut—one of those book-baubles that teach you how to swear in any language, although how useful it is to swear at local citizens is debatable.

Viktor's hired hands off-loaded tubs from dollies while Chitchee caught stray words from their mouthfuls of air like: *imbecile, idiot, scarface, porco, piggo, gordo, culo, cojo, cujo, cuco*; whatever they said, it sounded like *gringo sucko . . . calderon, pendejo,* and *gallipoli. Veek-tor Cor-tez* was pronounced by drinking rancid, grimacing cream.

Chitchee felt miserable, cold, and cramped. He dreaded the long January in Minneapolis when the deep freeze sinks into your bones and seeps into your blood, when one can't even imagine the sweet and indolent lilacs of April—and even in April you wake up shivering after going to sleep cold. MPG has turned off the heat before Earth itself has warmed up, so you have to go outside and scrounge sunlight to warm your marrow bones.

"Why is that light on?" asked *Veek-tor Cor-tez*, blowing his nose openly onto the floor next to Chitchee's couch—a foot away from his own nose.

Chitchee began a sneeze and stotted off the floor when he suppressed the urge.

"*No say, Pee-zorro,*" shrugged one of the sarcastic Ecuadorian dishwashers Victor recruited. "*My name Hohe Hee-menace.*"

When the Club Miami workers let the door slam behind them, Chitchee crawled out of his crawlspace. Curious, he unclasped the tight-fitting snap lids from their brand new plastic gray tubs: at first he saw gamma-hydroxybutyrate in gallon milk jugs. He fingered the neatly-packed, stacked Ziploc baggies. Each baggie held either gray-and-blue pills or white powders. And each baggie had a plastic sticker of an alligator with a squirrel in its mouth. In another corner, crates as big as steamer chests were marked POLICE, MPD, and FRAGILE.

Every night, dolly after dolly of gray tubs wheeled into the BookSmart basement, each containing one 16-ounce, surgically-wrapped cocaine brick, one kilogram of methamphetamine rocks, one ounce of fentanyl in a sealed container, one heroin stack of little white pillows, one snub-nosed shotgun, and one brown bag containing from $1,000-$10,000 cash.

"Value paks," said Chitchee, examining the allegorical alligator with a squirrel in its mouth.

This was big. This was headlines. This would be the biggest drug bust in Minnesota history. Would there be a reward? That this would result in the FBI's offering Chitchee a permanent position, which he would turn down as tactfully as possible, was foregone in Chitchee's excited forebrain, crackling with an illusory fame.

"I appreciate the offer, Director Mueller, but I have other icons in the fire . . ." said Chitchee, pacing with his hands crossed behind his back. "Look Bob, I'd like to help you out, but I have other commitments such as lying in bed and staying warm."

Sweat flowed from his temples to his ankles in streams of dread. He knew he would face torture if Viktor discovered him snitching. What if Viktor had La Keillor Nostra connections? Or knew all the moles in Mossad? Or he and Putin whitewater-rafted together every St. Putin's Day to discuss their political enemies and how to kill them?

Chitchee curled up into a frightened medicine ball while his mind somersaulted. If he walked into the 5th Precinct with this fresh intel, he'd talk to the bored Desk Sergeant Weatherwax, noshing pistachios. Unwilling to complete an incident report, he'd dismiss Chitchee with: are you seeing flying monkeys on LSD now too? What color are their parachutes?

He did not find the pocket with Henry Hillswick's number in it. He jumped up in a panic.

Chitchee depended solely on a federal agency. In a legal sense, under the Constitution, he could deputize himself to federalize state and city law enforcement for the nonce and then bust all the suspects himself. Who needed thumpers? Chitchee lurched back to the couch, and he spread out a thin, tuna fish-smelling, linsey-woolsey sheet cut from a homespun blanket for a cover slip. He found a couple Afghans to suffice for the night's blankets. He lay on the cold, moldy cushions. He finally sneezed a whopper. He ended the explosion as if he had meant to *relish* the sneeze—as if Chitchee were a cartoon character to which he supplied his own sound effects. "*Four and twenty blackbirds baked in a pie . . .*" After bopping his noggin backward on the flexible, octopus-armed, octopoid brass floor lamp that toppled off a stack of hardcover *Lake Woebegone Days*, he clutched the bump on his head and heard the brazen crash, which cut the light bulb's filament like a firefly committing suicide. The floor lamp lay at a dead horizontal. There must be another 60-watt light bulb around with juice in it. As he scrounged, he reconfigured a universe with Viktor's brown bags of cash in it. Where could he go? Morocco, Montana, Mound? As he paced excitedly, his eyelids fluttered like black swallowtails. Unable to sleep, Chitchee sat up, hugged his knees, and dialed the FBI's local office number in Brooklyn Center. As soon as heard the confounded menu of options he cried at the new digital world order (for being out of order) and hung up feeling discombobulated.

He fell back to sleep on the couch and dreamed of dilapidated, operatic mansions whose staircases twisted like complex macromolecules leading to a stage set from *Turandot*, one of whose doors opened and led to Hooters. He sat in Hooters with Donald Barthelme—large wire rims, quizzical eyebrows raised, beard tufted to a gray vertex—when the server, Travis Bickle, asked them: "Who ordered the Perfect Whorehouse?"

"Leonardo," said Barthelme. "But he died in the pantry."

Another door slammed. Chitchee, eyes half-spinning out of their orbitals like fermions, stuffed himself like stuffing back into the stuffed couch. He scrambled back for the *Spanish Dictionary of Curse Words for Old Gringos*, stood up, pulled the dust bunnies parachuting out of his mouth, brushed a layer of dirt off his jeans, and re-darted back to his blind.

He crouched with his legs tucked up under him, all ears, inside the tomed walls of his book safe house.

"Why the fuck is that light *off* now?" asked Viktor. "Who turned that light *off?*"

"Where do you want her, boss?" asked Yakky, his breath soggy with dead apples and wounded bananas.

Viktor stood firmly planted in the BookSmart basement like the foreman of a construction site, face reddening into a heated pomegranate spitting out its own seeds.

"Everybody, get out! Vamoose!" said Viktor.

He slammed the Club Miami door behind him.

Chitchee scurried out the break room door, popped back into the basement proper, and scuttered up the BookSmart stairs. Chitchee heard a commotion behind him, which sounded like someone pushing a heavy couch across a concrete floor. Silence he witnessed, hearing nothing. Chitchee stood at the top of stairs in a frozen course of action. Curious, he moused back. He eared up to the break room and listened through the door, using his head like a suction cup.

"Take the picture, you fucking load, Yakky! Another one for the album! She's out cold," said Viktor. "Okay already! I'm going to shoot my load in her cooter! Okay, let's dump our little girl off the bridge."

The next day Chitchee reported the incident to Henry's voice mail:

"I'm on to something," said Chitchee on the voicemail's playback. "This is possibly bigger than the French Connection. Bigger than filling Pablo Escobar's face with a bullet salad. Even if Escobar were a flying monkey on LSD, he could never have hallucinated a criminal empire like the one we have in Minneapolis, right under our lilacs, dude. The corrupt powers that are the deep state of the Twin Cities constitute a parallel, paralegal universe opposite to the one presented to us in the evening news. The corruption reaches into the Fusion Center itself which implies you yourself Sausage Man—" it cut off.

Chitchee asked Aloysius if he had talked to Aubrey lately. He said he hadn't. She was recuperating from the flu, although she had planned to drive down to Northfield to visit friends (to borrow money Chitchee thought).

Night by night, more dungeon in the BookSmart basement added itself on. Tubs came and went. A body sling showed up, attached to the ceiling. Night by night, Chitchee dodged Viktor's incoming shipments of Ruger Mini-14s. On dungeon nights, Chitchee slept upstairs on the torn, black leather couch, the motion detectors turned off; in the morning, when Chitchee mentioned the commotions to Aloysius, Aloysius paled several phantoms white.

"Aloysius," said Chitchee, his eyes trembling, trembling before the earthquake of his own death. "What the hell is going on? Are you using me for human bait? There is an ongoing criminal enterprise in our basement. It's the Minneapolis Cartel down there. And now I am afraid of bumping into El Chapo down there. Don't you care?"

Aloysius pushed Chitchee into the wall.

"That's enough!" said Aloysius grimly. "I don't want to know anything about it! If it's too noisy, sleep upstairs on the couch! That noise is of no concern to you. Stay out of it. Less talk and more work, Chitchee. Otherwise, good job, buddy."

"Oh thanks, boss," said Chitchee.

That night, during Chitchee's bone china-delicate reading of volume 4, part 3 of Joseph Needhams's *Civil Engineering and Nautics*, Chitchee heard the voices of birds, no they were hybrid bird-girls, no they were cell's bells, no were they cell *belles* call-girling Larry's curly girlie phone? He set aside Larry's iPhone when he heard Viktor and—Spanish-speaking girls? And Hmong teenagers? Chitchee heard a lock throwing its bolt with a hoohaw of men's voices. The boxes, crates, and shipping containers were gone. The movers left nothing but a gym bag. Chitchee unzipped it: handcuffs, duct tape, bungee cords, chains, paddles, strap-on dildos, a whip, and a Polaroid camera.

Then all the jetsam of boxes, crates, and shipping containers floated back in a flotsam tide.

The BookSmart basement overflowed like the infamous Metro Gang Task Force's "evidence room" with top-of-the-line entertainment electronics, desktops, laptops, screens, sporting goods, exercise equipment, AKs, and a box covered with heart stickers, filled with dozens of labeled car keys to muscle cars and muscular trucks.

"RAMSEY COUNTY SHERIFF'S DEPARTMENT PROPERTY," said one gray tub, which when opened by Chitchee revealed stacks of baby human skulls.

His consciousness circled a darkening drain and he lost consciousness.

In the morning he awoke hungry. He traipsed to the Joyce United Methodist food shelf on Fremont Avenue South. He gave them his old address and lugged to his lair a Danish pastry drizzled with sugar frosting as large as Robert Smithson's *Spiral Jetty*.

It hit him that the BookSmart basement was both too dangerous *and* un-Emersonian. We had moved from the American Renaissance to the American Hegemony without so much as noticing that Thoreau had drowned. He chomped one more Danish mouthful—even if he had to have his stomach pumped at HCMC for $10,000. He sat down to work at the Dell upstairs to update his résumé when he realized he didn't have one. He sat in the front window. *Curriculum vitae*? He had to look it up.

He would not complain. He had his three meals a day—all at once and right before bed or right after bed or right before getting up from bed. His mother's death ran him ragged and turned him haggard. He always felt like a stool sample in a bomb calorimeter. Interrupted sleep all night long was punctuated by stacks of baby human skulls from the BookSmart basement to the Moon, thumping of tire chains, sharply canine laughs, groaning baboon vocalizations, and flesh slapped.

"Oh, get out of town, Viktor, you know you love to be tortured. It gets you going. It's your R & R. And all your Ground Zero thumper friends lining up like little adrenochrome bunnies to get their asses whipped and fucked by machines!"

"Bitch! You cut my throat! You drew blood!" he said.

"Oh, shit! Let me go! You're killing me!" she said.

Chitchee extruded his acorn cap from his black jean fob pocket. Chitchee blew a soaring coloratura not even Kathleen Battle could wring out of an acorn.

Chitchee burst into the overstock area. LaDonna, between all the *Kite Runners* and all the Jan Karons, stood still in stilettos, a latex mini-skirt, mesh bra, cuffs, and an opal choker. When she saw Chitchee, she carefully laid a double-handled machete for cutting pizza wedges at Shakey's Pizza Parlor on the floor. She slipped Viktor's wallet into her black mesh bra.

Viktor looked at Chitchee. Viktor spun around. LaDonna was not there and the door to Club Miami was wide open. Chitchee darted past Viktor into the tunnel after LaDonna, who tossed the wallet.

LaDonna had ram-horned a corn cob up Viktor's hair-lined, splayed, and wart-bubbled cheeks. Viktor swam around the Booksmart basement naked, hairy-necked, saggily man-boobed, and bullhide buttocked with a slight fur. He was a Bronze Age man with a giant tattoo of Jerry Lewis (from *The Nutty Professor*) on his back, for which Skooge had paid the heavy price of permanent brain damage and goofy teeth.

"Wait!" said Viktor to the empty BookSmart basement. "Where did she go? Damn it! What the fuck! Hello? Call Izzy! God damn it! Wait, I'll call Larry!"

Viktor dressed. He pulled out his iPhone and punched the contact number for Izzy. He told Izzy to fetch a large duffel bag—something bad had happened—and to meet him in the alley behind Club Miami. When Viktor dialed Larry Sangster, Larry's ringtones rang like church bells in the same room. The bells echoed in the basement air like a reverberating medieval town. The smartphone, on the couch arm, where Chitchee had left it, insisted on an answer.

"What is Larry's fucking phone doing here?" asked Viktor.

He looked at Larry's phone. Viktor pushed down on the patches of warmth fading on the cold couch. Viktor stood over the couch and stared like a boxer at his opponent. He picked up Larry's long lost iPhone.

"What the fuck is Larry's iPhone doing down here?" asked Viktor. "FUCK! Larry is wearing a wire for the Feds! Fucking Larry was always the weakest link. I knew it! Izzy was right. We should have given fucking Larry two in the chest and one in the head. God damn it to fuck! Why, oh why am I such a nice guy? I've been the nicest guy in the world to everybody! My father, my son, and my best friends are always, always fucking me over! I'll show them who's boss. I'm the one who provides jobs. I'M THE BIGGEST JOB PROVIDER ON THE PLANET."

Viktor forced the snot out of both nostrils like a bombardier beetle warding off danger by spraying poisons from an anus hose. His furrowed forehead worried itself into trenches. Larry Sangster was a CI. For who? No. Weakling Larry had soft balls that melted like frying butter at confrontation, betrayal, danger, class-action lawsuits, mean bartenders, leaping muskies, loud alarm clocks, and female judges with crew cuts.

For some reason, the biggest drug bust in drug bust history had flatlined . . . Chitchee feared a leak, a mole, or a tip-off; somebody lost the evidence he had provided to the FBI. He needed more and more evidence, until he was becoming addicted to evidence. Chitchee snaked his way into Club Miami's main office with the copy he made at Ace Hardware of the stolen office key, which clove to his key ring. He plucked from his jean pocket a red, rubber-covered SanDisk 16 GB USB thumb drive. He plugged the flash drive into Club Miami's Apple iMac 27-inch screen state-of-the-art company computer. With Larry's passwords, he rooted up invoices, bills of lading, emails (some addressed to BookSmart), and documents incriminating Viktor, at least for shipping AR-15s to Manila in exchange for poor Filipina girls—hoodwinked, kidnapped, and exported like bleating lambkins to the butcher's block. Chitchee copied the documents to the SanDisk thumb drive, ejected the red thumb, and stashed it in his jeans pocket. On his way back to the BookSmart basement, Chitchee couldn't follow the direction of voices he heard. He couldn't see where he was going. His ears pricked up like SETI radio telescopes.

Viktor Martensen, Izzet Mutulugulu, Larry Sangster, Yakky Vorchenko, and BB talked in front of him now in the BookSmart basement, sounding like excited crows on a telephone wire.

Chitchee froze.

But for a crack of light containing Chitchee's eyeball, the manifold was infinite space expanding without planets, stars, or molecular motion. Chitchee filled the crack with more eyeball. He leaned his back like a weak ladder against the tunnel wall. He felt someone kicking his butt from mid-air. Which was impossible. He stepped on and squished something wormy, or mousey, or sausagey, which stuck to his salt-eaten Reebok.

Zalar swung from a water main by a pendulous meathook. Zalar's tongue had been cut in half. His eyes were gouged out so that they looked like enormous festering spider bites. Impaled, Zalar hung like empty armor.

"Ahhh!" cried Chitchee, covering his mouth reflexively in an expression between disgust and horror of horror.

"What the hell was that sound?" asked Viktor. "There are spies in the walls!"

"Somebody's losin' it," said Larry, venturing forth a chuckle. "That was just a squirrel."

Viktor grabbed a paper-hole puncher and punched a hole in Larry's earlobe with the other three holding him down.

"Don't tell *me* I'm losing it," said Viktor, giggling. "Hey, you guys, don't you think Larry would look great with earrings? Tee, hee. Let's get some beers down here! What should we get?"

"He'd look *better* anyway!" said Yakky.

Chitchee's scalp tingling, follicles puckering, and pupils dilating like little black umbrellas, Chitchee felt vomit flood his brain. The stress of disgust pounded his skull with revulsion. A migraine appeared in faint, vespertilian, shifting images. Toxins flushed through every capillary in his neck and face. He re-examined Zalar's mutilated, bloody, and puerile face, its mouth propped open by a baby human skull. Chitchee wobbled on fainting legs. The world drained down the holes beneath his feet. When he repelled a repulse to vomit, he noticed the brown extension cord tightened around Zalar's neck. Zalar's face was a split-open walnut at the forehead and below that the lumps and bruises looked more like a bracket of fungus. The little skull within the skull stuck out of the fungus of his once human face. He resembled photographs from secret police interrogations of political prisoners in Syria. The tip of Zalar's tongue had stuck to the bottom of Chitchee's Reebok. The worm he smushed was a tongue. He scuffled backward, hand up to his mouth. Then he scraped the bit of Zalar's tongue from the bottom of his Reebok and visualized Zalar's torture and Viktor's gloat.

"Blech!" crawled out of Chitchee's mouth like a spotted deer tick in a woodpile of forgotten, rotten, white pine wood.

"Blech's?" asked an apprehensive Viktor. "Who wants *Blech's*?"

"Larry," said Izzy, "book Viktor a flight to Miami."

"He has his own jet!" said Larry.

"This place is giving him the creeps," said Izzy.

"You, Viktor?" smirked BB. "You're creeped out? That's a new one! It's a squirrel in the wall stashing his acorns in the fridge. Viktor is afraid of a squirrel?"

"I'm not leaving town without Aubrey Aalgaard. That's the whole fucking purpose of tomorrow night. We're going to grab her by the cunt, dose her, and fly off into the sunset on my Lear jet offshore."

"But it looks like we're snowed in," said Izzy. "It's below zero."

"We're not snowed in!" said Viktor. "They always exaggerate the weather reports in Minneapolis to get higher ratings! Fuck them and their fake 'below zeros!'"

"We have to complete the book deal anyway," said Larry. "I agreed . . . under contract. It would look mighty suspicious if you canceled the reading and rushed out of town on your Lear jet, wouldn't it? Cool your heels. It's late and I have to get some sleep for tomorrow night's main event."

"I don't care about no fucking ghost-written book deal! I'm not going *anywhere* without Aubrey, and you're not going anywhere, Larry," said Viktor, "because you're the designated driver for tonight. How do you like that? Unless you want to wuss out, wuss. Let's get your pal Zalar. Here, Yakky— here's the machete Manual Noriega waved at the UN, which he gave to me for air-lifting a ton of high-class hookers to his yacht, stuffed to the gills with my Peruvian flake. Better yet, Larry, you can have the honors of carving up the turkey with Noriega's machete."

"Turkey!" laughed Yakky with the machete. "Gobble, gobble, gobblehead!"

"I think we need a circular saw for that," said Larry, "don't we?"

The five conspirators laughed like stiffs at a stiff family Thanksgiving.

"Somebody give Larry a hand!"

"Here's a hand, Larry!" gurgled Yakky, handing Zalar's truncated, ham-hock hand to Larry.

"Yakky, drive Zalar to the nearest compost site," said Viktor. "He'll make a great *mulch*."

"Mulch!" as if the room laughed to provide Viktor the laugh track to *Family Ties*.

Chitchee folded himself back into the safety of darkness as far as he could darken himself when Izzy, Yakky, BB, and a reluctant Larry thrust open the submarine door. After packaging Zalar's remains into cardboard file boxes, they stacked the four boxes of Zalar on top of each other by the submarine door.

"Yeah," said Larry unnerved, innervated, and deveined, "but whose car?"

"Hello, anybody home?" hallooed Noel down the stairs. "'Allo? Anybody home?"

"Yeah, the landlord! Who the fuck are you?" shouted Viktor from the open door of the storage area.

"Noel, Noel Schoolcraft," said Noel. "I work here. I want to get my *Hitchcock / Truffaut* out of the basement. You must be Club Miami? Aloysius gave me permission. I have k-k-keys. I'll be super quick, I'm d-d-d-double parked in the alley, engine running . . . it's just a Hitchcock . . . b-b-b-b-book."

"Come on down, Noel Noel Schoolcraft!" said Viktor, laughing and rubbing his tongue against his teeth.

Noel gingered down the stairs, but something did not seem level or on the square to him or conversely square on the level to him, and he suspected his not finding *Hitchcock / Truffaut* anytime soon.

Noel tightened his surgical mask. Viktor and his men snarled at him, because when they asked him why he was wearing it, Noel replied: he thought he might be coming down with the Spanish influenza and didn't want to have fifty million lives on his conscience.

"What's wrong with that?" laughed Viktor.

Despite this joke, Viktor reached out to introduce himself formally. Viktor grabbed Noel, spun him around, handcuffed him to a drainpipe, and kidney punched him a good one. Viktor wiped his hands on Noel's pants, eliminating all bogus viruses from Spain and Portugal from his medical future.

"You're my new chauffeur, pointy head!" said Viktor, reaching into Noel's pockets for the car keys to a Lexus.

"Hey, it's my dad's car!" Noel protested loudly through his surgical mask.

"It's *my* dad's car now," said Viktor, gurping down his falsetto chuckles.

"Noel? Where are you?" asked Ye Young down the stairs. "I had to park! I always hated park—"

At the twinge of a young woman's voice, the five men exchanged knowing glances, their faces cannibalized and cannibalizing.

Ye Young padded down the stairs slowly, an upright Siamese cat in her tan suede boots, and she parted her long black hair back to get a better angle into the draped darkness.

Viktor freed Noel. He threw Noel's car keys at Yakky's stinking face and told him to load up the trunk with the four boxes of "wild turkey."

"You know what to do," Viktor concluded. "Get it all outta here!"

Viktor, Larry, Izzy, and BB walked through the BookSmart basement door, walked up the stairs, looked around, walked outside, and re-entered Club Miami through the front door.

After showing Noel and Ye Young his rather demanding revolver, Yakky zipped up his gore-tex anorak and donned his silver Siberian-style, fox fur hat. He forced Noel and Ye Young to get into Noel's dad's Lexus and drive. Yakky sat in the back seat and necked with his iPhone, brown-fogging the screen of his Netflix cue, basketball scores, J Lo pics, and photos of one free (Viktor promised) Land Rover, Jeep, or 4 x 4 from BB's "garage sale."

"Siri, good burger?" asked Yakky.

"Where are we going?" said Noel, interrupting Siri's advice with a demanding tone. He repeated: "Where are we going?"

Noel's eyes winced at the air of sulphur compounds in the air—smelling a suck-egg snake's stomach contents.

"Never mind that, just drive," said Yakky. "Drive like everything's normal. You two talk like you two normally talk, so you don't fall asleep. It must be past your beddy-byes."

"Okay, but where were we?" asked Noel, gripping the wheel so tightly that Ye Young asked him if he was okay.

"Of course I'm okay," said Noel, driving with emergency lights and emergency brake on. "After we drop off this guy, we can go back to my place and try another Hitchcock. I thought you would have liked *The Birds*—that movie we watched last night. Melanie was Tippi Hedren. She's from Minnesota. New Ulm. And she modeled for Dayton's department store. Impressive, huh?"

"But why do the birds not like her?" asked Ye Young.

"It's unexplainable. It's just a dumb horror story, but the *cinematography*!"

"Get on 94 east," said Yakky. "Then 610 east."

"I'll need gas. I told my dad I'd top it off," said Noel, looking in his rear view when he thought he saw a shadow flit across the back window.

Noel couldn't see out the back because the silver Siberian-style, fox fur hat blocked his view.

Noel wondered whether a tree branch had fallen on the hood of the Lexus.

"Why is it *dumb?*" asked Ye Young.

"Because crows do not exhibit truly intelligent behavior," said Noel. "Especially at the level of group selection because only human beings act in an altruistic manner."

"But no such thing as group selection according to Dawkins," said Ye Young.

The warm barrel of a revolver lay like a cat's paw on Noel's cold neck.

"All right, quit 'dawking' and fucking drive!" said Yakky, his motorized tongue slick as an oil spill

"I'm almost out of gas," protested Noel.

"There's an SA," said Yakky, jerking his head to indicate a gas station glowing like an oasis in the night.

Noel wheeled into a deserted SuperAmerica, three crows flying after the bumper of the Lexus—ten meters behind and flying upward. Noel sidled out of the driver's seat.

He brandished his credit card, pushed it with his fingernails over the counter past the cash register to the clerk, and jacked his neck at the Lexus. When he peered into the stumpy clerk's acne, Noel inferred: *that* many pinched pimples must inevitably express a life-long resentment manifesting itself in credit card scams. Skimming, they called it. He had read about skimming on Reddit. Noel winked aside a sidelong glance. A crow landed on the hood of the Lexus, surveyed the area, flapped its wings, and lifted off. One crow and then two crows hopped down from the air onto the Lexus and stood on its roof, making a claim to it.

Drops of blood seeped from the car's trunk onto the oil-smudged, concrete pavement, the blood simulating motor oil from a leaky crankcase. Noel regretted making the trip to BookSmart for the *Hitchcock/Truffaut* book, making the idea of tutoring Ye Young on New Wave cinema look like grandiose hubris. Noel hurried back to the Lexus, bathing in a snowfall that made the Minneapolis skyline to the east appear like a mountain range in Colorado. Winter was exquisite to Noel (whose life might end at the very moment his panic set in). He took a last look at the skyline, moving in and out of a wayfaring mist like the oriflammes of an army.

Through the Lexus's frosty windows (windows gleaming), the streetlights' coronas beamed. Above the SuperAmerica parking lot on its snow-swept ledges, icy crows barked out of obscurity. Noel jumped into the driver's seat tumultuously and slammed the door covered with snow, which flaked to the oily, concrete pavement.

"Ye Young, I have a question."

"Ask it."

"Will you marry me?" asked Noel.

"Get off on the Maple Grove Parkway. Take a right on the Maple Grove Parkway," said Yakky, breathing over Noel's shoulder. "May-pole Grove!"

"Noel! Why?" asked Ye Young with imploring eyes.

"Get off on the first right," said Yakky. "The entrance will be the first dirt road on your right."

"Because—in the case we don't make it out of here—I love you, Ye Young," said Noel.

Noel drove the Lexus into the dream of an elf, dreaming in a hollow of lightly falling snow on birch, pine, and spruce. A barred owl cried from a hollow tree, deep in the woods, where only stillness interrupted stillness and the falling snow-motes captured the photons like sparks struck off an icy rainbow.

"It's closed," said Noel, braking and facing a chain-linked entrance gate locked with a thick chain over a STOP sign. "We can drive you home now."

When Noel glanced in his rear-view, he saw a "man" whose skin was so thick it looked tanned for hiding and whose head was so fat it looked gorged on the brains of a cow.

"No, it is not closed. Floor it," demanded Yakky.

"I protest," said Noel.

Yakky brained the top of Noel's head with the butt of the revolver.

"Shut the fuck up, college boy!" said Yakky. "I'll show you how to do it."

Yakky squirmed out of the Lexus, hordes of crows flocking down with talons and claws outstretched. The cacophony of a snappish street mob created a chaotic presentiment that a frenzy of violence was descending. A sky of crows gathered in the bare trees like Laplander sorcerors, who administer balsamic salves to the battle wounded.

When the crows detected the blood molecules of soft and wormy human creatures, one crow snatched the silver Siberian-style, fox fur hat off Yakky's head. So many crows laughed that more crows heard the contagion and laughed too. Yakky waved his gun and fired wildly into the sky. He didn't know a crow from a crowbar. He shielded his eyes. But the crows grabbed for his eyes and clawed for his iPhone.

Yakky scrambled under the Lexus to reload. Noel (adjusting his mask) and Ye Young, hand in hand, ran back to the dirt road and ran for their lives toward Maple Grove Parkway and flagged oncoming cars.

Chitchee scurried upstairs. He sat at the BookSmart Dell desktop, logged on (automatically autofilling), and uploaded the incriminating evidence from the red thumb drive onto the FBI website, care of Henry Hillswick, Agent of the FBI, Esquire. The taped Nagra itched like running poison ivy and it peeled/unpeeled. He re-taped it to his back and swathed it in girdles of medical tape. He practiced switching the recorder on by scratching his back nonchalantly. He bet ol' "Donnie Brasco" never thought of that one! Chitchee could not outsmart the computer. Shaky hands trembling, he wanted to restart the Dell, but he had no control over the mouse. Saami must have killed the mouse again. The cursor was a bat fluttering wildly in the LCD monitor.

Not what Ted Nelson and Doug Engelbart imagined the mouse would do for humankind, Chitchee thought when he powered the Dell off and on. The screen whooshed back. Chitchee typed on a Word document whose margins, spacing, and tabs rebelled at every turn of common sense. He said exactly what he did not want to say. Distracted, he sent an incident report in an attachment on BookSmart's Yahoo! email to the "Word people," who were all dead letters, which explained why they never answered any questions.

An alert message—a red exclamation mark—pulsated like arterial blood. The pulse beat inside the office of MPG upstairs, where a sleepy Corky Skogentaub intercepted the incriminating evidence meant for FBI Agent Henry Hillswick. Wide awake, Corky remote-viewed the bugged BookSmart Dell. It occurred to Corky to cover his tracks with Chitchee's tracks. Corky wasn't sweating for once.

Fingering Chitchee as the MPG hacker would send Viktor after a red herring and save Corky's neck. Corky grabbed a packet of French fries and ate them cold, excitedly.

Chitchee typed in the FBI's website again.

"I have some of it on tape, sir," typed Chitchee rapidly spewing typos:

And there's murder committed i the basement of Cub Miami. I saw body hangin and want to repot crim to the FFBII. I suspect murdrere knows Im here. Inside store. Im in delicate position must main anonimouse

Corky had learned the computer language Ruby to test the security of the Martensen People's Group IT infrastructure. While exploring Metasploit, Corky realized how easy it was to hack. After he told Viktor about the possibilities, the next thing Corky knew, he had Aloysius's IP address. He payloaded Meterpreting. Since Larry had already planted the trojan by clicking on Aloysius's email attachment, Corky, with his trusty distro Kali and a social engineering toolkit, redirected the already phished Aloysius to a cloned US Bank website, which sent Corky to a link that authenticated his US Bank ID. Corky hijacked Aloysius to the clone where Aloysius had secreted his business and personal accounts, his usernames, and his one password, which was always: joekapp69.

Corky ran a keylogger program in the Dell's Windows Vista background (an easy option on Kali) for getting into the Dell's "shell."

Corky commandeered the entire BookSmart terminal, transferred its hidden funds with a VPN via a server in Sichuan province and one in Bucharest, and stripped Aloysius of his hidden life savings and sinking college education fund for Aubrey.

Nested upstairs one flight above, Corky laughed at Chitchee! The babe in the computer woods, the babe struggling for words, let alone commands! And lol, the Dell's PF keys, some of which didn't work, fell out like loose teeth, which Chitchee clumsily wedged back into their qwerty sockets.

Corky watched the doomed Chitchee shoot darting looks over his guilty shoulder at Hennepin Avenue. Chitchee faced Hennepin Avenue like a movie. Thinking he had already busted Viktor, Chitchee lifted his busy head from the entrancing keyboard to look at the LED again and he felt joy.

"Al-*lah*, I'm good!" said Chitchee. "I should be working for the cops full time! Now I can save up and buy Ulysses & Sons. Do I call 911 to report a crime to the criminals committing the crimes because it's the law to report a crime or is it not a crime to not report the crimes of the law? That's what I want to know!"

A cascade of pop-up ads flummoxed Chitchee, which started when Chitchee clicked on an ad for a subscription to the Minneapolis StarTribune by mistake. The Dell fell into a free fall of offers, contests, coupons for miracles, virus alerts from a virus, and scam alerts from scammers.

Corky called Larry, whose iPhone vibrated in Viktor's pocket. Viktor, sitting at the Club Miami bar, handed it to Larry.

"Here's the fucking phone," said Viktor, "I paid a thousand bucks for. It's for you. Fucking Larry. I don't know what I'm going to do with you. You fuck things up royal."

When Larry grabbed his phone, Viktor slapped Larry's head from behind.

Viktor's iPhone vibrated.

"Yeah, Larry? Can you hear me?" asked Corky. "That big squirrely guy, he's in BookSmart right now! At the computer, leaving an anonymous tip for the jack-booted thugs in Brooklyn Park."

After several failed attempts that would allow his incoming call, Viktor, all thumbs, moved the green disc like a slippery blob of mint jelly, upward right.

"Yeah, what's up, Yakky?" asked Viktor, staring at the Tanqueray No. 10 gin gimlet Nestor mixed whose almond Viktor threw over his shoulder onto the floor. "I hate almonds, Nestor, you know that! They're Mongolian! Yakky? What? You're under the car pinned down by a flock of crows? Get the fuck out of here! What? Are you some sort of stupid fuckin' hoosier? Ya fuck!"

Servers buzzed by, assuring themselves that Mr. Martensen saw them working hard (rumors were that paychecks would be late). They danced attendant on his immediate needs with polite lies, but Viktor waved them off with the back of his hand, not looking.

"Go away!" said Viktor, clearing out a nostril.

"What's Corky saying, Larry?" continued Viktor, scratching his balls, which had stuck to his hair-covered thighs.

"He said that Chitchee guy," relayed Larry, "just attempted to blackmail Corky and upload all our financial documents to the FBI website."

"That Mongoloid fucker is going slam-dunk in the Mississippi with your slant-eyed Suzy Wong *chick*," said Viktor to Larry. "Boo hoo. Are you in love with her, Larry, you aging sex addict?"

Larry frowned, checked his old apps, and punched in old passwords.

"She only wants me for my money," muttered Larry, stiffening his heart to show no fear.

"That's about all you have," said Viktor, "isn't it? Where is that Chitchee guy?"

"He's at the book store's computer even as we speak, according to Corky," said Larry, not looking up from the mental coffin he wanted to die in.

"I can't hear a thing in here," said Viktor, blowing his nose across the bar's counter and looking without recognition at Alex, the EDM DJ from Pepsi Beaucoup who was on the stage. "Corky, can you come down to the bar?"

Only Alex's eyelids were visible to Viktor when his phone died or something. Intermittently Alex looked up with two ovoids of aqueous humor, mixing and scratching. His eyes were pinned to the turntable. Mermaids in Speedo swam in front of him. Pole dancers shimmied, one of which was LaDonna (camouflaged to fit right in). The dancers knew and greeted LaDonna, working her into the bass lines sampled from the Fifth Dimension's "Let the Sunshine In."

Alex looked apologetic and paused when Pepsi Beaucoup's manager, Mono Boondalicks, gripped the microphone.

"I'd like to introduce you all to Pepsi Beaucoup," said Mono Boondalicks, looking into a cavern at himself. "Pepsi Beaucoup is a soon-to-be famous musical band that has reconceptualized rock 'n' roll with their own brand of non-Western Other music. All our songs have been scrubbed in the interests of female and queer agency and have been written, full disclosure, from the perspective of a subaltern band that eschews the classical dissonances of classic rock (race/gender) by developing a metamusical style that combines the post-metaphysical rock of Nirvana with the political 'vibrato' of Gramsci's *Prison Notebooks*. Without relying on the West as a foundation for sexist grunge and post-musical, record-company music, which I refer to as Advanced Auto-Tuning 101 . . . Is this thing on? Hello? 1-2-3! Okay! As I was saying, *our* rock project challenges the 'Enlightenment' of the record companies and their hegemonic colonization of world music. Relying on the latest critical theory, Pepsi Beaucoup's *oeuvre* expresses this singularity of cognitive nervous tension. Even though our post-democratic world exists on the surface of a manifold that once isolated rock 'n' roll as a secularism that had to be marginalized, the religion of commodity now subsumes all rebellion—except Pepsi Beaucoup. That is because the plurality of their music distances itself from the Judeo-Christian axis of patriarchalism and the assumptions of Western 'reason.' Their music rebels against the loci of Eurocentric locationism and Western westernism, twin opposites of lateral and longitudinal thinking, the two halves of the bourgeois idea of the 'citizen' in the hermeneutical narrative derived from outmoded Newtonian laws of discourse and their Euro-discoursees. New breakthroughs in musical thinking have dissolved all the inconsistencies concerning Elvis. That the imperatives of Freudian analytics could not be expressed through Chuck Berry's hips but only by the establishment of a false universalism in the body of 'white boy Elvis' calls for redress, if not deep reflection. Music must de-appropriate the debt incurred by European exceptionalism and the false globality of Europe with a shift from the teleological "progressions" of the I-IV-V "classic" colonial rock to our subaltern counter-narrative of the more pentatonic I-II-III relationship, ridding ourselves of the major-minor/master-slave chord tradition derived from the canonization of the Western canon that resulted in a linear/anti-linear/binary/anti-binary exemplified recently by the stances of Karlheinz Stockhausen versus the Western-cum-narcissism dance project of Aphex Twin. Incidentally, in a post-Colonial sense, the irony of the abolition of the C major chord by its absence leaves a trace of its own false dichotomy on the absence of its own irony—"

Viktor said that "someone" should shut Mono that dumbfuck up. Izzy told BB, who took it to heart, stepped on stage, and punched Alex instead. Mono had dipped, dished, and booked offstage into the backscatter of pole dancers. LaDonna followd Alex backstage. Alex sat on the floor, crying a river. In the dressing room, LaDonna consoled him by rubbing his back and wiping off the trickle of individualized drops of blood, which dotted a line down his chin. Alex kindly gave LaDonna a change of clothes from one of the racks to sneak her out of the club.

"How did somebody get into the main office?" Viktor asked Nestor, tending the busy hive at the bar. "Somebody let the guy in. Who? I smell rats. Nestor? Someone is ratting me out! It better not be you!"

Nestor framed a stiff upper lip. Nestor, who had seen LaDonna disappear with his father, but not reappear, reflected and congratulated himself that his father was feeble-minded. Maybe he had a slight palsy of Parkinson's already and would stroke out soon due to a fattening, slobbering heart. LaDonna danced across the main stage behind pole dancers. She bounced like a hoop out the front door freely into the deep freeze of the winter's night. Nestor mixed intensely jealous drinks, one of which went to Sausage Man in a snowmobile suit and ski hat next to a fishing pole, next to Heinie Heinemann. Heinie received his Blech's beer with great gratitude, tipped ostentatiously, and intended to tell Nestor the history of ice, ice cubes, ice cream, and the Ice Capades, but the Chautauqua ended after two words.

"That Chinkee guy stole the keys," said Izzy, stating the epiphany into his cocktail while dreaming a horrible murder perfectly. "Viktor, seriously, I feel the heat closing in on us. It is safer in Florida. Let's cancel the book reading and—"

"What heat?" asked Viktor. "BB is racquetball partners with the President of the Policeman's Union, who is more powerful than Mayor Reebok. Or Dolan. Or whoever the fucking governor is. Do you know how I hire my security for the club? I see which thumper has the most complaints. That's my guy! Besides, elephant brain, we're going to abduct Aubrey, remember? We aren't going to Florida without her! She's a keeper, Izzy! Yeah! Keep her and kill her!"

Izzy swished his ice cubes and allowed the insult "elephant brain" to bounce like hailstones off his elephant back.

"Besides Izzy, you can have my sloppy seconds," nudged Viktor. "And then we can throw her in the alligator canal. So what did he download, Larry? Where is he?"

"Chitchee downloaded everything onto a SanDisk thumb drive," said Larry, distantly reading the writing on a screen, and continued, "drugs, guns, girls. Financial records. And actually all the money in our accounts."

Larry paused and took a draft and a deep breath.

"MPG is *wiped out*," continued Larry, slowing down his words and expecting a blow to the amygdala.

"What?" asked Viktor. "That Mongoloid wouldn't have known how to do that. What? WHAT? Who got into our computers? Corky doesn't know what he is talking about, the fat fuck!"

With the open mouth of a bowel movement, Viktor stood amazed. He snorted left and right, asking himself, "Why is my own son such a fucking whiner?" The bar fell silent.

Larry yelled in Viktor's mouth:

"Viktor! WE ARE WIPED OUT!"

Larry fell to the floor sobbing, his face in his hands—again obediently expecting a kick to the back of the head.

"Bullshit!" said Viktor. "You are LYING! Bullshit!"

Clinging to his bar stool's legs, Larry reseated himself. He finished his drink in one toss and shouted his heart out of his mouth:

"VIKTOR? DON'T YOU GET IT? MPG IS BROKE AND MUST DECLARE BANKRUPTCY. WE'VE BEEN HACKED!"

Viktor ignored Larry. He ordered Nestor to order Pepsi Beaucoup to play some "loud fucking garbage."

Nestor cranked the gain on all the TV sports channels at once, creating a titanic single event of all sports, while he dug around for a burned copy of himself playing a two-hour synthesizer solo sampled from his previous band, Bunch of Idiots, previously known as Bunch of Morons until he found out that another stupid band had already "stolen" that dumb name, which was when he went solo.

"And don't put on your music," said Viktor. "Your music sucks dead donkey dicks!"

"It's better than Pepsi Beaucoup," said Nestor, musically hurt, his eyes slitted for revenge. "It's better than Babes in Toyland. Better than Curtis A. Better even than—Tide!"

"Shut up, Nestor! I can't think! Larry! Delete everything, NOW!" continued Viktor. "Izzy, you take the Camry and find and dispose of Yakky. He jumped in the river, remember, another suicide. I'm going to cut through the basement and personally kill that chink with my bare hands."

Viktor ordered Nestor to hand him the bartenders' baseball bat (signed by Morganna) from behind the bar. Viktor, wielding the slugger like a hammer, plummeted downstairs and stomped through the Club Miami kitchen to the BookSmart basement.

Chitchee sat at the Dell computer in the front window of BookSmart, congratulating himself for finally conveying to FBI Special Agent Hillswick via voice mail the gist that Viktor Martensen was conducting an ongoing, worldwide criminal enterprise that noised abroad from Club Miami. What a racket. What a RICO racket. Not only that, MPG sported a *worldwide* network of RICO rackets, playing racket ball with innocent lives like they were all hollow, red rubber whackadoos to be whacked. Chitchee insisted he remain anonymous and be enrolled in a safe at home program once he had a home to be safe in. His Online Tips and Public Leads wouldn't upload. He yanked his little red, thumb-shaped flash drive out and heard an explosion that sent Chitchee spiraling upward from the swiveling office chair. Chitchee jumped to the Moon and back before he could catch his breath.

"Bang! Bang! Bang!" banged Lake Street Rodney, wearing a red plaid wool Pendleton jacket with matching red plaid ear muffs.

Chitchee peed himself before gaining bladder control.

"Oh, it's you! Thank you," said Chitchee through the window. "I thought you were another flash bang grenade of another Task Force gone rogue."

Rodney itched with nervous body jerks outside the frosty, white-knuckled BookSmart front window.

Chitchee stared at Rodney's lipless pitter patter, twitching neck, and eyeballs flickering in open-lidded REM. Rodney attached himself to the BookSmart front window. Gloves off, Rodney rapped on the plate-glass and looked onto the Dell computer station.

"Are you open?" asked Rodney. "Because you are usually open when I'm here! I see that it's *you* in there, so *you* must be open! But it's all dark in there like a dark room. What are you doing, developing photographs?"

"We're closed, Rodney, sorry!" heard Viktor.

Viktor thumped the signed-by-Morganna baseball bat on his open palm with slaps.

"I'm glad it's you," continued Rodney, "not the guy with the glasses, or the other guy who has no beard but looks like he might have had a beard until recently, but not you with no beard, not being the other guy, or the little guy who doesn't like me, or the other guys without the glasses, who I'm glad not to see, with or without my glasses on anyway. Chitchee! It's hard for me to grow a beard, but a beard with glasses? That seems to be 'the look' these days. And a black beanie. Beard, glasses, beanie. Are you really closed? For good? Oh my God!"

"No," said Chitchee. "Nobody works here. I mean——"

"Ow!" said Toby Pfeiffer walking straight into Lake Street Rodney. "Watch where you're standing! Where am I? Is this the the-A-ter? What? BookSmart? What kind of name is that for a name?"

Toby drifted into the snow drifts, blinded by blinding snow, causing tears to stream down his face inducing a desire to urinate.

"Anyway, I came to razzle your cage!" continued Rodney. "Razzle? Is that how you say 'razzle?' Or is it 'rattle?' I guess you're never ever busy in there. And you probably have all night to sit in your cage and write whole Moby Books! Did my *Smith of Wooten Major* come in?"

"I haven't seen it!" yelled Chitchee, "but if I do, I will assuredly put *Smith of Wesson Major* on hold and call for you at McDonald's."

"Did I tell you I invented a *plaid* language, based on Welsh syntax with borrowings from Middle-earth? Will you join me for a Dewar's and soda at Club Miami?"

Chitchee readjusted the Nagra taped to his back.

"Sure Rodney, let me close up shop here and I'll meet you over there! It's time to celebrate! Come on!"

Chitchee danced off his chain into a groove so deep you couldn't find him.

THE HEALTH INSPECTOR

Wouldn't you know it? As soon as Lake Street Rodney strode off, Chitchee saw a copy of J. R. R. Tolkein's *Smith of Wooten Major* sitting lazily on top of Rodney's hold pile. Instantaneously Chitchee knew Noel had set the book aside for Rodney, even though Noel looked down on Rodney as a Merlin looked at a mouse. Chitchee realized that Noel's act of kindness exemplified the true nature of a used book store, which was the unconditional love of learning. Happily, Chitchee skipped over to the front door of Club Miami. He reflected on humanity's innate goodness, altruism, mutual aid, reciprocation, and theory of mind. He would definitely offer Noel a job as a book scout at Ulysses & Sons. Aloysius would be a collectible in collectibles. Snorri and Saami would consult and advise at the front counter.

It would be a conference of birds.

"Do you have a reservation?" asked the Club Miami hostess Daisy Vang.

"No," said Chitchee, showing the hostess the cover of *Smith of Wooten Major*. "I'm the City of Minneapolis Health Inspector."

"OK, where's my husband?" asked Daisy, perking up. "I will definitely contact Viktor the owner and let him definitely know that Smith of Wesson Major, Minneapolis Health Inspector, is here for health inspection. Wait here."

TV screens bedazzled Chitchee. To order a drink, he competed with sporting events at high volume, announcers, replays, sports from around the world, play by plays, commentaries, interviews, and commercials for fast food. It was like being in Jersey Joe's Sports Bar during another Minnesota Vikings wild card miracle win. But Lake Street Rodney, where?

"Hey Chitchee, get your ass over here!" heard Chitchee.

He saw tipsy Dagny flapping her hand in a kind of ecstatic wave.

At her table, drinking umbrella drinks with Dagny, Astrid Eskola showed a glow and kissed a sore, stunned, and sobbing Alex. Mono's tongue traipsed over the table and wagged out sub-alternate after sub-alternate theory. He turned to his wife, who stroked his hair from a grooming reflex.

"I will . . . get . . . my . . . ass . . . over there but," called out Chitchee from the swirls and eddies of parched drinkers.

Chitchee looked cheerfully on. He was overjoyed to have a drink with his friends, having such an iridescent time. He had lost Lake Street Rodney in the kaleidoscope of drinks and faces formed from the tournament drinking and dancing to the sports channels. Nestor selected the music before Pepsi Beaucoup took to the stage. Chitchee ordered a gin from Nestor.

Winter storm warnings swept across all the screens like stormy petrels. Screens beamed at you from every angle—blowing and drifting snow across your face. Hazardous weather warnings. Records being set and re-broken. Ice bowl memories were replayed on NFL highlights.

Nestor watched Chitchee's Tanqueray No. 10 gin gimlet turn a little sea-sick green. He set the tumbler down on the bar and pushed it at Chitchee, who picked it up. Chitchee paid and tipped his longtime rival (Nestor blamed the "sick sixties," "polymorphous perversity," and "Mister Rogers Permissive Rights Movement" on Chitchee himself whenever he could).

Nestor liked but hated the idiot and dosed him—then spun his own demo-CD *Dunderheads On The Horizon*.

Chitchee barely sipped his tumbler. He ate the almond. He smelled something rank—or maybe it was a dirty tumbler! Poor Nestor couldn't even make a gin gimlet, pity the genius! Chitchee didn't want to complain about service. He was more eager to join Dagny, Astrid, Alex, Mono, and Mono's wife or whatever. He would order a Black/White Russian there.

Viktor tromped back from downstairs with the baseball bat (signed by Morganna), having smashed the Dell into glass tangrams.

"There was nobody there, Nestor," said Viktor, sweating enough to fill a shot glass. "He must have heard me coming. Did you tip him off? As far as you know, I never left my stool except to pee and never asked for the baseball bat, did I?"

Nestor nodded "no" back, leaned on the counter, and looked at his father with respect and hatred, with fate and blame, and with love and hope. Never moved and never moving, he had been emotional furniture to his old man *and* his old man's old man.

"How fucking thoughtful of you, Nestor," said Viktor, licked his thirsty lips, and quickly picked up Chitchee's gin drink. "Through thick and thin, shine or rain, I love my son who makes great gin drinks, if nothing else!"

"Thanks for the store-bought emotion! Hey, that's not—" said Nestor while his brain processed, re-processed, rehearsed scenarios, practiced lines, nodded "no" again, and whispered, "oh well."

Viktor tasted salt on the glass (but rushing for hydration he whaled down the gin in a gulp), which evoked a memory of the Caribbean's white broad beaches, his home and hearth. The sun always refreshed his soul, reminding him of family, duty, and honor killings. And honor killings gave him a sense of chivalry. A superb feeling of joy thrilled him on the backroads around Lake Minnetonka when he ran over rabbits caught in his Porsche's headlights.

Nestor's eyes and eyebrows formed a pyramid, which triangulated an inch above the bridge of his nose. Slowly a slight smile waxed like a moon on his red and rubbery lips. He held fast to the ironic, silver twinkle inside his gloat. He looked askance at his father.

The server Clara walked by and heard Viktor yell:

"BB, it looks like there was a burglary at BookSmart, so I expect the police will be here soon!"

BB didn't hear it correctly so dismissed it.

"Boss," said BB, cupping his hand to Viktor's ear for privacy. "The Health Inspector is here! Some guy named Smith!"

Viktor, with his dry throat swallowing that possible poison pill, split into two Viktors who sat mulling. Larry and Izzy looked at both Viktors, their faces anticipating Viktor's expectations.

"The Health Inspector?" asked Viktor. "There's no fucking way, there's never been a Health Inspector named Smith in the Twin Cities."

"Not even a Smith of Wesson Major, boss?" asked the ingratiating BB, wanting a scratch, scratch, scratch, scratch behind his wet ears or another promise of a free Porsche. "How about a Major Smith of Woodbury?"

Viktor, his eyes toward the ceiling as if stumped by a long division, looked overwhelmed to the breaking point.

"Soze," continued BB, "I don't need to tell the kitchen to get all the guns and ammunition out of the meat lockers?"

"WHAT? THE WHAT? That's impossible!" said Victor. "Where is this fucking Health Inspector? Get him out of here!"

Heinie Heinemann had read the buzz about Club Miami, which could lead to another article of note in Minneapolis world history, but only *if* Club Miami lived up to classics like Queen Anne's Kiddieland or the Cooper Theater or numerous other Seven Wonders of the Minnesotan World.

"Say, you fellas," said Heinie Heinemann, leaning into Larry's drink, "remember the Cooper Theater on Highway 12?"

Daisy Vang, the hostess, caught the eye of the vertiginous Viktor perched at the bar. She signaled him to follow her to her work station, where she informed Viktor that the Health Inspector had disappeared. Smoke rings started off the top of Viktor's twin-peaked, deciduously balding head. Daisy felt her pointy high heels crunch plastic. When she looked down, she saw a twisted flatworm trail of magnetic cassette tape.

"What is this?" asked Daisy. "That wasn't there before."

Unspooled magnetic tape from Chitchee's Nagra sprawled on the floor of Club Miami. Daisy tracked the magnetic tape from the hostess's station to her high heels to the crowd at Dagny's table, where the server, Clara, leaned into Dagny's table toward Chitchee.

"Hi, I'm Clara," she said.

Daisy disappeared.

"I'll have a Black/White Russian!" yelled Chitchee at Clara through the increasing entropy.

"Just wanted to let you all know," said Clara, ignoring Chitchee and looking down at the table, "my shift is over, the Health Inspector is here, the owner plans to murder him, and the cops are on their way."

Chitchee shrugged.

"Is there anything you'd recommend?" asked Chitchee.

"Just leaving," said Clara, leaving.

Chitchee waded through the crowd to the bar.

"Nestor! Nestor?" asked Chitchee sheepishly. "I feel guilty. I didn't drink that last drink you made. It tasted funny. How about a Black/White Russian? How's it going?"

"I killed a man and then I gave birth to the same man," said Nestor in a hurry. "Who am I?"

"Nestor! I hate riddles," said Chitchee.

"*Right*," said Nestor, handing Chitchee his drink. "It's on me!"

"IS EVERYBODY NUTS?" asked Chitchee. "Bunch of LOONIES in here!"

Chitchee, with a Black/White Russian in his hand, climbed over blushing alcoholics to his friends' table, cluttered by cornucopias of unfinished Greek cheese fries, Korean calamari, Polynesian enchiladas, Senegalese sushi, silverware, plates, and goochujang-soaking napkins.

The Health Inspector unbuttoned his shirt, revealing an old Nagra tape recorder tangled in his sweating chest hairs by medical tape. Chitchee itched his squirming back with his thumb. He tore the mini-tape recorder off his chest and planked the machine down on the table. He had hit the play button. Then the spindle had broken . . . the reel had fallen . . .

"Vik-Tor! Here the City Health Inspector, right here, this guy!" said Daisy.

Dwarves and elves with fake IDs slid past Daisy's station. Daisy pointed at Chitchee. She turned around.

Viktor, raising his arms and with his hand in the air, waved at BB. He pointed again and again at Chitchee over the heads of couples, who held insecure hands when Nestor's *Dunderheads On The Horizon* ended in perplexing silence.

Chitchee leaped and bounded on stage.

"I have an announcement to make, hello everyone!" said Chitchee into Pepsi Beaucoup's microphone. "Everyone in Club Miami! I want you to know that the owner of this club, Viktor Martensen, is running a date-rape club in the basement with protection provided by off-duty Minneapolis police. There is a prostitution ring importing underage girls from the Phillippines. Human trafficking is going on in the abandoned apartment buildings Viktor Martensen owns under the Martensen People's Group, which is under the Minneapolis Fiduciary Group, which owns practically all of Minneapolis—between Viktor and his father Marten they have the money and lawyers to corrupt local politicians, local cops, the DA's office—potentially all of Minneapolis. He is the guy with the baseball bat right in front of me. Author of *Quantum Biscuits*, I give him that—he was just literate enough to *hire* but *never pay* his ghostwriting team—Doe, Ray, and ME!"

Viktor rushed the stage (followed by Heinie (followed by Lake Street Rodney)), but he disintegrated. Viktor fell kneecaps toward the dance floor, then backward on his back. The disco floor went diagonal on him.

BB, having raced out to his first gifted Porsche 944 Turbo, ran back fully-armed into Club Miami.

Viktor's irreal thoughts spun a carousel of unicorns, lion-maned ponies, jumping Arabian stallions, liveried toads, polka-dotted cranes, monsters caparisoned in roses and blood-red jewels . . . horses . . . circles . . . blackouts . . . horses . . . vertigo made Club Miami spin. Heinie freely lectured Viktor (on his back, knees up) on the history of movie theaters in Minneapolis, especially the "big ones": the Suburban World, the Academy, the State, the Orpheum, the Heights, and twenty or so others . . . but especially the art deco, populuxurious, super Cooper Theater in St. Louis Park with its wonderful 35 mm., state-of-the-art, wraparound widescreen.

Viktor's eyes whited out white as snowballs. His body was clay. He foamed. Words died in his drool. All of Viktor fluctuated in the Heinemannian Force Field of Boredom.

Heinie's TONGUE AND LIPS in extreme close up: "Do you remember Cin-E-Ra-Ma? Cin-cin-cin-e-e-e-raaaaa-ma-ma-ma? Sensssssuuu-roundroundround arounddd?"

Heinie's tongue darted in and out of Viktor's consciousness, while Viktor spun on Catherine's wheel.

"Remember the COOOO-PERRRR? COOoOoOoOOOoOOOoper! CoooPPPEERR CinneRaaaaaaaaaaaaaaaaaaaaaaa-Maaaaaaaaaaaa!"

"I've . . . been . . . doped . . ." mummed Viktor.

"You'll be fine!" rattled on Heinie. "Probably just something you ate like organic soup! Like I was saying, the history of movie theaters in Minneapolis is a wonderful subject for a dissertation or two, but not as interesting as the history of the first telephones in Minneapolis, or the first ice cubes for that matter. You know, I was at the Minnesota Historical Society . . . guess how many digits the first telephone numbers in Minneapolis had?"

"What's wrong with him?" asked Lake Street Rodney, his face filling Viktor's sphere of consciousness. "Why are you on the floor? Are you the owner? I like to lie on the floor, but not in public places, which have chairs, and if not chairs, floors. Floors are good for people, but chairs are modern inventions—"

"Yes, quite recent," said Heinie. "Do you know when the first chair was introduced into Minnesota? Actually, the history of the first chair in the State of Minnesota took a lot of twists and turns in its evolution."

Viktor's eyes wobbled in their orbits. A befuddled puddle pooled behind his startled eyes. Slipping in and out of consciousness. In and out.

"The boss is down!" said BB. "The boss is down! Daisy, call an ambulance! Boss down!"

BB, with his biceptual lobster arms out and shiny penis face, rushed the crowd near the stage with his pepper spray canister and released the contents like air freshener. Then he frog-marched Chitchee, gripping his armpits, toward the front door, through the parting crowd, which looked on in amused horror.

"No!" said Viktor, getting up on his elbows. "I'm wo-kay! That ten thou'and dollar!"

He strangled Chitchee by the scruff of the neck and belt.

"Beat it, grandpa!" said BB, flexing his big guns.

Head first, Chitchee flew out the front door into the swift, strong wind racing up and down Hennepin Avenue like an invading army of icy Panamanian machetes.

Self-congratulatory BB walked back inside Club Miami.

"Wait!" shouted Viktor to the spinning disco ceiling inside his head. He stood up quickly, rubbing the nightmare from his eyes. "Don't throw that fucker out, I want that Mongolian idiot . . . dead!"

Ivan Von Volkov thought about smoking on the Moon. What would that be like? Oblivious to the gelid air, he peered in the BookSmart window. He had watched BB drill Chitchee like a SWAT team's battering ram into the snowbank. And Chitchee's landing at the feet of his snow-covered, unlaced boots.

Chitchee triaged himself for expensive, uncovered broken bones. A frozen lake of pain in his frozen skull expanded and produced a spiking ache. He staggered into Ivan, who stood aside and allowed Chitchee to splat again on the black ice. Ivan looked through his smoke rings and through the BookSmart front window at BookSmart's Dell computer, which was smashed.

"Are you open?" asked Ivan of Chitchee.

Snow plows passed, traffic passed, and pedestrians passed.

"I'm always open," said Chitchee, "what does it look like?"

"It looks like you're closed," said Ivan. "Hey, I'm looking for *Mutual Aid*! Do you work here? Excuse me for asking but, hell, hey, since I know you Chitchee, can you get me in? Are you hiring? Can I get an application? You, of all my friends, know that I am a true romantic like Dr. Chicago."

"I got thrown out of Club Miami, Ivan," said Chitchee, feeling bruised and nauseous. "And I can't get back into the building. I don't have front-door keys."

"Okay good, when can I start?" said Ivan, offering Chitchee two cigarettes of a discount brand, backed up by the same brand in an unopened, sealed, blank package inside his suede jacket (which had undergone some desuetude). Ivan's jacket blew open and flapped in the wind. And his not wearing a cap was foolish.

"I better check something first," said Ivan. "The funny thing is I'm not even French—I'm Finnished! I discovered Emily Zola in 1998, summer, July 14, 3:05 exactly. And I want to read all the *Rouge-Moulin* series. And then Ornery Balzac's *Old Gorey*."

Earlier that night, Ivan had gotten drunk alone on his bunk with strawberry wine, celebrating his self-published poetry release on CreateSpace, shouting, stomping, and hallucinating himself into *Petrouchka* (as Petrouchka) in a *pas de deux* by himself.

"Can I borrow your phone, sir?" asked Ivan, expecting a call from Sweden every Sunday morning (the wrong day) at six o'clock. "What day does Monday fall on in Sweden? Do you know? What's this?"

Ivan surprised himself when he pulled out an alarm clock, a gray-white square oblong electric Westclox from his pocket.

"Oh yeah, I was evicted by MPG for partying by myself," said Ivan. "Like I said, no one was there! I guess the neighbors could hear the music through my headphones."

A square-shouldered outline of a tabard-shaped body with a square head on it, one-story tall, approached Chitchee and Ivan from the blizzard.

"Hey," said Mjollnir, their last conversation never ending. "That bouncer in Club Miami is BB— the same thumper who broke my jaw at the RNC protests."

"You can't mess with the thumpers, Mjollnir!" said Chitchee. "Let it go. They own this town. They kill at will. It's provided for in the city charter. You could move to St. Paul—if that is safer now."

"Between Sheriff Robinson in St. Paul and Lieutenant BB Robbins in Minneapolis, there is no comparison, because they are exactly alike," said Mjollnir. "Even the good cops are like the buttons they button into their buttonholes. They fall in line and button all the way to the top. Hey, can I use your phone after Ivan? I didn't pay my electric bill. And I'm looking for weed. Seen Raven lately? Nestor said he saw him with Dougal who said he saw him with Nicky Fingers who said he saw him with Chameleon Slut Monster who said he saw him outside the Ordway, trying to get on the guest list for *Der Rosenkavalier*, but he didn't talk to him. Everyone I talked to said they'd seen him somewhere."

"Then he must be at home," said Chitchee. "You know Raven's very cautious about dealing and he makes visitors stay overnight, but he *does* feed them Cocoa Rice Krispies and bacon in the morning."

"Bacon?" asked Mjollnir ponderously and rhetorically. "How come I didn't get any bacon? I love bacon."

"We can go to my friend's house, Tiny," interrupted Ivan. "It's not as far as the crow flies—if you don't mind walking to the Mississippi River."

"Hey, get back here, Mongoloid!" yelled BB.

Bareheaded, BB's black hair stood straight up at attention, the deep wrinkles of a pumpkin lining his forehead. BB's eyes were red-hot coals (getting no response), the eyeholes burning through sheets of ice.

"Stop! Mongoloid! Stop or I'll shoot! Get on the fucking ground or I'll kill you!"

Mjollnir turned around with a bullet in his back.

Threatened by excited delirium, BB fired into Mjollnir's chest, which popped and shredded, but had no effect. Mjollnir grabbed BB's head and squeezed it until it was squishy-squoshy. BB's head rolled between Mjollnir's baker's fingers like a ball of dough. BB bit Mjollnir's thumb to bite it off. BB's baby fingers crumpled into balls and his crying eyes spit blood, when Mjollnir licked BB's ear, placed his entire mouth around it, clamped his teeth on it, and bit off BB's ear, which came off surprisingly easy, and went down like the liquefaction of a malted brown bat.

Mjollnir clasped his attacker in a banned Black Widower headlock, which he learned from a Moldavian grandmaster in chess at a youth hostel in Uzbekistan waiting to buy a little salt. He refrained from the Jindra Ankle Twist, which he had oathed to never use.

Mjollnir disarmed the thumper and threw his automatic into the intersection where a #6 bus ran over it. Mjollnir picked up the thumper by the belt and collar. Mjollnir's lifelong training in the hammer throw, a Rurik tradition going back to his ancestor Thor, kicked in. Thor precisely directed every ligament, tendon, and muscle in Mjollnir's body. Mjollnir spun like a dancer, released, and watched BB fly like a blue missile into the front plate-glass window of Club Miami, splat, and collapse. BB's wife Daisy Vang screamed.

Chitchee sneaked a quick look over his cold shoulder and dragged Ivan by the non-smoking hand into the lobby of the Uptown Theater.

"Chitchee!" said Felix. "Thank God! It's just you! I thought it was Garrison Keillor. Or not. Just kidding. Or not. Can you believe I have to work the blizzard? Or not. Ha!"

"Felix, help!" said Chitchee, opening the wind-slamming door for Mjollnir, who needed a phone to call Raven for weed. "We need to get into the storm sewer system again, Felix. The thumpers are on their way! The police are going to riot like they usually do when they start a riot."

Mjollnir had exhausted all his strength. He couldn't make it up the carpeted steps to the mezzanine to the men's bathroom. He lay face forward on his stomach, his arms above his head as if with a football over the goal line, snoring.

"'s-go!" said Felix, excited for some excitement. "Whoa! Life is better than Netflix, who knew?"

The manager, Emily, had gone home to watch a movie. She turned a blind eye to Felix's expeditions underground anyway as compensation for low wages and the gremlin customers always demanding their popcorn rights. The Uptown Theater movie, *Black Swan*, was not selling well; in fact only Toby Pfeiffer was watching it. Felix left his post to a co-worker who needed the hours so he could buy flu medicine for his flu at work. Felix said it would be all right if he punched out early too, because it would save Landmark Theaters money on the non-use of water from the drinking fountain.

"Hey! Hey! What kind of a theater is this? Let me out of there," whined Toby Pfeiffer, beating his head against the candy display case in a rocking motion. "*Black Swan*? What kind of a name is that for a movie without black swans? My head is spinning!"

TINY'S HOUSE

Felix thrust his boltcutter, a potpourri of tools, and flashlights into his backpack. Chitchee, Felix, Ivan, and Toby entered the underground storm sewer system. The 9 x 13 tunnels were endlessly labyrinthine, cloacal, and chilling as *Journey to the Center of the Earth*. Icicles formed the pointed teeth of dragons. It was a wandering worm. It was a ziggurat lengthened and straightened out on a path of munching gravel. It was a dream with trap doors that emitted the rotting, exhumed flesh of sweltering swine.

Highway 94 roared overhead with a waterfall of engines, the same I-94 that had sectioned off North Minneapolis like a black Alaska. The waves of cars beat inside the earth and sky. Felix's flashlight beamed collapsing ellipses of light, fringed with hoary rainbows that expanded into sudden giant ovals breaking apart into complete darkness. Felix's arm tired, his grip unsteady, he kicked the flashlight when he dropped it.

When Chitchee reached down for Felix's flashlight, his own cell phone fell out of his pocket.

"Where are we going, Chitchee?" asked Toby, nervously bumping into everybody, his head screwed on backwards.

"The river!" said Felix, recovering and flashlighting the way forward. "All for one and one for all! Guess not."

"The river? What river?" asked Toby. "Is there a bathroom down there?"

"The Mississippi," said Chitchee. "Ivan knows some guys who own a one bedroom cave we can hang out in."

"A one bedroom cave," sobbed Toby. "I thought I was going to see a R-rated nudie by that guy Mirror Max and his Playboy ballerinas that Frenchy always talks about!"

Ivan's boots plowed through icy puddles in deep concentration. He jotted down field notes on the network of sewers, drains, storm inlets, and mains for a stirring, love poem.

"I bet you they have ritualized murders down here," said Ivan, stroking his chin in the pose of deep thought.

"Why do you say that?" asked Felix, frowning with a nervous pout.

"Well, where else could you have them?" asked Ivan.

Four heads poked out of a storm sewer drain. It had stopped snowing. Flowing before them, the Mississippi River carried hundreds of millions of gallons of river. The old railway depot was deserted. Wharf rats stepped from the shadows. Gas lamps had once lighted Victorians to their opium pipes on the brick-sett streets of old Washington Avenue. It sounded like derelicts in a glass house fighting with glass bottles over a glass princess trapped in her own towering glass bottle. Ivan led the refugees through defunct flour mills; down dissipated, collapsed clay banks; by warehouses abandoned to rust; through a saw mill sawn through by time; by superannuated stables for trolleys and fire engines; and past the ghosts of exploded buildings, mission houses, and plush hotels for the once well-heeled, teeth-picking, getting-into-another cab, starlet-armed, smooth-as-silk suited, hair-oil-slicked back nightclub patrons of the roaring 20s.

They traipsed past water-softening plants, water works, barges, reservoirs, locks, and hydroelectric power stations flickering and shining like the empty lobby of Mystic Lake Casino. They trekked silently past brick lodging houses, which looked like stacked, crumbling boxcars, and hobos on front steps like giant flour weevils in sacks of bonanza wheat flour—the hobos' stubbled heads providing affordable housing for snow fleas.

"It was Jesus who made this wonderful night!" yelled Grover Gossick.

Grover greeted them on the Hennepin Avenue Suspension Bridge, a platinum-colored, gate-towered, rook-shaped, and cable-swooping bridge, next to which the Grain Belt Beer beer-cap glowed with noble gases. Grover paused. Looking very like a very squat lizard in a dull green parka, Grover stared at Chitchee as vacantly as an ad-less billboard.

"And you're the Chinee," said Grover, "who sells atheist science books at BookSmart, doing the devil's work!"

Grover called his handler, Detective Weatherwax in the MPD narcotics division (busy signal?) to report suspicious-looking "perps" on the Hennepin Avenue Suspension Bridge. Grover had refused the free ambulance ride, because he only had a headache; besides the Lord would take him soon anyway at the scheduled, appointed time. Grover distrusted all doctors, professionals, and so-called experts, who were all Freemasons, Knights Templar, and St. John's "Hot-spittlers." They made their blood money from harvesting organs and culling the population so that the Queen of England could sit on her throne and dump on everyone.

"And I heard there's lots of jobs for Somalian informants," said Grover. "I'm interested. I think I can bust all of them."

Grover walked down the concrete Grayco-painted stairs next to some old water main pipes. He entered his handler's special number again on his special flip phone.

Over a fence, Ivan, Chitchee, Felix, and Toby tumbled down an emaciated cliff. An apron of unrolled spilled cigarette stubs, broken chairs, shattered McCormick's vanilla glass, thorn bushes of Listerine bottles, and the litter of votive Marlboro boxes greeted their falls. Felix and Chitchee jumped up, hearing giant beavers on the shore thwacking their alarming tails. Toby's face grew round and Ivan surveyed the alders and the aspens in the area cooly.

"Watch out for the prehistoric, man-eating woodchuck, Toby!" said Felix.

The drumming of fomenting waterfalls beat the air in a frantic, but oddly peaceful background lion's roar.

Tiny's place was a house made of 2 x 12 foot popsicle sticks and a tarp. Dead watt bulbs hung every ten yards from wires and extension cables. A thick red side door lay obliquely propped against the hut, 15 x 30 feet, containing an altar, an *ofrendo* from *La Dia de los Muertos*.

"Hey, Tiny, remember me?" asked Ivan.

Tiny stepped forth, a gigantic African-American who looked soft as a baby.

"No," said Tiny.

"We met on the #21 bus in 2003, it was August 23rd, 5:05 p. m., and I read you my poems, and you sang me a song."

Tiny shook his head.

"Well, everybody," continued Ivan, "we'll just make ourselves at home. Does any of you know anybody who's looking for my autograph? Well, because I'm here!"

The group of liquored up souls (a group Mathew Brady could have crystallized and switched out as Civil War veterans of the Grand Army of the Republic) with long grey beards stood around a bucket of punch like a pitcher's mound at a relief change. They stared at Ivan when he neared the bucket of punch.

The ragtag Magi included the gigantic Tiny, the one-armed Jo-jo Joey, Dog Face, Rickety Jitters, Motherfuckin Green Eyes, Science of Moses from Sierra Leone, Mad Jack Apple Jack, Mad Jack Barley, Mad Jack Harry Snatch, and Undone Buttons. Chitchee recognized some of the others from raids at Hidden Beach on Cedar Lake and others from the Walker Library periodicals area.

"Got any hooch for us, Ivan?" asked Mad Jack Apple Jack.

"Actually, we aren't drinking," said Ivan. "I don't drink anymore anyway. I'm quitting for the night. But it kind of looks like you are booked for accommodations. I got evicted, and Chitchee is hiding from bouncers who want to kill him."

"Can we hide out here, Tiny? Please, Tiny!" said Chitchee. "Are we safe from the Minneapolis Police Department here?"

"Yeah," said Tiny in a falsetto blip. "They don't know I live here."

A bucket of punch, a pot luck for all who poured in the contents of their bottles into the large laundry bucket, stirred by the wooden spoon of Tiny, muttering a magic spell, or a blessing, or gibberish emitted from the fumes Tiny waved into his face.

And when Tiny declared ready, he pulled out a turkey baster and filled it to the mark. Each participant held out a dollar, which Tiny disappeared. He then squirted the reciprocal amount into the mouth of the investor.

"Anybody home?" asked Chester in his top hat, and his partner Marcia in a shawl, violin bow and violin in one hand.

Chester and Marcia shuffled up to the group, who welcomed the newcomers in silence.

Marcia played a tzigane of "Chester" and everybody relaxed with hand-rolled cigarettes.

Dog Face, a starved, bipedal gray wolf in ragged layers of wispy hoodies and fingerless gloves, his face blue with obscure, metallic band stencils, dance-stepped on a Naked Joy pomegranate bottle outside the circle of contributors, migrated, and later that night died of exposure, asleep in a snow bank.

"We should go back," suggested Chitchee.

"Oh, you're from BookSmart!" said Tiny, adjusting his Hopalong Cassidy floppy hat, not much more than a lump of felt over his ear muffs. "Remember me? We met on the bus. You gave me mouth to mouth on the back seat, because you thought I was having a heart attack."

"I meet lots of dying people on the bus," said Chitchee. "Let me think . . . was it the 17 or the 2?"

The Hennepin Avenue Suspension Bridge stood like an army ant. A duffel bag fell from the bridge. A scream and a splash. The scream had come from an onlooker, because the duffel bag plummeted like a lead sinker, and the scream came from Nicollet

Island. Flurries snowed upward like oscillating spangles. Brushing on the shore and drifting on the rocks, legs spindled outward like spin drift. A dead mutt lay in the water.

The stars, like white water lilies, unfolded lobes of blue atmosphere, although obscured by the acidic, carbon dioxide haze from industrial streets, bridges, and the cold wavelengths beaming from office towers.

"It must have been another old Indian alcoholic."

"It was probably a bag of garbage somebody dropped. I didn't see a body. Anyway Indians don't do themselves in like that. It's always white guys with beards who jump. Off *that* bridge anyway."

"There *was* a body. It fell out of the bag on the way down and waved."

"No, it didn't."

They replayed the event over and over, from beginning to end, backwards and forwards. "I was standing there, I heard something, I looked up, I saw . . ."

While some surmised maybe someone they knew had jumped from the Hennepin Avenue Suspension Bridge, others said this wasn't the first time they saw someone jump to their deaths, others were saying so what. A quarrel brewed on the sanctity of human life, some said yay, some firmly nay. Ivan argued loudly with himself about what he saw, iterating in his mind that a girl jumped. He knew it "through osmosis."

The Hennepin Avenue Suspension Bridge like abnormal catheters coming loose concentrated everybody's attention. Chitchee and Felix shared a joint. Chitchee looked North about three kilometers away at an angle of 45 degrees from where they stood.

Toby burst from his unaccustomed silence, hands thrust in pockets while he stamped his feet, and cried: "I want to go home, I want to go *home*. Are the buses running?"

"Nah, they cut the routes to save money on getting people to their jobs."

"Back in the day, all you had to do was whistle and a bus would come."

A lump floated in the icy Mississippi like a floe.

"There he is," said Tiny.

The bag snagged on the ghostly branches of a fallen cottonwood, jutting into icy, woolen-white eddies. Tiny fetched a gaff from his one-bedroom cave. He waded to the top of his bootheels in the Mississippi.

They dragged the duffel bag to Tiny's shore. Chitchee opened it. He gasped when he adduced Larry's girlfriend, the Filipina girl, Reina. She had sustained bruises around the eyes, cuts, broken teeth, and a split lip.

"What are you going to do with her?" asked Chitchee.

"Bury her with the others," said Tiny.

Chitchee heard the barking of hell hounds.

"LaDonna's curse!"said Chitchee, eyes shocked open.

Tiny grabbed his shotgun; but fumbling, he fired a warning slug into the sky by mistake. The bark of thunder and muzzle flashes of lightning accompanied the vested Minneapolis thumpers storming down the cliff. Hell hounds, in low to the ground stalking positions, growled and crawled like dragons. Chitchee was in an emptiness as if he were in slow motion. The hell hounds were in fast motion. He blew his acorn whistle at one hell hound—extremely powerful, low to the ground, and very short-legged—which then leapt at Chitchee's throat and froze in mid air. Chitchee smashed backwards against a brawny cottonwood tree, whose roots were like hooves thrust into the bank, and he slid down looking dead. A bullet ripped the night air like construction paper, and everybody scrambled for their lives as if in the front or back of an avalanche. A shotgun blast loosened the stars in their sockets, rattling the skyscrapers like pots and pans on a stove.

"Sarge!"

"You killed him!"

"He killed Sarge? Oh my god, Sarge, Sarge!"

"Who's Sarge?" Chitchee heard himself ask.

"Let's take this fucking garbage," said a thumper, pointing at Chitchee, "for a K ride! You guys get a stretcher, and tell the Animal Hospital you've got Sarge and he's on the way. We can't lose Sarge!"

"They got Sarge? Who did? This fucker killed *Sarge?*"

HENNEPIN COUNTY
MEDICAL CENTER

Chitchee felt a blow to the back of his head, and then a sharp jab in his arm like a razor cutting through his clothes. Then he lost all power over his own willful body and forgot everything, bouncing up and down in the trunk of a car, with the sound of spinning wheels on pavement the icy background of his consciousness. The car took a left from Lake Street into the North Calhoun Beach parking lot, which was empty. The driver got out and opened the trunk. The partner got out, and he took one end of Chitchee's limp body. They lay Chitchee on the ground and wrapped him in a Hudson Bay blanket. They carried him to the bottom of the hill facing Lake Calhoun, set him down, and the driver walked back and fetched a jerry can of gasoline from the trunk. He poured it on top of Chitchee's blanketed body. He reached for a lighter—patting himself down—then returned to the car and found an unopened book of matches from the glove. Pop, pop.

They both heard gunfire.

"Where did that come from?"

"It's that fucking guy who came out of that Porta Potty!"

Flakes of snow floated down like Kleenex—and before they walked away from the body, hurriedly, in dotted rhythms, the driver tossed a match.

A halo of fire danced on the blanket like the gold flames in Persian miniatures.

A bullet grazed the driver's earlobe, then his kneecap, and then his buttocks. They scrambled into the car, backed up, and floored it out of the parking lot onto the boulevard of semis and taconite gray cars.

Hawk Eye ran to the blanket, rolled the body, and damped out the flames.

Chitchee was not breathing. Ear to mouth, breathing into the mouth, tilting the head back, pinching the nose closed, Hawk Eye hovered over Chitchee. Hawk Eye felt for a pulse—neck and wrist. Hawk Eye rolled over the now breathing body (a puff of gray air crystallized in a silver cloud). Then he ran into the middle of West Lake Street and flagged a St. Louis Park squad car, which called for an ambulance.

Chitchee was a radar screen that sensed the traces of his vitals. Green and bleeping red buildings filled and emptied the room's blank windows with alpenglows, jack o' lanterns, and will o' the wisps in a Walpurgisnacht over white sheets. Chitchee gripped a metal bed. His head lay on a medical pillow. The light-barred Minneapolis skyline entered Chitchee's louvered blinds in zebra stripes of peripheral vision. Electronic water music flowed in the disinfected corners of ammonia, clorox, and bleach. The comfort of his body told Chitchee: rest, rest, rest, I'll be all right: and this comforted Chitchee when he opened his eyes and realized he lay in Hennepin County Medical Center.

"Do you remember anything?" asked Salah Mohammad.

"Oh, Salah! Am I ever glad to see you! Praise be to Al-*lah*!" said Chitchee.

"You overdosed on ketamine!" said Salah.

"But I've never *done* ketamine. Well. Okay I did it once. I was all rubber legs. I've read about it in John Lilly's works. Starting with *The Center of the Cyclone*. Did you know he went to St. Paul Academy?"

"Somebody," continued Salah Mohammad, "saw a car pull over to the side of the road, two men dragged your body out of a trunk; they poured gasoline on your blanket, and lighted you on fire; they were going to throw your burning body onto the ice. I guess someone called 911. You have the St Louis Park police to thank for saving your life."

"Thank God for the cops sometimes!"

Chitchee looked at his watch, which was missing and which had been missing for he didn't know how long. The nurse Salah exited.

"Where is my phone?" asked Chitchee, a note of panic, chords of anxiety, and fears of identity theft destroyed his slumber. "I left my phone at Tiny's!"

"*Ni hao,*" said Dr. Li Fan, clean-shaven, sunken cheeked, and black hair combed to the right like a stiff regulation. "Well, it is *All Men Are Brothers*, we meet. How are you feeling?"

"*Comme ci, comme ca,*" said Chitchee, his hand and fingers extended to which he gave an oscillation or two. "Did you read that Herman Hesse?"

"It was okay."

"Just *okay?*" asked Chitchee. "Hmmm . . . then try *Demian* or *Steppenwolf!*"

"Doctor, the police are here," said the nurse, Shuwen, returning and recognizing Chitchee with a slight smile and a slight bow. Two thumpers entered the room solemnly. Chitchee sensed they had been crying, but that seemed impossible.

Police? Here? Why?

The name plate read WEATHERWAX. And the other name plate read WEATHERWAX.

"Just some routine questions," said Officer Weatherwax.

"Are you guys brothers?" asked Chitchee.

"No, why?" asked Officer Weatherwax. "Oh, Weatherwax is a common name in Minneapolis—like Andersen or Rasmussen."

"Shoot," said Chitchee. "Maybe you're right."

"We lost our Sergeant last night," continued the other Officer Weatherwax. "He died at the Medical Center in St. Paul, and we have information leading us to believe you know something about it. We would like to ask you about your whereabouts last night."

The thumpers asked Li Fan and Shuwen to leave, but Li Fan shook his head, protesting that he had to run some tests and check some vital signs. They insisted and manhandled Dr. Li and his RN out the door.

"*The importance of a human life is as vast as the sky,*" protested the doctor. "That sentence determined me to become a doctor. And I must fulfill that vow."

"It's okay, Doctor Li," chirped Chitchee. "The last thing I remember from last night, I was at a party. Then there was a commotion, and the damnedest thing—there was a damn wolf at my throat! A wolf mistook me for a wolf!"

"That 'wolf' was our leader," said Officer Weatherwax. "That 'wolf' was Sergeant Hillswick."

"Got it!" said Chitchee. "K-9s are almost human beings and human beings are almost police dogs. And you guys have soft places in your hearts for killer pets like everybody else. But can I buy a gun from an actual store or do I have to shop underground? Next time I encounter a shootout, I want to be prepared!"

Their eyes drilled holes into Chitchee's eye sockets like oil wells: they had all rights and powers over his freedom, unspokenly, and they intimated they would wait to take down a statement when the person of interest was on his feet and coherent; so now Chitchee had to go to Police Headquarters at the County Courthouse for further questioning at the dawn of noon.

Discharged, Chitchee remembered to stop by the Police Headquarters, but thought better of it—that dog? That dog had had a good run. It assuredly was fed well, worked out, lived like a dog star, and enjoyed free rein of the female dogs at the local dog night clubs. Benefits, a retirement plan, vacations at Baden Baden, and a plot at a Lakewood Dog Cemetery.

"I'll skip talking to the thumpers," thought Chitchee, "and read Toynbee. Who has time for all their complicated questions? Sheesh! The book-signing party for *Quantum Biscuits* should start soon! I'll make a citizen's arrest of that arrogant pipsqueak, Viktor Martensen, YES, and blow away the whole corrupt Minneapolis Fiduciary Group—with just one whistle from my acorn, my acorn of just truth! Oh, this is going to be good! If I can get a book store out of this, my entire life will have suddenly fallen into place, looking backward!"

Chitchee whistled down Nicollet and then Lyndale past the icicle-fronted bars with their cavernous maws of patrons in dirty dungarees dressed like pioneers living in sod houses. The youngsters' beards lingered over their fussball games, and their scruffy-haired fussbellies protruded like fat white tongues. It was so funny. Billiard players chalked cues like nighthawks channeling Minnesota Fats. Lean drinkers leaned with cues over the pool tables. Pedestrians holding cases of beer hustled past the awning-and-brick bars. Early night and the falling snow made it so that Chitchee couldn't see the forest for the bars, or the empties for the alleys, or the bags of beer bottles for the overflowing dumpsters. The killed time had piled up and spilled onto the dog-pissed snow. The more drinking and smoking, the grubbier the schlubs aged in their plaid-thrifted flannels and drawn-down brimless caps, and the quainter and more picturesque Minneapolis appeared to Chitchee, who felt warm under a blanket of soft snow.

"I'll get Viktor to pay me what he owes me at his own book signing," said Chitchee cheerfully. "Good job, Chitchee! Yes, I have to do one brave thing before I start to live. Don't I? Maybe I don't. Does anybody? I don't know a thing. I want to reach my death point along a geodesic line with a minimum of pain and botheration and surrender peacefully like Epictetus, not Cicero. I can't afford to be a Stoic much longer."

He stopped to doubt himself. Then, walking in a dubious cloud, Chitchee concluded that no Ulysses & Sons was ever going to open its doors with Viktor and MPG buying up all the real estate in Uptown, Downtown, Midtown, and Pig's Town. Soon they would have ordinances against book stores, books, and reading in public. Literacy itself would be a battlefield in cyberspace.

Bewitching ice birds roosted under the awnings, lintels, and pediments. Utility poles with power lines of frosted vanilla, cocked forward to listen to Chitchee's thoughts, drowned out by the rosy snow plows, gearing forward and foisting mountains of snow up against parking-lot retaining walls. Mastodon red bulldozers with front blades curled the breakers of shoveled snow like surf frozen and smaller snow plows barreled down main avenues, kicking up shining sprays of crystals, enveloping eddies of shape-shifting drifts . . . oceanic snowwaves hove into higher and higher snowbanks, and crested drifts swelled around pockets of parked cars.

Resentful sloshes in their snow clothes tippled home—looking owned by adversarial landlords. For some, home was a rented rookery below the poverty line and a consciousness of being nobody at home with nothing, watching everything. Oh to live with only the love of a dive bar, or to live being loved only by one's own dive bar, if nothing else; if nothing else was the else, there was always the bar, the beer, and the snow of forgetting . . . snow fell down past those apartments where you perceived no future for yourself in the loveless brick of the loveless apartment building you always hated living in. But Chitchee never minded anonymous poverty like his friends minded, because he aspired only toward looking out a mirror-bright, clean shop window.

An invisible corn broom swept the snow banks up in the air like the sorcerer's apprentice while Chitchee created new jogs in his improvised paths. Down parkas parked over wood-handled, red shovels and blurred against spurs of snow, drifts, and buried sidewalks. Every cubic centimeter of space was jam-packed to the rims with snow, blanching the outlines of cars and trucks into ghostly bison of ice. Streetlights buoyed red, green, and yellow, and they swayed like Christmas ornaments hanging from fir trees. White evergreens (graphed against the horizonless white fields) formed a vast background of probabilities: probably a sluggish car, probably a man huddled to himself in a bent black overcoat getting out onto *probably* a street. Gales blew past the parked cars, swerving, spinning, and rutting in place, where only the buses were getting through like meandering snow geese.

As the city's disappearing skyline in discrete, collapsing distances faded, the sky switched on a mechanical thunder. Chitchee offered to help push a woman in her Hyundai Kia out of a snowbank, but she thanked and declined, unwilling to roll down her window, for fear. The cold air was pins and needles pricking his exposed flesh; but the headwind was the worst, which, walking into, breached his fortress of layered clothes and forced him to relinquish all hopes of the warmth of *tapas*. Instead, Chitchee warmed up in the Carousel Square entrance. Nicky Fingers jumped from a wrought-iron chair at Ragnarok's Choklit Stoppe and accosted Chitchee with another life-saving swindle.

"Chitchee," said Nicky, his mind racing to make a trade, a deal, or a swap, "I couldn't get you that Ecstasy you wanted months ago, but I went ahead and spent the money anyway. So the money is now gone. Don't worry about it, jeez, Chitchee. I plan to buy back the broken stereo I sold you to pay you back for the broken bike I sold you for the DVD player with no remote I paid you with for the buprenorphine I bought back from you and replaced with the crushed methadone tabs in the tiny plastic bag, stuffed with the one bud of schwag. Don't worry Chitchee, I've got your back! Jeez! You worry too much! You're getting old, that's all. Did you hear what happened to Dougal? He kicked the bucket last night, Chitchee, well you know that wasn't meant to be ironically. I mean he closed all his tabs. All his tabs are closed."

"Dougal is dead?" asked Chitchee. "Why?"

"Like you care?" asked Nicky. "He was desperate for a drink and drank that whole jar of formaldehyde, because that's all he had."

"I can't believe it," said Chitchee, breaking up. "I just saw him. Are you sure you have the right Dougal? He seemed okay, well okay for Dougal . . . is there a memorial or a concert?"

"Chitchee, don't get all sentimental on me," said Nicky. "To tell you the truth, I barely knew the guy, except as a first-class waste case. I heard his sister who lives in Winnibigoshish will cremate him and dump his crap off at the Goodwill in Hopkins, if they want it. To make a long story short, I stole his feet. Can I borrow five bucks, Chitchee? You know I'll pay you back. I can pay you back with Dougal's feet."

"Yeah, Nicky," said Chitchee. "I know you'll pay me back by not paying me back. So here's five bucks with which I'm paying you to not pay me back."

From Carousel Square's entrance, Chitchee saw that BookSmart was closed, but a mass of snowmobiles sat outside—so Viktor had not chickened out or canceled due to a little weather. A Carousel Square security guard named Weatherwax approached Chitchee and said:

"Just so you know, sir, Carousel Square will be closing early, due to a little weather."

Chitchee thanked him profusely and turned to Nicky Fingers, who absquatulated with the security guard's iPhone Infinity!

QUANTUM BISCUITS AT BOOKSMART

Viktor's friends and associates had parked their snowmobiles, one by one, approaching from all four directions, in front of the unplowed BookSmart like horses hitched in a Cormac McCarthy novel. Viktor didn't care about the buses. He hated buses and bicycles—besides, it snowed too hard for Club Miami's valets to park cars, but not too hard for regulars to park themselves in front of the bar. It was Victor's sidewalk. It was Victor's everything, because he had BB and his thumpers on his side.

Chitchee, blanketed with snow, entered Club Miami, which looked like a megaron, its stage a throneless throne of pole dancers, its murals Art Moderne boreal chariots with topless Dorian maiden murals, and the fish tanks emptied of the go-go girls who had all called in sick the night before, twelve hours in advance. He shivered the snow off his black overcoat, stamped his feet, and greeted the newly-hired teen hostess, Pakpao, who stood in for Daisy Vang and her hubby BB. Pakpao gave Chitchee her prefabricated smile that he x-rayed as: "I hate working here."

Chitchee sneaked into the Club Miami basement, neither looking up, nor looking aside, cut through the basement office area, prowled through the Club Miami kitchen, entered his BookSmart bedroom/overstock, and bridled before the BookSmart basement proper, eavesdropping on Viktor while Izzy and Larry absorbed the details of the abduction of Aubrey in silence. Larry joked:

"So you plan to leave the country for Las Vegas?"

The Martensen Peoples Group's Belated Christmas Party, which included a mandatory book-signing at BookSmart to celebrate the talent and skill sets of Viktor Martensen's genius, the American genius, and the genius of "the American genius." Also included was an after party at the Calhoun Beach Club.

Viktor considered himself a fan of the chipper "Gypper." And Viktor's success story was straight out of the American Dream playbook, co-written by the great Knute Rockne and his cupbearer Ronald Reagan. Viktor's followers had yet to appreciate him. His loyal MPG and MPJ employees filed into BookSmart dutifully, mandatorily, and grumpily—wearing Ralph Lauren- and Ghurka-designed snowmobile suits, John Lobb boots, L. L. Bean cardigans, Brioni gloves, and Charvet underwear.

Aloysius ushered for Larry Sangster, Hjalmar Halversen, Vinay and Thrania Deep, Corky and Gloria Skogentaub, Dan the Maintenance Man, Kennedy Kimani (looking like he was at a Travel and Boat Show at the Convention Center), Sausage Man, Yardley Singleton, Bobblehead, Courtney Kirkwood (gold dust might rub off—especially if Snorri was there), Libor Biskop (missed the bus), and a richness of others from the neighborhood who thought success was worth more than a million words. Viktor Martensen was famous and therefore immortal *in potentia*. Already he was as immortal as at least a Schlitz beer; but Viktor wanted more fame: movie star fame, rock star fame, and more immortal fame. Viktor knew scads of stars from the Portmans down to the Knightleys and from the Depps down to the Pitts. He wanted to fill his Hollywood movies with Hollywood movie stars so that he could be seen in the background stalking them someday, when their mysterious deaths by accident, involved him, and lurid TV crime shows connected all the connections to him—so the famous, glamorous, famorous, and glimmerous celebrities all were dying to have him as their powerful, influential Svengali, "the man who made it all happen in all the right and high places with all the right and high people."

Viktor supported his ego in a super down-puffy, snowmobile suit—a one-piece number of navy blue with five pointed symmetrical stars on top, red-white stripes, and a spice of stars thrown in from the waist down. He felt his feet warm as felt, warmed by his Korean War white bunny boots, which were worn by Clint Eastwood or Charles Bronson on Pork Chop Hill. Captain America had given him the sky blue helmet he claimed. Viktor disrobed down to his purple velour tracksuit, which Larry Bird gave him last President's Day in exchange for the sword of Humphrey, the Duke of Gloucester.

Aloysius handed Viktor a copy of *Quantum Biscuits*.

"Signed, sealed, and delivered, boss," said Aloysius.

"Wait, Aloysius, I thought it was going to be *Quantum Visions*?"

"Aubrey began writing it, but she ran out of time," said Aloysius unconcernedly, "because she had to work three jobs. So Chitchee Chichester wrote and edited it, and Aubrey self-published it and ordered all these copies. That's why it was so late."

"Who the fuck is Chitchee Chichester? The big squirrely-looking goonfart?" asked Viktor, lurking his neck around. "Hey, where is Aubrey? Isn't she adorable? Oh she's at the chalkboard! Hi Aubrey! Do you like to dance? Party at the Calhoun Beach Club later! Now I've been meaning to ask you, does Aubrey have a boyfriend yet?"

"If you had all the money in the world," said Aloysius, "in one hand and a revolver with one bullet in the other hand and offered me a choice, I'd take the revolver, spin the chamber, and fire—just to see the blank on your face."

"*You're* in a bad mood!" laughed Viktor, turning into a giggle. "Take it easy, Aloysius. We're going to make a mint off this book! What's the cover price?"

"Fifty bucks."

"So for every two thousand books sold," said Viktor, "we clear a 100,000 bucks! Not bad! And you'll get 30,000 dollars of that. Your *cut*."

"No," said Aloysius. "AuthorHouse gets half of that, and Amazon gets the other half."

"What do I get?" asked Viktor.

"You get screwed," said Aloysius, smiling a curse into Viktor.

"Nothing?" said Viktor as if he had a fly in his mouth. "We'll discuss it later."

"I earmarked the relevant passages for you," said Aloysius, raising his voice. "Now let's get on with your farce. Everyone dies without toys and you will too, *Wonder Wart-Hog*."

"Look Aloysius," said Viktor, holding Aloysius's elbow, "you have been a good friend. I'll get you a brand-new, mint Brothers desktop. That burglar did us a favor. What kind was it? I have some money for Aubrey. It's out in the Aston Martin. Where is Aubrey? I had to sell off some blue chips, but that's okay, that's okay. You know I would do anything for Aubrey. Aubrey will get her Master's Degree from Harvard Yard. I promise you Aloysius. I know lots of people there who can get her in. Would she want a brand new Bronco? Or Land Rover? 4 x 4? Something to muddy with? I can get them for free. The Land Rover was Charlton Heston's."

Viktor was brushed aside when Aloysius walked up to the dais, his back to Hennepin Avenue where the snowmobiles were illegally parked, where the wind's energy was like a brace of galloping horses. The front door would fling open and stay open, wedged by the wind, funneling frozen passers by into BookSmart to warm up, with their marshmallowed, swollen visages, dressed in their Muscovy feather-down jackets, in layers of tan and leather Slavic tunics, in stiff woolen floor-length coats, and in musty faded flannels, grubby Pendletons, and barnies— immediately roasting like potatoes. So the auditors in those roasting coats peeled off their baked layers and inhaled overheated air.

"Merry Belated Christmas," said Aloysius (awwwwghhhwgh). "As you all know, tonight's speaker is Viktor Martensen, who will be reading from his book, *Quantum Biscuits*. I regret to say that Pepsi Beaucoup had to cancel due to the weather."

"Pepsi, fuck you!" said Viktor.

When no one laughed, Viktor was mortally insulted, confused, and not consulted. Then he shrugged his shoulders and giggled.

"Hello, I'm Viktor Martensen," giggled Viktor in his purple velour tracksuit, "the author of *Quantum Biscuits* and multi-millionaire—"

"YOU STOLE THAT FROM ME!" said Libor Biskop, leaping up and pointing his compass at Viktor. "You stole my quantum biscuits! I coined that phrase. Where did you get that? From the big squircley guy? Fire, fire, fire!"

"Get him out of here, Izzy!"

Izzy with one hand tossed Libor Biskop into a bank of snow.

"As if there weren't enough loons out there," chuckled Viktor. "Welcome everybody from the Martensen Peoples Group and everyone else who wants to be a millionaire."

Viktor Martensen stood in front of the whiteboard on which Aubrey wrote:

1. *Lead. Lead. Lead.*
2. *Expect perfection and then play down and dirty.*
3. *Reward yourself for greatness with greatness.*
4. *Hire people who are self-sufficient and can take orders.*

5. *Make people hate you.*

6. *Write your own book about it.*

7. *Make sure it comes from the depths of your soul.*

Viktor cleared his nostrils, picked up a copy of *Quantum Biscuits*, and read from the text cold:

"*I am Viktor Martensen. And I am American born. I climb ladders and go at everything for the love of money or fame. I grew up poor on the rough side of Summit Avenue in St. Paul, Minnesota, the birthplace of one Francis Scott Fitzgerald, if you have heard of him.* [Am I supposed to? Viktor added.] *I learned the hard way that there is no justice for those below the ladder, and below the ladder I vowed to never be. My father raised me on those Horatio Algernon success stories. He taught me the ropes and dopes of real estate. Hang 'em high he always said. And my mother, bless her true blue Norwegian heart, instilled in me the love of country, duty, and the battle cry of nature.*"

The door flew openly like a goose of icy wind.

Ivan, as an ungroomed communard in an old storm coat with a mouton collar, shuffled in, farting, unwilling to lift his feet up when he slid forward. He tripped over the entire snakepit of electrical cords without noticing the wiry adders flying through the air.

"Can I read after you?" asked Ivan. "I just got out of jail where they starved me to death. I've written some poems about my humiliation. It's all because I told them I wanted to work in a book store."

"What?" asked Viktor, signaling with his eyebrows to Izzy. "No. Who is this snow hobo? This is my reading. Where was I?"

Raven stood outside the front window looking through binoculars, unable to understand why the store looked closed with so many people in it. He knocked on the window to get someone to let him in.

"*And now I am another example of the American success story.* And if you don't think America is the greatest success story of all time, you can leave my store right now, and what now?"

"Hey, it wasn't even locked!" said Raven and entered. "Good job!"

Raven, in mountaineering boots, carabiners, and a square-shouldered, blanket-thick checked jacket, stroked his long red square beard in a circular motion, but a look of disbelief prevented him from thinking that this reading would be better than *Der Rosenkavalier*. So he planned to keep a low presence and disappear like a grain of salt in a wind spout. He consciously re-configured the false smile of a deflated mouse.

"Hey you guys, did you hear?" said Raven. "Underwater archeologists have discovered what's at the bottom of the Bermuda Triangle!"

"What?" asked Viktor.

"Another Bermuda Triangle!" said Raven.

Viktor ran a hand backward over his twin widow's peaks and hair.

"Sorry, I'm late. Can I grab one of your books?" asked Raven. "*Wild Animus*, right?"

"I'm in the middle of a reading," said Viktor. "Have a seat in the back, way back."

Izzy stepped forward alertly.

"Wait a second," said Raven, squinting at *Quantum Biscuits: Six or Seven Keys to Success* by Viktor Martensen then at Viktor. "*You're* the guy who bought the Rainbow Cafe and went out and bought the kitschiest furnishings you could find, and turned that old boring bar into a Russ Meyer film set. That was genius! Oh yeah, I'll read this. For laughs!"

Raven two-finger stroked his auburn beard from its dorsal side, spied a seat, looked around, and sat down on a chair, covered in coats. He fluffed his beard out, relaxed on his fold-out chair, settled in, and then realized it was occupied.

"Why are you sitting on me?" asked Bobblehead.

"Aloysius!" said Raven, moving over to share the seat. "I told you, you should have assigned seating for big events like this! You should let me plan events for the store!"

Aloysius's bulging eyes bugged out.

"Sometimes you have to swallow the frog to eat the fly," said Raven to a serried rank of cold shoulders. "I'm not exactly feeling the love here."

"Seriously," said Viktor, lowering his eyebrows and steam flowing through his dilated nostrils. "Lock the front door, Aloysius.

We are at capacity (for idiots that is). No more room. Capiche? Okay, where was I? Somebody lock all the doors? *I have learned in my long prosperous life, age 46, that my honesty is my greatest asset. With honesty goes confidence. And I have so much confidence, that I don't really need to know all that much about honesty. In fact expertise, degrees, and economics can often get in the way of making money. You don't need a Harvard education for anything these days, which is good because you're not going to get a Harvard education unless you already have gobs of money*—so why go to Harvard? Good, gooey money. Really, the rental property business is about one thing: squirrels! Wait. It's about people, not squirrels. *Knowing people gives me about the knowledge of an acorn. Then I don't care if they hate me, as long as I can kill them.* What? Is this right? *I look at potential new hires, and I wonder what makes them tick and how much energy are they willing to spend on licking my balls.* Balls? What balls? Must be a typo. I'll try a different chapter. Aloysius could you fetch me a gin and tonic from next door? No almonds! I hate almonds, they remind me of Asia. He's my personal slave everybody. Aren't you, Al?"

"You don't know me as Al, pal," said Aloysius mechanically.

"There are a lot of typos in my copy, Al, pal," said Viktor on the verge of getting steamed.

"Fix them yourself," said Aloysius on the verge of getting steamed. "You know what to do."

"Don't mind him," said Viktor, looking around the peanut gallery at the peanut heads.

"His daughter never got into Harvard, so now he's whining about it—boo hoo! She had to settle for some shithole college in the Midwest."

Viktor ran his blackened tongue twice over the cold sores on his lower lip.

Aubrey's smile, frozen year round, thawed like open ice.

Viktor shrugged his shoulders, blew snot to either side, bowed down, and read stiffly from the page: *To earn respect you must never a-pol-ogize. Never apol-gize for being rich.*

"Can't you read your own handwriting?" interjected Raven from way back.

"*If you are rich, then you deserve respect, and people under you can feel the heat of your success. When people realize that you are successful, they will be motivated to follow you. Follow you to the moon professionally! But you have to have what I call 'quantum biscuits.' Quantum biscuits is the ability to perceive both the real and the unreal, the living and the dead, those in real time and those with time off for good behavior. Whatever good behavior is in today's competitive market depends on how much it costs! Now my advice to all you budding en-trep-en-ren-EARS, entrapenoors eternal pewers* . . . businessmen out there is: *never give up the sweat. Christopher Columbus once said, 'Take advantage of all the opportunities that arise in this life, because in the next life it's pretty likely you will be peeling potatoes in your underwear.'* What. *To fulfill the goal of your dreams, you must have the quantum biscuits. Having quantum biscuits consists not only of having the backing of the micromanagers loyal to your mission, but also the false front of executive officers in your mob-oriented corporation.* Mob what? What mob? I'm not a mobster. Okay, forget what I just said. Let's see. *To be a successful CEO and to live the American dream, you must demand support from those micromanagers who lack your confidence, who have no quantum vision of the quantum biscuit thing. If they have no quantum vision of your quantum biscuits, you must blind them with hot pokers like a King of England. Be direct and you can also use sharp needles. If you don't have killer instincts for business I guarantee you that you don't have the energy to stump a cow. Success breeds success like poor people with nothing better to do. Pyrrho the Maniac once said: 'I have butter for the biscuits gal, and a half a pint o' gin.'* Wait. Typo. Again. Lost my place. Energy. There it is. *The energy to breed a family, to be a big member in a conservative-looking church, and to participate in the community at all levels of criminal participation is what defines American energy. At the end of my day, I unwind, I paint, I play music, I meet whores and go out dancing at my favorite sex clubs, where I am known as 'The Elephant Man.' Yes, I am a workaholic, but I am above all a family-values man. My father always told me to believe half of what you say and half of what you do. Being a father to numerous monsters is like being a parent. Being a community leader in many ways is like being a door-to-door ice cube salesman, to quote the CEO of Ali Enterprises, Mon Sieur . . . Mass Anon . . . Man Sir . . . Al Hal Laj . . .* Who the fuck wrote this?"

"Oh look, *Good Morning, Minnesota with Skip Skiptown* is here too."

Good Morning, Minnesota with Skip Skipperton had been there for a while. They were the first ones there to set up their camera, but Viktor wanted his moment of fame to look spontaneous, which made it look staged like a white-teeth crime drama.

"Brady," said Viktor. "What brings you here? Brady! SKOOGE! Are you deaf?"

"Yes, I'm deaf, Mr. Martensen," said Skooge, not finding a seat in the first row, "on account you made me deaf when you cauliflowered my ears with a tire iron because I tatooed your back with the Nutty Professor instead of Frank Sinatra. Remember, when I was your chauffeur? And now I sleep in my car."

Skooge wept long tears from his face, which he hid, scrunched up tight. His chest sobbed so violently he allowed Izzy to escort him out of BookSmart peacefully.

"Where was I, God?" continued Viktor. "*Nothing exceeds like excess, and to be a commander of excess you must win over your deepest abscess. The loser will take your energy and bankrupt your red blood cells as they often say. Leadership wets itself. People have to see the Napoleon in your trousers. Nobody respects a dead mouse. If you want to be a dead mouse, you cannot win at your poker. Mice get fired. There is only you, with your burning ambition to get a nice fat juicy slobbering billion-dollar pony ride up and down. Whee! No more meatless and wheatless days. You are your own Money Maker. Ask the Man upstairs, who prints the checks.*"

"Hey, Man upstairs!" called Raven. "Who prints the checks?"

"*That is all you need to know about motivation. Do you want to be a winner who is laughing all the horses to the milk? Or do you want to cry for the rest of your leprosy over typos not made by the hand of man?* Oh fuck this shit! This is all fucked up. Aloysius! Look at all these typos. What the fuck happened to my book?"

"AuthorHouse happened to your book," said Aloysius. "Typos aside, the platitudes are a little hard to grasp; however, the quantum biscuits thing is brilliant. Who knew that a little word like 'quantum' was actually the placebo that could explain everything in the universe by your applying it to everything that slides under your runny nose? Hey, you! Quantum! See! You feel better already! Abracadabra! Quantum, Viktor!"

Viktor looked at Aloysius with the puzzled look of someone watching someone too slowly filling in a jigsaw puzzle, "Fucking Author OutHouse, I'm going to hunt them down to their fucking outhouse. I'll take three questions and then of course we have the dance party at the Calhoun Beach Club," said Viktor, slipping back into his Captain America snowmobile suit and bunny boots, "where I hope to see you, Aubrey! I rented out the whole club to show my appreciation of all you hard-working, honest-to-God Minnesotans from my favorite state. My home is where my heart started. Here in Minnesota. The state I hate, I mean I heart. I owe it all to the corn fields of Minnesota and then some, because this is where the Nordic gene pool is really strong."

"You're skating on thin ice, buddy!" said Raven.

"And I owe it all to my beloved America. Here in the winter wonderland of sky blue-eyed waitresses! Sky blue waitresses? Hello? Can you hear me in the back?"

"Have you ever been arrested for your torture of innocent sausages?" asked Sausage Man. "Sausages alone are certain good, don't you know?"

"Not you! Again? Can someone throw that wet brain out of here? Aloysius? Izzy?" asked Viktor.

His smile curdled after something he swallowed. He spit out the remains of a smile onto the floor.

"Am I late?" asked Heinie, brushing the snowman from his framed parka. "Is this for the lecture: 'On The History Of Washtubs in Wisconsin, 1890 to 1900,' inclusive?"

Viktor's eyes jerked back and forth watching the audience like Pong.

"Somebody lock the fucking door!" said Viktor. "What is it with you Minnesotans, the women are as corn fed as the cows, and the men are all cattle? I've had enough of this giant, fucking cornfield!"

"I'd also like to read from my recent award-winning book of poems," said Ivan Von Volkov shuffling forward in sloppy trudges. "And if there is time I'd like to fill out an application to work here. I guess I should tell you that to remain anonymous, I write under the name of Chilcote Carrothers."

Yardley Singleton, sitting next to his daughter Minerva and her partner Beda, stood up and fainted. Minerva screamed. Beda snapped a canister of bear spray from her utility belt.

"This is a poem I wrote last night, when I was deep in the bowels of the Deep State—before I came out on the other side, that is," continued Ivan, lucubrating under the distracting commotion. "It's called 'The Squirrel, The Rabbit, and The Marten.' I took it from a children's book, which I found in a cave I was hiding in. To get away from the cops who were coming to arrest me for subversive literature."

"Clear the area!" yelled Beda. "Give Yardley room to breathe!"

"Singleton down!" shouted Chitchee, appearing from the shadows, running up the stairs, and reaching for the cell phone in his inner overcoat pocket to call 911. "Yardley! Can you hear me? What's your name? Who's your favorite poet, beside Chilcote Carrothers? Don't die on us!"

Instead of his cell phone Chitchee pulled out Hawk Eye's Derringer.

"What is this doing there?" asked Chitchee. "How could I forget the gun?"

He held the Derringer up to the track lighting, which set the room in motion like a starting gun.

"Chitchee's got a gun!" yelled Vinay. "Don't panic! Run for your lives!"

Bobblehead stood up. Thrania, Minerva, and Bobblehead screamed together.

Chitchee recoiled from the screams, which clenched his fist and squeezed the trigger.

Vinay shoved Thrania into the wall to protect her and any potential Viking offspring, but her forehead banged into a bookshelf. Bending over to vomit, she screamed in pain like a wild jackal.

Extending all his fingers in a spider-web pattern around his holster, Sausage Man—metamorphosing—with his disguise tossed aside, his ugly nose thrust into his pocket—was FBI Special Agent Henry Hillswick pawned forward one square in his stead.

He paused to wonder whether his back up was stuck in the blizzard.

"FBI!" he shouted, flashing his FBI Special Agent badge and his identification.

All mouths yawned open.

The audience juggernaut toward the front door in a swallowing, deadly, helter-skelter, and flailing earthquake, reducing all directions to screaming holes of hell.

"VIKTOR MARTENSEN," shouted FBI Special Agent Henry Hillswick, "YOU'RE UNDER ARREST ON SUSPICION OF NARCOTICS TRAFFICKING, HUMAN TRAFFICKING, AND THE ILLEGAL SALE OF FIREARMS!"

"Ok," said Viktor quietly and humbly, "you traitor."

Viktor looked behind him with droopy eyelids to conceal his second thoughts. He glanced at the street. He shot a look at Izzy. Viktor, hearing more Feds clambering up the stairs, saw handcuffs coming at him like owl's claws around a sparrow's throat. The timing of the commotion of the Feds from the basement culminated in a man with a boy's voice saying:

"Does anyone have a toothpick?"

FBI Special Agent Hillswick, losing a second in the diversion and looking for his non-existent sidekick, felt Izzy grab his bad hand with the broken thumb. They wrestled for the 9mm Luger, which Izzy pointed at the ceiling and fired. Blast. Viktor jumped back into his Captain America-looking snowmobile suit as Izzy gripped the Luger's stock, cold-cocked Hillswick's head into pieces, and walked outside and out of Viktor's life forever.

"Is this the HalfSmart Books book store?" asked Toby Pfeiffer at the top of the stairs exhausted on all fours, sweating profusely, and urinating down his leg. "Can I get a toothpick from you guys?"

Slipping in a pool of Toby's urine that had dripped down the stairs, Viktor clutched, twisted his back, and fell down the stairs like a drunkard.

Straggling into BookSmart through the tunnel system were: Felix, Chester, Marcia, the one-armed Jo-jo Joey, Dog Face the Silent One, Rickety Jitters, Motherfuckin Green Eyes, Mad Jack Apple Jack, Mad Jack Barley, and Mad Jack Harry Snatch. Mad Jack the IV had moved to Phoenix to work in a warehouse, because he misread the ad he thought was for a whorehouse. Undone Buttons had a Timberwolves game to watch. Tiny had been beaten up so bad for killing Sarge, he couldn't even sit up in his own cameraless jail cell. Deprived of his medication for diabetes, he would be left to die by neglect on purpose. And he himself would be thrown in the river later.

"Is this HalfSmart Books?" asked Toby Pfeiffer. "What kind of a name is that for a furniture store that doesn't have toothpicks?"

"Whoa, I made a mistake," said Felix. "We went too far. I meant to take us to the Uptown Theater. I couldn't see!"

Face to face with Viktor, Chitchee pointed the quaking Derringer at him.

"Halt! You're under arrest, Citizen Marten! Citizen arrestee!" said Chitchee, helping Viktor get to his feet. "I've got all the goods on you! On this flash drive. So you might as well surrender before you try to go any farther. And we can sit here while I call someone. Can I use your cell phone? I can't find mine."

"Is this it?" asked Felix, dropping it. "It was in the tunnel! Probably where I lost the flashlight too. Sorry you guys for losing the flashlight!"

"I think this is mine," said Chitchee, bending down. "Yes, in fact it is! No one called, no messages. Like I said, we can sit here until the proper authorities arrive."

Chitchee stood up, dialed, and displayed the flash drive, pinched between index and thumb, shaped like a red thumb itself. Viktor snatched it from Chitchee as quickly as a reptilian picks off a blue-tail fly. Viktor sank a stabbing knife into Chitchee's stomach. Chitchee reeled back, thinking he had been punched, and fell into a heap of sobbing. Viktor thought he had stabbed himself, because FBI Agent Henry Hillswick's 9 mm Luger shrapnel had ricocheted into Viktor's right hand.

While the stampede mobbed the front door, bottlenecked amid screams and shouts, the newly-arriving, arm in arm Torg and Katrina stood in the doorway like dinner guests. Torg held an iced bucket with a bottle of Cold Duck sparkling wine potted in the chipped ice.

"Is this where the party of swingers is?" asked Torg. "It's Cold Duck time!"

Torg executed a dance maneuver resembling the Twist.

"Did we miss the swa-ray?" asked Katreena, drowned out by snowmobile engine noise.

Larry had run out back, sneaked around the block, keyed in the ignition, *wurr-wurr*, and started up his Polaris snowmobile.

Viktor had bunny-booted through the BookSmart basement and cut through Club Miami. If he could only snowmobile home, drive to the airport, private Lear Jet to Miami, elude the FBI, and cool his heels in the Bahamas! Viktor saw loyal Larry revving up, and he assumed Larry had had the courageous foresight to provide the getaway vehicle for Larry's beloved father figure, wearing the Captain America snowmobile suit over the purple velour tracksuit.

Viktor hopped on the back of Larry's Polaris.

Larry winced.

"Gun it, Larry!" howled Viktor. "To my house!"

LAKE CALHOUN

Chitchee flew outside. The assemblage of snowmobiles together sounded like a contest for the loudest chain-saw. More snowmobiles ignited their engines. Noise and exhaust disturbed the sleeping mall, Carousel Square, which itself reverberated like pistons and cylinders. Figlio's Restaurant's silverware trembled. Its linen tables vibrated, and the wine bottles in the wine racks chattered nervously. The chandeliers outside Ragnarok's Choklit Stoppe blinked. Everybody sitting at the wrought-iron tables blinked. Two stroke/four stroke engines attacked the night air like hungry wolves chasing cross-country skiers in a Loppet.

"Chitchee!" bellowed Kennedy over his Arctic Cat's engine. "Over here!"

Kennedy over-joyfully grinned—so eager to give his Arctic Cat the acid road-test of all time. Kennedy adjusted the nose guard on his X5 goggles, which cost a pretty copper, but now proved themselves worth all his extensive, exhaustive, and methodical machinations. The shivering wind blew snow off the snow drifts into the drifting streets, disappearing under so much snow that the scattering guests, news crews, and ambulances blended and disappeared into ganzfelds of white-on-white, barely-outlined blots. Contours dissolved and disappeared into the snow drifts, sculptured ocean waves of frozen foam breaking overhead.

Chitchee clung to the roaring Kennedy, and the snow burned like tears until Chitchee's eyeballs streamed down his cheeks.

Larry's Polaris drove point for a small cohort of Arctic Cats, Ski-doos, and vintage snowmobiles that skied and skidded like ducks and drakes through and over drifts into the trajectory of an arctic air mass, drawn down in vortices spiraling southward toward Minneapolis and colliding with rain dusting up from the Gulf of Mexico. After Viktor's followers ditched him, sloping down toward Lake Calhoun only two lion-roaring snowmobiles, the Polaris followed by the Arctic Cat, sped down the middle of Lake Street, where the snow-drowned cars resembled rows of Mycenaean beehive tombs.

"I'm going to live forever!" bellowed Viktor over the Polaris's engine's grinding. "Step on it, Larry, you lily-livered faggot! Don't tell me you are a liberal now! Get me home and to the airport. I've been shot in the hand. Fuck going to Calhoun Beach Club! Fuck this Minnesota bullshit! It's all bullshit farmers and bullshit cornfields!"

"BUNCH OF LOONIES OUT THERE!" yelled Larry.

Happenstance fishing shanties abruptly abrogated the snowy icescape. On the North side of Lake Calhoun, open water lay. The Park Board was aerating Lake Calhoun to provide more pike, perch, and sunnies for the hibernal fishermen, bleached to boredom by their clock-shaped holes, waiting for the recently-installed aeration system to oxygenate their lifeless game.

Plywood shacks on wheels and small ranch houses with aluminum siding faced little houses on little lanes. Some of the lake's structures were like outhouses, others like tents, log cabins, trailers, cabins, ramblers, yurts, and bungalows with propane tanks on the outside. Some had driveways of cars, trucks, all terrain vehicles, recreational vehicles, and Monte Carlos.

When the glacial ice boomed throughout the entire lake, Viktor heard a shotgun's gauge. He reached for his Glock 17 handgun strapped inside his purple velour tracksuit.

"WHAT WAS THAT?" asked Snorri, jumping up in his blue jean shorts with long white underwear underneath.

Snorri stared at the wall where he had mounted a gimmick plaque of a walleyed pike that talked. Obviously some depraved crook had knocked off the Big Mouth Billy Bass idea—that's how full of crooks the world was.

"Mother stumpin' snowmobilers," continued Snorri, shaking his head. "I'm going to investigate. Do I need gloves? Is it cold yet?"

"It's nothing to you," said Saami. "Don't sweat the sweaty stuff, Snorri! Who needs another Blech's? As long as I am getting up, I might as well get up. Don't get up. There's no use in our both getting up."

Saami had brought along the Amazon Kindle that Yardley paid Chitchee with, who gave it to Saami, who figured out how to turn it on and how to order a book from Amazon because that was the only thing it did. Saami had ordered a free book on ice fishing, *The Ice Fisherman's Bible*, but he stood flummoxed by the Wi-Fi connection's being co-opted by a local ComCast connection, whose password demanded itself in. Google couldn't connect to Google, so he couldn't get on Google to fix the Google. Saami, beside himself and running around in cyber circles, smacked his elfin head with the Kindle. Saami's absorption by the Amazon Kindle ruined his vibe.

Snorri's father Hjalmar spoiled the son he despised by giving him generous gifts in order to justify the act of shunning the ingrate every time the ingrate reached for bread or a glass of wine at the dinner table. They were strangers, if not enemies, which never would have been the case if Snorri had taken his father's advice to go to law school, pass the bar, and work for Faegre & Benson. Snorri did not love *enough* the ice house his father gave him and therefore, by analogy, the gift of life. Snorri owed his Abrahamic father his own life at any given moment. Snorri found fatherly love especially difficult to appreciate and express (although he thought about it to the brink of tears until the spiral of recriminations restarted at another family celebration).

"Relax, Snorri," said Madison.

"So what are we going to do about BookSmart?" asked Saami.

"I don't know," said Snorri. "Go fish."

"I was thinking," said Saami.

"What is that?" asked Madison.

"That's odd, " said Snorri.

"You know, I am capable of a thought or two," said Saami.

"Sounded like a Glock 17," said Snorri, taking back his held hand, Madison's hand floating for her can of beer. "Snowmobiles? That really *is* illegal. I should go out there with my flares and direct them off the ice! Probably a bunch of spoiled art school rich kids from MCAD. Art school hooligans are worse than slavophile soccer fans! It sure wasn't like that when I worked security at MCAD. I knew how to keep the little Picassos in line!"

"Can't we," said Madison, "have a nice relaxing night, Snorri, without your busting everyone's pork chops?"

"Glock 17," said Snorri. "That would be my guess. Or 19. You mean that's okay with you? A bunch of performance artists on their fathers' snowmobiles firing their Glocks, which they probably don't have permits for. That's okay with you? Hmmmm . . .?"

"Not really," said Madison. "Do you need another Blech's, Saami? Like I was saying, isn't this practically home sweet home, it's so cuuu-u-ute? Your father is really a sweetheart at heart!"

"Aaaw," said Linda, who loved Madison for moments like this. "Saami, why don't you show everybody what you got from your mother for Christmas?"

"What did your mother give you for Christmas?" asked Snorri, opening a Blech's beer although he didn't want it.

"A DNA testing kit," said Saami.

Snorri sat down and stood up anxiously—he didn't know why, but he felt irritated by every noise that knocked on his door.

"There's someone here!" said Snorri. "It's probably the cops! Stash the dank!"

"What is dank?" asked Linda.

"Who's there?" asked Snorri, turning to hush Linda.

"Jehovah's Witness," said the wilderness outside.

"Unless you got a warrant," said Madison, "you're not gonna come in!"

"Shhh . . ." said Linda, "don't piss 'em off! They're probably armed with smoke grenades and MAC-10 pistols."

When Snorri swung open the door, Katreena, holding an empty Cold Duck bottle, and Torg, stood exhausted in the portal.

"What are you doing out there," asked Snorri, "in the snow?"

"Say what? We're knocking on your fucking door, dumbass!" said Katreena. "Get this man a hot lemonwood tea!"

"Katreena! You found us!" said Madison. "Awesome as hell! I owe you fifty bucks for this!"

"You walked all the way out here?" asked Linda.

"It's not every day," said Torg, "I get invited to a party by a hot dame. I have to take a nap though. If I don't wake up, you can donate my good organs to the Science Museum."

Chitchee bounced up and down on the Arctic Cat.

Kennedy soared on eagle's wings over Lake Calhoun—he surveyed the expanse of ice-fishing huts and ice houses and gained ground on Larry and Viktor. Snow crystals, swooping around in fantastic floaters, obstructed Larry's vision. Kennedy was within twenty yards of catching up to the Polaris with his Arctic Cat. Larry spat curses and accidentally took a sharp right turn. Viktor nursed his right hand and almost swerved off the black leather seat. When Viktor heard Lake Calhoun's whalish wail again, he mistook the boom for a Glock 17. With his left hand, Viktor fired a starring round into the black Arctic Cat's windshield.

Chitchee fired the snub-nosed .22 Derringer.

"What was that?" asked Snorri. "Those MCAD art school students are coming back for more? I'll show them a little fucking Kandinsky, and they won't be coming back for Klee! I'm going to go out there and blow them off Lake Calhoun! Help yourself to the Blech's! Come on, Madison!"

"No Snorri, I'm staying right here, warm and cozy with my Blech's," said Madison, reading *The Wind in the Willows* (Pocket Book). "Toad is behind the wheel again."

"God, I fucking *hate* Kindles!" said Saami, guzzling a Blech's and wondering how to get the Wifi hotspot for the Amazon Kindle, but the device reached out for ComCast, demanding ComCast only—again, again, again.

Saami would have to join ComCast again. And after he had just canceled!

"Calm down, Saami," said Linda. "I'm sure God hates Kindles too, so you are in pretty good company. Here, let me try. Poor Saami!"

Linda immediately trouble-shot the glitch and handed the Amazon Kindle back.

"Fit as a fiddle-faddle," burped Linda, shaking out her feldspar hair. "Now you're connected to Snorri's hot spot. It looks like about five gigabytes left. You shouldn't have to check your email all the time anyway! You know? Can't we all relax, have a few laughs, and fish for walleyes in the middle of a winter wonderland and not watch porn?"

Saami, breezy as the air freshly bled from a tire, saamily gladdened himself with another freshly-opened Blech's. He gave Linda a big, smeary smacker on her lips, which rippled through her and bounced back in surprise and joy— only for Linda to witness Saami scrying his messages, hypnotized by the Amazon Kindle, which channeled him away from her again.

"Oh, what is this?" asked Saami aloud, trying to include Linda while Linda rooted through the ice of another Coleman cooler, unable to find a Blech's.

"Who is *this* guy?" Saami continued to ask. "Lord, the strangers you meet on Facebook!"

"How about a Blech's, somebody, anybody?" asked Linda, who hovered over Saami, rubbed his knotted back and tense shoulders, burped on him, and re-organized the coolers full of iced beers. Pfeiffer's Famous Beer, Schmidt, Gluek's, and Hamm's were left.

Dear Saami, by the time you read this I will have blown my brains out with a double-barreled shotgun. But I wanted you to know I was your real father. My name is Finkle Chichester. I knew your mother, Kristina Rolvaag, in the most biblical sense. We met when she was a waitress in Hibbing at a roadside restaurant called the Lingonberry Inn, owned by the famous Bok family. Many times over, when I was supposed to be on the road as a salesman selling food services to colleges to support my own family, I was with your mother. And you might be my love child. Kristina intended you for adoption. She didn't have the heart to abort you and bury your bones in the woods for the wolves to dig up. It was her secret. And I lost all contact with her until I found her on Facebook. I didn't believe her at first, so I suggested that she send you a DNA test kit. At last, I want to clear my conscience because I have recently lost an angel. My wife Paisley. I couldn't go on without her and will see her in heaven if I have to dynamite the gates to smithereens to be at her side again. I leave behind a small fortune (forty-five thousand dollars in gold coins), hopefully the GODDAMNED state doesn't take it all, to my adopted son, Chitchee, who although I begat him not, deserves as much, as my adopted son has proved to have been a source of love and comfort to his blessed mother, the angel Paisley, my Pug, who will live forever in my heart's eternity and heaven.

"Grain Belt Premium, Saami?" asked Linda, holding up the Grain Belt admiringly. "Diamond Clear. Ah! *I found a diamond clear . . .*"

"NOOOO!" said Saami, banging the Amazon Kindle into his forehead.

The pain incited him to retaliate against his own forehead. Nothing to attack, he smashed the Amazon Kindle against his smashed forehead and broke the Amazon Kindle. Chemical fumes poured upward and outward from the Amazon Kindle as from a Cyclops with a flaming brand in his eye.

"Saami!" screamed Madison.

Saami choked on a plastic cloud enveloping him like a djinn in an Orientalist flicker.

Viktor turned around and fired his Glock at Kennedy. Frustrated at their losing ground, Viktor with one hand squeezed Larry around the neck, raveled up Larry's scarf, and dog-leashed him backwards.

"Where are you going?" shouted Viktor above the lion's continuous and motorized roar.

"I'm going to kill you!" said Larry.

"Faster, Kennedy!" yelled Chitchee. "Pull up next to him!"

Larry's body fell like dead mass off the white Polaris.

Kennedy swerved, but skied over Larry who was only a scream lost in the roar of engines. Larry lay on the lake, the snow rapidly burying him, his legs unable to stand him up.

Kennedy regained purchase of his steering wheel. Viktor, steering one handed, tending his wound, holding his Glock, and describing a circle around Snorri's little house in a blizzard, fired a bullet that flew past Kennedy. The bullet could have blown Kennedy's heart through his back shoulder; instead the bullet zinged through Snorri's ice-fishing house and knocked the mounted walleye off its wall. The walleye landed on the floor, thudding and thudded.

A pink tongue stuck out.

"*The gin is mighty fine but them biscuits are a little too thin,*" sang the walleye from a tiny motor.

Viktor, having fired over his shoulder from a precarious posture, untwisted his torso, and saw before his snow-prowed Polaris, a snow-covered Snorri Halversen. Gloved hands out like blackbirds, Snorri signaled in semaphore something incomprehensible.

"No snowmobiles on Lake Calhoun!" shouted Snorri. "DIDN'T YOU READ YOUR DRIVER'S MANUAL? Head to shore NOW!"

Kennedy caught up to Viktor. Chitchee leaped like a flying squirrel onto Viktor's Polaris, causing Kennedy to lose his ballast, balance, and control of his Arctic Cat. Viktor and Chitchee grappled for the Polaris steering wheel, the Polaris approaching thinner and thinner ice towards more and more open, aerating water. The Polaris roared toward the north beach of Lake Calhoun.

"Give me my thumb drive! Private property!" shouted Chitchee through the driven snow that slashed his face and lashed his eyes with bull-whips of snowflakes. "That's nine tenths of breaking the law!"

Chitchee and Viktor on the Polaris clove-hitched. They knotted, unknotted, and then pretzeled into each other's pretzel. Chitchee pawed at the wheel and Viktor flailed for the Glock, neither seeing the rapidly-approaching open water opening ahead in opalescent expanding ovals. Chitchee reached into Viktor's pocket, plucked out the ellipsoidal flash drive, and the Polaris splashed into the black lake.

Chitchee arched his back backwards. His mouth was as wide and round as Grendel's.

Lake Calhoun's frozen water shot through Chitchee's layers of flannel shirts, Levi's, and socks—all of it could have been silk pajamas. He tread and kicked the water with his Reeboks on, but he couldn't breathe. His lungs sucked ice into his shivering lungs. The intensity of the cold and the suddenness of his paralysis icicled inside his blood vessels. Pressure on his head was Viktor's hand pushing him down to drown him. The Polaris snowmobile sank beneath them like an iron caboose filled with overstock *Lake Woebegone*s to the deep bottom of Lake Calhoun.

Viktor scrambled to the ice and held on to the shoring of the ice, but the shelf broke off every time.

Chitchee's corpse was piggybacked on Viktor, dragging both of them downward until Chitchee's entire body numbed up and froze shut.

Not breathing, Chitchee floated. Every muscle, tendon, and ligament had stopped. Each elongating second and each passing second was like an army being routed and rerouted on a battlefield. Only more suffering awaited him after what seemed a second day of death. Blacking out like lightning across a sky of moving storms, Chitchee's brain—with its arrows, darts, and javelins—re-animated, but a lightning stroke again struck him down.

Saami ogled the Amazon Kindle's melting plastic gush with blue smoke. The case rapidly heated into a hand-held, plastic inferno. It was melting like strange soot. It stuck to Saami's bare hands like a bowl of smoking resin. A blinded, screaming Saami was strangled by the blue chemical fumes pouring out of the splintered web of sharp glass from an endless cave of smoke.

"Toss it! Get rid of it! Get it out of here!" shouted Linda, Madison, and Katreena.

Saami's burning hands were unable to let go. The toxic smoke funneled pitchers of sulphuric stench into his little, hairy nostril holes, his nose flaring with ailerons for take off.

Katreena grabbed Torg and shook him awake, something which he found strangely pleasurable. Linda and Madison grabbed their jackets and they all ran outside to avoid asphyxiation, where they stumbled upon Larry. They dragged him by his broken ankles like a sled without scarlet runners into Snorri's ice house where Larry's broken bones stayed warm.

Saami, frozen outside the freezing ice house and freezing with the burning Amazon Kindle fire pinioned to his hands, relied on his vast storehouse of seen movies and sat-through TV shows to intuit that all burning things must explode. Settings, passwords, usernames, and users—to hell with all of it. Saami (in a back-handed tribute to Myron's *Discobolus*) spindled up and then unraveled like a discus thrower. The Kindle hurled itself toward the north shore of Lake Calhoun, where the open water's warning signs had been covered in snow.

Proceeding with the slow inexorability of a funeral for three blind mice, furry neighbors from their ice houses emerged with beers.

"What's going on? We heard gunfire! Not another police brutality case! Will they ever end?"

Viktor huffed for the cold air, soaked frozen in his "Stars and Stripes" snowmobile suit. A square black frisbee skated up to Viktor's outstretched arms and poured deadly fumes into his face. Viktor choked in a cloud of toxic blue Amazon Kindle gas. Viktor fell back into the icy water to certain death, but Kennedy had U-turned around on his black Arctic Cat, regained control, and sped toward Chitchee in the open water. Kennedy jumped off the Arctic Cat. He walked to the open water with the used safety picks he had matriculated from Treasures Await. He tossed the safety picks toward Viktor. Viktor ice-picked his way forward. Kennedy waited to give him a hand. Chitchee, delirious, shuddered in unbearable pain. Chitchee couldn't hear. His ear-drums had frozen.

The cell membranes in his heart tissue crystallized.

The olive-green vines of memory climbing trellises shrank back, withered, and vanished.

Viktor grabbed Kennedy's hand. Secure, Viktor stabbed Kennedy's hand with the ice pick. Then he tossed Kennedy over his Stars and Stripes back and into the icy, aerating water hole. Kennedy's screaming groan iced the whole lake over. The opposite end of Lake Calhoun by the drifted-over beaches and volleyball courts—the old Dakota woods reverberating in between booms of silence—heard Kennedy's last dying groan.

Hawk Eye, wrapped in a Hudson Bay blanket bestirred himself, his vigilant mind, superbly trained as a Navy Seal, intuited a discrepancy in the usual peaceful environment of his Porta-Potty. He ventured a look. A Captain America-looking Viktor sat violently shaking on an idling Arctic Cat. When the ice boomed again like a .12 gauge shotgun, Viktor fired his Glock toward the direction of the Porta-Potty. A zinging round nipped Hawk Eye's woolen cap. Hawk Eye bit his black-sored lip and remembered a long list of assassinations.

Viktor snapped on Kennedy's goggles. His face was green. His shivering mouth was open, breaking up the shocked look on his masky face. Hawk Eye aimed at Viktor's gas tank, read his purple lips through the infrared scope, and saw Viktor's Glock aimed at Hawk Eye. Viktor swallowed Hawk Eye's first bullet. The Arctic Cat tractored off on its own beneath him. The next bullet dug a hole through Viktor's right eye. His goggles swam in blood. Frozen blood congealed to his face when he threw off the goggles. Viktor fell backward from the Arctic Cat, but his Korean War bunny boots from the movie *Pork Chop Hill* hooked themselves to a strap and tangled up with the safety bar. The riderless Arctic Cat carved out smaller and smaller square circles in the snow, dragging the blood-blinded Viktor by one leg around Snorri's ice house. When the Arctic Cat straightened itself out, it slowed down enough for Viktor to crawl back onto its seat. Instinctively he gunned it toward the Porta Potty where he knew Hawk Eye sniped from.

"FUCK! IT'S THAT FUCKING BUM'S FAULT, HAWK EYE!" Viktor screamed. "KILL THEM ALL! KILL!"

Hawk Eye adjusted his fitted infrared scope. Since firing a rifle was so "ready to hand" for Hawk Eye, he grinned like a giant slice of Jolly Rancher watermelon.

Hawk Eye read Viktor's face like a map and pulled the trigger.

The Arctic Cat with Viktor at the wheel exploded in a fireball. The blast quartered Viktor limb from limb. His burning body parts scattered across the frozen surface of Lake Calhoun. From the flames of fireballs, continuously generating pulses of boiling fire, phoenixed out of the ashes Viktor Martensen appeared—a giant brown bat with black leather burning wings, oily burning ears, and jaw locked open in a scream, vomiting hells like an overflowing toilet-universe of infinite universes with backed-up toilets, vomiting into eternity after eternity.

Once Viktor's ashes had fallen from the air of the hereafter, every eagle that ever dreamed of his home in Minnesota felt the warmth of the earth returning. It was only a matter of time: the marshes, the cattails in the rushes, the redwing blackbirds on the reeds, the teal dabbling in the water lilies, and the mellifluous honeybees at the willows rejoicing. And the Earth shall be refreshed.

St. Louis Park Department police arrived in their siren-screaming cars to the north side of Lake Calhoun. The Fire Department arrived. The paramedics trudged through snow drifts toward the hole in the ice—the breath sucked out of their lungs from the below zero air—their heads bending and leaning into the snow, without a notion of success.

Snorri, Saami, Madison, and Katreena (Torg snored through it all) formed a slippery human ladder across the slippery ice. Kennedy shouted and stayed above water. Chitchee was gaining and losing consciousness, vaguely aware of Kennedy. Kennedy looked to Chitchee to keep him alive.

The wind swept over the open hole in the ice, creating frozen clouds.

There were shouts Snorri heard to clear the area.

"I can't! They will drown!" replied the sweating Snorri, prostrate. "I'm going in!"

Snorri tore off his clothes, recalling passages from *Beowulf*, jumped in the lake. He reached out to Kennedy, and shoved him onto the ice shelf. Snorri connected Chitchee's arms and legs so that Chitchee piggybacked on top of Snorri. From the icy water, Snorri pushed Chitchee into the arms of the EMTs. Chitchee needed compressions and mouth to mouth. Kennedy was given a warm compress around his torso and neck. They stretched Chitchee and Kennedy out as if sending them through giant rollers on the press of a titanic vise. EMTs started on the compressions. The defibrillator was next. The snow above described parabolas, and the wind, in Snorri's face, bounced crystals of ice off his closed eyelids, who walked point for Kennedy's stretcher all the way to the crystal-bright ambulance. Chitchee was as frozen as a frozen pike on ice in the seafood section at Lunds.

"It's the guy from BookSmart," said a paramedic. "I heard they have the complete *Field And Streams*. I wonder if I can still get those?"

The EMTs swathed Chitchee and Kennedy in blankets inside the snow-covered ambulance and treated them for hypothermia— at no cost. Snorri said he was fine but could use a Blech's; so he was going back to the ice house for a little rest and rehydration.

"Chichester! Chichester! Chichester!"

Chitchee floated through fields and streams, rolling down from frozen lakes of melting, silver snow and silver-throated birch and lindens until he heard, amongst all the birds that ever caroled the tales of creation, Melvin McCosh ask him a question.

"Chichester?" asked McCosh in his black flowing robes, his long red hair flowing, and his pale white skin the white light of death, beckoning with a flashlight's light cone, the very flashlight Felix lost in the tunnels when he found Chitchee's phone. Felix's flashlight enveloped Chitchee and blossomed upward toward a utopian used book store in a lotus-shaped manifold.

The sunshine of ten thousand rainbows flooded Chitchee's heart, which opened to the *shakti* of the universe and all human beings.

"Help you find a book, McCosh?" asked Chitchee, lifting his head for a second, which then fell back down, and his consciousness disappeared like a weevil into the quantum biscuits of spacetime.

"Yeah, I'm looking for *Perri And Her Friends*," said McCosh. "Not *Perri the Squirrel*. You got the title wrong! You worked in a book store, didn't you?"

McCosh turned and retreated.

"Sorry!" called out Chitchee.

"He's okay," said the paramedic. "You're going to be all right!"

"No, it's not all right!" said Chitchee. "I got the title wrong! I lost another customer!"

"You had a heart attack!" shouted a paramedic. "Don't worry about customers!"

"Hey, you guys, good job!" said Chitchee. "You can take me to the shelf now!"

ULYSSES & SONS

A leper's bell and death rattle penetrated everyone's ears. D-d-d-d-d-d-d-d-d-. Pause.

"Oh, Lord," said Saami. "Make it stop! Goddamn peckerwood!"

"I'd have to agree with Saami there! That woodpecker is driving off all our customers," said Snorri. "Wish I had my old BB gun! And some targets!"

"*The first circle is the literal sense, and the second is the inner sense, and the third is the allusion.* Allusion to what? The Tawhid?"

Chitchee was still skimming over *The Tawasin* he bought over thirty years ago at The Book House.

"Where is it?" asked Chitchee, leaning over BookSmart's old maroon counter.

"I turned it over to the 5th Precinct in an effort to promote gun safety," said Snorri regretfully. "God, I could shoot myself in the foot for that now, go figure."

"No, the woodpecker," said Chitchee. "Where is the woodpecker? It could be an endangered species. Let's not get myopic! We had better look up what the sentencing guidelines are for bothering it."

Chitchee, Saami, and Isatvastra craned their necks out the storefront's front window, blocked in with used books to look nested in with books.

Chitchee moseyed into the front window and straightened the CAROUSEL SQUARE pillow, also an artefact from BookSmart. He pushed the hard pillow back against the ribs of the tiny Windsor rocking chair. The sign on the overhead awning read: ULYSSES & SONS. ULYSSES & SONS, block- and gold-lettered on its green awning, hung down like bunting (used books planted in the frontage window to look like a used book store, even though it *was* a used book store). Tulips and daffodils fronted the painted bookshop upon the painted street, the charming street in a Paris of the Midwest, under a deep azure sky of rolling violet clouds.

Saami sallied outside and scurried back. Isatvastra fiddled with the old store's cash register. Chitchee picked up the old store's phone and listened for the old dial tone.

D-d-d-d-d-d-d-d-d-. Pause.

"What's the d-d-date today?" asked Isatvastra.

"It must be April," said Saami, perched in front of the store computer. "It's snowing."

"When it rains, it snows," said Chitchee.

"Seen any robins, anyone?" asked Torg, clinging to the maroon counter.

"I haven't exactly been extrapolating about town for robins," said Kennedy, laughing into his hand and stretching his legs from the relocated black leather couch. "Are they the red ones?"

"I thought I saw a picture of a robin," said Lake Street Rodney. "I mean a photograph, not a painting, because that would be a painting, not like a real robin in a photograph."

Kennedy, looking under the old couch, joked: "robins here somewhere."

"Don't you guys know what a robin looks like?" said Chitchee, pumping his chest out. "Where's the old store's bird calendar?"

Chitchee pulled out the old store's calendar and flipped frantically through the months.

"Ducks, sparrows, swans, herons, turkeys, owls, partridges, pipits, peacocks. How come there aren't any robins here? But here is a bluebird. So imagine this bluebird," said Chitchee, "is red and wears a livery of brown feathers. That's a robin."

"You sure we're on that there Craig List?" asked Isatvastra.

"Yeah, look!" said Saami.

ULYSSES & SONS, Seek Knowledge Even as Far as 1016 Dupont Avenue South.

Chitchee peered out the front window of Ulysses & Sons on 1016 Dupont Avenue South as a queen bumblebee roared by his nose.

A '65 Chevy Bel Air station wagon pulled up and overshot the curb.

"Here we go!" said Chitchee. "Our first customer! Okay all you regulars, look alive!"

He pulled an acorn out of his pocket and blew. He saw the seed hatching, waking up, yawning, stretching its leaves, sending a taproot down, and sending the green shoots up through the purple ephemerals. And out of that vision sprang another vision: the entire planet froze, reconsidered, stopped its useless massacres, and its waves of seas of bloodshed stopped.

"Incoming, Abba!" said Chitchee over his shoulder to his father Isatvastra. "Here comes our first buy! Knock on linoleum!"

A friend and a friend lugged, heaved, and dropped boxes taken from the back of the station wagon. Its doors were wingspread for flight.

"*Naaaaaa'aaaaaaammmm,*" said Chitchee.

"Hi Boss," said Isatvastra, opening the front door for LaDonna. "I hope you got some Gutenbergs in there! I hope and pray, hyuck! Hey, my friend had a car like that!"

"Yeah," said LaDonna, "I bought it from a guy named Skooge with 55 personalities. He sold it to pay for medical bills. Yeah so his ego bolts were a little loose. But it runs."

LaDonna wore a superfly hijab, hoop earrings, luxurious bracelets, red glasses, and faded blue jeans.

"Chitchee, are you still playing with acorns?" said LaDonna. "I saw your Craigslist ad. I knew it must be your dream come true! Congratulations! You've finally made it! And now you have it all."

They both looked around at the despondent clutter of unfinished shelving, the rare and the common books in heaps, the black leather couch (Kennedy, Lake Street Rodney, book pile), Torg staring into space, and Courtney coloring her *Junie B. Jones Coloring Book*. Her purple crayon broke, and she felt enough rage to spiral-throw her broken crayon into the waste-basket Chitchee had carried over to her like a bedpan. She pulled out a heart-shaped hand mirror, emoried her eyebrows, and replaced them with two swoops of a swallow in flight.

"Thank you, LaDonna," said Chitchee. "I am now the respectable owner of a successfully-failing used book store."

"This is what you always wanted!" said LaDonna soberly. "Anyway, these were my father's books."

"Wirt?" asked Chitchee, with a surprise that sounded uninterested but curious.

"No, my biological mother's second husband," said LaDonna with her wrist backward on hip and perspiration beads on her lip. "I finally tracked him down to right around the corner. I told you I had to find my true father someday. I did. But it was too late."

While Chitchee rummaged through LaDonna's father's books, she confessed she hadn't stolen goggles from New World Sunrise Massage And Spa, but grabbed two hundred dollars out of the open till and booked. And then she was arrested for that at Memory Lanes. After that, she was pulled over for a DWI and court-ordered into treatment again. Cleaned up, she counted her days of sobriety religiously.

LaDonna had found a form in a box her parents had stowed there and forgotten. It was from Lutheran Social Services. It contained a short biography of LaDonna's mother, Pembina, from which LaDonna gleaned that Pembina had a substance abuse problem too. Pembina Brisbee had attended Sleepy Eye High School in Sleepy Eye, Minnesota. LaDonna drove to Sleepy Eye, found all the yearbooks in the library, and pinpointed a graduation picture of Pembina Brisbee. LaDonna conducted a search on the Internet (Facebook) and Facebooked her. They agreed to meet at a Country Kitchen. Pembina had whiskers like a catfish and a basso profundo voice out of the bottom of the fourth movement of Beethoven's Ninth. They split some mashed potatoes and mashed peas and shared coffee with a bored waitress.

Pembina had married Arminius Weatherwax, the middle manager of a Mel's Fleet Farm. Arminius, a Golden Glove, with one punch broke his first wife Rhonda's jaw; later, she hanged herself (using Arminius's professional jump rope) from the branches of a maple tree in the backyard, the same maple stump pointed out to LaDonna when they drove up to Pembina's rambler. One night in another drunken quarrel Pembina shot Arminius in struggling to get drunken control of his hunting rifle. Pembina served time in Shakopee for manslaughter, sharing a cell with a woman who had thrown her own baby off a bridge. Pembina went back to college to start over. She met an exceptionally charming African poet-in-exile at Augsburg College in Minneapolis in the 1950s. Augsburg College, because mixed race couples were unusual at the time, demanded Pembina get a psychiatric evaluation. The marriage fell apart and they divorced. Unknown to LaDonna's father was LaDonna. Pembina, (once a summer slip of a girl, now a cowpea-eyed Juno) with no means of support, put her baby up for adoption with Lutheran Social Services, which contacted the ecstatic Wirt and placated Jen Jensen. And they adopted Donna. Wirt filed all the pertinent documents in attic boxes and forgot about them. Donna discovered them after her parents' deaths, having to sort through the estate.

"Lots of math and science here," remarked Chitchee. "French and African poetry . . . rare African Writers Series . . . and Buddhist books by the bushel . . . Aimé Césaire . . . who is read by only one person I ever knew . . . unless . . ."

"Obviously a teacher," said Kennedy, curiously curating the first stack of books and looking with concern and delight for that one magical book that would open his heart.

"Pile any ten books in a stack," said Chitchee, "and it will be the first thing everybody who walks in off the street touches."

The second box produced *Contributions to the Founding of the Theory of Transfinite Numbers* and *Feynman's Lectures on Physics* with underlining . . . "Go on, I'm listening."

He gazed at LaDonna and noted the rose petals of her perfume as "the light of the Unseen."

"What smells like a rose garden?" asked Chitchee. "A *Gulistan*!"

"It's attar," said LaDonna.

"*In ice I fry*," quoted Chitchee, "*in fire I freeze*."

His thoughts hopped from branch to branch as he watched two squirrels hop from branch to branch.

Rodney walked over and pawed through the priced piles Chitchee had set up.

"Any more *Smith of Wooten Major*s in there?" asked Rodney. "Or anything in Low or High Elvish?"

"I thought Elvish was always High," said Saami.

"High enough to volunteer for the DEA," said Chitchee, returning to the books. "Whose name is inscribed on the flyleaves of all the books? The Jung, the Stewart, and the Cantor, right there too. I recognize the Lion of Judah by his claw. You guys, these are Solomon's books. Solomon is dead! Long . . . live . . . the . . . king . . ."

He saw Solomon in his favorite chair, smiling benevolently. Such a smile would have only been more sublime if angels had brought it down from heaven.

"I have to take a moment," said Chitchee, vaporizing inside.

Crying, Chitchee crawled into a casket and nailed it shut from the inside. His ultra sensitivity to emotional currents carried him off. The sadness of Solomon's isolated passing fell on Chitchee's shoulders like a cloak, colored by silence and nostalgia for things unfinished unspoken.

"Rest in peace, brother," said Chitchee, bowing with his palms together.

"You knew my father?" asked LaDonna. "Wait. You knew Solomon? I never met him, because when I found his house and knocked on his door—he had *died*. There were only MPG Estate Management people. And I met Meski, his niece, there."

Solomon chose to die in the face of bodily decrepitude, unable to pay his medical bills, in fear of his possible medical bills, shunning medical attention, and not wanting to be a burden. He didn't tell anyone he was ill. He had diabetes and had allowed a festering wound on his foot to rot until it was too late for anything but his grandfather's advice: to meet his maker before his mind failed. Meski had found Solomon—dead in his sleep on his last bed of messy, swirled, eddying sheets, pillows on the floor, without his comforter.

"Sadness serves the purpose of humility," says St. Theresa of Avila.

"He left instructions to sell his books, and some of these are his grandson's books, which he used to read to him," said Meski. "Solomon wrote down his wishes on this sheet of paper: 'to sell if and only if there exists such a store called Ulysses & Sons, and if and only if there exists an owner who looks like a giant squirrel named Chitchee.' Does that make any sense?"

"Chester Himes, Richard Wright, James Baldwin—firsts, signed, inscribed—whew!" said Chitchee. "Aloysius! Aloysius?"

"Oh yeah, and there's this item I was supposed to give you," said Meski.

"Obviously," said Kennedy, moving the titles around, "this is the library of a man of immense ari-el-dition."

"What's up, buddy?" asked Aloysius, his throat dry as fishbone. "Did Ariel call?"

"No," said Chitchee, "but Lily did. Look at this gold mine! Noel will be floored."

"How does this sound?" asked Aloysius, the *kantele* cradled in his arms' cradle, unable to tune the pegs. He twisted a peg and the strung broke. "Solomon died? Oh no!"

Chagrin in a chain reaction clouded all the minds in the community of the room.

Meski pried a keychain from her jean pocket. She handed Chitchee the rabbit's foot that Raven had given Solomon.

"He remembered," said Chitchee, turning over the furry trinket. "*Dhikr* disembodied. Huh. Khaldun's *asabiyah*. He remembered me! If you are surrounded by love, you can only surrender."

Chitchee was delighted and danced like a thrown spider—he Charlestoned, knocked his knees together, cupped his kneecaps with his palms, alternated waving hands, and his face expanded with inflationary joy, his eyes big with tears.

"For I have known, loved, and celebrated Solomon," sang Chitchee, inspired by an owl's feather into dithyrambs. "Dance is human."

And the spirit of Solomon flew from Solomon into Chitchee—only the hand that erases can write the true word.

Chitchee saw illuminated words and ruminated: *Oh humanity you are lost, listen to the song of the reed.* Had Allah ever lived under his black knit-wool cap, he was wondering? He realized he had been slamming his head against the fire-wall of the transcendental all his life, and all he had gotten for his "spirituality" was the immanence of a weak ego. He had floated like a man of emptiness in a vacuum that stretched from the Big Bang until Now.

"I'm in a relationship now and I'm engaged," said LaDonna.

"No more *shirking?*" asked Chitchee.

"No more *shirking!*" declared LaDonna.

"If you find the *door*, LaDonna, let me know!" said Chitchee, who saw an excited LGBTQ walking Beda at the end of a hangman's noose of a leash—dragging Beda prisoner with Minerva behind her like a Cassandra offering to help, but not keeping up with the helping. Saami opened the door, when LGBTQ snapped the old leather—into frazzled, uneven halves. LGBTQ bit the CAROUSEL SQUARE pillow, clamped its soft red edges, and ran outside with the fluorescent splashes of fire on the eight-spoked wheel darting out of her mouth.

"She smells cocaine!" yelled Beda.

"Oh my god, drugs!" yelled Minerva. "She'll die! She'll die on drugs!"

"Cocaine-covered pillows?" asked Melusina from the Cookbook section. "What next?"

"Did you say somebody took a Cocaine by mistake?" asked Kriemhilde. "Shouldn't we call for someone?"

"Hey, hey, hey," Snorri blinked and hurried outside. "Stop that dog!"

Snorri chased the pit bull for the pit bull's pillow but was held back by a shortness of breath. He lost the scent in the purple ephemerals.

"AWWW," said LaDonna, "such a cutie! Look at her!"

Beda said nothing and looked at LaDonna funny.

"Yeah, so I'm thinning down, Chitchee, before the big move," said LaDonna.

"I'm on a book diet too," said Chitchee, peering out the front. "Only classics of World Literature from now on—and then everything else too. Look, Gudrun has the CAROUSEL SQUARE!"

"I'm engaged to an Iranian man I met on the Internet," said LaDonna in a hurry.

"Is he a Mu'tazilite?"

"Actually it's Feras al-Farsi. Our Arabic tutor from the U. He got a job teaching Persian at the University of Wisconsin, Madison. I'm turning my life around. I had to let everything go first, you know. And we're going to move to Madison this summer. I want to learn Persian now and read *The Conference of the Birds.*"

"Or Thirty Birds in Lake Calhoun," added Chitchee, hawk-eyeing out the window.

Gudrun bounced like a robin into Ulysses & Sons, hugging her crocheted pillow, her arms crossed, and gave Chitchee a bubblegum buss on the cheek, which afterglowed from his lips. She sang a song so high a little robin flew out of her mouth and took to the sky still singing higher and higher.

"Feras! Feras al-Farsi. You're in good hands or he is in good hands."

"*Inshallah!*"

Chitchee, thinking how language can unlock the potential energy of words from phrases—mawed and pawed over Solomon's books, and the sweet rays from Gudrun's eyes shone brightly when Chitchee hugged her shoulder, reciprocating her smile when she smiled. They were like two trees, oak and basswood, by Lake Calhoun, that grow and die together, not fearing, because they had and have each other forever.

" . . . in that Cote theyr fayth in youth had plight:
And in that Cote had spent their age."

"LaDonna, what are you doing tomorrow? *Hajj* to Mecca? Maybe we can hang out and go get a six-pack of zum zum water on Franklin. And after fifty years, I still have a crush on you! I'd like to say good-bye to my eternal crush. You never know which good-bye is the last."

"Oh, be quiet, Majnoon, you've bemoaned a thousand Laylas like a thousand Majnoons," said LaDonna, illuminating an allegory without knowing it. "Get real! Feras is waiting at Holy Land with baklavas for me. Can Solomon's books be worth anything? Who buys books? Nobody has time to read *books*. How much longer will this take?"

Chitchee popped open the third box. He saw the top book was the Little Golden Book, *Perri And Her Friends*.

I finished this book, *Carousel Square*, on March 24, 2021
Minneapolis, Minnesota
Chitchee Chichester